th

FADING
trilogy

FADING FREEING FALLING

*Julie
Always be fierce!*

e.k. blair

The Fading Boxset
Copyright © 2014 E.K. Blair

Compiled by Champagne Formats

Fading
Copyright © 2013 by E.K. Blair

Cover Design by Sarah Hansen, Okay Creations
Editing by Lisa Christman, Adept Edits
Interior design by Angela McLaurin, Fictional Formats
Photography by Maxim Malevich

Freeing
Copyright © 2013 by E. K. Blair

Cover Design by E.K. Blair
Editing by Lisa Christman, Adept Edits
Interior design by Angela McLaurin, Fictional Formats
Photography by Andrei Vishnyakov

Falling
Copyright © 2013 by E. K. Blair

Cover Design by E.K. Blair
Editing by Lisa Christman, Adept Edits
Interior design by Angela McLaurin, Fictional Formats
Photography by Andrei Vishnyakov

All rights reserved. No part of this book may be reproduced or transmitted in any form or by any means, electronic or mechanical, including photocopying, recording, or by any information storage and retrieval system, without permission in writing.

This is a work of fiction. Names, characters, places and incidents are the product of the author's imagination or are used fictitiously, and any resemblance to any actual persons, living or dead, events, or locales is entirely coincidental.

The author acknowledges the trademarked status and trademark owners of various products referenced in this work of fiction, which have been used without permission. The publication/use of these trademarks is not authorized, associated with, or sponsored by the trademark owner.

All rights reserved.

ISBN: 978-0-578-15593-7

FADING

a novel by
e.k. blair
New York Times Bestselling Author

For Gina
I've never been more pleased, and it's all your fault.

"And though she be but little, she is fierce."

~William Shakespeare

prologue

"WHAT DO YOU mean they cancelled? They've been on the books for weeks."

"I don't know. I didn't take the call, but we've gotta fill that slot in the next couple of days. Classes at U-Dub started today, so this weekend is gonna be busy as hell."

"Shit!" I pause for a second, frustrated as fuck. "It's too late to do anything about it tonight. I'll make some calls tomorrow and try to get another band booked. Oh, hey, if those fuckers call back, tell them to find another bar to play."

"Right, boss. You heading out soon? It's past midnight already."

"Yeah, in a little bit. I need to finish this paperwork and I'll be gone. Go ahead and go."

"See you tomorrow, man."

"See ya."

I try working on the inventory supply sheet that I need to get in to our liquor distributor, but my mind is elsewhere. I really need to call Gina and tell her to not come over tonight. She's starting to become so damn clingy. I can't stand chicks like that. The last thing I need to deal with is her needy shit. Gavin had warned me about her, but fuck if I listened. I was just looking for a one-night thing, but her stopping by my place and calling me all the time is getting annoying.

A clatter outside snaps me out of my thoughts. I look down at my watch to see it's nearing one in the morning. *Shit.* When I start packing my things up to head home, I hear more commotion from outside. I shake my head knowing it's probably just some drunk guys heading back home from a party. People are always cutting through the back alley.

I start locking everything up and make my way downstairs to the back door. "Crap," I whisper to myself, realizing I left my cell in my office. Walking back up the stairs to my office, I grab my phone off my desk. Then I hear screaming. A girl screaming.

"Fuck!"

Bolting out of my office, I quickly run downstairs to the back door and out to the small employee parking lot in the alley.

"God, please! Stop!" a girl shrieks.

Before my mind can process what I'm seeing, the bastard smashes his fist into the girl's face.

Adrenaline courses through my body, and I run. Yanking the guy off her, I start slamming my fist in his face over and over. I completely lose control of myself and relentlessly whale on him. My knuckles start to burn as the flesh begins to split open. He manages to get a few swift hits to my jaw and ribs, which allows him a quick moment to work out of my grip and flee.

Before I can charge after the guy, I catch a glimpse of the girl. It doesn't take but a split second for me to refocus. She lies there, completely unconscious, bare, with her clothes ripped off of her. My stomach clenches and my chest tightens as I slowly approach her and kneel down on my knees. Too scared to touch her, I take off my shirt and cover her naked, battered body. Her face is scratched and covered in blood and dirt. The side where the fucker's fist landed is already starting to swell and bruise, and her knees are ripped open and covered in gravel. My heart pounds and my gut is in knots.

I pat my pockets for my cell but it's not on me. I must have dropped it as I ran out here. Not wanting to leave her, I look around and spot her purse. I lean over and grab it in search of her phone. When I find it, I swipe the screen and dial 911.

As I sit next to her, she lies there, breathing peacefully. Whatever is running through her head right now has to be a million times better than the hell she's going to wake up to.

What the fuck just happened? I stare at her. I don't know what else to do. She is so small, and when I look at her tiny hands, there is bloody flesh under her nails. *Shit.* I notice a little heart tattoo on her lower hip that is still exposed. Sliding the shirt over a little to cover it, I finally hear the sirens.

"Thank God," I whisper.

chapter one

"WHERE DID YOU meet this guy?"

I stare at my hazel eyes reflected in the mirror and apply a little mascara to my already dark, thick lashes. "I ran into him at the country club."

"What the hell were you doing there? You hate all those pretentious tartlets," she says with a dramatic eye roll.

"I know, but my parents wanted me to meet them for brunch."

"How did that go?" Kimber asks.

I turn around to face her, "Oh you know, the usual. Mom is still up my ass for majoring in dance. Thinks I'm throwing my life away. I swear to God, the woman has got to get a life and stop trying to control mine."

Lying on my bed while I browse my closet for something to wear, Kimber says, "Ugh, forget about her. So tell me, is this guy hot, or is he a loafer-wearing, country club douche?"

Sliding on my favorite white pants and grabbing a sleeveless navy blouse, I shoot Kimber a smirk. "Hot, no loafers, clean cut, and a total mama's boy. So yeah, a bit of a douche."

"Seriously? Why did you agree to go out with him?" She rolls off of my bed and starts rummaging through my shoes. Kimber is like my sister. I met her my freshman year when we were randomly paired together to share a dorm room. She's very outgoing and has a flair for dramatics. Although her sense of humor can be a bit brash, her heart is sincere. After our freshman year, we ditched the dorms and moved into this house, which her parents own. The past three years have really bonded us, and I couldn't imagine my life without her.

"Because my mother was standing right there, and I just didn't want to deal with any more of her nagging. So, he asked, I said yes. We are just going out for a drink, that's all. No biggie."

"Here, wear these shoes."

"Thanks," I say as I slip on my gold Tory Burch sandals. I run a brush through my long, thick brown hair and give myself one last look in the mirror.

Smearing on some lip-gloss, I make my way toward the kitchen. When I grab my cell off the bar to check my texts, I see I have one missed call from Jase. I met Jason around the same time I met Kimber. I immediately connected with him and can tell him anything. I love Kimber, but for some reason, I'm able to let all my walls down with Jase.

There's a knock on the door, and I yell for Kimber to answer it. Quickly, I type out a text for Jase.

Heading out for a few hours. Come by later. Dying to see you.

Tossing my phone in my purse, I walk into the living room to meet Jack.

"Hey, Jack."

"Hi, Candace. You look great," he says, and I hear Kimber let out a tiny snort. I shoot her a look over my shoulder and mouth '*be nice!*'

I hop into Jack's car and we head to Prescriptions, a trendy upscale bar in downtown Seattle. Jack parks and then swiftly makes his way to my door to open it for me. Taking my hand, he helps me out of his small Audi.

When we walk inside, the bar is dimly lit and scattered with sleek leather couches and leather-upholstered coffee tables. The main bar runs along one of the walls and is made of a rich chocolate wood. Spanning the length of the wall behind the bar of lit-up bottles is a solid black chalkboard with the word 'Prescriptions' written across it with all the drinks listed below in a unique, artistic script. As we settle onto one of the couches, a waitress comes by; Jack orders a beer, and I order a glass of red wine.

Lifting his knee, he angles himself toward me on the sofa and asks, "So, how come I've never seen you at the country club before? I see your parents often, but never you."

"Not my scene, I guess. My mother serves on a few committees, so she practically lives there."

Jack narrows his dark blue eyes at me, and the edge of his mouth lifts into a slight grin. "You don't get along with your mother, do you?"

"It's complicated," I sigh. "We have very different views on life. She's really into appearances. Looking the part. Playing the role. I just don't see the point."

The waitress arrives with our drinks, and I take a generous sip of my wine. I can't help but notice how sexy he looks as he tilts his head back to take a drink from his bottle of beer. *Maybe I was wrong; maybe he's not a douche.* I let out a small giggle at my thought.

"What's so funny?"

"Oh, nothing. Just thinking about how maybe I had gotten the wrong impression of you the other day." I take another sip of my drink. "So, Jack, tell me about yourself."

"What do you want to know?"

"Hobbies? Major? What do you plan on doing after you graduate?"

"Well, I play on the lacrosse team, and I'm studying Political Science." He takes another swig of his beer and clarifies, "I'm pre-law. So after this year I plan on going to Stanford for law school. What about you?"

"I'm a Fine Arts major. Ballet. Another thing my mother doesn't approve of."

"So, what are your plans after this year?"

"Auditions, I guess. I mean, I'd like to dance professionally for as long as I can. Eventually I want to teach."

We fall into easy conversation as we continue to talk and get to know each other better. He seems genuinely interested in what I have to say. Jack isn't the typical guy I go for; he's a frat boy and comes from an upbringing such as myself, but he's really nice and for the most part, seems down to earth.

I tend to have a lot of first dates with guys but never find myself in a relationship with any of them. I don't really know the reason for that; maybe I just haven't found anyone that I care enough about to keep around. I'm not a slut by any means, far from it. I've only slept with one guy, my high school boyfriend. We dated off and on for over a year and wound up having sex the night of our graduation. I was young and stupid, but that was three years ago, and I haven't heard from him since that night.

After a couple of hours pass easily, I excuse myself to the ladies' room. I wash my hands and search my purse for a hair tie. The wine is starting to make me feel warm, and I need to get the hair off of my neck. I have always wanted short hair, but as a dancer, it needs to be long enough to secure in a bun on top of my head. So for now, I have long, thick, dark brown hair with natural golden highlights that hangs a few inches below my shoulders. When I finally find a hair tie, I quickly sweep my hair up into a ponytail.

When I return, Jack stands up and holds out his hand for me. "You ready to go?"

"Yeah," I say as I slide my hand into his.

Jack parks his car in front of my house, and once again, jumps out and opens my door for me. He walks me up to the front door and says, "I really had fun with you tonight. How about we do this again?"

"Umm, yea. That would be nice," I say as he leans in and lightly brushes his lips against my cheek. My neck heats, and I feel slightly embarrassed by the gesture.

"I'll call you so we can set something up."

"Okay, that sounds good. Thanks for the drinks. I had a really nice time."

"Me too. Goodnight, Candace."

"Night, Jack."

I watch him walk back to his car, and I turn to open the door. Instead, the door handle jerks out of my hand, and I stumble to my knees inside the house.

"What the hell, Kimber?!"

Nodding her head towards the door, she questions, "Mmm hmm . . . what was that all about?"

Pushing myself off the floor to stand, I look at her with an annoyed expression on my face, "What was *what* all about?"

"Him kissing you on the cheek. Lame." She scrunches up her nose in disgust. "Who does that?"

"God, whatever. And you didn't have to watch him kiss me. I swear your voyeurism knows no limits."

"Well?" she continues, staring at me with her way too curious, blue eyes.

"Ooh, leave me alone," I sigh. "I might have been wrong about him. He's a pretty decent guy. I think we might try and get together again. We'll see." I walk to my bedroom to change clothes, and Kimber follows me. She lies across my bed while I put on a pair of cut-off sweat shorts and a cami.

I watch Kimber as she stares up at the ceiling in deep thought with her wavy blonde hair fanned out around her. Kimber is beautiful, and she knows it. She's fit but has been blessed with feminine curves, where I have more of a straight, lean body. Typical ballerina form.

Still staring at the ceiling, she says, "Shit, Candace, do you realize that we are about to start our senior year, and I have yet to come across any decent husband material?"

I bust out into a fit of laughter. "Is this the crap that is constantly floating through your head?"

"Well . . . kinda. I mean, I have never had to work a day in my life, and I'll be damned if I have to work after we graduate. I mean, if I had a job, when would we ever hang out?" She gives me an evil smirk.

"You're crazy, but I love you so much." I lay down behind her and give her a tight hug.

"Hey, girls," Jase's voice booms through the house.

I jump up, run to the living room, and give him a big hug. Kimber quickly follows me and steps in for her hug while I take the two wine bottles out of his hands. I walk to the kitchen to grab a corkscrew and some wine glasses. When I return to the living room, I set everything down on the coffee table and make myself comfortable on the floor. Opening the wine, I pour myself a glass while I watch Kimber and Jase talk as they sit together on the couch. Jase is a very attractive guy. He has a hard, athletic build, and his skin is lightly tanned. He wears his thick, brown hair, which has turned more of a blond over the course of the summer, lightly gelled in a messy faux-hawk. His eyes are a unique shade of light gold that stand out against his dark lashes.

"So, how was your trip to San Diego?" I ask.

Jase finishes pouring his glass and says, "It was good. I hung out with friends, went out to a few bars, and saw some bands. You know, the usual visit home."

I take a sip of my wine and smile, "Well, we're glad you're back."

"You have no idea how happy I am to be back," he says with a straight face, and I can see a hint of tension in his eyes.

"Man, was it that bad, Jase?" Kimber asks.

"It's just not home to me anymore. Plus, I missed you bitches," he laughs, and his mood instantly shifts. "So, what have I missed?"

I get the feeling that Jase is hiding something about his trip back home. I look at him as he is downing his glass of wine faster than usual. Yep, he's definitely hiding something. I'm pulled out of my thoughts when I hear Kimber speak up.

"Well, Candace is dating a douche from Mommy and Daddy's country club," she says as she winks at me.

"I am not!" I say. "We went out for drinks. That's all."

"Are you seeing him again?" she asks even though she already knows the answer.

"You're seeing him again?" Jase questions, scrunching his eyebrows together. "Wait, who's *him*? Who are you seeing?"

"No. I mean, yes. God, really, it's no big deal."

"Must be if he's getting a second date," Jase says as he takes another drink. "Is that where you were earlier? On your date?"

"Uh huh," I nod.

"Where did you guys go? You never told me," Kimber asks as she folds her legs underneath her.

"We went to Prescriptions."

"I love that place," Kimber says. "Anyway. New subject. What the hell are we doing this week before classes start back up?"

"I have some serious studio time I need to put in. I also have to work."

"You always keep yourself so busy," Jase says. I don't even try to make excuses because he's right. I just shake my head and take another sip of my wine.

After a while, Jase and Kimber decide to watch some trash TV. I move to the couch and lie down with my head on Jase's lap while we all watch MTV. As he combs his fingers through my hair, it isn't long until I doze off.

I wake up to the feel of my bed dipping down and I smell wine. Jase lies behind me and wraps his muscular arms around my waist. I nestle back into his warm chest.

"Did I wake you?" he whispers.

"Yeah, but it's okay," I mumble quietly. "What time is it?"

"Around two. You passed out, so I carried you in here and hung out with Kimber for a while longer."

"Is she asleep?"

"Yeah, and snoring like a beast." We both laugh quietly at his words.

I roll over in his arms to face him in the dark, even though we can't see each other. I lay my head on his chest, and he wraps one arm around my waist and the other cups the back of my head.

"So, why did your trip really suck? I know something's bothering you."

Jase lets out a long sigh before saying, "I told them."

I wrap my arms tighter around him. "What did they say?"

"They threw me out."

My heart breaks and a quiet tear escapes my eye and rolls onto his bare chest.

"I'm so sorry. Why didn't you call me?"

"I don't know. I was embarrassed, I guess. I haven't told anyone what happened. I don't want the pity."

"You know I don't pity you, right?"

"Yeah," he whispers and kisses the top of my head.

"I'm sad because I love you. When your heart hurts, so does mine. Your pain is my pain."

We lie there together holding each other as my heart breaks to sync up with his already broken one. I love Jase. He's my best friend. We have a deep connection that runs through us and links us together. He has had a lot of pain in his life. He had a sister that was two years older than him. They were extremely close, but she died in a car crash the night of her senior prom. His parents still refuse to touch her room, like they are expecting her to come home one day.

Jase was extremely confused with his sexuality in high school. He said he didn't want to be gay and figured if he just slept with enough girls, maybe he would start to feel differently. So he slept around. A lot. He told me that growing up, he felt trapped as if he was living a lie—silently suffering on the inside as he held on to his secret. Until he came to college, no one ever knew he was gay. I'm happy he finally told his parents though. He needed to free himself of the secret he had been keeping from them. I hate that they turned their backs on their own son and would just toss him out of their home like he didn't even matter to them.

"You know this is your home, don't you? Right here with me. Kimber and I are your home. And we don't give a shit that you like guys."

Jase kisses the top of my head, and I grip my arms tighter around him.

"Jase?" I whisper.

"Yeah, sweetie?"

"I love you."

"I love you, too."

chapter two

I WAKE UP to the smell of bacon and coffee. "Thank God." I roll out of bed and make my way to the kitchen where Jase is cooking breakfast. Just another reason why I love him so much: he loves to cook, and I love to eat.

"Hey, lovely," he says to me over his shoulder as I pad into the kitchen.

I walk over to the stove where he is scrambling some eggs, and I lift up on my toes to kiss him on the cheek. "Morning," I say, then stroll over to grab a mug, and I begin to pour myself a cup of coffee. "What time did you wake up?"

"Early. I didn't get much sleep. Couldn't seem to clear my head."

I lean back against the counter and give him a side stare. It kills me that he's hurting so much. He peeks up at me and catches me staring.

"Don't."

"Don't what?"

He continues to whisk the eggs, "Don't look at me like that."

"I'm not. I'm sorry," I say as I walk over to sit at the bar. "So, what are you up to today?"

He turns around, dumps a portion of the eggs onto a plate, and takes several slices of bacon before setting it down in front of me.

"Not much. I need to pick up my books for my classes, and then I was going to hit the gym for a couple of hours. What about you?" Jase sets his plate on the bar and sits down next to me.

"Work," I say as I take a bite of my bacon. "I have to work all week. I also need to go up to the studio to get in some solo time before classes start."

We continue to eat in silence for a few minutes. When I finish my breakfast, I look up at him and tease, "My ass thanks you for the bacon." Winking at him, I walk around to the other side of the bar and rinse off my plate.

"God, you guys are up early," Kimber says as she walks into the kitchen with her eyes squinted as if the morning light is too much for her to bear.

"It's nine. Hardly early, Kim," I say sarcastically.

She grabs the box of Lucky Charms and pours herself a bowl, barely opening her eyes to do so, then sits on the barstool next to Jase. He stares at her with a smirk.

"Whaa?" she says with a mouthful of milk and a magical leprechaun concoction of cereal and marshmallows.

"You have this kickass kitchen to cook in, but you continue to eat like a six-year-old kid," he says, shaking his head and laughing.

"This shit's good," she says, using her spoon to point and emphasize her beloved breakfast cereal.

Jase and I laugh at her. I walk over and pour myself another cup of coffee before heading to my room.

"I'm going to hit the shower and get ready for work. I'll see you guys later."

"See ya," they both say in unison.

The weather is oddly nice today, so after I'm dressed, I decide that I will just walk to work. I've been working at Common Grounds, a local coffee house right off campus, for the past two years. I don't need the job for the money; I just like having the responsibility.

I pull out my phone as I walk to check my messages, and I notice I have a missed call and voicemail from my mother. Already annoyed, I go ahead and listen to her message.

Candace, I was hoping to hear all about your date with that young man from the club. I surely hope you didn't already screw this one up. It's your senior year and you should be taking your future seriously. I just heard Maggie's daughter got engaged to the Garrison's son. Well, anyways, I have a lunch date with the ladies, so I need to go. Please, call me back.

Deleting the message, I drop the phone into my bag. Of course she would think anything that didn't work out to her liking would be my fault. She's so unbelievable. I only wish I could have a decent relationship with her, with both of my parents, really. I know I shouldn't have those expectations, but I can't help hoping, that maybe one of these days things will change.

When I arrive, I am greeted with the familiar aroma of freshly ground coffee and muffins. I love working here. Everyone is really nice and my boss, Roxy, is great. She's in her early thirties and is extremely eccentric, with long, choppy colorful hair—purple this week—a pierced nose, and tattoos. She's always there for me when I need solid advice.

Roxy is working the espresso machine as I round the counter to grab my apron. I tie it on as she finishes with her customer.

"Is it just us this afternoon?" I ask as she is handing the customer his change.

Walking over to me, she sits down on a stool. "Yep. Brandon had to take care of some issue with his scholarship. But it's been pretty dead so far."

I pull up a stool and sit beside her.

"How was breakfast with your parents the other day?"

"You know, just the same old crap. Nothing ever changes. I don't understand my mother and why she just can't be happy for me. I keep holding on to the hope that she'll change, but I'm starting to get tired. If it wasn't for my father, I would probably never even see her." I look away from Roxy and focus on my hands. "God, that sounds horrible, huh?"

"No, hun, that sounds honest. Don't apologize for your feelings. You're allowed to be angry with her." Roxy stands up and walks back over to the espresso machine to make herself a drink. Talking over the loud grinding and hissing she asks, "So, did you do anything fun last night?"

"I kinda had a date," I said, peeking at her over my shoulder.

"Oh, yeah? How did that go?" She walks back over to her stool, sits down, and takes a slow sip of her drink.

"Fine, I guess. We just grabbed a couple of drinks. He said he wants to hang out again, which I guess would be okay. I mean, I might as well enjoy another date before the quarter starts and I get too busy."

Roxy shakes her head at me. "You take life too seriously, you know? You need to let loose and have some fun. You're never going to get this time back, Candace. Just enjoy it. Be young and carefree."

I know she makes a good point. I tend to have a hard time letting myself be free. I mean, I go to the occasional party with Kimber, and I go out on dates here and there, but mostly, I'm dancing, studying, working, or hanging out with Jase. I've been in college for three years, and I have yet to do anything crazy. Roxy is right; I'll never get this time back. After this year, I'm going to be focused on my dancing and trying to make it into a career. I need to relax and not take life so seriously all the time.

"Yeah," I sigh. I stare out at the front of the shop that is covered in floor to ceiling windows. I breathe in a deep breath and say, "Maybe you're right."

"I know I'm right. Every school year you get sucked into your classes and dance. You keep yourself so busy. Let go. Just for a moment—let go. Be a little spontaneous."

I stare her straight in the eyes.

"Just try," she says.

I'm not sure what it is about today that makes me actually listen to what she is saying. Maybe it's the fact that I am still irritated with my mother's crude voicemail. I've heard it all before, but this time, I feel it seeping into me. Roxy is right. What the hell was I doing? Kimber is always out having the time of her life while I have my head buried in books. I'm always striving to be perfect, but I know I will never be that in my mother's eyes. I try to do my best in school and with dance. Maybe if she sees how others look at me, she might start to appreciate me. She might even start to like me. *Screw it.*

"Let's go next door," I say as my lips start to turn up into a grin.

"Huh?"

"Come on. It's dead in here. Let's close up for an hour." I hop down from my stool and start taking off my apron.

Roxy gets an approving look on her face and smiles. "Hell yeah! No way I'm gonna give you even a second to back down. Let's go."

Next door to the coffee shop is the tattoo parlor that Roxy's boyfriend works at. We both yank off our aprons, and Roxy locks up.

The buzzing of tattoo guns fills the shop. The walls are painted black, and they are covered in tattoo flash. I don't even look because I already know what I want. I have thought about getting a tattoo in the past but was always too scared.

"Hey, Rox," Jared says as he walks up to the counter. "What are you guys doing here?"

Jared and Roxy have only been dating for a few months, but they are head over heels for each other.

"Candace wants to get a tattoo, and I need you to do it fast before she chickens out."

"I'm not going to back out," I say to her.

Jared looks at me surprised. "A tattoo, huh? Well, you're in luck. My next appointment isn't for another hour." Jared comes around the counter, takes my hand, and walks me back to his station. I hop up onto the table and he asks, "So, what are you wanting?"

Clasping my hands together nervously, I look down at him. "I'd like a tiny heart on my lower hip."

"Easy enough. Just lay down and relax while I get everything set up."

As I lie on the table, I suddenly get nervous wondering if it's going to hurt. I close my eyes and try to relax. Taking a few deep breaths, I feel Roxy grab ahold of my hand. I open my eyes and look at her.

"I can tell you're freaking out," she says.

"Just a bit. Does it hurt?" I ask as I eye the tattoos on her arms.

"Nah," Jared says as he wheels over to me on his stool. "Unbutton and pull down your pants a little."

Nervously, I do as he says.

"You ready?" he asks.

I look at Roxy as she gives me a reassuring look that reminds me of the conversation we had a few minutes ago. I want to do this. I need to do this.

"Absolutely," I say.

I feel Jared's fingers press down on my hip as the gun starts buzzing. The pricking of the needle stings slightly on the sensitive area, and I pinch my eyes shut.

"You doing okay?" Jared asks me.

Opening my eyes as I start to numb to the sensation, I look down at him. "Yeah, it's actually not as bad as I thought."

"Well, I'm just about done."

"Really?!" I say, surprised at how fast it was.

Roxy lets out a soft laugh, "Candace, It's just a tiny-ass heart. How long did you think it was going to take?"

"Done," he says and he rolls away on his stool to grab a mirror and then rolls back. He hands it to me, and I hold it up, staring at the reflection of my new tattoo. It's a simple black outline of a heart. Small and discreet.

"I love it, Jared. Thank you."

He rubs on a glob of cool ointment and adheres a bandage over it. I grab his hand as he helps me sit up.

"Here," he says and hands me a sheet of paper. "This will tell you how to care for the tat as it heals. If you notice anything unusual going on, call me."

I nod and tell him, "Will do. Thanks again."

Roxy grabs Jared around his waist to give him a hug. "Come over later?"

"Yeah, I get out of here around six," he says before leaning down to kiss her. "See you girls later."

"Bye," we both say as we head back over to the coffee shop.

Holy shit! I cannot believe I just got a tattoo. My act of rebellion is thrilling, and I like the energy that flows through me. I could get used to this excitement.

chapter three

"I STILL CAN'T believe you got a tattoo, and I'm still pissed that you did it without me," Kimber says.

"Honestly, it was a spur of the moment thing," I say as I sit on the floor and unpack my dance bag. I have been living in the studio for the past few days. Classes are about to start, and I want to make sure I'm prepared and on top of my game. Kimber had been upset when I told her about my rare act of rebellion, but she's since calmed down.

"I am so excited that you are coming out with us tomorrow. I'm not sure what has gotten into you, but I like it," she says as she sits on my bed and watches me as I rub baby powder into my pointe shoes and hang them on a hook in my closet to air dry.

I start stripping off my sweaty clothes. "I don't know. Roxy just finally got through to me, I guess. She's right; it's time to start having a little bit of fun."

I hear my phone chime, and I walk over to my desk to read a new text.

"Who's that?" Kimber asks.

"It's from Jack. I haven't heard from him since we went out last Friday."

Kimber jumps off the bed and is quickly hanging over my shoulder to read his message.

Got plans tomorrow night?

For some reason Thursday nights are big nights to go out around here. The bars and clubs are always packed.

"You should ask him to come with us," she says as she smacks my bottom and walks out of my room.

I sit down at my desk and text him back.

Going dancing at Remedy with some friends. You should come!

Remedy huh? What time?

Around 10:30.

Meet you there?

Yeah. See you then.

I hop up from my chair, excited about seeing him tomorrow, and throw on some clothes. I make my way to the kitchen to fix a salad. While I'm chopping some veggies, my phone begins to ring. I pick it up to see that it's my mother. *Crap.*

"Hey, Mom."

"Hi, darling. Look, there is a banquet this Saturday, and I am being recognized for my contributions to the Children's Foundation. I need you to be there," she demands.

I know she only wants me to attend for appearance's sake. One supportive, happy family. It's such a lie.

"I can't, Mom. I have to work that night."

"Well, take off," she says as if it's no big deal.

"I can't ask off work three days in advance. It doesn't work that way." I get so annoyed by her lack of consideration.

"Christ, Candace," she barks at me. "This is important. I don't even know why you have that little job."

"I like working, Mom. I'm sorry, but I just can't go," I say in the softest tone I can manage because I know she's about to flip. This is so typical of her.

"I swear, I don't know how to deal with you. You are such a selfish little girl. Here you are, playing around in college on your father's dime, and you can't even choose a respectable major. It's quite embarrassing. Then, when I ask you to do something to support me, you blow me off for some trivial job you don't even need. Where is your loyalty to this family?"

My face heats and I slam the knife down on the hard granite countertop. "Support you? You always want me to support *you*, Mother. What about supporting me? Shit, Mom, you have never once attended any of my shows. I work my ass off. You have no clue what it is I am doing here. I'm sick of this shit. I'm never going to be good enough, am I? What do you want from me? Please, just tell me so I know exactly what I need to do to make you fuckin' like me!" Disconnecting the call, I throw the phone across the counter. I am beyond pissed. My heart is racing, and I try to slow my breathing so I can calm down.

"What's with the screaming?" Kimber asks softly, knowing I rarely ever lose my temper.

My eyes begin to sting, and when I turn around to look at her, the tears start to fall. I feel so hopeless. I've fought with my mother my whole life, and I have no idea why she is the way that she is. She knows exactly what to say to me to set me off. I know it's only a matter of time before my dad calls to smooth things over and make excuses for her.

Kimber walks over and wraps her arms around me. "What happened?"

I let go of Kimber and wipe my face with the backs of my hands. "My mother. She went on another one of her tirades and thought it would be fun to belittle me. She just set me off, and I couldn't hold it in."

"Want to tell me about it?"

"Not really. I think I'll just take a quick shower and call it a night."

"You sure?" she questions me with concern.

"I'm sure."

Kimber heads back to her room, and I bag up the vegetables I was cutting and put everything back in the refrigerator. I can't even think about eating when I am this upset. I pick up my phone and decide to turn it off for the night so I don't have to hear it when my father calls. After a hot shower, I start to relax. I know I should probably check to see if my dad has called, but I don't have the energy to deal with it tonight.

Waking up the next morning, I'm surprised that I'm still pissed off about the fight I had with my mother. I throw the sheets off of me and walk over to my dresser. I pull out a pair of cutoff knee-length sweats, sports bra, and a loose fitting grey tank top. I get dressed, grab my dance bag, and throw in my pointes. After brushing my teeth and pulling my hair up in a messy bun, I go to the kitchen to grab a breakfast bar. I toss a couple bottles of water and an apple into my bag and make a cup of coffee to take with me. Throwing my bag across my chest, I head out to my car.

When I walk into the studio, I drop my bag onto the floor. I walk over to the stereo, plug in my iPod, turn up the speakers, and hit play. I sit on the floor with my legs stretched out, and I lower myself between them and begin to warm up my muscles. The melodic strains of Yann Tiersen's 'Comptine d'un Autre Ete' fill the room as I begin to stretch.

Feeling warm and loose, I grab my bag. I start taping my toes and stuffing my toe pads with new lamb's wool. Sliding on my pointes, I lace the ribbons around my ankles. This is what I love about ballet—the familiar rituals.

With the music filling the room, I grab the barre and begin to work. I start the very methodical routine: pliés, tendu, degagè. Feeling my muscles stretch, I continue to work the rest of the exercises, freeing my mind of all my stresses, and focusing on nothing but my turnout, posture, lines, and movement. Hearing the box of my toe shoes thudding against the worn wooden floor and the gliding of the shredded satin as I work my feet is soothing. I love this feeling of pure focus. Sometimes it's nice to shut out the world and be completely immersed in dance, feeling like there is no life beyond the walls of this studio. It's freeing.

After an hour or so, I end my barre work with grand battement, working on my high kicks. As I finish, I begin to feel slightly light-headed. I sit down and grab my water, downing it in just a few seconds. I remove my shoes and tape, lie on my back, close my eyes, and breathe. I know as soon as I walk out of here, the stress of my mother will creep in. So I just lie on the floor.

After leaving the studio, I sit in my car and call my dad. I just want to get it over with. I talk to him on my drive home and the conversation is the same as always. I apologize to him for my outburst, and he makes excuses for my mother. The conversation couldn't have ended any sooner. I was done with it.

'The Edge of Glory' by Lady Gaga is blaring throughout the house while Kimber and I get ready for our night out. I'm looking forward to seeing Jack, which is a bit odd for me because I never really take that much interest in guys.

I pick out a pair of cute white shorts, a sleeveless satin hot pink top with a white Moroccan pattern, and a pair of nude pumps. My hair is down in soft, wavy curls. I apply some lip-gloss before Kimber and I head out.

We arrive at Remedy, and the place is already packed. Kimber and I walk in and find a few of our friends sitting at a small group of couches that are set off from the dance floor. We make our way over to greet everyone. When I find Jase, he takes my arm and drags me to the bar with him.

"You thirsty?" I ask sarcastically.

"Not really. I just saw Mark," he says as we slide onto our barstools.

"Isn't that the hottie you used to see that plays guitar?"

"Exactly." He eyes me with a serious look. The bartender approaches, and Jase orders us four shots of tequila and two beers.

I shoot him a questioning look and say, "Okay, spill it. Clearly you're into getting drunk, so tell me what happened."

The bartender sets the drinks down in front of us, and Jase slides two of the shots and a beer my way. We clink our tequila shots together and down them quickly.

"He caught me kissing his roommate," he confesses.

I start laughing at him and take a swig of my beer. "You can be a slut sometimes, you know?"

"Trust me. I know," he says and hands me the second shot. We sit there for a while and continue to talk and laugh. Warm arms wrap around my waist, and I turn my head to see Jack standing behind me. He looks good in a pair of worn jeans and a simple black V-neck shirt.

"Hey, Jack," I say. When I stand up, I feel the effects of consuming the shots so quickly. Plus, I haven't eaten a lot today.

"Whoa, you okay?" Jack questions as he grabs ahold of my arm.

"Yeah, just stood up too fast." I turn to Jase and introduce the two guys to each other. When I sit down, Jack does as well and orders us another round of beers.

"So, what did you do today?" Jack asks.

"I spent the morning at the dance studio to get in some practice. Then I came home and took it easy for the rest of the day. You?"

"Been harassing the new pledges at the frat house." He laughs and takes a drink of his beer.

I sneak a quick glance at Jase and roll my eyes. Frat guys were never my thing. Maybe it's their arrogance, but I didn't catch that about Jack when we went out the other night.

Jack leans in close to my ear and whispers, "You wanna dance?"

Taking my hand in his, he helps me off the barstool, and we make our way to the crowded dance floor. I start to move to the beat of the music that blasts throughout the club. 'Push It' by Garbage is playing, and I lose myself in the sea of people dancing around me along with the flashing lights and loud music.

Jack is behind me, and I feel his arms as they slide across my stomach, underneath the hem of my top. He moves in sync with me as I dance to the rhythm of the song. I can already feel drops of sweat trickling down my spine, and it must be the tequila that is making me feel bold when I reach up behind me and wrap my hand around the back of his neck. I feel the stubble on his jaw as he glides his chin along my damp neck and takes a soft bite. *Shit, that's hot.*

Turning me around in his arms, I can see the heat in his darkening eyes. I rake my fingers through the hair on the back of his head as he pulls my hips tight against him, and he leans down and covers my mouth with his.

I'm not sure what has come over me. Since my conversation with Roxy, I have been a little bit bolder with myself. But here, in the middle of this dance floor, kissing Jack, is pretty damn bold for me.

Jack and I continue to dance through a few more songs when we decide to take a breather and get a drink. We walk over to our section and sit down on one of the couches. I take a long drink of my beer and nearly choke when Kimber suddenly yanks me off the couch.

"I've gotta piss," she says to me while looking at Jack.

"You're such a lady." I smirk at her and give Jack an apologetic look. "I'll be right back," I say to him. He nods back at me while stifling a laugh.

Kimber is nearly dragging me to the bathroom. As soon as she closes the door behind us she says, "What the hell was that shit on the dance floor all about, hooker?"

I start laughing. "What are you talking about?"

"What do you even know about this guy?" she questions.

"Well, nothing. I guess that's what makes it kinda fun," I say as I lean in to look at myself in the mirror. I lick my finger and swipe it under each of my eyes in an attempt to fix my makeup. "And why are you always spying on me?"

"Hey, can't blame me for watching. It was hot."

We both start laughing, and I shake my head, feeling a little embarrassed about the indiscreet show we gave her on the dance floor.

Kimber and I walk back, and Jack is laughing about something with Jase.

"What's so funny?" I ask as I make my way to sit in between the two of them.

Jack grips my thigh, giving it a little squeeze. He leans over and kisses me behind my ear and whispers, "I can't even remember now that you're here."

I look at him with a tiny smirk and shake my head. Sometimes Jack will say things that seem a little too fast, too soon, and it makes me feel slightly embarrassed. I turn away from him and ask Kimber how much longer she wants to stay.

She looks at her phone and says, "It's a little after one. I guess we can think about calling it a night if you're getting tired."

I look at Jack and give him an undecided shrug.

"Why don't we finish our drinks, and I'll drive you home," he says.

"Okay."

Kimber jumps up, "Great, well then I'm heading out. If I'm asleep when you get home, wake me up."

"I shouldn't be out too late, but I will," I say to her.

Kimber winks at me, then leaves. Jase says his goodbyes as well and heads out shortly after Kimber. I finish my beer and lean against Jack with his arm wrapped around my shoulders. We talk about what we have been doing the past few days. Most of our conversations are pretty easy, even though we don't seem to have a whole lot in common. But, it feels good to be next to him, so I don't really care what we talk about.

I'm pretty tired on the drive home. Leaning my head against the cold window, I close my eyes. It has been a crazy night for me, and I'm feeling a little confused about Jack but try not to think too much. I'm always thinking too much. When I feel the car start to slow, I open my eyes and roll my head to the side to face Jack.

It's now raining outside, and the trickling against the car is loud. Jack and I stare at each other in silence. I have missed having the affection of a guy, so I don't object when he leans in to kiss me. He touches the side of my face, and I wrap my hand behind his neck. His kisses are passionate and eager. I part my lips slightly, and he slides his tongue in my mouth and caresses it with mine. Grabbing my hips, he pulls me over the console and on top of him. With my legs straddled on either side of him, I can feel how turned on he is. He has both of his hands buried in my hair as he deepens our kiss. I am totally lost in him.

A soft moan escapes my lips, and I pull away. Suddenly, I'm thinking again as I look down at his flushed face. *What am I doing?* This isn't me. I don't act like this and especially not with guys I don't know and hardly care for. *Stop thinking, Candace.* I lean down and press my lips against his and we begin getting lost in each other again. Well, that's not true. I can't get lost because I can't stop thinking about how this is wrong. I'm only leading him on.

I manage to break our kiss and rest my forehead against his. My eyes are shut because I'm too embarrassed to look at him. As he runs his hands down my back, he whispers, "It's okay, Candace."

Pulling back, I look into his dark blue eyes. "Sorry," I whisper back and slowly shake my head.

"Can I see you again?" he asks as he continues to run his hands slowly up and down my back.

I know I should be honest with him and say no, but my hormones answer, "Yeah."

He reaches his hand behind his seat, and I wonder what he's searching for. He grins at me as he hands me an umbrella.

I laugh softly, "Thanks."

"Come on. I'll walk with you."

"No, it's fine. Don't worry."

He lifts up and plants a chaste kiss on my lips. "I'll call you, okay?"

"Okay," I say as I climb off of his lap and out of the car.

I make my way inside the house and slip off my heels.

"Kim, you awake?" I whisper loudly as I walk into her room.

She rolls over in bed and says, "Yeah. Come here, I want all the dirty details." She sits up and turns on the lamp that's on her nightstand. I walk over, sit down next to her, and let out a long sigh.

"I think he likes me."

"So, what's the problem?"

I look over at her, then flop back onto the bed and stare at the ceiling, "The problem is, I'm only trying to have a little fun, but it feels wrong. There is just nothing there, yet I keep kissing him, and I'm only leading him on. He asked to see me again, and my stupid mouth said yes."

Kimber lays down next to me, "So, see him one more time, and just tell him. Honestly, Candace, I think you're being hard on yourself and making this a bigger deal than it actually is."

I turn to face her. "You're right."

"I always am." She gives me a grin, and then asks, "Did you kiss him good-bye?"

"More like straddled his thighs, grabbed his hair, and let him shove his tongue in my mouth," I say, and then I burst out laughing as I cover my heated face with my hands.

"You little hooker!"

I jump off the bed, still laughing. "Good night, Kim," I say in a sing-song voice as I head to my room.

"Night, slut!" I hear her yell down the hall.

chapter four

I'M WORKING IN the back, restocking supplies, when I hear Roxy shout for me from up front. I stop what I'm doing, walk to the front counter, and see Jase. I spoke to him the morning after our night out at Remedy. He ran into Mark out in the parking lot and ended up talking to him for a while and Mark decided to give Jase a second chance.

"Hey, Candace," he says as he leans in to give me a peck on my lips. "I've been trying to call you."

"Oh, sorry. I was at the studio this morning and let the battery drain on my cell, and I never remembered to plug it in to recharge," I said. "I'll go do that now before I forget again." I run into the back and grab my phone and the charging cord. When I walk back up front, I plug it in by the register.

"So, I wanted to see if you and Kimber could get together with Mark and I later tonight?" Jase asks while he's leaning against the counter.

"I'd love to, but I'm working late tonight. How about tomorrow afternoon?" I ask. "We can do a cookout at our house."

"That sounds great. I really fucked up with him, and I want to make it right. Plus, I want you guys to meet him."

Resting on my elbows, I look up at him and say, "Of course, Jase."

"Great, I'll call him and let him know," he says, then leans down to kiss my forehead. I smile up at him as he turns to leave.

I notice my phone automatically turns on once it gets enough life in it. Picking it up, I swipe the screen to look at all my missed calls and texts. I see I have a missed text from Jack, and I tap to open it up.

You free Monday night? Frat house always throws a huge party after the first day of classes.

"What are you reading over there?" Roxy asks as she is steaming some milk for a customer's drink.

Looking up at her, I say, "I'm reading a text from Jack. He wants me to go to some party, and I'm not sure how to respond." I look back down at his text and stare.

After Roxy finishes up with her customer, she walks over to me. "What do you mean 'you don't know how to respond'? What's going on?"

I lift my arms off the counter and step away to face her. Crossing my arms in front of my chest, I say, "I need to distance myself from him. I think he wants more than I do. I mean, I don't want anything, so . . ."

"Just tell him you can't go. Or go, and tell him later that you just don't have time for a relationship right now," she says.

I pick up my phone to respond.

What time?

I walk over to pour myself a cup of coffee when I hear my phone chime. "That was fast," I hear Roxy say.

"No kidding." Walking back to my phone, I set down my mug, and tap on his message.

Pick you up around 10?

Okay, I'll see you then.

Miss you.

"Shit," I mumble quietly and set the phone down, wanting to pretend I didn't see that last text.

"What are you 'shitting' about?"

I take a sip of my coffee and then toss Roxy my phone. Sitting on my stool, I watch her closely as she reads through the texts. I notice her eyes get big, and I know she finally reached the text that is starting to make me panic slightly.

"Okay, it's not that—"

"You know I don't do well with this stuff. I never make it to date number two and now this guy says he misses me." I feel my heartbeat start to quicken and, yes, that is definitely panic I am feeling. I don't deal with intimate relationships well at all. In fact, I'm pretty closed off emotionally with guys. I've never had any closeness with my parents, then the one guy I thought at least liked me in high school turned out to be just another asshole. I feel like I'm emotionally moronic.

I look up to see that Roxy is laughing at me. "It's not funny!"

"It actually is a little bit," she says. "Relax, don't respond. He probably won't even notice. Guys are stupid anyway."

I hope she's right. I hope he isn't sitting there waiting for me to text him back to say that I miss him too. I don't like opening myself up like that.

The next day, Kimber and I get ready for the cookout. I'm in the kitchen preparing the burgers for the grill, and Kimber is chopping up veggies for a salad. Jase has never bothered to introduce us to any guys in the past, so I know he must really like Mark. I don't know much about him aside from the fact that he plays guitar for a local band.

"Hey, Kim, has Jase ever talked to you about Mark before?" I ask as I pound out another hamburger patty.

"Not much. He was pretty pissed off at himself when they broke up, so I figured he had really cared for him but didn't realize it until they split." Kimber slides the salad in the fridge then opens a bag of chips to pour in a bowl.

"Hmm..."

"What?" She eyes me as she pops a chip in her mouth.

I walk to the sink to wash my hands. "Nothing." I shake my head. "Just curious."

"We're here," Jase calls out.

I walk into the living room and give him a hug.

"Mark, this is Candace," Jase says as I pull away.

I turn to Mark, "Hey! It's great to meet you. Come on in. We're in the kitchen getting the food ready," I say as I start walking towards the kitchen.

"Hey, Jase," Kimber says with a mouth full of chips.

Jase looks at Mark then back at Kimber. "And this crazy girl is Kimber."

"Nice you meet you guys," Mark says with a grin.

Mark is good looking with an athletic build similar to Jase's. He has dark brown hair and striking green eyes.

"Will one of you start the grill?" Kimber asks the guys.

"Yeah, I can do that," Mark says, and Kimber leads him out back.

Jase and I grab the food and head out behind them. We are lucky to have a large backyard with a nice patio that is covered with a pretty white pergola. We have a table that seats six and off to the side, several chairs that circle around a fire pit. There is a small bar area with a built in grill that we only used when there were guys over to start it up.

Most students our age live in smaller houses or apartments, but Kimber's parents own this house. They bought it when they were having the house built that they live in now.

"This is a nice place you have," Mark says.

Kimber flops down in a chair. "I suppose," she says with a sigh.

I roll my eyes at her and look at Mark, "Please, just ignore her dramatics."

Kimber looks at me and laughs.

"Hey Jase, will you run inside and grab the case of beer that's in the fridge and bring it out? There's a cooler next to the door that already has ice in it," I say.

"Sure," he says and he walks inside the house.

I walk over to Mark who is standing next to the grill and hand him the plate of burgers. "So, Mark, are you in college too?" I ask

He grabs the plate from me and starts placing each patty on the grill. "Yeah, I'll be graduating after this year." He closes the lid and we both sit down as Jase walks over and hands us all beers.

"Same here," I say. "What are you studying?"

Mark takes a swig of his beer, "Same as Jase: Architecture." Looking over at Jase, he adds, "That's how we know each other."

We continue getting to know Mark and having good conversation. I really like him and we corner off for the majority of the night, talking and laughing, while Kimber and Jase drink and talk about who knows what. It's nice to have a relaxing evening with friends.

After cleaning up, it was starting to get late, and we decide to call it a night. I have an early class in the morning, so I need to hit the sack.

"It was so good to meet you, Mark," I say as I walk him to the front door.

"Same here," he responds.

I lean over and give him a hug, "You're welcome anytime, and you don't need Jase with you to stop by."

"Thanks," he says.

Kimber and I say our good-byes to the boys and they head out. Walking to their car, Mark holds Jase's hand and leans in to kiss him on the neck. When I close the door, I look at Kimber. "I love seeing Jase like that," I say.

"Like what?" she asks.

"Happy and comfortable," I say as I lean against the door.

Smiling at me, Kimber says, "Me too. He told me about his trip home."

"Sucks, huh?" I say as I push myself off the door and start walking towards the back of the house to our rooms.

"Yeah," she says and she follows me. "I love you, Candace."

I turn to her, surprised by the affection behind her words.

"I know I tease you a lot, but I just wanted to say it so you know," she says.

"I love you too, Kim," I say as I wrap my arms around her tightly. Kim and Jase are like family to me. They both love me and support me the way family should.

We pull apart and head to our separate rooms.

"Good night," I say.

"Night, hooker."

I shake my head and laugh as I close the door behind me.

chapter five

SO FAR MY classes have been uneventful. It's the first week, so I don't expect much until at least next week. I just left my Methodologies class and I'm on my way to the studio for my Ballet Technique class. When I walk through the double doors, I am greeted by a few of the girls.

The dance program here at the University of Washington isn't huge. You're in classes with the same people every quarter. I've been with these girls for three years, and even though we all see each other every day, I don't hang out with any of them outside of classes and studio. Everyone is pretty competitive, so I prefer to keep it strictly professional and not mingle outside of school.

This year will be exceptionally competitive because of our senior capstone, which is a self-choreographed solo. Only two solos will be selected to perform during the final production at the end of the year. It's an important performance for graduating seniors because there will be lots of agencies in attendance. Getting a solo can mean having a job after graduation.

Everyone is scattered around the studio, taping up their toes, banging new pointes on the floor to break in the box, stretching, and a few are even quietly chatting. I keep to myself and start taping my toes. The past three years that I've spent here have been good. I tend to get lead placements in dances, standout solos, and duets with the male dancers. We combine with the guys on Tuesdays and Thursdays for an extra hour on top of our normal two-hour class.

I look up and see Andrea Emerson walk in. She's our instructor for all technique classes, and she is hardcore. She has no patience for inconsistency and expects perfection. She's tough, but she's the best. I feel a little nervous upon seeing her, even though I put in studio time at least three days a week over the summer. If you are off your game, she will let you and everyone else know it.

Ms. Emerson is a seasoned dancer who has made a decent name for herself throughout her career. Although she is in her fifties, she can still dance like the pros. She has an intimidating look about her. She always wears her long blonde hair up in a tight bun with a black leotard, white tights, and a sheer black wrap skirt. She always has a stoic look, and in three years, I have yet to see her break a smile.

She claps her hands twice, and everybody goes in search for their place on the barre. We all look the same with our hair secured in buns on the tops of our heads, black leotards, white tights, and our pale pink pointes. The classical music of a piano comes through the speakers and fills the room. I place my left hand softly on the barre and wait for the signal to begin our exercises.

The routine never changes. I've been doing these exercises since I was eleven and was in my very first ballet class. It was my mother who first signed me up for ballet. She never imagined that I would want to make a career out of it, but I have always loved dance. The freedom you can find within the strict boundaries of technique makes me feel alive. I am happiest when I am dancing.

I work gracefully through the ninety-minute routine, and when we come to an end, Ms. Emerson calls for us to gather in the front of the room. She begins to talk about our solos for the year.

"Things will be different this year. Instead of you choosing your piece of music, you will be drawing it out of this basket. There is a different piece on each CD. You will randomly choose your CD and that will be the song that you will use to choreograph your final routine. Don't forget ladies, this could be the beginning of your career, and for some of you, the end," she says.

I slowly make my way up to the large, weathered black wicker basket. I look down at the pile of discs that have the potential to launch me forward or drown me. Picking the wrong song could be disastrous. I close my eyes and pull out a CD, all the while praying to the dance gods to bless me with the perfect piece of music. I stare at the blank disc as I make my way over to my dance bag that is lying on the floor. I sit down, shove it in my bag, and start to remove my pointes.

I walk out in the warm August afternoon and slide into my white Infinity coupe, setting my bag on the passenger seat. I take out the disc and push it into the CD player, turn up the volume, and hit play. I close my eyes as I wait for the music to start. I can barely hear the strings of a violin at first. They slowly and quietly begin to build with the low, deep hum of a cello followed by a dark, melodic piano. I recognize the piece as Clint Mansell's 'Lux Aeterna.'

This is an extremely dark piece of music. My stomach hollows and I feel anxious. I have never danced to, yet alone choreographed, anything this dark. I was hoping for something feminine and delicate, not this. All I can picture is Natalie Portman's psychotic character in 'Black Swan' as she bleeds out on stage. When the song comes to an end, I turn off the stereo and drive home in welcome silence.

I don't want to think about what I just heard. Instead, I try to focus on clothes. *Yes, clothes. Think about clothes, Candace.* Sorting through my closet in my head, I try to think about what I'm going to wear to the party tonight. It doesn't take long for my mind to fill with dread when I think about being honest with Jack and letting him know that I'm not looking for anything with him. And based on the music I just heard, my year is fucked. I am going to be living and breathing dance if I'm expected to choreograph a masterpiece to that song.

I wake up from my nap, and even though I took a shower when I got home after dance class, I decide to hop in for another. The bathroom fills with steam, and I open the glass door to the shower. I try to calm my nerves as I focus on the water beating against my back, but I don't think anything will take away these butterflies in my stomach. I give up on the shower and step out. I wrap a towel around me and see Jase fiddling around on my computer when I walk into my bedroom.

"What are you doing?" I ask while I walk over to my dresser and open the top drawer.

Staring at the screen, he says, "Nothing really, just messing around. I just finished my last class and thought I'd come chill with you."

I pull on my underwear and start to slip on my bra when he turns to look at me.

"You going somewhere?" he asks.

"Yeah, there's a party at Jack's fraternity tonight, and he asked me to go."

Jase leans back in the chair and sarcastically says, "You sound thrilled."

Grabbing my hair dryer, I look back at him. "It's just . . . I'm not into him aside from kissing. We have nothing in common, and I feel nothing towards him."

Jase grins at me.

"This should not be a surprise to you, Jase," I say.

"Nope, no surprise at all. Typical Candace, devoid of all things emotional. Well, except for me." He gives me a big smile then turns back around to the computer, and I flick on the hair dryer.

I see the lights of Jack's car pierce through the large windows in the living room. I grab my purse and yell at Kimber from across the house. "Jack is here. I'll see you later."

"Bye, sweetie, and good luck," she hollers back.

By the time I open the front door, Jack is already walking up to the house.

"Hey," he says, reaching out his hand for me to take.

Holding hands while walking to his car feels weird to me. I know it probably shouldn't since the last time I saw him I had my legs spread across his lap, but I guess it was the fact that I knew I was going to end things tonight. I feel like I'm being deceitful by holding his hand.

He opens my door and I slide into the car. When Jack gets in, he leans over to give me a kiss. I make sure to keep the kiss short. The silence is a little awkward as we drive to his fraternity house. I stare out the window and watch the streetlights pass.

"Is everything okay?" he asks.

I turn my head to look at him and say, "Uh huh. I'm just a little tired, that's all. I had three classes today plus my studio." With my head lazily leaning against the headrest, I continue to stare at Jack. I think about Jase's words back at the house: *Typical Candace, devoid of all things emotional.* Do I purposely avoid relationships or is it simply because I just haven't met the right person yet? Maybe I should try and give Jack a chance. Maybe that's it. I never see a guy long enough to give him a chance. Maybe if I gave him time, I might wind up really liking him.

I snap out of my thoughts when I feel Jack's hand run up my thigh. He cocks his head to the side and gives me a little smirk. I smile in return.

"You're beautiful when you smile," he says and then returns his gaze to the road ahead.

I don't say anything. I simply sit there with my head resting on the seat.

I can already hear the music as we pull up to the house. Jack pulls around to a small parking lot behind the house. We get out of the car, and the muffled music and voices become clearer the closer we get. Jack opens the door and there are throngs of people everywhere. It's a two-story house and the stairs are covered with students who already seem to be drunk. Everyone is shouting over the loud music to make themselves heard. Jack's warm hand grabs mine, and he gives it a squeeze as he leads me back to the kitchen where he is greeted by a bunch guys that are slapping him on the back and grabbing his hand the way guys do. He doesn't introduce me, which is fine; I'm feeling slightly uncomfortable. I look around and watch a group of girls that are sitting at a table playing some sort of drinking game with a few guys. The rest of the room is filled with people talking and laughing loudly. Everyone is drinking and having a good time.

"Want a beer?" Jack asks.

"Yeah, that sounds good. Thanks." Jack walks away to fetch our drinks, and I'm left alone. I lean back against the center island and continue to watch the drunken girls as they giggle and act stupid. Looking at them, I'm starting to feel underdressed. Most of the girls here are wearing little skirts and dresses with nice heels. I feel a little awkward in my black retro Vans tank top, worn tattered jeans, and a pair of black Chucks. I tried dressing it up a little by adding a fitted red and black flannel that I left unbuttoned, with a vintage gold necklace. But these girls look like they have a particular goal in mind for the night.

Jack returns with our drinks, and I take a long, slow drink. Wrapping his arm around my waist, he moves to stand in front of me. When he leans in and kisses me below my ear, I quickly move my head back.

"What's wrong with you tonight?" he snaps with his eyebrows knitted together.

I try and lessen the tension as I smile and say, "Nothing, I'm just a little uncomfortable, that's all."

Jack sets his beer down and places each hand on the countertop on both sides of me, locking me in. "Relax," he says in a soft voice.

But I can't. He backs away, takes my free hand, and walks us out to the main room where people are dancing and hanging out.

"I'll introduce you to a few people," he shouts over at me.

We walk over to a group of people and Jack introduces me. There are a couple girls that I have seen around campus, and we are able to strike up a light conversation. I'm not sure how much time has passed, but my head is starting to hurt from all the loud music. The girls suggest we go hang out outside. I let Jack know, and I leave him there with his buddies while I head outside with the two girls. We find a few chairs and sit down. They are carrying on a conversation while I rest my head back and close my eyes. I am somehow able to drown out the noise and focus on the light breeze that's sweeping across my face.

"You tired?"

I open my eyes to Jack's voice, and he is kneeling down in front of me with his hands on my knees. I look at him and nod my head. He stands up, takes my hand, and starts walking me back into the house. When he takes me upstairs, he leads me into a dark room with a couple full-sized beds.

"What are we doing in here?" I ask him and he moves to sit down on one of the beds.

"I figure we could just hang out and relax away from all the noise. Is that all right?"

I walk over to him and sit down. "Yeah," I say, and then I turn to look at him. "I'm sorry I'm being a drag. I've just had a long day."

"It's fine, Candace," he says as he lies back on the bed.

I shift and lie down next to him and close my eyes. My head is starting to throb with an oncoming headache. We just lie there in silence, and the peace feels really nice. Jack brushes his hand over my cheek, and my eyes flutter open. Leaning over me, he looks in my eyes, and I can smell an obscene amount of liquor on his breath.

"Jack," I whisper as he leans down and presses his lips against mine. I know this is wrong, and he has clearly had too much to drink, but I find myself getting caught up in the moment. I run my hand up the back of his neck and start kissing him in return. He rolls on top of me, and the weight of him presses me into the bed. Our kisses turn frantic, and my breath quickly becomes labored. He runs his hand across my stomach, hooks it into the waistband of my pants, and gently tugs down. I feel my stomach knot up, and I push away.

"I'm sorry," I say, closing my eyes tightly. "I shouldn't be doing this."

"What the fuck, Candace," he spits out, and when I open my eyes, I see the irritated look on his face. "What's the problem? It's like one minute you're all over me, and the next, you're pushing me away. You pulled this same act the other night."

I push back against his chest, but he doesn't move. "I'm sorry, I'm just a little confused. I don't want to lead you on, but—"

He crashes his mouth against mine and starts kissing me again. *What the hell is he doing?* I push against his shoulders, but I'm only pushing myself deeper into the bed. I feel his hand run up my inner thigh and between my legs. I gasp for air, but I feel like I can't get enough into my lungs. I jerk my head back and forth and manage to roll onto my side. The weight is gone. Taking a deep breath, I look at Jack who is sitting on his knees in the middle of the bed.

"What the fuck is wrong with you?" I shout as I stand up on my shaky legs.

Laughing at me, he says, "You can stop with the good-girl act, Candace." He says my name like it's dripping in disdain. He climbs off of the bed and starts walking towards me. "I just can't figure you out, and it's starting to frustrate me. I like you, but I get the feeling like you're playing me."

"I'm not. I'm just . . . I don't know. I just don't think this is going to go anywhere," I say as I stare at the floor.

Jack tightly grips my shoulders with both of his hands, pushing me backwards. I stumble a little when we hit the wall. My body turns cold, and I feel the skin on my neck prickling. I'm getting nervous, and my heartbeat quickens. *What is he doing? Is he pissed? Shit, I just want to leave.* I just want to go home and pretend this night never happened. It's been weird from the start, and it's only getting worse.

"Oh, no? And why's that? You must think it's funny to lead me on. Is this how you get your kicks?" He is inches from me when he speaks, his breath hot on my face.

My shoulders are trembling under his hands, and I feel the lump in my throat growing bigger, which is making it hard for me to breathe.

"I'm not jerking you around, I swear. Listen, I'm not good at this stuff. It's not you." My voice is shaky, and I hate that.

He pushes his body up against me and buries his face in my neck. I gasp for air and let out a whimper. I don't want to cry, but my emotions are all over the place right now. He thrusts his hips against mine, and that is my undoing. Tears flow down my cheeks, and I'm pushing my hands against his chest, but he won't budge.

"Jack, stop! What are you doing?" I am freaking out as he completely smothers me. Fisting my hands, I start smashing them into his chest, trying to get him off of me. I can barely see through my tears, and I wind up punching his lip. He takes a step back and wipes his mouth. It's bleeding. He looks up at me with a murderous glare, and I know he's about to lose it. I bolt for the door and run.

My heart is pounding against my ribs, and I struggle to breathe as I run down the stairs. Bumping shoulders with people in the crowded living room and stumbling over my shaky feet, I find the door that leads out to where Jack's car is.

I notice I don't have my wristlet purse that has my cell phone in it. There is no way I'm going back inside though. I quickly decide to just walk home and deal with the purse situation later. It won't take long for me to get home if I cut through behind a few buildings. I walk fast and try to grasp what just happened, but I can't clear my head enough to focus. My heart is starting to slow, and the tears return. I am overwhelmed, and I think it is so much more than what just happened with Jack. Confusion doesn't even begin to describe my current state of mind.

"Candace! Wait!" I hear Jack's voice calling from behind me.

I turn to see my tiny gold purse clutched in his hand, but fear creeps over me, and suddenly, I don't care about the stupid purse anymore. I run.

I run fast.

I hear his feet pounding against the ground, and I know he's running after me. *FUCK!* I will my legs to move faster but they won't. My throat is on fire, and I can't breathe. I don't turn around to see, but I know he's close. My whole body is burning with panic. Quickly, I cut behind a building and suddenly feel an intense stinging as the side of my face slides against the pavement. Jack is flipping me over onto my back while I desperately claw my nails into the road, pleading to break free from his grip on me. The flesh on my cheek burns as he slaps me across the face. I can't see. *Why can't I see?* I force out a weak scream and am instantly muffled by his hand.

"Shut the fuck up," he violently snarls in my face.

I can barely make out his face with the tears that flood my eyes. I squeeze them shut because they are burning intensely. My body is weighed down, and I can't move beneath him. I'm not sure what's happening, but the terror rushing through me is frightening.

He reaches down, rips open my jeans, and starts yanking on them. I try and kick my legs uncontrollably, but he's sitting on them. Somehow, he manages to pull them off of one of my legs, as he releases his hand from my mouth.

"Plea-hease. Stop!" I scream, and he quickly clamps his hand back over my mouth. I desperately try to bite him, but I'm too frantic. I'm sobbing and barely breathing. It takes everything I have to choke out any sounds. But, it's no use. I hysterically pound my fists as hard as I can against him, but he won't stop. *God, please stop!*

Grabbing the neck of my shirt, he jerks down, tearing the soft worn fabric too easily. With everything I have in me, I try to lock my knees together, but he's so much more powerful than me when he knees my thighs and forces them open. Consumed by rampant fear, I fight as hard as I can, screaming against his hand. I feel him pulling my bra down, and my breast begins to burn. I'm in such a panic when I realize that he is biting me. Shrieking in desperation as the pain shoots down to my belly, I dig my nails into his arms in response to the pain.

"Bitch!" He shouts through clenched teeth as he pulls back and backhands me across my face. The blood pools in my mouth, and my body heaves as I begin to choke on it through my cries. *Somebody help me!* The fabric of my underwear cuts into my skin and stings when he rips them off of me. "You're not gonna fuckin' tease me anymore, bitch."

He pins my wrists above my head with his large hand, and my body shakes in horror when I realize that I'm completely helpless. *God, please don't do this!*

I manage to let out another choked sob as I frantically try to jerk my body from underneath him, but my muscles are so weak, and the weight of him is too much for me to fight. He's so heavy on me. I wail when I feel a sudden burn as he violently rips and pounds into me. My whole body locks up.

What's happening?

Is this happening?

God, is this happening?

Is this really happening?

My head falls to the side, and my body goes limp aside from the involuntary twitches from each of his assaults. I focus every ounce of strength I have left on the corner of the dumpster that's next to me. It's painted dark blue, but maybe it's a lighter blue during the daylight. I can tell it's been painted five or six times . . . I can see every layer. It's chipping away, and the dark grey metal from underneath is exposed. The line along the chipped paint is ridged and there is a thin vein of white between the blue and grey. Gritty dirt clings to the wheel, and the wheel lock is beginning to rust. The dumpster is worn and full of dents . . . one . . . two . . . three . . . four . . . five . . . six . . .

I snap out of my thoughts when Jack grabs my chin and forces me to look at him. "Tell me you like this," he taunts, and my sobs are excruciating as I feel his body jerk into mine, and he stills himself, grunting loudly.

He yanks his pants up and starts running his hand down my naked torso. *What else does he want from me?*

"You're nothing but a cunt," he lashes when he abruptly jabs his fingers inside of me and then spits in my face.

I begin to yell and thrash my body, fighting to escape. "God, please! Stop!"

He lifts up, and suddenly, I see a flash of light that is devoured by darkness and silence.

chapter six

WHERE AM I? Why can't I see? I hurt.
   I try and move but something is holding me down. I feel my body rattling on something hard, and I sense that I am moving.
   Am I dreaming? I'm so confused. What's happening?
   I feel like I'm in a car or something, but I can't move.
   Why can't I move?!
   I'm panicking. I can feel it, feel my heart beating harder and louder.
   Open your eyes, Candace. Focus—open your eyes.
   "Miss?" I hear a man say.
   Someone's here. Help me! Wake me up!
   "Try and relax, Miss. We're almost there."
   Where? What's happening? Someone fucking help me!! Where am I?!
   Sheer fright shoots through me, and I feel the strain in my eyes as they start to open. I squeeze them shut immediately because they burn. I start to feel my body come to life and wriggle my wrists, but something is holding them down. I'm terrified and turn frantic as I keep trying to free my arms. The wriggling quickly turns into erratic jerks. I'm strapped down and I'm terrified.
   "Help me! Get me out of here!" I shriek out in a hoarse voice. I try to move my head, but I can't. I feel something is wrapped around my neck preventing me from moving.
   "It's okay, we're almost there. You're in an ambulance. You were knocked unconscious. We're on our way to the hospital."
   I try and open my eyes, but they still sting. I blink several times when I feel a damp cloth cover them. I start crying at the calming feel of the cool wet cloth. He presses it down gently on my eyes and forehead, then wipes softly.
   "Try opening your eyes," the man says.
   I do as I'm told, and he wipes one more time. After a few seconds the sting starts to subside.
   "You have a lot of dirt and sweat that has gotten into your eyes."
   Blinking a few more times, I start to focus on the man hovering over

me. I keep trying to move, but I can't get my limbs free.

"Just try and relax," he says in a soothing voice. "You are strapped down to a backboard and are wearing a neck brace until we can assess your injuries."

I stare up at the bright white light that is above me in the cab of the ambulance and focus on my breathing.

What just happened? Is this even real?

"Miss, how do you feel? Can you tell me if anything hurts?" he asks.

How do I feel? I don't know how I feel. I don't even know what the hell just happened. I feel scared and numb. I feel everything and nothing all at once. I feel like this is a dream—a very, very bad dream that I can't wake up from. I don't understand. I'm so confused. Fear and misery rip through me and create a new emotion that I can't even begin to describe. My heated tears roll continuously down the side of my face as I remain staring at the white light.

"Miss?"

"I don't know," is all I can manage to say, my only attempt at a response to his very confusing question.

I move my eyes downward to look at my body, and I am covered in a grey wool blanket. Suddenly, I remember that I am naked beneath this blanket. Embarrassment wells up inside of me, and I begin to sob uncontrollably.

"I want to go home!" I choke out. "I want to go home!!" I barely recognize my own voice. The panic I hear in myself is frightening.

We stop abruptly, and the smell of fresh air envelops the ambulance as the doors to the cab open. As I am rolled out, I watch the white light move up and over the top of my head. I want to cover my face with my hands, but they are still strapped down. I start choking on short breaths between sobs. *Where are they taking me? What's going to happen?* I feel completely out of control, and I live for control.

There is a lot of noise and people chattering while I am being wheeled into the hospital. I'm finding it hard to hear what they are saying over my crying and heaving breaths. But the whole world stops moving when I hear that unmistakable word. *Don't say that word.* I can't move. I can't blink. I can't do anything. This isn't me. This can't be me.

I am wheeled into a private exam room, and there are several nurses moving around and checking the IV that must have been put in place while I was unconscious. My legs and arms are finally unstrapped, but I no longer feel the need to move. I just lie there. Still. One of the nurses stands by me and asks, "Ma'am, my name is Allie. I need to ask you some basic questions. Is that okay?"

I nod my head.

"Can you tell me your name?"

I look at the nurse and she looks to be in her thirties. She's pretty, with a short blonde bob and almost emerald eyes. Her scrubs are green, which make her eyes appear extremely vibrant. She has flawless makeup, especially her black eyeliner. The stethoscope's cord that hangs around her neck is hot pink, and I figure that outside of work, she must have a flair for style. I don't really know, I'm just imagining.

I feel my hand warm, and I look down to see that she is now holding it. I look back up at her green eyes. "Candace," I whisper.

Taking her hand from mine, she starts writing on the clipboard she is holding.

"Last name?"

"Parker."

She continues through the questions as she fills out my chart with all of my information. When she finishes, she tells me that she is going to call another nurse who handles cases like mine to come in and talk with me.

"Would you like to call anyone?" she asks me.

I shake my head no. I don't want to talk to anyone. How would I even begin to explain this?

"Would you like me to call someone for you? Sometimes it's easier if you have a friend here with you."

Looking up at Allie, my eyes begin to fill with tears again. I do want my friend here. I want him here so badly, but I am so embarrassed. What will I even say? All I know is that I want Jase here.

"You'll call for me?" I ask, my voice shaky.

"Of course," she says softly.

"Jase. You can call Jase," I say. I give her his number, and she leaves the room.

I am only alone for a few minutes when a doctor wearing a white coat enters my room, along with another nurse who is carrying a white cardboard box. She sets it down on a table, walks over to me, and stands next to the doctor who is holding a steel box clipboard and is looking at it intently. When she looks up at me, she says, "Hello, Ms. Parker, I'm Dr. Langston. I am ordering a CT scan to rule out any evidence of a cerebral hemorrhage and a set of x-rays to be certain you don't have any fractures or broken bones."

I hear her words, but nothing makes sense to me. So I just lie there while tears stream down my temples and into my hair.

She sets the clipboard down, walks over to me, and assesses my face. She shines a small flashlight into each of my eyes then steps away as she puts the light back into the pocket on her white coat.

"This is Julia, and she is the Sexual Assault Nurse Examiner for the hospital. She's going to talk to you while we are waiting to run those scans, okay?" She says this all so matter-of-factly, and I'm not sure how to even react, so I just whisper, "Okay."

Dr. Langston proceeds to walk out of the room and closes the door behind her.

"Hi, Candace," Julia says in a soft, pleasant tone. I wonder if they teach everyone here how to talk to people like me, because they all sound the same. Gentle, as if they could break me with their words. "I need to know if you want to complete a sexual assault evidence kit examination."

I feel my heart rate pick up and anxiety kicks in. "I'm sorry. What?" I ask.

"A rape kit," she says. "It is an exam that is used to collect DNA evidence." She continues to talk to me and goes into more explanation, but her voice becomes distant. How is this happening to me? I don't know what to do. I look back at Julia to see her looking at me, and she's no longer talking.

I shake my head and say, "I don't know. I . . . I don't know."

"How about if we just talk? Can I ask you a few questions about what happened tonight?"

"Okay," I say unsurely.

She picks up her clipboard and pen, and then asks, "Do you know who did this?"

I hesitate before answering, "Uh huh."

"Can you tell me his name?"

"Why? What's going to happen?" I'm extremely nervous, and I'm not sure how much I should say.

"Nothing will happen unless you want to press charges."

"I don't," I immediately say. God, I don't want anyone to know about this.

The door slowly opens, and Allie pops her head in as she quietly says, "Jase is here. Would you like me to send him in?"

"Does he know?" I ask. "Did you tell him?"

Stepping in, she closes the door behind her. She walks over and sits down on a chair that's next to me.

"No. All he knows is that you were brought here by ambulance," she says softly.

"I don't know what to say." I look at Allie with a pleading expression on my face. There is no way I can tell Jase. I mean . . . I want him to know, I just don't want to be the one who tells him.

Nodding her head, she says, "It's okay. We will help you. Would you like me to bring him in?"

"Can you talk to him? Alone?" I ask. I don't want to hear what she is going to say, and I definitely do not want to see his reaction when she tells him.

"If you want me to, I will. How much do you want me to tell him?"

"Everything," I say softly.

"Okay. I'll be back in a few minutes." Allie stands up and makes her way out of the exam room.

I let out a sigh, and Julia continues asking questions about what happened. I don't tell her Jack's name, but I go ahead and tell her everything that happened tonight, starting from my house. She asks me to go into detail about the attack. She wants to know every part of my body that was touched, all the places his saliva could possibly be, and the questions seem to go on forever.

I look up when the door opens again, and Jase is there. I fall apart when I see the horrified expression on his face, and he rushes over to me and wraps my head in his arms. He keeps kissing the top of my head and repeating that he loves me as sobs wrack through my body. I slowly start to calm down, and the tears begin to subside. Jase sits down and looks at Julia.

"So, what's going on? Is she okay?" he asks her while holding my hand.

"We have just completed the written account of the assault." She looks at me and continues, "The next step, if you choose, is to complete a physical exam to collect evidence. We can do this whether you choose to press charges or not."

I look at Jase and shake my head, not knowing what to do.

Jase looks back at her and asks, "What's the exam?"

The nurse picks up the same white cardboard box that I saw her walk in with. "This is the rape kit. There are sixteen different pieces of evidence we collect. You are in total control of the exam. You say 'stop,' we stop. I will explain each step as we go so you know exactly what to expect."

"How long will this take?" I ask.

"It can take around four to six hours."

"What?! No," I say to her. I look back at Jase with wide eyes and sternly repeat, "No."

"Candace, I really think you should do it. I get that you're scared right now, but maybe in a few days you might feel differently about this." He turns and asks Julia, "If she does this exam, then what?"

"If she decides to press charges, we will hand over the kit to the police. If not, we keep the kit here. If she changes her mind about prosecuting, then at that time, we will hand the kit over to the criminal lab."

Jase squeezes my hand, "I'm right here. I think you should do this, sweetie." I have never seen this look on Jase before. I know he loves me, and I can trust him. I nod my head, and I fight back the tears that are threatening to spill over.

"Since the doctor has ordered a CT scan and x-rays, we will need to wait until after those tests are run. When you get back, we will begin the exam." She gives me a concerned look as she continues, "I want to let you know what to expect when you are taken for those tests. The nurses and techs will refrain from touching you as much as possible. I want you to try and stay calm and still. They will move you to and from this gurney by lifting the sheet that is underneath you. Okay?"

Nodding my head, I respond, "Okay."

"The scans shouldn't take that long, but your friend will have to stay here."

I look up at Jase before looking back at Julia, and ask, "He can't come with me?"

Shaking her head gently, she says, "No, I'm sorry."

Jase assures me that it will be okay, and all I can do is trust him. But I'm scared to be alone, even if it is for a little while. Feeling like I have lost control is making me very upset, when Dr. Langston returns to tell me they are ready to take me back.

When I am wheeled back into the exam room, both Julia and Jase are there waiting for me.

"You okay?" Jase asks as he comes to stand next to me.

"Yeah."

Julia picks up the white box and opens it, pulling out several white envelopes and lays them down on one of the stainless steel carts that are in the room. "We are going to start by collecting your clothes, okay?"

"Okay."

She walks to the private bathroom, and when she comes out she says, "Candace, I need for you to carefully remove all of your clothing, including your jewelry. I have laid down a large sheet of paper that is there to collect any evidence that may fall off of your clothes or body. Just stand on the paper while you undress, hand me each article of clothing as you remove it, and I will place each piece in a separate evidence bag. There is a hospital gown hanging on the door that you can change into."

"Do you want me to leave?" Jase asks.

I grab onto his arm tightly, "No. I don't want to be alone."

Jase nods and helps me off of the bed. I clutch onto the wool blanket that is still covering me, and I walk into the bathroom. I hand the blanket to Julia and step onto the paper that is lying on the floor. I look down at my body and start to cry. My shirt and bra are ripped and hanging off my shoulders. I quickly notice that I am bare from the waist down.

I jerk around and frantically ask, "What happened to my pants?"

"The EMTs collected them. We already have them."

I nod and look up at Jase as my body trembles.

"It's okay," he reassures me.

I slowly remove my tattered clothing and hand each piece to the nurse. The paper beneath my feet crumples with every movement as if it's taunting me as a continuous reminder of the misery I feel. The last item I remove is my necklace, and I watch as it is placed inside a ziplock evidence bag. When I turn to pick up the hospital gown, I catch my reflection in the mirror. My body freezes as I observe the face staring back at me.

My left eye is bruised and swollen and the whole side of my face is scratched and covered in dried blood and dirt. My eyes are bloodshot and puffy from all the crying. I hardly recognize myself. I turn away from my image in the reflection, slip on the hospital gown, and step off of the paper.

I walk straight into Jase's arms, and I let him hold me for a while as I hear Julia moving around the room. Jase rests his chin on the top of my head and runs his hands up and down my back. My arms are clutched tightly around his waist as I bury my face in his chest.

"Candace," I hear Julia say softly, "whenever you are ready, I need you to have a seat on the exam table behind the curtain."

I slowly pull away from Jase and lean the top of my head against him as I stare down at my bare feet. I realize I have no clothes here, and I look up at Jase and say, "I don't have anything to wear."

"When the nurse called me, she told me to bring clothes with me. They are in my backpack," he says.

I walk across the room and sit on the exam table, never letting go of Jase's hand. I go into a haze when the nurse begins to explain each procedure. I just nod my head as I feel cold metal digging under my finger nails; I don't watch anything in particular because I don't want to see what's happening. Everything feels like it's miles away from me. She begins swabbing my neck, my ears, my mouth, my breasts, my thighs.

When I lie back on the table, she begins to take samples. My body is being poked and prodded—everywhere. Turning my head, I begin to zone in on a tiny piece of thread that is beginning to unravel from Jase's shirt. I focus in on the tiny little holes that the thread used to occupy that are now hollowed.

I suddenly become very cold. My knees begin to quiver, and my heart is pounding. I look down and over my knees. I see Julia's lips moving as she is talking to me, but I can't seem to focus in on her voice. I watch as she opens yet another white envelope and pulls out a small black plastic comb. Jerking my feet out of the stir-ups, I clumsily shuffle myself back on the table and sit up. Pure panic. That is all I can feel. Panic.

"Enough!" I shout. I feel like I am losing control of myself, and I desperately want everything around me to stop. "Get out!" I yell at Julia as she looks at me in shock. I can almost taste the venom in my voice. "Stop touching me, and get the hell out!"

"Candace. Calm down, sweetie," Jase says. His eyes are wide, and I can tell he is freaked out.

"I'll be right outside," the nurse says, and she quickly places the sealed envelopes in the box and leaves the room.

I draw my knees up to my chest. "I want to go home."

"What happened?"

"I want my clothes, Jase," I say as I look him straight on.

He doesn't say a word; he simply walks over to his backpack that is lying on the ground next to the chair. When he picks it up, I see the door crack open.

"Candace, Detective Patterson needs to ask you a few questions," Allie says. "Can I send him in?"

"Can she at least get dressed first?" Jase answers for me.

"Of course," she says, and she gently closes the door behind her.

Jase walks over to me and sets the bag in front of me. Grabbing it, I walk into the bathroom. I pick up a hand towel that is folded up on the cold sterile counter and turn on the faucet. I soak the towel in warm water and begin to clean my face. I suck in a tight breath between my teeth at the stinging of the opened flesh on my face. I do my best to wipe the grime off. Taking a new towel, I pat my face dry. I slip off my gown and start putting on my bra and underwear. When I finish dressing, I walk back into the room, and Jase is standing next to some guy. He appears to be around my father's age. He is tall and fit with short greying hair. He's wearing charcoal slacks and a navy button up dress shirt with the sleeves rolled up toward his elbows. I notice a shiny gold badge that is clipped to the waistband of his pants. He looks up at me and takes a step forward.

"Ms. Parker," he says. "I'm Detective Patterson. Do you mind if I ask you some questions?"

Shaking my head slightly, I ask, "Right now?"

"Yes, ma'am."

"I've already told the nurse everything. Why can't you just ask her?" I am so exhausted and am starting to lose my patience. I just want to leave. "Look, I don't want to press charges or anything like that, so . . ."

"Ma'am, I know this is difficult, but there's a good chance we can catch this guy and the fact that we have a witness—"

"What?" I interrupt him.

"Yes, they called the police."

My mind is in overdrive, and I feel myself shutting down. "I just want to go," I say, barely whispering.

"Well, if you change your mind, here is my card. You can call me at anytime, okay? You might find that you feel differently once a little time has passed." He steps towards me, pulls out a card from his back pocket, and hands it to me. I don't even look at it before shoving it into my pocket. He takes a step back and nods his head, "Well, thanks for your time." He turns to look at Jase and reaches out his hand. Jase shakes his hand and gives him a nod in return.

As Detective Patterson is leaving, Allie comes back with a tray of bandages, ointment, and other small items I can't quite identify.

"I'm just going to clean up and bandage these cuts for you, okay?"

I silently nod my head and return to the table to sit down. I watch her as she washes her hands and puts on a pair of sterile latex gloves. She starts cleaning my wounds and covers them up. Once she is finished, she asks me if I want to take the morning after pill. My eyes dart to hers as I quickly try to think if I really need it. I feel my stomach hollow out, and I suddenly turn cold. *He didn't use a condom. Christ, he didn't use a condom.*

I whisper softly, "I think so." I can hardly move, let alone speak.

I hear Jase mutter an obscenity, and when I turn my head to look at him, he is sitting in the chair with his head in his hands.

"Okay, I will put in the order for that, and we can also take a few other preventive steps to safeguard against STDs," she says as she lays her hand on my knee. She gives me a reassuring look, and all I can do is continue to nod my head like an idiot.

About an hour later, Jase has his arm around my waist as we leave the hospital and head to his SUV. He unlocks the car and opens the door for me. He helps me up into the seat and shuts the door. I watch him in a daze as he walks around the front of the car and climbs into the driver's seat. I start to feel the anxiety build in my stomach at the thought of going home. I know when I get there I'm going to have to explain all of this to Kimber. God, I don't want anyone to know. I just want to pretend like this never happened. I want to hide from this nightmare.

"Can I spend the night at your place?" I ask as I stare at my fidgeting hands in my lap.

He reaches over, takes my hand, and gives it a squeeze. "Of course."

chapter seven

I WALK INTO Jase's apartment, and without a second thought, head straight toward the bathroom. I feel completely filthy, and the urge to scrub every inch of my body overwhelms me. I don't say a word to Jase as I close the door behind me. Reaching into the shower, I turn on the water. Purposely avoiding looking at myself in the mirror, I start removing my clothes. The bathroom quickly fills with steam. I open the large glass door and step into the scalding hot water. Standing underneath the showerhead, I let the water pelt against my body. I brace both of my hands against the wall of slick tile and let my head fall down. My face is hot, and I know I'm crying even though I can't feel my tears as they mesh with the water running down my face.

Time is frozen as I stand here in this position. My chest aches, and my whole body feels broken. My stomach burns, and I swear to God I can start to feel my soul begin to break. Piece by piece I begin to lose myself. My chest is crumbling into painful shards of what used to be me. Violent sobs wrack my body, and I slowly collapse on the wet tile beneath me. Sitting there on my knees, with one hand on the floor balancing myself, and the other pressed against my chest, I try desperately to gasp in breaths between my wails.

I know I am no longer alone when I feel arms wrapping around me and a heavy chest on my back. Jase holds me tighter than anyone has ever held me, and I begin to cry harder. I sit here, on the bottom of the shower, and everything I know about myself, everything I love, everything I am begins to fade.

My tears run dry, and Jase and I sit in silence under the water. He loosens his hold on me, and I continue to rest on my knees—frozen. Jase takes the body wash and starts to rub it into my skin. All of my energy has disappeared, so I don't protest; I just let him take care of me.

After he washes my hair, I open my eyes and look at him for the first time. He is soaking wet in his gym shorts and t-shirt. He turns the water off and strips out of his clothes, leaving them on the floor of the shower as he steps out. Wrapping a towel around his waist, he grabs another and drapes it over my shoulders as he helps me stand up. He walks me over to the toilet and sits me down.

"I'll be right back," he says as he walks out of the bathroom. When he returns, he is wearing a pair of dry gym shorts and is carrying a handful of clothes for me. Grabbing a hand towel, he kneels down in front of me and starts wiping my face. I look into his eyes, and I can see the worry in them. I reach up and rake my fingers through the wet hair on top of his head and grip tightly as I drop my head and begin to cry again.

"I'm so sorry," I manage to say through my tears.

He takes my hand from his head and kisses it. Leaning his forehead against mine and holding my face between his two hands, he says, "You ... don't you ever be sorry for this."

We sit like this for a while before he dries me off and helps me put on one of his shirts and a pair of his boxers. We walk to his room and slide into bed. Wrapping me in his arms, I lay my head on his chest and listen to the rhythmic sound of his heartbeat. I release a silent prayer that when I wake up, this will have never happened—it will have only been a horrendous nightmare. I hold on tightly to that prayer as my eyelids become heavy, and I slowly drift into a restless sleep.

I jolt awake and can hardly catch my breath. My hands are shaking, and when I look up, I see Jase on his knees next to me.

"Are you okay?" he asks, looking completely freaked out.

"I don't know," I say. I'm really confused, and my heart is pounding. "What happened?"

Jase lets out a deep breath as he falls back on his heels, sitting next to me. "You were having a nightmare. You scared the shit out of me, screaming and thrashing around."

"I'm sorry. I don't even know what I was dreaming about," I say as a slowly lie down on my side and try to calm my erratic breathing.

Lying down facing me, Jase asks, "How are you feeling?"

"Numb," I answer and close my eyes. Maybe I cried out all the emotions I had, because I can't seem to feel much right now. When I open my eyes, Jase is staring at me with concern written all over his face. I really wish he wouldn't look at me like that; it makes me feel weird, like I'm suddenly different now. I know that I am, but can we just pretend that I'm not?

"What time is it?" I ask.

He rolls on his back, reaches over to his nightstand, and swipes his phone. "It's almost three in the afternoon," he says as he rolls back to me.

"Three?"

"Yeah, we didn't even leave the hospital till after five this morning," he says, and then reaches his arms out as a request to hold me. I scoot over and allow the embrace. He kisses the top of my head before asking, "Do you want to talk about it?"

I haven't spoken one word to Jase about what happened last night. I'm not sure I can. But I know that I don't want to. I swallow hard against the lump in my throat and simply shake my head. How am I supposed to talk about it? What do I even say?

The tears start to well in my eyes; the tears I thought I no longer had. It's hard to fight them with the tightness in my throat. Jase must feel my body trembling when he kisses the top of my head and whispers, "I'm sorry, sweetie. I didn't mean to push you."

As the tears spill over, I silently curse my unanswered prayer. I try hard not to cry, but it only makes my body jerk as I try and hiccup the sobs back. Jase moves one of his hands up from my back, cups my head, and whispers in my ear, "Please don't hurt yourself like this, Candace. Just let it out. It's just me here."

I shove my head harder and deeper into his chest as a desperate attempt to hide. Hide from the cloud that is suddenly looming over me. He tightens his grip on me, and I let it out. I lie against his chest and just cry. I cry like a baby—helpless. I'm so desperate for someone to save me. To make it all go away.

The heat of Jase's bare chest against my wet, teary face suddenly makes my skin burn. I push back off of him and cup my cheek, unable to stop the free-flowing tears. He removes my hand and looks at the cuts on my face.

"I'll be right back, sweetie," he says as he jumps out of bed. I hear him in the bathroom, and when he returns, he's holding a large square bandage and some ointment. He sits on the bed in front of me and starts tending to the scratches on my face. Once he is done, he adheres the bandage to my cheek, then walks to his closet, and throws on a t-shirt.

"You hungry?" he asks.

"No," I say as I shake my head and lie back down. "I just want to go back to bed."

Walking towards me, he says, "You really should eat. Just try."

I lie there with my eyes closed. "Please, Jase."

He doesn't say another word. He simply crawls back into bed behind me and holds me until I fall asleep.

Drifting in and out, I'm finding it hard to shut my brain off. Every time I close my eyes I picture Jack on top of me. The more I try and fight the thoughts, the more vivid they become. He's right here with me, right here inside my head. I close my eyes again, and I can hear the ripping of my shirt as Jack fists the fabric. I quickly sit up in the bed and grab my breast where he bit me. I can feel the sharp pain shooting through me again. *Why can't he leave me alone? Why can't I get away from him?* My gut is in knots, and I am shaking. I jump out of bed, run to the bathroom, and empty the contents of my stomach into the toilet. Since I haven't eaten in over a day, there's hardly anything left in me. I begin dry heaving painfully. My whole body is convulsing, and tears are streaming down my face. I close my eyes, and I see Jack's murderous glare as he's ripping off my underwear. I hear frantic screams. My mind is in overdrive, and I can hardly focus, but the screams are piercing. I cover my ears and shuffle back into the corner on my bottom. I have no idea where all the noise is coming from, but it's scaring me.

Suddenly, the bathroom light turns on, and I see Jase run to me. He falls to his knees in front of me and grasps onto my wrists that are against my face. His lips are moving, but I can't hear him over the screaming. I try and focus on his lips to make out what he is saying, and his voice begins filtering through. I can hardly hear him when he says, "It's okay." I continue to focus and the more I do, the more I can hear him and less of the screams. "It's okay, Candace. I'm right here." He pulls me to him and slowly rocks me back and forth. The swaying feels soothing in the madness around me. As he whispers, "Shhh," into my ear, I realize that those screams I heard were coming from me. *How can I be so disoriented?* Terrified by what just happened, I feel myself being lifted off the floor. Jase scoops me up in his arms and carries me to the couch. I bury my head into his neck, fully embarrassed by what has just happened. I can barely comprehend it.

Setting me down, Jase walks into the kitchen and comes back with two bottles of water and a box of crackers. He twists the cap off of one of the bottles and hands it to me.

"Drink," he says.

I lift the bottle to my lips and take a slow sip. The water burns along my scratchy throat as I swallow it down.

I shift uncomfortably on the couch. My whole body is sore, and my back is badly bruised and scabbed over. It makes it nearly impossible to not think about what happened. I wish I could ignore it, but I can't because I hurt . . . *everywhere*. Sometimes when I move, I can feel the pain from his intrusion, and I want to throw up.

"What just happened?" he asks.

"I don't know. It felt like a nightmare, but I was awake," I say and take another drink.

Jase rests his elbows on his knees and clasps his hands together. Letting out a sigh, he says, "You scared the shit out me. I know you don't want to talk, but maybe . . ." He trails off as my phone rings.

"You have my phone?" I ask.

Standing up and walking to the kitchen bar, he says, "Yeah, the nurse at the hospital gave me your purse." He picks up my gold wristlet purse and hands it to me. I pull out my phone and swipe the screen to see that I have a few missed texts and a missed call from Kimber.

"Who was it?" Jase asks as he sits back down and starts opening the box of crackers.

"Kimber," I say, fiddling with my phone.

"You should call her, she's probably freaking out and wondering where you are," he says, as he eats a cracker.

"Maybe later." I set the phone down, lay my head back, and stare at the ceiling. I just want to hide here for a while longer. Maybe forever.

"She probably knows you're with me. She sent me a text earlier asking if I knew where you were. I figured you didn't want her to know just yet, so I didn't respond."

I let out a sigh, roll my head to the side, and look at Jase. I don't want Kimber to ask me any questions, but I know there is no way around that. One look at my face and she's going to flip. I can't hide all the cuts and bruises. I look like hell.

Jase holds a cracker up to my mouth and when I open it, he shoves the cracker in and gives me a smirk. Chewing it up, I turn my body and lie on my back with my head in his lap. I stare up at him and say, "I don't want anyone to know."

He looks down at me, starts brushing through my hair with his fingers, and says, "I know, but she's going to know that something happened. She's going to want to know how you got all these bruises."

"I don't know what to say."

"Why can't you tell her? You know she wouldn't say a word to anyone."

"I just can't. Even the way you look at me now is different." I sit up and turn to look at him. "It makes me feel weird. It just reminds me that it happened, when all I want to do is forget." I pull my knees up to my chest and lay my head on the back of the couch again.

Jase puts his hand on my knee and says, "You know you can't do that. It did happen."

The tears roll down my temples. "But why?" My voice is shaky as I speak. "I don't understand what I did that was so wrong."

Wiping away my tears with his thumb, he says, "You didn't do anything wrong."

"Then why did this happen to me?" I turn my head and look into his eyes, desperate for answers I know he doesn't have.

He shakes his head, and his eyes start to rim with tears. "I don't know, sweetie. But I do know that you didn't do shit to deserve this. This isn't your fault."

"But maybe it is. I mean, I really led him on when I had no intentions of . . ."

Jase cuts me off me off and snaps, "You mean Jack did this?!"

My whole body turns cold. *Oh shit! What is he going to do?* I quickly sit up and turn towards him. "Jase, you can't say anything," I plead in a stern voice.

"Christ, Candace. I thought it was just some random asshole. Why didn't you tell the police? Why didn't you say anything?"

"Because I can't. Everyone would know. Everyone, including my parents."

Jase rakes his hand through his hair, and I can tell he is pissed, which upsets me. I don't want him to be mad at me.

"Fuck," he spits out. Looking at me, I can see the rage in his eyes, and I start to panic. "I'm gonna kill that fucker."

"Jase!"

"What the hell happened?" he demands.

"Don't."

"Candace, you have to tell me."

"Please, don't." Slowly shaking my head, I begin to cry. I'm scared. Scared to talk. Scared of what Jase might do. Scared that people will find out.

Jase stands up and walks out to the balcony, slamming the door shut behind him. I sit in his living room, alone in the silence. The sun is starting to rise and Jase is leaning on his arms against the railing. I know he is pissed at me, which kills me inside. I can't stand to see him so mad and upset. I get up and make my way to his bedroom, leaving my phone on the couch.

I must have fallen asleep because when I open my eyes the room is bright. I sit up and look down at Jase who is sleeping next to me. I slip out of bed and make my way to the kitchen to get some water. I look at the clock and see that it's almost nine in the morning. I'm not too worried about the classes I missed yesterday or the ones I will most likely miss today. It's only the first week, so I know that classes are no more than discussing expectations for the quarter. But I'm worried about the fact that I missed my studio yesterday. I haven't looked at my face yet, but hopefully the swelling and bruising has gone down enough that I can attempt to cover it with makeup.

I open the fridge and grab a bottle of water. I twist off the cap and down the whole thing in a few large gulps. My head is throbbing slightly, so I begin to make a pot of coffee when I hear Jase come out of the bathroom. Scooping the coffee grounds, I look up at him as he walks into the kitchen. I don't say anything because I am unsure of his mood. I hope he understands where I'm coming from and isn't still mad at me.

He walks straight to me and turns me to face him. Cupping my cheeks with his hands, he says, "I'm sorry."

I can't find any words, so I simply nod my head. I notice his eyes are puffy and bloodshot before he pulls me in to hug me. I wrap my arms tightly around him and squeeze. It hurts to know that he must have been crying when he was out on the balcony earlier this morning. I press my head against his chest, and we just stand there, clinging to each other.

chapter eight

I SIT NERVOUSLY in Jase's car as we drive to my house. After coffee this morning, we decided that I would stay at his place for a few days. I emailed all of my professors and told them that I had gotten sick and wouldn't be attending class for the rest of this week. None of them seemed to mind. Knowing that I have always been dedicated to my classes in the past, no one even questioned me, not even my dance instructors.

I let out a sigh of relief as we pull up to the house and see that Kimber's car is gone. Giving Jase a kiss on the cheek, I thank him before hopping out and walking over to my car. We agreed that he would go in and get my things in case Kimber showed up. As I slide into my car and turn the key, guilt begins to wash over me. I feel like I'm lying to Kimber by avoiding her, but Jase is the only one who knows, and I'd like to keep it that way.

I call Roxy while I drive back to Jase's apartment and tell her the same thing I told my professors. I ask if I could have a few days off, and she doesn't even hesitate. Lying to everyone feels horrible, but I just can't tell them the truth.

Pulling up to the apartment, I hear my phone chime. I pick it up and read Jase's text.

Got everything you asked for and more. On my way now.

Thank you so much. See you in a bit.

I am in the bathroom putting more ointment on my face when I hear Jase walk in. Wiping off my hands, I make my way into his bedroom where he is unzipping the bags that have my toiletries, clothes, textbooks, and dance gear.

Looking up at me, he says, "I grabbed more clothes than what you had asked me to."

"Thanks," I say as I walk over to the bed. I start unpacking, hanging up my clothes, putting my makeup and other toiletries in the bathroom, and throwing my books and dance things in his closet. Jase sits on the bed and watches me as I move around his room. When I turn and look at him over my shoulder, he has that look in his eyes. The look I can't stand. The look that reaffirms the fact that I need to keep this private.

"Stop," I say.

"What?"

I walk over and sit down next to him on the bed. "Stop looking at me like that."

Lowering his head to stare at the floor, he says, "You know Kimber is going to flip when she comes home and sees that a bunch of your things are gone."

"I know," I sigh out as I lie back on the bed and close my eyes. "What am I going to tell her?"

Lying back and turning his head to look at me, he says, "We'll figure it out."

As we lie here, staring at each other with no words, Jase holds my hand and laces his fingers through mine. This simple gesture comforts me in a way that only Jase can do. We have always been very affectionate with each other, but it has never felt weird. It was our natural chemistry from the moment we met our freshman year. And now, I feel like he is my only lifeline.

I lift up slightly and rest my head on his chest, and he wraps me in his arms. We decide, without spoken words, to remain in bed for the afternoon and nap. But just before I am about to doze off, I hear someone enter the apartment. Before I can sit up, Mark appears in the doorway of the bedroom.

I notice a shift in his eyes as he says, "Oh my God."

I think for a moment that maybe he is upset that I'm cuddling in bed with his boyfriend, but that thought is quickly replaced with anxiety when he asks, "What the hell happened to your face, honey?"

Shit! I quickly try to cover what he has clearly already seen with my hands. Turning to Jase, I see he is already sitting up next to me, looking at me with the same worry that I feel. Mark's eyes dart back and forth between Jase and I as we sit there, not knowing what to say because we never got around to discussing it.

"Um, hey. I'm sorry, but could you give us just a minute?" Jase asks.

Mark looks at me and then back at Jase before responding. "Yeah, man. Sure, I'll just be in the other room."

Mark turns and closes the door behind him, giving Jase and me some privacy.

"Shit, I'm so sorry," I say as I rake my fingers through my hair.

"What for?"

"I don't know, for having your boyfriend see us in bed together."

"Don't worry about it. I talk about you all the time. He knows how we are; it doesn't bother him," he says, reassuring me. He shifts his body to face me and continues, "Candace, I don't know what to do here. I just got back together with Mark, and I can't lie to him."

I stare at him for a long while. We sit there, looking into each other's eyes, and we don't say a word. I can't be selfish with Jase; I love him too much, and I know how happy he is to be with Mark again. But I can't help to be terrified out of my mind. I lower my head and look down before I hesitantly nod.

Lifting my chin with his finger, he says, "Mark would never say anything. He isn't like that, Candace."

I am so scared and begin to cry at the thought of anyone else knowing. Jase wipes my tears and leans his forehead against mine.

"Don't cry," he whispers.

"I'm so embarrassed."

Pulling me into his arms, he sighs, "I know you are, sweetie, but you shouldn't be."

He continues to hold me as my crying grows stronger. I bury my head in his neck and let it pour out of me as I feel him slowly rocking me back and forth. I don't know how long I've been crying when I feel the bed dip down next to me and another hand on my back. I know that it's Mark, and now I'm even more embarrassed that I can't even look up. So I just stay there, in Jase's arms, and cry.

As the tears start to slow and my body grows tired, Jase slowly pulls away. Fixing his eyes on mine with his eyebrows knitted together, I feel the bed shift again. I turn my head to see that Mark is kneeling beside the bed in front of me. I look down at him as he stares at me with nothing but concern. I'm no longer crying, but the tears keep falling, and I don't know how to stop them.

He takes my hand before speaking. "Who did this?"

It's pretty obvious that this didn't happen by some accident by the way I was just sobbing for what felt like an hour. I can't find any words though. I no longer feel the intense anxiety; I feel defeated. So, I just continue to stare at him.

Jase clears his throat before I hear him say, "Um . . . Candace was attacked Monday night."

Hearing those words knocks the air out of me, and I lower my elbows to my knees and hide my face in my hands. Jase never takes his hand off of my back, but I now feel two more hands on my legs.

"What happened?" Mark asks.

I hear Jase let out a long sigh, and I start shaking my head in my hands. I know he's about to say it. I'm scared to hear the words I know are coming any second. My body turns cold, and I tense up as I try desperately to hold onto the sob that is threatening to escape my chest.

Jase slides his hand up my back to my shoulder and squeezes tightly.

"She was raped."

I feel Mark's forehead fall to my knees, and the pain I was trying so hard to contain suddenly rips out of me, and I can do nothing but sob. My body begins to jerk when it becomes difficult to breathe.

The three of us sit there and cling to each other. How the hell did this become my life? I am not a weak person. I am strong and hold my emotions tight. I hardly recognize the weakness that is pouring out of me. Defeat. I am so tired and worn out. Exhausted.

I wipe my eyes with the backs of my hands as I take in a slow shaky breath and let it out slowly. Looking up, I see Marks eyes staring into mine.

"I won't say anything, if you were worried about that."

I nod my head. "I'm so tired," I say, not knowing what else to say really.

"I told her she could stay here for a few days," Jase tells Mark. "She doesn't want anyone to know, and if Kimber saw her face, she would question her."

"I think that's a good idea," Mark responds, then looks at me and says, "I know we don't know each other that well, but I am here if you ever need me. I feel like I know you well by how much Jase speaks of you. The both of us are always here for you."

I nod my head and say, "Thanks."

We sit in the living room and eat a late lunch. After my embarrassing breakdown, Mark offered to go and pick up some Chinese food. While he was gone, I took another quick shower. I have been taking a lot of those in the past few days. There's something about the hot water against my skin. It makes me feel clean, but only for a short while.

"I've gotta get out of this apartment," I say as I pick up an egg roll and take a huge bite. With my emotions running on high and the lack of sleep, my hunger finally caught up with me.

"Okay. What did you have in mind?" Jase asks.

"I don't know. Some place quiet."

"Why don't we go to my house? Change of scenery," Mark says while twirling a fork full of lo-mein.

I look at Mark and say, "Perfect."

We sit there quietly and continue to eat our greasy food when I hear my phone ring. I walk over to the bar and see that it's Kimber calling. Suddenly nervous, I let it continue to ring until it goes to voicemail.

"Who's that?" Jase asks.

I turn around to look at him and answer, "Kimber." Before I can set the phone down, it chimes with a text from her.

I'm starting to wonder if you're mad at me. Where's your stuff?

I don't respond. Instead, I turn my phone off and leave it on the counter.

"The more you ignore her, the worse it's gonna get," Jase says, picking up his plate and walking into the kitchen.

I watch him as he starts to rinse off his dish in the sink. "Drop it, please. Can we just forget? Just for today?"

The truth is, I don't want to drop it just for today. Call me the Queen of Avoidance, but I hate dealing with issues head on. I get really anxious and nervous, so I tend to just ignore and let things slide. But I know this isn't going to just disappear. And Jase is right: the longer I wait, the worse it will be. I just don't have it in me right now.

After lunch, we hop into Mark's car and head over to his house, first stopping to pick up some beer at the store. I stay in the car with Mark while Jase goes in. I'm very self-conscious about the scratches on my face, so I'd rather avoid public places.

Mark lives right off campus in a small house. After the fiasco with his roommate and Jase, Mark kicked him out and got another roommate. Mark assured me he wouldn't be home though.

The patio in the backyard is surprisingly large, so we decide to relax outside and drink for the afternoon. I'm not in the mood to talk, so I just listen to Mark and Jase. I begin to tune them out as I start on my second beer. Sitting back in my chair with my eyes closed, I enjoy the heat of the sun on my face. I keep dozing in and out of a light sleep, and I can faintly hear the boys talking about Mark's band and how they just got a new gig to play this weekend at a local bar. I have never heard them play before, but they seem to be popular around UW.

"Hey, Candace?"

Squinting my eyes against the bright sun, I look over at Jase. "Kimber just texted me."

Closing my eyes again, I say, "We're pretending, remember?"

And with that, the subject is dropped.

The next few days pass in a bit of a haze. Jase has classes during the day but stops by to check on me when he can. I spend most of my time in bed trying to sleep. Nights are rough. Something about the darkness. I have been having nightmares—bad nightmares. Jack is constantly in my dreams, tormenting me. I wake up in a state of confusion, screaming and crying; often having to run to the bathroom to throw up. I know I'm freaking Jase out, but he stays calm and holds me while I cry until I fall into another fit of sleep. He suggested that I call my doctor to see about getting on a sleeping pill. I will do just about anything to get Jack out of my head to get some rest. I'm exhausted, and it shows in my eyes.

By Sunday, the scratches on my face are hardly noticeable, which is a relief because I have to work this evening. I decide to go to the studio since I know it will most likely be empty, and I can have the place to myself. I haven't danced all week, and I'm hoping that being back in the studio will make me feel a little more normal. Before I leave the apartment, I put on some makeup just in case I run into anyone. I am able to cover up the light scars on my face pretty well now that the ugly scabs are gone.

I breathe a sigh of relief as I pull into the studio's parking lot and see that it's empty. I head inside and proceed with my normal routine. Once my pointes are tied up and I'm stretched, I plug my iPod into the stereo system and decide against the barre for some much needed center work. I start going through various adagio and turn combinations. As I begin working the floor, I am relieved when my mind begins to emancipate, as it always does when I dance. All I think about is my turnout, posture, port de bras, and lines. Gliding through my movements and hearing the thuds of my pointes against the wooden floor are therapeutic in a way. I listen to the music that fills the room and move through several combinations that I know by heart and repeat them over and over. I don't want this serene feeling to end, so I keep repeating the combinations. I feel surprisingly flawless for being out this past week, and I continue making my way through the different combinations.

A crash of thunder quickly brings me out of my euphoric state. I walk to one of the windows and look up into the sky to see dark clouds rolling in. I decide to pack up and head back to Jase's before the storm hits. Taking off my pointes, I powder them and my feet before sliding them into my flip-flops. I sling my bag over my shoulder, run out, and hop into my car. When I turn the key, I look at the time on my dash and am shocked when I realize I've been dancing for over two hours. I don't know how the time slipped away so fast.

As I drive, reality slowly starts creeping back in, and the weight in my chest returns. The thunder continues to rumble, and I feel like the weather fits my mood perfectly. The clouds open, and the rain begins to crash down on my windshield. I turn my wipers on high, but I struggle to see the road ahead. I pull into one of the empty parking lots on campus to wait until the rain lightens up. While sitting in the car, I listen to the rain beating violently against the steel.

For some reason, I get the urge to get out of my car. I open the door and step out into the rain. Closing the door, I lean against the car, and within seconds, I'm drenched. The beating of the raindrops against my delicate skin feels good, almost painful in a way—but good. I lean my head back and feel the pellets as they strike my face. I enjoy the biting sensation. With my eyes closed, I just stand there, wishing I could live here, in this vacant lot, alone, focusing on nothing more than the stinging pleasure of the storm as it batters me. Knowing that this will soon end, that the sun is lingering behind the clouds and I will be faced with the hell that is my life, my body slides down the side of my car, and I sit in a puddle of water on the dirty ground and cry.

Why didn't I fight more? Why did I just lie there? I am constantly replaying that night in my head, wondering what I could have done differently. What happened at the party that made his mood suddenly shift? I know that I led him on, and I shouldn't have. If only I could have just been honest with him from the start. Now I'm constantly haunted by his eyes, his voice, and the feel of his hands clamped around my mouth, keeping me from screaming.

He took so much from me. He took everything that wasn't his to take. I had only been with one guy, and that experience was far from a loving one. Preston was drunk off of keg beer, and the whole thing lasted less than a few minutes before he passed out on top of me. Why is this my life? Why did I allow this asshole to take all that was good in me? I feel like nothing.

When the rain lightens up, I drag myself off the ground and slide back into my car, leaving puddles of dirty water on my leather seats. I drive the rest of the way in a complete daze, feeling drained and emotionally exhausted.

I wander aimlessly into the apartment and head straight to the bathroom to strip out of my soggy clothes and grab some towels. I wrap one of them around me and lie down on the floor, enjoying the cold tile against my face. I savor the numbness I currently feel and drift off.

chapter nine

AFTER MY UNEXPECTED nap on the bathroom floor, I'm finishing up my makeup and getting ready to go to work. I have managed to pull myself together as much as possible to try and resume my normal routine, but the knots in my stomach won't seem to go away. I am nervous about seeing Roxy. I'm not sure what I will say if she notices the healing scars on my face. I think I have done a pretty decent job with my makeup, but I'm still nervous.

Walking out of the bathroom, I grab my purse and jacket then head out. Luckily, Jase hasn't been home today. I really needed the alone time. He and Mark are spending the day together, but they said they would be here when I get off work in a few hours.

Before I pull out of my parking space, I swipe my phone to see how many more missed calls and texts I have from Kimber. Her texts have turned rude and so have her voicemails. I really can't blame her though. Jase told me she came over the other afternoon when I was out running errands with Mark. She was pissed off and demanded to know where I was. Again, I told him to drop it, but I could tell he didn't want to. I don't want her mad at me, so I decide to finally send her a text.

Hey, I promise that I'm not mad at U. Just needed a little time away. Will explain later. Love U.

If only I knew what the hell I was going to explain. I know I have to resolve this quickly because I will be going back to our house in a few days, and I really don't need any more awkwardness.

Mark and I have been spending time together when he isn't in class. I can see why Jase loves him. They are alike in many ways, and we have bonded pretty effortlessly. He's wanted to stay over, but I am too embarrassed for him to witness the nightmares that seem to come every night.

As I drive to work, I listen to music and try my best to act normal. I'm not even sure what that is anymore, but I desperately crave it. I feel different, and I don't like it. When I pull up to Common Grounds, my nerves intensify. I haven't seen any of my other friends all week. Only Jase and Mark. Will Roxy be able to see right through me? Will she ask questions? My heart is racing, and I start taking slow deep breaths to calm myself. Getting out of my car, I walk straight in and towards the back to put my things away and get my apron. I pass Roxy, and she is busy helping a customer. When I reach the back room, I take a minute to try and pull myself together.

I take one last look at my face in the small compact mirror that's in my purse before walking back out. Looking around, I notice that the place is dead. I really wish we were busy so that my interaction with Roxy would be limited. I'm nervous and want nothing more than to get back into my car and drive to Jase's apartment. I walk slowly to one of the stools by the front counter and sit down.

"You feeling better?" Roxy asks.

Nervously, I lift my head and answer, "Yeah, thanks," hoping she can't see what I am hiding under my makeup.

"That's good. I missed having you up here." She walks over to sit beside me and continues, "So, I never did hear what happened with Jack."

My body turns cold when she says his name, and I blurt out, "What do you mean?"

"The party? You telling him you weren't interested?" she questions. "How did it go?"

"Oh, um . . . yeah, it was fine," I say, stumbling over my words and hoping that will be enough to satisfy her, but I know that it won't. I really want to be left alone right now. Maybe being normal isn't what I want because all I want to do right now is run back to the bubble I just came out of. It's safe there. No questions.

Roxy chuckles and says, "That's all I get? Girl, you were freaking out. Seriously, what happened?"

I suddenly feel my ears heat, and before I can stop myself, I snap at her, "Nothing, I already told you. Can we drop it?"

I immediately feel bad, but I can't do this. I stand up and walk straight back to the bathroom to try and compose myself. I lock the door behind me, and the tears are back. I quickly wipe them away and rest my hands on the sink. Staring at my reflection in the mirror, I start thinking about what excuses I could use to get out of here. How am I supposed to do this? I spend a few minutes settling my nerves before returning.

"I'm sorry," I whisper as I sit back down next to Roxy.

She slides me a coffee and says, "Here. It's okay. I won't mention it again."

"Thanks."

After about an hour, the place starts to pick up, and I enjoy the much needed distraction. It's been a little tense and uncomfortable as Roxy and I struggle for conversation. But now the place is full, and there is a line of customers. Roxy is working the register while I move about quickly, making various versions of lattes and espressos.

When the line dies down, I finally get a chance to lift my head and realize that it's dark outside.

"What time is it, Rox?" I ask while I begin wiping down the counters.

"A little after ten," she says over her shoulder as she is replacing the receipt tape in the register. When she finishes, she walks over and starts helping me wipe down the machines. We are both silent as we clean up and prepare to close.

When eleven o'clock rolls around, we shut everything down and lock up. Before I can head toward my car, Roxy pulls me in for an unexpected hug. The gesture makes my eyes prick with tears, but I quickly blink them away. When she pulls back, I can see concern in her eyes, and I know that she knows something is going on. How could she not? I have been acting weird all night.

"Have a good night, okay?"

"Thanks, you too," I say, trying to avoid eye contact.

We both walk to our cars, and in an attempt to make this less weird, I look over my shoulder, and in a fake perky voice, I say, "See you Tuesday!"

"Yeah, see ya."

When I walk into the apartment, Jase and Mark are in the kitchen cooking dinner. They have music playing loudly, so they don't hear me when I enter. I stand there and watch them move around the kitchen, flirting with each other. Jase approaches Mark while he's standing over the stove and wraps his arms around his waist, kissing him on the neck. A part of me feels a little sad—envious. Maybe I'm just not meant to ever have that. When Mark turns around to look at Jase, he sees me.

"Hey!" he says excitedly. "We're making Italian tonight. You hungry?"

"Yeah, a little," I say, walking toward the bedroom. Why am I suddenly feeling sad? I wish I could get a hold of my emotions. I should be happy for Jase and Mark, not pitying myself. God, I am so selfish.

Closing the door behind me, I toss my purse on the floor. Walking across the room, I sit on the edge of the bed and take a moment to myself to just be sad. I need to get it out now before going back out there. I am sure the boys are sick and tired of my depressing moods.

I hear the creak of the door opening while I'm sniffing and quickly wiping away my tears. I really don't want to put a damper on the evening, so I paste on a smile before looking up to see Mark walking in the room.

"Hey, what's up?" I say in a fake cheerful tone, pretending that I wasn't just crying.

He closes the door and starts walking over to me. "What's wrong?"

I watch him as he moves across the room and sits down beside me. He places his hand on my knee and gives a light squeeze. "Nothing, just a weird day at work. That's all."

With a friendly smirk, he teasingly says, "You lie."

Not wanting to pretend, I just confess what's got me in my mood. "You're right," I softly chuckle. "Honestly, I love you and Jase, so don't take this the wrong way, okay?"

"Okay."

"I see how happy the two of you are, and I can't help but wonder . . . why not me? I know it's selfish, but . . ."

I don't finish, when Mark cuts me off and says, "You are *not* selfish." Shifting on the bed, he turns his body to face me. He looks extremely serious as he stares into my eyes. "I know what you're thinking, but stop. You will have that, I promise. Look, I can't even imagine how much everything sucks for you right now, but this does not define you."

Tears rim my eyes when Mark rests his hands on my shoulders and repeats himself sternly. "This doesn't define you." Leaning in, he kisses my forehead, and the tears slip out. He takes his thumbs, and wipes them off my cheeks. "It doesn't, okay?"

"Why does it feel that way? Maybe you believe that, but . . ." Looking down, I shake my head before looking back into his eyes. "None of this makes sense to me."

Tucking a lock of hair behind my ear, he says, "One day, this pain will make sense to you." He pulls me in for a hug, and I try to believe his words, but it all sounds too good to be true.

I pull back and attempt to lighten the mood as I grin and ask, "So, what are you boys cooking for me?"

Mark smiles, but I clearly see the concern in his eyes. "Jase is the one who is doing everything. I'm not much of a cook. I'm trying to look helpful, but all I'm doing is stirring the pasta." Laughing, he stands up, grabs my hand, and pulls me off the bed. "Come on, let's devour the bruschetta while we admire Jase's sexy ass moving around the kitchen."

I smile, thankful for the humor, and say, "Absolutely."

Walking into the kitchen, Jase strides over to me, pulls me in for a hug, and gives me a quick kiss. "Hey, sweetie. How was work?"

"Weird at first, but it wound up being a busy night, which was good," I say as I walk over to the wine rack and select a bottle of Nero d'Avola. I uncork the bottle and pour three glasses of the floral Italian wine. As Mark and I settle at the bar, Jase picks up his glass and stands next to us. No toast is needed when the three of us clink our glasses before drinking.

Mark and I sit, chitchatting, while Jase slices up a baguette for the bruschetta. This is exactly what I needed tonight: a relaxing evening with my guys, good food, and wine.

"So, what are you cooking?" I ask Jase as he's stirring a few pots on the stove.

"Lobster tortellini, vodka sauce, pan-fried asparagus, and roasted garlic bread," he says as he moves around the kitchen.

"God, that sounds good!" I look over at Mark and ask, "Hey, didn't your band have a show last night?"

"Yeah, we played at Blur. It was a great gig; the place was packed."

"I've never been there before," I say.

Jase looks over his shoulder at me and jokingly says, "Candace, you haven't been anywhere." He chuckles and then adds, "You should really hear them play sometime. You'd like their sound."

The conversation halts when there is a knock at the door. Mark walks over to open it, and my stomach sinks when I see Kimber standing in the doorway. I jump off the barstool, and Jase is immediately by my side.

"What the hell is going on?" she asks. She is pissed, and understandably so. Walking in, she throws her purse on the couch, and with her hands on her hips, she continues, "You two have been avoiding me all week, and I have no clue what I did to piss you guys off!"

"We're not pissed at you," Jase reassures her, but by the look on her face, she's not buying one word. "Candace just wanted a little time away, that's all."

"From me? I'm supposed to be your best friend?!"

I've seen Kimber worked up before, but not like this. She is visibly not only pissed, but I can tell that her feelings are hurt as well, which hurts me in return. It's not my intention to hurt her at all. I love Kimber, and we have never had secrets between us until now.

"Why won't you talk to me?" she demands.

"I'm sorry," I say, as Mark heads back into the kitchen. I walk over, sit down on the couch, and quickly think of any reason to give her. She moves to stand in front of me, and I know she is waiting for an answer. Nervous, I start to speak again, "Jack and I got into an argument at the party. I was upset, he was drunk, so I called Jase to come pick me up."

Jase butts in and adds, "I suggested she stay here in case he showed up at your house. That's all."

"So why couldn't you just call me and tell me?" The look in her eyes is calling *bullshit* on our lie.

"I didn't want you getting involved. You can sometimes overreact, and I just wanted everything to die down without any drama. It's no big deal, and I haven't heard from him. It's over, so can we just drop it?" My hands are sweating; I hate even mentioning his name. I really want this conversation to be done with. I look up at Kimber, and she is shaking her head at Jase and me.

"Bullshit!" she snaps as she grabs her purse off of the couch and heads for the door.

Jumping up, I say, "Kimber, wait. Please don't be mad at me. I'm coming back home this week. It's not a big deal, please don't make it into one."

She takes a step towards me and says, "You're the one who made it such a big deal when you decided to avoid me all week. We have always been honest with each other, but if you really want me to believe your story, then fine. I believe you." With that, she turns her back to me, walks out, and slams the door behind her.

chapter ten

"ARE YOU SURE everything is all right?" Jase asks as he is helping me unpack my bags.

After my fight with Kimber, I stayed a couple more nights with Jase. It was nice to have him there when I got home from classes on Monday. I didn't think returning to school would be as stressful as it turned out to be. I didn't miss much, so I wasn't stressed about that part. I guess it's more paranoia than stress. Truth is, I am terrified of running into Jack on campus. I know the likelihood of that happening is slim, considering I have been here for the past three years and our paths have never crossed before, but I can't help constantly looking over my shoulder while I walk around campus. The feeling consumed me every day, and when I got back to Jase's apartment, he was there when I broke down from all the panic I was trying to keep bottled up all day. He had asked if I needed him or Mark to help out by trying to meet up with me on campus, but none of our schedules matched up enough for it to be possible.

"Yeah, Jase. I can't stay with you forever, and you and Mark don't need me around all of the time." I start piling my dirty clothes in the hamper and get a load of clothes separated to wash. In all honesty, I don't want to be here. But I feel like a burden to Jase. He keeps assuring me I'm not, but I know he and Mark really want some privacy. I don't blame them. Plus, I haven't heard from Kimber since Sunday night when she showed up at Jase's, so my being back here at the house is unsettling.

Tossing my empty bags in the closet, Jase asks, "What time do you get off work tonight? Do you want me to meet you afterward?" I know he's worried about me since my new feelings of paranoia have surfaced. He met me yesterday after I got off work to simply walk me to my car and follow me home. But I really don't need him to keep doing that since I always walk out with Roxy or another employee.

"I close tonight, so I'll leave around eleven, but you don't have to meet me there. I'm working with Roxy, so I won't be alone," I say as I grab the basket full of clothes and walk out of the bedroom. I dump the basket off in the laundry room before heading to the living room. Jase takes his bag, and

I walk him to the door. "Thank you."

Looking at me, he asks, "For what?"

"Everything." I barely get the words out when I feel the tightening in my throat. I'm not really good at expressing how I feel, but I wish I could because everything Jase has done for me this past week and a half has been beyond anything anyone has ever done for me. The compassion and love he gives me every day means the world to me.

"Sweetie, I feel like I haven't done nearly enough," he says. But he has. He couldn't have done anything more.

I shake my head and start to cry. He knows me well enough that no words are even needed. He pulls me in, and we hold each other tightly. I press my head into his chest, and the tears keep coming. Jase combs his hand through my hair while I cling to him.

"You keep the key to my place, okay. Come over anytime you need, even if it's the middle of the night."

Nodding my head, I pull back and look into his eyes. I lift up on my toes and give him a quick kiss. "I love you."

"I love you, too," he responds as he opens the door. "Text me tonight when you get home."

"Okay." Shutting the door behind him, I walk back to get my laundry started and to start reading for one of my classes.

As soon as I get into my car, I pull out my phone and text Jase to let him know that work was fine, and I am heading home. Kimber had classes all afternoon, so I didn't see her before I left for work, but I know she will be there when I get home.

Roxy is starting to get a little concerned about me. She keeps asking me questions and wanting to make sure everything is all right. I try assuring her that everything's fine, but I know she doesn't believe me. I can't blame her really. Just like at school, I keep fearing that Jack is going to walk through the doors at work. Every time the little bell over the door rings, the anxiety builds in my stomach, and I know Roxy notices.

Pulling up to the house, I see Kimber's car out front. I didn't tell her I was coming home today. Walking inside, I make my way to the kitchen to grab a bottle of water before I go to my room. I see Kimber sitting at the bar when I enter.

Looking up at me, she says, "Hey, I didn't know you were coming back today."

"Yeah," is all I manage to say as I open the fridge and grab a water. The silence is very awkward, and I just want to go to my room and not deal with this tension between us. "Well, I'm really tired, so I'm going to head to bed."

"Yeah, okay," she says quietly.

I really hate that things feel so strained between us, but I am not sure what to say to her. She knows I'm lying to her, and I feel bad for that but not bad enough to tell her the truth.

I brush my teeth and slip on some sleep shorts and a tank top before taking my sleeping pill that the doctor prescribed to me. Since I started taking them, I haven't had any more extreme nightmares. I lie down in bed and grab my phone off the nightstand to text Jase one more time. I've gotten used to sleeping with him in the same bed, so lying here alone feels strange, almost scary. I've been clinging to Jase as my life support lately, and not having him here with me makes me wish I was back in his bed, in his arms—not alone.

Goodnight. I miss U.

Miss U too. Did U see Kimber?

Yeah. Didn't really say much. It's awkward.

I'm sorry, sweetie. Hopefully it will get better and things will get less weird for you guys.

Maybe. Is Mark with you?

Yeah.

Tell him I said HI. Love you guys.

We love you too.

2 weeks later

Things are still tense with Kimber. We hardly even talk anymore aside from the civil greetings when passing by. I keep apologizing, but she is still mad at me. I wish we could move past this and go back to the way it used to be. But I'm beginning to think that the way it was is the way it will never be. Things are starting to get a little more comfortable at work. Roxy has never mentioned Jack again since that first night back. I've been having issues with being alone at night, so I have been spending a few nights a week with Jase. Either he comes over or I go to his apartment. Once I'm asleep, it's pretty restless. Lying in the dark, waiting for sleep to come, is the hardest part. Every time I close my eyes I am back in the alley, on the ground, with *him*.

Ms. Emerson, my dance instructor, has been making my life hell lately.

I never miss a class; in fact, I have been clocking in a lot of after hours studio time. My moves are flawless, but she is on me about feeling the dance. She keeps telling me that she's watching a perfect dancer, but I'm dead. There is nothing behind my movements. The problem is, I don't know how to fix that because frankly, I feel like I am wasting away. But when I dance, it's the only time my mind feels free of the pain that is constantly consuming it.

4 weeks later

Kimber found my sleeping pills. She needed to borrow my hair dryer when hers bit the dust. While she was in my bathroom, she saw the bottle that I had accidentally left out. When she kept questioning me, I told her I was taking them because the stress of school was keeping me up at night. I don't know whether she believed me or not, but it really doesn't matter since our relationship seems to be drifting further apart.

I fought with my mother this morning when she called to bitch at me for not being a better daughter and returning her phone calls. I hadn't spoken with her or my father since the blowout about me not attending the banquet that honored my mother. Every time either one of them calls, I just let it go to voicemail, but this time I answered. My lack of conversation ticked my mother off, and she went on another one of her tangents about how childish and disrespectful I am. I didn't argue back. I didn't have the energy, so I just sat there and let her say everything she needed to say. If it wasn't for her pushy attitude, I would have never agreed to go on a date with Jack, and none of this would be happening. I know what he did isn't her fault, but I hate her for it anyway. So when she finished lecturing me on her expectations, I simply disconnected the call without saying anything.

6 weeks later

Yesterday was a horrible day. My mind has been consumed with flashbacks, and the stress finally caught up to me. After dance class, I came home. Kimber was still on campus, so I thought I would take a quick nap before having to go into work. I woke up screaming, and I couldn't calm myself down. My heart was racing, and I must have been hallucinating because even though my eyes were open, Jack was right there with me, muffling my mouth with his hand and ripping my clothes off. No matter how much I fought, he wouldn't stop. I huddled down in my closet and tried shielding my eyes from the images of him, but he was there too. With me in the dark. I felt like I was going to die. The pounding of my heart made my chest hurt, and I could barely breathe.

I managed to call Jase when I started to calm down. He came over right away and sat with me in my closet while I sobbed uncontrollably. It seems that no matter how hard I try to let go of it all, Jack finds a way to creep into my head and remind me of everything I want to forget.

I decided to go ahead and go into work, even though Jase wanted me to call in sick. But I really needed the distraction. It was a busy night, so I didn't have much time to think about anything other than making lattes. In fact, I barely even noticed the taunting bell above the door, which usually has me in a constant state of paranoia. The busier I keep myself, the less time my mind has to wander. So when I am not at Common Grounds, I'm buried in schoolwork: dancing and studying.

8 weeks later

Jase has been trying to convince me to see a therapist. He believes my erratic behavior is post-traumatic stress disorder. The last thing I want to do is talk, so I brush him off and pretend like it's no big deal whenever he brings it up, which is often. All I need is a little more time to pass, and things will get easier. I keep telling myself this every day, but so far, nothing has changed. I can do nothing but hope that one day I will wake up and things will be different.

Ms. Emerson told me to report to her office this afternoon at three o'clock. I have never been to her office before; I hadn't even been singled out in class like I have been lately. She's constantly barking at me in class, telling me to *feel* more. I can only imagine that this meeting will be more of the same.

When I pull up to the studio, I take a deep calming breath before getting out of the car. Feeling nervous as I walk into the building, I head down the hallway to all the instructors' offices. When I reach her closed door, I take a few moments before lightly knocking on the door.

"Come in," she says loudly, and I slowly open the door and peek my head in. "Ms. Parker, please, have a seat," she says as she motions to the large leather chair with weathered nailheads.

Sliding my purse off my shoulder, I plop it on the floor next to the chair before sitting down. I look at Ms. Emerson as she folds her hands together on top of her desk and clears her throat.

"Ms. Parker . . . Candace?"

"Please, call me Candace," I answer as I fidget with my watch.

"I can't help but notice a decline in your performance lately, and it's beginning to concern me."

"Oh . . ."

" I've never had to worry about you in the past, and frankly, I never thought I would be needing to have this conversation with you, but . . ." She backs her chair away from her desk, stands up, and walks around, leaning against the desk as she now stands directly in front of me. "Is there something going on? Something that has caused this sudden shift with your dancing?" Her voice softens when she questions me. I'm surprised by her tone of empathy.

Shaking my head, I say, "No. I'm not sure what's causing this struggle." Only I do. And the knowing causes me to swallow back hard and fight to keep the tears from pooling in my eyes.

When I look at Ms. Emerson, I see the concern. An emotion I thought she couldn't possibly possess. My body betrays my act of strength when I feel my chin start to tremble as the emotions build inside my tightening chest.

Slightly tilting her head to the side, she pushes, "You sure?"

There is no way I can speak right now, so I simply nod my head.

She pushes herself off the desk and sits down next to me in the matching leather chair. Shifting her body to face me, she continues, "Dancers like you don't often walk through these doors. When I first saw you three years ago, I knew I was seeing something special. You are destined to have a successful career, and I've never had to worry about you. You breathe this." Hearing her words, I lose my composure and let the tears escape. "But it's almost November, and your time here is limited. Whatever *this* is . . . we need to fix it. I see perfection, but I no longer feel the passion in you. I feel emptiness."

Agreeing with her last statement, I nod my head and say, "I'm sorry. I don't . . . I don't know what to do to fix this."

She reaches over and covers my hand with hers. "Whatever is making you shut down, allow it to come to life inside of you."

Her words are my greatest fear. Would she be telling me this if she knew? I know I have to find another way—I have to.

"I believe in you, Candace. I wouldn't have called you in today if I didn't."

I am taken back by her candidness, and I know she isn't saying this for my sake. She means it. Wiping my tearstained cheeks, I say, "Thank you."

She stands up, and I lean down to grab my purse before doing the same. As she walks back behind her desk, I make my way to the door. Holding the door handle in my hand, I turn over my shoulder and assure her, "I'll fix this."

"I know you will," she replies as she sits down.

chapter eleven

WRAPPING MY PLUSH black scarf around my neck, I head out the front door into the brisk and rainy October evening. It's Halloween, and everyone at work wanted the night off to go to various parties, so I volunteered to work. Roxy will be there for a little bit, but I will be working most of the night and closing by myself. It should be pretty slow with it being a Wednesday and also a party night. Most people will be opting to drink liquor rather than coffee.

When I arrive, Roxy and her boyfriend, Jared, are the only ones in the shop. Sporting her new flame-red hair, she looks up and says, "Hey, Candace! How was your day?"

Shaking off my wet jacket, I say, "Busy. I've been trying to choreograph that solo I told you about." I shrug off my coat and scarf and hang them on the coat rack by the front doors.

"Hey, Jared," I say as I approach the counter.

"Haven't seen you in a while, girl," he says.

"Yeah, I've been keeping busy with school."

Eying my backpack, he says, "I see."

I sling my backpack off my shoulder and drop it on the floor behind the counter. "I figured it'd be dead tonight, so I thought I could get some reading done for my classes."

Roxy walks up to me, leaning against the counter, and asks softly, "You sure you're gonna be okay here by yourself?"

"Roxy, I've worked alone before. No biggie."

"Yeah, but—"

Interrupting her, I repeat, "No biggie, Rox," giving a slight nod and looking her in the eyes. I know exactly what she's thinking, but I just want her to drop it. We both realize I haven't worked alone since she's been noticing my strange behavior these past couple months. She knows something is up, but I tend to cut her off every time she starts to insinuate concern.

I walk over to the espresso machine and begin making myself a double shot latte.

"It was nice seeing you, Candace," Jared shouts over to me while I'm grinding the coffee beans.

"You heading out already?" I ask.

"Yeah, I gotta run." He turns to Roxy and asks, "I'll see you in an hour?"

"Yep, meet you at your place," she replies before kissing him.

I turn around, not wanting to look at how happy they are and focus on steaming the milk. I add a pump of vanilla flavoring and quickly wipe down the counter before turning back around. When I do, Jared is walking out. Leaning against the counter, I blow on my hot drink before taking a slow sip. Roxy is staring at me, and I can read her thoughts clearly. I know she doesn't want me here alone, and she is worried. Before she can say a word, I try to place the focus on her, not me.

"So, what are the two of you doing tonight?" I ask.

"A friend of ours is in a band, and they are playing a show at The Crocodile."

"That's a huge gig," I say excitedly.

Roxy and I start talking about her friend's band, and before I know it, she's grabbing her things and getting ready to leave. A part of me is starting to feel jittery, and it isn't the caffeine. The thought creeps into my mind: *What if he comes in tonight?* I have never seen him here in the past, and to my knowledge, he has never been here, but it still makes me nervous.

"You okay, hun?" Roxy asks as she stares at my hands that are tightly clenched together.

Immediately, I loosen my grip as I feign a smile and say, "Yeah, fine. Must be the two shots of espresso, that's all." Truth is, I'm not okay, but I need to be. I need to function and be able to go about my daily routines without freaking out. The only way I know to get to that point is to keep forcing myself.

"Okay," she responds in a weary tone. I assure her I'm fine and tell her to not worry about me and have fun. Before walking out the door, she turns around and says, "Call me if you need anything, or . . . just call me, okay?"

Waving at her in mock exasperation, I say, "Just go."

It's a little after ten o'clock and the rain is now pouring down outside. The evening has been pretty slow as predicted. Only a handful of people are sitting around drinking coffee, visiting with friends, or studying. I have been able to get a decent amount of reading done and am now finishing up some research for a paper I need to write by next week.

My heart skips a beat, as it does every time the bell above the door rings. I look up to see a guy with dark, wet hair walking in. I hop off my stool and walk over to the register to meet him.

"Hey, what can I get for you?" I ask.

Looking at the drink list on the wall behind me, he says, "Uh, just a twenty coffee. Black."

Roxy didn't feel like she needed to give her drink sizes any special names like other coffee establishments, so it's simply a twelve, sixteen, or twenty.

"Easy enough," I say, and before he can look up at me, I am over pouring him his cup of coffee. When I return, he is typing something into his phone. "That's one ninety-three," I say as I slide the drink towards him.

Looking up at me, he hands me a five, and I open the register to get him his change. I feel him staring at me, and when I shift my eyes up, sure enough, he's staring at me with a confused look on his face.

"Everything okay?" I ask as I hand him his change. He doesn't take his eyes off of me, and I'm starting to freak out inside. I can feel the rate of my heart as it increases, and I nervously ask, "Anything else?"

He finally blinks and shakes his head as he says, "Um, no. No, that's all," never taking his eyes off of me.

Who the hell is this guy? I take a few steps back and accidentally kick the barstool I was sitting on, and it makes a loud scratching noise against the floor. He turns around and starts walking out but looks back over his shoulder at me a couple times before finally leaving.

Panic shoots through me, and my breathing becomes erratic. Does that guy know me? Does he know Jack? My paranoid thoughts start to overtake me, and I quickly announce to the few people who are still here that we are closing immediately. My voice is trembling, and it doesn't take long for the place to empty out. As soon as the last person leaves, I lock the doors and turn off the outside lights. I walk back behind the counter, scared, not able to slow down my pounding heart. Sitting down and pulling my knees to my chest, I once again feel defeated and hopeless as the tears start to fall.

As soon as I get home, I take a sleeping pill, strip off my clothes, and lie down in bed. I hate that I have become so weak and can't get my shit together. It shouldn't be like this. I shouldn't be feeling this miserable every day. It's been two months, and I know I am stronger than this pathetic girl that lives inside of me and is consuming me.

It's sometime in the middle of the night when I wake up to Kimber loudly stumbling through the house. She's giggling, and I hear a guy's voice before her door slams shut. *Great.* I am just about to fall back asleep when her moans echo though the walls. My stomach knots up when the guy starts grunting out her name.

I can't take this. I am a mix of emotions: pissed, disgusted, jealous, and scared. Throwing the covers off of me, I grab my coat and slide on my Uggs. I need to get out of this house and away from what's going on in Kimber's room. So, I grab my keys and leave.

Quietly, I slide my key into the lock and open the door. Shutting it softly behind me, I walk through the living room while stepping out of my boots and tossing my coat on the couch. When I open the door to Jase's room, I see he is alone. *Thank God.* I pull back the covers and slide in behind him. It isn't long before he rolls over and wraps me in his arms. It is then when my stomach finally unknots, and I fall asleep.

"So what happened last night?" Jase asks when I walk into the kitchen.

Pouring myself a cup of coffee, I walk into the living room, which is adjacent to the open kitchen, and curl up in a blanket as I sit on the couch. Jase walks in and sits next to me, propping his feet up on the coffee table.

"Kimber brought some guy home last night, and the pervert wouldn't stop shouting her name," I say.

Chuckling, Jase asks, "Who was it?"

"I have no clue. I was asleep until they came stumbling in and woke me up." I take a sip of my coffee before adding, "It was gross!"

Jase cocks his head to the side and says, "It's not gross, Candace."

"It's gross," I insist before taking another sip of my coffee.

Jase just laughs at me, but I can't help it. Hearing those two last night was disgusting.

"Anyway, new subject. How was last night?" I ask. Ever since Mark's band played at Blur, they have become somewhat of regulars and played another gig there last night.

"It was fun. You really should've come with us."

"I told you, I had to work," I say.

"Nooo, you volunteered to work," he responds and gives me a smirk.

I have been avoiding going out with Jase and Mark. The thought of going anywhere aside from my normal spots, where I feel a little safer about not running into *him,* scares me. So I stick to school, work, and home.

"You live in a bubble, Candace," he says and then grabs the corner of the blanket that I am under and pulls it over his lap as he scoots up next to me. "You need to get out."

"I am out."

"You're not. I always know where to find you because you have the same routine every week. It never changes." He drapes his arm around me and pulls me closer. "I'm worried about you."

Sighing, I respond, "You don't need to be. I'm fine."

"Don't pull that act with me. I know you're not fine. It's been two months, and you are no more fine than you were back in August." Kissing the top of my head, he continues, "I worry because I only know what you tell me. But I wonder how much this really consumes you that you hold in and don't tell me about. You won't do anything to help yourself."

Taking my coffee mug out of my hand, he reaches over and sets it on the end table. I hate that he's right. I hate that I am stuck. I hate that I am scared. I hate everything about my life. Every day is so goddamn hard, and all I can do is just focus on going through the motions just to get to the next day, which is the same thing all over again. But, it's all a façade. Truth is—I'm drowning.

"I'm constantly scared," I confess to Jase, and his arms tighten around me. "I'm scared I'm going to see *him*. And I know this sounds absolutely crazy, but . . . most days . . ." I stop in my thought, my almost confession, which might make Jase drag me straight to a therapist if I tell him. So I lay my head on his chest and take a deep breath when he says, "You can tell me."

"I feel like I'm going to die."

The place is packed when I walk into work Saturday morning. Brandon and I are busy trying to keep up with the drink orders while Roxy deals with the customers. Brandon and I hardly ever work together because our schedules at school are opposite of each other. He's on a soccer scholarship and is a year behind me. He's laughing about something when I accidently knock the iced mocha I just made all over me.

"Crap!" I grab a towel and start wiping the sticky drink off my arms and hands.

Brandon is laughing at me, and I shoot him a mock 'go to hell' look. "Go clean up, I'll take care of this," he tells me, and I holler to Roxy that I'll be right back.

Luckily, most of the drink spilled on my apron. I wash my arms in the sink and wipe down one of the chocolaty brown spots on my top. When I walk back out, the line is down to only two people. Roxy decides to move off the register and make drinks, so I take her place.

I look up to take the last customer in line, and there he is. The guy from the other night. Only this time, I'm the one staring and not speaking.

"You okay?" he asks, and I snap out of my daze.

"What can I get for you?" I ask. He looks at me intently, which makes me nervous and orders the same drink that he had a few days ago. I turn around and walk over to pour his cup of coffee when Roxy sides up next to me and whispers, "Who's that guy?"

"I don't know, why?"

"Well, he's hot, and he can't seem to take his eyes off of you."

I peek at him over my shoulder and catch him staring. Turning back to his coffee, I snap the lid on and whisper, "He's creepy."

Roxy laughs, and I walk back over to the register. "One ninety-three," I say as I hand him his drink. When I give him his change, in a moment of bravery, I ask, "Do I know you or something?"

"I don't think so. Why?"

I notice his striking eyes. They are almost clear with a slight hint of blue. I don't think I have ever seen eyes that color before. Shaking my head, I say, "You stare." *What was that, Candace? You stare?* "I'm sorry, that was rude of me," I quickly apologize.

Not acknowledging my apology, he asks, "You go to school here?"

"Yeah."

Taking a step back from the counter, he thanks me for the coffee and leaves. I don't know what to make of the exchange we just had, but decide not to give it anymore thought.

"What did he say?" Roxy asks.

"Nothing really. Just thanked me for the coffee," I say as I walk over to Brandon and help him finish wiping down the counters.

When I get home and pull into the driveway, I notice a red Jeep in front of the house. Walking in, I expect to see Kimber, but she must be in her room. I grab a bottle of water and an apple from the fridge, and when I start heading to my room, Kimber is walking out of hers and shutting the door behind her.

"Hey," she says when she turns around and sees me.

"Whose car is out front?" I ask.

"Oh, that's Seth's car." She says this as if I should know who Seth is. I give her a confused look when she clarifies, "The guy I've been seeing."

Nodding my head, I softly say, "Oh," when she walks off. I turn around and walk into my room, closing the door behind me. How could I not know she's dating someone? Sadness washes over me at the realization that Kimber and I are hardly friends anymore. She has a boyfriend, and I had no clue. I just figured that guy she brought home with her the other night was a one-night stand. I never thought I would drift so far from my best friend. How can we live in the same house and not know each other at all? What's worse—this is all my fault.

chapter twelve

THE NIGHT IS cold and misty, and Mark and I are sitting by the fire pit in my backyard roasting marshmallows while we wait for Jase to come over. I am curled up in a blanket as we sit and eat our sugary treat and share a bottle of red wine.

"Where's Kimber?" Mark asks, as he stabs another marshmallow onto his skewer.

Looking over at him, the only light coming from the glow of the fire, I say, "At Seth's, probably. She spends most nights over at his place, so I've been here alone for the most part."

"Does that bother you?"

"Not really . . . well, kinda." I grab my skewer, loaded with two marshmallows, and place them directly into the flame. I watch the glow of the fire brighten as my marshmallows ignite into a mini fireball. Pulling them out of the yellow crackling blaze, I blow out the flame on my now scorched confection.

"That's disgusting," he says while eying my bubbly, charred marshmallow.

Sliding off the burnt shell and leaving the remainder of the uncooked marshmallow on the skewer, I shove it in my mouth and crunch down. "It's fabulous," I jokingly say with my mouth full.

Mark laughs and shakes his head at me. "So . . . ?" he questions, still wanting a confirmation to his previous question.

I shove the remainder of the marshmallows that are left on my skewer back into the blaze to repeat the process. "I mean, I like that I don't have to feel awkward when she's around, but at the same time, it makes me sad that she's not around and that we hardly speak." Eating the last of my marshmallows, I lay the skewer down and continue. "It hurts. Kimber has never been serious with a guy, and now she has a boyfriend I know nothing about. She's seems really happy, and I wish I was a part of it."

"So, why don't you just talk to her?"

"Because she knows I'm hiding something and lying to her. She told me that she doesn't want to be friends with someone who can't be honest."

Shrugging my shoulders, I take another sip of wine and tighten the blanket around me.

"Maybe you should . . ."

Mark is cut off when the door opens and Jase comes outside to join us.

"Hey, guys," he says as he walks over and kisses Mark, then turns to me and kisses my cheek. "What are you guys doing out here? It's cold."

Mark holds up the half-eaten bag of marshmallows and says, "I'm fattening up your rail-thin girl over there." He eyes me with a smirk and winks.

"Good luck, fatty," I respond playfully.

Jase sits opposite me and starts, "So, I want you to come out with Mark and I Saturday night."

"Jase," I say as I slowly shake my head. I don't go out. I never go out.

"It'll be low key, promise. Spines is closing early to have a private concert, and I was able to snag three tickets for us."

"You want me to go to a concert?"

"Candace, seriously? It's at a book and music store. It's a private show, but forget about that. You won't turn me down when I tell you who's playing," he says as his smile grows. He reaches in his back pants pocket and pulls out a ticket. He hands me the solid black ticket with two white X's on it.

"Are you serious?" I ask as a snatch the ticket from him. "How did you get these?"

"A friend of Mark's," he says.

"Who?" Mark asks.

"Ryan. I ran into him at the gym earlier today. We got to talking about music, and he mentioned the show. When I told him my best friend is a huge fan of The xx, he gave me a few extra tickets that he wasn't using."

Looking at Jase, I ask, "Who's Ryan?"

Mark answers for him and says, "He owns the bar that my band has been playing at."

Holding the ticket, I really want to go, but I am nervous. I sit there quietly, staring into the bright fire, when Jase reaches over and takes ahold of my hand.

"I really want you to go. You'll be with the two of us. Nothing will happen," he assures me.

Looking at him, I let out a sigh and say, "I don't know. It makes me nervous."

"I know," Jase whispers. "But nothing will happen. You have to start trying."

I look back at Mark, and he shrugs his shoulders and nods in agreement. Letting out a slow breath, I turn back to face Jase. "Okay," I say with a shaky voice. I need to do this. I know I do. I'm just scared. Paranoid really. I tell myself everyday that I need to function, so I will push down the fear that is already rising inside of me, and try.

Sitting back, Jase quietly says, "Thank you."

I stare at the black and white ticket that lies on my desk. Every time I walk past it, I try and reassure myself that I can do this. Jase and Mark will be picking me up shortly. I walk into my closet to find something to wear. Looking around, I decide on simplicity: jeans, a long sleeved white V-neck shirt, brown knee-high boots, and my brown crew-collar leather jacket.

I hear the guys when they come inside the house and shout, "I'll be out in a sec. I'm just finishing straightening my hair." Taking a huge gulp of the wine I've been sipping, I look at myself in the mirror. My eyes look a little glassy, but I'm not surprised. I've been drinking since I got home from work a little bit ago, hoping the alcohol will help calm my nerves.

I turn off my hair straightener, grab my cell, and slide it in my pocket along with my ID and credit card, and I walk through the house to the living room where the guys are.

"You look great," Jase says with a smile. "You ready?"

I nod my head, grab my leopard scarf that is lying on the couch, and tie it around my neck before walking outside. I don't say much on the drive; I just listen to Mark and Jase talk about school and football. When we arrive at Spines, a trendy book and music store, I begin to panic when I see all the cars.

"I don't know about this," I say quietly.

The guys get out of the car and Mark opens my door. Holding his hand out for me, he says, "No worries, okay?"

I slide my hand into his and step out of the car.

When we walk inside, there is a gathering of around one hundred or so people. There is a bar set off to the side that is serving drinks with tables and chairs scattered about. The lights are set low and there are candles everywhere. I stay with Mark, still holding his hand tightly, as Jase goes to the bar to get us drinks.

Mark and I browse through the section of vinyl records. Flipping through them and admiring the artwork on the old cardboard cases, I am starting to feel a little more at ease. Jase finds us and hands Mark and I each a bottle of beer.

"Come on, they're about to start playing," Jase says. We walk over, and decide to stand next to another group of people by a low shelf of books. I set my beer down and lean my elbows on the bookcase as Jase and Mark stand on either side of me. I watch as the band takes the small stage that has been set up for them and starts getting their equipment ready. I have loved The xx for years but have never seen them live before.

The strum of a guitar fills the dark room as they ease into their song 'Infinity.' Listening to the slow soothing sounds, I lean into Jase—a non-verbal *thank you*. He wraps his arm around me and pulls me in closer, and I know exactly what he is telling me with his actions.

After a few songs, I am ready for another drink. I go with Jase to the bar to get another round for the three of us. When we walk back, I see Mark talking to some guy who has his back to me. When we approach, the guy he is talking to turns around, and I nearly choke on the beer that I just took a sip of.

He looks shocked to see me as he stares at me with his clear-blue eyes. He doesn't say anything to me, so I decide to speak up. "You again."

"You two know each other?" Mark asks.

"Not really," he responds as he blinks his gaze away from me.

I look at Mark and add, "He's come into Common Grounds a couple times to get coffee. How do you guys know each other?"

"He owns Blur, where the band has been playing lately," Mark says.

"And the guy who gave me the tickets," Jase says to me before turning his attention to the guy, whose name I still don't know, and adds, "Thanks, man."

"No problem at all."

I stand there awkwardly as the guys continue to talk, so I turn my back to them and focus in on the band as they begin to play 'Missing.' I haven't heard this song in months, and it begins to affect me. What I used to consider a desperate love song now breathes new meaning when I hear the words about how the heart beats. Sadness creeps through me, and my body tenses up as I try desperately not to cry.

"Hey, let's go sit down," Jase whispers in my ear, and I am snapped out of my tormenting thoughts.

Looking at him over my shoulder, I nod, not sure if I am able to speak just yet. He lowers his head and looks me in the eyes. I know he sees it—the hurt—so I quickly shake my head and give him a reassuring grin that I've got this under control. He takes my hand and leads me to a table where Mark and his friend are already sitting.

Taking a seat and setting my beer down, I say, "I'm sorry, but I never caught your name."

Giving me a half smirk, he says, "Ryan. Ryan Campbell."

I give him a slight nod and introduce myself. "I'm Candace." Eying his cup of coffee, I add, "Ever drink anything besides coffee?"

"I work a lot of late nights," is his vague response to my question.

"So, Ryan," Jase says, "Candace will be graduating this year as well. She's a dance major."

What the hell is Jase doing? I look over at him and give him a snide look, but he just grins at me.

"Dance. What kind?" Ryan asks.

"Ballet," I say and then take another sip of my beer.

"Can't say I know anything about that," he responds with an honest chuckle.

"It's okay. Nobody ever does."

"So, I take it you're the best friend who loves this band," he says as he nods his head towards the stage.

Feeling odd about this interaction, I reply with a simple, "Yeah." I start to feel the need to close myself off. It feels weird talking to someone new. My life is very secluded, and I like it that way. It's safe. So being here, out, listening to music, talking to a new person, suddenly makes me want to run back home.

I know I can do this. I have to do this. I reach under the table and rest my hand on top of Jase's leg, in a way, using him as my anchor while I try to pull my thoughts together. He looks over at me as he lays his hand over mine and gives me a reassuring squeeze. I keep repeating in my head: *Get it together, Candace. Just function.* I say it over and over in a desperate attempt to will it to happen. I tell myself to act normal, but I'm not even sure I know what that is. I push the uncomfortable feeling aside, knowing that nothing will happen because Jase and Mark are both here with me. Everything is fine.

I'm peeling the label off my beer bottle when Ryan starts to talk. "So, Candace, what do you plan on doing when you finish school?"

I look up at him and take a deep breath before answering. "I hope to dance professionally while time allows. Not sure where that will happen. New York was always the plan, but I'm not so sure now." Why did I just tell him that? *Please don't ask why.*

Looking over at Jase, he and Mark are lost in their own conversation, not paying any attention to Ryan and me.

"I love New York. You ever been?" Ryan asks.

"Yeah, several times. It's a great city. I actually lived there the summer before my senior year of high school. I had a scholarship to one of the conservatories in the city."

"So, your parents just let you live there alone for the summer?" he asks with a hint of concern in his eyes.

"Umm, yeah. My parents are . . . well, not your typical involved parents," I say.

"Sorry."

I shrug it off, and we continue to talk about our love of New York City. I'm surprised with how easy it is to talk to this new person. He's laidback and makes me feel comfortable.

Time continues to pass pretty effortlessly as we talk. Mark and Jase are engrossed in their own private conversation about who knows what.

"What are you two talking about?" Mark asks, when his conversation with Jase has died down.

"New York City," Ryan answers.

When I hear the band begin the intro to another one of my favorite songs, I excuse myself to walk over to the bookcase where we were standing earlier so that I can listen and enjoy the song. A few moments later, Jase, Mark, and Ryan join me. Jase is on one side of me and Ryan stands opposite. Leaning forward, resting my elbows on the bookcase, Ryan lowers himself next to me, and I instantly feel Jase's protective hand on my back.

I shift my eyes slightly to look at Ryan, and he is watching the band. I know I shouldn't be looking at him like this, but I find it intriguing that he doesn't make me feel scared. He turns his head and catches me staring at him. Cringing inside, I try and play it off by giving him a slight grin and refocusing my attention back to the band. When they announce their last song for the evening, Jase leans into my ear and whispers, "Mark and I will be right back."

Looking at him curiously, I ask, "Where are you going?"

"Don't worry about it. We'll be back in a second." He kisses me on the temple, and gives me a reassuring nod before he turns and walks off with Mark.

Standing here alone, next to Ryan, we listen to The xx play an extended version of 'Intro.' The languid plucks of the guitar are soon interlaced with the ever thumping of the bass drum. The song begins to intensify into a fusion of haunting and seductive sounds. I push back off the bookcase while Ryan remains leaning on his elbows. I watch him. I shouldn't be, but I am. His hair is a rich dark brown that falls slightly over his ears. He has a strong, well-defined jaw and a muscular frame that is evident through his dark grey shirt. Looking back at me over his shoulder, a small lock of his hair falls over his forehead. *What am I doing?* I take a step back as he pushes himself off the bookcase and looks at me. Turning around quickly to walk away, I run smack into Mark's chest.

Tripping over my own feet, he catches me and asks, "Whoa, everything okay?"

"I wanna go," I say softly so that no one can hear me but him.

Clutching both of my arms, he looks back at Jase and gives him a nod. When Jase walks over he asks, "You ready to go?"

"Hey, man. It was good seeing ya. We'll catch up later this week," Mark says to Ryan.

I turn around as Ryan approaches Mark and they give each other a tight handshake as Mark slaps Ryan on the side of his shoulder. "Catch you later," Ryan says before holding his hand out to me. "I'm glad I ran into you again," he says.

Sliding my hand into his, I say with a slight hesitation, "Yeah, it was nice."

As Jase and Ryan say their goodbyes, I walk out into the drizzly, cold night and take a deep breath. Jase walks out, hands me my coat, and I shrug it on before getting into the car.

"What was that all about?" Jase asks me.

Leaning my head against the window, I quip, "You tell me. Where the hell did you two run off to?"

Turning around in his seat, he adds, "Just thought you two should talk without Mark and I around."

"Why?"

"Just got that feeling. You two kept staring at each other with that look."

Sitting up, I ask, "And what look would that be?"

"Candace, the guy is hot. You know what look he's talking about," Mark adds as he drives back to my house.

"Doesn't matter," I say as I lie back against the seat.

"What do you mean it doesn't matter?" Jase asks.

I shake my head and stare out the rain-covered window.

"Candace?"

"It just doesn't matter, Jase. It's wrong."

"It's not wrong for you to find someone attractive."

Turning my head to look at him, I say, "Yes, it is."

I feel the car slow down and can see that Mark is pulling into a random parking lot. He turns the car off, steps out, and opens my door. Sliding in next to me, he shuts the door behind him. "Stop punishing yourself."

I open my mouth to speak, but he immediately cuts me off and repeats slowly, "Stop punishing yourself."

Facing me, Jase adds, "Nobody says that you can't enjoy life. You can. You should. You just won't allow yourself."

"How can I feel like that after what happened? It feels wrong."

"It's not wrong," Mark says. "You need to let yourself feel happiness and not run away from every good feeling that comes over you."

"It doesn't feel right."

"Why?" Jase asks.

"Because . . . it makes me feel cheap—dirty." My stomach is in knots talking about this. I don't want to be talking about this. I never want to talk about this.

Mark places his hands on my shoulders and looks me straight in the eyes. "You aren't either of those things, not even close. What happened doesn't make you cheap or dirty or whatever else you're thinking. It happened, and you have been punishing yourself ever since."

"Candace," Jase adds, "He's right. You can't keep doing this to yourself. You can't keep taking this wound and ripping it further open beyond repair. You have to try and leave it be, and allow it to heal."

"I don't know," I say.

"I'm proud of you," Jase says. "I honestly didn't think you would come out with us tonight. Thought you might back out." He smiles at me, and I lean forward between the seats to hug him.

"I'm glad I came," I say as I sit back.

Mark takes my hand, kisses it, and says, "Think about what we said."

Nodding my head, I say, "Okay."

Mark hops out, gets back behind the wheel, and drives me home. When he pulls up to the front of my house, Jase asks, "You want us to stay over?"

"I'm fine, Jase. Thanks again, guys." I give them both a kiss and step out of the car. When I walk inside, Kimber is gone. I go to my room, strip off my clothes, throw on a pair of pajama pants and a cami, and take a sleeping pill before climbing into bed.

chapter thirteen

"I HATE YOU!" Roxy shouts, a few octaves above normal, while she teasingly shoves my shoulder. "I love that band! How did you even get tickets?"

"Jase got the tickets from one of his friends," I say as I shrug my shoulders as if it was no big deal that I got to see The xx in a private concert last weekend.

"Man, I need to meet this *friend* so that I can score some tickets too."

Looking up at her while I'm refilling the coffee beans in the grinder, I say, "You have met him. Well, you've seen him."

"Who?"

Securing the burlap bag with the remaining beans, I tell her, "That guy that came in the other day, the one you said was *hot*."

Giving my shoulder another playful shove, she says, "You're kidding?!"

"Nope," I huff out as I carry the heavy bag into the back stockroom. When I walk back out, Roxy is standing there staring at me with her hands on her hips and an evil grin on her face. I roll my eyes when I walk past her and continue cleaning up before my shift ends in a few minutes. I can feel her stare when I finally turn around and snap, "What?"

"That's it?"

"Yes, that's it." I turn back around and continue wiping down the machines.

Roxy sidles up next to me, leaning her hip against the counter with her arms crossed in front of her. "Was he there?"

"Yes, Rox, he was there," I say as I continue to busy myself with cleaning.

"You're driving me crazy here. Talk to me, girl."

Turning around, I say matter-of-factly, "There is nothing to tell. We went out, ran into him at Spines, had a drink. There is no crazy story to tell."

I start untying my apron when I notice Roxy eying me with a strange look on her face. "Really? No story to tell," she says as she tilts her head toward the entrance.

I look up to see Ryan walking through the shop, heading to the counter. *What is he doing here?* Looking at Roxy, I shake my head at her as I make my way over to him.

"You're gonna get an ulcer," I jokingly say, even though I'm a ball of nerves on the inside.

He lets out a soft chuckle as he says, "I didn't come for coffee."

I look at him with slight confusion when he lifts his hand, which is holding my leopard scarf. The scarf I was wearing last weekend that I thought I'd lost.

"Oh," I say as I reach out and take it. "I thought I had lost this. Thank you."

"No, you left it on the table, but you rushed out so fast, I didn't have a chance to catch you."

Looking down, embarrassed about my sudden exit that night, I quietly say, "Sorry."

"No need to apologize."

With my apron still clutched in my one hand, I lay it on the counter and start backing away when he asks, "Are you taking a break?"

"Um, no. My shift is over."

"Perfect timing," he says with a grin. "Want to have a quick drink?"

Before I can decline, Roxy butts in and answers for me. "She'd love to."

"Actually, I . . ." I don't finished my sentence because I can't think of an excuse fast enough, and I am totally busted. Letting a slow breath out of my nose, I reluctantly agree. "Sure. Let me go grab my bag."

When I walk into the back room to get my purse, I'm feeling very uneasy. Heading back out, Ryan is sitting down at one of the tables by the front window. I walk over and sit down. He already has a drink for me, and as I eye it he says, "Your co-worker said you like hot tea."

Sitting down in front of him, I say, "Oh, thanks. She's actually my boss. Roxy." I sound like an idiot with my voice slightly trembling. I pick up the tea and take a long drink, focusing on the hot, floral infused liquid as it slowly heats my chest. The rain is pouring down outside, and I watch the raindrops as they trickle and twitch down the foggy glass window.

"Did Mark tell you we are heading down to Mount Rainier on Saturday?"

I look up at him and reply, "Yeah, Jase mentioned something like that to me."

"You should come with us."

The nerves I thought I had just gotten under control return. Why is he inviting me to go hiking with him?

"I don't know," I say. "I have a lot of studying I need to get done." This is my go-to excuse when I want to back out of something. But I notice him staring at me with a look that screams *I know you're lying.*

"Well, if you change your mind, we are heading out in the morning around eight."

Nodding my head, I take another sip of my tea.

"How did you know I would be here today?" I ask.

He grins at me before replying, "I didn't. I just thought I would stop by, and if you weren't here, I was just going to leave your scarf with whomever was working."

"I didn't mean for that to come out rude," I apologize.

"It didn't."

As we sit there in awkward silence sipping our hot drinks, he finally speaks and asks, "So, what are your plans for the rest of the day?"

"I have class in a couple hours, then I go to studio until five o'clock."

"Studio?"

"It's dance class," I explain.

Nodding his head, he asks, "You do that every day?"

"Yep. Two hours a day except for Tuesdays and Thursdays, which are three hours. But I tend to go in on the weekends as well for extra practice."

"That's a lot. When do you have time for anything else?"

Pressing my lips together and shaking my head, I say, "I don't"

"That bother you?"

"No . . . Why?" I ask.

"I don't know. When do you ever get down time?"

Down time isn't an option for me. The more occupied my time is, the less my mind tends to drift. "I don't. But I love dance, so I consider that my down time. It relaxes me."

Ryan continues to ask questions about dance and school as time begins to pass gently by. When I finish my tea, he notices and offers to get me another. I decline, knowing that I need to head home and clean up before going back to campus. He walks me out to where my car is parked and reminds me to think about the hiking trip the guys have planned. I tell him I will before getting into my car.

Storming out of the double doors of the studio, I head straight to my car, slide in, and slam the door shut. Frustrated, I grab the steering wheel and lay my head against my hands. My heart pounds fast, and I can still here the echoing of Ms. Emerson's hasty remarks in my head: *Get it together, Candace! Where is your head at?* CLAP! CLAP! *Feel it! Come on!*

I am so humiliated. I have never been yelled at like that in class before, but I feel like what she is asking for is outside of my control. My feet are flawless, I have no doubts about that, but I know what she's wanting, and I just can't give it to her. Inside that studio is the one place, the only place, where my head is free—where I am free. I don't want to lose that, lose the escape, the freedom, the nothingness.

She hammered me for nearly the entire two hours. I kept my eyes focused, but I could hear the sneers from a few of the other girls.

As I'm driving home, my phone rings from inside my dance bag. Digging through it, I grab my cell and look at the screen that reads: MOM CALLING. *Ugh!* I decline the call and let it go to voicemail then toss it back into my bag. That woman is the last person I want to talk to right now. Who am I kidding? She is the last person I want to talk to most of the time.

I haven't spoken with either one of my parents in over a month. Thanksgiving is a week away, and I'm certain that's why she's calling me. I'm dreading having to go home and spend time with them. For now, I'll just avoid her, because with the mood I'm in, there will be no way to avoid a fight with her.

Pulling up to my house, I see Kimber's car and Seth's jeep parked out front. I was hoping she wouldn't be here. I really just want to be alone right now instead of having another awkward and tense interaction with the girl who used to be my best friend—who I wish still was.

When I walk through the door, the house is quiet, and I assume they are in Kimber's room. I walk back to my room and begin powdering my pointes. I hang them up in my closet to air-dry before hopping into the shower.

As I am rinsing the last of the shampoo out of my hair, I hear the sounds that are becoming all too familiar from Kimber's room. "Are you kidding me?" I mumble in frustration. All I want is some peace and quiet to ease the stress I'm feeling.

Shutting off the water, I step out of the shower and quickly dry myself off. I throw on some underwear and a white tank top then walk into my closet to grab my black velour sport pants and matching zip-up hoodie. Standing in front of my mirror at my dresser, I shake out as much water as I can from my hair before throwing it up into a messy, loose bun on top of my head. I quickly apply some powder and swipe on my lip-gloss before sliding into my Uggs.

Hearing Kimber and Seth is making my skin crawl at this point, so I throw my sleeping pills in my purse, grab my keys, and get the hell out. I figure I can just spend the evening at Jase's apartment. I really need a little space to clear my head and relax.

When I arrive at Jase's and let myself in, I'm shocked to see Ryan sitting on his couch. I stop in my tracks and stare, unsure of what to say. *What is he doing here?*

"Hey, is everything all right?" I hear Jase ask from the kitchen.

I turn my head away from Ryan and focus on Jase. Taking a few steps further into the apartment, I respond, "Umm, yeah . . . I mean no." I'm stumbling over my words like an idiot, but I am so caught off guard that Ryan is here. And then realizing that it wasn't but a few minutes ago I was in the shower and here I stand with my wet hair that's tied up in a hair tie is making my head swirl.

Jase walks around the bar with a couple bottles of beer and heads over to the couch to hand one to Ryan. "What's that mean?" he asks.

"Nothing, never mind." I let out a deep sigh and walk over to take a seat in the oversized chair that is next to the couch. I flop down and lean my head back. "I didn't know you would have company, or I would have called or something."

Laughing, Jase says, "Candace, I gave you a key so you wouldn't have to call. You can come over whenever."

"You okay?" Ryan asks me.

I turn my head to look at him, then back at Jase, whom I know is wondering the same thing. "I don't want to talk about it," I say as I shift my eyes to the TV, which is playing SportsCenter. "Where's Mark?" I ask as I continue to zone out on the football highlights that are currently playing.

"He's finishing up rehearsals with the band. He should be here shortly, then we are heading out to Malone's to shoot some pool and chill," Jase says. His cell begins to ring and when he answers it, he grabs his jacket and excuses himself to the balcony.

"So, I take it the rest of your day didn't go well?" Ryan asks.

Looking over at him, I say, "Not exactly."

Even though I was extremely uncomfortable the other night at Spines, I'm feeling a little more at ease after hanging out with him this afternoon at work.

"Don't want to talk about it?"

I shake my head and turn my attention back to the TV when Jase walks back in.

"Who was that?" I ask

"Just Mark. He's heading over now."

"Hey, did you get a chance to think about Saturday?" Ryan asks. When I look over at him he is taking a sip of his beer.

"Saturday?" Jase questions.

"Yeah, I asked her to come with us."

I wish he wouldn't have brought this up because I know Jase will hound me until I say yes. He is on a mission to get me out more.

"Oh yeah? You coming?" Jase asks me.

Eying him, I say, "I have a lot of studying to do before finals."

"Please, we both know you are way ahead in all your classes," Jase says. "You should come. We are hiking up to the Tolmie Peak Lookout."

Not wanting to argue with Jase in front of Ryan and make him wonder why I am so anti-social, I appease him with a simple, "Fine."

When I look up at Jase, he has a big grin across his face, and I shake my head at him. Honestly, I don't really feel uneasy about going hiking. It's November, so there more than likely won't be too many people there, and it's not that often that I go to Mount Rainier. I went over the summer to go running a few times. I have never hiked to this particular lookout, but I have heard that the peak has an amazing view of the Sound.

I hear my phone ring from my purse that is sitting on the floor next to me. Reaching down, I pick it up and see that it's my mother again. I hit decline as I did when she called earlier and toss it back in my purse.

When I look up at Jase, he is giving me a questioning look, so I go ahead and answer his unspoken curiosity. "My mother."

By the time Mark arrives, I am ready for sleep. Having been at work this morning by six, I'm exhausted. As the guys get ready to leave, I ask Mark, "Do you mind if I stay here tonight?" I feel like I need to ask Mark most of the time instead of Jase because Jase will never tell me no.

"Of course not. I was going to go back home anyway. Thursdays are early days for me, so it's better if I'm not here," he explains.

As I nod my head, he gives me a long hug, knowing that something must be bothering me or I'd just go back to my house. When we pull apart, I catch a glimpse of Ryan over his shoulder, and he is watching me with a curious look on his face. He's probably wondering why I have a key to Jase's place and why I'm sleeping here tonight. I'm sure it must look weird to him, but for me, this is my normal.

chapter fourteen

THROWING AN EXTRA set of clothes into my bag, along with a few toiletries, I go to my closet and grab my black hiking boots. It's another chilly and misty grey day, but that is nothing new for this time of year, and it doesn't stop people from being outdoors either. The plan is to hit a few of the trails before hiking up to Tolmie Peak. Afterwards, we are going to hang out at Mark's house for pizza and beer.

Today feels a little strange for me. I haven't gone out like this since this past summer. But, it also feels nice, and it is keeping my mind busy and focused. I've been warming up to Ryan as well. He blends nicely with Jase, Mark, and I. Last night, Ryan ended up hanging out with us over at Jase's. We just laid low and watched a series of 'Ridiculousness' reruns on MTV. It felt nice to laugh like that. I honestly can't remember the last time I laughed so much. Last night, even if it was just for a moment, I felt a little normal—and it felt good.

When I pull into Mark's driveway, all three guys are tossing their shoes and backpacks into the back of Mark's white Range Rover. I grab my bags, step out of the car, and lock it before walking over to Mark.

"Hey, Candace," he says as he pulls me in for a hug.

"Hey, here's my backpack," I say, and I hand it to him to put in the car. Holding up my other bag, which has an extra set of clothes and toiletries, I say, "I'm just going to run this inside and leave it in your room."

"Sounds good."

Saying 'hi' to Jase and Ryan, I walk inside the house to drop my bag in Mark's room so that I can shower and change when we get back. When I make my way into the kitchen, I run into Ryan.

"Hey," I say as he is pulling out several bottles of water. "Can you grab me one of those?"

"Yeah, here you go," he says as he walks over and hands me one.

"Thanks."

"No problem. So, are you ready?"

"Yep. I haven't been out to Rainier since this past summer," I say and then I open my water and take a sip.

"I didn't know you liked to hike."

"I like most things athletic, although the majority of that is inside the confines of the ballet studio. I mainly just run the trails there, but I've been hiking a few times as well."

Picking up the waters, he says, "You're a runner too? I'm impressed," while walking towards the door. I walk over and open the door for him when he says, "You should come running with Mark and I sometime. We've been going early Tuesday mornings before hitting the gym."

We walk out, and Ryan tosses the waters into the car. I still haven't responded when he questions, "What do you think?"

I look down before looking back at him. "I haven't been out running in a while. I'd probably just slow you guys down. It was always something I did alone anyway."

Jase comes up to me, puts his arm around my shoulder, and asks, "What do you do alone? Besides everything."

I elbow him gently in the ribs and smile as I walk around the car and hop in the back seat. "I'm ready to go," I teasingly announce before closing the door and putting on my seatbelt.

Ryan gets in the front with Mark, and Jase slides in next to me. For most of the two-hour drive, the guys talk amongst themselves as I doze in and out of sleep. I have been spending a lot of overtime in the studio, and last night I was there pretty late, so I didn't get much rest.

When my body suddenly jerks out of a restless sleep, and I gasp in a loud breath, all eyes turn to me, but Ryan's are the only ones filled with questions. Mark turns around and starts talking to Ryan to take the attention off of me while Jase undoes his seatbelt and slides up next to me, wrapping his arm around my neck. Resting my head on his shoulder, he whispers in my ear, "You okay?"

I nod my head, close my eyes, and concentrate on my breathing. I feel embarrassed, and attempt to force out the thoughts that are creeping through my head. I just want to have fun today. I need to have fun today. For the remainder of the drive, I sit in the comfort of Jase's arms.

When we get to the turnoff, we have to drive about twenty minutes on a pot-holed gravel road to get to the Wonderland Trail that will lead us to Tolmie Peak. When we finally arrive and park the car, Mark opens the hatch, and I sit on the bumper while I tie up my hiking boots. It is lightly raining, and I pop the hood on my raincoat up and over my head. This time of year, the lower trails can become extremely muddy with the increase in rain. Ryan hands me an extra bottle of water to throw into my backpack before I sling it onto my back and wait for everyone else.

Once the guys are ready, we start making our way over to the trailhead.

Mark told me the hike should be around four hours. The terrain isn't too difficult to navigate as we start on the trail. We are all keeping a pretty decent pace and Mark is talking about the last show they played at Ryan's bar. I have never been to Blur. Jase has invited me a few times to go watch the band play, but has never pushed too hard.

A couple hours into our hike, the clouds open and it begins to rain. As we continue to trek on, the ground becomes marshy beneath our feet. I start to fall behind a little, but I yell to Jase to keep going and I'll catch up. I pull the hood on my jacket further over my head, so I don't realize that Ryan has stayed back until I almost pass him. Stopping, I look up at him, and he doesn't have his hood over his head. Rain is dripping off the ends of his hair, and it reminds me of the first night he came into the coffee shop with his rain soaked hair.

"You don't have to hang back. You can hike on ahead."

"Don't worry about it," he says as we continue to make out way through the trail. "I would hate for you to fall and hurt yourself and nobody be around."

Turning to look at him, I give him a grin and say, "Thanks."

"This shit's freezing."

I start laughing and agree with him. The rain is really cold.

After about a half hour, the rain finally lets up, and at this point, I am soaked from head to toe. I stop for a moment, take the hair tie that is around my wrist, and pull up my stringy wet hair on top of my head. Ryan walks closer to me. Laughing, he swipes his hand across my cheek, and the gesture makes me a little uncomfortable, until I see the brown mud on his fingers, and I laugh with him.

"You are covered in this shit," he chuckles, and all I can do is shrug my shoulders. You can't expect to not get dirty when you are hiking in the rain.

"Yeah, well, you're covered in it too," I say as we keep moving forward.

We manage to catch up with Jase and Mark near the incline to the peak. It's a mile hike up, and there is a light dusting of snow throughout the trek. When we reach the top, I climb the stairs to the lookout house and take in the view. I look out at the Sound and just stare. It's a breathtaking view. I walk back around the lookout, sit on the stairs, and grab a protein bar out of my backpack. Jase sits down behind me and kisses the top of my head. I look down to Mark and Ryan who are standing down below and catch Ryan looking up at us before he walks around to the other side of the lookout.

"Having fun?"

Turning my head to look at Jase, I say, "I actually am."

"Good." He wraps his arms around my shoulders, and I lean back into him as I eat my snack and rest.

"We should start heading back," he says after ten minutes or so.

"Okay."

We walk back down the stairs and find the other two.

"You guys ready to head back?" Jase asks them.

Everyone agrees, and we start the trek back down after we have all taken in the spectacular views. The walk down the peak is a slippery one from all the rain earlier. It isn't long before my feet slide out from underneath me, and I fall back into the mud.

"Crap!"

Reaching out both of his hands, I grab tightly onto Ryan's wrists as he pulls me out of the soggy mud.

"You're a complete mess."

"Yeah, I know," I say with a muddy face and now a muddy ass. I feel absolutely disgusting.

I keep ahold of Ryan's arm until we finally reach the bottom and let go. Jase and Mark are several steps in front of us, apparently lost in their own conversation, and it's not long before Ryan and I start talking about his job.

"So, how did you come about owning a bar?" I ask.

"Just kind of fell into it. When I graduated college, the economy was starting to decline, and I couldn't find a job. So, when I found out that the previous owner of that bar was about to shut the place down, I worked out a deal with him and was able to do a slow buyout."

"You went to U-Dub?"

"Yeah, I graduated back in 2007."

"So, that makes you . . . ?"

Laughing at me, he says, "Twenty-eight."

"What did you study?"

"Business Finance. So, it wasn't too far out of reach that I would come to own my own business."

"You enjoy it?"

"I do. When I did the buyout, I changed the whole place out and created a new vibe for it. It wasn't before long that the business was taking off quicker than I expected. At this point, the staff pretty much runs the place, and I have a trustworthy manager, so my schedule is very flexible."

"Sounds like the perfect job."

"You ever been there?"

Looking over at him and smiling, I say, "No. I don't really ever go out." I shake my head and continue, "I'm sort of a work-a-holic. Jase is always nagging me about that."

"Well, you should stop by sometime."

"Yeah. Maybe."

He laughs and says, "You're full of shit, aren't you?"

"Yeah. Maybe," I say, chuckling back at him.

Still laughing, he shakes his head at me as we continue the hike back.

When we finally reach the car, all of us are a mess, wet and covered in mud. I grab one of the towels that is in the back of the Range Rover and attempt to clean myself off, but at this point, most of the mud has dried and is now a hard, crusty matting on my clothes and face. Not wanting to drive all the back in these clothes, I ask Jase if he brought any extra. He tells me that Mark keeps a bag full of clean clothes in the back for when he goes to the gym. I reach in, grab his gym bag, and pull out a t-shirt and athletic pants, along with a dry pair of socks. I wouldn't think twice about changing in front of Jase, but I tell Mark and Ryan to go sit in the front so that I can change. Mark laughs at me, but gets in the car along with Ryan. I quickly strip out of my soggy clothes and Jase hands me the clean ones. Once I am good to go, I hop into the back seat and snuggle up tightly with Jase to try and warm up.

After everyone has showered and cleaned up, we all sit around the living room and tune into the Washington vs. Colorado football game. Mark throws a few logs of wood into the fireplace, and I go to get a bottle of wine from the kitchen. Mark and I have the same taste in wine, so we decide to share a bottle while the other two drink beer.

"What kind of pizza do you want, Candace?" Ryan hollers to me from the other room.

While I am opening the wine I shout back, "I don't care. I'll eat anything at this point."

As I walk back in with the wine and two glasses, Ryan is on his cell ordering dinner, and Jase is already finishing his first beer and watching the pre-game show on TV. We sit around, talking about our day and begin planning our next hike and the other trails we want to explore.

After a couple hours and way too much pizza, I lie back on the couch and laugh at Jase who has had a few too many beers and is screaming at the TV at a penalty call. Enjoying the entertainment of his theatrics, I hear my phone ring from the kitchen. Before I can get off the couch, Jase runs in and answers it with an obnoxious slur. When I stand up, he is walking my way, holding the phone out and mouthing 'I'm sorry' to me.

"Who is it?" I whisper as I take the phone from his hands, and he quietly says, "Your mother."

I walk out to the back patio when I finally say, "Hi, Mom."

"Jesus, Candace! I have been trying to get ahold of you for over a week. Why haven't you returned any of my calls?"

"Sorry, I've been busy and I guess a little distracted lately." Truth is, I have been purposely avoiding her calls. Thanksgiving is this Thursday, and she loves putting on a show at the country club. God knows the woman would never lift a finger in the kitchen, so for my whole life, every holiday dinner has been at the club.

"Well, your father and I were wondering when you were coming home?"

"Umm... I have a lot of schoolwork to get done, so I won't have much time," I lie. "What time are the reservations for?"

"That's it? You are just going to come for dinner? We haven't seen you in three months!"

Why does she do this? She always wants me to call her and visit her, but when I do, all she does is criticize me. "Mom, I'm really pressed for time, plus I am not sure when I have to work." Another lie.

"Well, that's just great! I had invited the Anderson's over for brunch Saturday morning. Now, I will have to rudely cancel."

My heart skips a beat when I question loudly, "Why would you do that, Mother?"

"What do you mean?"

"Mom! I haven't spoken with Jack in months." God, I hate saying his name. My stomach is knotting up just talking about this. But what the hell is she thinking? Why would she invite his parents over and just assume I was involved with that asshole?

"Well, what happened?"

"Nothing, Mom. We just didn't have anything in common."

"So, you ruin yet another possible relationship. What did you say to him?"

"Of course this is my fault, right?" I yell at her. "You are unbelievable, Mother!"

"I just have to wonder why, at the age of twenty-two, you have yet to meet anyone." Her voice is like ice to me, and I lose it.

"Why does it matter? Why do you even care? I wish you would show as much interest in me as you do my non-existent dating life." My voice is harsh and loud.

"Candace. Please. This is so childish of you to always yell at me when you don't like what I have to say. I'm just concerned, that's all."

"Well, Jack's a fucking asshole! I'll see you Wednesday, Mother," I spit out then hang up before I give her a chance to respond. God, she drives me absolutely crazy.

Shoving the phone in my pocket, I sit down on one of the chairs and stare up at the black sky. I take a moment to quell the tears that are threatening and breathe. I need to collect myself before going back inside. When I do get up and turn back to the house, I see Ryan watching me through the double French doors. He opens one of the doors and asks, "You okay?"

Not wanting to let this ruin my evening, I brush it off and laugh. "My mother's lost her mind, that's all."

"Wanna talk about it?" he asks when I walk past him.

Turning around to face him, I casually say, "Nothing to really talk about." Then I walk back into the living room and lie back down on the couch next to Jase.

"What did she want?" he asks.

"She wanted to know when I would be home for Thanksgiving."

"When are you going to leave?" Mark asks.

I watch Ryan walk back into the room and take a seat on the fireplace stoop. Looking back over at Mark, I say, "I told her I would be there Wednesday night. I'll probably leave Saturday morning." Turning my head to Jase, I ask, "When are you guys heading out?"

"Our flight leaves around noon on Tuesday," he says. Mark is taking Jase home with him to meet his parents in Ohio. Jase has been nervous about meeting Mark's parents, but I know it'll be fine. From what Mark has told us, his family is more than accepting of his sexuality. I am so happy that Mark and Jase were able to work everything out between them because they are so happy together.

"When do you guys get back?"

"Late Sunday afternoon."

I roll onto my side and ask Ryan what his plans are for Thanksgiving.

"I'm going to go spend a few days with my family down in Cannon Beach in Oregon. My aunts and uncles always come to my mother's house with my cousins for a big dinner."

"Will you be there for the weekend?" I ask.

"Nah, I'll come back home that night. My mom and her sisters spend the day plotting for Black Friday, so I always come back home and just lay low."

"Sounds like you have a big family," Jase says.

"Yeah, man, five cousins and between them they have seven little kids. I love them, but shit they're loud," he says, laughing.

"Must be nice though. I'm an only child with no cousins. Small family," I say.

I wish I knew what it was like to have a family like that. I had always wished I had a brother or sister growing up. I always felt lonely. My father worked constantly and my mother was never around. Always too busy attending all of her charity functions to pay attention to me. I know now that I will never have that close family that I had always dreamed of.

chapter fifteen

I GRAB MY last pair of shoes to put in my suitcase before driving to my parents for Thanksgiving. Kimber left Monday to go stay with her parents who live in Redmond, and Jase and Mark left Tuesday to fly to Mark's parent's house in Ohio. Everyone seemed excited for the break before they left while I have been dreading it.

I try to avoid my parents for the most part. Growing up with them wasn't easy. My mother is a social bee and is concerned more about herself and her family's image than happiness. She is a very stern and critical woman, and to please her is nearly impossible. Everything in her world has to be simply perfect so that others will envy her.

My father, being an orthopedic surgeon, was never around much. Both of my parents are influential and well-respected. But they were always so busy that I was left alone for the most part. When my mother was around, all we ever seemed to do was fight. We still do. It has always bothered her that I never participated much in her endeavors. She is involved in many charities, fundraisers, and other social events around town. I know she dreams of a daughter that would follow in her footsteps among her friends and be more concerned about my, as she puts it, 'social standing in the community.'

So now I am making the short twenty-minute drive to Shoreline to spend Thanksgiving with my parents. I plan to leave Saturday morning so that I can have a little down time before classes start back up on Monday.

As I enter through the gates of The Highlands, I make the slow winding drive that leads to the house I grew up in. Pulling up the drive to the two-story coastal house that is reminiscent of a Hampton beach house, I park, grab my suitcase, and walk up to the front door.

When I walk in, I can hear my mother talking on the phone, and I follow her voice to the kitchen to let her know I'm here. She stands there, leaning her hip against the center granite island, in her houndstooth pencil skirt, cashmere sweater, and black pumps. She acknowledges me with a slight nod before picking up her glass of wine and walking to the living room to continue her conversation.

I drag my suitcase to my bedroom, flop my purse onto the floor, and lie down on my bed. I turn my head to look through the French doors that look out over the Sound. I have always loved this view, even as a little girl. I used to spend hours sitting up here and staring out this very window wondering what my life would turn out like.

"Candace, dear," my mother calls from downstairs, and I am snapped out of my reverie.

Making my way downstairs, I meet her in the kitchen as she is refilling her glass of wine.

"Candace, there you are. How was your drive?"

"Not too bad," I say as I take a seat at the kitchen table.

"Did your friends already leave to go home?"

"Kimber did. Jase is actually spending Thanksgiving with his boyfriend's family."

"Candace, you know how I feel about that boy," she says in her judgmental tone.

Looking at her, not wanting to begin arguing with her ten minutes into my visit, I brush it off. "Yes, Mother."

"Well, then, your father got called into the hospital, so it's just us for the afternoon. I thought we could go over to Bellevue and do a little shopping."

"Yeah, that sounds great, Mom," I say as I stand up and walk to the fridge to grab a bottle of water. If there is one thing my mother is good at, it's shopping.

Standing in front of the three-way mirror in the fitting room, I slip on a beautiful lace and tweed Karen Millen shift dress. I smooth down the pencil skirt with my hands and admire the detailing.

"How does the dress fit, darling?" my mother asks from outside my fitting room.

"It's perfect." The one thing, possibly the only thing, my mother and I have in common is our love for fashion. I have always admired my mother's elegance and flair, and thankfully, it has always been something we have agreed upon.

My mother pulls back the heavy curtain to my dressing room, holding a pair of black platform pumps. Handing them to me, she says, "Here, try these on."

I slide on the shoes and turn to her to see her approval of my outfit.

"Stunning," she says and then turns to walk back out into the store.

I carry the outfit, along with a few tops and several pairs of pants, to the register and set everything on top of my mother's selections. As the sales clerk begins to ring up our items, my mother asks, "So, did you hear about Olivia's engagement?"

Keeping my eyes focused on our clothes, I respond, "No, I didn't hear."

"Yes, to William Lewis. He just partnered with his father's law firm.

And she is heading up the new division for the Children's Foundation."

I am trying hard to keep myself in check. I know exactly what my mother is doing, but I am determined to let it go. I know my mother wishes I were more like the Olivias of the world.

"That's great," I say as I grab our bags and start heading toward the exit.

"Before we leave, let's go to Neiman's for a little while. Maybe we can indulge in a glass of wine at Mariposa as well."

"Sounds great, Mom." I could really use a glass to help with the nerves that she is beginning to pinch.

While shopping through the racks, my mother continues, "I spoke with Sheila the other day, and she told me that her daughter was accepted into Columbia's graduate program for Museum Anthropology."

"Mom," I say as I eye her over the rack of clothes.

Shrugging her shoulders as if she is clueless, she says, "What, dear?"

I tilt my head to the side and give her a knowing smirk.

"Fiiine," she surrenders.

We finish up, purchasing more clothing than necessary, and go find a seat at Mariposa. Aiming to keep the focus off of me, I ask her about how the planning is coming along for the annual Christmas party at the Seattle Golf and Country Club that she heads every year. She begins to ramble on and on about it for the next hour before we decide to drive home.

"Bunny!" my dad exclaims as I walk into the house. He has called me 'Bunny' for as long as I can remember. When he pulls me in for a hug, I inhale his familiar scent. Since I was a little girl, he has always worn the same clean-scented cologne. I oddly find comfort in that smell. Although my father and I are far from having a close relationship, we never fight like my mother and I. Even though my father won't go against what my mother says and will always make excuses for her, I think that on some level, he might actually understand me.

"Hi, Dad," I say with my arms wrapped around him.

When he pulls away, he takes the bags from my hands, carries them into the kitchen, and sets them on the center island. He turns to kiss my mother on her cheek and says, "So, I see you ladies had fun spending my money today."

My mother laughs at him, and retorts, "Lots of fun, honey."

"Well, I am sorry that I had to work so late. We had a few emergency cases come in, but I have all of tomorrow off to spend with you," he says as he walks up to me and kisses me on my forehead. "Come on. Let's go have a drink before heading out to dinner." He takes my hand and leads me to the living room.

We all sit down, and I instantly become invisible as my parents begin to talk about anything and everything concerning them. I sip on my wine and tune them out as I pull out my cell and text Jase.

How's your trip so far?

I only have to wait a minute before he responds.

Good. Mark's family is oddly great!

LOL! What's that like? :)

Take it you're not having a good time.

It actually hasn't been too bad. Went shopping with mom, all the while bragging about how great her friend's children are doing. As if I'm slumming it at UW.

Sorry. Just a couple more days.

I really miss you. I'm so happy for you though!

Thanks. I miss you too. Text if you need me.

"Well Bunny, are you ready to go get something to eat?" my dad asks me.

Looking up at him, I grin and say, "Yeah, let me go freshen up really fast."

I quickly shoot Jase one last text before heading up to my room.

I will. Love you!

Love you too.

Dinner last night was surprisingly pleasant, although my parents continued to talk all throughout dinner as though I wasn't even sitting there. I have learned, with them, that sometimes it is better to be invisible than not.

I am finishing getting ready for our four o'clock reservation at the club. I have been keeping to myself most of the day with a run first thing this morning and then studying in my room. No one has said anything about my avoidance, but that's nothing new.

Wearing the dress that I got yesterday while shopping with my mother, I slide on the black pumps and put in a pair of pearl earrings. I take one last look in the mirror before grabbing my wool coat and going downstairs.

My parents are sitting in the library having a drink when I walk in.

"Don't you look lovely."

"Thanks, Dad," I say as I stand in the doorway. "It's almost time to go. You ready?"

"Yes," my father says. He stands up and takes my mother's hand before helping her up as well.

When my mother walks towards me, she doesn't say a word, and I wonder what's got her strung so tight. I shake it off and follow my parents out to the drive.

"Oh, hey. Do you mind if we take separate cars? I was thinking about visiting Katy after we leave the club. I haven't seen her since summer."

"Of course, darling," my father says as he opens the car door for my mother.

"Great." I walk over to my car and hop in. Katy and I grew up together and we try to see each other when we are both home from college on breaks.

When I pull up to the prestigious Seattle Golf and Country Club, I am greeted by one of the valets. He opens my door and helps me out of the car where I am rejoined with my parents. Walking in, I plaster on a smile as people begin to say hello to my parents and myself. The faces never change, only the occasions.

When we are seated at our table looking out over the immaculate greens, our waiter approaches, and I quickly order a glass of wine. Looking down at the menu card that is placed on the center of my place setting, I let out a sigh of relief that this year they are actually serving turkey instead of the dreadful duck they had last year. But of course, it's not your traditional turkey, not that I even know what that is since I have spent every holiday dinner here in this very room. They are serving a porcini-soy stuffed turkey with shallot-truffle gravy. Nothing can ever be simple.

When the waiter returns with our drinks, my father orders some hors d'oeuvres before our main course. My father lifts his glass and makes a quick toast before we clink and take our sips.

"So, Bunny, how is this school year going for you?"

"It's been really busy, but I am managing to maintain my four point GPA, which should make you proud."

I hear my mother softly chuckle as my dad says, "You know how important grades are to me, and it shows that you care. Of course I'm proud."

"Thanks, Dad."

My mother clears her throat, and I eye her when she says to my father, "She's a dance major, honey. How hard can it be to have a four point?"

Clearly she had one too many cocktails in the library back home, because she is being more bold than usual. I tell myself to let it go so that this doesn't wind up in an argument.

My father doesn't say anything when she continues, "Sorry if that came out rude, but have you given any thought as to what you will do after graduation this spring? Have you applied to any graduate schools yet?"

"Graduate schools?" I ask as I shift my look to my dad and shake my head feeling like this choice of conversation was premeditated.

"Yes, well, your mother and I were concerned about your next step."

"You know I have always planned on dancing. That has never changed."

In a much softer voice, my mother says, "We were assuming that you would be taking a more serious outlook on your future. I mean, we have allowed you these past four years, hoping you would grow out of this little ballerina dream of yours." She says this as if I'm a child with foolish dreams, like when a little girl says she wants to be a fairy princess when she grows up.

I take my time to respond when my father speaks up. "Your mother's right, dear. It's time we start making some serious decisions. Although I have been fine with letting you direct these past four years, it's time to get on track and get focused."

I look at these two people sitting in front of me. My parents. The two people that should know me the best, love me, support me, and encourage me. But they don't know me at all. My stomach twists at the realization that they have never known me. Deep down, I've known this all along, but I guess I've been fooling myself to believe that I was wrong about them. How can they be so oblivious to who I am?

"I thought you guys knew what I wanted. This was never something I have wavered on." I begin to feel my eyes sting, but I refuse to cry. Although I'm aware that they disapprove of my choice of major, I never really thought they would try to step in and change my dreams.

"You can't seriously think that you can make a respectable career out of dancing, do you?"

"Yes, Mom. I do." I snap back.

"Your mother and I just want to help you avoid having regrets."

"About the only thing I regret was believing that you two supported me," I whisper harshly. "How can you do this?"

"Honey, look at yourself. Your choice of friends is a little concerning, you don't participate in any extracurricular activities, you don't have a steady boyfriend, you never call us or visit when we live only a few miles away. I look around and see the girls you graduated high school with and they are either getting married, furthering their education, starting their careers, and I just have to wonder what went wrong?"

"Nothing went wrong!" I say a little louder than I should have. Lowering my voice, I continue, "Is it so hard for you to believe in me? To trust that I am making the best decisions for myself? And as far as my friends go, at least they understand me and love me anyway."

"Bunny, we do love you."

"No. You may think you do, but you just want me to be someone I'm not. I've never been that person. How can you not see that?"

"Candace, calm down."

"No, Mother. What did you expect? That you and Dad could just trap me here and I would willingly let you step in and take control of my future? That's not going to happen. Thank you for paying my way through college, but we're done."

"Your mother and I are not going to stop supporting you, Candace. That's not what we are saying. But this idea of yours . . . it's just not realistic—"

My father is cut short when my mother interrupts. "I can't deal with you anymore. I simply cannot figure you out and why you can't be more responsible. Do you know how embarrassing it is for me when people ask me what my daughter is studying in college? The looks I get when I tell them you're a dance major, knowing you have no intentions on going to grad school and finally getting a respectable degree. And your attitude is just very unbecoming lately—"

She stops talking when I stand up and throw my napkin down on the table. "What's unbecoming is *you*, Mother. You are nothing but a self-centered woman who never even put her education to use. You married rich and frolic with all the other housewives, and you justify your lifestyle with your charities, but I see right through you." I look over at my father and quickly apologize for my abrupt departure before turning my back to them and walking out of the dining room.

The tears begin to fall as I feel another part of myself breaking, a part that I have held onto so tightly with hope, hope that my parents, behind all their shit, really loved me. But I just realized that to them, I am nothing more than a tarnished accessory.

chapter sixteen

I FEEL LOST, like I'm floating around and there is nothing to grab onto to ground me. Today did not go as I thought it would. Sure, I often argue with my mother, but today was more than another fight. Today was my realization, a culmination of everything, finally clear and right in front of my face, staring into my eyes.

After I walked out on my parents, I drove back to the house and grabbed all of my belongings. There's nothing left for me to say, and there's nothing they could say to dull the pain that's shooting through my chest. I finally see that I'm a failure in my mother's eyes and a disappointment in my father's. So, I just left.

Pulling up to my empty house, I sit in my car for a little while and listen to the rain beating against my car. I close my eyes and lean my head back on the headrest. Everyone is probably having a great time, eating dinner, and visiting with family and friends, laughing. And here I am, alone, sitting in my car in the pouring rain. Pathetic.

I step out into the rain, pull my suitcase out of the trunk, and walk slowly to the front door not caring that I am getting soaked. It's dark and quiet when I walk inside. I drag myself to my room and head to the bathroom to shower.

When I am cleaned up and in my pajamas, I unpack my bag and hang up all of my new clothes. While I am sorting through my closet I hear my phone chime. I rush over to my bed to grab my cell when I see a text from a number I don't recognize. Swiping the screen to open the message, it reads:

Got your number from Mark. Wanted to see how your Thanksgiving went.–Ryan

I hold the phone in my hand, staring at the text for a minute before typing my response.

I think we managed to fall into the universal tradition of holiday drama. :)

That bad?

Kinda. Now I'm home with no food.

It takes a while for Ryan to text me back as I continue to hold my phone and stare at the screen. I have never considered Ryan one of my friends, more of just Mark or Jase's friend that I hang out with on occasion. But being able to sit here tonight, when I feel like crap, and text him, feels nice.

Sorry, saying bye to everyone. About to head home myself.

Did you have a good time with your family?

Yeah, I did. Ate way too much. Feel like I need to hibernate.

LOL. Drive safe. Is it pouring where you are?

Not too bad. Try and have a good night.

Thanks.

Before I set my phone down, I store his number into my contacts then hop up to go rummage through the kitchen. I find an old bag of popcorn. No one went grocery shopping since we all were supposed to be gone for the week, and now there is nothing to eat. I decide to heat up the bag, get comfortable on the couch, and turn on the TV.

The chiming of my phone wakes me. Squinting my eyes against the sunlight that is filtering in through the windows, I grab my phone to see that it's almost eight in the morning and that I have a missed text from Ryan. I shift and sit up on the couch, then read his text.

I am heading out for breakfast. Wanna join?

Grocery shopping is the last thing I want to do, so with no food in the house, I type my response.

Sure. Where?

The Dish Café. 9:00?

See you then.

I hop off the couch to take a quick shower and get ready. I wasn't planning on coming back home for a couple days, so it'll be nice to hang out since I have nothing to do otherwise.

After smearing on some lip-gloss, I slide on my leopard rain boots under my boot-cut jeans. I clasp on my watch and make my way out into the rain to get into my car.

When I walk into The Dish, a small dive café, I see Ryan is already sitting at one of the tables. He looks up from his menu as I approach the table.

"Hey," he says.

Shrugging off my coat and draping it over the back of the chair, I sit down and say, "Hi, thanks for inviting me. I literally have no food at the house."

"So, what did you wind up doing last night?"

"I ate an old bag of popcorn and passed out on the couch."

Laughing at me, he says, "That's pathetic."

"My thoughts exactly," I say grinning.

"I ordered you a hot tea."

Surprised that he remembered that I like hot tea, I say, "Oh, thanks."

I pick up the menu and quickly decide on the blueberry pancakes. When I set my menu down and look up, Ryan is staring at me. I know the obvious question that must be lingering in his head is what happened yesterday that made me come home early. Before giving him an opportunity to speak, I quickly turn the focus on him and ask, "So, how was your Thanksgiving?"

"It was good. We did the typical family thing like we do every year. Mom and her sisters being loud and gossipy, cooking all day. I hung out with the guys and watched football while the kids ran around screaming and playing. My head was pounding by the end of the night."

"That actually sounds nice."

"Yeah, it is. It's not too often that everyone can get together, so when it does happen, it's fun. Crazy, but fun," he says then picks up his cup of coffee to take a sip.

When the waiter stops at our table, I tell him I want the blueberry pancakes, and Ryan orders the heuvos verdes.

"So how many nieces and nephews do you have?" I ask as I sip my tea.

"Three nieces and four nephews all under the age of five. I'm not lying when I say it's loud and crazy!" I can see by the smile on his face that he loves the kids regardless of his comments.

"So, you're an only child?" Ryan asks.

"Yeah. I have a pretty small family. My grandparents on my father's side died when I was in high school, and I have never met my mother's parents or her sister. My father is an only child as well, so it's just the three of us."

"Quiet."

"Hmmm . . ." I don't even want to begin to explain my family's dysfunction, so I ask, "Is your mother out with the crazy Black Friday crowd today?"

"God, you have no idea. She and my aunts go bat-shit over the sales."

The waiter comes and drops off our food. I let out a pleased sigh when he sets down my pancakes that are bigger than the plate they are served on. I pick up my fork and knife and look up at Ryan as he says, "That's a shitload of food. You gonna be able to eat all that?"

Putting all manners aside, I cut a chunk of pancake that is obscenely large, shove it into my mouth, and chew while nodding my head at him in response. His smile broadens and he laughs out loud at my gesture.

We continue to chat as we indulge in our food. Ryan is a really easy person to talk to, even without the company of either Jase or Mark. We talk mostly about his family, and I do pretty well with keeping the focus off of myself. When I can't eat another bite, I lean back in my seat and groan with the discomfort of being entirely too full. I close my eyes when I hear Ryan laughing at me and saying, "I can't believe you ate all that. You sound like you're about to die."

"You have no idea."

"You gonna be able to walk, or will I have to carry you?"

I open my eyes to look at him, when I say, "Honestly, I really need to walk this off."

"Come on, let's get outta here." Ryan stands up, throws some cash on the table, and reaches his hand out to me. We walk out into the rain, and he nods his head towards a four-door black Rubicon.

"What?" I ask as I wonder what he's thinking.

"I know you don't have shit to do today, so come on." He walks over to the large jeep that sits high on its wheels and opens the passenger door. "Come on."

I stand where I am and ask, "Where are we going?"

"I'll figure that shit out when you get in."

I can't help but laugh at his apparent love for the word 'shit.' Walking over to him, he takes my hand again to help me into the seat and closes the door behind me. When he gets in, I shake my head at him as he begins to pull out of the parking lot. He turns onto the main road and asks, "You like Thirty Seconds to Mars?"

"Love them."

He smirks at me and questions, "Really?"

"Yeah, why?"

"You just don't strike me as the type of girl who would like that kind of music."

He turns on the stereo and 'Northern Lights' begins to play when I ask, "And what type of girl is that?"

"First impression I got was that you're really quiet. I thought you were just shy, but the more we hang out, it seems like not much embarrasses you.

When I look at you, I see this tiny little ballerina, so I figure you sit around and listen to Mozart and shit."

We both start laughing and I say, "Mozart and *shit?* I'm not *that* refined, so you can relax. But I've never been loud and obnoxious, so yeah, I'm quiet."

He quickly glances my way and grins at me before returning his focus to the road.

"So, where are we going?"

"Someplace I haven't been to in a long time," he says then reaches over and turns up the music. I lean back in my seat, and we don't say anything else. We just sit and listen to music. After a few minutes, he turns into a waterfront parking lot, and I am surprised at where we have wound up.

"The aquarium? I haven't been here since I was a little girl."

"Me neither."

"Why are we here?"

"To have a little fun. Come on," he says as he gets out of the car.

When we go inside, the place is full of kids and their parents. I feel as if we are the only adults that are here by our own free will because this place is a madhouse. We walk up to a huge underwater viewing window that greets you as you walk in. I go right up to the window and press my hand against the cool glass and watch as the fish swim by. I remember coming here on a field trip once before when I was in the fifth or sixth grade. Even though I grew up here, I never really did many touristy things unless it was through school. My parents rarely ever took me out to explore the city.

I look down to my side at a little boy, maybe around six years old, who is looking up at me. He has his hand on the glass just as I do.

"Hi."

"You're pretty," he says, and I smile down at him and respond, "Thank you. You're not so bad yourself."

His face lights up with a huge smile when Ryan walks up from behind us and asks the little boy, "Do you think I can steal your girlfriend away from you, buddy?"

The boy looks up at him and laughs. I can tell he is embarrassed as he nods his head.

I say 'bye' to my new friend and follow Ryan as he navigates us all the way to the touch pool. I hesitate as he starts to walk up to the exhibit.

"Come on."

I slowly walk up to the edge of the tank.

"You scared?" he asks.

"Kind of, yeah"

Pulling me up to the tank next to him, he dips his hand into the water and starts touching the orange and purple starfish.

"They're not going to attack you, Candace," he says with a smile.

"No way."

"We aren't leaving until you touch something in this tank," he teases me.

I look around, and kids that are elbows deep in the water surround us. Pushing up my sleeve, I very slowly start to move my hand toward the water, but when I see a hermit crab crawling in the tank where I was just about to put my hand, I jump back and squeal. Several of the kids start laughing at me, and Ryan joins in.

"Really nice!"

"What?" he says through his laughter.

"You're making fun of me."

"You're such a baby. Come here," he says and takes ahold of my hand to pull me back up to the tank. He shifts his hand to grip the top of mine and I shout, "Wait a second!" when my hand almost hits the water.

I don't look at him, but I hear him laughing at me.

"Relax."

He moves our hands down to the top of the water, and I nervously start to shift my weight between both of my feet when I feel the cold water on my fingertips. I know I am bouncing up and down like a scared little girl, but I don't care. I am terrified of these little sea creatures, especially the spiky sea urchins. The few kids that are near us are giggling at me, and when I finally feel the course, rough texture of the starfish on my fingers, one of the little boys claps and screams, "You did it!"

I look up at Ryan, and he is laughing along with me at the excitement of the little kid.

"See, not too scary," he says as he takes his hand off of mine and goes to grab some paper towels to dry our hands.

We take our time exploring the aquarium and all the exhibits while laughing and having a fun time. After an hour or so, we head downstairs to the underwater dome. We walk through the small tunnel that leads into the concrete and glass enclosure. The room is a little dark because of the weather outside; the sun isn't out today to filter its light through the water. We find an open seat along the perimeter of the dome that faces the windows and sit down. I lean back and prop my feet up on the concrete ledge and watch the schools of fish swim by. This day has turned out to be really fun. I never go out like this with my friends, and I'm starting to wonder why. Being here has kept my mind free from the way I left things with my parents yesterday.

"What are you thinking about?" Ryan asks.

"Nothing really."

He doesn't say anything; he just sits back with me and stares out into the water. When we finally decide to leave, we stop and grab a coffee at the café before heading out to the car. It's a pretty cold day, so I basically use the coffee to keep my hands warm as we walk to Ryan's jeep. Again, he helps me step up inside the car, and I set the coffee down in the cup holder and shove my hands into my coat pockets.

"Damn it's cold!" Ryan says as he hops into the car and starts it. He turns up the heat and begins to drive.

Feeling tired, I rest my head on the back of the seat and shut my eyes. Our drive is quiet and peaceful. When I finally hear the car turn off, I open my eyes and wonder why we are parked in front of a grocery store.

"What are we doing here?" I ask.

"You said you don't have any food at your house."

"Yeaaah?"

"Well, let's go buy some food so I don't have to hear about you eating stale popcorn again," he says as he laughs at me.

He gets a cart and starts following me around the store. Feeling a little uncomfortable and embarrassed, I throw in a couple bags of lettuce and some apples.

"No wonder you were starving at breakfast, you eat like a rabbit."

I roll my eyes at him and continue grabbing food for the week. Once I purchase everything and we load the car, I give him directions to my house. When he pulls into my driveway, I become nervous. I don't like the idea of having him inside my house. I try to calm myself down, but I can't help feeling scared. Hanging out with him all day has been fine, but we have been surrounded by people. I don't like the idea of being alone with him in my home. Knowing there isn't really much I can say to make him stay in the car, I hesitantly get out and grab a few bags as he grabs the rest, and I unlock the front door.

"This is a pretty nice house for a college student," he remarks.

"Yeah," is all I say in response as I lead him into the kitchen. Trying to keep calm and not overreact, I silently and quickly put everything away. When everything is in its proper place, I immediately start walking to the front door, and thank goodness Ryan follows without questioning my strange behavior.

As we are driving back toward the café, I feel bad for my rude behavior, so I soften it by saying, "Thanks."

"For what?"

"Today. I had fun hanging out."

"You should say 'yes' when I ask you to go running with me tomorrow morning."

"Is that you asking me or telling me?"

He turns to look at me and smirks, not saying anything. Giggling at his invitation, I say, "Okay then."

"Okay then," he repeats.

By the time we arrive back at the café, the parking lot has emptied out and the rain is now falling hard. Ryan reaches over and turns down the music before saying, "I didn't want to say anything earlier, but I can't help but wonder about what made you come home yesterday."

Being worn out from our day, and feeling more at ease around him,

I don't hesitate much when I decide to answer. "I got into a fight with my parents. Some pretty nasty things were said, so I just left."

He shifts in his seat to face me and I do the same, as he asks, "You guys fight a lot?"

"My whole life. My mother is a difficult woman to be around. She doesn't approve of the way I want to live."

"What do you mean?"

"My parents are more concerned about their social standing than my happiness. So, having a daughter who wants to be a dancer and is unengaged is not a good look for them."

"That's pretty shitty."

"I'm used to it," I quietly say and lean the side of my head against the seat.

"No one should be used to that," he says in a soft raspy tone. "They should be proud of you. I've only just met you, but you're pretty great from what I know so far."

His words are so sweet, but at the same time, a little unnerving. What's strange is that I can say the same about him. I have only known Ryan for a short while, but our friendship feels very natural.

"I had always hoped that somewhere beneath their hard exterior that they would be proud of me, but after last night, I now know that they aren't. My mother actually said she was embarrassed by me."

Ryan lets out a long sigh and leans in closer to me. I look down to see him reaching over and sliding his hand over the top of mine. When I look up at him, he is staring at me with a hint of sadness in eyes.

My heart starts to race, and I feel myself wanting to close off. It hasn't really bothered me when he's taken my hand in the past, but something about being alone with him now and opening up to him is beginning to overwhelm me. I sit up, pull my hand away from his, and start fiddling with the door handle. I hear the click of the locks and thank him with a shaky voice for hanging out with me. I hesitantly turn around to look at him when I get out of his car and give him an apologetic smile because I don't know what else to do, but I need space, and I need to be alone before I start to really freak out. I dig out my keys from my purse and unlock my car door. I take another quick glance at him before driving away, and he is sitting there watching me with a confused look on his face.

Embarrassed by my moment of weakness, I pull away and start driving home. Anxiety begins to course through my body, and I cry. How can I be so weak and show it in front of Ryan? I'm disappointed in myself for not holding it together better.

When I pull up to my house, I just sit in my car and continue to wipe the tears that are falling down my cheeks. I slowly inhale a deep breath and am able to gain a little bit more control over my emotions.

Why am I acting like this? I had such a great day, and Ryan has become a good friend to me. I know I need to just pull myself together because he will be coming over tomorrow morning to run, and he will think I'm a total basket case if I call and cancel on him after what just happened. *God, Candace, get your shit together. You can do this.*

chapter seventeen

AFTER I LACE up my shoes, I go to the kitchen to get some water when I hear the doorbell ring.

"Hey, you ready?" Ryan asks when I open the door.

"Yeah. Here, hold these." I hand him the waters and turn to grab my hooded running jacket off the couch. Zipping it up, I say, "Okay, I'm ready. Let's go."

I take one of the bottles of water and tell Ryan to keep the other. Locking the door behind us, we start off with a brisk walk through the neighborhood.

"I figured we could run around campus and through some of the surrounding neighborhoods. How are you with distance?" he asks.

"I'm good for around six or seven miles, but it's pretty cold out today, so I'm not too sure how long I'll last."

The morning is bitterly cold, and the sun has just started to rise. The streets are empty aside from a few other runners we see as we start walking toward the UW campus. We begin with a light jog for about a half-mile before we break into our run. The streets are wet and soggy with dead leaves that are piled along the curbs and scattered over the lawns. A slight mist is in the air, which isn't anything new, and it looks like we are due to have another rainy day. It has rained every day this month, and the news keeps talking about the city hitting the big 'four-oh' this next week when the yearly rainfall will reach forty inches.

When we finally hit the campus, the sidewalks are completely empty, and it's abnormally quiet.

"Next weekend Mark's band is playing another gig at the bar. You should stop by," Ryan says as we run through the quad that is lined with now-bare cherry trees.

"Thanks, but I have to work."

"Would you come if you didn't have to work?"

"Probably not," I answer a bit more honestly than I intended. He knows I don't go out much, well, ever. Jase is always teasing me about being a hermit around Mark and Ryan, so it shouldn't be any surprise to Ryan when

I say that.

"Have you ever heard Mark play?"

Jogging up a flight of stairs, my breath is short when I answer, "No."

"Never?"

"God, don't make it sound like I'm such a bad friend, Ryan," I say sarcastically.

Ryan starts to laugh. "No, I'm not. I'm just surprised, that's all."

When I look over at him, he meets my eyes, and I say, "No, you're not," with a grin.

"So, why don't you ever go out?"

"I'm normally busy with either school or work. I've never gone out too much. In fact, the past few weeks have actually been a big stretch for me. But, Jase has been on my case, so instead of butting heads with him, I haven't been putting up much of a fight."

"I should thank him then."

"Why's that?"

"Because I really like hanging out with you," he says openly, and I immediately feel my face heat despite the frigid weather. I don't respond as we continue to run. If I'm being honest with myself, I really like hanging out with Ryan as well. He's been a great distraction for me since the fight with my parents.

"So, what are your plans for today?" Ryan asks after a while.

"I need to study. I was also thinking about going up to the studio since nobody should be there and working on my solo."

"Your solo?"

"Yeah, graduating seniors have to choreograph a solo and audition for our final production at the end of the year." I say as we begin to veer off into another neighborhood. "It's kind of a huge thing."

"Why's that?"

"It's the one time that agencies come out to watch. So if you get one of the solos, then you have a good chance at having a job after you graduate."

"Will it be hard for you to get a solo?"

"I honestly don't know. My piece of music isn't the best, so I'm having a hard time feeling it, and my instructor is noticing, which is never good. Plus, all the girls are insanely competitive." I say with labored breath.

The cold air is starting to burn my lungs when Ryan asks, "You doing okay?"

"My lungs are burning."

Looking over at me with a slight smile, he says, "No more talking, just run."

I smile back and nod my head as we continue to weave through the quiet streets.

We are making our way back to the house when the rain starts to fall. The drops feel like tiny pieces of ice on my face as we pick up our pace to get back to my house. Ryan turns to look at me, and I see that he's laughing.

Barely able to breathe at this point, I manage to huff out, "What the hell's so funny?"

"Us."

I stare at him until he continues, "Always getting stuck in this freezing ass rain."

Smiling in agreement, we start sprinting to my house as we round the corner onto my street. Running up the sidewalk and the few steps to the covered front porch, I lean over and grip my knees with my hands as I gasp for air. I begin to feel lightheaded when Ryan steps in front of me, placing both his hands on my shoulders. He walks me over to the large bench on the porch, and we both sit down. Still feeling slightly dizzy, I lower my chest down toward my knees and lay my head in my hands.

Ryan places his hand on my back, leans down to my ear, and says, "Slow your breathing, Candace." He begins to rub my back when he repeats, "Slow."

I take in one long, deep breath and let it out gently. When the dizziness begins to subside, I slowly lift my head up and lean back into the seat.

"Here," Ryan says as he unscrews the cap to his bottle of water and hands it to me.

My throat burns, so I'm only able to take in a small sip before thanking him.

"I shouldn't have pushed you like that by sprinting," Ryan says.

"It's fine, I just haven't been running very much since summer, and the cold air got to me. I'm okay," I say with chattering teeth. I look at him, his long hair dripping with water, and I know I would be a total bitch if I left him like this to drive home. So, with hesitation, I say, "We should go inside and dry off."

When we walk in, I show him to the guest bathroom and run to grab some of Jase's clothes that are in my room for him to change into. I leave him be while I go into my room and change into some dry clothes and tie my wet hair into a messy bun. When I walk out of my room, Ryan is sitting on the couch in the living room. He stands up and starts thanking me for joining him on his run. A huge part of me is relieved that he isn't trying to stay here and hang out. Being alone with him inside my house still makes me feel very uneasy.

"You still going to the dance studio after that run?" he asks while walking to the front door as I follow him.

"Yeah, honestly, I'm fine. I didn't eat before we left, so I'm sure that's why I got lightheaded. I'm going to fix something to eat, then study for a while before I head up there."

"I'll catch you later then?"

"Yeah," I say.

Once Ryan leaves, I make a pot of coffee and grab a breakfast bar. I go back to my room, pick up my phone, and call Jase. When he answers, he's concerned that something is wrong. I assure him that I'm fine and that I just miss him. He can't talk for long because he is out with Mark's family for brunch. I'm used to always having Jase around, but I am happy that he is so content with Mark. They have become very serious in these past few months; I know Jase really loves him. Both of them come back home tomorrow, so Jase and I make plans to hang out after Mark goes home.

Dancing was just what I needed today. After Ryan left, I spent the majority of the afternoon stressing about my parents rather than studying. I'm used to my father calling me after a fight and trying to smooth things over, but he hasn't tried contacting me at all. My mother and I said some pretty harsh words to each other, and I'm just not quite sure how we are going to move past this.

Going to the studio helped clear my head and relaxed me as it always does. I was able to focus on and choreograph several eight-counts for my solo. I am starting to get some direction with the piece, and it feels good to be making progress with it.

After I worked on my solo, I decided to stay a while longer to work on my center floor technique. I ended up being at the studio for a little over three hours. By the time I got back home, my head was clear, so I decided to make good use of it and get the schoolwork done that I couldn't focus on earlier.

Finishing up some research for a paper, I check my phone to see that it's past eight o'clock. I decide to call it a night and quickly change into a pair of pajama pants and a t-shirt. I pop a sleeping pill and walk to the kitchen to grab a quick bite to eat before heading to bed.

The doorbell rings just as I am opening the fridge. I'm beyond surprised when I open the door and see Ryan standing there with a pizza and beer.

"What are you doing here?!"

Giving me a slight smile, he steps around me and comes inside. "I ran out to grab some dinner and knew you weren't doing anything tonight, so I drove here instead of back to my place."

"Oh . . ."

"That a problem?"

He starts walking to my kitchen, and all I can mumble out is, "Ummm . . . no. I just . . ."

"Just what?"

"Just surprised that's all. Why didn't you just text me?"

He sets down the pizza and beer and starts opening drawers until he finds the one with the bottle opener. "Because I figured you would probably tell me you were studying." He pops the cap off the beer, hands it to me, and winks as I press my lips together and agreeably nod. He takes his beer bottle and clinks the neck of it to mine then takes a sip.

"Plates?" he asks, and I nod my head over to the cabinet they are in while I take a long sip of my beer. "So, how was the rest of your day?" he continues while he moves with ease around my kitchen.

"Good. I got a lot done actually."

"Great, let's eat then," he says as he stacks the plates and napkins on top of the pizza box and heads into the living room. "Do you mind grabbing the beer?"

"No problem."

Setting everything down on the coffee table, he plops down on the couch and watches me until I move to join him. The past two times he has been here made me very uncomfortable, but his playful attitude tonight is amusing me more than anything.

I am pleasantly surprised when I open the pizza box to see that he got a Hawaiian pineapple pizza. I look over at him and ask, "How did you know I like pineapple on my pizza?"

Leaning forward and grabbing a slice, he says, "I didn't. Like I said, I got this for me before deciding to come over."

"Oh."

He smiles at me before taking a bite, and I grab a slice and join him. Sitting here, eating pizza and drinking beer, feels a lot like the times Jase and I have done this—comfortable. Then I remember that it probably feels comfortable because I already took my sleeping pill, which always helps relax me. Enjoying his company, I brush it off.

"So, you know what I did with my day. What about you?" I ask.

"After our run, I went to the gym to do some lifting. Then later, I went to the bar to work. Had to sign off on a bunch of paperwork and inventory orders. That's pretty much it."

I grab another beer and hand it to him so he can pop off the cap. When I start to take a drink, Ryan suggests finding something to watch on TV. I grab the remote for him, and he starts flipping through all the channels before stopping on some old black and white movie. He sets the remote down and leans back on the couch, content with his selection.

"What the heck is this?" I ask facetiously.

"You don't know this movie?"

"Does anyone know this movie?"

He smiles at me and says, "Candace, it's a classic."

I shake my head at him, completely clueless.

"It's 'Double Indemnity' from the 1940's. It's a great movie."

"You watch a lot of these movies?"

He shakes his head at me in mock disapproval. "Sit back and just watch. You'll like it." I sit back into the couch, and he points to the TV as he continues. "See that girl? Her name is Phyllis and that guy is an insurance agent that she is trying to seduce."

"Why?"

"Because she wants him to murder her husband so she can collect the money from his policy."

"Oooh, I like her already," I tease.

Ryan laughs at me and says, "Just watch."

Kicking our feet up on the coffee table, we lean back and watch the movie.

"Candace . . . Candace, wake up."

Opening my eyes, I look up and see Ryan as he is whispering at me to wake up. I lie there, confused in my sleepy haze, and it takes me a moment to realize that I am lying on the couch with my head in his lap. The haze instantly disappears as I jump up, startled at the scenario. *What happened?* I must have completely passed out. Mixing my sleeping pill with the beer was a huge mistake.

"Are you okay?" Ryan asks as he stands up and takes a step toward me.

Feeling a bit flustered, I hold my hands out to gesture to him not to come any closer.

"I'm sorry, I didn't want to leave you without you locking the door behind me. You fell asleep, and I didn't want to wake you, so I let you sleep for a while."

"I'm sorry."

"For what?"

"Startling easily. I didn't know I fell asleep. I'm just . . . I was just disoriented." I put my hands down and feeling abashed, I apologize again.

"Candace," he says as he takes a step toward me and reaches his hand to brush back a lock of my hair off of my forehead. My body stiffens at his touch, and he quickly pulls his hand back.

"I'll lock the door behind you," I say to rush him out.

"Let me help you clean this up."

Looking at the pizza box and beer bottles, I say, "I'll do it. It's all trash anyway."

"You sure?"

"Yeah."

We walk to the door, and he turns back to look at me. He is standing so close that I have to look up at him. I have never noticed our height difference before now. I'm a little over five feet, so he stands much taller than I do. Looking me in the eyes, he quietly says, "I want you to feel comfortable with me."

There is something about the look on his face that's telling me he feels strongly about this, and I whisper, "I know," because I think I feel the same way.

"Okay. So, we'll talk later?"

Nodding my head, I say, "Yeah."

I lock the door behind him after he leaves, and I let out a long sigh. I grab all the trash and dump it in the garbage can then go crawl into bed.

Feeling confused about Ryan, I have a hard time settling back down to sleep. My mind is all over the place, and I am not sure how to sort my thoughts out. Thank God Jase is coming back home tomorrow because I really need to talk to him. For now, I lie in bed, confounded by my thoughts as I stare into the darkness.

chapter eighteen

BEING ALONE IN the house all day is driving me crazy, so I decide to head over to Jase's even though his flight doesn't get in for another two hours. The quiet is just a reminder of how much I miss my roommate. It's almost as if I live alone because we hardly ever interact anymore. I do know that she will be coming back today, I just don't know when. Before this year, we were like sisters. Even though I never really went out with her and her other friends, we always made time for each other and would constantly call and text each other. Now—nothing.

When I get to Jase's apartment, I go lie down in his room. It has been a couple weeks since I have slept here, so his bed is a welcome comfort. I think it will always be a comfort to me. I still have trouble sleeping alone in my bed. Even with the sleeping pills, my nights are restless and filled with night terrors, and I often have flashes of that night when I close my eyes. The flashes aren't nearly as bad as the nightmares, but they are still a constant reminder of the turmoil in my life.

My new friendship with Ryan is not something I expected. Then again, that's what's got me so confused. How can I be so closed off to the world around me, yet feel comfortable with this new person? The fact that he has become good friends with Mark and Jase eases my mind, but the past few days have me questioning a lot.

I jump off the bed when I hear Jase walk through the door. I practically knock him over when I run into his arms. I didn't realize how much I missed him until now.

"I am so glad you're back."

"Everything okay?"

Letting go of him, I smile and say, "Yeah, I just missed you." I take his arm and pull him toward the couch as I say, "I am dying to know everything about your trip. Where's Mark by the way?"

"He just dropped me off. He has an early morning tomorrow, so he needed to go home, unpack, and get laundry done," he says while we sit on the couch.

"Sooo . . . ?" I say and Jase just smiles at me. Nudging him in the arm,

I demand, "Come on! Tell me. How was it?"

"Great, actually. His family is nothing like our families."

"Thank God for that," I tease.

"We had a great time. His parents were so accepting of me, which made me comfortable from the moment I arrived. His sisters are a little crazy. We went out with the two of them one night, and they got totally shit-faced, so Mark and I had to sneak their loud asses into the house so they wouldn't wake up his parents. It felt like high school." Jase laughs, and he seems genuinely happy.

"They sound great. I am so happy for you, even though I missed you."

"I missed you too."

"So, it seems you and Mark are pretty serious now."

"I really love him. I was a dick before and thought I had screwed everything up, but I'm glad he gave me another chance. He's pretty perfect for me."

I can't help but smile when I hear Jase talk like this. He has been through a lot to get to this level of happiness.

"Well, for what it's worth, I really love Mark too. He's been a good friend to me, and he has never questioned our friendship, which means a lot to me. He totally gets us," I say.

"I know. He really does, and that makes me love him even more."

I lean in and give him another tight hug and then he asks, "So tell me about your break? How did Thanksgiving go?"

Leaning back, I sigh. "It didn't. I left before the food came to the table."

"What happened?"

"Honestly, it was pretty bad," I say, and I continue to tell him all about the fight and what was said. He shakes his head, but I know he isn't shocked. He has gotten to know a lot about my relationship with my parents over the past three years.

"So has your dad called you?"

"No, which worries me. He always calls to try and brush everything under the rug."

"So, you've just been laying low then?" he asks.

I fidget when he asks, and he picks up on it immediately when he questions curiously, "What's going on? Why are you nervous?"

"Not nervous . . . confused really."

"Tell me."

"I actually spent the past couple of days with Ryan."

"Alone?"

I nod my head, and he looks a bit stunned when he asks, "How did that happen?"

"I guess he got my cell number from Mark, and he texted me. We wound up spending all of Friday together and then some of yesterday as well."

"What'd you guys do?"

"We grabbed breakfast, then we went to the aquarium, but I kinda freaked when I left to go home."

"What happened?"

"We were alone in his car, and I was telling him about the fight with my parents, and when he reached over to hold my hand, I panicked."

Jase turns his body to face me when I continue. "He had held my hand earlier, but it was different. We were at the aquarium, and he was trying to get me to touch the sea creatures at the touch pool, but the way he held my hand in the car was just . . . I don't know. Anyway, I acted like a maniac. I couldn't get out his car fast enough. I just left without really saying anything."

"What did he do?"

"Nothing. He didn't say anything. But I was really shaken and cried the whole drive home."

"Because he touched you?" he questions.

"I mean . . . I felt panicky when it happened, but I think I was more upset because I felt that way. Am I making any sense?"

"Yeah. I just don't like that you beat yourself up for having feelings," he says, and he takes my hand in the both of his.

"I hate that there are these random moments that come out of the blue, and I can't hold myself together. But that isn't the worst of it."

"What?"

"He surprised me at my house last night after I had taken my sleeping pill. We ate dinner and were watching a movie, and the next thing I knew, I was waking up with my head in his lap. I totally freaked, Jase."

"What did Ryan do?"

"He just apologized, then I apologized, and then we had this weird moment when he was leaving. I just don't know what to think."

Shaking his head in confusion, Jase asks, "Let me get this straight, so he comes over and you let him stay with you . . . alone?"

"I know, but he actually made it comfortable for me. I mean, we had a fun night, but before he left, he brushed some hair out of my face. I know this may sound stupid, but it felt extremely tender, and now I'm confused because he's my friend."

"Are you confused because he's your friend, or are you confused because it feels wrong?"

Jase is still holding my hand, and I lean the side of my head on the couch. Sighing, I say, "I know you don't understand, but it doesn't feel right. It just doesn't feel right to be having any feelings like this."

"So, you like him?" he quietly asks me.

Whispering back in hesitation, I say, "I don't know." I close my eyes and sit there for a moment. My thoughts are all over the place, and when I open my eyes back up, a few tears fall. "I just can't be feeling like this."

"Why not, sweetie? I mean, if Ryan makes you feel safe enough to be alone with him, why is it so wrong to feel something for him, if for only that?"

"Because . . . he can't even touch me without me constantly freezing up and being scared. I feel so pathetic and weak, and I hate it. I hate that I feel like this—every day. I try so hard, Jase." I feel myself cracking as I cry and continue to say, "Every day I do everything I can just to hold myself together, and when I think I'm finally getting past this, something happens, and I am reminded just how weak I am. And I don't know what to do. I just wish I knew what to do, but I don't." Jase pulls me into his arms as I cry harder, and he just holds me. "I just want to move on, I want to feel like I used to. I mean, it's been three months of hell. I just want to go back. I should have never gone to that party. All I want is to forget. Just forget everything."

"Three months isn't enough, sweetie. It's just not enough. No amount of time will ever be enough for you to forget, for you to go back completely." Jase pulls back to look at me, and I can't stop myself from apologizing. Shaking his head at me, he gives me a smile, and suddenly I feel a little stupid for my tears. I know he is trying to cheer me up and lighten the mood when he teases me by saying, "So, Ryan has a thing for my girl."

"Shut up," I tease back.

"Seriously though, I want to see you happy. And if hanging out with Ryan makes you feel good, then you shouldn't question it. Don't stand in the way of your own happiness."

Cupping my face with his hands, he gives me a kiss. Hopping off the couch, he pulls me up and starts walking to his room.

"What are you doing?" I ask.

"Sleeping. I'm so tired, and I've missed you."

"But I've got an early class tomorrow."

Jase starts getting ready for bed when he says, "Skip."

I stand there and laugh at him, but I comply because I've missed him too.

This week has gone by really fast. I did wind up skipping my morning classes on Monday to spend time with Jase instead. Aside from that, I have been really busy with the quarter coming to an end shortly. Ryan has been texting me throughout the week, and we went running again Thursday morning. We decided to make it a routine to run together on Thursday mornings before I go to school.

Yesterday, he had some free time before he had to go to the bar, so we met up for an early dinner at a sushi-go-round restaurant near my house. While we were eating, we made plans to go running again when I get off work today. So, I am quickly finishing up my end-of-shift routine so I can change before he gets here.

It's been a busy morning today, and I haven't had much time to stand around and think, which is good because I feel like I have been thinking too much lately. Jase told me to relax a bit, and that's what I am trying to do. I'm texting and hanging out with Ryan the way I would with any friend. But I'd be lying if I said that there wasn't something about him that intrigues me. Lately, I've been having that fluttering feeling in my stomach when he's around. I haven't had a relationship with a guy since high school, and I'm not sure that one even qualified.

I don't feel right even thinking about this. How can I? Plus, who would even want me if they even knew who I really was? I'm still a mess, and that damn bell above the front door reminds me of it every time someone opens it.

Jase brought up calling the detective the other day. He has never mentioned it before, but he said he never wanted to because he knew I wasn't ready. I'm not sure why he thinks I'm ready now. I'm not. I don't want to be. All I want is to lock that horrific memory up and burn it to ashes, not be forced to relive it over and over for others to hear. I told Jase to drop it, told him it would never happen, so he didn't say another word about it.

"Hey Roxy, I'm gonna go to the back to restock a few things before I leave, okay?"

"Yeah, thanks," she says over the hissing of the steamer.

I grab a box cutter and start opening boxes of flavored syrups and stocking the shelves. When I move on to the sugar boxes, I see Roxy come through the door with a huge smile on her face.

"So, that hot-ass guy is back and asking for you."

Sitting on the floor, surrounded by scraps of cardboard boxes, I say, "His name is Ryan."

"Well then, that hot-ass guy, Ryan, is here for you," she says teasingly with her hands on her hips.

"Thanks. Can you tell him to give me ten minutes?"

"You guys have a date or something?"

Standing up, I say, "What? No! He's just a friend."

"Mmm hmm." Roxy turns on her heel to walk back out to the front, and I pick up my bag and go to the bathroom to change into my running clothes.

When I walk out, Ryan is chatting with Roxy. He looks up at me as I'm walking over to him and says, "Hey."

"What are you guys talking about?"

"Your friend, Ryan, was asking about my tattoos." I silently thank her for leaving out the *hot-ass* part.

Ryan takes a step towards me and asks, "You ready?"

"Yeah, I just need to put my bag in my car."

Reaching out, he takes the bag out of my hand and starts walking to my car. I say 'bye' to Roxy as I follow him out.

I zip my keys up in the pocket of my running jacket, and we take off for our run from the parking lot. We head around the perimeter of campus before making our way through a few neighborhoods. I am mostly quiet as I listen to Ryan talk about work and the new bands that have been playing there during the week. Turns out that we pretty much have the same taste in music, and I find his reaction funny each time he discovers I like another one of his favorite bands.

We start making our way through some streets we haven't gone down before. I follow him and keep my pace by his side. My throat is beginning to dry out when I realize that neither of us brought any water, and I know we've already run at least three miles. I am more quiet than normal, and I'm sure Ryan notices when he turns his head and asks, "You okay?"

"I'm thirsty. We forgot water."

"No worries," he says as he picks up the pace, and we turn down another unfamiliar street.

I don't have time to question him when he slows down and starts walking up a driveway to a three-story building.

"What are you doing?"

"Getting you some water. Come on," he says while nodding his head toward the building.

I walk a few steps behind him, and he pulls out a key fob from his pocket. When he clicks the button, the garage begins to open.

"Do you own this building or something?" I ask.

Ryan turns back to look at me and grins. "This is my loft. I live here."

"Oh," I mumble, but I stop following him, not really wanting to go into his home. I try hard to control the anxiety that begin to race through me. I have been spending a lot of time with him and feel like he is trustworthy, but I can't seem to shake my nerves right now.

He motions for me to come, and I don't want him to think I'm some sort of basket case, so I swallow back my apprehension and follow him into the garage to the staircase leading up to the loft.

When we reach the top of the stairs, he unlocks the door, and we head inside to the large open space. The main room is completely open with a large kitchen along the back wall of exposed brick. The finishes in the kitchen are industrial and sleek, and two of the walls are lined with floor to ceiling windows. There are exposed beams on the ceiling, and the wooden floors are a rich wide-planked espresso. I wonder how he came to own a place like this; the square footage alone would cost a fortune.

"Here you go," he says as he walks back to me and hands me a bottle of water.

I take a sip and say, "This is a great place. How long have you lived here?"

"About five years."

He pulls his cell phone out of his jacket when it begins to ring. I can tell it's something about work when he starts talking. Telling the person on the other end to hang on, he puts the phone down to his side and tells me, "Make yourself comfortable. I need to take this call really quick. I'll only be a few minutes, okay?"

I nod my head, and he walks down the hall and into one of the rooms. I stand there in the middle of his house, not sure what to do. As I drink my water, I make my way over to Ryan's living room. It's filled with overstuffed furniture and a TV that is mounted to the wall above a large fireplace. I walk over to one of the windows near the corner of the room. I accidentally kick a stack of books, and when I bend down to straighten them back up, I see several large black photo mats. Leaning down, I flip one over and look at the beautiful black and white photograph that is a close-up of the curve of a woman's bare back. The lighting of the photo is exquisite.

I kneel down to flip through the others when I hear him walk back into the room. Before I can stand up he is at my side. I look up at him and say, "I'm sorry." Setting the photos back where they were, I stand up and he asks, "For what?"

"I wasn't snooping or anything, I just noticed these and was curious."

"Candace, I have nothing to hide. I told you to make yourself comfortable, and I meant it." He steps aside, sits down in one of the large, overstuffed chairs, and takes a swig of his water.

"Where did you get those?" I ask, referring to the photos.

"They're mine," he says.

"Yours?"

"Yeah. Sometimes I get bored and like to mess around with my camera," he says casually.

"That's pretty amazing for just messing around. You only shoot people?"

"For the most part, yeah," he says as he gets up from his seat and walks over to me by the window. He picks up the picture of the woman's back and looks at it as if he hasn't seen it in a long time.

"She a model?" I ask about the woman in the photo.

"No, just some chick I used to know." He sets down the photo and walks to the couch while motioning for me to join him.

I walk over, sit down next to him, and ask, "So, when did you get into photography?"

"When I was in college I took some art classes. So, one day I just decided to buy a camera and started taking pictures. Like I said, I pretty much have no clue what I'm doing. Just a little hobby of mine I mess around with every now and then."

"You ever do anything with them?"

"No."

"Maybe you should," I say, and he turns to look at me and repeats my words back to me quietly, "Maybe I should."

"You sure you don't want to come out to the bar tonight to see Mark play?" he asks.

"I told you, I have to work."

"I just picked you up from work."

"I know, but I have to go back. One of the girls quit and Roxy hasn't hired anyone to replace her, so I've been picking up extra shifts," I explain. "Plus, I'd probably be tired and no fun to be around."

"I can't imagine it not being fun to be around you," he says as he looks at me intently, and I begin to feel uncomfortable with his words. "You ready to finish the run?"

A smile crosses his face when he stands up and reaches out his hand to me. I sit there for a beat before I hesitantly place my hand in his. When I do, he gives me a slight tug and pulls me off the couch. He never lets go of my hand as he locks up and we walk down the stairs and out to the driveway. This closeness has my nerves twisted up, and I'm sure he can feel sweat on my hand. As we walk out to the street, hands still connected, he asks, "Wanna make it a long run, or are you ready to head back?"

I take a hard swallow before saying, "Long."

He gives me a squeeze before he unwraps his fingers from around my hand, and we begin to run.

chapter nineteen

SCHOOL HAS BEEN really busy. It's the last week of classes before finals. Aside from work, I have been buried in my books and getting everything wrapped up before the quarter ends. I'm going into all my finals with perfect grades, so I am sure I will still be able to maintain my four point GPA.

I did manage to meet up with Ryan Thursday morning for our run. I was starting to get really stressed out, so the run was just what I needed. Ryan was considerate and let me ramble on and on the whole time about my classes and everything that I needed to do to make sure I was ready for my exams.

But now that classes are officially over until January, I can start to wind down a bit. I only have three finals next week and a studio final. Everyone has learned the same routine, and we will perform in groups of four for our final grading. I have the dance memorized and perfected, so today when I go to the studio, I plan to just work on my solo. Ms. Emerson will be meeting me up there in a little bit to critique what I have so far. I am surprised that she offered to do this for me since she never gives anyone private instruction. So when she offered, I immediately said yes.

Ryan said he would meet me at the studio around four o'clock to grab a coffee before he has to go into work. I shoot him a quick text as I am heading out.

Leaving now. See you in two hours?

I'll meet you in the parking lot.

OK, catch you later.

When I arrive at the studio, Ms. Emerson is already there waiting for me.

"Hi, I hope you weren't waiting long," I say when I walk in and set my bag down.

Walking over to the stereo, she says, "Not at all. I just got here. Did you stretch at home?"

"Yes, but I need to warm my muscles up a little more." The cold temperatures make it hard to keep my muscles loose, so after my pointes are on, I slide on some leg warmers and loose long pants.

"Well then, let's do a little floor work before we begin." She flips on the music, and she joins me in the center of the room as we do a few adagio combinations.

I have never danced alone alongside Ms. Emerson. She is as focused as I am on arm placements and bodylines. We move gracefully together through the movements and repeat the combination a few more times before she asks for my music. I hand her the disc, and she gets the music set up as I take my spot on the floor in fifth position. When I hear the strings, I slowly relevè on my pointes and begin a series of chainès across the floor. I continue through my choreography, and when I get to the peak of my developè, I begin spotting my head as I go into a variation series of fouettès. I hear Ms. Emerson beating the counts by loudly clapping her hands. When I come to the end, all she says is, "Again." She clicks the remote, and the music cues back up.

I repeat my steps, and I focus in on the movements as I hear: "I need more, Candace . . . Hit that position, and hold!" *CLAP CLAP CLAP* "Piquè! Piquè! Come on! I need more from you!" I hear her stern voice through the loud music and follow her commands. When I come to the end, she repeats, "Again."

We go through this process countless times before taking a break only to continue repeating this routine over and over. I keep pounding out the moves harder and harder, but she continues to yell and demand. We do this for over an hour, and I begin to grow exhausted when she shouts, "Again!"

The music repeats, and I go through the steps over and again. "Pick it up, Candace! Hit! Hit!" She claps the counts loudly and continues, "I'm not feeling it! Come ON! Feel it! Watch that port a bras. Demi second, make it strong!" I focus on her commands, trying to keep my emotions tight, although I feel like I'm at my end. She's relentless. "Again. Last one," she says, and she starts the music again.

"This time . . . *feel* it, Candace. Really feel it. Let it out."

I nod my head and silently take my position again as the music pounds through the room. Making my way through the steps, my toes are aching, but I push through again. I can hear the frustration in Ms. Emerson when she yells over the music. "Feel it, Candace! You're dead behind the movements . . . Make that spotting stronger!" *CLAP CLAP CLAP* "Hit those fouettès . . . Smooth out that demi right there. I'm getting nothing! Feel, Candace!"

She shuts off the music, and I stop, standing in the center of the floor when she walks toward me.

Speaking softly, she says, "Whatever walls you have built this year, you need to break them down. I'm getting nothing from you. You feel nothing."

"Yes," I say breathlessly as I nod my head.

"We spoke about this earlier, but I'm not seeing any changes. This is a powerful piece of music. In my opinion, the best piece of all the girls, but you're wasting it. Whatever this is . . . fix it."

"Okay." And before I can say anything else, she turns to leave.

When the door closes behind her, I let out my pent up frustration and scream through my clenched teeth. Ripping off my pointes, I throw them hard across the room. I lie back on the floor, taking a few deep breaths and feel the tears welling up. My emotions are on edge after being so harshly berated for the past two hours. I squeeze my eyes shut and feel the tears as they roll down my temples and into my hair. I throw my arm over my head and continue to breathe in and out slowly.

Letting a few minutes pass, I grab my things and leave. I just want to go home, shower, and try not to think about this disastrous rehearsal. I slam the door open when I walk out, and I'm shocked when I see Ryan leaning up against my car. *Shit!* I completely forgot that he would be here. Quickly, I wipe the tears off my cheeks and try to pull myself together fast. But before I can start walking, he's standing in front of me with both hands cupping my face.

"What happened?"

"Nothing, honestly. Just a tough rehearsal." My voice comes out wobbly, and I hate that.

Ryan stares down at me with a clenched jaw. Taking his thumbs, he wipes my damp cheeks. The tender action breaks my strong façade, and I fall into his chest allowing the comfort of his arms as they wrap around me. He cradles the back of my head with his hand the same way Jase does when he hugs me, but this feels different. His hold is strong and tight, and I let myself soften into him. Aside from Jase and Mark, there is no one that I ever let touch me like this. I know it isn't much, but it's difficult for me. Being in Ryan's embrace feels safe, so I wrap my arms around his waist as we stand in the empty parking lot.

When I start to pull back from him, he asks again, "Are you sure you're okay?"

I nod my head, uncertain of how my voice might sound.

Ryan takes the bag off of my shoulder and drapes his arm around me. "Come on," he says as he starts walking me to his jeep.

I don't ask where we are going, and honestly, I'm too worn out to really care. He helps me into his car, and when he closes the door, I rest my head against the back of the seat and close my eyes. Ryan doesn't say anything; he doesn't even turn on the music as we drive. It's only a few minutes later when the car stops in front of his loft.

When we get upstairs, I sit on the couch in his living room while he gets me a bottle of water from the kitchen. He sits down next to me, and I gulp the water down quickly.

"Feeling better?"

"Yeah, I'm sorry. After being yelled at for two hours, I just . . ."

"Don't worry," he says as he puts his arm around me and draws me closer to his side.

Leaning my head back on the couch, I say, "No . . . It's embarrassing."

"Don't let it be," he says.

"Can I ask you a huge favor?"

"Anything."

"Do you have dry shirt I can change into? I've been dancing for the past few hours, and I'm sweaty and stinky."

He laughs at me and says, "You don't stink at all actually."

"Liar."

"I'll be right back." I watch Ryan as he head up the stairs, to what I presume is his bedroom.

"You need socks?" he yells down.

"Please. It's cold," I say.

When he comes back down, he hands me his clothes and shows me to the guest bathroom. "Thanks. Just give me a few minutes."

"Take your time."

I turn on the faucet and wait for the water to run hot. I open the linen closet and find a washcloth. When I take off my clothes, I wet the washcloth and freshen up as best as I can. I slip on his old UW shirt and a pair of his pajama pants, leaving my dirty clothes folded on the side of the sink. His clothes are huge on me, and I have to tug on the ties of his pants to cinch up the waist and rollup up the waistband several times, but the pants still drag on the floor.

Walking back into the living room, Ryan is sitting back on the couch, flipping through channels on the TV. I sit down next to him, and he grabs the bun that is still secured on the top of my head and laughs. "This is cute," he teases me.

I swat his hand away. "Whatever."

"Come here," he says, and I lean back on the couch with him. "So, what happened?"

"I have this tough piece of music, and I'm having a hard time connecting with it. My instructor keeps telling me what I need to fix, but I don't really know how. It's frustrating. I can perfect my moves, but I don't know how to get into this piece."

"So she just bashed you the whole time?"

"It's how she is. But the fact that she even came in to work with me is unheard of. She's extremely stern, but she's only trying to help me."

"I didn't like seeing you upset."

Looking up at him, I say, "It's not a big deal, really."

"I didn't like it." He says this intently as he looks down at me, and I have to look away from him because when he says things like this, it makes me feel too much. I know Jase likes Ryan, but the other night Mark had mentioned that he has a bit of a reputation for hooking up with random women. It's hard for me to picture him that way because I don't see him like that, but at the same time, it makes me feel like I should be even more cautious around him.

"You want that cup of coffee?" he asks, and I am pulled out of my thoughts.

"That'd be great, I'm still really cold."

"There are some blankets in the trunk by the fireplace," he tells me as he walks into the kitchen. I hop up and grab a large blanket, wrapping it around me before I sit back down.

"How do you take it?" he asks from across the room.

"One sugar and really blond."

Ryan hands me my mug and sits down next to me with a grin. "You getting warm?"

"Trying too."

He picks up the remote and turns it to TCM. I shake my head and laugh at him.

"What's so funny?"

"You. I don't know anyone who watches the classic movie channel, aside from you."

"You want me to change it?"

Pulling my feet up on the couch, I say, "No, it's fine. I'm only teasing you."

He turns up the volume and we sit back and watch 'The Blue Dahlia.' He knows I'm only half paying attention because every now and then he will make commentary to keep me up to speed.

By the time the movie ends, Ryan has to get ready to go to work. I grab my clothes from the bathroom, and we head downstairs to his jeep. When he pulls in the studio lot, he asks me to come out tonight. When I tell him that I can't, he doesn't push.

"I'm sorry, but I'm just really tired and will probably go to bed early," I say. I know Mark's band has become the regular Saturday night house band and that Jase is often with him, but the thought of being in a crowded bar, and possibly crossing paths with Jack, is too much for me to think about. "Plus, I have the early shift at work tomorrow."

"Your boss doesn't strike me as the type who would mind if you came into work a little hungover," he jokes.

"You're probably right about that, but I've never drunk enough to have ever been hungover."

"Never?"

"Don't act surprised."

"I'm more relieved," he says

"I'm not even going to ask why. But, thanks for today."

"Any time."

"Tell Mark and Jase I said 'hi' when you see them tonight, okay?" I open the door and hop out of the car. Looking back at him before I close the door, I say, "Thanks again for being there today. It probably would have ended up being a crappy day if I just came home."

"Thanks for letting me be there," he says.

I close the door and get into my car.

When I arrive home, Kimber is sitting in the living room flipping through a magazine as I walk in.

"Hey," I say.

Looking at the clothes I'm wearing that are entirely too big, she asks, "What are you wearing?" I'm surprised that she is speaking to me.

"Oh, um . . ." I stutter as she nods her head. By the look on her face, she seems annoyed. She closes the magazine and starts walking toward her room.

"Kimber," I call out after her, but she just ignores me and slams her door shut.

I dump my clothes in the laundry room before I go into my room. I brush my teeth, take my sleeping pill, and slide into bed. I am still wearing Ryan's clothes, and can smell the warmth of his scent with a hint of amber-wood as I start to grow tired.

chapter twenty

"WHAT ARE YOU going to do for the next few weeks?" Ryan asks as we unload some firewood from his jeep. I figured since I was going to be alone for Christmas break, I could at least make it as festive as possible with a tree and wood for the fireplace. I called Ryan to go with me to the tree lot since his jeep is big and could hold everything I wanted to buy.

"I don't know. This is the first year that Jase isn't here with me. We normally spend most of the break together when I am not at my parents.'"

"How is that going?"

Stacking the firewood in the garage, I say, "It's not, really. I spoke with my father for the first time since Thanksgiving a few of days ago, and he wants me to come over for dinner Christmas Eve."

"You haven't spoken with them for all this time?"

"No."

We walk out to grab another load of wood. Kimber and Jase both left as soon as they were finished with finals, so I have been picking up a lot of extra shifts at work this past week to keep myself busy. Ryan and I have been spending more time together. He continues to show affection with me by holding my hand or putting his arm around me while watching TV, but that's about it. I'm not sure about my feelings for him, but I'm pretty sure that he sees me as more than his friend. Sure, I'm affectionate with Mark and Jase, but they are non-threatening to me.

When Ryan and I were out getting coffee earlier this week, we ran into a girl that Ryan must have dated in the past. He seemed really uncomfortable talking to her in front of me, but she seemed more than comfortable with him. It didn't make me jealous, but it made me a little more guarded. Ryan is a good-looking guy, so I shouldn't be surprised that he has dated a lot of girls, I'm just not sure what *a lot* actually means. Part of me doesn't really want to know.

"So, you're going over to see them then?"

"Well, yeah, I don't really want to, but it's Christmas and all. I'm just a little scared about how it will all go. The last time I saw them, we said some pretty nasty things to each other, and I have never gone this long without talking to them."

"What are they so upset about?"

Back inside the house, I pour a glass of wine, and Ryan takes a beer from the fridge.

"Everything. Turns out I've been nothing but an embarrassing disappointment to them all along."

Ryan lets out an irritated sigh as we take our drinks and head into the living room. We sit down on the couch, and Ryan slides his arm around my shoulders, pulling me next to him.

"I'm sorry, babe," he says quietly, and I notice his term of endearment. I try not to act flustered, but he has never said anything like that to me before. It's things like this that he does that confuse me. The friendship that we have has been eased into pretty naturally; I have never questioned him about it, and I find myself liking it.

"Honestly, it's nothing that I didn't already know deep down, but it was the first time that it actually hit me that these were their true feelings toward me."

"I don't want you going over there." His statement catches me off guard, and I look up at him. I can see it written all over his face that he's nothing but serious.

"Ryan, I have to. They're my parents."

"I don't care. I don't want you going over there for them to treat you like shit."

Letting out a sigh, I lean back and rest my head on his chest. I'm not sure why this upsets him so much, but I can't not go see my parents at Christmas. "I have to go," I softly whisper. "It's Christmas, and I really should be there. I'm only going for dinner. That's all."

"Then I'm going with you."

I pull away from him and turn to look at him straight on. "What?"

"I don't want you going alone, Candace. I'll go with you."

I shake my head and say, "I don't think that's a good idea."

"Well, I don't think it's a good idea that you're going. So, we can argue about this, or you can just say 'okay.'"

I sit there looking at him, surprised that he would even care so much about this. But, he's right, I don't see him backing down, so instead of fighting him on this, I turn and lean back into him. "Okay."

"And I don't want you spending Christmas alone either, so why don't you come with me. I could use the distraction at the madhouse."

"What?! No. Thanks, but I'll be fine."

"I'm sure you will be fine, but I don't like the thought of you sitting here alone, so you're coming with me."

"Ryan, it feels weird."

"Why?"

"Because. It just does. I know you have a big family, and I just don't want to intrude."

He shifts to face me, and says, "It's not an intrusion. My family isn't like that."

I look down and take a moment before saying, "Okay, but no gifts. It makes me uncomfortable."

"Why's that?"

"I don't know. It just always has. Please," I say in a serious tone.

"Okay. No gifts. But just so you know, I have a shit-ton for the kids," he says with a chuckle.

I smile and we sit back, kicking our feet up onto the coffee table. "So when did you start making all the rules?"

"When you started making me worry about you."

I don't respond to his statement; I don't know how to respond. The protectiveness of his words confuses me, but they make me feel good. Instead, I just sit there next to him and stare at the undecorated tree by the front window and worry about Ryan meeting my parents.

I have been on edge all day thinking about how dinner will go tonight. I'm nervous because the last time I saw my parents, it didn't go so well, and nothing has been discussed or resolved. I'm also nervous about Ryan meeting them. I know my mother will jump to conclusions and assume we are dating, and that will not go over well since I know she will be judging him and measuring him up to her unreachable standards.

When I see Ryan's black Rubicon pull up in front of my house, I slip on my coat and head out. He gets out of the car to help me into my seat. When we pull away, he must have picked up on my nerves when he says, "Relax."

Feeling the need to warn him, I say, "Ryan. You need to know that—"

But he doesn't let me finish when he interrupts me and repeats, "Candace, relax."

"They're just very judgmental people."

"There is nothing that they can say that I haven't heard before," he says, and I wonder what he means by that. Is he referring to his parents? I know he is close with his mother, so I assume maybe his father has something to do with his statement. Ryan has never mentioned his dad. I figure his parents are divorced and he just isn't close with him, but I have never asked.

I start fidgeting and twisting my hands when he pulls into the gates of The Highlands. He reaches over and lays his hand on top of mine to calm me, but it doesn't help. When he pulls into my parents' circle drive and shuts off the car, I don't get out. We both sit there for a moment when Ryan asks, "You ready?"

"Yeah," I breathe out.

"Bunny," my dad beams as we walk through the door. His candor is not what I expected, and he pulls me in for a big hug. "You look beautiful, dear."

He turns to Ryan and shakes his hand. "And you must be Ryan. Thanks for joining us. Come in."

Turning back to me he says, "Your mother is finishing getting ready. She should be out shortly."

We walk back into the kitchen and my father asks, "What can I get you two to drink?"

"A beer is good, Mr. Parker."

"Please, call me Charles."

My father hands Ryan a bottle of beer and pours me a glass of red wine.

"Why don't we go to the library and visit while we wait for your mother?"

As we are walking through the house, Ryan keeps a supportive hand on my back, and I appreciate the gesture.

"So, Ryan, what is it that you do?" my father asks as we all sit down.

"I own a bar right off campus."

"Oh, how did you get into that type of work?"

"Long story short, after I graduated college, I couldn't seem to find a job with the economy, so I just sort of fell into this business deal. It's been working out nicely though, so I can't complain."

"What did you study in college?"

"Finance."

"Now that's a respectable degree," my mother says as she walks into the room, heels clicking against the wooden floor.

I cringe inside at her passive-aggressive statement. When she approaches, I stand to give her a quick embrace.

"Hi, Mom."

"Good to see you, darling. And Ryan, welcome."

Ryan stands to take her hand, and says, "Thank you for having me."

"Of course. It isn't every day that our daughter brings a man home."

I roll my eyes, and Ryan sits down next to me and squeezes my knee. I know this is going to end in disaster already. My mother's words are like poison, and I'm beginning to question why I even came.

"Ryan was just telling me about the bar he owns," my dad tells my mother.

"A bar?"

Before I allow my mother to make some snarky comment, I jump in, "So, when are the two of you leaving for Colorado?" My parents own a cabin in Aspen and go there every year after Christmas.

They begin to talk about what they have planned for their trip this year, and I sit back and listen to them go on and on. It's pretty much the same every year.

As I take the last sip of my wine, my father says, "Bunny, why don't you show Ryan around. I need to talk with your mother about something. We will leave in about thirty minutes."

"Okay, sure."

I walk Ryan around the house and then outside to show him the view of the Sound.

"I'm sorry about that," I say.

"About what?"

"They can be a lot. They're pretty pretentious."

"Candace, no one has perfect parents. Everyone's flawed in some way."

We walk back to the covered patio and sit down on one of the benches. I tie my scarf tighter around my neck, and Ryan wraps his arm around my shoulders.

"So, you grew up here in Shoreline?" he asks.

"Yeah. In this very house. The Kelley's, who live across the street, have a daughter that's the same age as me. We used to be best friends when we were growing up."

"And now?"

"And now all I really have is Jase, Mark . . . and you."

"What about your roommate?"

"Kimber? We used to be really close, but not so much anymore."

"So what happened to all your friends from high school?"

"They've moved on. Applying to grad schools, getting married, making a life for themselves. Most of the kids here wind up becoming people like my parents. More concerned about their image and what social circle they are in. It's not me, so I never cared enough to stay in touch with anyone."

I feel Ryan squeeze my shoulder and pull me in tighter, and I'm starting to feel uncertain about all this. Him. Having him here with my parents. Talking about myself. Him touching me. I pull away and stand up, needing a little space to try and calm my nerves.

"We should go back inside," I say.

Walking back into the house, my father calls from the library, "Candace, could you come in here?"

"Yeah, just a second," I holler back. I turn to Ryan and say, "I'll be right back. Make yourself at home."

"Do you want me to come with you?"

"No, it's okay."

When I walk into the library, both of my parents are waiting for me, and my father tells me to shut the door behind me. I do so, anxiously wondering what this is all about.

As I walk further into the room, my dad says, "Well, I just got off the phone with a friend of mine who works in admissions at Columbia. He owed me a favor and was able to pull some strings to get you a conditional acceptance for the fall semester."

"What?"

"This is wonderful news, isn't it, darling?" my mother says.

"I'm sorry, but what is this all about?"

"Well, we know that you've been busy finishing up at U-Dub, so your father and I thought we would help you out by taking care of this."

"Taking care of what?" My head is spinning, and I can't believe what I am hearing. Are they serious right now?

"Honey, you look upset. You should be happy—"

Raising my voice I say, "Happy about what?! Happy that you don't trust me to make decisions for myself? Happy that I know you don't think I'm good enough? Happy that you feel I am so pathetic that you have to go behind my back to try and control me?"

"Candace, lower your voice please," my father says sternly.

"No! I can't believe you did this!"

"I would have hoped Thanksgiving would have given you something to think about, but clearly you are determined to make a fool out of yourself. And to top it all off, you bring home a boy that works in a bar. Honestly, I don't know what you're thinking."

"He owns that bar, Mother," I spat.

"It's not you. This path you're leading yourself down is not for you," my mother says.

"It's not for *you*. You're too goddamn judgmental to ever live like I do. I'm happy. I wish you could just see that and accept that." I look to my dad to try and grasp why he would do this. I always thought that he understood me, but he just stares at me with an unfaltering look. I slowly shake my head in disbelief and ask him, "Why?"

"Your mother is right, dear. We thought you would come to your senses, but clearly you are stuck in this fantasy of yours. You have a name to uphold."

My eyes start to blur, and when I blink, the tears fall.

"I just don't understand you. You should be thanking your father, not pouting."

"You are unbelievable, Mother!" I continue to yell as I say, "I'm not a child! You can't just step in and take away everything I have worked so hard for during these past four years! How can you call yourself a mother? You're nothing! You say you're embarrassed by me, well it goes both ways." When I stop to take a breath, I see Ryan rushing in.

Holding out his hand, he says, "We're leaving. Now."

"Excuse me, but this is a private matter," my mother says to him condescendingly.

Looking at Ryan and the anger in his eyes, I can't seem to stop the tears that are falling. I'm shocked that he would care enough to come in here and stop this fight.

"Candace, if you walk out, it's over. Don't come back. We refuse to sit back and watch you ruin your life." I look at my mother and can't believe she even went there.

I shift my eyes to my father's. "Daddy?"

"We're done letting you play games, bunny. No more."

I look at the both of them, and I feel myself falling apart. My own parents, threatening me and trying to control me. Looking at them is actually making my stomach turn, so I do the only thing I know to do. I grab Ryan's hand and let him take me away.

His grip on me is tight as he walks us through the living room, grabbing our coats, and leading me outside to his jeep. He doesn't say a word, but the look on his face tells me he's pissed. He opens the car door for me, and I begin to feel lightheaded. I reach forward and brace my free hand on the side of the seat, trying to hold myself up and clear the haze in my vision when Ryan grabs me and pulls me into his arms. I cling to him tightly and start sobbing into his chest. I can barely grasp what just happened. But, I know I can't go back. They made that clear.

After a few minutes, I'm able to calm myself down enough to stop the tears. My breathing is still erratic, and I'm so embarrassed that Ryan had to see all of that. I can't even look him in the eyes, so I keep my head down when I finally loosen my grip on him and pull away. He kisses the top of my head before gripping my waist and helping me into the car.

The drive home is quiet. I'm still trying to process what happened back there. I never thought my parents would ever go that far. I don't need their money or their lifestyle, and the fact that they thought it meant that much to me that they could threaten me with it proves that they don't know me at all.

When we get back to my house, I am thoroughly drained. I curl up on the couch and kick my heels off and onto the floor. Ryan walks into the kitchen, and when he comes back out, he has a beer and a glass of wine. He hands me the glass, and I gulp half of it down quickly before setting it on the coffee table. Sitting down on the couch, he leans back on the side armrest, pulling me between his legs so that my back is resting on his chest. He wraps one arm around my waist while his other hand is threading through my hair. I can feel his steady breathing by the rise and fall of his chest.

This closeness that I feel with Ryan is a lot for me to process. Closing my eyes, I take a slow, deep breath and shift to my side, resting my cheek on his sternum. I listen to his heart as it beats rapidly.

"You okay?" His words are the first spoken since we left my parents house. I know I can't talk around the huge lump in my throat, so I just shake my head. Ryan rests his chin on the top of my head, and when I begin to cry again, he tightens his hold on me.

I feel safe enough with him to finally have this release. I've spent years making excuses for my parents, just brushing off and accepting their behavior. But, this . . . this cuts deep. My whole life I've been trying to make them proud of me, but I just can't be what they want me to be. I can't even think about trying to bottle up this pain, so I just let it out.

chapter twenty-one

RYAN STAYED OVER for a few hours before leaving me last night. We barely spoke at all as he held me, but we didn't need to talk. I never feel as if I need to be anything I'm not when I am with him. I don't even want to think about what last night would have been like if he hadn't been there.

He told me I didn't have to go with him to his mom's house, that he would stay with me. But I really need the distraction. So, we are making the four-hour drive to Cannon Beach in Oregon to spend the next few days with his family. I'm nervous about meeting everyone. Ryan has a large family, something I have never been around. All I know is the dysfunction I grew up around with my mother and father.

"You're quiet over there," Ryan says as he drives through the tall, thick pine trees of the mountains.

"Just a little nervous."

"Don't be." He gives my knee a soft squeeze of reassurance.

On our long drive, I try not to worry too much about what they will think of me. Ryan does a good job of distracting me with conversation and listening to music. After a while, I decide to lean back and take a nap since I had a restless night of sleep.

When we pull up to the large, two-story, dark grey beach house with a driveway and street full of cars, I start wringing my hands and fingers together. He parks the jeep, steps out, and walks around to my side, opening my door.

Grabbing both of my hands, he says, "Don't be so nervous. Just relax."

I nod my head, but I worry they might think I'm weird or rude if I'm too quiet. I worry that I don't look nice enough, or maybe that I look too nice. Ryan helps me out of the car, and when I start smoothing down the pencil skirt of my black cap-sleeved dress, he starts laughing.

"Why are you laughing at me?"

"Because I've never seen you so wound up before."

He reaches in the jeep and grabs the bottle of Pahlmeyer Merlot that I bought for his mother. We start walking to the front door when I tug against his hand. Turning around, he cocks his head slightly and gives me a concerned look.

"Ryan . . . I don't do well around a lot of people," I hesitantly confess to him.

He places his hand on my shoulder and says, "My family will love you, but if you feel that uncomfortable, we can go. Just say the word."

"No, I want to meet them, I'm just . . ." I feel like I am stumbling over my words when he says, "Hey, I'm right here. No worries, okay?"

Letting out a sigh, I say, "Okay."

He takes my hand in his and starts leading me up the wet drive. When we walk in, I'm almost knocked down when two little boys dart through the foyer, chasing each other with plastic swords.

Ryan chuckles at the kids and says to me, "Come on," as he takes me through the house. The walls are filled with family photographs. It's a beautiful house, not extravagant like the one I grew up in.

Laughter echoes through the large house, and as we turn the corner into the kitchen, I see three women huddled over the counter looking at a tabloid magazine. One of them looks up as we enter the room, and a warm smile crosses her face when she sees Ryan.

Stretching out her arms and wrapping them around him, she says, "Finally, you made it. We missed you this morning."

Never letting go of my nervous hand, he embraces her with his free arm. When I start to loosen my grip to allow him his other arm, he tightens his hold on me.

After she lets go of him, she turns her attention to me, and Ryan introduces us. "Mom, this is Candace."

"I am so glad to finally meet you, dear." And just like she did with Ryan, she pulls me in for a warm hug, but I'm a little distracted by her word *finally*. Has Ryan mentioned me to her before a few days ago when he called to tell her he was bringing me? Before I can think about it too much, Ryan's hand leaves mine as the other two women are hugging me and introducing themselves as his aunts. Little kids start flooding into the kitchen screaming for their Uncle Ryan. His mother starts calling off the names of all the children, but I can't even focus on what she is saying because I'm overwhelmed. I look over to Ryan, and he's holding two little girls, one in each arm. One of the girls is tugging on his hair while he is pecking kisses on the other one's ear, making her squeal loudly. Seeing him like this makes me laugh at how fun and easygoing he is. Although he shows these traits around me, he has started to become more protective lately.

It's a whirlwind as I'm introduced to all of Ryan's cousins and their spouses, along with his two uncles. Everyone is talking and hugging me, and I know there is no way I will remember anyone's name aside from his mother's, which I'd already known.

All the noise and touching is beginning to overpower me, and when I look to see where Ryan is, he is engulfed in a conversation with two of his cousins while he is still holding one of the little girls.

Needing some space to regroup, I turn to his mother and quietly ask, "Excuse me, Donna. Where is the restroom?"

She directs me to one that is on the other side of the house, and I quickly make my way through the chaos. When I shut the door behind me, I walk over, sit down on the lid of the toilet, and embrace the calm. I take a few minutes to compose myself when someone knocks on the door.

I stand up to go open the door, and when I do, Ryan is standing there.

"Everything okay? When I looked up you were gone."

"Yeah, just needed a moment to myself."

"Sorry about that," he says.

"It's okay. I'm just not used to . . ."

Ryan runs his hands down my arms and says, "I know. Do you need a few more minutes?"

"No, I'm fine."

Holding my hand, he begins to walk me back to the kitchen where all the commotion has died down a bit. Most of the little kids are now watching a movie in the other room as a few of the guys sit on the couches, drinking and laughing about whatever they are talking about.

I turn my attention to Ryan when he hands me a glass of red wine, and I give him a smile. I appreciate that he does things like that for me without needing to ask, that he pays attention. I used to feel uneasy around him, but over the past month or so, that feeling has waned, and I have become more relaxed when we're together.

"Come with me," he says in my ear, and he leads me out of the room. We wander through the house as he shows me around. The house backs up to the beach, and the view is absolutely breathtaking. When we walk past the formal dining room, two of his cousins are sitting at the table chatting. One of the girls looks up at me and invites me to join them. I look to Ryan, and he says, "I'll just be in the other room helping my mom out."

I nod my head and walk over to sit down as he leaves the room.

Not remembering their names, I say, "I'm sorry, but with all the introductions, I can't remember your names."

"I'm Tori, and this is Jenna."

"So, you live in Seattle too?" Jenna asks.

"Yeah, I grew up there. What about you, where do you guys live?"

"We both live in Astoria, but my sister, Katie, lives in Portland," Tori says.

The three of us begin to talk and get to know each other. The two of them, along with Katie, are the daughters of Ryan's two aunts. They are all married with kids and live in Oregon. They told me that Ryan is the only one in the family that lives in Washington, that he moved there after high school to go to college and just never came back. They seem genuinely interested in me and ask a lot of questions about college and my dancing.

"Tori, Madison's sick," her sister says as she comes into the room.

Tori asks, "What's wrong with her?"

"She was upstairs throwing up. I know there has been a stomach bug going around at her preschool, so I'm hoping that's all it is. I laid her down in Ryan's room, and she's sleeping now."

"Well, just let her rest. As long as she isn't running a fever, I wouldn't worry too much. I think Aunt Donna actually has some leftover Pedialite from when Connor got sick."

Turning to me, she says, "I'm sorry, it's been so crazy today, and I didn't meet you earlier. I'm Katie, Tori's sister."

"I'm Candace."

"So, Ryan finally brings a girl home. I can't believe it," she says.

I see Tori give Katie a wide-eyed, annoyed look, and Katie dramatically says, "What?!"

Jenna and Tori both shake their heads at her, and I'm beginning to feel awkward, so I just ask, "What do you mean?"

Surely he's brought girls home before. From what Mark has told me about what he's heard from Ryan's friends, he has been through a slew of women.

Jenna tells me that all the women in the family are constantly giving him a hard time for never bringing a girl home, that I'm the first one.

"Well, we're just friends. Honestly, I think he only invited me because he felt bad that I was going to spend Christmas by myself."

The three of them give each other curious looks when I say this, which doesn't do much for my comfort level. I feel like they know something I don't, so I just come right out and ask, "Am I missing something here?"

Tori shakes her head at Jenna as Jenna leans in and quietly says, "I don't think that's why he invited you."

"What do you mean?"

Before anyone has a chance to say anything, Ryan's mom walks in and jokingly says, "You girls look like you're up to some gossip." Looking over at me, she says, "I've been so busy all day, I haven't had a chance to visit with you. Let's go chat."

Donna's personality reminds me a lot of Ryan's. She's not intimidating and seems fairly laidback and casual. She has a cute short bob of light blonde hair, and is tall and slender. She's dressed casually for the day in black pants and a red cable-knit sweater.

I stand up and grab my glass of wine as I follow her through the living room where I see Ryan helping one of his nephews put together a puzzle. When he looks up at me as I pass through, he gives me an endearing grin as I smile back. His mother and I walk out of the room into a quiet study.

She makes herself comfortable on the couch with a cup of coffee in hand while I sit in one of the plush chairs. Setting my wine down on a little round table next to the chair, I thank her for having me as a guest.

"You are more than welcome. I have been wanting to meet you for a while now."

I am flustered by her words, especially after the conversation I just had with his three cousins. "A while?" I ask.

"Yeah, ever since he first called me to tell me about you, I've been wanting us to meet."

Not wanting to sound like I'm snooping, I just let her comments be. "Well, I'm glad we got to meet. Ryan's been a good friend to me. I feel like I'm imposing a bit, but he insisted that I come."

"You're not imposing at all! When you have as many people over here as we do, adding one more to the mix is nothing," she says with a giggle. "Ryan tells me you have a fairly small family."

"Yeah, it's just me and my parents." Although I say this, I'm not so sure that's even true after last night. I kind of feel like Jase is my only family now, and at the same time, I wonder how much longer I will have him. He and Mark are very serious, and I have no clue what will happen after we all graduate this year.

"I hope you don't mind, but Ryan has told me a little bit about your family dynamics. I just wanted you to know that Ryan and I have a close relationship and he talks openly with me."

"I don't mind. I figured the two of you had a tight bond. You guys are lucky. I never had that with my parents." I take a sip of my wine when I start to feel the lump in my throat return. I have always wished for that type of closeness with my parents, but it never came. And now we couldn't be any more divided.

"So, Ryan tells me that you're studying ballet at school. It sounds like such fun, to have the opportunity to turn a passion into a career."

I can't contain my smile when I respond, "I can't imagine doing anything else with my life. I've taken ballet since I was a little girl, so when I graduated high school, there was no doubt what I wanted to do next."

"That's great to have that desire and focus. Not a lot of kids your age do."

Donna and I talk and get to know each other. She wants to know me better, and I find her to be warm and very easy to talk to. We are deep in conversation when we hear Ryan yell from across the house, "Mom! You're slacking in the kitchen! I think the ham is done!"

Donna and I look at each other and laugh.

"Can I help you in the kitchen?" I ask.

"I have it covered. You go and enjoy yourself."

"Really, I'd like to help."

Donna looks at me, and I can see in her eyes that she probably understands why. Taking my hand, she says, "I'd love that."

Before we ate dinner, Ryan finally let the kids open their gifts. He wasn't kidding when he said he had a lot. He clearly spoils his nieces and nephews rotten, and it was fun for me to sit back and watch him. He's just so relaxed with them. Ryan sat on the floor with Zachary, his nine-month-old nephew, in his lap and helped him tear off all the giftwrap, and then laughed in amusement when all Zachary wanted to do was play with the paper, waving it around in his hands.

Dinner wasn't like any Christmas dinner I have ever had. The kids ate at the bar and breakfast table, with Jenna sitting next to Zachary who's in a high chair. And everyone else spread out between the formal dining room and the living room. We couldn't all sit together with there being eighteen of us. The evening was casual with loud conversation and lots of laughter. Ryan's family made me feel as if I'd known them all forever. I really get along well with Tori and Jenna. Katie has been upstairs with her sick daughter most of the day, so I haven't had much time to get to visit with her.

After a while, the commotion and noise start to overwhelm me. Needing to take a little breather, I offer to take Katie a plate of food since she missed dinner. Walking upstairs, I quietly knock on the door to Ryan's room. I crack the door open and Katie is lying in bed next to Madison.

"I brought you some dinner," I whisper.

Katie gets out of the bed, and I hand her the plate.

"Thank you so much, Candace. That's really sweet."

Looking over at her daughter, I ask, "How's she feeling?"

"She doesn't have a fever, just an upset tummy mostly. I can't get her to go to sleep though."

"Well, I have no experience with kids, but do you mind if I try?"

"God, pleeease," she chuckles. "She has books in her bag by the bed if you want to try reading to her."

"Thanks. Why don't you go downstairs and eat? I'll stay with her."

"Are you sure?"

"Yes, go," I say with a smile.

"Okay. Thank you."

Walking over to the bed, I sit down and Madison rolls over with a tiny groan.

I tell her that I'm a friend of her Uncle Ryan's, and she immediately starts babbling about him and asking me questions. When she begins to slow down, I reach over to her bag and take out two books. They're both ballerina princess books.

"You like ballerinas?" I ask.

"Mmm hmm, I wanna be one. Mommy says when I turn four that I can go to dance class."

"I think you'll make a beautiful ballerina." She smiles up at me and I say, "Do you know that I'm a ballerina?"

"A real one or pretend?"

"A real one."

"You wanna be my friend?"

"Best friends."

She giggles as I open one of her books and begin to read. It isn't long until she is sound asleep with her head on my lap. Not wanting to wake her, I keep still and allow her to sleep.

Setting the books down, I finally take a moment to realize I am lying in Ryan's bed. I look around the room that he grew up in. He has a couple of surfboards leaning against one of the walls and a large flat screen mounted on the wall facing the bed. Something about being in his room makes my heart beat a little faster. I don't want to be feeling this way, but I am. The way he was with me last night makes me feel as if I want to like him more. I have never felt this way about any guy in the past, and that scares me. I only wish he knew me before this year, before I was so screwed up.

Light filters into the room when the door opens. Ryan walks in, looks at me, and laughs. "Are you stuck under Maddie?"

"I didn't want to move and wake her up. What time is it?"

"Past eleven. Everyone has gone to bed. I told Katie to go on to bed and that I would check on you and Maddie."

"I wanted to thank your mother before she went to bed."

"Don't worry about it. Here's your bag. I made a big pallet of blankets and pillows downstairs in the living room. Since Maddie is in my room, we're just going to sleep down there. We can watch a movie or something if you want." He sets my bag on the floor and walks further into the room.

"Oh . . . ummm . . ." I mutter nervously. I was supposed to sleep in this room and Ryan was going to stay on the couch.

Sensing my hesitation, he says, "Don't worry. I'll take the floor and you can have the couch."

I smile at him as he walks over and grabs some clothes from his dresser. "I'll be downstairs. You can use my bathroom to change."

"Okay," I say as I slowly slide out from underneath Madison, careful not to wake her.

I grab my bag and go into Ryan's bathroom. I quickly take my sleeping pill, brush my teeth and hair, and then change into a pair of pajama pants and a black cami.

When I walk downstairs, I see Ryan in the kitchen wearing only a pair of flannel pajama pants that are hanging low on his hips. I'm surprised when I see a half-sleeve of tattoos on his right arm that spans a few inches onto his chest.

When he spots me from across the room, he says, "Grabbing some water. Want a bottle?"

"No, thanks."

I notice all the blankets and pillows piled into a big fluffy makeshift bed in the center of the living room.

"You mind if I take the floor?" I ask.

"You sure?"

"Yeah. It looks more comfortable anyway."

"Okay."

Suddenly feeling nervous about spending the night here in the same room as Ryan, I apprehensively walk over and sit down, sliding the covers over my legs. He walks across the dark room, the only light coming from the last of the burning embers in the fireplace. I try not to stare at his bare chest that is revealing the tattoos I never knew he had. He sits down next to me and turns the TV on.

"TCM?"

I laugh at him and say, "It's all we ever watch. Why switch now?"

"I think you're starting to like my movies," he teases.

"Maybe."

We sit back and start watching a movie when Ryan turns to me and says, "Were you okay today?"

"I was. You're really lucky; you have a great family."

"Well, everyone really likes you, especially my mom."

"She's really nice. We had some time to visit earlier."

His words are sweet, but at the same time bring sadness. I only wish it was my parents who felt this way. But being here today, with his big family, has made me realize just how cold my family is. You can't even compare the two. Feeling the emotions tugging at me, I lie down and lay my head on the pillows sitting next to Ryan. He starts playing with my hair, and it's only a matter of minutes when I begin to feel the effects of my pill and drift off.

Gasping for breath, I thrash up out of a dead sleep. My breathing is loud, and I'm confused about where I am until I hear Ryan say, "Candace," as he jumps off the couch and is by my side in a second, pulling me into his arms. "You okay?"

My body is stiff, and I'm shaken, panicked by what just happened. I have no idea what I was dreaming about. I start taking deeps breaths.

"What happened, babe?"

"Bad dream," I quietly whisper through my erratic breathing. I have no idea what brought that on.

"Slow your breathing down, okay?"

I do as he says and concentrate on his heartbeat as he holds me against his chest. Wrapping my arms around him, he begins to stroke one of his hands up and down my back. Once I'm calm and my breathing has steadied, he asks, "Wanna talk about it?"

I don't speak; I just shake my head no. Truth is, I don't know what I was even dreaming about, and the last thing I want to do is try to remember it.

Ryan slides under the covers with me and lays us down, both on our sides facing each other. I look up into his eyes, and he is staring back into mine. Holding me tightly against his warm body, looking into his clear-blue eyes, my heart begins to quicken again, but in a completely different way. He brings his hand up and gently places it on the side of my cheek. My breath catches, and I am so close to him that I can hear his breaths as they begin to increase slightly. Everything about him is calling me. I'm too scared to even move, but at the same time, I want to move. He's all around me, and I still want more. Never taking his eyes off of me as we lie in the darkness, I grasp onto a thread of bravery and bring my hand up to cup his cheek as he is doing mine. Wrapped up in each other, his gaze slowly moves down to my mouth. I shouldn't be wanting to do what I know he wants to, but when his eyes flick back to mine, I keep my eyes locked on his as I nod my head, my timid way of letting him know what I want.

Lowering his head slowly, my heart begins to pound in my chest as he gently presses his soft lips to mine, and my eyes fall shut. My body starts to tremble under his arms, and he grips me tighter. His kisses are slow, but purposeful. When I begin to move my lips softly with his, he glides his hand from my cheek to the back of my head, weaving his fingers into my hair and holding me close.

He brushes his tongue across my upper lip, and a soft noise escapes my throat. I want this, and I want this with him, but I'm scared. I've never felt this way before, and I don't know what it is about him that makes me feel like this. I take my hand from his cheek, slide it under his arm, back up around his broad shoulder, and grip tightly. My heart is all over the place as our lips meld together.

Without breaking our connection, he shifts me onto my back. He begins to softly nip and suck, taking his time and not rushing our kisses. I slide my hands down his shoulders and hold tightly onto his muscular arms. When I feel his tongue brush across my lip again, I part my lips more and allow him to deepen the kiss. He dips his tongue into my mouth and caresses it against mine.

My emotions are running high, and I'm not used to the feelings that course through me. Suddenly, the thought creeps in that I'm too damaged for him to ever want to be with me. And what if I'm just another girl to him? I can't do this. I realize that I'm feeling too much, and he now has the potential to hurt me.

I push my hands against his arms, and he pulls back."I'm sorry," I barely whisper, keeping my eyes closed because I'm embarrassed to look at him.

He continues to hold me tightly in his warm arms. "Look at me, Candace," he breathes out.

I take a second before I hesitantly open my eyes and look into his. Supporting himself above me on one elbow, he takes his hand and brushes the back of his fingers along my face.

"I don't want you to feel sorry for that."

Another small noise escapes me as I nod. I can't speak, because holding on as tightly as I am to keep my tears from falling is taking up all the strength I have. So, I wrap my arms around him, clinging to his warmth, to the belief that I didn't just do something stupid—clinging to my hope that he won't hurt me.

Leaning down and resting his forehead against mine, I can't help myself when I tilt my chin up and gently kiss him. His lips fall slowly onto mine, pushing my head into the pillow. I cup his face between my two hands before he languidly pulls his lips from mine. Lying back on his side, he pulls me into him, and for the first time in my life, I let someone besides Jase hold onto me through the night.

chapter twenty-two

MY LEGS ARE tangled with Ryan's, and he's lying behind me with his arm draped around my waist. His warmth is wrapped around me and although I feel nervous about seeing him after our kiss last night, I also feel relaxed in his arms as he sleeps.

My stomach is full of butterflies, and I haven't even opened my eyes yet. What does this all mean? I wish I knew where his head was at, what he's thinking. At the same time, I feel like I'm not guarding myself like I probably should be. What if that kiss didn't mean anything to him? What if that's something he just does with any girl? Did he feel what I felt?

Taking in a deep breath, I hold it and try to clear my head of all these jumbled thoughts. When I let out my breath, I open my eyes and see two round blue eyes staring into mine.

"Night night over."

"It's not over, Bailey," Ryan mumbles behind me in a sleepy raspy voice.

I look at Bailey, Ryan's two-year-old niece, and give her a grin.

"I eat bweakfast. Night night over," she says to me in her sweet toddler voice.

"Okay," I whisper to her as I start to wriggle my way from underneath Ryan's arm.

He pulls me back down and with his eyes still shut says, "Where are you going?"

"To go get her something to eat." I slide out from under the pile of blankets and walk to the dining room while Bailey follows.

Pulling out a chair for her at the table, she takes a seat and says, "I eat ceweal."

"Sounds good. Where's the cereal?" I say to myself as I walk into the kitchen and open the door to the pantry. I scan around and see a box of Cookie Crunch.

"How about this?" I ask her as I hold up the box.

A big smile covers her face, and I start opening and closing cabinets to find her a bowl.

"The kid's things are in the cabinet by the fridge," Ryan says from across the room.

I look over my shoulder at him as he is walking toward me. His hair has a messiness to it that just adds to his appeal. I shake off the thought and turn around to pour the cereal in the bowl.

I walk over to the table and set it in front of the little girl and then peel open a banana for her as well.

"Fanks," she says around a mouth full of cereal.

When I walk back into the kitchen, Ryan is starting a pot of coffee. The house is quiet and we are the only ones up.

"Want some?" he asks as he is opening the cabinet to grab the mugs.

I lean back against the counter opposite of him and nod my head. I don't know what to say to him, and I'm a bundle of nerves as I watch him move around the kitchen.

"Umm, I'm gonna sneak upstairs and get cleaned up." I need space to regroup and watching him move around wearing nothing but a loose pair of pajama pants is way too distracting for me.

"Here," he says as he pours the creamer in my coffee and adds one sugar.

"Thanks." I take the cup, and avoid eye contact. *What am I doing? Why does this make me so uncomfortable?* Even the fact that he remembers how I take my coffee feels like too much.

It's always been difficult for me to connect to people, to let them in. Jase says it's because of the lack of affection I had when I was growing up. Maybe he's right. I've only ever truly let one person in—Jase. Guys have always made me feel awkward. I don't know how to respond to affection, and I wind up feeling embarrassed and shy. For the first time, I don't want to feel that way. Not with Ryan. Maybe it's because he has seen a part of me that no one besides Jase has.

Fighting with my parents has been my life. I am used to the chilled air that surrounds them. But having Ryan witness that, and then watching me fall apart, is something that no one has seen. I've always kept that hidden within me.

"Hey," he says, and I am snapped out of my thoughts. "You okay?"

No. I'm confused. I don't want to be, but I am. What happened last night? What did that mean?

"Yeah, I'm fine. I just want to get ready before everyone wakes up."

"Okay."

I turn and make my way upstairs and quietly sneak into his room, careful not to wake Madison.

I take my time showering and getting ready, needing to pull my thoughts together before going downstairs. Yesterday was overwhelming, being around Ryan's large family. I am so used to calm and quiet. I can already hear the kids playing as I slip on my jeans and one of my old UW sweatshirts. Wrapping my hair on top of my head in a messy bun, I hear a knock on the bathroom door.

"Come in," I say. When the door opens, Ryan walks in and leans up against the sink right next to me. I look over at him while I'm swiping on some lip-gloss and start putting everything away. He watches me as I pack my things up, and when I pass him, he takes me by the waist and pulls me in.

"What's wrong?" he asks.

"Nothing. Really."

Cocking his head slightly to the side, he says, "You wanna get out of here for a while?"

Without thinking too much, I nod my head.

He takes my hand, but this time it's different. He laces his fingers through mine and leads me downstairs. Everyone is moving about, eating breakfast, and tending to all the kids. He walks us into the formal dining room where his mother and cousins are sitting. I see Donna's eyes go straight to our hands, and I quickly try to pull my hand away, but he grips me tighter.

"Good morning, Candace," she says as she stands up and gives me a hug. "How did you sleep last night?"

"Good, thank you."

"Hey, Mom, we're going to go to Indian Beach for a while," Ryan tells her.

"Oh, okay. Well, the girls and I are heading to Astoria for the day to do some shopping, so we won't be around. But the guys are going to stay here with all the kids."

"What are the plans for dinner tonight?"

"The kids really want Fultano's Pizza," she says.

"Text me when you're driving back, and we'll go pick it up," Ryan tells her.

"Thanks, dear." She leans in and kisses him on the cheek. "You guys have a good day."

We head out to the jeep and start driving towards Ecola Park to the beach. The drive is quiet as we weave through the lush trees on the narrow, winding road. The surroundings are absolutely stunning, considering the dark grey skies and rainy weather. When we make our way out of the canopy of trees, Ryan parks the jeep, reaches into the back seat, and grabs me a hooded raincoat.

"Here, wear this," he says as I take the coat from him.

When we get out of the jeep, I shrug on the huge coat and pull the hood over my head. The wind off the water is strong, and the chill is biting. He takes my hand again and starts walking us down the wooden stairs to the wet puddled sand and rocks. This place is beautiful in a dark and moody way. We are the only ones on the beach aside from a few surfers in wetsuits out in the water. I follow Ryan and we walk along the uneven stacks of black rocks toward a few logs of driftwood. We sit on one of the logs, and he wraps his arm around me as I shiver in the rainy cold. The view of the deep cliffs around us and the sea stacks in the water are awesome.

"This is amazing," I say.

"Yeah, I love it out here. I used to surf here a lot growing up."

I nod my head, remembering the surfboards in his bedroom.

"Candace," he says as he turns his focus on me. Looking into my eyes, he asks, "What's bothering you? And don't say nothing, because I know something is."

Looking away, back at the water, I try to find my words. If I don't talk to him, then the awkwardness will just continue. But, what do I say? There are a million things racing through my head, and I am finding it hard to hone in on just one. And what if he thinks I'm crazy for reading too much into a kiss that was probably something so casual to him?

"Candace," he says, and I turn to look back at him.

I let out a breath before admitting, "I just don't really know what we're doing." It's all I can say.

Shifting his one leg over the log, he turns to face me straight on. "Tell me what you want."

What? Why can't he just tell me what he wants?

Not wanting to look at him, I stare out into the water again when I confess, "I'm not good at this stuff, Ryan."

"Come here," he says as he tugs on my leg, and I shift my body slightly to face him. "I've wanted to kiss you since the night of the concert. I don't know where your head is at, but whenever I'm not with you, I want to be."

My heart begins to race as he says this to me. It's what I was hoping to hear, but also what I was scared to hear.

When I drop my head, he says, "Talk to me, babe."

"I just . . . I don't do this well."

"Do what?"

"This . . ." I stop talking when he cradles my face in his hands and moves me so that I'm looking at him.

"Whatever *this* is, I want it. I just need to know if you do." His eyes are serious, and he never takes them off of me as he speaks. It's intimidating and makes me anxious. Hearing him speak so honestly makes my stomach flutter. I'm scared. I'm happy. I'm all over the place when I finally look up at him. And with trepidation, I nod my head yes.

A smile breaks across his face as he pulls me in and kisses me. I wrap my arms around him, underneath his coat as his cold, rain soaked lips cover mine. He draws me in tight, and I melt into him. Pushing my fears aside, I focus solely on him. His hold on me is strong, which contrasts his gentle kisses. He's in no rush as he takes his time, dragging his tongue across my lip and slipping it inside my mouth. When our tongues slide across each other, I tighten my grip on him. His lips are soft, and I can taste a hint of mint on him. He holds my head and guides me with him as we move with one another. I've never been kissed the way Ryan kisses me. He's slow and deliberate, and I can feel that it's more than just a kiss to him, which settles me because it's more than that for me too.

His hands still on my cheeks, he breaks our kiss, and I stare up into his eyes when he says, "Should we get out of here?"

"Let's stay." I'm in no hurry to go back to his house, and I don't want this moment to end just yet.

"Come here." He pulls me onto his lap, and I hook my arms around his neck. He is much larger than I am, so I fit perfectly in his hold.

"Can I ask you something?"

"Anything," he says as he turns his head to look at me.

"I never asked before because I didn't want to intrude, but . . . where is your father?"

He lets out a slow breath and shifts his focus out to the beach. "He died about ten years ago." He turns to face me again, and I feel awful for asking.

"I'm sorry, I shouldn't have asked," I say when I drop my head, feeling bad for bringing it up.

Lifting my chin to look up at him, he says, "Candace, you can ask me anything. I don't want you to feel like you can't, okay?"

"Yeah," I quietly sigh and turn my head away from him, still feeling like I shouldn't have asked him that.

After a moment he begins to speak. "My dad was an asshole." When I look at him, he continues, "He drank way too much and was never around, but when he was, he was a total dick. So, don't feel bad for asking, because I don't feel bad that he's dead."

His voice is hard when he speaks, and I have no idea how to respond to his harsh words. I want to know more, but I don't dare ask. Whatever is underneath this is something that seems painful, so I let it go.

I look up at the cliff that is behind us and notice a roped off ledge. "Is there a trail up there?"

Turning his head to see what I'm looking at, he says, "Yeah, it's a pretty decent path if you want to go up there."

Needing to cut this intensity, I say, "Yeah, let's go."

He eyes my leopard rain boots and asks, "Those have enough traction?"

"We'll see." I giggle and hop off of his lap and grab his hands to pull him off the log.

He smiles at my laugh and leans down to give me a chaste kiss before bending down and grabbing me behind my knees, scooping me up over his shoulder. I squeal as he starts hauling me up the stairs while I hang upside down. I don't even think to tell him to put me down because I love this feeling of playfulness. I honestly can't remember the last time I have felt like this; I don't think I ever have.

We hike along the path and explore the area for a couple hours. I was apprehensive about coming on this trip with him, but I'm so glad I did. My discomfort has dissipated, and it feels like it always has with us—light and easy.

We start walking back to the jeep, thoroughly wet and windblown.

"You up for shopping?" he asks me with a smirk.

"Shopping?"

"Yeah, everyone is leaving tonight, so I need to get the kids hopped up on sugar before they go," he jokes. Opening my door, he helps me up into my seat before walking around to the other side. When he gets in, I ask, "Where are we going?"

"Seaside. There's a cool candy shop called The Buzz."

I laugh at his excitement. "Your cousins are going to hate you, you know?"

"I'm their uncle, it's my job to spoil the shit out of those kids to spite their parents."

He makes me laugh, but his love for his nieces and nephews is apparent. I get the feeling that is how they all are with each other. It feels so abnormal to be around them, but I know it's because I've never had that in my life. It's always just been me and my parents, and there was never any warmth between us.

Ryan reaches over, laces his fingers with mine, and holds my hand. I smile when I look over at him. I sit back, with our hands connected, and enjoy his quiet company as we drive.

Pulling onto the Broadway Strip of Seaside, there are throngs of people walking on the sidewalks, going in and out of the shops that line the street. When we find a parking spot, we walk to the candy shop. He leads me to the back of the store, and when I see what he is eying, I start laughing and say, "You cannot let those kids eat this stuff!"

"Watch me," he says with a devious smile.

I just stand there next to him, shaking my head as he tells the sales clerk to bag up chocolate-covered and peanut butter-covered Twinkies, chocolate covered bacon, and a chunk of peanut butter foam rock.

Looking over at me as he pays for the diabetic-coma-in-a-bag, he innocently says, "What?" as if he doesn't understand the absurdness of his purchase.

"Nothing," I say in a high-pitched mock defensive tone.

After grabbing lunch, we continue to shop around before deciding to head back. The rain has been constant all day, and we are both in desperate need of clean, dry clothes, especially since we decided to hike in the mud earlier.

Ryan's mom calls to let us know that they are on their way back to the house, so we stop by Fultano's to pick up a few pizzas for an early dinner before everyone leaves.

We arrive home before his mother and aunts do, so Ryan stashes the pizzas in the oven and offers to take the older kids upstairs to play to give their dads a little break. There is a large playroom that he takes the three kids into and has me shut the door behind them.

"Can you guys keep a secret?" he asks them.

Madison, Bailey, and Connor, his four year-old nephew, all say 'yes' in excited unison when Ryan pulls out the bag of sugary junk. I sit back on one of the couches in the room and laugh as Ryan and the kids dive into everything. Watching how he is with these kids, laughing and playing on the floor, is another reason for me to like him even more. I know he owns a successful business and works hard, but it's nice that he has this lighthearted side to him as well.

Ryan comes over to sit next to me with one of the pieces of chocolate covered bacon.

"Here," he says as he tries to hand it to me.

Pushing his hand away, I say, "Gross. I'm not eating that."

"It's surprisingly really good." He takes a bite out of it and holds the leftover piece to my mouth. "Just try it," he says, and I open my mouth and bite it out of his grip.

I'm amazed that it is actually good. The salt and smoke of the bacon blends well with the sweetness of the chocolate.

"Okay, you win. That was actually really good," I admit.

Ryan looks out the window that's over my shoulder then back to the kids.

"Guys, eat fast. Our mom's just pulled up."

The three of them giggle as they try desperately to scarf down the rest of the sweets. Ryan and I laugh while watching them in their simplicity of fun. We get up, and Ryan wads up all the wrappers.

Holding out my hands, I say, "Give them to me. I'll hide them."

The kids run downstairs and Ryan hands over the wrappers as I walk to his room. He follows me in and closes the door behind us. I walk into the bathroom and toss everything in the trashcan. When I walk out, Ryan is sitting on the edge of the bed.

"Come over here," he says.

Walking over to him, he pulls me between his legs and slides his arms around my waist. Because of our height difference, we are almost level. Looking at me, he says, "I'm glad you're here with me."

I smile at him with my hands gripped on his shoulders. "Me too."

Placing his hand behind my neck, he draws me in so he can kiss me. He keeps the kiss short then pulls me down to sit on his knee. The room is dark as we stare at each other with our foreheads resting together. Being like this with him, in this quiet room, is peaceful. Neither one of us speaks as we sit here together.

"We should go downstairs," I whisper.

Whispering back, he says, "Not yet."

We stay like this, me on his knee, foreheads together, when Connor comes bursting through the door.

"Busted!" he shouts.

I jump up, and Ryan turns to him. "What do you mean?"

"Bailey had chocolate on her face and Mom is blaming you."

"Okay, kid, let's go face the firing squad."

When Connor starts running back downstairs, Ryan and I follow.

"What did you feed these kids?" Tori asks Ryan.

"I'll never tell, and neither will they," he jokes as the kids start laughing uncontrollably. "Call it a going-home present," he says with a wink.

"Payback's a bitch. Just remember that, Ryan. One of these days, when you have kids, you'll see."

Ryan laughs at her, and I try to stifle my laugh as well. Watching their playful banter is pretty funny.

The house is quiet and still. Everyone left about an hour ago, and I have been curled up on the couch, reading one of my favorite childhood books I found on the bookshelf, since I got out of the shower. Ryan is upstairs, getting cleaned up, while I drink a cup of hot tea and read as the rain trickles down the large windows that look out to the beach.

"Where's Ryan?" Donna asks as she walks into the room.

"He's taking a shower."

She grabs a couple blankets and joins me on the couch. "Here, cover up. It's cold."

Draping the blanket across my lap, I set the book down and say, "Thanks."

She wraps up in her blanket and asks, "How are you doing, dear?"

"Good actually. I'm sorry I wasn't around much to visit with everyone. I hope no one thought I was being rude."

"No one thought that. Please, no need to apologize."

"It's just . . . I'm not used to being around a large group. It's a little overwhelming for me."

"You don't need to explain. Everyone loves you. It was a nice surprise to have you, and Ryan seems really happy."

"Oh," I say, not sure how to respond to her statement.

"Ryan said he went to meet your parents on Christmas Eve. I've been so busy, I haven't had a chance to ask him about it. How did it go?" she questions.

Looking down at my tea, I shake my head. "Not well."

She reaches over and places her hand on my knee. "What happened?"

I sit there, trying to figure out where I should begin. I've been so busy the past few days that I haven't had much time to think about our fight. Now that I am searching for the words, the finality of our fight plays back in my head. I swallow hard against the lump in my throat, and when I open my mouth to speak, I can't seem to get anything out. I close my mouth and stare into Ryan's mother's eyes.

"Oh, sweetie," is all she says when she scoots closer and wraps me in her arms.

How is it that this woman I just met yesterday seems to read me better than my own mother? Why can't my mother just love me? Why has she never loved me? My thoughts become too much, and I begin to weep quietly as Donna rubs my back. My mother has never comforted me like this, not even when I was a little girl. When I was younger, it was always the nanny who would lie with me when I got sick, or put Band-Aids on my knees when I would fall off my bike. Why couldn't I have had a loving family like Ryan's?

"Do you want to tell me about what happened?" she asks as she pulls away.

Wiping my tears, I decide to open up to her. "We got in a bad fight. It wasn't good. They told me they were done with me and not to come back."

"My God," she says quietly in shock.

"What's worse is that Ryan heard it all."

"Ryan would never judge you for that."

"I hope not, but it was embarrassing nonetheless."

"What were you arguing about?" she asks.

"The same thing we always fight about. They aren't happy with my choices. I'm not good enough. I don't measure up to the name they work hard for." Donna leans over to the end table and hands me a box of tissues. I pull one out and wipe the tears from my cheeks. "It's always been this way, but then at Thanksgiving my mother told me that I was nothing but an embarrassment to her."

"I'm so sorry, dear. No child should ever have to hear that."

"Hear what?" Ryan questions, and when I look up, I see him walking down the stairs. He crosses the room and comes to sit next to me on the couch as I face his mother. I try not to look at him as he wraps one of his arms around me.

"Candace is telling me about what happened the other night."

"Mom."

"It's fine," I say.

Covering my hand with hers, she asks, "Do you have any other family at all?"

"No. It's only ever been the three of us since my father's parents' passed away."

"What about your mother's family?"

"I've never met them. I have never known them to speak. I'm not even sure they know about me." Wiping my cheeks again, Ryan rests his other hand on my leg. He doesn't say anything, he just sits there, letting his mom and I talk.

She shakes her head as if she can't believe what I am saying. Leaning forward, she takes me in her arms again. The comfort I am getting, being held by both Ryan and his mother is almost too much for me, but I know this is what I've been missing my whole life. I wrap my arms around Donna as more tears fall.

Letting go of me, she says, "I'm glad you're here with us," as she brushes her thumbs under my eyes. "I'll let the two of you be," she says to Ryan then kisses my forehead. When she leaves the room, Ryan pulls me back onto his chest.

"Don't cry, babe," he says softly in my ear.

"I'm tired. I don't want to talk anymore."

Ryan gets off the couch, and I follow him upstairs. Walking into his room, I go into the bathroom to take my sleeping pill and brush my teeth. When I walk out, he is still standing by the door. I crawl into his bed and don't even question him when he slides in behind me. He pulls me into him and curls himself around me. Neither one of us moves, we just lie there, snuggled up together. I've never had this before. But there is something about Ryan, about the way he makes me feel, that makes me want this—with him.

chapter twenty-three

"MORNING, BABE."
Lifting my head and looking up at Ryan, in the still-dark room, he has me tucked tightly against him. Trying to wake from my sleep, I let my head fall lazily back down on his chest. His thumb is stroking my shoulder, and I blink a few times before fully opening my eyes.

The room is cold, and I sink further down in the bed beneath the covers. I hear Ryan chuckle under his breath as he says, "What are you doing?"

"I'm cold," I whisper.

"You're always cold."

I roll over onto my stomach and look up at him. "I know."

He reaches down, pulls me back up against him, and wraps the comforter around me.

Aside from Jase, I have never slept a full night in bed with any other man. I thought it would be weird; maybe it would be with anyone else, but with Ryan it feels safe.

We are supposed to be driving back to Seattle later today, and I'm not quite sure how Jase is going to react to this new development. He knows I'm here; I texted him after the fight with my parents to let him know I was going to be with Ryan, but I haven't spoken with him since I have been here.

"Why are you so quiet?" Ryan asks me.

"Just thinking."

"About?"

Snaking my arm around his waist, I say, "Jase. He and Mark will be back Saturday."

He rolls on his side and props himself up on his elbow. Looking down at me, he says, "Stop thinking," as he leans down and nuzzles his head in my neck, lightly nipping on the sensitive flesh. Goosebumps begin to prick on my skin. Raising his head, my hands holding his face, he says, "Do you know how beautiful you look right now?"

His words make my heart quicken, and I pull his face down to me and kiss him.

"Are you guys all packed up?" his mother asks as Ryan pulls out some cold pizza for us to eat.

We spent the morning lying in bed, dozing in and out of sleep, and just enjoying the calm of being alone.

Handing me a slice, he turns to her and says, "Yeah, I have to go to my office and get a bunch of paperwork done, and Candace has to work tonight."

The three of us sit together at the table, eating cold leftover pizza. I sit and listen to Ryan and his mother talk to each other. They have a natural flow and connection between them, and it's apparent that the two of them are really close.

"Candace, will you take a quick walk with me on the beach before you go?" she asks.

I look up at Ryan, and he smiles at me before getting up from the table. Turning to look at Donna, I answer, "Yeah. Let me go grab my rain boots."

The mist is light this morning, as we walk along the firm puddled sand. The wind is kicking hard, and the waves are rough as they crash along the shore.

"I'm sorry if I pushed too much yesterday," she says, looking at me over her shoulder.

"You didn't. I don't ever talk about that stuff with anyone, but it felt nice to unload a little of it."

"I feel just awful about what you've been through, and I want you to know, that even though we just met, you can talk to me whenever you want. I'll give you my number before you leave. Call me, please."

I nod my head and say, "Okay."

"Everyone needs a parent they can depend on, including you, dear."

I'm taken back by her words. Donna has such a warm and maternal demeanor.

She stops and turns to face me when she says, "He hasn't always had it easy, you know? He doesn't let a lot of people in, but I know you're special to him, which makes you special to me. From what Ryan has told me, he's really lucky to have you."

We stand there, facing each other, and I'm at a complete loss for words. Where have these people been? Why are they just now in my life? Why couldn't I have met Ryan years ago? I could have possibly been saved from so much, and now I feel like I could destroy this if he knew my secret. Standing on this beach right now with his mother, I vow to do everything I can to bury this deep down. If he knew, he would never look at me the way he does now. He would be disgusted, and everything would crumble. I can't have that happen. I've lost Kimber, I've lost my parents, I've even lost myself; I can't lose anyone else.

When Ryan pulls up to my house, I quickly jump out to stretch after the long drive. Ryan gets my bag and walks me inside. He follows me back to my room as I go to put my bag away. I turn to look at him standing in the doorway. He's looking around my room as if he is taking in every detail.

"What?" I question, feeling a little too self-conscious of my belongings.

He walks right up to me and scoops me up in his arms. I love it when he holds me like this, I think he gets a kick out of how light I am and picks me up often. I wrap my arms around his neck and giggle as I look down at him.

"You've got a lot of ballet shit in here," he says, and I can't help but laugh at him.

"Yeah, I do."

Leaning my head down, we spend the next few minutes kissing each other. He is always so patient with his kisses, never rushing. It's perfect. He walks over to my bed and lays us down. He doesn't push to go any further than kissing, and I thank God for that because I don't think I am capable of doing anything else. He just holds me.

"What time do you have to be at work?" he asks.

"At seven. I have to close, so I won't be home till midnight."

"Come to my place tonight."

"I don't . . . I," I stumble over my words, not really knowing what to say, but stop trying when I hear Ryan chuckle at me.

"Why are you nervous? You've slept with me for the past two nights."

"Stop laughing at me," I say as I nudge him in the ribs. "And that was just a little different."

"Why?"

"Because your mother was there."

He starts laughing again, and I know he's not doing it to be rude, but I'm scared. This makes me nervous, and I don't know how to explain it to him. I'm sure most girls wouldn't have an issue with this. Most would be doing more than kissing like a couple of kids, but I don't know what I'm doing, and this scares the shit out of me.

When he realizes that I'm no longer talking, he shifts over me, and in a more serious tone asks, "What's going on?"

I shake my head, because what could I possibly say to a twenty-eight-year-old man that isn't going to sound completely pathetic.

"Talk to me."

"I don't know what to say," I tell him honestly.

"Say what you're thinking, babe."

"I told you that I don't do this well. I just . . . I don't." Taking a deep breath I close my eyes and continue, "I don't do this, I'm . . ." *Shit. Why can't I get my words out without sounding like an idiot?*

"Open your eyes. Don't hide from me." When I look at him, he brushes his hand through my hair and says, "We'll move as slow as you want. But, I want you in my bed tonight. I want you next to me."

"Okay," I whisper.

"I want you to talk to me though. I need you to tell me what is going on in your head. I'll never judge you."

God, why does he have to say these things to me? His words pierce through me and melt me, but they also intimidate me. How can I be open with him when I have never opened up to anyone besides Jase?

He brings me out of my thoughts when he says, "I'll never hurt you. I just need you to trust me."

I nod my head at his words, but how can I trust him like that when I don't trust anyone?

"Come on," he says as he stands up and pulls me off the bed. "I have to run and take care of things at work. You'll come over tonight." He doesn't ask, he just tells me. Not allowing a response, he leans down and kisses me before leaving.

After I unpack, I call Jase. I need to talk to someone about everything, and when he answers the phone, I break at the sound of his voice. My emotions are all over the place, but Jase is my rock, and I really need him right now.

"What's wrong?"

"I don't really know where to begin. I wish you were here. I just really need you right now." My voice trembles as I try hard not to cry.

"Sweetie, you're scaring me"

"I think I may be getting in way over my head with Ryan."

"What are you talking about? What's going on with Ryan?"

Not sure where to begin, I just start rambling uncontrollably, and I'm sure I'm not making any sense. "He kissed me, and I kissed him back. We've been sleeping next to each other. He told me he wants to be with me, and I foolishly agreed. Now we're back home, and he wants me to spend the night at his place. And I just have no clue what the hell I'm doing. And you're not here. And I'm freaking out. And . . ."

"Whoa, you have to slow down," he cuts me off. "Go back. He kissed you?"

"Uh huh."

"What happened?"

"It was late Christmas night. We were lying down, and it just sort of happened. I don't know. We just kissed, then we fell asleep together."

"Well, how did you feel when you woke up?"

"Really confused. I mean, I know we've been hanging out a lot, but I feel like I don't know a whole lot about him. And then everything Mark told me about all the girls started freaking me out."

"But he told you he wants to be with you?"

"Yeah, we went to the beach, he just came out and told me, and then I agreed with him. We ended up sleeping together again. And then his mother was insinuating that he's talked to her about me in the past, and that kinda intimidates me."

"Why?"

"What do you mean? You know I have zero experience with this shit. I have no clue what I'm getting myself into. I have never felt this way about anyone before, and I'm scared."

"What are you scared of?"

"Everything. He hasn't done anything more than kiss me, but what happens when he wants to do something else? Knowing what Mark told me, I feel like I just can't handle this. I'm scared he's going to touch me, and then what?"

"Ryan doesn't seem like the kind of guy who would push you."

"What? How do you know?"

"Because, he told me how he feels about you."

"What?!" I squeal out. "When?!"

"He called me Christmas Eve to tell me what happened with your parents. He told me that he's been having feelings for you for a while and wanted to know if he was wasting his time."

"What did you say?"

"I told him I thought he should tell you. But I told him not to fuck with you if he wasn't serious, that you've been dealing with a lot, and that I didn't want to see you get hurt."

I'm shocked. My heart is racing, and I don't know what to say.

"Candace?"

"Yeah, I'm here. Why didn't you tell me?"

"I'm telling you now."

"Don't joke with me, Jase."

"Because if I told you, you would have never let this happen. You would have completely shut him out, and you need to start living again."

"I have been living."

"You've been existing. There's a big difference."

His words cut into me. I can continue to make excuses, but I know he's right. Tears well up in my eyes, and when I sniff, Jase is right there with me.

"Don't cry, Candace."

"I'm scared."

"I know. But it's okay to feel that way. You have to feel this. You have to start opening yourself up again."

"Am I going to lose you?" Wow, that came out of nowhere. But, I have been thinking a lot about what will happen after this year. Plus he's with Mark now. What if Mark gets a job out of state? Will Jase go with him?

What if Jase gets a job out of state? And where will I get a job?

"Never. I promise."

"I want you to come home."

"Two more days. Don't cry. It'll be fine."

"Okay."

When I hang up the phone, I take a deep breath and pull myself together. I throw a load of laundry in and repack my bag before heading out to work. I try not to think too much about all the possible outcomes of what I am getting myself into. I like Ryan, and Jase's reassurance gives me the push I need to move forward, to try to open up to him. That's all I can really do—just try.

chapter twenty-four

IT'S A LITTLE past midnight when I pull into Ryan's driveway. The lights are on up on the second floor. I grab my bag, walk to the side of the building, and up the flight of stairs that lead to his front door. I stand there for a while and think about what Jase told me earlier. Based on what he said, I shouldn't be nervous about Ryan, but I am.

Aside from everything else, this is new to me. The guy I dated in high school hardly counts as a relationship. We barely even knew each other, and he didn't care enough about me to really even pay much attention to me. It was a relationship of convenience; he served as a distraction from my home life, and that's it. Aside from graduation night, we never had much of a physical relationship. I am completely inexperienced, and I know it. The fact that I am almost twenty-three makes it even more embarrassing.

I am startled when Ryan opens the door.

"What are you doing out here?" he asks.

"Umm, nothing. I was just about to knock," I lie.

He takes my bag out of my hand and steps to the side so that I can come in. I walk to the living room but don't sit. I stand like an idiot in the center of the room, not sure what I should be doing. I don't know why I feel so awkward tonight. Ryan was right; we have spent the past two nights together, so why do I feel weird about a third? Maybe it's because I am in *his* home. How many girls have been here? How many girls have slept in his bed? God, why am I even thinking about this?

He sets my bag down by the stairs that lead up to the third floor where his bedroom is, and starts walking toward me.

"Did you eat?"

"I did before I went to work."

When he reaches me, he wraps his arms around my waist, and the touch alone is enough to relax me a little bit. I clasp my hands together behind his back and lean my forehead against his chest.

Kissing the top of my head, he says, "Better?"

"Mmm hmm," I hum.

"Good. I'm wiped, what about you?"

"Yeah." Driving back from Oregon and then having to work so late, I'm drained.

Taking my bag, we go upstairs to his room.

"The bathroom is right over there," he says, and he points past his large closet.

Closing the door, I lay out my clothes and turn on the shower so that I can rid myself of the smell of coffee. That's the downfall of working at a coffee shop: you leave work smelling like an old pot of coffee.

After drying my hair, taking my sleeping pill, and brushing my teeth, I walk back in the room at the same time Ryan is coming back upstairs holding two bottles of water.

"Here," he says as he hands me one of the bottles.

"Thanks."

Ryan wears a pair of pajama bottoms with no shirt, and when he crosses the room, I notice another tattoo that looks like scripted words that is inked on the side of his ribs. He walks over to the large king-sized bed and starts pulling back the covers. I hop up on the bed and slip under the sheets. Ryan sits next to me, leaning his back against the dark leather headboard. When he lifts his arm to wrap around me, I can finally make out the words of his tattoo:

pain is a reminder
you're still alive

Laying my hand over it, I ask, "What's this for?"

He looks down at my hand and says, "A reminder." He takes my hand off the tattoo and holds it against his chest.

I then notice a jagged scar under the tattoo. I want to ask, but I don't. When Ryan sees what I'm looking at he says, "Like I said, my dad was an asshole." I shift my eyes to his when he begins talking again. "He was a drunk and liked to take his anger out on me and my mom. I took more of it than she did. The drunker he was, the worse it would get. He was like that for as far back as I can remember. It was all I knew. Then one night, I beat the shit out of him when he was wasted, and when he got in his car and left, he never came back. His car was found wrapped around a tree, and that was it. He was dead."

I'm sure my eyes are filled with horror as I listen to him speak because he pulls me tight and comforts me instead of me trying to comfort him. I am speechless; I can only tighten my grip around him to let him know how I feel. How could I have droned on about how shitty my parents are? I've had it pretty good compared to what he had to grow up with. And Donna, God, I had no idea. She is such a wonderful person. My heart hurts for what they must have gone through.

"You're the only one who knows that, outside of my mom and me," he tells me. He is only giving me more reasons to trust him.

"I feel really stupid. I'm so sorry about complaining about my parents."

"Candace, you're far from stupid. Your parents treated you like shit. They filled you full of misconceptions of yourself and fucked with your head. Anyone would be devastated. Don't dismiss your pain because you don't think it's worthy. It is."

Raking my fingers through the hair on the back of his head, I pull him down to kiss me. He slides down in the bed and hovers his body over me. He drags his lips from my mouth, across my cheek, and down my neck, taking little sucks along the way. I hold him close to me when he starts trailing kissing across my collarbone. Taking his face in my hands, I guide him back up to my lips. I begin to slip away to a place where nothing exists but us. His soft lips caress mine as we move at our slow pace. Taking one of my hands in his, he laces his fingers with mine and presses my hand into the mattress as I feel myself falling for him even more.

When Jase got back in town, we spent some much needed alone time together. Ryan has been busy this past week with work, and we haven't had much time to hang out during the days. In the mornings, we have been running together. Aside from that, I've been in the studio almost every day and picking up extra shifts at work.

Somehow I let Jase and Ryan talk me into going to Ryan's bar to hear Mark's band play tomorrow night. Still nervous about the possibility of seeing Jack out one of these days, the fact that I'll be there with Jase and Ryan was comforting enough for me to say yes.

Ryan is working late tonight, so Jase and I are spending the evening together at his place. After grabbing some tea and coffee at Peet's on the ground floor of Jase's apartment building, we head upstairs for the night.

Making ourselves comfortable on his couch, we talk for quite a while about Mark and Ryan. This is the first time that both of us have had boyfriends we can talk about, and I'm enjoying our newfound pastime for gossiping. But, the conversation takes a more serious tone when Jase asks, "Can you hear me out on something?"

"Sure. What's up?"

"I know I've brought this up before, but I want to bring it up again because you seem to be in a better place now."

"What are you getting at?"

"Have you thought about calling the detective from that night?"

"What? Why would I do that?"

"Because Candace, you know who did this, and the hospital has the evidence."

"I don't want to talk about this."

"What if he does this to someone else?"

"Drop it, Jase."

"Candace, think about it. If he could do what he did to you . . ."

"I'm serious, Jase. Drop it." My hands are shaking, and I cannot believe he even went there. Getting off the couch, I storm off to the bathroom and slam the door behind me. I have been trying so damn hard to not think about that night, and now when I close my eyes, I'm right back there. How could he do this to me? I turn on the faucet and splash cold water on my face, but the anger keeps coursing through me. Looking at myself in the mirror, I realize I'm crying, and when I see the tears, I get more pissed.

The door swings open, and Jase is standing there with guilt all over his face.

"What's wrong with you?!" I scream at him.

"Shit, Candace, I had no idea," he pleads. "I honestly thought you . . ."

"Would be over it by now?! I can't. He won't ever let me," I sob out. "I can still feel his hands all over me, and I hate it."

"God."

"All I have ever asked is for you to drop it, and now you bring this shit up?! Now?!"

"I thought . . ."

"I just can't. And God, Ryan would find out."

"He doesn't know?"

"No! He'll never know. He can't."

"Why?"

"Because I'd lose him. He'd run away. Who would want me?"

"You have to tell him."

"No, I don't. This is my secret, and I plan to keep it that way."

"Candace, I'm sorry. I didn't realize." His voice is hurt, and I feel horrible for blowing up at him like that.

"I'm sorry," I say then hug him. "I'm sorry."

"I never thought you'd be over it; I know you better than that. I just thought that you'd be in a little bit of a better place."

"Can we just forget about it?"

"Of course. Forgotten."

I decide to call it a night. Jase wanted me to spend the night, but I really need some space.

Seth's car is parked out front when I get home. As I walk past it, I notice for the first time that he has Greek letters on his back window; the same Greek letters of Jack's fraternity.

Oh my god.

Does Kimber know this? She'd almost have to know. I start to panic a bit, wondering if she's talked to Jack, and if so, what was said. Did he say anything about me?

I feel uncomfortable when I walk in and see Kimber and Seth watching a movie in the living room. I quickly walk through the room. Kimber doesn't say anything; she simply sits on the couch and looks at me when I walk to my room. This tension with Kimber hurts and the fact that Jase and I just had an argument, when we never argue, has me emotionally exhausted. God, I hate this.

Ryan seemed excited this morning on our run that I was finally going to come by his bar and hang out. After everything that happened with Jase last night, I am more apprehensive than ever, but I stuff it down deep because I know Ryan wants me at the bar with him tonight.

He's already there—he's been working all afternoon—and Mark drove with Chasten, the drummer, for a quick sound check. So, I'm getting ready and hanging out with Jase. The tension between us has dissipated and neither one of us mentions our fight.

Sliding my black boots on over my jeans, I say, "Okay, I'm ready."

"Finally," Jase teases as we start to head out.

I pull my hooded black raincoat over my plum satin swing top and lock the door behind me. When we get in the car, I text Ryan to let him know we are on our way.

"Mark is really excited that you're coming tonight."

"I feel bad that I've missed all of his shows," I say.

"Don't. He gets it."

Jase turns in down an alley, and I give him a look as he says, "We're parking in the back employee lot."

As we drive around the building, I'm surprised at the size. I had no idea he owned a place this big. Although it's dark and rainy out, I can see that the front lot and side streets are lined with cars.

Jase turns the car into a small empty spot in the back. When I get out and turn around, away from the car, my heart freezes—I can't breathe.

Holy shit.

I zone in on the blue chipped paint. I see those chips that expose the dark metal underneath almost every day. I'd know them anywhere.

When I take a step back, the heel of my boot snags on a divot in the asphalt and I trip, falling on my bottom. I begin to panic when I hit the ground. All I see is that dumpster, and I can't get up fast enough.

I can't even hear Jase as I see his lips move as he squats in front of me. Quickly, I pull myself up and Jase follows, grabbing my shoulders, he puts me back in the car. I lower my head to my knees and begin to sob uncontrollably.

When Jase gets in the car, I start screaming, "Get me out of here! Go! Get me out of here!"

He doesn't say a word as he starts the car. I sit up, with sobs wracking me. I'm still screaming when I see the back door open, and Ryan comes out. His eyes meet mine, and I can see the shock in his face as I'm crying and screaming at Jase to drive.

He rips out of the parking lot as I hear Ryan yelling my name.

Covering my face with my hands, I continue to wail.

Jase pulls the car into a gas station and throws the car in park. Getting out, he comes around to my side, opens my door, and kneels down beside me.

"Candace, I need you to breathe. Calm down, okay?"

But I can't. That night keeps replaying in my head. That dumpster. Jack ripping off my clothes. Digging my nails in the asphalt, trying to get away. It all flashes through me.

"Candace, look at me. What's wrong?"

Letting my head fall in my hands, I say, "That's the alley. That's the alley Jack . . ." I still can't bring myself to say that word, but no words are needed when Jase pulls me into him and holds me.

"Oh God," he mutters over and over as I cry.

My sobs begin to weaken, and fatigue overcomes me. I release my hold on Jase and fall back into the seat, thoroughly drained and exhausted.

"Let me take you back to my place, okay?"

My eyes sting from the mixture of tears and makeup, so I keep them closed and nod my head.

Walking into Jase's apartment, I head straight to his bedroom and lay my head on his pillow. My head is pounding, and my body is weak. Jase lies down next to me and holds me.

"What can I do?" he asks hopelessly.

"Just make it go away," I mumbled. If only he could, I just might have a fighting chance to be myself again. Instead I lie here, as I have so many times before: pathetic, weak, and broken.

Letting out a sigh of defeat, he tells me, "I wish I could. I would. I would do anything to take this away from you."

I know that he would too, but hearing the pain in his voice brings on another slew of tears.

We both jump when there is a loud pounding on his door. I sit up when Jase gets out of bed.

"Stay here," he says as he shuts the bedroom door behind him.

I soon hear Ryan's loud voice demanding to know where I am and Jase yelling at him to give me space, when the door suddenly opens.

Still crying, I look up at Ryan, and he gently closes the door behind him and rushes over to the side of the bed where I am sitting. Kneeling between my legs, he holds firmly onto my knees. I hate seeing the pain and confusion in his eyes. I continue crying and repeating, "I'm sorry. I'm sorry, Ryan. I'm . . ."

Grabbing me behind my back, he slides me off the edge of the bed and onto the floor with him. "What happened, babe?"

Hiding my face in my hands as I cry, I keep apologizing. He pulls me tight against him, and I wonder what I could possibly say to excuse this breakdown. He's going to want to know, and I don't know what to do.

He takes my wrists and pulls my hands away from my face, "I need you to talk to me."

Looking down at my lap, I say the first thing that comes to my mind, "I just . . . I got myself too worked up and had a panic attack. I know you wanted me there tonight, but I couldn't."

"Why couldn't you just tell me?"

"I was embarrassed. This has happened a few times in the past, but only Jase knows that I have these."

He wraps me up in his arms, and I feel horrible. I didn't lie, but I still feel guilty.

When I'm calmed down, he backs away and looks me in the eyes when he says, "You could've come to me. Jase isn't the only one you have, you know?"

The hurt in his eyes is too much, and I have to look away, but he lowers his head to catch my dropping eyes. "I need you to trust me enough to talk to me." Nodding my head he continues, "I understand you and Jase, but I know how I feel about you." He takes a moment before softly saying, "I want you to need me more than him."

Feeling the need to defend myself, I say, "He's all I've ever had."

Taking my hand in his, he places it against his chest when he tells me, "You have me now too."

I feel myself falling for him even more when I hear the sincerity in his words. Fisting his shirt in my hand, I wrap my free arm around his neck and hug him.

"Let's go home," he says into my ear, and I know that when he says home, he means his place, and I like that.

chapter twenty-five

SCHOOL STARTED BACK up this past week and so far, it seems that apart from my dance studios, classes should be fairly easy. Leaving my Technique Instruction lecture, I text Ryan to let him know I'm coming over a little earlier than planned since all we did was go over the syllabus.

The other day I was looking at the matted photos that I had seen back in November and when I asked to see more, he offered to show them to me this afternoon. I have been fixated on the photo I originally saw of the curve of a woman's back. I've been trying to not let my curiosity get the best of me, but I can't help but wonder who the women are in his photos.

When I arrive, the door is unlocked, so I let myself in. I don't see Ryan when I enter, so I call out, "Ryan?"

"Back in my office," he yells.

Walking down the hall to his home office, the door is cracked. I lightly knock before I enter.

"Hey, babe," he says as he leans back in his leather chair from behind his desk. "Come here."

I walk around his large desk as he scoots his chair back. He stretches his arms out and envelops me as I sit on his lap.

"How were your classes today?" he asks as he brushes my hair off my shoulder.

"Uneventful, but it's only the first week. Nothing but going over the syllabus for the most part."

"I'm glad you're here. I've missed you," he says as he brings my head down so that he can kiss me.

I've been working more while Roxy rearranges the calendar to accommodate everyone's new class schedules. When I'm not working, I have been in the studio adding choreography and rehearsing my solo. Auditions for our final production are next month, so there hasn't been much time for Ryan and I to spend together.

"So, don't be mad, but . . ." I start when Ryan interrupts, "Oh, God."

"Just listen," I say. "When I was on campus today I ran into Stacy Keets who works at the Henry Art Gallery. She was telling me that one of her pieces got picked up for a gallery show next month."

"So, you want to go?"

"Yes, but I was thinking that you could submit one of your photos."

"Babe," he says as he cocks his head to the side. "Those are just a hobby that I hardly even take seriously. I'm far from having them displayed in a gallery of all places."

Rolling my eyes at him, I continue, "Well, I happen to love the few photos I've seen. They're a lot better than you think they are."

"You're cute," he teases.

"I'm serious, I think that you should at least submit something and see if it gets accepted. If not, nothing lost, right?"

"And if they are?"

"Then you can take me as your date for the showing," I say with a sly grin.

"If I say I'll think about it, will that suffice?"

"Yep."

Laughing at me, he buries his head in my neck and starts nipping the curve of my shoulder, which he knows is my ticklish spot.

Giggling uncontrollably as he playfully assaults my neck, I manage to push him away and hop off of his lap.

"Show me all your photos so I can pick out the ones for you to consider submitting," I tease.

Rolling his chair back to the wooden credenza on the wall behind his desk, he slides one of the doors open and pulls out a stack of mattes.

"Here, boss," he says with a wink and then follows me as I start making my way to the living room.

"Want something to drink?" he asks.

"Yeah, anything hot."

Taking a seat on the couch, I cross my legs under me and make myself comfortable as I look at the first photo. It's a black and white image of a woman's neck and collarbone. It's backlit so everything is black except for the outline of the curves. Flipping to the next, it's another similar sensual photo. Then a photo of a naked woman lying on her back with her legs seductively crossed. I keep flipping, until my stomach is knotted up so tightly that I can't look anymore.

I set the stack facedown on the coffee table and stand up.

"I'll be right back," I say as I rush to the bathroom and shut the door behind me.

Seeing the one photo a few months ago seemed so harmless compared to all the ones I just saw. Who are all those women, and why is every picture so sensual? What is he doing with me? I could never be what those photos are, and I know he can't possibly see me in that way. I don't think I want him to see me that way. No, I definitely don't. It's not me. I'm . . . no, I can't even finish my thought.

Thoughts begin to flash quickly through my head, and I can't tell if I am overreacting. If he looks at women like that, then what is he doing with me? I have never really felt unsure of Ryan, but maybe I should be.

My thoughts seize for a moment when I hear Ryan tap on the door, and I wonder how long I've been in here going crazy. Apprehensively, I open the door.

"What are you doing?" he asks suspiciously as he takes a step in, and I take a step back. He can read my apprehension and gives me a confused look. "Babe, what's wrong?"

"Nothing."

Dropping his head, he lets out a breath of irritation at my lie.

"Is it the photos?"

I don't respond when he asks, but I know it's all over my face.

"Candace, you asked to see them. You knew what they would be of."

"I know, I'm sorry. I didn't think they would all be like that."

He walks in front of me and leans against the sink and says, "They're just pictures, that's all."

Sitting down on the closed toilet seat, I say, "But . . . they just seem so intimate."

"Babe, don't."

I look up at him and ask, because I need to know, "Did you sleep with them?"

"Yes," he responds honestly.

"How many have you . . . ?"

"A lot."

"And you photograph them?" I say with a tinge of disbelief.

"No. I've only photographed a couple women. Most of those photos are the same person."

"Oh," I say as I drop my head, now more worried than ever. I feel uneasy sitting here in front of him when he's just told me all of this. I can't help but think what those women must have meant to him. Did he talk to them the same way he does with me? Were they all in his bed, the bed I sometimes sleep in? And what am I to him?

He crouches down in front of me and says, "I know what you're doing, and you can stop. None of them meant what you mean to me. I never had or wanted a relationship with them."

"Then why?"

Holding my hands, he admits, "Because for most of my life I've been lost. I dealt with a lot of shit growing up, and I used women as a way to escape. But when I met you . . . you're just different. I wanted to know you, really know you. You're nothing like those women. Nothing. I've never looked at them or wanted them the way I do you."

"I don't know what I'm doing," I shamefully confess.

"I don't either."

"I mean . . . I haven't . . ."

"Been with anyone?"

When I cover my face with my hands, he grips me behind my waist and brings me down to the floor with him, sitting sideways between his legs. Holding me, knowing I must be embarrassed, he says, "Talk to me."

"Only once, but he was really drunk and it . . . well, it was pretty much over before it begun."

"Sounds like an asshole."

"He was, but it kept my parents off my back. They really liked him and his family, so we would go out every now and then, but that was about it. So, I can't help but sometimes wonder what you're doing with me." *Crap! Did I really just admit that?*

"Look at me," he says, and when I do, he continues, "I don't give a shit how inexperienced you are. In fact, I prefer that because the thought of another guy touching you pisses me off. That guy was a dick for treating you like you were disposable. But don't devalue yourself because of that. I won't rush you into anything. You know that right?"

When I nod my head, he says, "You're what I want. No one else, okay?"

"I just get scared, and I feel like you might start thinking you're wasting your time with me. I know you'd prefer that I stay every night here with you, but that's what scares me. I just need to move slow with this."

"You're not a waste of my time. You're worth every second."

Sighing with a mild feeling of relief, I smile as he leans down and gives me a slow, soft kiss.

When I let a giggle slip out, he breaks our kiss and asks, "What?"

"Can we get off your bathroom floor now?"

Laughing, he stands up and holds out his hand to help me up.

"Let's get out of here," he says.

"Where are we going?"

"Let's go hang out at Zoca's and get some coffee."

"Perfect."

Regardless of the rain, we decide to sit outside, drink our coffee, and listen to an insanely grungy street performer. Standing in the rain, he strums the somber chords of 'Something in the Way' by Nirvana as he sings the doleful lyrics. Listening to this stranger sing one of my favorite songs, I get lost for a moment at the familiar words.

"You know this song?" Ryan asks, and I pull myself out of my daze.

I turn to look at him, and respond, "It's one of my favorites."

"I used to listen to this a lot when I was younger."

"Hmm . . ."

"What?" he asks.

"I did too." When the corner of Ryan's mouth turns up in a small half smile, I say, "Go give him some money."

Snickering, he says, "What? Why?"

"Because I want him to keep playing, and he deserves to be paid." I say as I smile back at him.

He shakes his head at me in amusement when he walks over to the desolate man and drops a few bucks in his open guitar case. When he returns and sits down, he gives me a smirk. "Happy?"

Lifting my mug to my mouth, I murmur, "Mmm hmm," as I take a sip of my coffee.

"I've been wondering about something."

"What's that?" I ask.

"I need to know that you're okay with money. Since your parents aren't helping you out and you just work part-time at a coffee shop, I've been worried."

"Don't be. I'm fine. When I turned twenty-one, I gained access to my trust fund, and my parents resigned as trustees."

"I didn't want to overstep, but I needed to know you're okay."

"I am."

"Ryan, man! Where've you been?" a guy yells as he's crossing the street toward us.

Ryan stands up and walks toward him, clasping their hands together before leaning in for a quick hug as they slap each other on the back. "I've been busy keeping the bar going."

"Shit, man, last I heard that place was raking in the money."

"Something like that."

The guy looks down at me and back to Ryan. "Sorry, I'll let you get back to your friend."

"No worries. This is Candace."

He reaches out his hand, and I stand up and shake it, when he says, "I'm Gavin."

"Hey."

"Sit down and grab a drink, man," Ryan says, and Gavin pulls up a chair to our table. Ryan turns to me and says, "Gavin and I've been friends since I moved here for college."

"Oh, yeah?" I say.

"Yeah, this guy left my ass behind when he decided to buy that fuckin' bar."

"So what do you do then?"

"I work in promotions and marketing at Sub Pop Records."

"Really? That sounds like a lot of fun. Working with anyone good?" I ask.

"Ever heard of Washed Out?"

"Yeah, I have their album actually."

"Within and Without?"

"Uh huh. So they're your client?"

"Yep, one of them. We're trying to get a tour set up right now, but that shit takes forever. Before this guy got so tied up with work, he used to always come out and listen to all the bands play," he says, nodding his head at Ryan.

"You should give me a list of some of your guys, and I can check the lineup and see if I have space for any of them to perform," Ryan says.

"Yeah, man. That'd be great."

"So, Candace, what do you do besides hang out with this loser?" he says while laughing at Ryan.

"I'm a student, actually."

"U-Dub?"

"Yeah."

"What are you studying?"

"Dance. I'm a Fine Arts major."

"No shit?!"

"Yeah, man. No shit," Ryan jokes with a hint of possessiveness, and I have to laugh at his demeanor.

"Well, hey, I gotta run. I was actually on my way to a meeting, but I had to stop when I saw you."

"I'm glad you did. Sorry I've been out of pocket for the past couple months."

"No worries, but, hey, I'm throwing a party next month at my place. Everyone will be there. You should come by."

"I will. I'll call you next week."

"Oh, and if you're still around, you should come too," he says, cocking his head my way, "At least you have decent taste in music." He winks at me before saying, "Seriously though, it was nice meeting you."

Ryan looks at me and jokes, "Just ignore him."

"It was good to meet you too, Gavin."

"Take it easy, man," he says to Ryan as he starts walking off.

Turning to Ryan, I say, "So, why haven't you been hanging out with your friends?"

"I've been a little distracted for the past few months," he says with a grin, and I know he's referring to me.

Grinning, I say, "Well, don't let me keep you from your friends."

"Don't worry about my friends, I see most of them a lot 'cause they hang out at Blur to hear bands play."

"Oh." I feel like I have isolated myself from a part of Ryan's life because I never go to his bar. Maybe if I did, I would know his friends. Instead, there's this disconnect. Ryan knows my friends, albeit, only Jase and Mark, but he also chats with Roxy frequently when he stops by the coffee shop when I'm working. Although I've met his family, it would be nice to get to see him with his friends as well.

"I didn't mean how that came out," he says.

"No, I understand. You guys hang out, I just didn't know that."

Reaching over and taking my hand in his, he says, "Would you think about coming up again? We can just go together during the day. No people."

I stare at our entwined fingers, and I know that night bothers him. He hasn't mentioned anything since or questioned me about it, but I know it hurt him that I bailed with Jase and didn't turn to him. But, I don't know if I can ever go there again.

When I don't answer, he simply says, "Just think about it, babe."

"I will. I promise."

chapter twenty-six

H*EY! YOU HOME?*

On way now. Leaving gym.

Mind if I stop by?

Not at all. Be there in 10.

See ya!

"Hey, Roxy," I holler over the coffee bean grinder. "I'm heading out, okay?"

"Yeah, okay. Thanks for covering the shift this morning."

"No problem. Have you found anyone to replace Brandon yet?"

"I have another interview today," she says as she hands a customer their drink.

"Well, I'll be in tomorrow."

"Okay. See you then."

"See you," I say while putting on my coat and popping the hood over my head before heading out into the rain.

I've been taking over Brandon's shifts after he had to quit a few days ago. I'm not taking as many hours in school right now, so I have the free time. Now I need to run by Ryan's and pick up that photo so that I can submit it to Thinkspace Art Gallery. I didn't bother selecting photos when I was over there last Thursday. That sort of turned into a mess that led to confessions on the bathroom floor. Not my finest moment, but let's face it, those are few and far between these days.

But, I only need that one photo that originally caught my eye. When I walk into his loft, I can hear the shower running upstairs, so I go into his office. Sliding the door open to his credenza, I notice the mattes aren't there. I head back into the living room to look around, but I can't find them.

"Hey, babe," Ryan says while he's walking down the stairs. He's dressed, but his hair is still wet from his shower.

"Hey."

"What are you scrounging around for?" he asks as he cradles my cheeks and kisses me.

"Your mattes. I can't find them."

Kissing me again, he briefly pauses to say, "That's because they're not here," before covering my mouth with his again.

"Where are they?" I mumble against his lips.

Pausing again, he says, "I tossed them," and then he kisses me again.

I pull back in surprise. "What?! Why?"

"Because they made you uncomfortable."

"But I was looking for the photo of the woman's back so I could submit it to the gallery."

"I don't have it. I threw them all away."

Flopping down on the large leather chair behind me, I let out a defeated sigh.

Ryan sits on the coffee table in front of me, elbows resting on his knees, and asks, "What's wrong?"

"Nothing, I was just excited to submit that photo." Leaning my head back on the chair, I mumble, "Maybe it was a stupid idea."

"Is it that important to you?"

"I just thought if you saw one of your pieces in a showing, that you would see the art in it."

Giving me a smile, he says, "It wasn't difficult to capture or enhance. I can recreate it if you want."

"We don't have time for you to find someone to pose. It needs to be submitted tomorrow by the end of the day."

"We don't need to find anyone. Let's go upstairs. I'll shoot *your* back," he suggests and I feel my face flush at the thought of him photographing me.

"No."

"No, what?"

"I'm not taking my top off for you to photograph me."

He leans in and rests his hands on my knees. "You don't have to take anything off, promise. It's an extreme close-up; you only need to hike it up a little."

His original photo was so beautiful; there is no way he could capture that with me.

Standing up, he takes ahold of my hand and lifts me out of the chair.

"What?"

"We're going upstairs."

I tug my hand away. "Ryan, no."

He turns around to look at me. "What's wrong?"

"It feels weird to me."

"Don't let it."

"You just can't say that and expect me to be okay," I say and fold my arms across my chest. "I'm not like the girls you took those pictures of. I'm . . ."

"No, you're not. You're nothing like them, which is why I threw them in the garbage." Cupping my face again, he kisses me before assuring, "I only want you. No one else. The only photos I want are ones of you."

When we walk into his room, my heart starts beating faster. I sense the dampness on my palms and they begin to tingle with nerves.

Ryan goes into his closet and pulls out his camera. Walking toward the windows, he pulls the drapes shut and the room darkens. He takes my hand and leads me over to the bed.

"Just lie on your stomach."

I swallow hard against the lump that's lodged in my throat and lie on the bed, folding my arms beneath my head. Staring at him as he climbs onto the bed next to me on his knees, my body tenses when I feel him touch the hem of my shirt.

"I'm just going to lift it up a little."

Taking a deep breath through my nose, I close my eyes and feel his hand graze my back as he pulls my shirt up and tucks it under my bra.

"You okay?"

"Mmm hmm." My heart is still racing, and I'm very aware of myself.

The bed shifts, and when I open my eyes, Ryan is kneeling beside the bed, focusing on his camera and adjusting the settings. I take a calming breath and concentrate on what he's doing to take my mind off of how awkward and exposed I feel right now.

Holding the camera up to his eye, he sets the flash and starts fidgeting with the camera again. He repeats this a few times, then tells me, "I'm gonna take a few test shots to get the shutter speed right, okay?"

I nod my head and watch him as he leans in close to me, his camera up to his eye. The loud clicks of the camera startle me slightly, and my body tightens as I flinch. I'm hyperaware of everything around me as I lie here in the dark.

He reaches over me and picks up a pillow. "Here, lean up," he says and I push my chest off the bed as he places the pillow under me. "I just need a little more curve to your spine. Just lay down and relax."

He kneels back down and moves in close to me with the camera back up to his eye. "That's perfect," he mumbles, and I begin to hear the fast clicking of the camera. The flash pulses in pops of light in the dark room. And before I know it, it's dark and quiet again. The bed dips back down as he sits next to me, untucking my shirt from my bra and pulling it back down over my back.

Bracing his arms on the mattress on either side of my shoulders, he hovers over me and lowers himself to kiss my cheek.

"Thanks," he says with a soft rasp.

I shift to my side, and he lies next to me, pulling me closer to him. He lightly brushes his lips against mine before pressing into me. Weaving my fingers through his hair, I pull him even closer. My stomach starts to flutter, and an overwhelming need for closeness takes over. Being with him like this makes me want to open myself up. I feel safe in his arms and the feelings that come with it are intense. Feelings I have never had for anyone else before. I want to be close to him, but I'm so uncomfortable with myself. I worry I'll embarrass myself if he touches me in a way I can't handle. I worry that I'll be a disappointment to him.

Rolling me on my back, he begins to trail his warm damp kisses down my neck and along my shoulder. I grasp onto his arms and feel the flexing of his muscles under my hands as he moves across my collarbone. He reaches down, placing his hand on the side of my thigh, and squeezes as he starts to glide it slowly upward. My breath catches, and I quickly clamp my hand around his wrist. Pulling his head back, he studies my face, and I whisper, "Sorry."

"You don't ever have to be sorry."

I gently nod my head.

In a whisper, he says, "God, you're beautiful."

"So, you have to tell me what's going on with you and Ryan," Roxy says as we move around, making drinks for the line of people waiting.

"I don't really know."

"You like him, right?"

I look at her as I steam some milk for a customer's latte and she prompts me, "Right?"

Snapping the lid on the cup, I walk over and hand it to the girl who's waiting on the other side of the counter. Roxy steps next to me as she hands a drink to another customer. We walk back over to the machines and I finally admit, "I do."

When she looks at me, I clarify, "Like him. I do."

A sincere smile slowly creeps across her face and I become embarrassed. "Stop!"

"Oh, come on Candace! Give me a break here. I've known you for almost three years and you have never shown an interest in anyone. Let me enjoy this."

"You're embarrassing me."

"Sweetie, everything embarrasses you. Get over it," she says with a sincere smirk.

As we continue to fill drink orders, Roxy begins asking a multitude of questions, all of which I avoid answering. When the last drink is made and the shop calms down, we both take a seat and relax from the Monday morning rush.

"Well, even though you won't tell me anything, I'm happy for you."

"Thanks. Now will you stop?" I tease.

"For the time being, I'll stop," she says with a grin.

My phone chimes from under the counter. When I retrieve it, I see I have a missed text from Ryan.

Your photo from yesterday is almost finished. Touching up the lighting.

Getting off work in 30 min. Can I stop by?

Yeah.

"Ryan?" Roxy pries.

"Didn't you just say you would stop?"

Laughing, she teases me again. "So secretive."

"I'm going to the back to refill the syrup bottles. Yell for me if it gets busy."

"Yeah, yeah," she says as she waves me away.

It's nice to be able to joke around with Roxy again. The tension has definitely lightened in the past few weeks, and I know the reason for that is waiting for me at his loft right now.

I can't contain my smile when I think about us in his bed yesterday. The way my skin tingles when he kisses me, the way I soften when he holds me, the fluttering I feel when he whispers his words to me. Even though it's all so new, it's also so comforting.

I could tell he was disappointed when I didn't spend the night with him, but he understands that I don't feel comfortable being there every night. Although I love being with him, I'm still scared about moving forward.

When the bottles are refilled, I walk back into the store and put them back on the shelf. I start to gather my things and clock out.

As I'm walking out the door, Roxy can't help herself when she says loudly, "Tell your hot-ass boyfriend I said 'hi.'"

I roll my eyes at her as I open the door to leave.

Leaning against Ryan's desk, he hands me the large matte, and I cannot believe how well the photo turned out. Everything is black except for the curve of the back—my back—which is a striking muted grey with a shadow cast along the spine—my spine.

I stand there, staring at the photo, every detail of the photo. When I do look up, Ryan is focused on me with a grin on his face.

"What?" I ask.

"You."

"Me?"

Stepping in front of me, he takes the matte out of my hands and places it on the desk behind me. He slides his arms around my waist and pulls me into him and says, "You're fucking amazing," and kisses me with an intensity I haven't felt from him before. I let myself fall into him as his lips tangle with mine. When he dips his tongue in my mouth, I can taste the coolness that is left over from the mints he's addicted to. I feel so connected to him right now, and I never want to lose this feeling. So, when he breaks our kiss, I can't help the moan that creeps past my lips.

He closes his eyes and rests his forehead against mine, and I can hear his heavy breaths. Placing my hands on his face, I move in to selfishly kiss him, to feel the warmth of his touch on me. Gripping my waist, he lifts me onto his desk as he stands between my legs. Holding the back of my head, he intensifies our kiss, and I let him take more control than I have in the past.

When his shoulders tense up under my hands, he pulls away. I know it's hard for him to stop himself when we are together like this.

"Do you know how hard it was to concentrate on touching up that photo of you?"

As I shake my head, he tells me, "You're so fucking beautiful."

I believe him when he says those words to me. I might not feel that way in a day from now, or even an hour from now. But right now, in this moment—I believe him.

chapter twenty-seven

AFTER STUDIO ENDS, Ms. Emerson asks me to stay so that she can watch how my solo is progressing. Last time I rehearsed with her, it was a disaster. I'm beginning to feel the power of the piece when I dance. I know she wants me to focus on myself when I hear the music, but I just can't go to that place yet. Instead, I think about Ryan and everything he's told me about growing up and the violence in his house. It's been enough to help me better connect with the piece.

"Okay, Candace. Are you ready?" she asks as she grabs the remote to the stereo and takes her place at the front of the room.

"Yes." I walk to the center and place my feet in fifth position, waiting for the music to begin. When the strings begin to echo through the speakers, I slowly relevè on my pointes and begin my series of chainès across the floor. The low hum of the cello vibrates within my chest as I work through the movements. My heart thumps harder with the staccato brushes of the violins, and I'm spot on when I turn into my fouetté sequence. I flow through the progressions and the twinge in my stomach courses through my body as the music slowly fades into nothingness.

The room is quiet except for the breaths flowing in and out of my lungs. When I look over at Ms. Emerson, she's walking toward me. Standing in front of me, she says without any inflection in her voice, "That's better."

She says nothing else, and turns to walk out of the room. When the door closes behind her, I let out a puff of breath and allow myself the relief of a huge smile. Replaying her words, those two simple words, in my head, I spend the next hour dancing and feeling. Even though I am feeling someone else's pain, I'm still feeling.

When I leave the studio and get into my car, I decide to stop by the loft and surprise Ryan before he has to go into work for the night.

"Hey, babe!" Ryan says when he opens the door. "What are you doing here?"

"I wanted to see you before you left for work."

Picking me up in his arms, I laugh before he kisses me.

"I've missed you this week," he says as he sets me back down.

"Sorry. Auditions are in a few weeks, and then I won't be living in the studio."

"Candace!"

Leaning over to look around Ryan, I see Gavin walking over.

"Hey, Gavin. What are you doing here?"

"Just stopped by to bullshit with Ryan."

I look back at Ryan and say, "I'm sorry, I should have called before stopping by."

Gavin grabs my hand and pulls me inside. "Wanna beer?"

"Um, no."

Walking past me, Ryan says, "I'll get you a water."

"Thanks." I love that he knows exactly what I need without having to ask.

Gavin and I sit down in front of the TV where they have been watching *SportsCenter*.

Pointing the neck of his beer bottle to my head, he jokes, "What's with the hair, grandma?"

"Don't be a dick," Ryan says as he hands me a bottle of water and sits down next to me, wrapping his arm around my shoulder.

I shake my head at their banter and unscrew the lid to my water. "I was in the dance studio all day," I say and then take a long drink of water.

"How'd that go?" Ryan asks. He knows I've been having a lot of bad studios and rehearsals lately.

"It actually went pretty well. My instructor complimented me on my solo."

"Really? That's great, babe."

"Well, actually all she said was 'that's better' but coming from her, that's huge."

"You coming out with us tonight?" Gavin asks me.

"Umm," I say, turning my attention to Ryan, wondering what Gavin's talking about.

"Gavin's just coming by the bar tonight with some friends, that's all."

"Oh," I say and turn my attention back to Gavin. "No, I've got plans."

I feel left out of Ryan's life with his friends. I know it's my own doing, so I try to not let it affect me. I know it's just me being over-sensitive, but I can't help the feeling of being left out.

"What are you doing?" Ryan asks.

"I'm going to Jase's to hang out. We haven't had a lot of time to see each other lately."

"Come with me to my office before you go," he says as he stands up and takes my hand.

"If you guys are gonna fuck, I'm out," Gavin says.

"Dude!" Ryan snaps at him.

Shrugging his shoulders, he says, "What? It wouldn't be the first time."

I look at him in disbelief when he says, "Just sayin,'" as he leans back on the couch and turns up the TV.

Ryan starts leading me to his office, and when he closes the door, he turns around, placing his hands on the door, caging me in.

"Sorry about that. The guy has no filter."

The fact that he isn't denying what Gavin said is making my stomach turn. I want to run out of here, get some space, but I know he won't let me do that. I can't even look at him right now, so I keep my eyes focused on a stack of papers lying on his desk.

"Candace," he says quietly, and I turn my head and look to the floor.

He drops his head and sighs, "I'm sorry."

"Did you really do that?"

Our eyes meet when he looks up and by the look written all over his face and his creased forehead, I can tell he's ashamed to answer me.

He nods his head and says, "Yes."

I feel sick, and I look back down, not knowing what to say. Even though he didn't know me back then, it still hurts. It hurts to know that he has shared something so intimate with those girls. An intimacy that we don't share.

Tears begin to flood my eyes, and I look at him when I ask, "Is that what you want?"

He gently takes my face in his hands, and when I blink, I can feel the heat of my tears rolling down my cheeks.

"No. I was miserable then. None of them ever gave me what you give me."

"That's the problem, though. I can't give you what they could."

"You give me everything." Taking his thumbs, he wipes the tears from under my eyes. "You have more of me than any of them ever had. And when you're ready to move forward, I can promise you that it won't be like what I had with them. It was just empty with them."

He leans his forehead against mine and even though I feel upset about the way Ryan was before he met me, I'm also upset for me, that I can't give him what I want to. I can see the pain and regret in his face.

"I shouldn't be upset. I didn't know you then."

"You have every right to be upset."

Not wanting to drag this out, I wrap my hand behind his neck, draw his head to mine, and kiss him. I don't want to think about it anymore; I just want to have peace with Ryan.

"I've missed you," he mumbles over my lips, and when he does, I pull him closer to me and cover his mouth with mine. "Stay with me tonight?"

Parting our lips from each other, I whisper, "I can't."

"Why not?"

"I promised Jase I'd stay with him."

Ryan lets out a deep sigh, hanging his head down, and I know he's frustrated, but I don't ask. I haven't spent the night with him since last Sunday, and I'm sure it's bothering him.

"You have to work anyway," I say.

"I want you in my bed when I get home."

I release my hands from his neck and look down, feeling guilty, that I'm not giving him the closeness that he wants. I know he'd prefer moving this a lot faster than we are, but I feel like I'm pushing myself as it is.

"Ryan . . ." I whisper.

"I know," he says as he leans his forehead against mine.

I know he doesn't really understand my feelings of apprehension, and it hurts me that he's feeling this way because of me.

I cup his cheeks and pull up on my toes, pressing my lips into his, and when I do, he holds my head in his hands as well. We hold the kiss for a few seconds before pulling away.

"I should go."

"I'll walk you out."

We walk through the house and Gavin looks up and asks, "You heading out already?"

"Yeah, I gotta go."

"Good seeing you again."

I smile and turn toward the door with Ryan and say goodbye.

"Ryan's frustrated with me."

"What makes you say that?" Jase asks while chopping up the peppers for the stir-fry he's making.

"I just get the feeling that he is. I mean, we've been together for a few months and haven't done anything more than kiss. He has to be getting annoyed with me."

"But he hasn't said anything?"

"No, I don't think he would though."

"Do you trust him?"

Taking a sip of my wine and setting down the glass, I say, "Yeah, but I'm scared he's going to compare me. I mean, how could he not? It's only natural, right?"

"No, it's not. It's not like that. You're someone new to him, and he clearly loves you. He would be a total ass to compare you."

I widen my eyes when he says that Ryan loves me, and he catches the look on my face when he sets down the knife and questions me, "What?"

"God, Jase, you think he loves me?"

"Candace, have you seen the way he looks at you? Yes, the guy loves you." He scoops up the peppers and onions and dumps them into the hot skillet, shaking it around and flipping the vegetables. When he turns back around, he laughs. "Why do you look so surprised?"

"Because, I just . . . I mean . . ."

"Do you love him?"

"Jase!"

"Seriously. Do you?"

"At times when we are together I feel like I do. I mean . . . I think I do. Honestly, I am overwhelmed most of the time. But I'm scared. All I know is that I have never felt this way about anyone else."

"What are you so scared of?"

"Everything."

He turns around, picks up the skillet, and pours the stir-fry onto our plates. We walk into the living room and set them down on the coffee table to cool when he continues, "Explain to me what *everything* is."

I empty out my thoughts with Jase because I know I can tell him anything and he will never judge me. "I'm scared I might freak out on him, and he'll think I'm weird and won't want to waste his time with me. I'm scared I'm not enough for him. I'm worried he will somehow know what happened to me, and he'll be disgusted by me. And I'm scared of losing him, for whatever reason. What if this thing ends up badly and I'm left hurt?"

"If that does happen, you'll be okay. You're strong. I know you don't see it, but I do. You're the strongest person I know."

"I don't feel like it."

"You are. And everyone has fears in a new relationship. It doesn't make you weak; it makes you real. I was scared when Mark and I got back together. Scared that somehow I would screw it up again. That I would fall for him and then he would realize what a dick I was and leave. Scared that his family wouldn't like me. I was scared of a lot, but I still wanted him more than I wanted to give up."

"But everything that Mark was telling us. The stuff about all the girls. It's true."

"What did he say?"

I don't tell Jase everything, because what Ryan told me is private, and I want to keep it that way, so I say, "He said it was a rough time in his life, and he used women as a distraction. I asked him how many and he just told me it was a lot. But today when I stopped by his place, one of his friends was there, and he made a comment that's really been bothering me."

I pick up my plate and start moving the food aimlessly around as I continue, "So, Ryan and I were walking to his office to talk, and his friend made a remark about us having sex in there and that it wouldn't be the first time Ryan has done that."

"God."

"I know. So, when we were alone, I got upset, but then I felt bad for him. You should have seen the look on his face, Jase. It was horrible. I know he felt embarrassed, so I let it go and didn't say anything else."

"That's probably best. I mean, what is there really to say?"

"I know. It just makes me uncomfortable to think about that stuff happening at his place, and now I'm hanging out there."

"That sucks, but you can't think about all that. It's just going to eat at you."

I take a big bite of food, tilt my head back, and say, "I know," so that none of it falls out of my mouth.

Laughing at me, he jokes, "Is that how they taught you to eat at the country club?"

We both laugh and enjoy our dinner, dropping all serious conversation aside.

After dinner we simply hang out like we used to, watching trash TV and relaxing. We decide to call it a night around midnight. We lie down in his bed to sleep. We have been sleeping together for the past four years. I have always found it to be comforting, not sexual at all. Being able to have that closeness with Jase has really bonded us together. I know I can totally be free and open with him, and I need that. I don't have that with anyone else. He's seen me at my absolute worst, and has never abandoned me.

I've been studying and trying to get ahead in my classes this afternoon. Knowing that my audition is in a couple of weeks, I have been spending most of my free time at the studio. Kimber has been at her parents' house all weekend, so I have the house to myself.

I've been working on a project for one of my classes for the past few hours when Ryan drops by. I welcome the distraction as we hang out in my room and talk. I can tell something is bothering him, and I just assume it has something to do with what Gavin said yesterday at his place.

But before I can say anything, he says, "I need to talk to you about something."

Sitting on my bed, I cross my legs and say, "Okay," feeling a little nervous at the seriousness in his tone.

"Look, I get your relationship with Jase, and I haven't ever had any issues with it, but I don't like that you guys still sleep together."

"But, it's not like that."

"I know, but I still don't like it."

"But . . ."

He turns to face me, placing his hands on my knees, and says, "I know it isn't like that with you two. I get it. But I don't like the thought of you in bed with another man holding you. I want to be that guy. I want you to want me to be that guy, not Jase."

When I hear the crack in his voice, I know that this is really affecting him. Returning the honesty, I tell him, "I want you to be that guy, but I don't know how. Jase is so unthreatening to me because he's just my friend."

"Why do you think I'm threatening?"

My hands begin to fidget when I tell him, "Because you could easily walk away from me." I have to look away from him because the honesty I just put out there is too much for me.

He scoots right up next to me and says, "You think it would be easy for me to walk away? It wouldn't be easy, babe. And I doubt there is anything you could say or do that would make me want to walk away. It kills me that you're so scared of me."

When I look up at him, I confess, "You're the only person I've ever felt this way about, and I don't want to lose you."

He shifts on his knees and leans into me until I am lying on my back. He's supporting himself above me on his one elbow and wraps his other hand around my head, pulling me in for a slow kiss. I hold his face in my hands as his lips dance across mine. When he pulls back, he takes his time staring at me, and I get lost in his clear-blue eyes for a moment before he says, "You're not gonna lose me, babe. I love you too much to let you go."

The pounding of my heart is all I can hear as I try to digest his words, and I know that I love him too. I just can't bare myself that much to him, so I clench my need to say it back to him. The love I feel for him overtakes me, and I start to blink out the tears that fill my eyes. When I nod my head, he leans down and melds his mouth to mine, gliding his tongue across mine. I pull him down on me as I grab his hair with my other hand. I need to be close to him, to somehow show him that I do love him, even though I can't say the words yet.

He reaches down and skims the skin between my pants and my top with his knuckles, and I begin to quiver under his touch, but I allow it. I need to give him more. He flips his hand and begins running his palm up my stomach slowly. My breaths become short, and I try to focus more on his kisses than his wandering hand.

Holding him tight against me, I lean my head forward and nestle it in the crook of his neck. His hand stops right below my bra, and he keeps it there. I know I have to try, so I whisper with a tremble, "It's okay." Dropping his mouth on my shoulder, he grazes his lips across my sensitive skin, kissing and gently sucking as he covers my lace-covered breast with his hand. Pushing my head harder into his shoulder, I hold on tightly to him.

"God, you're perfect," he mumbles between his kisses, and when I feel his thumb skim across my nipple, a whimper escapes my mouth.

Lifting his head up, he says, "Don't hide from me, babe."

I slowly let my head fall back onto the pillow and open my eyes. A few locks of his hair have fallen over his forehead, and his eyes are locked on mine. Keeping his hand on my breast, I pull him down for a kiss. He hooks his finger under the lace of my bra and slides it across my bare skin. Our legs are tangled together, and when he starts to tug at the fabric, I get a flash of Jack tugging at my bra, and my body tenses up. "Please, don't."

Ryan doesn't say anything as he slides his hand from underneath my shirt and moves it to my head, threading his fingers through my hair.

"I'm sorry."

"Look at me," he demands, and when I do, he continues, "When we're together like this, I don't ever want you to be sorry for anything, okay?"

Nodding my head, he kisses me lightly, barely brushing my lips with his when he says one more time, "I love you, babe."

chapter twenty-eight

SITTING AT MY desk, I finish emailing a paper to one of my professors when there's a soft knock on my bedroom door.

"Come in," I say as I hit send and close the lid to my laptop.

Kimber opens my door and asks, "Can I come in?"

"Umm, yeah."

She walks in and takes a seat on the end of my bed, and I turn my chair around to face her, when she says, "I need to talk to you about after graduation."

I have hardly spoken to Kimber in months, so sitting here with her in my room makes me a little nervous.

"Okay."

"Well, I didn't know what your plans were."

"My only plan is to try and find a job. I've always had my heart set on New York, but I will go wherever I get an offer from. Why?"

"I was thinking that it might not be a good idea if you lived here after we graduate."

"Oh." I feel a lump forming in my throat and I want to cry, but I don't. We used to be so close, like sisters, and now she wants me out. How could I let things get this bad between us where she doesn't want me here?

"It's hard having you around and us not talking. I just don't feel like we are even friends anymore. It's been five months, Candace."

"I don't know what to say."

"I wish you would just talk to me. But, honestly, I don't even know if it would do any good at this point. I don't want to continue walking around here with this tension every day."

"Okay," I say. I'm hurt and pissed at myself for causing this fracture between us and now I wonder if this is even fixable.

Neither one of us says anything else, and it's only when she leaves that I begin to cry. When I pick up the phone to call Jase, it starts ringing in my hand. Being upset, I answer it without looking to see who is calling.

"Hello," I choke out.

"Jesus, what's wrong?"

When I hear Ryan's voice I start babbling. "Kimber asked me to move out. She doesn't want me here. She doesn't feel like we're friends anymore. She'd rather I went somewhere else, and I don't know if I can fix this."

"Breathe, babe. I'm in my car heading to the gym. I'm right by your house. I'll be right there."

"Okay," I say before hanging up.

When Ryan arrives, we go back to my room. Sitting on the bed with his back against the headboard, he holds me in his arms as I curl up beside him, still upset.

"So, what happened?" he asks as he starts threading his fingers through my hair.

"What I told you. That's all that she said. I didn't say anything because, you know me, I just shut down."

"What the hell happened between you two anyway?"

Shit! What do I say?

Thinking quickly, I tell him the truth, but leave out what I can't have him know.

"At the beginning of the school year, I stayed with Jase at his place for a while and Kimber thought I was avoiding her for some reason. But she didn't believe me when I told her it had nothing to do with her. So we got into a fight and she called me a liar. That was it. We've literally been avoiding each other ever since, and now so much time has passed that we're barely friends anymore."

"I don't understand you chicks, but I hate to see you so upset over this."

"I just miss her. We used to be close like sisters."

"Can't you just tell her that?"

"It won't do any good," I say.

"You know you can always stay with me."

"Yeah, I know."

Ever since Ryan told me he loved me a couple weeks ago, I have been more comfortable talking to him and opening up more. But I have yet to tell him I love him. Something about being that vulnerable still daunts me. He told me he knows I love him and to not worry about the words. I know I'm getting there; it's just taking a little while.

Quickly changing the topic he says, "Come to the gym with me."

I sit up and look at him bemused. "What?"

"Yeah, come with me. We haven't been running much because of your deranged fear of breaking your legs. You can ride the bikes, or if you're feeling risky, run on the treadmill," he jokes with me.

Smacking him in the arm, I say, "Stop laughing at me. And it isn't deranged. Seriously, what if I broke my leg before this audition? It would ruin everything."

Raising his hands in defense, he says dramatically, "I know. You've been telling me this all week."

Needing to get him off my back, I say, "Fine. I'll go ride the bikes. Let me go change."

When I walk out of the bathroom, Ryan is standing there waiting for me. Bending down, he scoops me up, over his shoulder and playfully grabs my ass. I can't control my laughter as he hauls me through my house. I return the favor and grab onto his ass as he carries me out to his jeep. When he sets me down, I have to grab hold of his arms until the dizziness subsides. He opens my door and helps me up into the car before leaning in and kissing me.

When we arrive at the gym, I make my way over to the cardio machines and Ryan follows closely behind.

"What are you doing?" I say as I turn around to face him.

"Your ass looks hot in those tight pants," he says with a wicked smirk.

I roll my eyes and before I can turn around, he grabs me by said ass and pulls me against him. Swatting his hands away, he laughs as I make my way over and sit my ass on a bike.

"Now what the hell am I supposed to look at?" he complains.

"Go lift your weights and stop harassing the gym's clientele."

I spend the next half hour riding the bike and then decide to run on the treadmill. At least there's a bar I can grab onto if I fall. Ryan has been getting a kick out of teasing me about my fear of breaking anything that has to do with my legs.

I increase the incline and set the speed for a quick-paced run. I scan the gym until I spot Ryan by the free-weights. He's lying on the incline bench doing sets of chest presses. While he's focused on his workout, I take a moment to ogle over his muscular body. When his eyes flick to mine and he catches me gawking, he gives me an egotistical grin, which I shake my head at.

We spend the next hour going back and forth like this, although I catch him a lot more than he catches me. Walking across the gym, he stands in front of my treadmill, leaning against it while I continue to run.

"You trying to kill yourself?"

"No," I say breathlessly, "Just building endurance."

His cocky grin returns, and when I side-step off the tether, I smack him and clarify, "Not for that! For dancing, you perv."

I take his hand as he helps me off the machine, and we walk over to grab some water. I drain my bottle quickly and toss it in the trash. After I towel off my face and neck, we head outside, and I welcome the cold drizzle that's falling.

On the drive back to my place, Ryan mentions the party that Gavin is throwing this weekend. Wondering if I still wanted to go, he assures me it'll be a small crowd, so I tell him yes.

We've hung out with Gavin several times in the past few weeks. He has since apologized to me for making that comment to me at Ryan's loft.

I could tell he felt bad about it, so I brushed it off. He's very crass with his words, but he's really funny at the same time. The party, if nothing else, will at least be amusing with him there.

Walking into Gavin's house, Ryan is greeted by several people. Keeping a firm grip on my hand, he introduces me to a few guys before Gavin walks up and throws his arm around me.

"It's about time you guys showed up. Help yourself to whatever is in the kitchen."

"Hey, Gav."

"Hey, gorgeous. I can't believe you haven't left this ass-hat for me yet."

"If it weren't for your delicate language, I might consider it."

"Leave her alone," Ryan says as he pulls me away and into the kitchen to grab a couple of beers.

As he's opening my bottle, I notice a tall blonde eying him. When he hands me my bottle, he leans down and gives me a chaste kiss then leads me back to the living room. We sit on the couch and Ryan begins chatting with two guys that he knows. I sip on my beer and only catch bits and pieces of their conversation. I like that he never takes his hand off of my knee while talking to them; that he's always so aware of me.

I scan the room and spot Gavin who is talking with the blonde I saw in the kitchen. Her hair is long, about the length of mine. She wears her make-up in a sultry way, opposite of my simple mascara and lip-gloss.

When both she and Gavin turn their heads and look at me, I immediately shift my eyes to Ryan. Looking back at me, he squeezes my knee, and Gavin flops down next to me.

"What's up?"

"Were you talking about me?"

"God you're paranoid," he teases and nudges my leg.

"I'm gonna go get another drink." Scooting forward on the couch, I ask Ryan if he wants another beer.

"Yeah, babe. Thanks."

I grab his empty bottle and make my way into the kitchen, tossing them into the trash. Opening the fridge, I grab two more and when I turn around, the tall blonde is standing next to me.

"Hi, I'm Gina," she says politely and holds out her hand.

Sticking one of the bottles under my arm, I reach out my now free hand to shake hers.

"I'm a good friend of Gavin and Ryan."

"Oh. I'm Candace."

"They've never mentioned you before."

"I just met Gavin a few weeks ago," I say.

"So are you and Ryan . . . ?"

"What?" I question, not quite sure what she is trying to ask me.

A grin begins to spread across her face when she leans in and says, "He's good, isn't he?"

I back away from her face and say, "Excuse me?"

"Oh, come on. Everyone knows what he's like."

What the hell is this girl's deal? Did he sleep with her? Thoughts start flooding my mind, and I just want to leave. Jealousy fills me when she says, "I'm a little surprised by you though. You don't seem to fit his type."

"Excuse me," I say as I start to walk away. I don't know this girl, but I hate her nonetheless.

"Oh my God. That's so cute," she says before I can get too much distance between us. When I turn around to look at her, she's laughing at me and says, "You think he loves you? Ryan doesn't know what that is. Trust me, I've been with him enough times to know that."

I feel sick and fire rushes through my veins, and if I wasn't so small compared to her, I'd slap the shit out of her. I set the beers on the counter and turn around. Walking through the living room, I pass Ryan and snap at him, "Take me home," and then make my way outside. My hands are shaking as a multitude of emotions runs through me: jealousy, anger, embarrassment.

"Candace," Ryan says as he rushes behind me.

I turn around, angry, and shout at him, "Did you sleep with that girl in there? Gina?"

He lets out a deep breath, and I shake my head and say, "Forget it. Just take me home."

I open the door before he can open it for me and hop up onto the seat. It's one thing for me to hear about his past, but to have his past right there in my face, taunting me, is more than I can handle.

When we start driving, Ryan finally speaks up. "I didn't know she was going to be there. When I saw her, I didn't want to say anything to draw attention."

I don't respond. I'm too upset to respond, so I pull my knee up to my chest and shift my body toward the door, leaning the side of my head against the cold leather seat and stare out the window. I want to cry because I'm embarrassed and hurt, but I don't.

"Candace, say something."

I don't.

To be honest, I'm upset with that girl, not Ryan. I know Ryan has been nothing but open with me, so I can't fault him for that. But, it doesn't make it any easier. I wonder if everyone in that house thought I was just another girl like Gina. I hate that thought.

When he pulls into his driveway, I softly say without moving, eyes still looking out the window, "Ryan, I really just want to go home."

He doesn't say anything when he gets out of the car and walks around to my side. Opening the door, he takes my hand and helps me out. I don't protest because I'm too tired to argue with him. We walk inside, and he takes me upstairs to his room.

I stand in the doorway as he walks over to his dresser and starts pulling out clothes.

"Ryan, what are you doing?"

"You're not going home. Here," he says as he hands me a pair of his boxers and a t-shirt.

I stand there for a moment and watch him as he begins to undress, then I turn to go to his bathroom and change myself. Realizing I don't have my pills, I call out for Ryan to bring me my purse.

When he knocks on the door, I open it and thank him when he hands it to me. I quickly brush my teeth, and when I walk out, the lights are off, and Ryan is already in bed. He didn't pull the drapes shut, and the moon casts a muted light through the room.

When I slide under the covers, Ryan instinctively pulls me in, facing him.

"Talk to me," he says with a soft voice.

"I'm sorry. I'm not mad at you, and I shouldn't have snapped at you. I just . . . I don't like feeling the way she made me feel. It's embarrassing."

"She was nothing to me."

"When did you . . . I mean . . . How long ago?"

"August or so."

I sigh and close my eyes, not wanting to talk about this or think about this anymore.

Brushing my hair back with his hands, he tells me, "They were only there to distract me, but when I saw you, you faded everything I needed distracting from."

Opening my eyes, I look up at him and ask, "Did you love any of them?"

"No."

Hesitantly, "Do you love me?"

"I've only ever loved you."

He rolls on top of me, staring down into my eyes. I pull him down, and I kiss him with an intensity I haven't felt before. Crushing his lips with mine, tasting each other, and feeling each other, I grab his hair, keeping him close to me. He trails his hand down the center of my sternum, between my breasts, over my stomach, and when he reaches the hem of my shirt, I feel the heat of his hand as he slides it up, making my body shudder beneath his. When he cups me in his hand and squeezes, my body bows up to him, and he lets out a deep moan.

"God, I want you," he whispers.

Sitting back on his heels, he pulls me up to him. He reaches down and slowly begins lifting up my top. Raising my arms up, he peels the cloth off of me and tosses it on the floor. He takes his hands and slides them down my sides. "Babe . . ."

He lays me back down and grazes his lips down my neck and over the thin lace of my bra. I hold tightly onto the sides of his head when he covers my nipple with his mouth and drags his tongue across the fabric. I begin to feel the anxiety build inside my stomach. I can't do this.

When he hooks his fingers under the waistband of my shorts, I clench my eyes tightly shut, panic coursing through me. I choke back a silent sob, and when I open my eyes to stop him, I see a pained look on his face. He's sitting back and slowly brushing his thumb over my tattoo, staring at it intently. His touch is jittery on my skin, and when his eyes shift to mine, I can't take the panic that is still coursing through my body.

I quickly shift up to my knees and throw my arms around his neck, just needing to feel safe in his hold. It takes him a while, but he eventually wraps his arms slowly, almost hesitantly, around me. I grip him tightly, trying hard to not freak out in front of him, and I notice his body trembling under my arms. I don't say anything because I am still so consumed with anxiety and wondering if he can tell how scared I just got when he touched me like he did.

Silently freaking out, neither one of us moves. We cling to each other and let time pass.

Eventually, I feel my heart slow, and I begin to soften in his arms.

"Candace."

"Please, don't say anything."

And he doesn't as he lies us down and pulls the covers over us.

When we wake up the next morning, Ryan is really quiet and seems tense. I notice his eyes are a bit bloodshot, and I ask him, "Did you not sleep last night?"

"Not too much," he says while pouring me a cup of coffee to take with me before he drives me home.

We've barely spoken this morning, and he hasn't been his usual affectionate self with me. In fact, I feel like he's avoiding me. I'm feeling extremely self-conscious; not only because of what happened last night, but also the way he is acting today. I'm sure he's getting tired of me always pushing him away. From my run in with Gina last night, I can tell he's used to getting what he wants without having to wait.

"You ready?" he asks.

"Yeah." I'm surprised when he takes my hand as he walks me to his jeep.

When he pulls up into my driveway and parks, I turn to him and say, "I'm sorry about last night, and I get that you're mad, but—"

"What?" he interrupts. "Why would I be mad?"

Suddenly feeling very unsure of the situation, I say, "Because I keep pushing you away. You've hardly said two words to me this morning. So, I just figured . . ."

He turns away from me and gets out of the car. I watch him, confused, as he walks around to my side and opens the door. He reaches over me and unclicks my seatbelt, turning me toward him.

"Everything you give me is perfect. You have to stop feeling like this. I'm here with you, and I'm not going anywhere." He leans in to kiss me, and his words bring me relief. "I'm sorry if I've been a dick, I just didn't get much sleep."

"It's okay. I overreacted."

Helping me out of the car, he kisses me again before leaving.

When I walk inside, Kimber is studying on the couch, and I've never felt more awkward around her since she asked me to move out.

"Who was that?" she asks as I walk across the room.

Turning to her, I ask, "Who?"

"That guy you just kissed in the driveway. I wasn't spying or anything, but you're right outside the window."

I look out the large bay window then back at her. She looks sad when I say, "Oh, um, his name's Ryan."

"You dating?"

"Yeah," I say, and I can tell that she is upset. I'm guessing it's the same sadness I felt when I found out about her and Seth. I want to talk to her, to tell her all about him and how great he is, but I can't. We aren't like that anymore, and I know she's hurting more than me as each day we grow more distant.

"Well, I have to go get ready for school," I softly say and then walk out of the room.

Seeing her now, after yesterday, is awful. I hate knowing that I've hurt her this much. I feel like I've lost her, and it's hard to be in the same house as her when we both feel the way that we do.

When I pick up my phone, with apprehension, I type out my text.

Can I stay with you?

I hold my phone with nervous hands and wait for the reply.

Of course babe.

chapter twenty-nine

AFTER I HAD texted Ryan about staying with him, he came over later that night when I got off work to help me pack a few bags. Thankfully, Kimber wasn't home. It was hard enough trying to pack when I was so upset. But I know I need a little time away from this house so that emotions can settle.

I thought it would be weird staying with Ryan, but he's been able to keep the weirdness away. I know he's happy that I ran to him instead of Jase. But after knowing how he feels about Jase and me sleeping in the same bed, I knew I couldn't stay with him.

My sleep has been a little more restless lately and filled with night terrors since I stopped taking my sleeping pills last week. Taking them was always hard for me; a daily reminder of why I need to be on them and it was only becoming worse. So I hoped that enough time had passed, and I wouldn't need them anymore. I haven't had another nightmare though, which has been a relief. My restless sleep worries Ryan, but I just told him it's because of stress with school, graduation, and my issues with Kimber. I know it's a lie, but I told him that regardless.

Jase and Mark have been spending more time at the loft as well, now that I'm there. They tend to come over, or at least Jase does, when Ryan goes into work at night. They have both been scouting out firms to start applying to in a few months. I try not to think about what graduation will mean for Ryan and I. He hasn't ever said anything or asked, so if it's been on his mind, he doesn't want me to know. Truth is, I could wind up staying if this is where my job is. I have no idea where I will wind up, but for the moment, I want to enjoy being right where I am.

Ryan makes me happy, and I desperately need that. I still have my moments where I think I'm going to see Jack at school, or that he's going to walk into the coffee shop. And I know he's the cause of my restless sleep. Every time I take off my clothes, I'm reminded of him, of that night. He left a scar on my breast where he bit me so hard that he broke my skin. I can still remember the pain that shot down to my belly. Ryan has never seen it because the few times he's taken off my shirt, I never let him take off my bra.

But he's seen my tattoo; the foolish tattoo I got when I thought it was time to abandon my cautious ways and have a little fun. Who knew fun would have left me battered, lying on a street by a dumpster? But, when I'm next to Ryan, he takes almost all of that away from me. I only wish he could take it all away.

"Candace Parker, please take the stage." My name echoes throughout Meany Theater. Nerves course through me, as they do every time I walk across this stage. Walking to the center, I find my spot and posture myself in fifth position. The thump of the spotlight being turned on is loud as it casts its glow down on me. And as it does, like all the times in the past on this very stage, my body relaxes and I am free when the music begins.

I let go, and do what I have been training for during the past six months. My body knows exactly what to do as I work the floor. The comforting sounds of my ripped satin pointes gliding across the stage, and the thuds of my boxes only add to the peace I feel when I am on this stage. I know I don't have to concentrate on my turnouts and port a bras, my body does it for me.

One haunting beat after another, I feel it pouring out of me: the pain, the darkness, the weakness; it's all there on the smooth black floor beneath my feet. My spots hit hard and sharp, and I know my lines are perfection when I feel the pinching in my back. My ankles are warm and loose when I move into my fouettè combination during the peak of the music. When I flow out of it, naturally leading with my heel to further push my turnout, I progress through the piece. The return of the staccato brushes of the violin pushes the music to its drop into silence.

The spotlight thumps off, and I can finally see the panel of instructors as they are taking notes. There are nine of them. I've been with them for the past four years, dancing in their classes and learning from them.

None of them look at me, and when I hear the voice of Sergej through the speakers announcing the next dancer, I walk off the stage and hope it isn't the last time I will grace it alone.

My heart races the whole drive back to Ryan's. I can't get out of the car fast enough when I pull into his driveway. I run up the stairs and burst through the door, throwing my bag on the wooden floor. When I see Ryan walking down the hall from his office, I run like a child and jump into his arms, wrapping my legs around his waist.

"I take it you kicked ass?" he asks through his laughs.

I can't wipe the cheesy smile off my face. "I totally kicked ass. It was amazing!"

My legs are strong around his waist when he takes his hands off of my hips, places them on my cheeks, and kisses me. I slam my mouth onto his as he pushes me up against the hallway wall, but we don't stay connected for long because I cannot stop talking and laughing, telling him each detail when I know he has no clue what the hell I'm saying, but I don't care and I know he doesn't either. He just watches me in my excitement with his beautiful smile.

He never moves me from the wall, and I keep my lock around his waist as he lets me ramble on.

"I'm so proud of you, babe. I wish I could have seen you," he says when I finally stop talking.

"I know. I'm sorry. Auditions are always closed," I say as I run my fingers through his hair.

"When will you find out?"

"March first."

"Next week?"

"Yeah, Friday."

Pulling his head in, I kiss him again, and he begins to mumble over my lips that don't want to stop. "I've got news too."

Still not willing to break my lips from his, I mutter, "What's that?"

"Thinkspace Gallery called."

I snap my head back as a new wave of excitement begins to flow through me. "And . . . ?"

"They accepted your photo."

"Your photo?!"

"No, *your* photo, babe," he says softly and he rests his head against mine.

I smile at his words. I can't help myself. He knows how tense I was when he took that picture that he refuses to take credit for it.

"Congratulations," I say when he changes our pace and slowly presses tighter against me, tenderly pressing his lips over mine. I rake my fingers through his hair, and I am overcome with happiness. Happy about having a great audition, happy that Ryan's photograph will be displayed in an art gallery, and happy that I am sharing this moment with him. Everything about Ryan floods my being, and I want no one else.

He pulls back and looks into my eyes and when he does, I see it all. I see it clearly; he loves me, and I know I'm safe.

"What is it, babe?"

Brushing my hand down the side of his face, I give him a part of me that I've been holding tightly to.

"I love you."

I know he's been waiting a long time for me to get here, but I know it's okay when I look into his clear eyes and see the lines appear at the corners when his smile grows.

"You'll never know what those words just did to me," he says and he carries me over to the couch, where we proceed to make out like a couple of kids. This might not be typical for anyone else our age, but it's us, and I love us.

I'm not sure where I am when I wake up. I try to sit up, but I'm paralyzed. Looking up, I see the dark sky filled with tiny sparkling specks of stars.

"Ryan?"

There's no answer in the stillness. When I roll my head to the side, I see a rust covered wheel and lock. It's familiar. I inhale the damp summer air.

Wait. It's supposed to be winter.

"Ryan?"

Where is he?

I focus my attention back on the rust, and when I finally realize why it looks so familiar, I jerk my head back to the stars, but they're gone, and my heart stops.

His taunting laughs fill the silent night as his devilish eyes peer into mine.

"Ryan!"

Leaning in, his hot breath on my face, his voice a quiet firm growl, "Shut the fuck up."

He strikes my cheek with the back of his knuckles, and my face burns when the tears begin to prick out. Trying with everything I have in me, I can't move. I'm frozen on the rough concrete as he stares down at me—laughing. He starts to unbutton his pants, and I begin to lose control and shriek for Ryan, but no one is here to help me. My heart is pounding in my chest so hard my ribs ache. The terror singes through my veins, and I scream, "Please, not again."

"This time, you're gonna fucking like it," he sneers as he pulls my shirt up and rips my bra down. All I can do is dig my brittle nails into the cement. My blood-covered hands shake and sting as I cry helplessly on the ground. His mouth is all over me as I beg him to stop.

I turn to find the dumpster, but it's no longer there. I need that dumpster to take my mind away and it's not fuckin' there!

My stomach convulses with each button he pops open on my jeans.

"Get off of me!"

Ripping off my underwear, he slides his hand between my legs, and I begin shrieking out violent sobs.

Gripping my upper arms, he holds me down as I keep screaming through my labored breaths, "Get the fuck off of me!"

Panic and confusion hit me hard when I see Ryan's face above me instead of Jack. Suddenly, I feel my legs moving, and I begin to kick in a frenzy to get out of his tight grip. When I look back up, I see Jack again. He dips his head and licks up my throat.

"God, please stop!" I wail.

"Candace, wake up."

Thrashing under Jack's grip, I'm no longer paralyzed, and I'm no longer being pinned down.

I hear myself screaming as I shuffle back in a panic, trying to escape. I feel myself fall on my hip. Not able to get to my feet, I clumsily continue to shuffle on my hands, desperate to get away.

All I hear is Jack laughing at me.

When the wall hits my back, his hands are on my shoulders, and I scream, "Don't fuckin' touch me!" as I curl into a ball, covering my face with my hands. I continue to scream the same thing over and over until I no longer hear Jack, but Ryan.

Ryan!

"Candace, open your eyes."

But I can't. I don't know what's happening, what's real. My breathing is erratic, and I am engulfed in fear. I'm still sobbing. I don't know how to stop.

"Candace, please. Look at me. It's only me here with you."

My arms are stiff when he touches my wrists to move my hands away from my face. I don't want him to see me—not like this. When he moves my hands, I turn my face away from him, wanting to somehow disappear.

"Babe, please don't hide from me."

Trying to take in some air through my cries, I choke on my breath, and when I do, he pulls me close, and I just fall into him. His arms are so tight around me, and I know it's only him.

I don't know what I was thinking not taking my pills anymore. How could I be so stupid to think I was strong enough to be okay without them? Now I'm consumed with worry and dread. What the hell is Ryan going to do or say? What am I going to do or say? What do I do?

God, what do I do?

I'm curled up tight in Ryan's lap, and he is stroking my hair with his fingers. I'm so embarrassed. But, he doesn't give me a choice from eluding this when he leans back to look at me.

Closing my eyes, he says, "You have to look at me. Please."

When I feel the heat of his hands on my face, I blink my eyes open and slowly shift my eyes to him. His expression is worried as he scans my face.

"You okay?"

I nod my head.

"What happened?"

I drop my head and rest it on his chest as he rubs my back. I just want to hide and not have to look at him.

With hesitation, I ask, "Can you please call Jase?"

"What?" he says in disbelief, and I don't blame him. "Shit, Candace, no."

A new round of tears begin to flow, and I hear the desperation in my voice when I urge, "Please."

"Candace, no. You can't always run to him. Need me for change. Talk to me."

"I can't," I cry out.

"Yes, you can."

"No, I can't. Please. I just can't"

"But you can with Jase?"

I'm sobbing now, but Ryan never lets go of me.

"I want you to need me," he says.

"I do."

"You don't; you cling to him for everything." He takes my hands and presses them against his bare chest, over his heart. "Look at me," he demands, and when I do, he tells me, "Cling to *me*. Love me enough to *need me*."

"I can't . . . I . . ."

"Why?"

I know he's not going to drop this, and I begin to get angry. Angry that I'm even in this position right now.

"Because, you'd leave me."

"Not happening, babe."

"Ryan, please," I plead.

"I'm not leaving you. Nothing you could say would make me want to leave you."

"I'm just too fucked up."

"We're all fucked up," he says. "I want you to let me in."

I know there is no way out of this. But how? How do I do this?

He grabs my hands again when I try to cover my face as my cries quake through me.

"I can't! You'll never look at me the same. You'll run away."

When I say this, he slides his hand around the back of my head and pulls me against him as he sighs out. I cry in his chest as he says, "I promise you, nothing will change the way I look at you. Nothing will change what you do to me when you're next to me. You make my heart beat in a completely different way—nothing will ever change that."

I finally wrap my arms around him, hanging on with everything I have. "I'm so embarrassed," I confess around my cries.

"God, babe." I can hear the pain in his voice. "Please, don't be."

I have never said the words. Not ever. Not to anyone. Not even to myself. Maybe I foolishly thought if I didn't say it, then maybe it wasn't really real.

When he strengthens his hold on me, I let it out on a whimper, "I was raped."

Releasing a heavy sigh, he lays his head on top of mine, and I continue to cry. I feel so weak and tired, like I'm drowning. I keep treading water, but I can never seem to get my head high enough out of the water to take in a full breath of air. I've been drowning since that night. There are times I feel like I can make it, but then I'm pulled right back under.

Ryan says nothing as we sit here on the floor. I feel guilty for the lies and mistruths I've told him to try and hide this. When my sobs soften into whimpers, I speak.

"I've been lying to you," I say quietly.

"I don't care. It doesn't matter."

"I feel horrible."

"Candace, don't do this. You have every right to lie."

But I need to tell him.

"I can't go to see you at work because . . ."

"Shhh . . ."

"Because it happened in your parking lot. By the dumpster. That's why I freaked out. I didn't know where I was until I saw the dumpster."

When I tell him this, I feel a breath thud in his chest. I loosen my hold and pull back. I break when I see the tears streaming down his cheeks. Looking into his eyes, as the tears begin to fall from mine again, I cry, "I'm so sorry."

"Don't ever fuckin' say that again. Don't ever be sorry for anything again."

"I'm just so far from what you thought."

"You're not."

"I am. Every day is a struggle. Everything. I'm scared every day." I drop my head for a moment, and when I look back up at him, I finally admit what I've been feeling for the past six months. Ever since that night, the night Jack left me broken and desperate. The night he took everything from me: my trust, my peace, my security, my faith—my light. He took it all and left me with nothing.

"I'm fading." I feel the heat of my tears as they linger down my cheeks. "He took all my light, and I've been fading ever since."

Cradling my face in his hands, he says, "You're not fading. I won't let you."

I nod my head, fold myself into his arms, and let him hold me.

"That's why Kimber is mad. I didn't go home after it happened. I stayed with Jase and never told her why. She knows I'm lying."

Ryan doesn't say anything. He simply lets me talk and get it all out. I love him even more for that because I need to get it out.

"I've been taking sleeping pills, but I stopped last week. That's why I haven't been sleeping." I take a second before continuing. "I dream about that night—about him. All I see are his eyes." I confess as I weep out, "He made me watch him."

Ryan doesn't say anything as a new slew of sobs wrack my body. He just bands his arms tighter around me and I finally speak again, "So, I take pills to keep him away."

"Babe, why did you stop taking them?" he asks as he brushes my hair back behind my shoulder.

"Because every night when I take them, it's only a reminder of what happened. I just want to forget, but I can't."

"Have you told anyone?"

"No. Only Jase and Mark. Jase was with me in the hospital. Mark only knows because he walked in and saw my face. It was pretty banged up."

"Your parents?"

"God, no. It was because of them that I went out with that guy at all."

He pulls his head back and looks at me in disbelief. "You knew him?"

I nod my head and he asks, "But you didn't do anything?"

"No."

"I wanna fucking kill him," he says through gritted teeth.

It takes a while, but when I finally feel Ryan's tense chest relax, he pulls back and looks me in the eyes as he says, "This changes nothing for me. Okay? Nothing. No one will ever love you like I do."

When he leans down and gently kisses me, I release my worry. Worry of him leaving, of him being disgusted, worry of him running away from my dark side. I relax in his arms, knowing that we have no more secrets.

chapter thirty

"HE KNOWS."

"You told him?" he says in surprise.

"I didn't really have a choice," I tell Jase. "I had another nightmare last night."

"What happened?" he asks as he shifts on the couch to face me.

"I freaked out with him in the bed. It was humiliating. So, I had to tell him."

Jase reaches over and grabs my hand, holding it tightly when I continue. "I've never said it before. I never wanted to say the words. I mean, I have silently in my head, but never out loud."

"Are you okay?"

"Yeah, I think so."

"What did he do?"

"I mean, what could he do? He listened and assured me that it doesn't change anything with us. I was scared he'd want to leave. I wouldn't have blamed him."

"God, Candace, I'm sorry, but he needed to know. I'm glad you told him," he says with sincerity.

"I told him I loved him." A grin spreads across his face and I say, "Don't embarrass me, Jase."

"I won't. I swear."

Taking my hand from his, I grab my glass of wine from the coffee table and take a sip when he asks, "Do you know what he's doing for your birthday?"

"Jase, you know I hate parties and presents. It's all awkward and uncomfortable. Plus, I haven't told him it's my birthday."

He laughs at me and says, "You're so weird."

"Seriously, we have never done anything before, why start now?"

He takes a swig of his beer, then suggests, "Let's at least get together. We can go do dinner at Mark's. No birthday cake. Promise."

"Fiiine," I whine and then give him a tiny smile. "I'll let Ryan know. And no presents. It's just stupid."

"None."

We sit together on his couch and continue to drink and catch up on what's been going on in each other's lives. It's Friday night, and Ryan is at work. One of Gavin's bands is playing there tonight, so he and his friends decided to make a night out of it. He wanted to cancel when we woke up this morning, but I told him that it would make me more uncomfortable if he didn't go because of me. Plus, Jase and I had already made plans to get together, so Ryan agreed, although with much hesitation.

I nearly finish the bottle of merlot by myself and am drunk for the first time in my life. Maybe it was just everything that had happened yesterday that has me wanting to drink way more than I normally do. I'm barely coherent when Jase calls Ryan to come pick me up.

"Youuuu take me home," I slur out, and then burst into a fit of giggles.

"I can't. I've had too many beers. He'll be here in a bit. He just left the bar."

I lie down on the couch and close my eyes when the room begins to sway in a hazy way. Jase is talking to me, but it sounds like an echo at this point. When there is a knock at the door, I pop up on my knees, looking over the back of the couch as Ryan walks in.

"You're heeeere!" I scream and throw my arms into the air.

"Shit, man, what the hell did you give her?" he laughs out.

"She inhaled a bottle of wine," Jase tells him.

Pointing to Ryan, I shout, "You'rrre hot!" and then burst out into another fit of uncontrollable laughter.

"Okay, party's over, babe," he says as he walks toward the couch shaking his head humorously at me.

"Noooo!" I pout as I jump up to my feet on top of the couch and feign authority.

He grabs me behind my knees and throws me over his shoulder as I continue to giggle.

"Alright, let's go."

I reach down, grab his ass, and squeal, "Niiiice!"

"Oh yeah. You like that?" he says through his chuckles, and I can hear Jase laughing as well.

Looking up, I wave to Jase, "Byyyye, buddy!"

"Call me tomorrow when you sober up."

"Bye, man. Thanks for calling me," Ryan says before hauling me to the elevator.

When we get inside, he sets me down, and I turn to the buttons and laugh while I swipe my hands over them, lighting each one up.

"Woohoooo!"

"Shit, babe! Do you know how long it's gonna take us to get to the lobby?"

"A looong, looong time," I say extremely slow.

He holds onto my hips to steady me and then smiles down at me. "You're so fuckin' cute when you're drunk."

"I'm druuuunk?!"

"Yeah, just a bit."

Slinging my arms around his neck, I hang my head back and look up at him. "You'rrre so tall."

"I don't think so. You're just really small."

"I like it!" I chirp out. "It's sexxxxy."

"You think so?"

"Ooooh yeaaaah." Lifting high on my toes, I slightly lose my balance and give him a sloppy kiss before cracking up in giggles.

He wipes his mouth and mumbles, "That was interesting."

While the elevator slowly makes its way down to the lobby, stopping on every floor, I decide to make myself comfortable on the floor.

Sitting in the corner, Ryan looks down at me and smirks as he leans against the wall.

"Can we some cake?" I mumble out.

"Babe, you're missing some words in there." The elevator dings again, and this time, the doors open to the lobby. "Come on," he says and he scoops me up, cradling me in his hold. I wrap my arms around his neck and say, "I wannn cake."

"It's the middle of the night. You have ice cream in my freezer. Just eat that."

"I told Jase nooo cake for my birrrthday, But I wannn some."

Setting me in his car, he says, "Birthday, huh? Why am I just now hearing this?"

"It'sss Thursdaay."

"Hmmm." He reaches over me to fasten the seatbelt, and I lay my head down on the center console.

When he gets into the car, he brushes my hair back. "How're you feeling?"

"Sleepy."

"Just close your eyes."

My head grows heavy, and I begin to drift while Ryan strokes my hair during the drive back to his place. He carries me inside and up the stairs to his room. Sitting me down on the edge of the tub, he goes to get me my clothes.

"Here. Do you want me to help you change?"

"No. I can do it," I say, not wanting Ryan to see me without my clothes on.

"Okay. I'm gonna run downstairs. I'll be right back."

"Okay."

I slip into my pants and cami, brush my teeth, then go to slide into bed. I don't open my eyes when I hear Ryan come back in and change.

"Candace," he whispers.

"Hmmm . . ."

"Babe, where are your pills?"

"Purse."

When he returns, I take my pill and some aspirin with the bottle of water he set on the nightstand. I roll over into his arms and curl up.

"Thanks," I whisper in the darkness.

"For what?"

"Staying."

Turning on his side to face me, he pulls me in flush against him. "I told you, I'm not going anywhere."

"I know, but that was before . . ."

"I love you. I wanna be that person you can bring anything to; the good and the bad."

"I love you, Ryan."

He kisses me slowly and then tucks my head under his chin. "I love you too."

Time passes and I hear Ryan's breaths as they slow into a soft rhythmic pattern as he falls asleep. My head is woozy, and I try to fight the sleep that is threatening to take over. My dream last night fills my head and haunts me. I don't want to close my eyes because I'm afraid Jack is on the other side. I toss and turn in my restlessness. Reaching over, I grab Ryan's phone to see the time is almost two a.m., and when I roll back over, Ryan is awake.

"What are you doing?" he asks in a sleepy rasp.

"Nothing."

"How are you even still awake?"

I lay my head on his chest and don't respond.

"Babe . . . ?"

"I don't want to sleep just yet."

"Why?"

"I'm just . . . I'm scared I'll have another bad dream."

He kisses my forehead and says, "Try not to think so much about it. It's just you and me. Think about us. If you could go anywhere, where would you go?"

"Back to Indian Beach with you." I think about that morning; him telling me that he wanted to be with me, us kissing in the cold rain.

"Close your eyes and go back there. You and me sitting on the driftwood."

"Talk to me," I request, and he does. He replays our morning on the beach and tells me everything he was feeling. Confessing how nervous he was and how much he was already falling for me. His words chase away the fears of Jack, and I drift off before he finishes talking.

I've had more free time to spend with Ryan since my audition last week. We've started running again, and I even let Ryan photograph me. He said he wanted to get a few shots of my legs. He's been working on them for the past couple days while I'm in class. He showed them to me this morning, and they are incredible. It's pretty amazing what he can capture and enhance. I love that we can do that together. The way he looks at me when he takes my picture, it's an intimacy I haven't ever felt before.

When I get back from work, Mark's car is already parked in the driveway. We decided to have my non-birthday dinner here at the loft tonight. I told Ryan to not make it a big deal, and explained how my mother would always throw these extravagant birthdays for me, but how they were really her way of one-upping her friends.

My parties had more of her friends there than mine, and we never got to do what I wanted. They were always so formal when all I really wanted was a simple white cake and to play silly games. Instead, for my sixth birthday, I had a tea party at the country club. We all wore frilly dresses and fancy hats. So, ever since I left home, I prefer to do nothing for my birthday since the day only holds dismal memories for me.

When I walk in, I am happy to see the guys watching TV and drinking beer. I love each of them in very different ways and smile when I see them sitting there.

I walk in and give Jase and Mark a hug and a kiss and when Ryan motions me over, I go sit on his lap.

"I missed you," he says quietly in my ear and runs his nose down my neck. "Mmmm . . . coffee," he jokes.

I laugh and hop off his lap. "I'm gonna take a quick shower. I'll be back."

"Pizzas will be here in a few minutes," Mark calls out to me when I start up the stairs.

"All right."

After I shower and dry my hair, I decide to take it easy and throw on my pajamas. When I hear the doorbell ring, I hurry downstairs because I'm starving.

When I turn the corner, I see Ryan hugging his mom.

I'm surprised when I say, "Donna?"

"Candace," she says with a smile.

I walk over to her, confused, and give her a hug. "What are you doing here?"

"I wasn't going to miss your birthday. But I'm a little disappointed that I had to hear about it from Ryan when you and I talk every week."

When I look over at Ryan, he gives me a wink and a chaste kiss.

"Sorry, I . . . I don't normally do anything for my birthday, but I'm so happy you're here," I say and hug her again. "I can't believe you drove all this way."

"It's a few hours, dear. Hardly a chore." She takes my hand and walks us into the living room.

I introduce her to Mark and Jase, and they all exchange hugs.

"Mom, what do you want to drink?"

"A glass of wine will be good."

"Me too," I say.

"You're not gonna get drunk, slap my ass, and tell me how sexy I am, are you?" he teases.

"Ryan!"

I look at Donna with an apologetic look while Ryan is laughing at my expense in the kitchen.

"I didn't . . . I mean it wasn't . . ."

"Honey, we've all been there," she says with a hint of laughter.

Ryan walks back in, hands his mom and I our glasses of wine, and sits down next to me while his mom and I chat. Ever since Christmas, she calls me once a week to check in. At first it was a little uncomfortable, but we've grown close. She knows that I've been staying here with Ryan and how I feel about him. She's never once been judgmental or snarky like it was with my mother when she would call me. The relationship I have with Donna is one that I have been needing, now more than ever. She's nothing but supportive and encouraging, and I love her for that.

When the pizza arrives, we all sit around the living room and eat straight from the boxes. Ryan and I share the box with the pineapple pizza. I love that I can spend a night like this, in my pajamas, with people I care about.

Mark and Ryan gather all the boxes and take them to the kitchen when we are done. When they come back in, Ryan is holding a cheap grocery store birthday cake.

"Don't get upset, but you told me in the elevator that you wanted cake, so here it is."

He smiles at me as he sets it on the coffee table and Mark hands everyone a fork. We all sit on the floor, around the table, and eat. We don't bother cutting it; we just eat straight from the cake. When I can't take another bite, I throw my fork in and lie back.

"I'm gonna die," I moan out in discomfort.

"I don't get how you can be so tiny when you eat like a horse," Mark teases.

"Because I work my ass off."

"Please, you twirl around on your toes," he chuckles out.

"Oh yeah? When I find a pair of pointes in size Yeti, I'm gonna make you wear them, and then you can see what a workout it is."

"I'd pay to see that shit," Jase says.

Ryan and Donna clean everything up while Mark, Jase, and I continue to tease each other.

When we decide to watch a movie, Donna calls it a night. She's tired from the drive, but we will have all day tomorrow to hang out. While Ryan gets her situated in the guest bedroom, Jase, Mark, and I get comfortable on the floor and turn out the lights. We pull the pillows off the couch and chairs and huddle under blankets. Ryan returns and slides under my blanket, and we cuddle as we watch 'The Breakfast Club.'

By the time Allison throws the bologna and cheese on the statue and proceeds to make a sandwich out of Captain Crunch and Pixie Sticks, Jase and Mark head out. Once they're gone, I roll over and face Ryan, the only light being the flicker of the TV. I tangle my legs with his and snuggle in close.

"Thank you."

"For?"

"Your mom and the cake," I say with a grin.

He kisses my nose and says, "Anytime."

I slide my hand under his shirt and run it up his smooth back. "I love you."

He doesn't say anything; he only kisses me. It's all I need as I melt into him. I can taste the sugar from the cake and he caresses his tongue with mine. I grip onto his shoulder and wrap my leg around his hip. Grabbing onto my thigh, I tangle my other hand in his hair. He rolls on top of me and runs his palm up my side, under my shirt.

We've done this before, and I let myself relax because I know that he knows when to stop with me. I trust him, and I know he would never push me. I feel warm under his touch, letting him wrap me up in it. He makes my heart beat faster, and I just want to be close with him. I love what we have together, and I love him.

It's been two weeks since I told him my secret, and he hasn't once looked at me differently. When he said to me that it didn't change anything, I didn't believe him at first, but now, all I can do is trust him and what he says.

Ryan runs his soft kisses up my neck and then pulls away. "Come on," he says as he holds out his hand for me. "I want you in my bed, under my sheets."

I smile up at him before he grabs me and takes me upstairs.

chapter thirty-one

DONNA INSISTED WE go to Common Grounds for breakfast while Ryan goes to the gym. She said she wanted to see where I worked, so when Ryan left, we got ourselves ready and I drove us to the coffee shop.

The place isn't too busy when we arrive. We walk up to the counter and I introduce Donna to Roxy.

"So, you're Ryan's mom?" she says with a smirk, and I know she wants to mention his hot-ass, as she does every time his name comes up, but thankfully, she keeps her couth.

"Yes, it's so good to meet you."

Donna doesn't look fazed at all by Roxy's unique style and her cobalt-blue hair.

"Likewise. So what are you girls up to today?"

"We're just here for breakfast," I tell her.

Donna and I give Roxy our order and when she hands us our drinks and muffins, we make ourselves comfortable on one of the cozy small loveseats.

"Thank you for driving up here. It really means a lot me," I tell her as I sip my hot tea.

"Well, I'm glad Ryan called me to tell me it was your birthday."

"Sorry, if it was last minute notice, but he didn't even know until last week."

She gives me a warm smile and says, "Well, I'm happy to be here. It's so good to see the two of you. I've never seen him so happy. All he seems to talk about when I call him is you. So, I take it you guys are getting more serious?"

It's not awkward for me to talk to her about Ryan. We talk about our relationship almost every week. Even though I haven't known her very long, she gives me the maternal support I've never had. She's been easy for me to let in.

"Yeah, I mean we love each other. I try not to think about it too much, but I sometimes worry about what will happen after I graduate."

"Well, have you thought about where you want to go?"

"I don't have a whole lot of choice in the matter. I have to go where the job is, and I have no clue what company will offer me a spot. That's what's so unnerving."

Swallowing a bite of her muffin, she asks, "What does Ryan say?"

"We haven't talked about it. I've never mentioned it."

"You have to follow your dreams. I don't see Ryan standing in the way of that."

"I really do love him."

"I know you do," she says as she reaches for my hand.

"I don't know if I could ever leave him."

"Don't let your dreams fade away. Whatever happens, I know you two will find your way through it."

I smile at her words and hope that she's right. I know Seattle has a few outstanding ballet companies. I've expressed interest in a couple; I just hope that one of them will offer me a spot, but at the same time, I've always dreamed of New York. Ever since I was a little girl, I've been fantasizing about dancing in the city.

"Well, dear, Ryan told me to not get you anything, but . . ." She reaches in her purse and pulls out an old weathered box. "I didn't wrap it, so technically, it's not an official present."

When she places the box in my hands, I look at her in disbelief. "Donna, I can't."

"I've had it for years, dear. It's just an old, dirty book, but I saw you reading it at Christmas, so I thought you wouldn't mind having a copy."

I open the box, and I know it's the original publisher's box. Pulling out my favorite book from my childhood, I open it up to see the publishing date is 1935.

Shaking my head, I say, "But this is a collector's edition. How . . . ?"

"When I was a little girl, I loved this book. My grandmother bought this for me when she found it in a rundown antique shop. I bought a current published version for the kids that I keep out, and when I saw you reading it, I figured you would appreciate having this version."

When I start to shake my head again, she places her hand on top of one of the original prints of Frances Hodgson Burnett's book, 'A Little Princess,' and says, "Like I said, it's an old book that has been sitting at the top of my closet for years, doing nothing but collecting dust."

Tears prick my eyes when I think about what this book was for me when I was growing up. In a way, I felt a lot like the girl, Sara. She believed herself to be a princess, and even though her world was falling apart at the hands of someone else, she pulled through, despite the cruelty she suffered. I hadn't read it in years, but when I saw it at Donna's house, I read it again and found it to be just as meaningful as an adult as it was when I was a child.

I set the book in its box on my lap and lean over to hug her. "I can't tell you what this means to me. Thank you."

"Thank you for accepting it."

When she sits back, she smiles and says, swiftly taking the focus off of her non-present, "So, tell me, when do you find out about your audition?"

Placing the cover back on the box, I say, "Today, actually. It should be posted this afternoon around five."

"Either way, I am so proud of you."

Hearing those words from her, every time she says them, fills little empty places in my heart. I never got to hear those words from my parents, so hearing them now does tremendous things to me.

"Tell me about this production. How many dances will I get to see you in?"

"You're coming?" I ask.

"Are you kidding me? I can't wait to see you dance."

Again, filling up little pieces of my heart.

Smiling, I tell her all about the three ensemble pieces I will be dancing. While I talk, she asks questions and is sincerely interested. We continue to enjoy each other's company and relax in our slow lazy morning. When we finish up, we decide to walk around the block and into some of the little boutique and fragrance shops. We both buy a few things here and there as we hop from store to store.

When I look at the woman Donna is, it's hard for me to imagine what her life used to be like with Ryan's father. Ryan told me that the night his dad died, he had beaten Donna pretty badly, smashing a coffee mug into the back of her head. Ryan was just coming home from a party and walked in on it. He said he lost all control of himself and started throwing punches. His dad managed to grab a knife from the counter and that's how Ryan got the scar on his ribs.

Once his dad died, Donna was determined to put that life behind them. Seeing them now, you would never know the hell they lived with. I know that Ryan still deals with the memories of it all. He told me that he's scared that he'll wind up like his father, and that's why he's never wanted to get serious with a girl. So he got pretty good at shutting down when he was with women. I hate to think about him being like that; I can't even picture him as that person because all I have ever known is the way he's always been with me.

Leaving the last store, we make our way back to the loft so that Donna can pack and start driving back to Cannon Beach. It's a little after twelve by the time we get back, and Ryan is waiting on us.

"Damn, that was a long breakfast," he says when we walk through the door carrying all of our shopping bags. Walking over to us, he kisses his mom and then me before taking the bags and setting them on the table.

"Sorry, time got away from us. If I didn't have to go home, I would have spent the whole day with her."

Ryan throws his arm around my shoulder and teases his mother. "Well, thanks for bringing her back, I'm sick of sharing her."

"Ryan!" I say as I nudge him playfully in the gut.

"Sorry, babe, but it's the truth," he says, then starts facetiously ravaging my neck.

"Okay, kids. I've seen enough. I'm going to go pack," Donna says, as she's already halfway down the hall.

"Ryan, that tickles," I chuckle out, trying to wriggle out of his arms, but it only encourages him. Picking me up off the ground, he carries me to the couch and lays me down. Softening his kisses, he asks, "Did you have a good time this morning?"

"Uh huh," is all I can manage to say when he licks the hollow of my neck.

"Ryan, we should stop."

"Why?" He says this without taking his lips off of me.

"Because your mom is about to leave, and you should go spend a little time with her before she goes."

He lets out a sexy groan and pulls away. "Okay, but I'm not done with you," he says as he starts to walk away.

I give the two of them some alone time to visit while I start unpacking my new purchases. After hanging up my new dresses in Ryan's closet, I put my new bottle of perfume on the bathroom counter. When I look around his room and see my things, it makes me happy to be sharing this space with him, but it also reminds me that I'm not at home with Kimber. I've been so wrapped up in Ryan these past few weeks that I haven't thought much about her, but now I wonder. Wonder how she's feeling about everything, wonder if she's mad that I left again, wonder if I can mend this fracture between us.

"Candace," Ryan hollers from downstairs.

"Coming," I say, and when I get to the door where Donna is standing with her bags, I suddenly feel a twinge of sadness creep over me. A part of me doesn't want her to leave. She's become someone special to me, and having her near brings a peace that I've been missing all my life.

I don't say anything when I reach her, I just let her hug me, and when I feel the tears puddle in my eyes, I pull back. When she sees my sadness, her face pains. I blink, and the tears roll down my cheeks.

"Dear," she says softly before pulling me back into her arms, and I feel Ryan's supportive hand on my back.

"Come see me, okay?"

When I let go of her, I nod my head, not able to speak around the knot in my throat. Ryan wraps his arms around me from behind, and I lean back into him.

"When is your next break?"

Ryan answers for me, knowing that I don't like to talk when I get like this. "She has the last two weeks of this month off before her last quarter."

Looking at me, she says, "You and Ryan come visit, okay?"

As I nod my head, she picks up her bags, and Ryan says, "Mom, let me take those out for you."

"That's okay. I've got it. Stay in here with her."

"Thanks for coming, Mom. Call me when you get home."

"I will, and call me when you find out about the solo."

"We will," he responds.

When the door closes, Ryan turns me around in his arms and holds me until I can compose myself enough to pull away.

Cupping my head in his hands, I look up at him when he asks, "You okay, babe?"

"I hate that she lives so far away. I really like having her around."

Wiping my tears with the pads of his thumbs, he says, "I know you do. We'll go visit her when you're on your break."

I rest my head back against his chest, and I take a moment before saying, "My parents never even called me."

He runs his hand up the back of my head and grips me close when I add, "I mean . . . I knew they wouldn't, but it still hurts."

"I know it does."

I inhale a deep breath and let it out when he says, "Come on, let's go grab something to eat before we go to the campus."

"Sounds good. Give me a few minutes to freshen up?"

"Of course."

We have a long lunch at Eastlake Bar and Grill before driving to UW. We park and walk to Meany Theater. Walking up, I can see a crowd of fellow dancers walking inside to see if their name is one of the two that will be listed. I feel the butterflies in my stomach and turn to Ryan, "Can we just go for a walk first?"

"What? Don't you want to find out if you got it?"

"Yeah, but not around everyone else."

Holding my hand, he turns the other direction. By the time we walk through the quad and back to the theater, the crowd has dissipated, and we walk inside. My palms start to sweat when I see the white sheet of paper taped to the wall. When I step closer, I let out a loud sigh in disbelief. Shaking my head, I turn to Ryan and say, "I can't believe it."

"Believe it."

My rapid breathing slowly turns into laughter, and I sling my arms around Ryan's neck as he picks me up. Wrapping my legs around his waist, I squeal out, "I really can't believe it!"

Looking up at me, he smiles, wide and gorgeous. I lean my head down and kiss him, but it doesn't last long with my excitement. When I look up, I see Ms. Emerson and Sergej walk through a set of double doors. I jump out of Ryan's arms and try to reel in my emotions, but I can't seem to wipe the cheesy smile off my face.

When they walk past me, Ms. Emerson stops to face me. I notice a small twitch in the corner of her mouth as she gives a slight nod of her head before turning and walking out the door. Spinning around to Ryan, I can't contain myself, and I cover my face with my hands as I feel a weight being lifted from my chest that I never knew was there.

"Come over here," Ryan says, and I walk to him, straight into his embrace. "You're amazing, you know that?"

Looking up at him, I confess, "Because of you."

"No, babe. It's all you."

Today has been a mixture of emotions, and after I finish brushing my teeth, Ryan slides his arms around my waist from behind and starts kissing my neck. We watch each other in the reflection of the mirror, and when I turn around to face him, he picks me up and sets me on the edge of the sink. Tilting my head back to look up at him, he says, "You're fuckin' gorgeous."

He makes me laugh as he leans down to kiss me. My legs wrap around his waist, and I twine my fingers in his hair when he picks me up. When we fall into bed, he trails his kisses down my neck, and my body starts to shiver. He slowly pulls back and gazes down at me with an intensity burning in his eyes. Sliding my hand up his chest, I wrap it around his neck and pull him back to me.

Our kisses are slow and with a passion I haven't felt before. I thrust my tongue into his mouth and taste him, throwing myself into our kiss. His arms band tightly around me, and I've never felt so safe. My mind blurs, and I begin to lose myself in his touch.

When he lifts my back off the bed, I'm barely thinking when I pull off my top as he lets out a low groan. Lowering me back down, he shifts his hips between my legs and drags his head down to my breasts.

We've never moved quite like this before, but a part of me doesn't want to stop. What I feel for this man is more than I ever thought I was capable of feeling. For a while, I thought I would never truly laugh again, but with Ryan, I'm my happiest. He gives me what I have been desperate for. Feeling him on my fingertips is enough to take me over, and I now want more.

Dragging his mouth from me, he pants, "We should stop."

I'm not sure I want to though. I know I will never love anyone the way I love him; he's all I want.

"Don't."

"Babe," he says in heavy breath, searching my face.

When I look up in his eyes, I see all I ever want to see. He loves me in a way I never thought I could be loved.

"I don't want you to stop."

"I need you to talk to me."

I can tell he's unsure, I see it in his face.

"I don't want to stop tonight."

He closes his eyes and drops his head to mine. "Please tell me this is okay." When I nod my head against his, he says, "I need to hear you say it, babe."

Cupping his face in my hands, I say, "It's okay. I want this, with you, I just . . . I don't know if I can."

There is a worry in his eyes that I don't want him to have. Although I'm scared, I know I want him.

I take his hand with my trembling one and place it back on my breast and whisper, "Just touch me."

He leans down and kisses me, long and slow while he slides his hand underneath my bra strap and slips it off my shoulder. I've never taken my clothes off in front of him before, and I feel the anxiety pool in my belly as he slides the other strap down, kissing my bare shoulder along the way. Pulling the fabric down, my pulse quickens, and in a moment of nervousness I confess, "I'm scared. I've never . . ."

Sweeping my hair back, he assures me, "It's just you and me. You're all I'll ever want."

He wraps his arms around me and unhooks my bra, dropping it on the floor. When he looks down at me, he sees my scar.

"He bit me," I say on a hush.

I hate that I have Jack's mark on my breast. It torments me to look at. It surprises me when Ryan leans down and kisses the scar.

"God, you're perfect," he breathes against my skin.

He drags his kisses down my stomach then sits back on his heels. Taking my hand in his, he places it over his scar on the side of his ribs. With words unspoken, I hear what he's telling me. We're both still alive, together, and we're okay. Brushing his scar with my thumb, I bring my hands to his stomach, feeling his defined lines under my touch as my fingers slide up, around his neck, and tangle into his hair. I pull him down and lose myself in him.

My legs begin to quiver when he hooks his thumbs inside the waistband of my pants. He strokes his knuckles across my belly before gently tugging down. When I lift my hips, he pulls off my pants and underwear, tossing them aside. I watch as he removes his pants, and when we are both naked, he lowers himself back on me and my whole body is trembling. He pulls the covers over us, and I start to wonder if maybe I can't do this. I want to, but I'm so scared. I have nothing good to associate with this, and I'm not sure I can.

Holding himself up on his elbows, he says, "Babe, you're shaking."

"What if I can't do this?"

"Then we stop."

Nodding my head, I am filled with nerves.

"We'll move as slow as you need. You just tell me when to stop."

"I don't want you to stop."

Giving me a smile, he leans down and kisses me. I wrap my arms around his neck and part my lips for him. He slides his tongue across my lower lip before he dips it into my mouth. We meld together as I run my hands down his neck and over his chest. His muscles are hard and cut beneath my hands, and I've never really taken my time to explore him until now. He's a lot larger than me, and I feel tiny underneath him, sheltered. I take my lips from him, skimming them across his tattooed covered shoulder to his neck.

I need him when he grazes his hand over my breast and takes me in his mouth. I let out a soft moan when he slides his tongue over my nipple and gently sucks. My body heats, and I arch myself into him.

"Ryan," I breathe out.

He drags his damp lips up my neck before saying, "You sure?"

When I say yes, he takes a moment to make sure we're safe and protected. Resting his forehead against mine, he says, "Tell me that you want this, that you want me."

And when I say, "I want you to make love to me," he reaches down and slowly starts to push into me. I tense up at the touch, having never experienced it in this way.

He pulls back slightly and says, "Are you okay?"

I nod my head and whisper, "Yeah," before he continues to ease himself inside of me. Letting out a gasp of breath, he drops his head in the crook of my neck.

"Fuck, you feel so good, babe."

My legs are tense around his hips as he holds himself in me. Clenching my eyes shut, I can feel the few tears that have escaped and are rolling down the sides of my face. Tears of nerves and tears of overwhelming love.

"Open your eyes, Candace. Look at me."

"Don't make me look," I softly plead. I'm afraid if I watch him, it will remind me too much of watching Jack. I'm scared.

"Baby, please open your eyes. I need you to be here with *me*. It's only me."

When I cautiously open them, I can see the concern in his eyes.

I focus on him and gradually begin to soften myself into him and relax. He takes his time as he starts to gently move inside of me. The room begins to fill with our soft moans and breaths of pleasure, never taking our eyes off of each other. He wraps me up in his strong arms, and I cling my hands around him as we slowly move together.

"God, I love you," he sighs.

I lean my head up to kiss him, needing more of him. "I love you," I whisper against his lips.

He's all around me, and my breathing grows heavy as the air thickens. He takes my hand and laces his fingers with mine, holding on tightly to each other as he pushes himself deeper inside of me. Grabbing behind my knee, he pulls my leg up around him then runs his hand up my thigh, gripping onto my hip. I'm overcome with the closeness I feel with him on top of me, with him inside of me.

I push my hips against his hold, needing to move with him. Letting go, he runs his hand up my side and into my hair, threading, and gently grabbing. The pleasure he gives me runs from my thighs through my core and up my chest where my heart is enduring most of the intensity. I can no longer keep my eyes open when I begin to feel a swarm of sensations deep inside. I realize I've never felt this before, and my legs clench apprehensively to his hips.

"Relax, babe."

I hang on tightly around his neck as the feeling begins to build. When my hand jerks in his, he says, "Open your eyes. Stay with me."

They flutter open, and I see the want in his gaze. His face is heated and flushed, and when a whimper escapes me, my breath catches.

"Baby, let go for me."

'I lock my eyes with his as I fall and begin to shudder beneath him, giving him every piece of me as the intense pleasure radiates through my body. I feel myself pulse and tighten around him as he buries his head in my neck, grunting my name, and I feel his release.

Wrapping my legs tightly around him, I try desperately to hold back the tears that are threatening. I'm completely overwhelmed with emotions. To me, that was my first time. He's what I have always needed. Being with him like this, together in this special place that only we share, I know I'll never love anyone the way I love him.

When our breathing slows, he lifts his head, and brushes my hair back. I can feel the tears roll down my temples.

"God, baby, what's wrong?" he asks, as he brushes my tears away with his thumb.

I shake my head to let him know I'm okay. When I'm finally able to speak, I hand my heart over to him and bare, "Being with you . . . that's all I want."

Dropping his head to mine, he confesses softly, "You're the only one I've ever done that with. You're the only one I've ever made love to."

And with that, I pull his lips back to mine.

chapter thirty-two

WAKING UP, I am wrapped up in Ryan. Last night was incredible, being with Ryan in a way I never thought I could. I gave him all of me and have left myself entirely vulnerable to him. When he tells me he will never leave me, I believe him.

I gently ease my way out of his hold, careful not to wake him. I find my clothes that are strewn across the floor and quickly slide them on before walking to the bathroom. Brushing my teeth, I notice a necklace on the counter between the two sinks as I rinse the toothpaste out of my mouth. When I turn off the faucet, I pick up the thin, delicate silver chain that has a flat bar that horizontally connects the chain together. I see that the bar is etched with tiny letters that scribe: *And though she be but little, she is fierce.*

He had to have lain this here last night after I feel asleep, because I would have noticed it yesterday. Carrying the necklace in my hand, I open the door and see Ryan awake in bed.

He smiles at me when I hold up the necklace. "What's this?"

"Well, it's definitely not a birthday gift, because that was two days ago."

I can't help but laugh as I slip back into bed with him.

"I love it," I say as I hand it to him so that he can clasp it around my neck.

When he does, he crawls over me, forcing me down on my back. He drops soft kisses along my collarbone and back up my neck to my ear where he whispers, "Do you know how beautiful you are?"

"Mmmm," I softy moan.

"You were amazing last night."

Tangling my hands in his messy hair, I enjoy the shivers he sends through my body as he licks and kisses me while peeling off my clothes.

Last night was a first for me, and I know Ryan was being cautious, but lying here with him now, I am calm under his touch. I know he senses it, and when he removes my pants, he softly nips his way up my thigh. I watch as he makes his way up my stomach, and when he peeks up at me, I grab his face and pull him up to my lips.

He must have already been awake when I woke up because I can taste the mint when I slide my tongue over his. When I graze my teeth across his lip, he pulls back and says, "All I want is you, every fuckin' piece."

I melt into him and give him myself. We take our time now that my nerves are more settled and get to know each other in a whole new way. Ryan's lovemaking is slow and intent and when we can't hold on any longer, we lose ourselves entirely to each other.

Being curled up with Ryan in his sheets, I've never felt more secure. Folded up in his arms, we stay in bed for the rest of the morning.

Ryan went into work this afternoon to take care of some things so that he could stay home tonight. While he's gone, I drive over to Jase's place to hang out for a while. I know I need to tell him everything that's happened since seeing him the other night. When I get there, Mark is there too.

"Hey, what's up?" Jase says from the kitchen.

"Not much. I'm so glad you're home. Ryan had to go into work for a few hours, and I had nothing to do."

"Is he not working tonight?" Mark asks.

"No, he's taking the night off to hang out at the loft."

"So . . . ?" Jase hints.

"What?"

"You never called. Did you get the solo?"

"Oh! God, I'm sorry I forgot to call. Yes, I got it!"

"That's awesome!" Mark says, and when Jase walks in the living room with beers for all of us, he sets them on the coffee table before giving me a hug. "Congratulations, sweetie."

"Thanks."

"Is Ryan's mom still in town?" Mark asks, and then takes a swig of his beer.

"No, she left yesterday. But hey, I have to tell you something, but you can't embarrass me and get all crazy, okay?"

"Shit, this sounds good," Mark teases, and when I eye him, he says, "Sorry."

"Promise. We both do," Jase says.

"Okay, so last night . . ."

"Holy shit! I knew it!" Jase yells.

"What?" Mark and I ask in unison.

"Oh, come on. It's written all over her face," he says to Mark while gesturing to me with his hand.

Mark looks at me and gets a wicked grin on his face.

"What did I just say about embarrassing me?"

"Candace, you're always getting embarrassed. Spill it," Mark says with a hint of laughter.

"Seriously, guys."

"Okay, serious," Jase affirms. "I had no idea you were even thinking about going there."

"Well, yeah. I mean, we love each other and I've been wanting to, but I've always been too scared. It's not like I've had anything good to associate with sex."

"So, how do you feel about it now?" Jase asks.

"Happy. He's what I've been missing my whole life."

Leaning in, Jase hugs me and whispers, "He's lucky to have you."

"Thanks."

"So what kind of lover is he?" Mark asks with gossipy intent.

"Mark!" I say in shock. "I'm not telling you."

Jase starts to laugh and when I narrow my eyes at him, he defends, "What? You know that Mark thinks Ryan is hot. He's not gonna stop asking."

Mark shrugs his shoulders, laughing. "Gross," I say to him.

"Why's that gross?"

"Cause he's my boyfriend."

"So! I let you sleep with *my* boyfriend," he says, tipping his head at me and lifting an eyebrow.

"That's different," I argue.

"Candace, it's not that different," Jase chuckles.

"Aren't you supposed to be on my side?"

Jase and Mark laugh at my childish remark, and I give them an equally childish eye roll.

The three of us continue our playful bickering and hang out for a couple of hours. I never reveal anything to Mark even though he keeps pestering me. Jase, being as levelheaded as he is, just laughs at Mark's crooked curiosity.

When I get back to the loft, Ryan still isn't home, so I decide to get some schoolwork done. I have two exams next week before the end of the quarter that I need to prepare for. Spreading out my books and notes on the coffee table, I make myself comfortable on the couch. I lose track of time as I flip through my books and study some of the dance terminology that I need to know for one of my classes.

When I notice the grey, misty sky beginning to darken as the sun sets behind the clouds, I wonder why Ryan isn't home yet. Picking up my phone, I call him and he sounds stressed when he answers.

"Babe, hey."

"Hey, I didn't think you were going to be working this late."

"I wasn't, but one of our distributors stopped by today and notified me that we are now a COD contract. When I went back, I saw that Michael hadn't been paying the fucking invoices. So, I've been going through the back logs making sure there aren't any outstanding."

"Have you found any?"

"No, but this shit pisses me off. I need a manager who is more organized. This shit's a mess in his office."

"I'm sorry."

"It's fine. Just been a long day. I'm about to pack up and leave."

"Have you eaten anything yet?"

"Yeah, I had one of the bar girls run out and pick up some food."

"Okay, well, I'll see you in a bit."

"Love you."

"Love you too."

When Ryan gets home about a half hour later, we decide to camp out downstairs and watch a movie. We change into our pajamas and Ryan pours me a glass of wine then gets himself a beer. Moving the coffee table out of the way, Ryan lights the fireplace while I throw a pile of blankets and pillows on the floor.

Wrapping up in the blankets together, Ryan puts on one of his old black and white movies, and I can't help but smile in amusement when he does.

"What? You wanna watch something else?"

"No," I say and I settle my head on his chest, getting comfortable. "I love watching these with you."

"I thought you hated them. You're always making fun of me."

"I know, but secretly, I've always loved it."

Kissing the top of my head, he wraps his arms around me as we watch 'Out of the Past.'

About halfway through the movie, I remember that I need to run upstairs and take my sleeping pill. When I return to Ryan, I curl in beside him and he rolls over to face me.

"I need to run into work tomorrow and sign off on a few things Michael is redoing tonight."

"Okay."

"I was thinking you could come with me."

"Ryan . . ." The last time I went there I totally panicked. The last thing I want to do is go back just to be reminded of what happened.

"I know, but I hate that you can't come up there to see me. I mean . . . it's where I work, babe."

"I understand what you're trying to say, but I just . . . I can't."

"I know, I just think if you tried . . . we can go in the morning, before we open. You and me. We'll park in the front."

Letting out a deep breath, I close my eyes. I want to be able to go up there and see Ryan. I'd love to hang out with him and his friends and see where he works. And it bothers me that I've never seen Mark's band play. I'm just not sure if I'm ready to push myself that far yet. I know I can't avoid that place forever since Ryan owns that bar.

He cups my cheeks with his hands and whispers, "If you're not ready, I get it. It was just a thought."

I open my eyes and look up at him. "Ryan, it just takes me back farther than I want to go. There have been times I've wished that I would've just died that night."

He releases a hard breath and tucks my head under his chin as he holds me.

I know what he's trying to do, and a part of me loves that he pushes me and doesn't baby me. The fact that he thinks I'm strong enough to go there shows me that he views me in a way I want to truly be—strong. But another part of me is terrified to stir up those memories again. I love Ryan, and I know that he cares for me. I want to show him that I can push myself.

"Okay," I whisper softly.

"What, babe?"

Pulling my head up, I say, "Okay, I'll try," when he looks at me.

"Are you sure?"

"No, but I'll try."

Cradling my face in his hands, he says, "Do you have any idea how amazing you are?"

"Ryan, I'm not saying I will. I'm only saying I'll try."

"And that's all you need to do. The fact that you're even willing to is one of the reasons I love you so much. You're so unbelievably strong."

Before I can deny his words, he captures my mouth with his.

I'm a bundle of nerves as I drink my coffee and wait for Ryan to finish getting ready. I had agreed to make an effort to go with him to the bar this morning. The place doesn't open for a few hours, and he wants us to go when no one else is there.

When he comes downstairs, he takes my hand and reassures me that all I have to do is say the word and we'll come back home. But I don't want to be that person. Ryan sees me in such a strong way. I wear his necklace that he gave me that is engraved with the word 'fierce.' He chose that Shakespearean quote for a reason. If he believes that about me, then maybe I should try to believe that about myself as well.

My stomach is in knots as he drives, and I don't say a word. His hand is laced tightly with mine, and I turn cold when I see us approaching the building. He does as he promises and parks along the curb in front of the bar. I know there is no way I could handle being in the back lot with that dumpster.

I'm lost in my thoughts and don't even notice that he's gotten out of the car until I turn to see that my door is open and Ryan is standing there with his hand on my knee.

"Just try," he says as he takes my hand and helps me out of the car. I'm not familiar with the front of this building, so I don't find it terribly difficult to walk with him. I keep telling myself not to think about what is on the other side.

When we get to the door, he takes his keys, unlocks the door, and opens it for me. When I step inside, I am surprised that the place looks completely different than what I had envisioned. The interior is dark and masculine. There is a huge rich mahogany bar that runs the length of one of the walls with exposed brick and wooden shelves that hold a variety of liquors. On the opposite wall there is a fairly large platform stage. Sleek leather bar stools flank the high top tables that are scattered throughout the place.

I follow Ryan as he walks me down a small hallway that leads to stairs.

"My office is up here," he tells me before he takes me up.

Still holding my hand, we walk up the wooden stairs. When we reach the top he tells me he's going to get the papers from Michael's office. When we walk in, I instantly turn around and stumble into Ryan. Behind Michael's desk is a large window that looks over the back lot.

"Babe?"

"I want to go."

Reaching around me, he picks up a folder from the desk and walks me out, shutting the door behind us. We walk into the office across the hall, and he tosses the folder onto his desk. I'm shaking when he turns to me, running his hands up and down my arms.

"I'm sorry, I didn't think."

I don't even need to explain what's got me startled, he just knows.

Leaning against the edge of his desk, he pulls me between his legs and hugs me. I lay my head on his chest and listen to his heart while I focus on slowing mine down to match the rhythm of his. I don't speak because I'm trying not to get myself worked up.

After a few moments, I look up and over Ryan's shoulder. His view is out the front of the building. I watch the mist collect on the glass and slowly trickle down.

"You okay?"

I nod my head and lean it back down on his chest, letting out a slow sigh.

"I hate seeing that dumpster." His arms tighten around me, and I find myself continuing to talk. "It's weird because I also love it in a messed up way. It's all I had to focus on."

"I'm so sorry."

"When I dream about that night, it's always taken away from me. There's nothing to distract me."

"I wish I knew his name," he says with spite.

Ryan has asked me once to tell him who the guy was, but I refused. I know he'd only kill him if given the chance. It doesn't matter anyway;

what's done is done, and it can't be fixed.

When I look up at him, his jaw is tightly clenched. Sliding my hand along his jawbone, I lift up on my toes to reach his mouth and give him a soft kiss. I hate that he feels this way—helpless.

He pulls me closer to him, and I feel him relax under my hand.

"I'm glad you're here," he says when he breaks our kiss.

"It isn't anything like I'd thought."

"How's that?"

"I don't know . . . I didn't expect it to be so nice." I chuckle, realizing how rude that just sounded.

"Wow. Thanks, babe," he says, with mock annoyance.

I smile up at him. "No, that's not what I meant. I like it. I should have known it would be nice like this by the way your loft is."

"It's okay. Let me just sign these papers and we can go, all right?"

"Okay."

I watch him as he stands over his desk and finishes signing the orders. I'm relieved that I can be here and not be having a total freak out. Of course, we are here alone, which helps, but realizing that I can come here feels good. I don't fight the smile that starts to spread across my face. When Ryan sets his pen down and turns to look at me, he grins, and asks, "What?"

"I thought this would've been a lot harder."

"Thank you for doing this," he says as he runs his hands down my arms.

"Thanks for pushing me."

When we leave and get into his jeep, I know I just did something huge. I did it, and I was okay. I've been avoiding this place for months, and it feels slightly empowering that I don't feel that same level of fear. It isn't completely gone, but it's a big step for me.

chapter thirty-three

"WHY DON'T YOU come with me?"

"Because I just rehearsed for an hour on top of my two-hour studio. I've also been getting painful cramps in my calves.

"When did that start?"

"This week. I upped my calcium and have been using Tiger's Balm, but I don't really want to put anymore strain on my legs right now."

"Okay, well, I'll be back in a couple hours. I'm gonna run after I lift," he says as he's mixing his protein shake.

"I'm going to go pop by Jase's while you're gone since I won't see him much during the break."

He takes a gulp of his shake, sets it down on the kitchen counter, and brings me into his arms.

"Text me when you're on your way back, so I can be here waiting for you," he says in a sexy low voice as he grabs my ass and sets me on the countertop.

When he leans in to kiss me, I push against his chest. "Don't kiss me after drinking that crap."

"What?" he says as he chuckles.

"That stuff is nasty. I don't know how you can stand it."

Laughing at me, he ignores my words and plants a big kiss on my mouth. I try to turn my head to the side when he kisses me, but his hold is tight, and my outburst of giggles makes me too weak to push him off. He tastes like chocolate dirt.

"Ryan! Gross!"

He releases me, takes a few steps back, all the while laughing, and then picks up his cup and chugs the rest of his shake.

Wiping my mouth with the back of my hand, I jump off the counter and jab my finger in his ribs as I walk out of the kitchen.

He follows behind and locks up as we head out to our cars.

"See you later?" he asks as he opens my car door for me.

"Yeah, I'll text you when I leave."

"Love you, babe," he says before he leans in and nips me on my neck.

"Love you, too." I slide into my car, and he shuts the door before I start backing out of the driveway.

When I hit the elevator button in the lobby of Jase's apartment building, I'm caught off guard when the door slides open and Kimber is standing there. She looks equally shocked to see me.

Stepping out, she says, "Hey. Where have you been?"

When I called Ryan to stay with him, I only planned on a week or two, but it's been over a month since he came over to help me pack my bags.

"With Ryan."

"You living with him now?"

"Um, no . . . I mean, kinda." I shake my head and gather my thoughts. Being honest, I tell her, "I could tell you were upset after we talked, and I was upset too. So, I thought I would give us both a little space. I didn't intend on being gone this long."

"Whatever," she says softly as she hangs her head and looks to the floor. "I guess it doesn't really matter." That's all she says before turning to walk outside.

"What are you doing here?" Jase says when I walk into his apartment.

"Just thought I would stop by. You busy?"

"No," he says as he scans my face. "What's wrong?"

Upset from seeing Kimber downstairs, I let out a sigh and fall onto his couch.

"Was Kimber just over here?" I ask him when he sits down next to me.

"I didn't want to say anything because I didn't want to upset you."

Looking over at him, I say, "I'm not upset."

He cocks his head and says, "Sweetie, I can tell when you're trying not to cry. You get all squeaky."

Taking a deep breath and puffing it out, he continues. "She texted me a few days ago wanting to know where you were. When I called her, she was upset. I felt bad, Candace. She was my friend too, and I have felt real shitty about how I've treated her."

I wipe the tears from my cheeks as I listen to him talk, and I feel like a horrible person for causing all of this.

"She asked if she could come over and talk. Candace, she's really upset. She misses you."

Trying to stop the tears, I begin hiccupping back my breaths. Jase scoots over and wraps his arm around my shoulder.

"Do you think you could talk to her now? Be honest with her?"

"I can't. Her boyfriend is in the same fraternity as Jack."

"What? How do you know that?" he asks as he looks at me with surprise.

"I saw the Greek letters on his car one day."

"Did you say anything to Kimber?"

"No, why would I?"

"Are they friends?"

"I don't know. I never brought it up because I didn't want to draw any attention to him."

Jase leans his head back on the couch, and I feel envious that he can still be friends with her.

"I'm not upset. I understand that she's your friend. I'm sorry I ever put you in that position."

"Sweetie," he says as he rolls his head to the side to look at me. "I love you. Even though I haven't been a good friend to her, I would have done that to anyone for you."

I smile at his words. There isn't any way I could ever express exactly how much they mean to me. Jase has always been so selfless with me, and I try to give back to him what he gives to me.

"So, what did she say?" I ask.

"She just talked about you. How hurt she is. How much she misses you. She wanted to know what's going on in your life. I told her about Ryan and that you're really happy with him."

As I nod my head, he adds, "If you won't talk to her, then I think you should at least start spending some time back at your place."

"Yeah . . . okay."

I sit back on the couch next to him and rest my head against his shoulder. After a few minutes pass, Jase switches topics and asks me about the gallery show at Thinkspace on Friday night. Ryan's photograph will be on display and up for sale. Jase and Mark are going along with some of Ryan's friends as well. I haven't told Jase that the photo is of me. I don't want anyone to know, and Ryan doesn't either.

"So what time should Mark and I be there?"

"It starts at eight, so anytime around then."

"Sounds great. And when are you guys heading out to Oregon?"

"We're going to leave the next morning. I'm not sure when we'll be coming back. Ryan wanted to leave it open. He's taken the week off, so we will just play it by ear."

"Mark and I will be around, so when you get back, let us know."

"I will." Sitting up on the couch, I turn to look at Jase and say, "Hey, you wanna go down to Peet's and grab a coffee? We can walk around some of the shops."

"Yeah, let's get out of here. Give me a second to throw on another shirt."

We spend the next couple of hours shopping around the vintage stores on Fremont after stopping by Peet's. While we roam around, I think about what Jase said. I know I need to talk to Ryan and let him know that I should go back home. I never intended on staying at his place for as long as I have.

We just kind of fell into it. I love him, and I love being there, but I have my own place and a friend that I sort of abandoned, even though we aren't really talking and haven't been for months. I can't tell her about Jack. After telling Ryan, I don't ever want to go through that again. Plus, I'm not even sure of Seth's connection with Jack. It scares me to think what Kimber would do, being that she is, in a way, linked to him. I don't know what I can do to salvage my relationship with Kimber, but I do know I should at least try.

I've been gone most of the day, so when I return to the loft, Ryan is more than eager to have me back. We spend the rest of the day being lazy and listening to demos from bands that are trying to get spots at Blur. I know I need to talk about going back home, but I know Ryan isn't going to like that idea very much. I've spent most of the evening putting it off.

Ryan pulls me out of my thoughts when he says, "Something's been bothering me today." When I walk across the room to Ryan, who's sitting on the couch, he holds out his arm and tugs me down onto his lap. "I've never seen you dance."

"Oh . . . yeah, I guess not. But you will in May when we have our production. You'll see me a lot. I have three ensembles plus my solo."

"It just bothers me that there is a huge part of your life that I've never seen."

"Well, I can grab some videos at the studio of past performances. They have also recorded some of our studios this year. Would that suffice for you, watching me on video?"

Grabbing me behind my waist and neck, he flips me back onto the couch and just before he buries his head in my neck, he says, "Nothing about you will ever suffice for me. I'm always gonna want more."

So I give him more, right there on the couch. Truth is, I feel the same way. I don't think I'll ever get enough of him. Tonight, he's more playful with me and being able to giggle while we make love, I realize that he's finally giving me pieces of myself that have been missing for a long time. I relish in the closeness we have.

Ryan wraps us up in a blanket as we lie in each others' arms on the floor. Stroking his hand lazily up and down my back, we chat about random nonsense and continue with our fun banter from this morning. But I know I need to be honest and talk to him about what's been on my mind all day.

With hesitation, I say, "Ryan, I ran into Kimber today. She was leaving Jase's when I walked into his building."

"Did you guys talk?"

"She just asked where I've been, and I could tell she was hurt. Jase told me she reached out to him and that she's really upset."

"I'm sorry, babe. I know how much this bothers you. Have you thought anymore about talking to her?"

Ryan and I had discussed Kimber the week before. He felt that maybe she wouldn't react the way I initially thought she would since I'm in a better place now. If she could see that I was happy, she might be less likely to be reckless with her reaction. I agree with him, but I also didn't tell him about Seth being Jack's frat brother. I haven't told Ryan anything about Jack because I know how much he hates him and worry about what he might do if he ever found out.

"I just can't. I don't trust her enough to not do something."

"I don't know what to tell you to do. Just try talking to her and see if you guys can move past this rift."

"I think it would help if I went back home."

"Candace . . ."

"Ryan, I was only supposed to be here for a week or two. I never intended on moving in like this. But, we are about to graduate, and I'd like to see if this is fixable. I can't do that if I'm not there."

"I still want you here."

"And I'll still be here. Just not *every* night."

He releases a deep breath and says, "Okay. We can go tomorrow and take some of your things back."

Sliding my hand over his cheek, I tell him, "Thanks for understanding," before pressing my lips into his.

The next day, Ryan helped me pack up my things and take them back to my house. He insisted I leave some of my belongings at his place, so I did. It was strange being back home after being away for so long. Kimber was home when we got there, so I introduced her to Ryan, but they really didn't talk.

Ryan wanted to stay here with me that night, but I thought it would be best if he didn't for the first night I was back. If Kimber was uncomfortable, I didn't want to make it worse. He wasn't happy with it, but he understood.

Tonight is the gallery showing at Thinkspace. I wanted to look nice, so I had gone out and bought a dress. Standing in front of my mirror, I smooth down the sheer nude lace of my sleeveless pencil skirt dress. The lace is offset by the black satin underlay and has a bateau neckline. Although the necklace that Ryan gave me doesn't go with the dress, I wear it anyway. I love the quote and that those words make him think of me, something I haven't thought about myself for a while.

When he comes to pick me up, he has an effortless style about him that I find alluring. Ryan often dresses in simple t-shirts and dark jeans. Even though his closet is filled with nice dress clothes, he never wears them. But tonight, he wears dark charcoal slacks, a sports coat, and a white collared dress shirt leaving the first few buttons undone. His clothes are tailored to him perfectly and accentuate his broad shoulders and chest that 'V' down to his narrow hips. Ryan spends a lot of time in the gym, in addition to running, and his frame is near perfection. His dark hair is slightly messy, like he just ran his hands through it, but in a sexy way.

"We need to skip this whole thing tonight," he says as he approaches me and slowly slides his hands from my neck to my shoulders down my arms. He pulls me tight, grazes his nose up my bare neck, and kisses me behind my ear.

Cinching up my shoulders from the ticklish spot he kisses, I laugh. "Ryan, stop."

"I'm serious. Fuck everyone. I just want to stay here with you," he whispers in my ear.

"The deal was, if you got your picture accepted, then I got to go as your date. So, whether you like it or not, I'm dressed and ready to go."

"Okay, but tonight, you're sleeping in my bed. I didn't like not having you next to me last night."

"Ryan."

"I know, I get it. I understand the whole Kimber thing, but I'm taking you home with me tonight."

I slip on my knee-length black wool coat before we walk out into the cold misty night. When we arrive at Thinkspace, a chic and contemporary art gallery in the heart of the city, I look over at Ryan and say, "I'm really proud of you, you know?"

"Babe, the only reason that photo is on display is because you're in it. You're perfect."

I don't even try to convince him of his talent because I know he would simply deny it. So, I let it be as we walk through the open doors. I immediately spot Stacy Keets, the woman that originally told me about this showing.

"Candace."

"Stacy, hi," I say as I give her a hug.

"That dress is amazing."

"Thank you."

"And this is . . . ?" she asks as she glances to Ryan.

"Ryan." I say.

"Ahh, 'Nubile.' Beautiful photograph," she says as she shakes his hand. "I'm Stacy Keets. I work at the Henry Gallery."

"Ryan Campbell."

"Well, your piece is great. I saw a couple eying it a minute ago. Do you have more pieces?"

"A few. It wasn't ever something I intended to show anyone or have displayed, but Candace insisted."

"I'm glad she did. I'd love to see more of your work." Looking at me, she asks, "Do you still have my number?"

"Yes, I do."

"Give me a call," she tells Ryan. "We have some wall space opening up soon, so if you're interested, we can discuss the possibility of displaying some of your pieces."

"Will do. I'll have Candace give me your number."

Turning to me, she says, "And I owe you a congratulations. I heard about your audition from Sergej."

Sergej has been dating Stacy since I met her over two years ago. He has instructed my partnering studio since I first came to UW. He's originally from Russia, but moved to the States and danced for a company in New York before retiring and relocating here to teach.

"I hope it was all good."

Lowering her voice, she tells me, "He thinks people will be fighting for you to sign with their companies."

"I can only hope."

"No hoping. I'm looking forward to seeing you perform in May."

"Thank you. I'll be sure Ryan calls you," I say.

"Enjoy your night."

"You too, Stacy," Ryan says as he starts walking us to the bar.

Mark and Jase are already drinking and mingling when we walk over. I knew they would have a good time and they'd know several people here with them being architecture majors and art snobs.

"Hey, man," Mark says when he spots Ryan.

We all stand around and visit. After Gavin and his friend Chris arrive, I excuse myself and take a glass of wine from the bartender. Jase and I separate from the group and start to stroll through the gallery, looking at all the pieces. I know Ryan is here merely for my sake, so I don't mind that he spends the evening with his buddies. When we find ourselves in front of Ryan's photograph, which he'd titled 'Nubile,' Jase says in a quiet voice, "You're beautiful." He speaks to the photograph, not me. I stand there for a moment and only respond when he slightly turns his head to wink at me.

"How did you know?" I ask.

"Because of what he titled it." He turns to look back at the photograph and adds, "It could only be you."

I don't know how I would live without Jase. He's my rock. He's always stuck by my side and has been my strength when I had none left. I step closer to his side and hold his hand, and when he looks over at me, I tell him, "I love you, so much."

"I love you too, sweetie." He squeezes my hand and we continue through the gallery, admiring all the art on display. We don't speak with anyone else; we just spend our time together and enjoy each other's company. Eventually we find a bench and take a seat to give my feet a break in my platform heels.

"There you are," Ryan says from behind me.

Jase takes my empty wine glass and excuses himself to give Ryan and

I time together.

Sitting down next to me, he says, "Where have you been?"

"Just walking around with Jase."

"I heard someone bought your photo," he tells me, and I'm so excited for him.

"Really?"

He doesn't respond, he just smiles at me and takes my hand. "Walk with me."

Sliding my hand into his, I follow him through the gallery and down one of the halls to a roped off area.

"What are we doing back here? We're gonna get in trouble."

Laughing at me, he says, "You're so cute."

We turn to go behind a wall, far from everyone else. He turns to me, pressing my back against the wall, hands on either side of me, caging me in. He doesn't even need to say anything when I reach for his face and bring him down to me. He's eager and passionate, and I know if he had it his way, he would take me right here against this wall.

"We should go," I say breathlessly between our lips.

He pushes himself against me as I grasp his shoulders, and I know it's *really* time to go.

"Ryan."

When he finally drags his lips off of me, he takes my hand and walks us out of the back exit, not saying goodbye to anyone.

When we arrive at his place, he opens my door and scoops me out of the car, cradling me with his arm behind my knees. Kicking the door shut, he carries me up the stairs to the front door and once we are inside, straight up to his bed.

He lays me down and runs his hands down the length of my body slowly, down my thighs, wrapping around to the backs of my knees and then slides past my calves. He slips off my heels and I hear them as they clatter onto the floor. Standing by the edge of the bed, Ryan stares down at me as he takes off his shoes and socks and shrugs off his jacket.

My heart is racing as I watch him, and when he lowers himself on top of me, he gently kisses me. The rushed intensity that I felt earlier is gone.

"I love you so fuckin' much."

Brushing my fingers through his hair, I smile and study his face, the way it looks right now in this moment.

"I love you, too."

"Make love to me, babe."

I know what his words mean. I've always let him be in control, not feeling confident enough in myself. But I love this man, and I want to give him what he wants, which is to give myself to him in a way I haven't yet.

Wrapping my arms around his neck, I nod as he pulls us up to our knees. I kiss him and caress his tongue with mine. Sliding his hands up my back, he catches the zipper and slowly pulls it down, loosening the lace on my body. One by one, I unbutton his shirt, and when I hit the last one, I run my hands up his cut stomach, over his chest, around his shoulders, and down his arms, sliding the shirt off. He covers my mouth with his, and when he does, I let the lace fall off of my shoulders. I sling my arms back around him and he lays me down, slipping my dress the rest of the way off.

His lips and tongue slowly drag against my heated skin as he makes his way up my legs, dropping kisses here and there along the way. He grabs onto my panties and starts pulling them down, taking his time as I lift my knees to help him. Leaning back over me, he runs his hands over my knees, up my inner thighs, and my breath hitches when he pushes his palm over my sex and up my stomach. I catch his hips with my legs, wrapping them around his waist, pulling him firmly against me.

He takes one of my legs and pulls it down from his hip as he unhooks his pants. When they land on the floor with the rest of our clothes, he leans over to the nightstand and puts on protection.

He reaches behind my back and pulls me up, sitting back on the bed as I'm straddling his lap. When he unhooks my bra, the last piece of clothing between us, I lift up on my knees, wrap my arms around him, and gently slide myself on top of him. I feel my body instinctively tighten around him when he enters me, and I have to drop my head in the crook of his neck with the profound pleasure that is coursing through my body.

His breaths are heavy, and when I lift my head and look into his blue eyes, I slowly begin to move. Giving myself to him as never before, I lace my fingers through his hair and fist it in my hands. I can't help the moan that escapes me, and I don't even try to hide the waves of pleasure I feel from being with him like this.

"God, I love you," he says through his panted breaths, and when my hips rock into him, his head drops to my chest.

Grazing his hands along my sides, he begins kissing my breasts, and I start to feel the intensity building. Our moans become louder as they fill the room. When he grips me tighter in his hold, I rock into him again, clinging to him when he says, "Look at me, baby. I want to watch you come."

Leaning my forehead against his, our eyes lock onto one another. My body begins to shudder and clench around him, and when I hear Ryan moan my name, I know he's right there with me. Never taking our eyes off of each other, we ride out our pleasure until we have nothing left.

He's hot to my touch, and I can feel the sweat beading down my back when he slowly begins to kiss me. Laying us down, I brush a few locks of his hair from his damp forehead.

"'I love you' will never be strong enough for what I feel for you."

Pulling the covers over us, he wraps me in his arms, still inside me, and I know I'll only ever have this with him—I'll only ever want this with him.

chapter thirty-four

"I CAN'T FIND shit in here," Ryan says from deep within my closet.

He offered to help me pack since I didn't get much sleep last night. I was so wrapped up in the moment that I forgot to take my sleeping pill, and I kept waking up all throughout the night. I'm starting to wonder if I'll ever be able to sleep without them. My dreams weren't terribly vivid, but when my mind would begin to drift, Jack would find me.

Ryan suggested that I should talk to someone about what happened, but I quickly shut him down, same as I did with Jase when he brought it up months ago. Sitting around and hashing out what happened when all I am trying to do is move on doesn't sound like it would be beneficial at all.

"Just grab a few pairs of jeans."

"Which ones? You have like fifty pairs in here."

Laughing at his dramatics, I say, "It doesn't matter."

He walks out of my closet and puts them in my suitcase while I am going through my dresser.

"Could you grab everything that is sitting on my bathroom counter?"

"Yeah."

When I dig back in my top drawer to find my wool socks, I come across something I haven't seen in seven months. Pulling it out, I look at it, and I'm immediately taken back to that sterile hospital room. Jase was with me, never letting go of my hand, while the nurse scraped Jack's bloody flesh from under my nails. I can still feel the stinging of my eyes as my salty tears flowed effortlessly.

I stash Detective Patterson's business card back in the drawer and close it when I hear Ryan walk out of the bathroom.

"Is this everything?" he asks.

"Umm . . . yeah," I say as I continue to stand at my dresser, but when my voice comes out shaky, Ryan doesn't miss it.

"Babe," he says, and he walks over to me. Placing his hands on my arms, he continues, "I'm sorry about last night. I should have made sure you took your pill."

I don't correct him when he assumes my mood shift is due to my lack of sleep.

"No, it's not your fault. It's fine."

Kissing my forehead, we move around my room and finish packing my bags. I put in my dance DVDs that I picked up from the studio the other day.

"Okay, I think that's everything." I zip everything shut and Ryan grabs both bags off of my bed, and I lock up as we head out.

I sleep most of the drive to Oregon, but Ryan wakes me up as he exits the highway.

"Where are we?" I say, still groggy.

"Portland."

"Why?"

"Because I want to stop by Voodoo Doughnut. I'm starving."

"Do we really need to drive all the way into the city to get a doughnut?" I groan.

Looking at me with all seriousness, he says, "Yes."

Giving him a half smile, I shake my head. We drive through the city and when we find a parking space, we walk, and get in the line that wraps around the building.

Standing in line with a variety of sugar-crazed Portland hippies, we finally make our way inside the artsy grunge doughnut shop. I stand next to the glass display and stare at the insane doughnuts that rotate on the round trivets. I look over at Ryan and ask, "You're really going to eat one of those?"

"You are too. What do you want?"

"None."

"Okay, then, I'll pick for you."

Shaking my head, still feeling tired, I let him choose for me.

Looking down at me, he gets an evil grin and says, "I'm getting you the cock and balls doughnut."

"Ryan!" I elbow him in the ribs and start looking at the menu behind the registers.

He's still laughing at me when the girl behind the register starts taking our order.

I carry the pink box and set it on one of the tables outside. I pull out my doughnut that is covered in Fruit Loops, and Ryan takes his creepy voodoo doll-looking doughnut with a pretzel stick that is stabbed through the heart. I laugh at him when he bites off the head and winks at me.

We take our time as we get wired on sugar and laugh together. When the light mist starts to thicken into heavier drops, I toss the remainder of my doughnut that I'm too full to finish, and we head back to the car to resume our drive to Cannon Beach.

We get to his mom's house about an hour later, and it's close to dinnertime. I am so happy to see Donna, and she is sweet enough to help Ryan unpack my bags when she sees how tired I am. Ryan explains to her that I had a rough night, and she goes downstairs to get me some hot tea.

Running his hands up and down my arms, he asks, "Are you hungry, babe?"

"No, I'm just so tired my head hurts," I say as I rest my forehead on his chest.

"Why don't you change and lie down?"

When I get into bed, Donna knocks on the door and sets the tea down on the nightstand along with a couple of aspirin.

"Ryan said you had a headache."

"Thanks. I'm sorry to come and just crash."

"Sweetie, please. Don't worry about me." As she closes the blinds she tells me that Ryan is eating a quick dinner and will come up when he's done. I take the aspirin along with my sleeping pill, and after a few sips of the hot tea, I doze off.

Waking in a haze in the middle of the night, Ryan is wrapped around me. I roll over to face him, and when I do, he begins to stir.

"Everything, okay?" he whispers as he tucks me closer to him.

"Mmm hmm." I weave my legs with his and close my eyes again, drifting easily back to sleep.

"How are you feeling?" Donna asks as she sits down with me on the couch and hands me a cup of coffee.

"Much better, thanks."

"Hey," Ryan says as he comes down the stairs, already dressed for the day.

"Good morning," his mom says when he walks over and sits on the couch with us.

"So, you two are going to have the day to yourselves. Marci called me this morning and I have to drive into Portland to go over and sign off on some tax documents. While I'm there I'm going to meet with a friend of mine for a late lunch, so I won't be home till around six or so. But I have no plans for the rest of week. This just popped up yesterday."

"Don't worry about it, Mom. I was going to see if I could convince Candace to hop on a surfboard with me."

"What?!" I say as I jerk my head to look at him.

"I just checked the weather and the waves should be pretty good at the beach we went to the last time you were here."

"That water's going to be freezing, Ryan."

He laughs at me and says, "That's why you wear a wetsuit, babe."

His mother interjects and says, "Well, have fun with that, Candace," dripping in playful sarcasm. "I need to go get ready. I'll see you guys later tonight."

Ryan and I head up to his room, and when I get out of the shower, I wrap a towel around myself to go grab some clothes.

"Fuck, babe," Ryan says as I walk into the bedroom.

"Don't start," I say as I lay my hand on his chest, keeping him from coming any closer. "Your mother is downstairs."

"I don't care who the fuck is downstairs when the only thing covering your wet body is that towel."

"That's why I'm getting my clothes."

I quickly grab my clothes and run back into the bathroom before Ryan can strip the towel off of me. Once I'm dressed and walk back out, he says, "Tori has an extra wetsuit in my closet that should fit you okay."

"What?"

"Surfing. You and me."

"I'm fine with trying anything new, but that water is freezing."

"I promise, when you're in that wetsuit, you'll be fine. Tori loves to surf, so she has her wetsuit here and some swimsuits in my closet."

When we get to Indian Beach, the wind is just as strong as the last time we were here. The mist is thick, and the skies are dark and heavy with clouds today. I grab one of the blankets that Ryan put in the car before we left the house and wrap it around me when I get out. Ryan unhooks the boards from the top of the jeep, and we head down the wooden stairs to the wet and rocky beach. I stop and watch the rough waves as they crash along the shore. If ever there was a time I worried about breaking a leg, it's now.

Holding out his hand for me, he says, "Come on."

I shrug off my blanket, toss it on the stairs, and follow him out.

"Ryan, I'm going to hurt myself."

He chuckles and says, "No, you won't."

"That water looks rough. There's no way I'm getting up on that board."

"You're getting up, babe."

When we get to the water, he drops the boards on the ground and starts telling me everything I hope I need to know to not kill myself. He shows me how to pop up on the board, and I have no problems showing him I am fully capable.

I take the hairband from my wrist and tie my hair up on top of my head, as Ryan straps the cord around my ankle.

When he stands up, he gives me a quick kiss and says with a big smile, "I fuckin' love that you're doing this."

"You know I'm willing to try almost anything, but don't get your hopes up. I don't think I'll be able to get up."

Grabbing me and pulling me up against him, he leans down to my neck and says, "If you get up, I'll get up for you later," and then starts sucking on my neck.

I smack his arm and push him away as he's laughing.

"You're so gross!"

"Pick up your board. Let's go," is his only response.

I ended up having a pretty great time with Ryan in the water. When he wasn't trying to get frisky with me, I managed to get up on the board a few times. After several hours, we decide to head back to the house. I've been wrapped up in blankets since we got in the car to try and get warm again.

When we get back to the house, I run upstairs to take a shower while Ryan makes us sandwiches.

I turn the water on and step into the large glassed-in shower when steam begins to fill the room. My body is freezing and even though the water is scalding on my skin, I'm still shivering. I close my eyes and let the water wash over me as it slowly starts to warm me up.

I'm startled when I hear the door open.

"What are you doing?!" I squeal when Ryan closes the glass door behind him and wraps his arms around my waist.

"It's time to ante up, babe." Dipping his head under the running water, he pushes me against the cool wall, and slides his hand back through his wet hair.

Running my hand up and around his neck, he lowers his head to mine and kisses me. He easily pulls me up, and I wrap my legs around his waist, locking my ankles. The air is thick with steam, making my breathing labored as Ryan nibbles playfully along my neck and ear.

I've been wishing that there was someone just like him, and now that he's found me, I feel like he has the power to pull me though this madness that has been consuming me.

His wet hand lingers down my neck to my breast, and he presses into me harder. Dropping my head into the curve of his shoulder, I breathe, "I want you."

"I don't have anything with me in here."

"It's okay. I've been on the pill for a while. I trust you."

He pulls his head back and gives me a confused look. "When did you get on the pill, babe?"

"I've been on it. I got it . . ." I drop my head for a second and when I look back up at him I tell him, "I got on it after what happened."

He goes on to assure me that he's always been safe and that he's never had unprotected sex. I know he would never hurt me, and I trust him, so I don't hesitate when I reaffirm that I want him.

As his bare flesh touches mine, a ragged breath leaves his chest.

"Fuck, babe, you feel so good."

I love knowing I can give this to him, that he can have me completely, with nothing to separate us. We proceed to spend a lengthy amount of time in the shower making love to each other.

After we eat lunch, we decide to spend the rest of the day being lazy in bed. I pull out the DVDs that he had asked for, and as we lie in bed, we watch a production from last year. I show him the two ensembles that I had lead placements in and one of my duets with Maxim.

As he's watching one of the ensembles where I have a standout solo, a hint of a smile appears, and for some reason, that tiny gesture has the biggest effect on me. I scoot down in the bed and nestle my head on his chest as he watches me dance.

"I don't know shit about dancing, babe, but you're amazing," he says as he continues to watch.

I can't help but laugh at him and wrap my arm snuggly around his stomach. When the clip changes to my duet, I know it won't take him too long to make one of his possessive comments, so I close my eyes and just wait for it.

"Hmm . . ." is all I hear him say for a while, and then it comes. "I don't like that dude's hands all over you."

"Ryan, his hands have to be on me for all the lifts."

"His hands are on you for more than just lifts, Candace."

A giggle escapes me and he says, "I'm serious, his hands are all over you."

"He's gay!"

"I don't give a shit. I still don't like it."

He is really unbelievable, but I love him all the same, so I simply laugh it off.

When the video ends, he tells me again and again how amazing I am, then proceeds to tell me how incredibly turned on he is, so we get a little playful before opting for a nap in the middle of the day. Having this time to be with him like this is making the thought of graduation that much harder. I love him, and I'm pretty sure I would never move away from him. I push all that aside for the moment and simply relish him.

Ryan and I decided to spend the rest of the week at his mom's. Both of us have enjoyed the down time. I love spending time with Donna. We have made a couple days out of shopping and dining. But it's the best when we stay home for dinner, and I can help her cook and clean up. It feels very comfortable and normal, and I crave that feeling at this point.

Ryan took me surfing again, and another day we took his jeep to Long Beach in Washington. We had fun driving up and down the sand along the water. We spent the day out there, building a small fire pit and wrapping up in blankets. I could have spent hours in his arms, staring out at the ocean.

I can't help but feel like part of his family when I'm with him and Donna. I'm sad to be leaving today, but so happy we got to have this week together. As I'm finishing getting ready in the bathroom, Ryan is packing our bags.

When I slip on my sweatshirt, my jeans tug down enough so that I can see a hint of my heart. I don't like what this tattoo reminds me of, and for some reason, I don't think Ryan likes it either. I've never asked him, but sometimes when we make love he covers it with his hand.

I shift my pants down slightly to look at it in the mirror. I've considered having it removed, but I've never done anything to look into what that would involve.

When Ryan opens the door, I quickly yank my shirt down and turn to face him.

Cocking his head, he questions, "What are you doing?"

"Nothing."

He steps over to me and places his hand over mine, which is still holding onto my top. He only looks in my eyes as he lifts my hand and exposes the heart.

I know he's curious, so I admit, "I don't like it."

He lowers my hand and shirt. "Why?"

"Because it's not me. I was trying to be someone different, and it only led to bad things."

He looks confused and asks, "What do you mean?"

"I got it in a moment of rebellion, I guess. It was stupid, really. I got it and started acting foolishly, which led to . . . umm . . ."

Ryan stops me so I don't have to finish. "I get it. But, babe, nothing you did led to that."

I can't look at him because I know if I'd never behaved that way, if I'd never led *him* on, it wouldn't have happened. When I walk out of the bathroom, he follows and grabs my arm.

"Wait. You know that, right?"

When I look at him, I know he can read it all over my face. And by the look on his face, he hadn't known that I felt the way I do.

"Come here," he says as he sits on the side of the bed and pulls me next to him. "Tell me you don't think that."

The way he says his words almost make me feel stupid. Like somehow I don't understand, but I do.

When I don't speak, he says, "Babe, there is nothing you could have possibly done to deserve that."

My throat begins to tighten when the tears come, and I begin to get upset at myself for showing this weakness. I shift away from Ryan and begin choking back breaths to stop the crying, which is actually making it worse. He pulls me back to him, but I keep my head turned away.

"Shit, babe. I had no idea this is how you felt."

My voice trembles when I say, "Please, don't."

"I need you to talk to me about this. You have it all wrong. What that guy did was fucked up, babe, and you didn't do shit to deserve what he did to you."

I don't even bother trying to stifle the tears, and I'm pissed that I can't hold myself together. I yell at Ryan through my cries, "You don't get it, Ryan! What I did was stupid, and I completely led him on. It wasn't right, and I knew it, but I did it anyway."

"What the fuck could you have possibly done, because I know you, Candace, and I know you couldn't have led him on that much. But that shit doesn't even matter because you could've stripped down in front of him, and you still didn't deserved to be raped."

"Don't say that fucking word, Ryan!" I sob out and then begin crying uncontrollably.

He pulls me into his arms and begins apologizing when I lose control and tell him, "I didn't even really like him, but I was stupid and lonely, so I would let him kiss me, knowing that I didn't like him. And I fucking hate my mother for this, because if it wasn't for her being such a bitch, I never would have gone out with him."

Ryan tries to get me to stop, but I continue. "You just don't get it. I did lead him on, and I pissed him off. I never should've acted like that. I should've just been honest."

"This isn't your fault," he says sternly, and I snap back, "Yes, it is!"

Not releasing his hold on me, he says again, "It isn't your fault, Candace."

Turning into him, I fist his shirt in my hands and cry, "But it is."

He doesn't say anything else. We wind up lying down in bed for a while until I calm down. We lie face to face, and with my eyes closed, I finally speak. "It's been seven months, Ryan."

"I know, babe."

"I just want it to go away."

"I know. But it's never going to get easier if you keep blaming yourself. It kills me that you feel this way. It fuckin' kills me that I can't take this away from you."

I close my eyes for a while, and when I feel myself start to drift, I ask, "Can't we stay another night?"

"Anything you want."

chapter thirty-five

ON THE DRIVE back to Seattle, Ryan suggests that we talk to Jared to see about changing the tattoo. He thinks that it will help if I don't have to look at the heart every day just to be constantly reminded about everything, give the tattoo a new association.

I hold Ryan's hand the whole drive home, feeling like I need him close. I hate that he saw me so weak when I try to be so strong. I push myself so much with him, and then last night, I fell apart. I know he loves me regardless because he has never wavered, but I want to prove to him that I'm not this sad, pathetic girl, but I'm as fierce as he believes.

When we get back to my house, he carries my bags in for me. Since we didn't come back yesterday like we had planned, Ryan has to go into work tonight. Feeling a little needy, I tell him I don't want him to go.

"Baby, I have to. It's Saturday night, and I've been gone all week."

I fold myself into his arms and stay quiet.

"Come with me," he says, and when I look up at him, I ask hesitantly, "What?"

"You don't even have to be around everyone. Stay with me in my office."

Knowing how he just saw me last night, I know what I need to say.

"Okay."

He's right; I can just be with him and not around all those other people. I went there the other week, and I was fine. I can do this. I *need* to do this.

"Really?" The stunned look on his face tells me he wasn't expecting the response I just gave him. The look makes me smile, and I'm glad I don't have to be alone tonight.

"Just park in the front, okay?"

"Of course. You'll finally get to hear Mark play."

"Oh. I didn't even think about that. Could you do me a favor?"

"Sure."

"They've been kinda embarrassing me lately with . . . things. Um . . . could you just text them or something and tell them to not make a big deal about it."

Smiling at me, he holds my face and kisses me hard with intent. Keeping his hold on me, I let him control the connection and when it's broken, he says, "I love you so much. You're always surprising me."

As we walk into Blur, Ryan has a firm grip on my hand. When I was here the last time, it was empty, but tonight it's packed. I never expected this many people to be here.

"Where's Max?!" Ryan shouts to someone I can't see. I feel really overwhelmed with the amount of people in here, all of whom tower over me. I wrap my free arm around the arm that is holding my hand, and hold tightly onto him

"Right here, boss," a low voice calls from behind us. Turning around, I come face to face with an extremely large man with a shaved head wearing a black shirt that reads 'BLUR' in white.

Ryan shouts over the noise, "Max, hey, this is Candace."

Max looks down at me, and the warm smile that covers his face doesn't really match his overwhelming appearance. Whereas Ryan is muscular with long, strong, athletic cuts, Max is big, bulky, and very intimidating, but he has a soft smile.

"Nice to finally meet you," he says and shakes my hand.

"Nice to meet you, Max," I have to practically yell.

"You want to help us get upstairs?" Ryan says.

Probably noticing the tension written all over my face, Max says to me, "Not good with crowds?"

I shake my head, and he puts his arm around me, tucking me tightly to him with Ryan still holding my hand on my opposite side as he pushes his way through everyone. Feeling a bit uncomfortable with the closeness of being in Max's hold, I cling myself tighter to Ryan. He looks down at me, and all I know to do is give him a slight shake of my head, and by the look in his eyes, I know he understands what I'm trying to tell him. When we get to the back stairs, Ryan tells Max, "Thanks, man."

"No problem, boss. Let me know when you guys are ready to come down, okay?"

"Yeah."

We walk up the stairs and when we get into his office, he asks, "You okay?"

I nod my head, when he assures me, "Max is a good guy. I've known him for years."

"It's just uncomfortable," I say.

Walking us around his desk, he pulls me down on his lap when he sits in the chair.

"Is it always this busy?" I ask.

"On Fridays and Saturdays, yeah." When his cell buzzes, he pulls it out of his pocket and says, "Mark and Jase just got here." Setting it down on his desk, he tells me, "I love that you're here," and then kisses my shoulder.

When there is a knock on the door, Ryan says, "Come in."

"Hey, guys," Jase says as he walks in. When he demands a hug, I get up off of Ryan's lap and walk over to him.

He folds his arms around me and leans in close to my ear, whispering, "I'm proud of you."

I sigh and squeeze my arms a bit tighter around him. Pulling back, I ask, "Where's Mark?"

"Downstairs. He said he'd find you before the band goes on."

"Oh, okay."

"Are you coming down to watch?"

"I . . . well, Ryan has some work to do, so I was just going to stay up here."

Jase tilts his head and shakes it.

"What?"

"Candace, at least go down for a couple songs."

"Did you see how many people are down there?"

"Yeah, sweetie. The same amount that are always here, and nothing has ever happened."

Looking over at Ryan, he shrugs his shoulders in agreement, and says, "I'll have Max stay with you."

I flop down on one of the chairs in front of Ryan's desk and think for a moment before saying, "I don't want everyone touching me."

"If Max is with us, trust me, you'll have breathing room."

"He's right," Ryan assures.

I take a moment before saying, "All right."

Ryan smiles at me as he picks up the phone and pushes some buttons before saying, "Hey, Mel, send Max up to my office."

I turn around when the door opens and Mark bounds in excitedly. "Hell, I thought it was a lie. I can't believe you're here."

"Tone that shit down," Ryan says to him as I stand up and give Mark a hug.

"I just wanted to see you before I go on. You coming down?"

"Yeah."

"Awesome. Well, I gotta go. Love that you came." He leans down, kisses my forehead, and then heads out at the same time as Max walks in.

"Hey, Max, Candace is going down with Jase. I don't want you to leave her side, got it?"

"What about the door?"

"I'll get Chase to take care of it." Ryan gets up from his seat and walks over to me. "You want me to come down with you?"

"No, it's fine. I haven't talked to Jase all week, so . . ."

"Are you okay with Max?"

"Yeah. It'll be fine." Even though it makes me uncomfortable, I know Ryan is protective over me and wouldn't leave me with anyone that's less than completely trustworthy.

"Okay. Let me take care of a few things, and I'll come down in a bit."

Nodding my head at him, he leans down to kiss me. When we walk out into the hall, Ryan calls for Max to come back to his office.

"Stay here, I'll be right back," he tells me and then walks into Ryan's office and shuts the door. It's only a short minute when he walks back out and leads me back downstairs into the throngs of people. Holding me safely under his arm, he moves us across the busy room, and I see him nod his head at some people who are sitting at a table. They quickly grab their drinks and free up the seats for us.

"Shit, Max, why have you never helped me out like that before?" Jase jokes.

"Because you're not the boss' girlfriend," he responds with a condescending kiss in the air.

I laugh at Max as he sits down next to me, and Jase leaves to go to the bar and grab some drinks.

"So how long have you worked here?" I ask.

"About three years. Ryan and I go to the same gym, so we were friends before he hired me."

"Here we go," Jase says when he returns with a bucket of beers. Popping the top for me, he hands me a bottle.

Max sits silently beside me as Jase and I start talking about this past week. I tell him everything that we did, and we talk a little about Donna when Mark's band takes the stage. When they start playing, I am impressed with their sound. It reminds me a lot of the Silversun Pickups.

"They're really good," I yell over at Jase.

"Yeah, I know. I knew you'd like them," he yells back.

We continue to sit there and drink our beers while listening to the band. I can't believe it took me so long to come here. I feel happy and relaxed being here with Jase and finally getting to hear one of my closest friends play. The room is chaotic and noisy and I have no concept of time, but when I feel Ryan's arms wrap around my waist from behind, I know I've been down here for a while.

He nuzzles my neck and gives me a nip before saying, "You having fun?"

"Yeah. I had no idea how good they were."

"They've really been bringing in the crowds since they started playing here. Been trying to figure shit out because they aren't sure if they are still going to play after this summer. A couple of the guys are graduating with Mark, so we'll see."

A girl in a tight black tank top with the word 'BLUR' written across her chest, like Max's, approaches the table with a beverage tray in her hands.

She sets the tray on the table, and while she is placing our empty bottles on it, she says, "So this is the girl that finally took you off the market," while looking at me. She doesn't give my stomach a chance to knot up when she gives me a warm smile. "I'm Mel." She reaches over to shake my hand and continues, "It's great to finally put a face to the name. Ryan never shuts up about you."

She laughs as she rushes away, not giving Ryan a chance to say anything.

He leans down to my ear and tells me, "She's worked here for years, you'll like her."

When I give him a side stare, he says, "Don't worry, she's married."

I shake my head and turn my attention back to the stage as I lean back in Ryan's arms.

It feels good to finally be here in Ryan's world. It's always felt weird to me to not be involved in such a big part of his life. I guess it must be the same way he felt about never seeing me dance. Finally being able to link these two missing pieces, I feel more connected to who he is.

For the past several weeks, Ryan has been good with me only staying with him a few nights a week, and although he complains, I know he understands. Kimber and I still don't really talk that much, but she has asked about Ryan and I have opened up to her a little about him. She is still dating Seth, even though she says it's not too serious. She told me he was accepted into graduate school at UCLA, so there is no reason for her to get too attached. She's convincing when she says that they are both just having fun together at this point.

I talked to Roxy the other day about changing my tattoo. She wanted to know why I wasn't happy with it, so I just told her that I wanted it to be more of a reflection of who I am now. She didn't really understand, and of course, I didn't expect her to. But I came to the decision to simply have the heart shaded in. I didn't want to add to it to make it any larger than what it already is. I like that it's tiny. I didn't realize until I fell in love with Ryan how full my heart could actually be, so having the empty heart on my hip filled in only makes sense. Ryan loved that idea and went with me yesterday to get it done.

I was a nervous wreck, the same as I was when I first got it. Jared was quick, and it didn't hurt too bad. Ryan held my hand through the short process, and now I have a solid black heart instead of the empty outline. Even though it's the same, it feels very different to me. I love Ryan for helping me transform something that was filled with such bad memories into something that now makes me happy when I look at it. I think of him when I see it, and I love that he was able to give that to me.

While I was going through my drawers and getting rid of old clothes,

I ran across Detective Patterson's card again. I held it in my hands and thought about how I first met Jack and how quickly it spun out of control. I'm not even sure if too much time has passed to call. Not that I would call. I don't really know what to do about it all. I have always just assumed I would leave it be and move on.

But then the thought crept into my head that if he did that to me, then he has the potential to do it to someone else. What if he already has done it to someone else? What if I wasn't the first? What if there is a girl out there just like me? I wondered if he was seeing anyone; if he had a girlfriend now. She has the right to know what kind of guy she's with. But the thought of having people know what happened to me, having to talk about it, I'm terrified it could break me. Even though Ryan assures me that I did nothing wrong, I still feel responsible for sending Jack over the edge and leading him on.

After a while, I give up on thinking too much about it all and slip the card back into my sock drawer. If I was going to do anything about it, I should have done it already. I need to just let it go, but for some reason, I can't bring myself to throw the card away.

chapter thirty-six

RYAN AND I jog up the steps of my house after our morning run. It's still early out, and the sun is just starting to rise behind the grey clouds that blanket the city. Once inside, we each grab a bottle of water and go back to my room so I can clean up.

Shutting the door, he walks up behind me and starts planting kisses on the back of my neck. I reach up and wrap my hand behind his damp neck. His kisses make me shiver, and he grazes his lips over my ear and says, "I want you in your bed."

It may sound weird, but we haven't ever had sex in my bed, but then again, Ryan rarely spends the night here with me and the few times that he has, Kimber was home, and it made me feel uncomfortable with her in the next room. But she is gone this morning, and the way his kisses are affecting me, I don't want to say no.

Turning around in his arms, I start tugging up his shirt. He reaches over his head and pulls it off at the same time I take mine off. We stumble over to the bed and when we collapse on it, we are a tangled mess, fumbling to get each other's clothes off. Running my lips down his neck and along his broad shoulders, I taste the salt on his skin. I knot my fingers in his sweaty hair and pull him down on me.

My body bows into his when he grinds his hips into me, pushing himself deep inside me, and we begin to move together. Reaching behind my back, he pulls us onto our sides, and I wrap my leg around his waist pulling him closer to me. We lie face-to-face, flushed and panting, as he grips tightly onto my thigh.

We don't speak, and with our foreheads connected, we keep our eyes locked while he takes his time with me. Never rushing. Never in a hurry.

I'm alone for the day while Ryan is at work. Tonight, Blur is hosting a concert for one of Gavin's bands and they are expecting a huge turnout. I agreed to go since Mark and Jase will also be there. My car is still over at Ryan's house from last night. When we left for our run this morning and found ourselves here, I told him I didn't need to go back for my car. I would just stay here for the day.

It's nearing the end of April, and I decide I should start sorting through my belongings and slowly start packing. I still don't know where I'm going, but with graduation a little over a month away, I need to start getting organized. New York has always been my dream, but I know I'll never be able to leave Ryan behind—I'll never *want* to leave him. Plus, Seattle has produced many world-renowned dancers and choreographers. Pacific Northwest Ballet is here in Seattle and is internationally recognized as one of the elite. Even if they're not interested in me, I know if I stay here, I can still have a successful career.

After I pack up a box of books, I start thinking more and more about Ryan and how I never thought I would have what I found with him. Jack destroyed everything in me, and to be able to trust someone again is something I didn't think would ever be possible. Is it selfish of me to not want to save someone else from that theft? I know that it has probably been too long, but maybe I should just call and get some information on what could be done. Hell, for all I know, I could even remain anonymous. But, I will never know if I don't call.

Opening the top drawer of my dresser, I fish out the card that I was given now eight months ago. I keep telling myself that it's just a phone call; I just want to ask some questions.

Picking up my cell, I swipe the screen and with nervous fingers dial the number while my heart beats at an insanely rapid rate. After several rings, I am half relieved when I get the detective's voicemail. I leave him a quick message with my name and number and set the phone back down. All of a sudden I consider the possibility of Jack finding out. If I did do anything, would he come after me? Would he try and hurt me? I resolve that it's probably best if I don't say anything. I shouldn't be calling and talking to Detective Patterson. I really do need to move on and just let it be.

"Babe, you ready?"

"Yeah, I just need to grab my jacket," I say as I walk back into my closet.

"So, it's going to be busy. A lot busier than the past few times you've been. You sure you're okay with that?"

"I mean, if it's too much then I can always go upstairs until you're ready to leave."

He takes my hand and laces his fingers through mine, pulling me to him, and suggests, "Or we could just stay here and break in your bed a bit more," as he nuzzles my neck.

I smile at the memory of being with him this morning and give him a kiss. "I think we should go now and break in the bed later."

Nipping my lip, he walks us out to his jeep.

When we pull up in front of the bar, there is a line wrapped around the building. Max spots us from the door and is standing next to me when we walk in. The music blasts through the bar as Ryan and Max lead me to the side of the bar that curves around to the back wall. We told Mark and Jase to meet us here and see them waiting for us. When we approach them, Gavin and several of Ryan's friends are there as well. Jase orders me two shots, and I feel relaxed over in the corner with our group of friends. We all drink and laugh and eventually Mel comes by to chat with me a bit while the guys are busy talking about things I couldn't care less about.

Mel has always been really sweet to me. She's a little older than I am and reminds me a lot of Roxy. Her husband is a drummer for a band that just got signed to a label in L.A. I've only met him once when he was in town during a break in recording his album. She decided to stay here in Seattle so that she could have the support of her family instead of being alone in L.A. where she doesn't know anyone. Personally, I think she isn't too happy in her marriage and that's why she stayed.

A few hours later, the band returns to the stage after taking a short break and begin to play a cover of the Imagine Dragons' 'Radioactive.' Ryan tells me he needs to run upstairs to grab some inventory sheets to give Mel before we leave. Holding my hand tightly, he tries to lead us across the bar. The door has been busy, so Max is back at his post outside.

Bumping shoulders through the crowd, Ryan wraps his arm around me and we slowly walk through the swarm of people. I stumble a little when I suddenly spot Kimber out of the corner of my eye. I had no idea she was even here. My body jerks and freezes when I think I'm seeing things. Running his nose along some girl's neck, when he turns his head back to the stage, I know I'm not losing it. I see Jack's face. My vision begins to tunnel as panic shrieks through me, and I start tugging in the opposite direction that Ryan is going, pulling back against his arm that is around me. My eyes are locked on Jack, who doesn't see me from across the room.

"What are you doing?" Ryan hollers over the crowd as I keep stumbling back. When he shifts his body, I fall out of his hold and tumble onto the floor.

In shock and terror, I keep trying to shuffle back when Ryan picks me up. He turns to see what I'm staring at and looks back at me as I attempt to turn my back and run. He grabs me around the waist, not letting me escape and leans over my shoulder, yelling over the music, "Babe, what's wrong?"

Trying to peel his grip from me, all I can do is shout, "It's Jack!"

"Who?"

"Get me out of here!" I scream in a panic, jerking to get out of his grip. "I can't breathe! Get me out of here!"

Tucking me tightly against him, he moves us quickly to the door, yelling at Jase to follow, but Jase is too far away.

When we finally make it outside, my breathing is labored and my whole body is shaking. I run to Ryan's car, wanting to get as far away as I can from Jack. Aside from my dreams, I haven't seen him since that night.

"Babe, what the fuck happened in there? Who the fuck did you see?"

Leaning my back against his jeep, I grip onto Ryan's shirt as I start to cry and gasp for breath.

"Jack is in there. We have to leave."

"Who's Jack?"

"Him! Jack is . . ." I'm cut off when I hear Jase holler my name as he runs toward me, and I'm sobbing hysterically.

"Candace, what happened?"

All I can say between my panting breaths and tears is, "Jack's inside."

"Oh, shit!"

"Who the fuck is Jack?!" Ryan yells and Jase tells him, "The guy that attacked her."

Ryan snaps his head to me, grabs my shoulders, and says in a low stern voice, "Get in the car. Now." He reaches in his pocket and hands his keys to Jase and yells, "Get her in the fucking car!" And then he takes off back to the bar while I sob uncontrollably.

"What's going on?" I hear Mark ask Ryan as they pass each other. Ryan says nothing as he goes through the door.

Jase turns around and yells at Mark to go in after him.

"What the hell is going on?" he asks.

"Jase, he'll kill him," I cry out and he turns back to Mark. "Jack is in there! Ryan's gonna fuckin' kill him!"

"Shit!" Mark yells as he starts to run back in, and I see Max following right behind.

"Jase, you have to go get him!"

"Sweetie, get in the car," he says softly.

"What?! No!" I thrash in his arms and wail, when he wraps his arms over mine, locking them down and lifts me up into the jeep. He stands outside the car with the door open, and I lower my head to my knees and cry. Rubbing my back, he assures me that Mark's going to get him.

My mind is racing, and I can't seem to focus on anything in particular aside from what Ryan is doing inside. I cry as Jase keeps reassuring me and trying to calm me down. When I hear Ryan's voice, I sit up and watch him as he walks over. His hands are covered in blood, and blood is splattered across his face. When he walks past Jase, he quietly demands, "Keys."

Jase hands them over and quickly leans in to kiss me and says, "Call me."

I nod as he closes my door, and I turn to look at Ryan as he gets in the car. He doesn't say anything and neither do I. He starts the car and begins to drive. His jaw is clenched hard, and his breaths are slow and heavy. Ryan's grip is tight on the steering wheel, and his knuckles are cut open and covered in blood.

Neither one of us speaks the whole drive to his loft. His breathing has slowed and softened by the time he shuts off the car. My tears haven't stopped flowing. Getting out, he walks in front of the jeep to my side, opening my door. When I shift myself to face him, he drops his head to my lap and grabs onto my hips. Weaving my hands through his hair, I fist them closed and lean my body over his. I know he's crying when I feel his back begin to heave.

I let go of his hair when he pulls back. The pain in his eyes is almost unbearable. Wiping my thumbs across his cheeks, I brush the tears away from his bloody face. I look over him, and I know it has to be Jack's blood because Ryan doesn't have a scratch on him. I don't ask what happened because I don't think it really matters.

He takes my hand and walks me inside and up to his room. While he's in the shower, I grab my purse and take my sleeping pill. I can't stop crying as I change into a pair of his boxers and a t-shirt and wait for him in bed. He walks out with a towel slung around his waist and goes to throw on his boxers. Getting into bed, he scoops me in his arms as I continue to cry.

All I can see is Jack. He's there when I close my eyes; he's there when they're open, staring into the darkness of the room. I cry because I don't know how to get him out of my mind. I just need to be close to Ryan, to feel safe and to know everything will be fine.

I lay my hand on his cheek and turn him to me. Pressing my lips against his, I pull back for a moment and whisper, "Make love to me," before kissing him again.

"Baby, you're crying."

"I don't care." I bring him to me and begin running my kisses down his neck. Ryan doesn't move, so I pull away and look at him. "Kiss me."

"Candace, you're upset."

"I need to be close to you right now. I want to get him out of my head, and you're the only one who can do that for me."

He rolls on top of me and lets out a sigh, resting his head against mine. "Are you sure, babe?"

"Yes," I say through the tears that won't stop.

I cling tightly to him as he slips his hand under my shirt and squeezes my breast while kissing my neck. I reach down and tug on his boxers, just wanting them off.

"Candace."

"Please, Ryan."

He pulls down his boxers, and I lift my hips so that he can remove mine. I quickly pull off my top, and when he slides into me, I close my eyes, letting the tears seep out. Ryan has a thing about watching me when we make love, but tonight, he never asks me to open my eyes. I cling to his body as he pushes into me unlike any time before. Without words, he continues to thrust inside of me until we both find our release.

When he rolls off of me, he pulls me snug against him, and he reaches down to grab my hand, holding it tightly. He never lets go of it, and I suddenly feel bad for using him like I just did when he's also so upset.

"I'm so sorry. I shouldn't have done that."

"Don't be. You take whatever you need from me."

chapter thirty-seven

THE RINGING OF my phone wakes me up, and I climb out of bed to dig it out of my purse. Not wanting to wake Ryan, I step out into the hall, closing the door softly behind me. I don't recognize the number, so I answer with a hesitant, "Hello?"

"Is this Candace Parker?" a man's voice asks.

"Yes. Who is this?"

"Detective Patterson, ma'am. I got your message and was returning your call. How can I help you?"

The anxiety slowly builds in my stomach as I'm caught off guard by the phone call, especially since last night's events. A flash of the girl's face that Jack was with crosses my mind, and I decide that maybe this is what I need to do.

"Oh, yeah. I . . . umm, I'm not quite sure where to begin."

"It's okay. Did you have a specific question you wanted to ask me?"

I walk further down the hall and sit down at the top of the stairs. "I guess I was just curious about what would happen if I wanted to press charges; if it was too late . . . or . . ."

"Well, I have your file here. It seems the hospital went ahead and had your rape kit sent over to the criminal lab where it is being stored. That, along with the eye-witness report, well, you have a solid case."

"Umm, so there was someone there? I don't remember . . ."

"Yes, ma'am. Let me pull up his statement." It takes a few seconds before he continues, "Okay, according to his statement, he heard screaming in the alley. When he came into view, you were knocked unconscious. He was the one who called 911 and waited with you until the ambulance arrived."

My hands begin to tremble as I think about someone being there with me. It makes me almost feel embarrassed just thinking about someone seeing me like that—beaten and naked. That night begins to replay in my head: the screaming, the weight of him on top of me, his grunting, watching his fist before he slammed it into my face.

"Umm . . ." I mumble out in a shaky voice and wipe away a few tears that are now rolling down my cheeks. "Do you know who? I mean . . ."

"Give me one second." I hear him tapping the computer keys when he continues, "Last name is Campbell. Ryan Campbell. Seems he owns the building where this happened."

Suddenly the air is sucked out of me, and the sensation of pinpricks overtakes my body as I turn cold.

"Ma'am?"

The phone slides out of my trembling hand and tumbles down the wooden stairs. I'm frozen and I'm shocked. *Ryan?* I begin to wonder who the man is in the other room; the man I trust. *Why didn't he ever tell me? Was this all a game to him?* My stomach churns, and I feel like I'm going to be sick. How could he lie to me, deceive me?

I start taking deep breaths as I reach my hand up, grab onto the banister, and pull myself onto my wobbly legs. I need to get out of here.

Gently easing the door open, I quietly pad across the room and pick up my purse. I look down at Ryan, who is still sleeping, and I feel pieces of my heart crumbling and falling hard into the pit of my stomach. I'm so embarrassed. No wonder he was so patient with me; he knew all along. *How could I be so stupid? How could I have let my walls down like this?*

I fumble with the necklace around my neck, and suddenly, everything feels like a lie. If he truly ever thought I was fierce, it was just a product of his deceit. I clench the bar of the necklace and yank on it, breaking the delicate chain. I look down at the engraving, and I feel like an idiot for allowing another man to strip me bare.

When the tears begin to fall, I set the necklace on the nightstand, and I turn my back and leave. Quickly running down the stairs and out the door, I run to my car as fast as I can and throw it into reverse. All the wounds I've tried so desperately to mend are slowly starting to rip open as I start putting together all the pieces. The way he looked at me the first time he walked into the coffee shop. He knew me. He never pushed me because he knew exactly who I was. It was all a lie. It was all a sick game, and I was the fool who fell in love. *What the fuck is wrong with me?*

As soon as I get home, I run into my room and shut the door behind me. Still trying to make sense of everything, I fall onto the bed and cry. I cry for a long time. I've never felt so hollow, so completely hopeless. When I can move, I roll over and grab my pillow to bury my head in it while I sob. Gasping for breath, I smell the remnants of his scent that linger on my pillow. I jump out of the bed and frantically start ripping the covers and sheets off, slinging them across the room.

"Candace?"

Startled, I turn to see Ryan walking into my room and closing the door behind him.

"Get out," I seethe.

"Babe, what's going on?"

Holding my arms out in front of me, I tell him, "Stay away from me."

His brows are knitted together as he looks at me in confusion. "Baby, what happened?"

I begin to cry harder and back myself against the wall. "You know exactly what happened. You know exactly who I am!"

Standing in the middle of my room, he doesn't say a word as his face slowly turns to shock, and I know he knows exactly what I mean.

"How could you?!" I scream.

Shaking his head, he says, "Babe, let me explain."

"Explain what?! That you've been lying to me this whole time? That you've just been using me? Why?!"

"No! It's not like that. I didn't know."

"How could you not know? God, I'm so fucking stupid."

"I didn't know when I first met you. I didn't know until I saw your tattoo."

"What?!"

"Babe, please let me explain."

"Get out!"

When he doesn't move, I scream, "Get the fuck out! I don't ever want to see you again." My legs can no longer support me, and I fall to my knees, sobbing—breaking.

"Just leave me alone."

"I'm not leaving," he says as he moves and kneels down in front of me.

"I fuckin' hate you. You made me fall in love with you, and it was all a goddamn lie."

"God, Candace. Please let me explain."

When he reaches out to touch me, I snap. "Get out! Get the fuck out!"

He jerks around when Kimber bursts through the door. Our eyes meet, and she turns to Ryan and demands, "Get the fuck out and away from her before I call the cops."

He turns back to me and pleads, "Babe, please. I love you so fuckin' much. Let me explain. Don't do this."

"I didn't do shit, Ryan!" Covering my face with my hands, I wail and scream, "Just go. It's over!"

"I'm serious. After the shit from last night, you better get the fuck away from her and leave. Now!"

All I hear through my cries is Ryan's voice echoing when he screams, "Fuuuck!" from across the house and then the slamming of the door as he leaves.

I fall into Kimber's arms when she rushes down to her knees in front of me. She holds me in her arms as I cry harder and harder. It's been so long since Kimber has hugged me, and her touch is almost too much for me. Ryan just took everything, and I feel like dust, like at any second I could be blown away into nothing. I grasp tightly to Kimber, desperate for her. I can't lie to her; I need her too much.

"I'm so sorry. I'm so sorry that I've been lying to you."

"Candace—"

I cut her off and let everything out. Everything I've been hiding.

"I didn't want to lie to you. I love you, but I was scared. I was scared you would tell someone, and I was afraid to trust you."

"Sweetie—"

"Jack raped me. That night of the party, he raped me. And I stayed with Jase because I didn't want you to know. I didn't want anyone to know, and I was scared you would go to Jack and do something stupid. So I hid from you. I lied, and I hurt you. I lost my best friend and I'm so sorry."

"Candace, you didn't lose me," she says as she begins to cry. "I've always been here."

"I'm so sorry."

Kimber doesn't say anything as we both cry. I don't know how long we are on the floor, but when exhaustion hits, I lean my head back against the wall and release a hard sigh. When I look back at Kimber, I apologize again.

"Let's get off the floor, okay?" she says and then stands and helps pull me up. We walk out to the living room, and I sit on the couch as Kimber gets us some water. Sitting down next to me she asks, "Candace, what happened?"

"With Jack or Ryan?"

"Jack."

"He got pissed at me that I led him on and when I ran from him, he . . ." I don't finish my thought, because I can't, and I know I don't need to. "I was taken to the hospital, and I went home with Jase. I couldn't come back here because Jack had banged up my face pretty bad."

"Fucker," she hisses.

"Kimber, you can't say anything."

"Ryan beat the shit out of him last night."

"I know, I was there. That's Ryan's bar, he owns it."

"Is that why you were fighting? I don't understand."

Shaking my head, I start to cry again. "God, it's so messed up."

"Candace, I know you didn't think you could, but you can trust me. I love you."

"The thing with Jack happened in the back lot of Ryan's bar. I didn't know it, and I didn't know him when we met. But I spoke with the detective this morning, and he told me that Ryan had witnessed it." Hanging my head down, I struggle to get my words out. "I don't know what to think. He knew me all along and never said anything. God, I broke down like an idiot and told him what had happened to me and he already knew."

"That's fucked up," she says as she hugs me.

"I fell in love with him. How could he make me fall in love with him? I feel so stupid."

"You're not stupid. He lied to you. He's a dick face."

I can't help but chuckle through my tears at her words. I've missed her words so much.

"I wish I would have known," she tells me. "I wish I could have been there for you. I had no idea. I thought you were mad at me, and I couldn't figure it out. I couldn't figure any of it out, so I just gave up trying. Then I just got mad at you."

"I'm sorry."

"I don't know what to do. I mean, last night was the first time I've hung out with Jack, but he's one of Seth's friends. They're frat brothers and all."

"You can't say anything. Please, Kimber."

"I won't. I promise. I just don't know what to do."

"I don't know."

"Are you pressing charges?"

"No."

"Why were you talking to a detective?"

"He was at the hospital. He gave me his card. Jase had tried a couple times to get me to call him, but I didn't. I came across it the other day when I was starting to pack my room and I . . . I don't know, I guess I wanted to see what my options were. I don't know."

"You can't let him get away with this, Candace. He has a girlfriend, you know?"

"Kimber, I just can't. This year has been a nightmare, a never-ending nightmare, for me. I thought I was stronger. I thought Ryan was real. I don't know, Kimber. I feel so lost. More lost than before."

There's a knock on the door and Kimber gets up to answer it.

"Hey, Jase," she says as he walks into the house and straight towards me.

"I've been trying to call you, sweetie. What happened?"

I must have forgotten my phone when I rushed out of Ryan's place.

"He lied to me."

Sitting down next to me, he asks, "What do you mean 'he lied?'"

I start to cry and he takes my hand. "Remember when the detective told us there was a witness to what happened?"

"Yeah."

"It was Ryan. Jase, he saw it and never told me."

Kimber sits down on the other side of me as I lean into Jase's arms, and I hear Kimber tell Jase that I told her everything. And for the first time in a long time, the three of us hold each other. I'm so hurt and so lost, but at the same time, I feel like I'm finally back with the people who I have always considered my family.

When Jase pulls back, he wants to know how I found out, so I tell him about calling Detective Patterson and everything that he said.

"What did you say to Ryan?"

With a new slew of tears breaking free, I say, "I ended it. Jase, I don't know what to do. I just don't know what to do. How could he do this to me?"

"I don't know, sweetie."

"You're gonna have to go over to his place. All my things are there and my phone. I left it all there."

"Don't worry about any of that. Jase will take care of it," Kimber assures me.

"I'll go over there when I leave here. But I don't want to leave you like this."

I lie down, rest my head in Jase's lap, and let him console me. I listen to him and Kimber talk about everything while Jase answers all of her questions. I don't say anything. I just lie there until the tears dry up and I have nothing left in me. I never thought I could feel as low as I do right now. I didn't think it was possible, but I feel like the depths of my despair can't sink any lower. If ever I wanted to lose myself and disappear, it's right now. I'm so empty and nothing Jase or Kimber can do or say could take away the stabbing pain inside me.

When Jase leaves, Kimber takes me into her room, and I crawl into her bed. I tell her I can smell Ryan on my sheets, and she goes into my room, grabs all of my bedding, and tosses a load into the washer. When she comes back, she lies down with me like we used to do and pulls the sheets over us, hugging me from behind. I've missed this, having her, my best friend, my sister.

chapter thirty-eight

THESE PAST TWO weeks have been such a daze. I'm miserable. I can't sleep. I can't eat. I try to keep myself consumed with school, but I can't even focus. Ryan calls me every day, and each time he does, it's just a reminder of how alone I am. I can't even read his texts. I delete them as soon as they come through. When Jase went over there to get my belongings last week, he came back and suggested that I talk to Ryan. But I know there is nothing he could possibly say to lessen this pain. I gave him everything I had to give. I bared it all to him, and the whole time he was lying to me. I feel so betrayed and so used. And the most sickening part of it all is that I still love him. I hate myself for that. I don't know what's wrong with me; I don't understand how I can still feel this way about him after everything.

Mark and Jase still talk to him and see him. I told them that I understand. After all, Mark's band plays at his bar. I can't expect them to not be his friend. But I've been keeping my distance from them because I can't help but feel hurt at the same time.

When Roxy kept asking about Ryan and why she hadn't seen him around, I just didn't have the energy to deal with it, so I quit. I know it was a total overreaction, but all I really want to do is escape from everything. I'm trying hard to be strong and put the pieces back together, but Ryan didn't leave me with pieces—he left me with ashes.

Since I no longer have anything aside from dance to distract me on the weekends, I'm home alone most of the time. Kimber is at her parents' this weekend. She wanted me to come with her, but just the thought of pretending to be happy around her family was enough to exhaust me. Jase called earlier to try and get me out of the house, but I told him I wasn't feeling well. I know he didn't believe me, but I don't care.

He's worried that I'm not taking care of myself, and I guess he should be. I know I look awful. It's only been two weeks and my clothes are all loose on me, but I can't rid my stomach of the knots that consume it. Ms. Emerson has been riding my ass again, and I know I need to pull it together and quick because our production is a mere two weeks away.

When the doorbell rings, I drag myself to the door. I look out the living room window, and I can't swallow against the lump in my throat when I see Ryan's black Rubicon. Leaning my head against the door, I say, "Go away."

"You won't return any of my calls, babe. Please, let me talk to you."

I turn away and start walking back to my room when I hear a key slide into the lock and then the door opening.

Snapping back to face the door, I yell, "What are you doing?!"

"Jase gave me a key."

"Ass," I mumble under my breath. "Ryan, please go. I don't want to talk."

"I can't *not* talk to you. It's killing me."

"It's killing *you?* What about me?" I can barely get the words out over the sob that starts to threaten. "Ryan, I can't do this. I can't even look at you. Please, just go."

"I can't stand to see you like this."

"Then go! I will do almost anything to make you leave."

"Just let me talk to you. Please, babe, just let me talk."

"Fine, say whatever you need to say, then leave me alone."

He motions for me to sit on the couch and when I do, he sits next to me. I can't control the tears that free fall down my cheeks. Seeing his face and being next to him is too much for me. If I had never loved him so much, then he never would have had the power to destroy me like he did. More than anything, I want to cling to him, but I don't. I know I can't ever allow anyone to get that close to me again. I can't give another person the power to hurt me like he did.

"I'm worried about you," he says as he looks me in the eyes.

I turn my head so I don't have to look at him. "Don't."

"When was the last time you've eaten?"

"Ryan, don't. Just say what you need to say."

He reaches for my hand, but I pull it away as he says, "I love you. I know you don't believe me, but I do. No one has ever affected me the way you do, babe. I swear to you . . . I swear I didn't know. I didn't, Candace. Not at first." When I hear his voice crack, I look up at him and see the tears that fill his eyes, and I have to look back down.

"When I saw you at the coffee shop I thought it was you. I thought you were *that* girl. But then I kept thinking, 'What are the chances?' I didn't know because you looked so different than from that night. And then I found out that you were friends with Mark. Every time I saw you, I felt myself being drawn to you in a way I've never felt before. I had myself convinced that my head was playing games with me, and I honestly did not think you were that girl. It wasn't until I saw your tattoo when we were in bed. That's when I knew. When I found that girl, I saw her tattoo—*your* tattoo."

"Ryan, please," I whimper, but he doesn't stop.

"When I saw it, I broke. I didn't want you to be her. I had already fallen so hard in love with you and realizing that it was you fuckin' killed me.

Everything started making sense to me. How scared you always were with me when we first met, how afraid you were when I tried to touch you. Everything made sense. But, I didn't know how to tell you. And then you told me you loved me, and I know how hard that was for you. I just couldn't hurt you," he says, now crying.

"But you did. You lied to me. I let you see all the parts of me that weren't pretty, but you knew all along. And when I finally opened up to you, you already knew." Lowering my head into my hands, I cry. I cry hard. "You let me give everything to you. You had to have known that you couldn't hold on to that secret forever. I would've eventually found out, and you still let me fall for you like I did. I feel so stupid and used, like you just felt sorry for me or pitied me."

"I never pitied you, babe. I have only ever loved you. I just didn't want to hurt you."

He reaches out to hold me, but I push him back and stand up from the couch.

"I can't do this. You can't say those things to me."

Standing up and taking a step toward me, he says, "I know I fucked up. I fucked everything up so bad. I know all you wanted was someone you could trust. I wanted to be that for you, and I fucked it all up. But, I didn't know what to say; I was scared. You'll never know how fucking sorry I am."

"I knew better. I knew I shouldn't have let you in like I did. But, I can't see you anymore. You have to stop calling and texting. I need you to just not exist for me because I can't do this. It hurts more than I thought anything possibly could."

"Candace, please."

"Just go."

He doesn't move. He just stands there. A part of me never wants him to move, but I know he needs to. I can hardly bear to see the pain in his eyes and the tears running down his cheeks.

"Please, you have to go. I can't do this," I plead with him.

Looking at me through his tears, he chokes out, "You have to know how much I love you."

"Please, Ryan," I say with closed eyes. I just need him to go because I can't take the excruciating pain any more. My eyes stay closed until I hear the click of the door as it closes behind him. I know I shouldn't, but I can't stop myself from watching him get into his jeep. I feel like I need to scream for him to come back, but I don't. I just let him drive away.

My heart hurts so bad, I swear it feels like I'm dying. I can't take this anymore. I know I can't live like this. I can't do this on my own. I've tried so hard. But I just can't do it anymore.

It's been just over a week since Ryan walked out of my house, and I finally hit my bottom. I finally had to surrender, and I knew I had to stop clinging onto people. I had to stop running to Jase. He would never be able to save me. And I no longer had Ryan to cling to. But even if I did, he wouldn't be able to save me either. I knew it was up to me to pull myself together and get help because all I wanted to do was fade away.

The first time I went to see Dr. Christman was the day after I saw Ryan. We decided that I would see her twice a week. During our first session, I basically told her everything that had happened since August: Jack, Kimber, my parents, Ryan. I told her about how I grew up and why I didn't seek therapy earlier this year when everything was falling apart. I really like Dr. Christman. She's helping me to see that what Jack did wasn't my fault. I still harbor guilt about it, but not as much as I used to. She's helping me learn how to tolerate my emotions and not avoid everything that I consider my triggers, like my fear of crowds or my thoughts of Jack.

Today is our fourth session. When I walk into her office and sit in my usual seat on the couch. "Hello, Candace. How are you feeling since we met earlier this week?"

"Okay, I guess."

"And what does that mean? What's 'okay'?"

"I've been trying to eat better, which I think is good. But, I haven't been sleeping well, so I've been really tired."

"What do you think is keeping you up?"

"It used to be Jack, but lately it's been Ryan. He keeps flashing through my head, and when that happens, I get really upset. I know I need to move on, but it's really hard."

"It's only natural that this will take time. You loved him, and that doesn't go away just because he hurt you. But it sounds like he also helped you. Would you agree with that?"

Shifting on the couch, I say, "I suppose. But, it really just seems like a façade. Like everything I thought he was helping me through wasn't real because the whole thing was a lie."

She flips a page over on her tablet and begins taking notes before asking, "But was it a lie? We know he held onto the secret of who he was to you, but were the feelings a lie?"

"I don't know. I mean . . . they felt real."

"If Ryan would have told you from the beginning who he was, if he was honest about that, do you think you would have let yourself feel what you felt for him?"

Taking in a deep breath and letting it out slowly, I say, "Yes."

"So, was it all a lie then?"

I shake my head and say, "I get what you're saying, but I can't go back."

"I'm not saying go back. There was a betrayal, and you have every right to guard yourself against that, but don't dismiss your feelings as a lie.

He was able to show you that you are capable of loving, and trusting, and having faith."

"I just don't know how to move past him."

She sets her pen and tablet down and leans back in her chair. "Well, that takes time, just like any loss we suffer. What is one thing you think you can do to help that process?"

"I don't know. I guess . . . I guess I need to stop spending so much time thinking about why I can't go back to him and just focus on the fact that I was already with him and it just didn't work. When I think about why I can't go back, it's like I'm trying to convince myself that I shouldn't, when I really need to focus on the fact that it just isn't an option. He's my past, and I need to start focusing on what I'm going to do about my future."

"And what about your future can you focus on?"

"My dancing. I have my performance this weekend, so hopefully offers will start coming in this next week. I need to focus on making New York happen. It's always been my dream."

She picks up her notepad and begins to write as she says, "I think you have a good plan."

We continue on to discuss issues about Jack and some of the paranoia I still feel about him for the rest of the session. After making my follow-up appointment, I stop by the house and grab my dance bag to spend the rest of the day rehearsing and focusing more on the thing I do have control over, which is my career, not Ryan.

When I get home, I decide to start taking more control, like Dr. Christman suggested. I can't keep avoiding situations that make me nervous and uncomfortable. I know I can't keep hiding from my emotions because I'm too scared to deal with them.

I take out my phone, scroll down to Roxy's name, and tap her number. After several rings, she answers.

"Candace, hey."

"Hey Rox, do you have a minute to talk?"

"Hun, I always have time for you. How are you?"

"I'm doing better, actually. I wanted to call and apologize for my behavior and walking out on you. I've been going through some stuff, and I was out of line."

"I've been worried about you. We used to always talk, but I feel like you've somehow gotten lost this year, and I wish I knew how to be a friend to you."

"You are a friend. And I love you. It's been a rough year, but I think I'm getting on the right track. It feels that way, at least."

"That's good to hear."

"But, I was calling because I wanted to know if you've filled my position yet."

"Your position will never be filled."

"So, I can come back?"

"Always, hun."

"Thanks, Rox. Can you get me on the schedule for next week?"

"Of course. Stop by in a couple days, and I'll have the schedule out."

"Great."

"And Candace . . ."

"Yeah?"

"I'm glad you called me. You know you can always call, anytime."

"I do know. Thanks again. I'll stop by later this week."

"Sounds good."

"Okay, bye."

"So, tell me how things have been going?" Dr. Christman asks as she pulls out her notepad.

"I called my boss and got my job back. She put me on the schedule for next week."

"What made you decide to do that?"

"You suggested that I stop avoiding situations that spike my emotions. Work has always been that place for me. It's always been a place I feared Jack walking into."

"What do you normally do when your anxiety peaks at work?"

"I go to the back room and restock."

"And what are you going to do now when you start to feel that way?"

"I know I need to stay out in the shop."

"Just remember that a spike in emotions is okay. They will spike, but they will come down again and you will be okay."

"When I get anxious, I feel that there will be no coming back down. I feel like everything is about to spiral out of control."

"That's very common after the kind of trauma you've been through. It's normal to be afraid of feeling, but whatever you're feeling, you need to understand that those feelings will not be permanent. Instead of running from your feelings, I really would like for you to stay in them. Try not to shut down. Think about your anxiety level, and when it gets high, I want you to see that you're still okay."

I nod my head and say, "I think that doing something like that at work is a good place to start. I'm not alone, and sitting here with you thinking about it, I can rationally say that nothing would happen. That I would be okay."

"Good. And how has your sleep been lately?"

"Restless."

"Are you still on your sleeping pill?" she asks.

"Yes. Honestly, I'm too scared to wean off of them."

"That's okay. You're making progress in other areas, and so we will keep focusing on that before approaching your nightmares."

After the session is over, I head over to Common Grounds to pick up my schedule for next week. When I walk in, I see Roxy behind the counter. She walks around it and comes to give me a hug.

"I'm so glad you decided to come back. I've missed you. I've been stuck working with Sarah, and all she talks about is her stupid dog."

I laugh at her and say, "Thanks. I'm so sorry for—"

Cutting me off she tells me, "Forget it. I'm just glad you're here, hun."

I walk to the back room with her, and she gives me the schedule for next week. It feels good to be back here. Even though Dr. Christman helped me to see that this place is a trigger for my irrational feelings, I feel like this will be a good starting point for me to try to overcome them.

chapter thirty-nine

"SO HOW ARE you and Kimber doing?" Jase asks me as we stand in the long line to buy our caps and gowns for graduation.

"Really good. We've both been busy getting everything wrapped up for graduation. But we spend several evenings a week hanging out."

"So are you excited about tomorrow night?"

"You have no idea. Excited and super nervous," I say as the line slowly moves forward. Tomorrow night is our final production, and I have been living and breathing dance for the past few weeks.

"Well, Mark has been dying to see you dance."

"I wasn't sure if he was going to be able to make it."

"Yeah, Ryan has a new band that alternates Saturday nights."

Looking down to the ground, I am a little caught off guard by the mention of Ryan's name. I know Jase is still friends with him, but he makes a point to not mention him around me.

"Sorry," he says.

I look back up at him and tell him, "It's fine, Jase. I know you're friends."

"So, can I go there?"

Letting out a sigh, I nod my head and he says, "He misses you. He hasn't been the same since."

"Neither have I. But, it's done. It's been almost two months."

"So, that's it?"

"In case you haven't noticed, I've been pretty busy trying to sort my own issues out," I tell him.

"I know you have. And I'm proud of you."

We take a few steps as the line continues to creep forward. "I just need to be alone right now. I realize how much I was clinging to people. I did it with you, and I did it with him. In a way, I guess I'm glad this all happened. It forced to me to finally find the will to try to pull myself out this hell. But, I had to do it alone."

"I understand. I really do. So, how is everything going with all of that?"

"We've been talking a lot about the attack. Dr. Christman really wants me to stay in the moment, feeling the power of those emotions without shutting down. The more we do those exercises the less scary it is talking about it."

"That's really good. I'm really glad that you're doing this. I always felt so helpless. I never knew what to tell you."

Grabbing his hand, I tell him, "You always said the right things to me. You always made me feel safe."

He kisses my forehead and asks, "How are your night terrors?"

"I'm still taking my pills. She told me that the more I can cope with my anxiety and triggers during the day and realize I'm okay, then the night stuff should work itself out naturally. But for now, I still take them."

He slings his arm around my shoulder and kisses my head. "You're pretty amazing, you know that?"

"Stop embarrassing me. So, tell me about you. Any job offers yet?"

"I have an interview at Dean Allen on Monday."

"That's great! So, you're definitely staying in Seattle?"

"Yeah. It's home for me. I love the city, and Mark is staying, so it only makes sense. What about you? I know you were thinking about the Pacific Northwest Ballet."

"That's when I thought I could never leave. But, I'm really hoping for New York. I think I can go now and be okay. I'll miss you like crazy, but if I got the opportunity, I'd have to at least give it a shot, you know?"

When we finally make it to the front of the line, we get fitted for our purple caps and gowns. I hand over my paperwork to order my honor cords and stole. Jase laughs at me and all the bells and whistles I have to wear. I just shake my head at him. I was still able to maintain my perfect four point this year, which makes a solid four years.

"Want to grab a coffee before we go?"

"Yeah, that sounds good."

While standing in line for our drinks, I spot Kimber from across the room. I shoot her a quick text letting her know we are here, and I see her start heading our way.

"God, this place is packed with every douchebag around!" she snaps as she joins us.

I laugh at her as we walk over to take a seat at an empty table. "Did you order your cap and gown?"

"No, did you see that line?"

"Kimber, you have to get it ordered today. It's the last day."

"Come with me," she begs in a whiney voice.

Taking a sip of my drink I say, "Too late, I just did it."

"Jase?" she says in a singsong voice, but her face drops when he tells her, "Sorry, I went with Candace."

"You guys are hookers! Why didn't you call me?"

"Because you were in class," Jase tells her while I laugh. She's going to be one pissed off chick when she has to stand in that line alone.

"Well, stand with me anyway."

"I can't. I have rehearsals in an hour. I have to run home 'cause I forgot my dance bag."

"You guys are really sucky friends, you know?"

"What are you doing tonight?" Jase asks Kimber.

"Aside from standing in that long ass line, nothing. Why?"

"Come out with Mark and I."

"Drinking?"

"When do they ever not drink?" I butt in.

"Then I'm in! I'll call you when I can find my way out of this fuckin' crazy ass vortex," she complains as she stands up.

"Where are you going?" I ask.

"To go get my cap and gown. Alone."

Jase and I laugh at her when she walks off.

"Well, I better run too. I gotta get to the studio."

"Okay, well I know tomorrow will be busy for you, but if we don't talk before then, I want to wish you luck now, sweetie. I am so proud of you, and we will be there to watch you."

"Thanks, Jase. Love you."

"You too."

"How have you been dealing with the blame?" Dr. Christman asks after I sit down on the couch.

"I don't know. I guess I still feel responsible in a way. I can't get past how my actions led to his actions. I know his actions were wrong, but I still feel responsible for leading him there."

"You can't hold your past responsible for your future."

"What do you mean?" I ask.

"You can't hold the past Candace responsible for the future Candace. You're holding your future self responsible for something your past self didn't know anything about. You can't judge your past behavior because of the way things turned out. You had no way of knowing what would happen next. It's only because you *do* know that you judge your past self."

"I struggle with that. I get what you're saying, but I can't seem to see past all the poor choices I made."

"Well, we will continue to work on that. For now, let's transition and talk a little about tonight. How are you feeling?"

"I feel good. I feel like everything you and I have done has really helped me finally connect to this piece the way I always should have. I used to use Ryan's pain to draw on, but I feel strong enough now to pull from my own."

"That's wonderful."

"I just have to remind myself that it's all right to feel it. It's just a feeling and it will go away, and I will still be okay."

"And the more you can deal with these emotions in a rational manner, the more your sleeping should start to improve. The goal is still to wean you off of the pills." She flips the page of her notepad and continues taking notes.

"I know. I'm just scared."

"But you just said that your emotions will come back down and you will be okay."

"The day stuff seems so much easier than the nightmares. They are so real to me." I don't have the vivid nightmares when I take my pills, but even on the pills my sleep is still restless and filled with night terrors. I'm terrified that if I stop taking them, the bad dreams will start up again.

Crossing her legs, she asks, "So, tell me, what do you think is causing your restless sleep?"

"At this point, it's a lot of things. I still feel like I'm mourning the loss of Ryan. I miss him. A lot. I miss what we had. I wonder what he's doing now. If he's seeing anyone. If he ever thinks about me. I know I shouldn't, but I do."

She leans forward, resting her elbows on her knees. "There is no right or wrong way. These thoughts are completely normal. Do you feel like you need more closure?"

"I don't know." I feel a lump form in my throat, and my eyes prick and sting with tears. "It's weird because he lives a few minutes down the street from me, but it feels like he's a world away."

"I want you to think about what you might need to bring you more peace over this situation."

"Okay."

I look at myself in the mirror. I have finished dancing my ensembles and am applying the last of my makeup before I take the stage for my solo. Adding a few extra bobby pins to my bun, I stand up and make my way backstage. I focus on keeping my muscles warm as I wait for my call.

I feel nervous, as I always do, but I know the nerves will fade as soon as I hit the stage. When the curtain drops, the dancers clear the stage, and I walk to center stage and place myself in fifth position. My heart is pounding, and I'm anxious for the curtain to rise. I know I've worked my ass off for this moment, now I just need to nail it.

The heavy velvet curtain begins to rise as I hear my music start. The heat of the lights sinks into my skin, as I feel the weight of everything I have been working so hard for in the tension of my muscles. Sliding into my chaînés across the stage, the music is loud and it fills the auditorium. When I feel the vibrations of the low cello in my chest, I let myself fall into the tortured piece. The music pulses throughout my body while I take myself to my dark places as I begin my footwork across the stage. I know every seat is filled, but right now, it's just me in this room as I glide effortlessly, always leading with my heel to show off my perfect turnout.

Everything about this year floods through me. I no longer need to take from anyone else; I only take my pain, my brokenness, my suffering. It pours out of me. Everything Jack did to me, and all the torment of losing Ryan. I let my heart bleed as I move through my piece. I throw it all out there and finally allow myself to truly experience this piece—I finally feel it.

When the staccato violins enter the piece, I hit my fouettès one by one with a double pirouette on every second and sixth count. The applause rises as I finish and slide out. The spots are sharp on my piquès and I know I've nailed the routine when the music hits its second high then drifts away.

The crowd is almost as deafening as the music was. I stand and pas marchè to center stage. With a strong port a bras, I take the final curtsey of my college career. Ms. Emerson catches my eye as she walks onto the stage, looking as stoic as ever, and hands me a bouquet of long-stemmed pink roses. I thank her, and I can barely hear her over the applause when she says, "I knew you could do it," and then steps aside, giving me a reverence, and I curtsey one last time before the curtain drops.

I stand there for a moment while dancers for the next ensemble run and rush all over the stage and around me. I soak in the moment and then walk off stage, back to the dressing room. I'm overcome by the congratulations from my fellow dancers and friends.

When the show ends, I wash my face and change into my old yoga pants and UW sweatshirt. I tie my running shoes and throw my bag over my shoulder as I make my way out of the building. Everyone is coming over to the house tonight for drinks to celebrate. Nothing big, just hanging out as we usually do. When I turn the corner, I have to do a double take when I see Donna standing there against the wall.

"You were amazing, dear," she says as she walks toward me.

I haven't spoken to her since Ryan and I broke up. She has called several times, but I knew it would hurt too much to answer. Donna filled a place in my heart that was only hers to fill. She's the mother I'd always wanted—the one I'd always needed.

"What are you doing here?"

Pulling me into her arms, I savor her embrace as she says, "I told you I would be here." Leaning back, she adds, "I couldn't miss seeing you dance. You were beautiful. I knew you were amazing, but I just had no idea you were that amazing."

"Thank you," I say as a smile breaks across my face. "I still can't believe you're here."

"I tried calling a few times, but—"

"I'm sorry. I know you called. It just . . . It hurt to lose Ryan, but it hurt to lose you too."

"You didn't lose me. I love you, dear. You will always have me whenever you need me. I know Ryan hurt you, and I understand it might be easier if I'm not around, but please know that I am always here for you."

Her words hit where they always hit: deep inside. My chin quivers as I try not to cry, and I go in for another hug. When she wraps her comforting arms around me, I let the tears free. "I'm glad you came. I've missed talking to you." When I step back, I add, "But you're right, it hurts. You were the best gift Ryan ever gave me, but I need the space right now."

"Of course. I understand."

"I'm sorry."

"You have absolutely nothing to be sorry about. I am so proud of you. You will do amazing things. Just keep following that strong heart of yours."

"Thank you, Donna. Really . . . thank you for everything."

"Well, I better get going. Congratulations."

I smile at her one last time as she turns to walk out of the building. Another pang of loss eats me from the inside and I cry. I don't fight it; I just let it envelop me. After a few minutes, I walk outside into the cold rainy night and welcome the chilling drops that plunk down on me and mix with my hot tears. I keep telling myself it'll be okay, because I know it will be. I have to believe in that.

chapter forty

A FEW DAYS after the production, the calls started coming in. I was offered placements in five companies. Pacific Northwest Ballet here in Seattle was one of them, but when the call came from the American Ballet Theatre in New York, one of the most respected ballet companies in the world, I couldn't say no. My dreams of dancing full-length classics such as Swan Lake and La Bayadere at the Met are about to come true. I can hardly believe it. Life has been a total whirlwind since I accepted their offer.

Graduation is in two weeks, so I have been busy packing up my room and researching apartments in New York City. I found a flat in a walk up that is close to Lincoln Center, where I will be dancing every day. I rented a storage unit here in Seattle to store some of my furniture and the boxes of things I don't need or won't have space for. Once I'm more settled I will figure out what to do with everything.

Everyone is out of town for Memorial Day weekend. I stayed behind because I just had too much to do. Kimber is still seeing Seth even though he is moving to California for grad school. She says they aren't in love or anything, just having fun. They went to Whistler for four days while Mark and Jase went to Vegas.

It's Saturday night, and while everyone is on vacation, I am sitting on the floor of my trashed room, trying to sort through all of my things, deciding what to throw away, what to take with me, and what to leave behind in storage.

My phone rings and when I pick it up, I see it's Kimber calling and that it's already past midnight. Swiping my phone, I answer, "Hey, Kimber."

"Candace, hey." Her voice is shaky and slow.

"Is everything okay?"

"Yeah. Uh . . . Candace, Seth just got a call from one of his fraternity brothers, and I need to talk to you about something."

My mind immediately goes to Jack. Why else would I care about any news from Seth's frat house?

"Okay. What's up?"

There is a long pause before she speaks.

"Jack's dead."

I swear my heart stops when she tells me this, and I have to remember to breathe.

"What?"

"Yeah. It happened earlier today. A drunk driving accident."

"Oh." I don't know what to say. I feel numb.

"Look, I can come home if you need me to. I just wanted to tell you before you saw it on TV or something."

"No, I'm fine. Really." For some reason, I feel tears threatening, and I rush to get off the phone. "You guys have fun. I'm about to go to bed. I'll talk to you later."

"Are you sure?"

"Yeah. Bye."

When she hangs up, I set the phone down. I feel the tears run down my face, but I don't make a sound. *Jack's dead.* I keep saying it to myself over and over. *He's dead.* The more I say it, the more my emotions well up. I want to shut down, but I know I need to force myself to feel whatever it is that is brewing inside of me.

When I choke back a breath, that's when I begin to cry. I'm not sure why I'm crying. I'm so confused. I don't know what I'm feeling, but it feels a lot like sadness. But why am I sad? Shouldn't I be happy? But I'm not happy. He's dead. God, what's wrong with me? I shouldn't be feeling sad for the guy who raped me. I should be relieved—relieved that I don't have to be scared of him anymore. I begin to sob, my emotions overtake me, and I know for sure: this is hurt and sadness.

I pick up the phone to call Jase, but it just goes to voicemail. I hate that I'm feeling this way. I lie on the floor in the middle of my messy room, and curl into a ball. I try to slow my breathing, but everything about Jack starts flashing through my mind: meeting him for the first time at the club, dancing with him at Remedy, kissing him in his car. Why am I thinking this way? I should be thinking about the asshole that raped me, broke me, destroyed me. He ruined my life, and I'm sobbing on my floor because I feel bad for him.

I need to run away. I know I shouldn't, but I just need to escape. I throw on my running shoes and walk outside. It's the middle of the night, and the streets are quiet. It's raining, but I don't care. I just walk. I walk and cry as the drops fall from the sky. I don't know how long I've been walking or where I'm even going. My running shorts and t-shirt are soaked through, and my hair is drenched in a bun on top of my head. I wander through the streets, unable to calm myself down.

When I turn onto yet another street, my vision blurred by my tears, I start walking up stairs—familiar stairs. When I knock on the door and no one answers, a fresh wave of tears break free. I feel so alone.

Hearing the click of the lock, I look up as the door opens, and my stomach clenches when I see his clear-blue eyes staring at me. I start sobbing and fall into his chest. He quickly wraps his arms around me, and I cling desperately to him. It's been months since I've touched him. I melt into him, and he reaches down, slipping his arm behind my knees and scoops me up, cradling me in his arms as he walks me inside.

When he sits us down on his couch, I remain in his arms, curled in his lap. I lay my head on the curve of his shoulder as he holds onto me tightly, as if he's scared I'll slip away. When my cries soften into short breaths and hiccups, he asks, "Baby, what happened?"

I lift my head and look at Ryan. He reaches up and strokes my cheek with his knuckles.

Shaking my head, still confused, I tell him, "Jack died tonight."

He lets out a deep breath and leans his forehead to mine. When he does, I let out all my thoughts in a blubbering mess. "I'm sorry. I didn't know where to go. I'm so confused. I don't know what's wrong with me."

"Slow down, babe."

"Should I be happy? Or relieved?" I ask, desperate for someone to tell me how I should be feeling.

"Well, what do you feel right now?" he asks as he tucks a lock of my hair behind my ear.

"Sad. And hurt. I don't know why. It's like all I can think about is Jack when he was good. Or when I thought he was. But I know he wasn't. I know I should hate him. But, if I'm sad, does that mean I don't hate him?"

"I think you're just in shock. I think you need a little time to sort this out in your head."

I lay my head back down on his shoulder, when he says, "Let me go get you a towel. You're freezing."

I nod my head and scoot off his lap and onto the couch. He returns with two big towels and wraps one of them around my shoulders. Sitting next to me, he pulls me back into him.

"You need anything to drink?"

I lean back forward and let my head hang down. Wrapping my arms around myself, I shake my head no. Ryan's hand runs up my back and onto my shoulder as he tugs me back.

"Talk to me."

I sigh and say, "I'm sorry. I didn't even realize I was here until I was in front of your door."

"I'm glad you're here." He cups my cheek with his hand and says, "I've missed you so much."

His words hurt. They hurt because I know how he feels. I've missed him too. I've been trying not to. Trying so hard to not think about him, but he's always been there. Without even thinking, I reach up and run my hand down the side of his face as I feel my own face scrunch up, and I start to cry again.

"Baby, don't cry," he says as he brushes his thumbs over my cheeks.

Being here, in his house, on this couch where we've made love, and in his arms, I just want to go back to when it was all good. When I didn't know about the lies. When I was safe and we were so in love. But, I can't. I can't go back there again and make myself that vulnerable.

He leans down and presses his lips to my forehead, and I have to force myself to not take more. Pulling back, I shake my head and say, "I can't."

"Babe."

"I can't. It hurts so bad, I just can't"

"I swear to you, I will never hurt you again."

"But you swore you wouldn't hurt me before and you did."

Lowering his head slightly to look into my eyes straight on, he affirms, "I love you. God, I love you so much."

He moves his head in slowly. I can smell his sweet minty breath. I've missed that smell. His lips barely skim mine when I pull back slightly.

"I'm moving," I say on a hush.

Lifting his head up, he looks at me with his brows knitted together.

"I got a job. I'm moving to New York in two weeks."

He looks down and shakes his head slowly as I say, "You can't kiss me." My cries begin to intensify. "If you do . . . I'll never want to leave you."

"Then I'll come with you."

"Ryan . . . I just can't. I'm too scared you'll hurt me again. I just need to be on my own. I've been working so hard to pull myself out of the hell I've been living in."

"I know you have. I ask Jase about you all the time. He's told me how well you're doing. I just wish I could be around to see it, babe." He chokes on his words and drops his head. When he looks back up at me, his eyes are rimmed with tears. "All I ever wanted was for you to be okay, to be happy."

"I'm okay," I affirm.

We sit there while time slowly passes. I thought I would always be with Ryan. I thought he was it for me. I wanted him to be it for me. A part of me stills does, but I push that part deep down, because it hurts to feel it. I love Ryan. Despite everything that happened, I still love him. I'm not sure how long it will take for these feelings to fade, but I really wish they would because missing him is excruciating.

"Do you think you could drive me home?" I ask after a while.

"Yeah," he whispers, and I know he doesn't want to.

He helps me into his jeep and drives me the few minutes to my house. When he pulls into my driveway, he asks, "Can I walk you in?"

"Ryan," I sigh out.

He nods his head, understanding that I don't think it's a good idea.

When I grab the handle to open the door, he says, "I'll never love anyone the way that I love you."

I turn my head back to look at him, and I know my face is reflecting the pain that is wracking me as my tears fall. I nod my head, my only way of letting him know I feel the same way toward him. I can't speak. I don't know how. My sobs start to break through when I open the door and walk away from the only person I never wanted to walk away from.

Leaving Ryan last night was the hardest thing I have ever had to do. I sit up in my bed and look at the chaos in my room. All my belongings are strewn all over the place. I feel like this room is a reflection of how I feel inside: chaotic. I need order in my life. I resolve to pull my life together and move forward, starting with this room.

I spend the day packing and sorting. By late afternoon, I can finally see the floor again when I stack all of the boxes along one of the walls. When my phone chirps at me, I read a text from Roxy.

Drinks?

When and where?

Prime. 7:00?

Perfect.

I hop in the shower to wash all the grime from packing off of me. After drying my hair and putting on a little makeup, I slip on a pair of dark wash jeans and a short-sleeved black peplum top.

When I walk into Prime, I am relieved to see that it's not too busy. I still tend to get nervous around crowds, especially since I don't have Jase or Ryan with me, but Roxy is already there, with her newly platinum blonde hair, waiting for me with a martini in hand. I smile at her appearance as she places her bright red lips on the glass and takes a sip, while all of her colorful tattoos are exposed on her sleeveless arms.

"Hey, hun," she says as I take a seat next to her at the bar.
"You been waiting long?"
"No, just got here."
I order a glass of red wine and Roxy asks, "So, are you all packed?"
"Pretty much. I spent all day working on my room."
She scans my face and says, "It shows. You look like shit, girl."
"Thanks," I chuckle.
The bartender sets my wine down in front of me, and I pick it up to take a long sip.
"Thirsty?"
Setting the glass down, I open up to Roxy about last night.
"It's really over with Ryan," I sigh.
"What?"

Resting my elbow on the bar, Roxy does the same when I start, "Yeah. I saw him last night. It was awful."

"What happened?"

"Nothing, really. I mean nothing was really said that wasn't said months ago. He did say that he wanted to go to New York with me."

"God, he really loves you."

"I really love him too. But I can't go back there again. Besides, New York is my dream, and if I didn't go, I would always be wondering 'what if.'"

She leans back and takes another sip of her drink. "That's understandable."

Last week I decided to tell Roxy about Jack. My therapist told me that the more I deal with it, the easier it will become, and the less power it will hold over me. She's right. It was hard, but not unbearable. I did it, and I was okay.

"Jack's dead," I slip out.

Almost choking on her martini, she shouts, "What?!"

"God, you're loud."

"Sorry," she says, and then whispers, "What?" in exaggeration.

"Yeah, last night. Car wreck. Kimber called and told me. I went for a walk to try and calm myself down, and I wound up at Ryan's house. I shouldn't have gone there. I know it only hurt him to see me again, just to have me walk away."

"Why didn't you call me?"

"I don't know. I was a mess."

"Shit," she says as she sits back and downs the rest of her martini.

"I'm ready to move on though. I'm ready for New York."

She shakes her head at me, and I ask, "What?"

"I don't think you are."

"What's that supposed to mean?"

"Nothing. Forget it. I'm happy for you. I'm gonna miss the crap out of you."

"I'm going to miss you too."

"You think you'll come back?"

"I honestly don't know. I have no idea where my life is going to take me. But I think I am finally ready to explore it on my own."

chapter forty-one

I TAKE ONE last look around the room that has been mine for the past three years. The walls are bare and everything that is mine is now in boxes sitting in storage. I dropped my car off at Kimber's parents' house last night. They are going to keep it in their garage until I figure out what I'm going to do with it. I already shipped out my boxes, and they should be waiting for me to pick up when I arrive in New York later tonight.

"You ready?" I turn to see Jase walking into my room, and he sits down on my stripped bed.

"I'm sad," I say as I sit down next to him and lean my head on his shoulder.

"Me too. I can't believe you're leaving."

"I know. Me either." My chest aches knowing I will soon be leaving everything I know and hopping on a plane to go where I don't know a single person. Jase has always been my rock. He's my best friend, and I swear he's the breath that kept me going this year. I'm scared to not have him.

Jase is moving in with Mark next week. They both got jobs here in the city and since Mark's roommate is moving out and he'll have the place to himself, he asked Jase to move in.

Kimber also got a job at a local magazine working in the marketing department. She told me she refuses to get another roommate, but that's just her being stubborn. She told me she didn't want to live with anyone if it wasn't me.

"Hey, guys. We need to leave soon," Kimber says as she stands in my doorway. She looks around my room and shakes her head. "This shit makes me sick." She walks over and sits on the other side of me. I still feel so guilty for wasting all that time not speaking to Kimber. I wish I could get every second back.

"Have you even told your parents where you're going?" Kimber asks.

"No. I haven't spoken with them since Christmas Eve. And when I never heard from them on my birthday or graduation, I figured, why bother?"

"That really sucks ass," she says.

"Yeah."

She wraps her arm around me and Jase does as well. Kimber is the first one to break down and start crying and I follow shortly after.

"I'm going to miss you guys so much."

"We are too," Jase says. "Come on, girls, we need to head out."

Jase stands up, walks over to my two large suitcases, and starts wheeling them out of the room. Sitting alone with Kimber, I say, "I'm so sorry that I didn't trust you enough to talk to you. You're my sister, and I shouldn't have avoided you like that."

"Candace, you have already apologized enough for all of that. It's okay. It's in the past."

"I hate that I'm leaving just as we are talking again."

"I know. Me too." She gives me a squeeze before standing up. "We'd better go."

The drive to Sea-Tac Airport is a quiet one. No one speaks, and the somber mood is thick in the car. I sit in the front seat with Jase and grip his hand the whole way there. I never thought I'd leave him. I never thought I'd be strong enough to. I keep reminding myself that this has always been my dream. This was the goal all along. I just got really sidetracked this past year.

Ryan keeps breaking through my thoughts. I tell myself moving will lessen the pain I feel every time I think about him. I know once I get to New York that I will be busy learning the ropes at ABT and learning a lot of new choreography. I'm already jittery thinking about it.

When Jase pulls the car around to the departures drive, I can feel the fear in the pit of my stomach. I tighten my hold on Jase's hand, and when I do, he looks over at me. "You're going to be fine. Everything is working out the way it should."

I nod at him, unable to speak, and he smiles at me. He pulls up to the curb, and the three of us get out of the car. I turn around to hug Kimber and breakdown at the same time she does.

"I love you," I choke out and I feel her nod her head in response. We hold tightly onto each other and when we finally loosen our hold, I turn to Jase and just fall into him and cry. His arms have been home for me. He's everything to me, and my heart breaks to think about not having him. He kisses the top of my head and says, "I'm so proud of you. I'm going to come visit you in a few weeks, okay?"

I pull back and nod my head. As soon as I accepted my offer in New York, Jase booked a ticket to come visit me at the end of June. So, I only have a few weeks until I see him again.

We all say our goodbyes and cry a little more before I grab my bags and wheel them to the luggage counter to check them. Once they are checked, I make my way through security and walk to my gate. My mind is consumed, and a part of me wants to hop in a cab and run back home. I start doubting myself, and I'm not sure I can do this alone. Maybe I should have taken the job in Seattle. If I did that, everything would be different.

I sit down on one of the chairs facing out the window. My plane is already here, and I watch as the carts drive up next to it with everyone's luggage. My insides are twisting with anxiety. I think about how everything has changed in the past two months, ever since the morning the detective called. It took me a while to understand why Ryan did what he did. Dr. Christman helped me sort out all of my thoughts and I know, in Ryan's mind, he only did it because he didn't want to hurt me. I know he never meant to deceive me, and in my heart I have forgiven him.

Going to New York has always been my dream, but now that it's actually happening, I'm suddenly questioning if it still is. Would I be this sad if it was? Shouldn't I be happy? I wonder if I should even be doing this. Maybe I'm just stuck on the dreams of my past. Dreams change; maybe mine has. I thought I had everything planned out, but this year took me in a completely different direction. Meeting Ryan and falling in love was the last thing I ever expected. The last thing I thought I ever deserved.

I've been working so hard in therapy, but now I think this whole New York thing is just something I'm forcing, to try and prove to myself that I am strong enough to do it, to stop clinging and be independent. But what if what I am actually clinging to now is the dream? A dream that really isn't my dream anymore. Because when I close my eyes it's never there. It's Ryan. What if the choice that takes the most strength is not the choice to get on that plane, but the choice to know that I shouldn't get on that plane? I snap out of my thoughts when realization suddenly hits me. *What am I doing?*

Grabbing my purse, I stand up and start pushing my way through the crowds in the terminal. I run by the security check and find the exit. I fly down the escalators and when I run out the sliding doors, I hail the first cab that I see. I hop in the back seat and give the driver the address.

Pulling out my phone, I go through my call history and find the number I'm looking for. I tap it and after a few rings a woman answers, "PNB. How may I help you?"

"Is Peter Kirchner available?"

"May I ask who's calling?"

"Candace Parker."

"One moment please."

Butterflies swarm in my stomach as I wait. I'm on hold, hoping that I still have a chance to sign with them.

"Ms. Parker, this is Peter. How can I help you?"

"Hi, Mr. Kirchner. I was actually wondering if it was too late to be considered for placement in your company."

"What happened to the American Ballet Theatre?"

"It wasn't the right choice for me."

"Why don't you come in on Monday, and we can get all those papers signed? We would be honored to have you."

"Thank you. Really. I will see you Monday."

"See you then."

When the cab stops, I hand over the money, get out, and start walking up the drive to the stairs that lead to his front door. I ring the bell and immediately start crying, feeling a total overload of emotions.

When the door opens, my breath catches, and he takes one look at me and asks, "What are you doing here? I just got off the phone with Jase. He said he dropped you off at the airport."

"I can't go. I'm so sorry. I can't do it."

"What do you mean you can't do it?"

"Because . . . I love you too much to leave. And I miss you. And I made a huge mistake by leaving you. I'm so sorry," I cry out.

When he wraps me in his arms, I know this is where I belong. This is my dream.

"Baby, you didn't make any mistakes."

"I did. And I know I hurt you. But, I'm so sorry. I can't go because I can't leave you. I don't want to leave you."

Pulling me inside, he closes the door, and he walks me over to the couch. When we sit down, he says, "I can't let you give up on your dream. I can't."

"But, it's not my dream. I was just hanging on to it because I was scared to see that it really wasn't what I wanted. It's you. It's always been you."

When he crushes his lips to mine, I wrap my hand around his neck and climb onto his lap, straddling his legs. Ryan bands his arms around me and holds on tight. He pulls away for a moment and tells me, "I've missed you so much, babe. You have no fucking idea."

"I love you. I'm sorry I've been so stupid and wasted all this time when all I really wanted was to be here with you."

"You have nothing to be sorry for. I fucked up. I hurt you, and you'll never know how much I regret it."

"I don't blame you, Ryan. I did, but I don't anymore. I just want to be with you."

He cradles my cheeks and wipes my tears with his thumbs. "I don't ever want to lose you again."

"You won't. I'm yours."

Our affectionate kisses are laced with passion, making up for lost time. Picking me up, I lock my ankles around his waist as he carries me upstairs. He lays me down on his bed and crawls on top of me. I've missed this bed, being wrapped up with him in these sheets, smelling his scent all around me, feeling his warmth.

He reaches back, pulls his shirt off over his head, and tosses it aside. I look at the tattoo that's on his ribs and read the words again: *pain is a reminder you're still alive*. I sit up and brush my fingers across his scar and over the words. I tilt my head back to look up at him and he says, "I couldn't breathe without you."

I reach up and run my hand along his jaw. "I need you."

And with words unspoken, he presses me down with his weight wholly on top of me, and I soften into him. I let my arms float above me as he takes his time peeling off my shirt. He slides his hands from my neck, over my breasts, along my stomach, and when he gets to my pants, he unhooks them and pulls them off, along with my heels. When he removes his pants, he lies down next to me, and I wrap my leg around his hip as we are face to face.

We move slowly as we reclaim each other after being apart for these past two months. Our hands explore, and I relax into the heat of his body. I feel the peace that had been missing since I left him return to my heart, and I'm whole under his touch.

Ryan unhooks my bra and drops it to the floor with the rest of our clothing. He trails his lips over my sensitive flesh and licks my nipple with his hot tongue before covering it with his mouth, sucking gently. My head rolls back into the pillow as my body lifts and presses into his, needing more. When he reaches down and drags his hand between my legs, feeling what he does to me when we're together, I release a moan. His touches are intimate and exactly what I need right now.

Shifting between my legs and running his hands up my knees and down along my inner thighs, he looks down at me, "God, you're so beautiful." I reach up and bring him to me, melding my mouth with his. When I feel him enter me, he parts my lips with his tongue and licks slow and deep, freely exploring each other's mouths. My arms wrap around his neck as his hips roll over me, pushing himself deeper inside. Our breaths are labored, and our moans fill the room.

He rolls us over, and I'm spread across his lap as he sits up to keep our bodies close. He wraps his hands around my shoulders as I slowly begin to roll my hips into him. We take our time with each other. I love that Ryan can be this way with me, open and vulnerable, never rushing. He's the only one who can make me feel so safe when I bare my entire self; he's the only one I want to.

With one of his hands on my hip, guiding me, and the other on my cheek, I wrap mine behind his head and weave my fingers into his unruly hair as my body begins to climb.

He doesn't even need to ask as we look into each other's eyes. I know he likes to watch me. My body begins to quiver beneath his hands as my hips rock into him, and I grip his hair in my fists. "Let go, baby." I drop my forehead to his as his blue eyes pierce mine, and I fall apart in his arms. A carnal moan escapes the both of us as he pushes himself deep inside of me and finds his release too, gripping his fingers tightly onto my body.

I fuse my lips with his, never wanting to let go as he lays us down on our sides, bodies still connected, facing each other. I've missed this so much, and I don't even try to hold back my tears. I love this man from a place inside that I never knew existed. He's saved me in a way I never knew a person could be saved. He holds me close, and it's only when I sniff that he pulls back from our kiss. "Babe."

Looking at him, I take my time before saying, "I never want to know what life is without you."

He reaches down and pulls the sheets over us as we tangle our legs. "You won't ever have to."

We continue to hold each other and kiss until we drift off together.

I wake from our afternoon nap, and the mist from earlier is now coming down harder. I lay in Ryan's arms for a while as I watch the raindrops trickle down the windows. I never knew home until now. It's with him, in this house, in this bed. My mind and body are free of doubt. This is my dream. He is my amazing.

Looking back over my shoulder at him, his eyes still closed as he sleeps, I know I will never love as powerfully as I do with him. I reach down, grab his discarded t-shirt, and shrug it on as I make my way to the bathroom. I flick on the light and before I can close the door, I see my necklace lying next to his sink. Walking over and looking down at it, I see that he got the chain fixed from when I ripped it off my neck. I run my finger along the etched letters: *And though she be but little, she is fierce.*

Looking up, I see that my toothbrush is still next to the other sink along with a bottle of my perfume. Warm arms slowly snake around my waist as his lips press into my neck. Our eyes meet in the reflection of the mirror. "I could never let you go."

He picks up the necklace and clasps it back around my neck where it belongs. I will never be close enough to him to satisfy me. Maybe it was supposed to be like this all along; maybe I needed the pain of losing Ryan to make me finally pull myself out of the madness. Maybe I just had to lose him for a moment to keep myself from fading.

Every 2 minutes, someone in the U.S. is sexually assaulted. Approximately 2/3 of assaults are committed by someone known to the victim. And only 46% of assaults are reported to the police.

You just read about Candace who suffered from Post-Traumatic Stress Disorder, Flashbacks,
Sleep Terror Disorder, and Nightmares.

These are only a few of the effects one can experience after being sexually assaulted.

There is help.

National Sexual Assault Hotline
1.800.656.HOPE

National Sexual Assault Online Hotline
www.ohl.rainn.org/online/

Visit http://www.rainn.org to find more information and resources.

FREEING

a companion novel by
New York Times Bestselling Author
e.k. blair

For my son and daughter
You need to know with every fiber of who you are that when you walk through the front door of your home, you are safe, and you are loved.

"In the end, there doesn't have to be anyone who understands you . . . There just has to be someone who wants to."

~Robert Brault

prologue

THE RAIN FALLS hard as I drive back home. I'm a goddamn mess, and I can't get my head to stop tormenting me. I don't know what the hell is wrong with me or why this is happening. I couldn't even force myself to come this time, and I was such a dick that I made her believe it was her fault. It was a shit thing to do, but I knew if I didn't embarrass her, she would go open her mouth to all her friends.

I pull up to my house and head inside. It's dark as I quietly make my way upstairs to my bedroom. Shutting my door, I lie down on my bed and stare at the fan on my ceiling making its rotations over and over. How is this my life?

I'm so twisted that the only reason I wanted to fuck that girl was because I knew Tyler had. It was my sick way of connecting with him. I hate myself for doing what I did. I hate myself for so many reasons.

I grew up in church, going to Sunday school and Bible study summer camps. I believe in God, and was taught that this way of life is wrong. It isn't what He wants; it isn't what I want, but at the same time . . . it is. This shouldn't be happening to me. I've done all I can to force these thoughts and feelings away. I've pretty much screwed every girl in my graduating class at La Jolla High. Nothing is working though; in fact, it's only making everything that much worse.

Nobody knows. I'm not sure anyone will ever know. I've spent the last few years praying that this is just a phase, fighting the thoughts that skate around in my head. Pretending to be someone I'm not in an attempt to escape this sick person who lives inside of me.

The only person I need right now—the only one who would listen and not judge me—is gone. I feel like God is punishing me for some reason. He took away the only one who could help me. The only one I could confide in. It's been almost two years since Jacie died. She was in the car with her boyfriend on prom night when an overly tired truck driver hit them head-on and killed them. She was my best friend. Everyone even called us by the same name: Jase for Jason, and Jace for Jacie. We never went through any sibling rivalry and did everything together: exploding mud pies with firecrackers when we were little, and later, learning to surf. Surfing was our thing; we would always go out early on Saturday mornings and stop at the In-N-Out Burger on the way home. Mom and Dad still haven't touched her room, and I'm not allowed to mention her name.

I miss her.

I miss everything about her, and now I need her more than ever. I need her to tell me it's okay, that I'm okay.

When I got my acceptance letter from the University of Washington the other week, I knew it was where I was going to go. I need to get the hell out of California and away from everything I know. I need to free my mind of the constant taunting. I just need to be free to find myself. To figure all this out. To understand why, when I was banging Carly tonight, all I could think about was Tyler. *Fuck.*

I'm not a fag. That shit is sick, and it's not me. I hate myself for even thinking that it could be. Just three more months before classes start at UW. August is when I will escape from here and finally get the headspace I need to work everything out.

chapter one

"KIMBER, WHAT'S TAKING you so long?"

"Stop bitching. Just let me get my boots on, and I'll be ready. Man, what has your panties in a twist?" she whines as she sits on the floor of her closet, zipping up her boots.

"I'm going to say goodnight to Candace real quick. Hurry up, okay?"

"Uuugh!" I hear her grunt as I walk down the hall to Candace's room. When I open her door, she is sitting on her bed studying. Typical Candace. She's focused and quiet, and she's the sweetest girl I know. I love her more than anything. She was the first person I met and became friends with when I moved here to Seattle three years ago. We had an instant connection. In a way, she reminds me a lot of Jace in her sincerity. She made it easy for me to decide to open up to her about being gay, and she was the first person I ever told. She didn't even think twice about it when I told her.

"Hey, Jase," she says as I walk into her room and sit down next to her.

"You really should come out with us. This band is supposed to be really good."

"I have a lot of reading to do. Besides, I have to be at work by six tomorrow morning," she tells me as she closes her books and slides them to the foot of the bed.

"You know your excuses are lost on me, right?"

She smiles, and I kiss her forehead before hugging her.

"Stop molesting my roommate. I'm ready," Kimber says loudly as she enters the room, flipping her bright blonde hair behind her shoulder.

"You guys have fun. Call me tomorrow, Jase."

"Will do. See ya later."

When we arrive at Level One, the place is packed. Kimber and I head straight to the bar and waste no time downing a couple shots. The band playing tonight has brought in a large crowd. It's the busiest I have ever seen this place.

"They're really good," Kimber shouts over the music.

Picking up the bottle of beer the bartender hands me, I nod my head and take a sip. Mark, the guy who plays guitar, is in a few of my classes; he's an Architect major like me. We've never talked much, but he was the one who told me about this gig tonight. It's hard to tell, but I get the sense that he's gay too. I guess he's a lot like me. Kimber and Candace told me that there's no way they would've ever known unless I told them. But there's something about Mark that makes me think I'm not wrong about my assumption.

Kimber and I get comfortable at the bar and sit back to listen to the band play for a while. I met Kimber around the same time I met Candace. She's a wild chick but fun as hell. I tend to go out more with Kimber, although we aren't as close as I am with Candace. I don't think many people have the connection that Candace and I have.

After a couple beers and a round of pool, we find ourselves back at the bar as the band takes a short break.

"Jase, man, you made it," I hear from behind me.

Setting my beer down, I turn and Mark has sidled up next to me. "Yeah, I've been here before. Never knew you played here."

He nods at the bartender and then looks back at me. "Dude, we play everywhere we can get a decent gig. We've been here before, just not a lot."

The bartender hands him a bottle of beer, and I catch myself staring as he takes a long swig. His build is similar to mine, so I know he must hit the gym as often as I do by the way his sweaty shirt is clinging to him. *Damn.* I take another sip and look down the bar at Kimber, who is scoring a free drink from a loser who thinks he has a chance with her. I laugh and shake my head when I hear Mark ask, "You here by yourself?"

"No, but she's left me to sexually harass anyone she can," I joke.

"My type of girl."

Shit. I was wrong.

After taking another gulp of his beer, he sets his bottle down and cocks his head before saying, "If I was into girls."

"No?" I ask for clarification.

Turning to lean his back against the bar, he looks at the stage as he says, "Nah, man."

"Good to know," I respond, and when he looks back at me, he gives a sexy side grin that lets me know he understood what I meant.

"So, you sticking around?"

"Yeah."

"Good. We have one more set for the night." He turns around and calls for another beer. When he gets it, he looks my way. "I'll catch you after?"

"Yeah."

He nods before heading back to the stage to join the rest of the band that is already up there.

Ever since I moved away from La Jolla and came to Seattle, I have been trying to figure out who I am. I was really confused before coming here, but after seeing the reaction from telling Candace and then Kimber, which was hardly even a reaction at all, I felt a huge boulder being lifted off my shoulders. Candace encouraged me to be myself and not hide while I was here. No one knew me, and it was a fresh start.

Putting myself out there was difficult at first. I didn't know what the hell I was doing and always felt awkward. But I figure that is how most people are when they start dating, even straight people. Even though I screwed around a lot in high school, it was never what I really wanted. I barely felt anything, other than disgusted. I think I was more disgusted with myself for using all those girls. Now that I'm here, I've been more comfortable with myself. The misery that I used to feel back home isn't so mind-consuming.

I've casually been with a lot of guys but haven't found myself in any serious relationship yet. I have been having fun and enjoying college life, not taking anything too seriously. But watching Mark on stage with his guitar slung low on his body, working the fret board, I wonder what it is about him that makes me want to keep my eyes fixed on him.

"He's fucking hot," I hear Kimber say. I didn't even know she had sat back down next to me; I've been so zoned out.

"Who?"

Rolling her eyes, she says, "Don't be stupid. The guitarist you haven't taken your eyes off of for the past five minutes."

"His name's Mark."

"You know him?"

"We have classes together," I say as I turn my attention back to him.

"Gay?"

"Uh huh."

"Well that sucks," she pouts, and I have to laugh at her.

"Only for you," I playfully tease.

She nods her head as she continues to listen to the song they're playing. They have a unique alternative sound and can clearly draw in a crowd. As they finish the song, Kimber turns to me while asking, "How much longer do you want to stay?"

"A while. I told Mark I'd stay to the end of their set. Why?"

"I'm a little tired. I think I'm just gonna grab a cab. It's getting late."

"You sure?"

Looking at me and smiling, she teases, "Yeah. I'm not gonna stick around and cock block you like you did me the other night."

"You're full of shit," I laugh as I shake my head at her.

She smiles at me and gives me a hug before she heads out.

About a half hour and several songs later, the band is packing up their equipment before the next one takes the stage. Walking over to me, Mark hands his guitar case to the bartender who sets it against the back wall and then hands him another beer. He introduces me to Chasten, the drummer, who comes over to say bye before he leaves with the rest of the guys.

"So, are you from around here?" he asks.

"California. I grew up near San Diego. What about you?"

"I'm from Ohio. All my family is there. I just really needed a change of scenery, mostly people, so I came here."

Nodding my head, I tell him, "Sounds like me, man. You go home often?"

"Try to. I have two younger sisters that I'm close with, so I like to get back there a few times a year to visit. What about you? Any brothers or sisters?"

"A sister," is all I say. Mentioning her always brings a burn to my tightening throat. So, I leave it and move on. "You guys are pretty good. How long have you been playing?"

"We've played together for a couple years now." He takes a swig of his beer and continues to talk about how the band got started and some of the gigs they have played.

Talking with him is easy and we casually go back and forth, getting to know each other. I've never really noticed his green eyes until now, not that I've ever had the chance to. We've had some classes together for the past three years, but our paths never crossed enough to allow for more than just brief interactions, but he's sexy as hell.

After a while, we realize it's getting late, so Mark grabs his guitar as we head out into the parking lot to leave. He walks over to his white Range Rover that is parked a few spaces away from my SUV. Following him, he slides his guitar into the back seat and turns to face me when I ask, "So, you got any plans this weekend?"

Shutting the door and leaning against his car, he says, "No, not really."

"You wanna get a bite to eat tomorrow?"

"Yeah, that sounds good. Dinner?"

"Eastlake?"

I see a hint of a smirk when he says, "Sure."

God, I want to kiss him, but for some reason I'm hesitant, so I don't. We exchange numbers and say goodnight before I turn to my car. When I hop in and turn the key, a pang of anticipation hits me, and I wonder what's different about this guy that is sparking this eagerness in me.

chapter two

"SO, WHO'S THIS guy you're going out with tonight?" I ask Candace as she flops down on the couch next to me.

"Kaleb. He used to work at the coffee shop a while ago. We ran into each other the other day."

"Hmm."

She tilts her head at me and asks, "What?"

Candace is a serial dater. One date then she is done. She's always been closed off with guys and never really cares enough to get to know them.

"I don't know why you even waste your time." I try and soften my remark by reaching my arm around her and bringing her closer to me.

"Honestly . . . I don't know either."

Kissing the top of her head, I joke, "I think you just like free dinners."

We both laugh while we shift to lie down on the couch. I love this girl; I always have. I can share things with her that I never could with anyone else. She never judges.

Our physical relationship has always been a part of who we are together. We often sleep in the same bed, and I honestly think I give her something she has always lacked in her life—affection. I've never met her parents, but from what she has told me, they are pretentious assholes and have always treated her like shit. Although she dates a lot, I know I'm the only man in her life that she allows this affection from.

"What do you have going on tonight?" she mumbles with her head on my chest.

"I've got a date myself."

"Really? With who?"

"This guy named Mark. We've had a few classes together. He plays guitar in the band that Kimber and I went to go see last night."

"That's hot," she says with a giggle.

"I know."

Just like Candace, I'm a serial dater too. Hookups are kinda my thing. I've never even brought a guy around Candace. It's one thing for her to know I'm gay, but I feel weird having her see me that way. I know this is who I am, but in a way, I still don't think I've completely accepted it.

"So what are you guys doing?"

"Just grabbing a bite at Eastlake," I say.

Shifting herself tightly against me, she laughs a little when she says, "So, tell me how hot he is."

"Hot enough that you'd take a second date with him if he were straight." I turn into her before saying, "Now shut up, and let's take a quick nap before you have to go."

"Fine," she whines, and I lean down to give her a quick kiss on the head.

Hopping out of the shower, I feel that pang of excitement again. I sling my towel around my waist and head into the kitchen to get a beer to try and settle what's going on inside of me.

I throw a little gel into my hair and grab a pair of jeans and an old UW t-shirt. I down the rest of my beer, take my keys, and head out towards the elevator. I shoot Candace a quick text.

Call me when you get home tonight.

It doesn't take her long to reply.

Okay. Have fun. I love you.

Love you too.

On the drive to the restaurant, I can't get the images of Mark last night out of my head. Normally, I would have gone in for a kiss, but something about him made me nervous. I try not to think about it too much when I walk in and spot Mark already sitting at a table. I make my way over and take a seat.

"Hey. Been here long?" I say.

"Nah, just got here. I ordered a couple beers."

"Thanks." God, he looks good in an old, worn Mudhoney shirt that fits snug across his chest.

"So, what did you do today?"

"Not much, man." The waiter comes by and drops off our beers as I continue, "Just hung out with one of my friends. That's all. You?"

"About the same. Hit the gym and hung out."

"What gym do you go to?"

"I'm doing Crossfit at The Rock right now," he says before taking a swig of his beer.

"Yeah, I've heard about that place. I'm a member at the Athletic Club.

It's a little closer to me."

"I need to check that place out now that the summer is winding down. I usually workout on campus during the school year, but always do Crossfit in the summer."

Knowing that I already want to see him again, I offer, "You should tag along with me Monday morning."

"Really?" he asks as he sets his beer down.

"Yeah, I'm normally up there by seven."

He nods his head and says with a slight grin, "I'll meet you there."

Conversation with him is comfortable as we continue to talk about school and what our plans are after we graduate this next year. I never really care to chat too much with the guys I see, but Mark is pretty cool.

"Did you have a busy summer?" I ask after the waiter drops off our food.

"Not too bad. We've been playing a lot more gigs, so it keeps me busy. What about you?"

Setting my beer down, I say, "I pretty much hung low. Took some day trips down to Westport to do some surfing."

"How long have you surfed?"

"My whole life. I grew up next to the beach, so it has always been a part of me. I don't do much of it anymore though since it takes almost three hours to get to a decent spot to paddle out," I tell him and then ask, "You ever been?"

"Surfing? No," he laughs. "I'm from Ohio, remember? The only thing we do in the water is sail and fish."

He has a beautiful smile, and I can't help the one that crosses my face when he looks the way he does right now. "Well, maybe one day I'll get you on a board."

"Don't get your hopes up," he chuckles.

We eat a long dinner and take our time getting to know each other.

After paying the tab, we walk out into the misty night, and I follow Mark to his car. Before he opens his door, he turns around, and says, "So, I guess I'll see you Monday."

"Yeah," I respond as I step closer to him and brace my hand on the car next to his shoulder. I wanted to kiss him last night, but fuck if I don't feel those same nerves again right now. Nerves I never feel when I'm with a guy. Shoving them down, I lean in, and I'm relieved when Mark wraps his hand around my neck and pulls me into him, pressing his lips against mine. We stand there in the light rain and kiss, all the while, the anxiety that rushes through me has me on edge. He crushes his mouth against mine, and I thrust my tongue past his lips and slide it against his. My body is pressed firmly against him, and I'm getting myself too worked up, so I pull back.

Not releasing his grip on my neck, I stare at him, and he gives me a slight grin when he brings me back to him and kisses me again. This time, soft. Our lips just rest on each other's for a moment before he drags his off of mine.

"See you Monday?" he says in a low voice.

Stepping back, I nod and respond, "I'll call you."

He smiles and then turns as he opens his door and hops into his SUV.

The intensity that's rolling through my body makes me want to drive straight to his house and continue what we just started here in this parking lot. I get in my car and am knocked out of my indecent thoughts when I hear my phone chime. I take it out of my pocket and read a text from Candace.

Just got home. How was your date?

Usually I tell her about my dates, but there's never been much to say because I haven't ever clicked with anyone before. But this is different, and I'm nervous to tell her. I wish that I wasn't, but I am, and I'm not entirely sure why.

Good. Heading home now.

That's all I get? No dirty details? ;)

Nothing to tell. We ate. We kissed. What are your dirty details?

I laugh as I hit send because Candace never has dirty details. She's pretty straight-laced, but I love to tease her nonetheless.

Went to The Bar Method. It was weird. He tried kissing me, but I dodged it. Awkward!

Poor guy.

Whatever. I'm going to bed.

Night, sweetie.

Driving home, my mind starts to consume itself with Mark again, and for the first time, I think that maybe I could give this a chance.

Maybe it's time.

Maybe.

chapter three

AFTER LIFTING WEIGHTS for the past hour with Mark, I desperately need a cold shower, but instead, he suggested a run, and I somehow agreed. So now we are making our way through the streets of a neighborhood that is not too far from the gym, and I'm dying 'cause running with a semi is not all that fun. God, I have to get these thoughts out of my head, and fast.

"So, you plan on going back to Ohio after you graduate?" I ask, trying to refocus my thoughts on something else besides his cut body that's covered in sweat.

"I don't think so. I really love it here. Although I miss my family like crazy."

"You guys close?"

"Yeah."

Must be nice. It's been years since I felt close with my parents. Ever since Jace died, they just avoid me. Back when I was in high school, it was as if I was no longer their son, but some dude that just occupied a room in their home. We barely even speak now.

"What about you? You close with your family?" he asks as we turn onto another street that happens to have an incline so steep, I swear to God, if I didn't have decent traction on my shoes, I would slide down it.

Huffing out a short breath, I tell him way too honestly, "No. We hardly ever talk."

"Why's that?"

I take a second to gather my thoughts because I immediately want to tell him the truth. I'm not sure why since the only person I have spoken to about my sister is Candace. She had already told me how demeaning her parents are and how hard it was for her growing up in a house with them, so when I finally opened up to her, I knew she would be able to relate to me. I decide to go with my gut and reveal, "I have a sister, but . . . she died five years ago. And, in a way, my parents did too. I'm pretty much invisible."

"Shit. I'm sorry, man."

Hearing the regretful tone in his voice makes me feel bad for making him uncomfortable, so I brush it off quickly. "Don't be. It's life."

"So I take it you'll most likely stay here after you graduate?"

Finally making it to the top of the hill, we turn the corner, and I sigh when I see we have hit a flat street. Mark laughs, and I turn to look at him and say, "That bitch of a hill nearly kicked my ass."

I laugh with him for a moment before answering his question. "I doubt I'll ever go back home. So, yeah, I plan on staying."

A smile crosses his face, and we both power run back to the gym. Once we hit the parking lot, I am thoroughly drained. I open the back door to my car and grab a couple bottles of water from my gym bag. Tossing one to Mark, I down mine quickly.

"Thanks for the workout," he says as he moves to lean against my car next to me.

"Yeah. Anytime."

"So, hey, I'm gonna be up on campus later this week. I have to shift one of my studios around, and the online enrollment isn't letting me make the change. You wanna meet up for coffee or something afterwards?"

"Sounds good. Just give me a call," I say as Mark steps in front of me and leans in, giving me a slow kiss that lingers long on my lips.

I wrap my arm around his waist, fisting his damp shirt, and pull him closer to me. I'm not exactly sure what we're doing, but I want it. I've never been this way before with anyone else, drawn to them like I am with Mark. Getting to know each other—I like it—and I like him, but at the same time, I'm wondering what this all means.

Mark slides his tongue across my lower lip before dipping it into my mouth. Licking and exploring, I have to break the kiss before he can tell just how turned on he's making me. Something about Mark tells me he isn't into just screwing around, so I tell him, "You can't keep doing this to me in parking lots."

Chuckling, he smiles and responds with, "I agree. I'll call you later?"

"Yeah."

"You want a glass of wine?" I ask from the kitchen.

"Please."

I pop the cork and pour Candace a glass of Merlot before getting myself a beer and joining her on my couch. She's laughing her ass off, watching an episode of 'Ridiculousness' on MTV. We often get together in the evenings and watch these shows. I love that she has the same humor as I do.

"Thanks," she says as I hand her the glass of wine.

I sit down in the corner of the couch as she leans back into me. The bond that we share has only grown tighter through the years. She's always been so honest with me; she's an open book. I try to be just as open as she is with me, but there are some things that are just too difficult to admit—even to myself—but she's my family. She's the one person I know I can always depend on to be there for me because she always has been.

"So what's Kimber up to tonight?" I ask.

As she scoots around to get comfortable, she tells me, "She's at home with some of her girlfriends just hanging out."

"You're so anti-social," I tease with a soft laugh.

"No, I'm not," she responds with mock defensiveness and pinches my side when she continues, "I'm here with you, aren't I?"

"You're either with me or Kimber. That's it."

Shifting to her side, she sets her glass down on the coffee table and inches her way down on me, laying her head on my lap.

"Her friends are annoying. And you know I don't really like being around a whole bunch of people anyway."

"I know. I'm just giving you a hard time, sweetie," I say quietly, knowing that this is how she's always been.

"Plus, I spent the other evening with Kaleb."

I laugh at her, and joke, "Your date that you didn't even like? That hardly counts."

"It counts," she tries to defend, but it's lost on me.

Finishing my beer, I set the bottle next to her glass and slide down so we are face to face. "So, what was it about this one that you didn't like?"

"We just didn't have anything in common."

"You say that about all of them."

Letting out a sigh and closing her eyes, she says, "I know. I just . . . I have a hard time looking at guys that way."

"You wanna know what I think?" I ask, and she opens her eyes to look at me again. "I think you don't know how to accept or give affection because you've never had it. Your parents never gave it to you, therefore you never learned how to give it."

"But I accept it from you," she whispers.

"You do, but I don't think you view me as someone who would ever hurt you."

Candace looks down for a minute before returning to my eyes. "Is that a bad thing?"

Kissing her forehead, I wrap my arms around her and whisper, "No, but it does prevent you from having other real relationships."

"And what about you?"

"What about me?"

"Well, aren't you doing the same thing?"

She's right. Except now I find myself wanting to change that. I surprised myself when I told Mark about my sister this morning when I don't talk to anyone about that stuff. There is something different about him that makes *me* want to be different with him. But I don't want to tell Candace. I'm not really sure what I'm doing, but I don't think I'm ready to reveal to her that I might want something more with him. So I simply say, "Yeah, sweetie, I am."

She looks up at me as I give her a quick peck and then rolls over on her other side so that she can continue watching her show. I lie behind her, combing her long, thick brown hair with my fingers as thoughts of Mark start to flood my mind.

chapter four

"JASE, ARE YOU coming out with me tonight?"

Looking up at Kimber, who is standing in Candace's doorway, I say, "I don't think so."

"Are you serious? Why the hell not?" she barks as she sits down next to me while I lie on Candace's bed.

Propping my hands behind my head, I tell her, "I'm supposed to be meeting a friend later."

"What friend?" Candace asks as she walks out of her bathroom. She makes her way over to her dance bag and takes out her ballet shoes to start powdering them.

"So, I've been watching you do this routine with those damn shoes for years and have never had a clue why you douse those things in powder."

She looks up at me and says, "Because your feet sweat when you dance and the powder absorbs it. It also keeps the shoes from smelling like crap."

"Ahhh."

"Don't change the subject on me. Who are you seeing tonight?"

"Mark."

"You're going out with him again?" Candace asks in surprise and then Kimber pipes up and adds, "That guy from the other night?"

Looking between the both of them, I answer, "Yes, and yes."

"You're such a slut!"

I just laugh at Kimber.

"I didn't know you were seeing him," Candace says as she stands up and starts walking into her closet.

"I'm not *seeing* him. We're just hanging out, that's all." But I know that's really not all. It's not like we're dating or anything—we are in fact just hanging out—but a part of me really does want more.

Kimber jabs me in my ribs. "Fine, ditch me for ass."

Laughing at her, I tease, "Has anyone ever told you how delicate your mouth is?"

Hopping off the bed, she kisses the air while flipping me off. When she walks out of the room, I continue to laugh at her crudeness as I hear her call from down the hall, "Text me later, bitch."

Walking out of the closet, Candace strips out of her sweaty dance clothes and throws on a pair of shorts and a t-shirt. She turns to me and lies down beside me.

I wrap my arms around her when she softly questions, "Do you like him?"

"We're just grabbing coffee, that's all."

A few moments later, I feel my phone vibrate in my back pocket. Candace giggles and she reaches under me to retrieve it. When she hands it to me, I swipe the screen to see the missed text from Mark.

"I gotta run. He's leaving campus now."

"Okay. You wanna spend the night here tonight?"

"Yeah, I'll text you when I'm on my way," I say as I get off the bed. I lean back down and kiss her cheek before I leave.

Walking into Café Allegro, I see Mark standing at the counter chatting with one of the staff. I step up next to him and he says, "Oh, hey. Jase, this is Nathaniel."

I nod my head, and Nathaniel reaches over the counter to shake my hand. He's an older guy with a bit of a gnarly look about him. "Nice to meet you," I say.

"Any friend of Mark's is a friend of mine."

Mark laughs and tells me, "He owns this place."

"Thirty-seven years," he proudly says.

We visit for a couple of minutes, and then Nathaniel makes our drinks before we find an empty table to sit down at.

"Did you get your schedule fixed?" I ask him.

"Yeah, I really wanted to get into Gibson's studio, but when I first went to register, it was full. But I hopped online the other day and saw that someone had dropped and there was a seat open."

"Gibson's Tuesday/Thursday studio?" I ask.

Taking a sip of his coffee, he sets the mug down and says, "Yeah."

"That's my studio."

"Really? That's cool. Yeah, originally I was signed up for Professor Walter's."

"Oh, man, he's so traditional. I had him sophomore year, and he criticized everything I did. He was a dick about it too."

"Well, since we have our capstone this year, I really wanted Gibson 'cause our design styles are similar."

We wind up hanging out for over an hour, drinking coffee and talking about school. Afterwards, he invites me to come back to his house, so we head out and I follow him in my car as we drive to his place.

Mark rents a nice two-story house that's not too far from campus. When we walk in, there is a guy standing in the kitchen.

"Hey, Kyle. You heading out?" Mark asks.

"Yeah, some guys I know are throwing a party," he says and looks at me. "I'm Kyle, Mark's roommate."

Before I can say anything, Mark says, "Oh, sorry, this is Jase."

"Good to meet you. I gotta run though."

"Yeah, nice to meet you too," I respond as he takes his keys and heads out the door.

Turning to me, Mark nods his head for me to follow him. We walk through his house and when we turn into his room, I don't even wait to grab his arm and pull him into me, crashing my mouth against his.

Mark slides his hand behind my neck and holds me close as he starts to step us back toward his bed. He breaks the kiss when he lies down, and I crawl on top of him. Lowering my head, I take my time when I kiss him again. He rakes his fingers through the hair on the back of my head. Pushing my tongue past his lips, I slide it against his, tasting him, before pulling back and gently biting his bottom lip.

His touch is hot when he runs his hand up under my shirt, and my abs tighten at the excitement of being with him in this way. I lower my mouth to his neck and drag my lips up, kissing him behind his ear. When his hand grazes over my chest, I sit back on my knees and reach over my head, tugging my shirt off. Mark sits up, removing his shirt as well.

He looks so goddamn hot, staring up at me. His chest is defined, and his abs are sculpted with deep cuts. I begin to swell up and grow hard as I watch him beneath me. Wrapping his arms around me, he brings me back down, and I try to relieve a little of my ache as I grind my hips into him. I can feel that he is just as hard as I am, which does nothing but turn me on even more. Our breathing is labored, and I want him so bad right now. Sliding my hand down his stomach, feeling each groove of his muscles, I don't stop when I hit his pants. Resting my forehead against his, I slip my hand under his waistband and grip him tightly in my hand.

Mark lets out a low growl at my touch, and I push myself into him again, needing more relief. Before I can move my hand, he grips my wrist and says, "Wait."

I pull my head back and take my hand off of him. "What's wrong," I pant.

He scoots back, and I roll onto my side when he says, "Look, I really like you, but I've heard a little about your reputation from a couple guys at school. You need to know that I'm not like that. I don't do the whole casual thing. I just want to make sure we're on the same page here."

I look into his eyes, not quite sure of what to say. I have only ever been casual with guys. Hell, even before I was with guys, I was only a fleeting moment with girls as well. I've never really looked beyond that. I go ahead and admit, "I like you . . . a lot," but I'm not sure I'm on the same page as him. It's unexplored territory for me, and something about being in an actual relationship with another man freaks me out a bit.

My mind starts to spin, and now I'm questioning if this is really me. Am I ready to do this? Am I ready to be defined in this way? I haven't even come out to my parents. Anxiety and fear begin to rush through me, and I suddenly need space.

"Maybe we should take a breather tonight before we take things too fast," I tell him.

Nodding his head, he says, "Yeah, I agree."

I reach around his neck and draw him in for a slow kiss. I can't deny how good he feels and how good I feel when I'm with him. I want him, but I'm scared shitless at the same time.

When Mark breaks the kiss, he asks, "Can I see you Saturday?"

"Yeah." Apart from being so unsure about our relationship, one thing I am sure of is that I have to see him again.

Stripping down to my boxers, I slide into bed with Candace. Lying behind her, I tuck her tightly against me. I'm conflicted in my thoughts about Mark, but I don't reveal these worries to her. I simply absorb the comfort she gives me just by being with her.

"So what did you guys do?" she whispers into the darkness.

"We grabbed coffee. That's all." I want to tell her. I want her to know my fears, but for some reason, I can't get enough courage to go there yet.

"You gonna see him again?"

"Probably not," I lie, and I have no idea why. Why am I doing this? It's Candace. She would never judge me; I know this. Why am I acting like such a pussy about this?

Snapping me out of my self-destructive thoughts, she says, "We're hopeless, huh?"

I hear her giggle under her breath when I kiss the top of her head and agree. "Totally hopeless."

Lacing her fingers with mine over the top of my hand, she sighs as she softens into me. I lie there in her bed, listening to her breathing slowly leveling out as she drifts off to sleep. Emotions begin to well up inside of me as I try and sort through my thoughts.

I like Mark, there is no doubt about that, but the anxiety I've had since we started spending more time together is stirring up this shame I thought I had let go of. I've been fine just playing the field and having fun, not bothering to question myself or what this all really means. This is almost too much for me to deal with. I thought that maybe I was ready for this; I thought I knew who I was, but it turns out, I'm still confused as shit.

chapter five

TOSSING MY GYM bag into the back of my SUV, I text Mark when I hop in and shut the door.

On my way.

After the other night, Mark had called and wanted to hit the gym with me. I probably shouldn't have agreed; I know he wants something more than what I think I'm able to give him—what I know I'm not able to give him. But I can't help the feelings that overwhelm me every time I talk to him, or hell, even think about him. So when he called and suggested getting together, I couldn't say no.

Hey, I'm running late. Meet me at my house and we can ride together. Kyle is home.

Okay. See you in a bit.

When I arrive at Mark's house, Kyle answers the door and lets me in.
"Hey, man. Mark just called and said he was on his way."
"Oh, okay," I say as I follow him into the living room. "What are you up to today?"
"Nothing really. Just hanging out, watching TV," he says as he picks up his beer from the coffee table and sits back on the couch.
I sit down next to him as he starts flipping through the channels and asks, "What are you guys going to go do?"
"Gonna hit the gym for a couple hours."
Taking a swig of his beer, he stays focused on the TV when he asks, "So you guys dating?"
"No," I answer way too quickly. God, why can't I face this? Why can't I just be comfortable enough to say yes?
Tipping his head to look at me, he smirks and repeats, "No?"
I know that look. I give that look. A lot. When his eyes shift to my

mouth, I suddenly feel like I'm back in my all-too-familiar territory, so I maintain, "No," with a slight shake of my head.

Meeting my eyes again, I know what he's thinking. Knowing Mark is on his way home, and as much as I like him, these feelings I'm starting to have for him bring up all the shit I don't like to think about. Being numb and emotionless with guys is just easier, so I take this bait as an easy out from my conflicting situation with Mark. When Kyle leans in, I take the rope he is offering and hang myself.

I kiss him.

Grabbing his face with my hands, I tangle my lips with his, knowing that once Mark walks through that door it will all be over, and I can bury this self-hatred that only he has been able to dig up.

There is nothing behind this kiss aside from pure destruction. I feel sick to my stomach, and when Kyle thrusts his tongue in my mouth, I'm consumed with guilt. But I don't stop. Instead, I push him down and hover over him. He's running his hand up my shirt, and I don't stop kissing him when I hear the door open. My stomach sinks when Mark's voice pulls Kyle away from me.

"What the fuck are you doing?"

"Shit, man," Kyle says as he jumps off the couch.

I know what I've done, and really, there is nothing I can say. So I don't speak. I get off the couch and walk to the kitchen to get my car keys.

"You're not gonna say anything?" Mark questions as I walk past him. He's visibly pissed, just as I expected. He isn't like me; I know that.

Grabbing my keys, I walk to the door as he persists, "Jase! What the hell, man?"

I can't fuckin' look at him. I feel like complete ass for what I just did, but I'm a coward. He doesn't deserve it; he's better off without me anyway, so I leave. I walk out the door and straight to my car without ever looking back at him. I hate myself for this. All that anguish I've been hiding so well finally surfaces, and I fuckin' lose it. The tears that are blurring my eyes spill over, and I slam my fists into the steering wheel as I speed back to my apartment. I can't even begin to sort my thoughts out. Hopeless—Candace said it the other night, and I couldn't agree more right now. Why can't this be easy? Why do I have to be this way? I can't stand this shit.

I hate that I just hurt Mark. The first guy—the only guy—that I've ever had real feelings for and I destroyed it before I gave it a chance. What the hell is wrong with me? Trying to understand why I hate myself so much is ever consuming, and I honestly don't think I am strong enough to handle the reality of it. So I let the animosity eat at my flesh, right down to my bones.

When I walk into my apartment, I get a beer and go lie down in my bed. My phone chimes, and I'm scared to look at the text message that I'm sure is from Mark. Reaching over, I pick it up and swipe the screen. I sigh in relief when I see it's from Candace.

Getting off work soon. Can I stop by later?

Feeling like a total dick, I don't want to see anyone right now. I love her, but I can't talk to her. I can barely stand being in the presence of my own thoughts. Here I believed, for the past three years, that I've been an openly gay man, but truth is, I'm still hiding. I didn't see it until Mark came along. He made me realize just how scared of these feelings I actually am. I don't want a relationship with him because I'm afraid that will make it too real for me. Define me. Gay. Fag. Queer. *Fuck.* Am I ready for that?

Is this the life that I'm meant to have? No woman? No wife? Immediately, I know that it is. I have never been attracted to women the way I have always been to men. I know I could never have those feelings for a girl. I've only ever wanted guys. It seems so easy for Mark to be who he is, as if it doesn't even phase him. Doesn't even bother him. I wonder if it ever has.

I pick up my beer and down it. Getting up, I walk back to the kitchen and just grab the whole pack and bring it back into my bedroom. I open another bottle before finally texting Candace back.

I'm out. Maybe tomorrow?

I can't deal with this right now. I have no idea what I'm doing and feel more confused than ever. Lost.

"Can I get my tab, man?" I ask as one of the bartenders passes by.

Moping around my apartment after what I did to Mark this afternoon was driving me crazy, so I decided to walk to 9 Million, a local bar in my neighborhood. It's getting late, and I'm about to hit my limit with alcohol.

Sitting here alone, trying to think about anything other than what a total dick I am has proven to be harder than what I was hoping. *What the hell is wrong with me?* I'm sick of the self-pity, wondering why *I* have to deal with all of this. Why can't my life just be simple—simple choices. Hell, who am I even kidding? I know this isn't a choice. I wish it were. None of this would even be an issue if I were just straight. Maybe I was better off just being numb, taking what I wanted from guys and not having to worry about what it all means for me.

"Here you go," the bartender says as he hands me my receipt.

I don't even look at it; I just hand him my credit card and turn around in my seat. It's a busy night and people are packed in here. Everyone seems so carefree—happy even. I'm envious of them.

Before I turn back in my seat to finish off my drink, I spot familiar tattoos on arms I vaguely remember. Making his way through the crowd, I definitely recognize his face as he pins his eyes on me and approaches.

What's his name? I can hardly filter through my intoxicated brain to remember who this guy is.

I swallow the last of my beer when he leans onto the crowded bar top and says, "Jase. It's been a while, mate."

His Australian accent is his tell and it clicks. "Hey, Preston."

"Haven't seen you around lately. You just disappeared on me."

I disappear on almost all the guys I hookup with, and Preston is no different. In fact, this was the very bar I met him in the night we messed around several months back.

"Didn't disappear. Just been busy," I respond, not really in the mood to talk.

When the bartender hands me back my card, I stand up, shoving it into my pocket.

"You headed out?"

His accent is more than appealing, then I remember how even more appealing it was in bed. No question, this guy is hot with his short, messy hair, hard build, and the almost cryptic winged tattoo I know is splayed across his shoulders underneath his shirt. Needing to dull the anguish in my head, I find myself return to my not-so-old habit. "Yeah. Wanna come with?"

We head out into the Seattle mist and walk the couple blocks to my building, staggering as Preston drones on about whatever it is he's talking about. I can't focus because my mind is still with Mark. I need to rid the thoughts of him; they're only making me feel worse.

It's not long before we step into my apartment. I toss my keys towards the coffee table with shoddy aim and hear them hit the floor as I walk to my room. Preston follows and when I clamber into bed, I look up to see him stripping off his shirt before he climbs on top of me.

I'm a fumbling mess, trying to remove my shirt, needing to move quickly in an attempt to clear my head. He doesn't seem to want to waste any time either when he pulls my pants off and tosses them across the dark room. His kisses are rough and aggressive, and I find it distracting because it's such a contrast to Mark. *God, stop thinking about him.*

Returning Preston's intensity, I flip him over, tear open a condom, and almost immediately find myself regretting this hookup when I slam myself inside of him. This used to be fun, but now it feels wrong. I grip his shoulders, and my emotions start to spin out of control until irritation pervades.

Frustration takes over, and I can't do this. I don't want to do this. Quickly, I push off of him and fall on my back onto the bed. "You need to go," I pant out.

"What the hell's your problem?" he snaps back, and when he does, I roll out of bed, rip off the wasted condom, and yank my boxers on.

"Just get out," I throw over my shoulder as I walk out of the room and to the kitchen in search of some aspirin. I used to be able to do this, no problem. Pushing feelings aside, and just taking the moment to be in a place of pure physical indulgence. It hits hard when realization affirms that this isn't what I want. It's *him*. How could I be so stupid—weak? Why is it that Mark, in an instant, made everything I thought I knew about myself irrelevant?

"This is really fucked up, you know?" Preston slings with ill temper as he walks into the living room, and I can't blame him; I'm an ass.

I can't say anything else, so I just agree. "Yeah, I know," I mumble before taking another sip of my water, back towards him.

"What, you can fuck me but you won't look at me?" he yells, becoming more pissed.

"It doesn't even matter," I say in a low, defeated voice as I turn to face him. And to me, he doesn't matter. I'm not even sure I matter.

His words are mixed with threat when he laughs and says, "It doesn't matter to you *now*," before slamming the door behind him.

My phone reads that it's a little after two in the afternoon when I pick it up off my nightstand. Running my hand down my scruffy jaw, thoughts of what happened last night run through my still sleep-induced head. How is it possible that I feel even worse than I did yesterday?

I should have accepted Candace's offer to come over last night; it would have saved me from making a complete ass of myself. I'd much rather be waking up with her than alone in the bed where I completely used Preston when all I really wanted was to go back in time and erase screwing things up with Mark. And now—now all I want is *her*. Truth is, I need her, and I know her well enough to know she won't pry. With Candace, I'll be able to relax a bit; she has a way about her that, no matter what, just makes me feel good.

Can you come over?

After I text her, I drag myself out of bed and into the kitchen to mix up some Gatorade. My phone chimes with Candace's incoming text.

Heading to the studio. Everything ok?

Yeah, just want to spend time with you.

See you in a few hours?

Sounds good.

Knowing that she'll be coming over, I force myself to pull it together. If she saw me like this, she'd worry too much, and I don't want her to worry. So I decide that tonight will be like any other night for the two of us. We'll hang out, cook, and just relax . . . God, I need to find a way to relax.

I decide to forego the self-loathing and hit the pavement for a much-needed run and try to do some productive thinking for a change. I toss back my Gatorade, chugging it before throwing on some clothes and heading out.

I run around Fremont before drifting into the surrounding neighborhoods. Pushing myself, my mind starts to drift again, but this time, I try and focus my thoughts on how to make this right. What I did to Mark was wrong, no question about it. But if I'm ever going to get to a place where I can stop living a lie and face the truth that deep down I know is me, I need to do something. I am so damn torn up about Mark. *Why did I have to be such an idiot?*

I think about what my parents would say if they knew. What would they do? Pounding my feet against the ground, I take long strides as the thought of baring myself to my parents sends chills through my ragged body while sweat trails down my back.

Fuck that. It will never happen. I just need to get away—get out of Seattle for a while and get some space away from this mess. As much as I don't want to, I do need to go back home. Check in with my parents. It's been almost eight months since I went back. We haven't spoken in a couple of months, so just the phone call alone will be uncomfortable. I know they'll leave me alone for the most part, and that's really what I need right now. Space. Get out in the ocean and do some surfing, maybe hang out with some of my old buddies.

Calling my mom was awkward, as predicted since we go long spans of time without speaking. She was a little surprised when I asked if I could come home for a visit. When they said it would be fine, and that they would be there, we decided I would leave at the end of this week and spend a few days with them.

Once that conversation was over, I ran down to the market on the ground floor of my apartment building. I decided to cook fajitas for Candace tonight. Cooking has always been my thing; I love it and find myself cooking for her a lot, since she is normally a bottomless pit. She's a dance major at UW and spends hours in the studio nearly seven days a week, so she always has an appetite when I cook for her since her idea of cooking is grabbing an apple from her fridge.

As I'm slicing the peppers, I hear a knock on my door.

"It's open," I holler.

Her hair is still in a bun when she opens the door and walks in.

"Hey, you mind if I take a quick shower? I came straight from the studio."

"Go ahead. Dinner will be ready soon."

Walking into the kitchen, she kisses my cheek and says, "That smells so good. I'm starving."

"Hurry up then."

"Okay, give me ten minutes," she says as she rushes off to the bathroom.

While she showers, I finish chopping the peppers and onions, and toss the sirloin into the skillet of hot oil. When I take the last heated tortilla from one of the skillets, I place it in the oven and look up to see Candace walking in, wearing a pair of my boxers and a t-shirt.

"What are you making?"

Turning off the stove, I pull out two plates as I say, "Fajitas. I made a lot, so you better be hungry."

She laughs and picks out a bottle of wine for us. Once we have our plates made and drinks in hand, we make ourselves comfortable on the couch.

"So what's bothering you?" Candace asks, catching me off guard.

"What are you talking about?"

"I see it in your face. I know you well enough to know when something is weighing on your mind," she says and then takes a bite of her food.

What's weighing on my mind the most is Mark, but I appease her with saying, "I called my mom today."

"Really?" She's surprised. She knows we don't talk and barely even have a relationship. "What did you guys talk about?"

"Nothing really, but I'm going back home for a quick visit at the end of this week."

Setting her tortilla down, she gives me a curious look and asks, "Why?"

"I haven't seen my parents since last Christmas. We just thought it was time for a visit."

"Are you worried at all . . . I mean, being back home when you guys are so distant with each other?"

Taking a sip of my wine, I say, "It's not like it'll be different than any other trip back home."

"True. I just worry, that's all."

"I know you do, but it's just a short visit to catch up." I don't tell her the real reason why I'm going because I'm not sure I'm ready to admit all of my insecurities to her just yet. I don't even want to admit them to myself, but I hate keeping secrets from her; she's my best friend.

"When do you leave?"

"I booked my flight for Wednesday."

"You want me to drive you to the airport?"

"No, I'm just gonna leave my car there. Who knows if I'll come home early or not, but if I do, I want to have my car."

Setting her plate down, she shifts to face me. "What's really going on?" she questions.

"Nothing, but I've told you about my parents. I just don't want anything to keep me from coming back here in case I want to leave."

Letting out a deep sigh, she says, "Okay, well, when are you supposed to be back?"

"Saturday."

"I feel like there's something you're not telling me."

Setting down my plate, I pull her next to me, and we lean back on the couch. "You know I love you, right?"

She doesn't speak; she just nods her head against my chest.

"Let's not talk about my parents anymore, okay?"

Looking up at me, she grins and says, "Okay. I'm sorry."

"Don't be. I like that you worry about me." I kiss the top of her head and promise myself that I will tell her everything when I can find a way.

chapter six

THE TWO AND a half hour flight to San Diego felt like time was standing still. But as soon as the plane landed, it suddenly felt all too short. My father was already there waiting to drive me back to the home I grew up in. Mom had stayed behind, and when we arrived, we said our uncomfortable greetings before she went back to doing whatever she was doing before I walked through the front door.

Tossing my bag in my bedroom, I take out my phone to call Candace and let her know I made it. She can't talk long, so we cut it short, and I tell her that I might be out of pocket for the next few days so she won't worry if she doesn't hear from me.

This house feels exactly the same. Nothing ever changes. It's like my parents have been put on pause ever since Jace died five years ago. Like suddenly the world stopped spinning. I walk down the hall to her room and open the door. Everything is still untouched. Photos still displayed on her pinboard above her desk of her and her boyfriend. She really loved him. They had both been accepted to Cal State. She was so happy that they were going together, and I was happy that she would be less than two hours away from me. I close the door on those memories, head back to my room, and lie on my bed.

I miss her. I miss her so damn much. I think the reason I am bonded so tightly with Candace is because she reminds me a lot of my sister. Sometimes, I swear Jace gave her to me so I would always have a piece of her with me.

I swallow hard and slide off the bed. I've got to get out of here for a while. Packing up my wetsuit, I head downstairs and borrow the keys to my father's truck. I load up my shortboard and head down to the beach. I need some space to clear my head.

I spend most of the afternoon in the water, but La Jolla is a small town, so it isn't long before I run into some of my buddies I went to high school with. They're home from college for the summer, and I don't get home till late.

The next two days pass by with me dodging my parents. I fill most of my time at the beach, surfing, and hanging out with old friends. Last night, a few of us went to a local bar to hear a couple of bands play.

But now, here I am. I have six hours until my flight leaves to take me back to Seattle, and I feel no better about the mess I caused with Mark than I did when I got here. I find myself wandering down to my sister's room. Walking in, I go over to her dresser and pull out a small photo album she had made of the two of us. She was going to take it to college with her. I look at these pictures every time I come home. I sit on the floor and lean my back against her bed. Flipping the album open, I look at a photo of her and I together on the beach. My eyes are the same light golden color as hers, and as her eyes bore into me, I wonder what she would tell me to do.

I just want to be happy; I don't want to feel ashamed or embarrassed. Because I feel this way, I screwed up something that had the potential to be good. I know Jace would want me to be happy. She wouldn't want me to be carrying around this secret. Maybe that's it. Maybe this lie needs to end where it began. *Here.* My sister would want me to be honest with my parents, but it's more than that. I think she would want me to finally be brave enough to be honest with myself.

What do I really have to lose by telling them? It isn't as if we speak; we don't. Ever since Jace died, I've been nothing but an afterthought for them, and they hardly even acknowledge me.

Coming out to my parents may be just the thing I need to do to erase this gray haze I've been living in. The reality of being *out* with my parents might be my defining moment . . . my freeing moment.

As much as the thought of having that conversation with my parents terrifies me, I think it's time that it happens.

I focus in on my sister's eyes in the photo, and I know she'd have my back no matter what, but I fear that telling my parents could possibly be the end of my family. They are all I have, and I'm pretty sure when I get on the plane to go back to Seattle, I will be going back to the only thing I have left in the world—Candace.

My mind is in overdrive, dreading and fearing what I am about to tell my parents. I think about Mark; honestly, I can't stop thinking about him. I want to call him. I want to explain why I did what I did.

Standing up, I walk over to the dresser and slip the album back into the drawer. I turn around and stare at her bed while I try and muster up all the strength that I feel is failing me in this moment. Jace would tell me to do this. She wouldn't want me to hurt, and right now, that's all I'm feeling. For many reasons.

My stomach is in knots, and I feel sick as I start walking out of the room. Making my way down the stairs, I feel like I am losing control with each step I take. What they say or do is completely out of my hands, and I'm scared. I don't want to hurt them, but I don't want to hurt myself more than I already have. I hate feeling the shame and embarrassment. I hate the lies. I hate that these feelings caused me to hurt a really decent guy who didn't deserve my shit.

When I walk into the living room, my mother is reading a book on the couch next to my father, who is working on his laptop. Taking a deep breath and trying to grab on to any shred of courage I can find, I sit down in one of the chairs that's across from where my parents are sitting.

Looking up, my mother acknowledges me and says, "Hi, dear."

"Hey, Mom. Umm, listen . . . I need to talk to you guys about something," I stammer out, and I can't believe I am about to tell them this. My hands are shaking and my heart is beating at an insanely rapid rate.

"Is everything okay, son?" my father says as he closes the lid to his laptop.

"Yeah, I mean, no." I take a second to try and compose my thoughts, but they are all over the place, and I can't seem to find a coherent one floating around my head. "It's just . . . something has been bothering me, and I think you should know."

My mother sets her book down on her lap and focuses on me. "Is everything okay at school?"

"Yeah, it's not that. School is fine." I take a deep breath and let it out slowly. I know the words I need to say, so with my head down, I repeat them over and over in my mind, trying to force my mouth to actually speak them. *I'm gay. I'm gay. I'm gay.* Lifting my head up, I look to my mother. "I'm gay." *Fuck! I take that back. God, why did I just tell them?*

"I'm sorry, what?" my mother says with her brows cinched together in confusion.

God, don't make me say it again.

"What did you just say?" My father speaks in a tone that's none too friendly.

Looking between them, I swallow against my dry throat and repeat, "I'm gay."

"Is this your idea of a sick joke?" my father says with harsh intent, and I know what's coming. I knew they wouldn't be happy. I knew I'd most likely lose them. But the reality of it feeds the anger within me, and I can feel it boiling inside.

"No, it's not a joke."

"I don't understand. You've always liked girls. In high school, you were always dating," my mother says.

"I know, Mom, but I have always liked guys more."

"Enough," my father snaps. He stands and begins to quickly pace back and forth across the room, rubbing his head and staring at me with fury.

Stopping in front of me, he seethes, "No son of mine is a faggot. I don't know what the hell is going on, but I've heard enough."

His words sting. "I had to tell you; I'm sick of lying about who I am. I needed you to know so that I can stop hiding."

"But, you haven't actually . . . well, I mean . . ." my mother can't get her thoughts out when my dad butts in.

"God, of course not, Sharon!"

His condescending tone is fueling me to throw it all out there. Standing up, I snap. "What? Kissed a guy? Slept with a guy? Yes."

"Get out of my house," my father demands in a low stern voice.

I look to my mother, who is sitting there in shock. With her eyes fixed on me, she shakes her head and says, "Listen to your father." Tears begin to fall down her cheeks as she stands next to my dad and continues, "I thought losing your sister was bad, but you . . . knowing that you're going to hell, come in here and shame what's left of this family . . ."

"You need to get your things and go. Until you can sort yourself out, you're not welcome in this house. You hear me?"

"I'm your son!"

"No. You're not. Not anymore," he asserts sternly.

I don't say another word. There is nothing for me to say. Why would I want to beg these people to accept me? Why should I have to? I turn around and walk back upstairs to my room to pack my bags and call a cab. Pain rips through my chest, knowing that I've just lost the only family I have. It's another burden I'll have to carry with this life that chose me. I've always blamed the lack of love they have for me on the agony of losing their daughter. But now I know, that regardless of whether Jace was dead or alive, they still wouldn't accept me for who I really am.

I walk down the hall to her room and open the door. I go into her closet and take her La Jolla High cheerleading shirt she always used to wear. Closing the door, I walk over to her dresser, open the top drawer, and grab the photo album.

Taking both of these items, I walk back to my room and pack them into my bag. I just can't walk away from here without taking pieces of her with me. I zip my bag and let my fears, my worries, my sadness rip out of me. I sit on the floor, against my bed, and the tears fall. I'm so fuckin' lost right now. I don't know what to do or where I belong. I feel like everything is crashing down on top of me, and the pain in my chest is almost unbearable.

With my head in my hands, I cry. Being in this house is agonizing. What once held good memories, now only holds burning ones. Knowing my cab will be here any minute, I take my bags and head downstairs. My parents are still in the living room, and they don't even look up when I walk through and make my way to the front door. It's as if I don't even exist.

I'm thoroughly drained when I finally get off the plane and get to my car. As weak as it sounds, I just want to go back to the only home I know. I just want to crawl into bed with her and tell her all this shit and let it out, knowing that she loves me regardless of anything I could possibly say.

I shove my luggage into the back and slide into the driver's seat. When I turn my phone on, I see I have a missed text from Candace.

Heading out for a few hours. Come by later. Dying to see you.

Knowing that she thought about me enough to even send this text is all I need. I breathe in a sigh of relief and head straight to her house when I see that the text was sent a couple hours ago. Even if she isn't home yet, hopefully Kimber will be. I just need my friends right now.

I stop by the liquor store first and pick up some wine before driving to their place. When I pull up, Kimber's car and Candace's little white Acura are in the driveway. I've always had a key to their house, so I don't even bother ringing the doorbell. I just unlock the door and walk right in.

"Hey, girls," I call out, and before I can make it to the kitchen to set the wine down, Candace runs into the living room and gives me a big hug. God, this feels good. It's only been a few days, but I've missed her like hell. She looks up at me, and with a huge smile on her face, she gives me a kiss and takes the wine. Kimber steps in and wraps her arms around me as I watch Candace walk into the kitchen.

Kimber starts chatting about some band she saw last night as I make myself comfortable on the couch. Candace walks back into the room and sits on the floor, opening the wine and pouring herself a glass.

Looking up at me, she hands me the bottle and asks, "So how was your trip to San Diego?"

Pouring my wine, I say, "It was good. I hung out with friends, went out to a few bars, and saw some bands. You know, the usual visit home." I don't tell her what really happened because I want to talk to her about it in private, away from Kimber. Not that I won't tell her, but I just want to talk with Candace first.

"Well, we're glad you're back," Candace says with a smile and then takes a sip of her wine.

"You have no idea how happy I am to be back," I say in all seriousness.

"Man, was it that bad, Jase?" Kimber asks.

"It's just not home to me anymore. Plus, I missed you bitches." I laugh in an attempt to shift my mood from its current somber one. "So, what have I missed?" I ask and then down my wine faster than I should, but I'm desperate to take the edge off.

"Well, Candace is dating a douche from Mommy and Daddy's country club," Kimber says as she winks at Candace.

"I am not!" she practically squeals, and I really do wonder what the hell

I've missed in the past few days. Candace looks at me and explains, "We went out for drinks. That's all."

"Are you seeing him again?" Kimber questions, teasing Candace, and I can tell she's getting under her skin.

"You're seeing him again?" I ask in utter shock. Who is she giving a second date to? "Wait, who's *him?* Who are you seeing?"

"No. I mean, yes. God, really, it's no big deal."

"Must be if he's getting a second date," I say as I take another drink. "Is that where you were earlier? On your date?"

"Uh huh," she nods.

"Where did you guys go? You never told me," Kimber asks as she folds her legs underneath her.

"We went to Prescriptions."

"I love that place," Kimber says. "Anyway. New subject. What the hell are we doing this week before classes start back up?"

"I have some serious studio time I need to put in. I also have to work."

"You always keep yourself so busy," I say. I wish that she wouldn't. I feel like Candace hides too much behind her school and work.

We kick back for a while, and I enjoy this much-needed distraction from what happened earlier today. We talk about school and what our schedules are going to be like this next quarter. I can tell that Candace is tired, so when Kimber and I decide to turn on the TV, I tell Candace, "Come here, sweetie," as I motion for her to sit next to me.

Kimber turns on some trash show and Candace lies down with her head on my lap. I comb her hair with my fingers as I sit back and only half pay attention to the TV. After a while, I look down, and Candace is passed out.

"Is she asleep?" Kimber whispers in my direction, and I nod my head yes.

I let her sleep for a little bit longer before I decide to go lay her down.

"I'll be right back. I'm gonna try and get her to her room without waking her," I tell Kimber.

"Okay. I'll go grab the other bottle of wine."

I nod my head and scoop Candace up in my arms. This chick is tiny and barely weighs anything, so getting her into her bed is no problem. She's already in her pajamas, so I lie her down and pull the covers over her before heading back out to the living room.

Kimber and I drink the second bottle of wine, and wind up hanging for a couple more hours. When she passes out on the couch, I head to Candace's room and strip out of my clothes. Sliding into bed behind her, I wrap my arms around her and draw her in close to me. She presses into me, tucking herself tighter against my chest.

"Did I wake you?" I whisper.

"Yeah, but it's okay," she says softly. "What time is it?"

"Around two. You passed out, so I carried you in here and hung out with Kimber for a while longer."

"Is she asleep?"

"Yeah, and snoring like a beast." Candace laughs, and the sound makes me crack up as well.

She rolls over and lays her head on my chest, and I band my arms tightly around her. I feel like I'm clinging to the only person I have left to depend on.

"So, why did your trip really suck? I know something's bothering you," she questions, and I love that she can read me so well.

I let out a deep breath and say, "I told them."

Her grip on me tightens. "What did they say?"

"They threw me out." When I tell her, my chest begins to ache, and each breath I take almost feels like painful stabs.

I know she is crying when I feel her tears roll onto my chest. I hate that she's hurting for me, but in a way, it comforts me to know she cares so much.

"I'm so sorry. Why didn't you call me?"

"I don't know. I was embarrassed, I guess. I haven't told anyone what happened. I don't want the pity."

"You know I don't pity you, right?"

"Yeah," I whisper and kiss the top of her head, feeling a little more free now that I've told her. I know I have a lot more to tell her, but I won't tonight. I don't want to make her more upset, and honestly, I just don't think I have it in me right now. I'm tired and have had way too much to drink.

"I'm sad because I love you. When your heart hurts, so does mine. Your pain is my pain."

Each of her words lifts more and more weight off my chest. We lie there and I just hold her.

"You know this is your home, don't you? Right here with me. Kimber and I are your home. And we don't give a shit that you like guys."

I kiss the top of her head again, and she grips me even tighter. I allow her words to comfort me, the words I wish my parents would've said. The heat of my tears roll down my temples, and I try to keep my emotions under control so she can't see how upset I really am.

"Jase?" she finally whispers.

"Yeah, sweetie?"

"I love you."

"I love you, too." More than anything in this world.

chapter seven

I HAVEN'T SPENT much time with Candace this past week. She's been picking up a lot of extra shifts at work and spending more time in the dance studio before classes start back up next week. I've been dreading having to face Mark since we have a couple of classes together this quarter. I think about him a lot and feel terrible for what I did. I've thought about texting him, but have no clue what I could possibly say at this point.

Since I came back home, I haven't spoken to my parents, so I can only assume they meant what they said. It hurts. It hurts to know that I might never see or speak to them again. I just don't understand how you can turn your back so easily on your child. It makes me think that everything with them, all of the good, was nothing but a lie. Maybe that's where I learned it from. Maybe pretending comes so easily to me because it's all my parents ever did.

I don't really know what I gained from telling them. It didn't give me what I was hoping for. I'm not sure what it'll take or what I have to do to be more at peace with myself. I've been trying to keep busy so my mind doesn't wander too much. I've been spending a lot of time in the gym and running.

I was shocked when Candace said that she was coming out with Kimber and me tonight. She never goes out with us, but lately, she's been coming out of her shell a little more. I think all the fighting with her parents has finally taken a toll on her and she's looking for some sort of release. She even said that the guy she went out with the other day is coming along. I'm not sure if she even likes him, but I'm happy she's giving it chance.

I decide to head out a little early, needing the distraction. When I arrive at Remedy, I spot some of my friends that are already here. We sit around and talk for a while before my eyes catch Mark as he's walking in. *Shit!* It feels like a brick falls in the pit of my stomach. God, he looks good, and a part of me, a really big part, wants to go over and talk to him, but I'm sure I'm the last person he wants to see.

Right behind Mark, Kimber and Candace walk in, and Candace can't get to me fast enough. I walk toward her and quickly grip her arm, rushing her over to the bar at the back of the club.

"You thirsty?" she asks with sarcasm.

Still freaking out, I say, "Not really. I just saw Mark." When we get up to the bar, we hop onto a couple of barstools.

"Isn't that the hottie you used to see that plays guitar?"

"Exactly." I give her a serious look. I still haven't told her what happened with Mark. I flag down the bartender and order us some shots and bottles of beer.

Eying me from the side, she says, "Okay, spill it. Clearly you're into getting drunk, so tell me what happened."

When the bartender sets the drinks down in front of us, I push two of the shots and a beer over to her, and we both knock the tequila back quickly before I confess, "He caught me kissing his roommate."

She immediately starts laughing at me, not knowing how I ever felt about him, and jokes, "You can be a slut sometimes, you know?"

"Trust me. I know," I say and hand her the second shot. We down them and I tell her, "He was really pissed off. I actually feel like total shit about it."

She lays her hand on my arm and looks at me a little concerned, but she is instantly distracted when a guy comes up from behind and pulls her into his arms.

She turns around to face him. "Hey, Jack."

I laugh to myself when she nearly stumbles off the barstool and into his arms. Candace never handles hard liquor too well, and it doesn't take much for her to feel the effects.

She introduces us, and I give him a handshake. I continue to drink my beer as Candace and Jack talk. This guy doesn't really strike me as her type. I can't help but feel protective of her. She really doesn't have anyone in her life to care for her other than Kimber and myself. I know that Candace considers the two of us her family, and there is no doubt that she is my family as well. When I turn back to look at her, she is rolling her eyes at something Jack just said, and I can't help but laugh at her.

He leans in and whispers something in her ear and the next thing I know, they're making their way to the dance floor. I order another drink when Kimber grabs the now empty barstool.

"Are we getting drunk?"

Looking over at her, I wink as I take a long swig of my beer, I wink at her.

"Perfect," she says with an evil grin and then yells at the bartender for a beer. When he slides one to her, she starts chugging the damn thing and turns around in her seat. "Holy shit!"

"What?"

Pointing the neck of her bottle in the direction of the dance floor, she says, "Our girl is giving her date a hard on."

I turn around and spot Candace dancing with Jack. I start laughing at her because she is acting so out of character. She is always so quiet and reserved, and she is nearly making out with this dude in the middle of the club.

"What the hell has gotten into her lately?" I ask Kimber.

"She said that she feels like she hasn't really let loose since coming to college. I guess this is her way of having some fun. It's pretty damn amusing if you ask me. Our quiet, little Candace, acting like a hooker."

I shake my head at Kimber. "You know damn well that Candace would never do anything with that guy."

When we see Jack's hands squeeze her ass, we both bust out in a fit of laughter, nearly doubling over at her crazy behavior.

"You sure about that?" Kimber says through her giggles.

I stay at the bar and continue to nurse my beer. Kimber has ditched me, and when I turn to see where she went, I spot Mark again. I watch him laughing with a group of his friends, and I wish I could be over there with him. I'm sure he hasn't seen me since I've been hiding out back here. I finally stand up and make my way over to the rest of our friends and see that Jack is sitting alone.

"Where's Candace?" I ask as I sit next to him.

"That crazy blonde girl dragged her to the bathroom."

"That would be Kimber. She's like a rabid squirrel on acid," I say with laughter.

When Candace comes up to us, she asks Jack what he's laughing at. She squeezes herself in between the two of us and he says, "I can't even remember now that you're here."

The look on her face is priceless, and I chuckle under my breath. She has no clue how to respond when guys say sweet things to her. She always gets so embarrassed, and Jack is completely clueless.

It's getting late, so Kimber and I call it a night. Candace decides to stay a little while longer with Jack, so we say our goodbyes and head out. Walking out to the parking lot, I notice Mark heading to his car. I turn to Kimber and say, "Hey, I'll catch you later, okay?"

"Yeah, have a good night," she says as she turns to her car.

I'm not sure what I'm doing or what I'm gonna say, but I call out, "Mark."

He turns around, and when he looks at me, he shakes his head and says, "We've got nothing to talk about, man."

"Wait. Just give me a second." I hate feeling like I have been for the past couple of weeks, and I figure if I can be honest with my parents, then I can be honest with him. He deserves an explanation and an apology.

He leans against his car and folds his arms across his chest as I approach. Clearly he's still pissed. But what he does to me when I'm around him is something that I can't explain. I feel it in my chest, it courses through me, and suddenly I'm nervous.

"Can I just explain myself?" I ask as I step in front of him.

"I don't really think there is anything you could say at this point."

Dropping my head, I take a second before looking into his eyes, and I instantly feel a need to beg him for another chance. I'm not quite sure where this is coming from, but I take a huge leap and follow my heart. "I know 'I'm sorry' isn't enough, but I am. I really fucked up."

I step to move beside him and lean up against the car next to him. Shoving my hands in my pockets, I make my confession. "I was scared."

When I say this, Mark finally turns his head and looks at me.

I continue, "I was scared because I've never done this before. I've never wanted to be around another guy the way I want to be around you. The thing is . . . I'm not sure what the hell I'm doing."

"Why couldn't you just talk to me?"

"Because it wasn't until I met you that I realized I was terrified to admit that I'm gay." I stop, trying to find the words to explain myself. "I mean, I've always known, but the idea of a relationship just seemed too defining, and I wasn't sure I was ready. I . . . a part of me is still really uncomfortable with this," I admit.

"So what does that have to do with you making out with Kyle?"

"I didn't know how to talk to you, so it was my fucked up way of destroying whatever it was that we had going on so that I didn't have to deal with it." I am nothing but honest with him, and although I could just be pissing him off even more, I feel like I owe him this.

He turns his head away from me and focuses straight forward. I notice his clenched jaw, but I stay quiet, waiting for some kind of response. Keeping his eyes ahead, he says, "I really liked you, you know?"

"I'm sorry."

He surprises me when he reveals, "I still really like you."

My heart thuds hard in my chest when he tells me this. He still doesn't look at me, but I decide to return his honesty and tell him, "I flew home and told my parents last weekend. I never told them before because I was afraid of what that meant for me."

He looks at me when I say this and takes a moment before responding. "You don't have to explain. I've been there. I felt the same way."

I nod my head and finally realize that if only I would have been honest with him, he possibly could have really helped me. Maybe he still can.

"What did they say?" he asks.

Shaking my head, I turn to look away from him when I say. "It's over. They threw me out, told me not to come back or call." When I turn to look back at him, the look in his eyes is of disbelief. "I wasn't completely surprised. I knew that would most likely be their reaction."

"Then why?"

"I hoped it would help me come to terms with all of this."

"Did it?"

"Honestly . . . I don't know, but at least I'm able to tell you everything I was too scared to say before."

We stand there without speaking when the mist turns into thicker sprinkles, but we don't move. I wish I knew what he was thinking. I'm feeling anxious and extremely exposed right now. But he gives me a little hope when he turns to face me and asks, "So what do you want now?"

"I know I don't have any right to ask you to forgive me, but I feel like absolute shit for what I did, and I'm so sorry." I swallow hard when I admit, "I really like you, Mark. I just want a chance to show you that I'm not an asshole."

"I know you're not an ass, but you really let me down. I'm not sure I can trust you."

"Let me show you that you can," I say, and I know with those words that I can't let my fears get in the way again. I need to face this. I need to learn to be okay with myself.

When I see him nod his head, I can't fight my smile. I want to kiss him. God, I want to kiss him so bad, but I don't. I just wrap my arms around him and pull him in for a hug. When I feel his arms band around me, I say once again, "I'm so fuckin' sorry."

"No more apologies. Let's just start over."

He leans back slightly, and I don't take what I want to take. I want him to know that I want something more than just that. So, I simply leave it with, "Coffee? Tomorrow?"

He smiles and responds, "Sounds good. I'll call you when I wake up."

I nod my head and take a step back when Mark opens his door and hops in the driver's seat. Before he closes the door, he says, "Jase . . . thanks for being honest with me."

"Thanks for giving me the chance."

chapter eight

MARK CALLED THIS morning like he said he would. I suggested we meet at Peet's on the ground floor of my apartment building. I'd be lying if I said I wasn't still anxious about all of this, but the feeling of not wanting to walk away from Mark is stronger than my fear of defining who I am to myself.

I shrug on a t-shirt and grab my keys before making my way to the elevator. I arrive before he does, so I go ahead and get a coffee before finding a seat by the window to wait for him. It's raining pretty hard today, and I watch as it falls from the dark sky.

I pull my phone out and shoot Candace a text. I really need to talk to her about everything that's been going on.

Can I see you later?

I sit for a while and drink my coffee before my phone buzzes with her response.

Yeah, I'll be home.

Okay, I'll text you in a bit. Love you.

"Hey, man," I hear Mark say, and I shove my phone in my pocket as I stand up to give him a hug. I'll take all the touches I can from this guy.

Seeing his coffee already in hand, we sit down and he says, "How's it going?"

"Good. You?" I ask as he nods his head and leans forward, resting his elbows on the table.

"I was thinking about what you said last night. About your parents and all."

I shake my head. "Don't worry about it."

"Are they all the family you have?"

"Yeah, but we haven't been close for a long time. It's not like we really ever spoke."

He takes a long sip of his drink and sets his cup down. "So what are you gonna do?"

"There's nothing I can do. It's done with. They were pretty final with what they said. I know them well enough to know when they shut down, they don't open back up."

He shakes his head, and I know this bothers him. So I assure him, "I'm not alone, if that's what you're wondering. I have a really close friend that I've always considered my family."

"Oh yeah?"

"Yeah. Actually, I should probably talk to you about her." I need to explain our relationship to him because I know it isn't typical. He needs to know how we are, and I need to know if this bothers him.

"Okay? You're making me nervous," he says with a chuckle.

"No, it's nothing crazy, we just have a strong relationship, and I want you to understand that it's nothing beyond friends."

"What do you mean?"

Leaning back in my seat, I tell him, "We're really close. I mean, we're physically close as well. It's just always been that way with us. Her name's Candace. She's a sweet girl, but in many ways, extremely closed off. Her parents are dicks to her. But, anyway, I just need you to know that we spend a lot of time together . . . we spend a lot of nights together in each other's beds. But it isn't like what most people would assume at all. She's just a friend . . . well, family really. She's all I've had for a long time."

He nods his head, but doesn't say anything at first. I worry that he might not be okay with this, but when he says, "I think it's good that you have someone like that in your life," I relax a little bit.

"Are you sure you don't have a problem with it?"

"Look, I don't know much about you, but I hate that you don't have a family that supports you," he says, and I know his words are genuine. "So, if this girl can give you what you can't find from anyone else, then yeah, I can be okay with it."

Curious about his family, I ask, "So how did your parents react when you told them?"

"They took it pretty well. I didn't tell them for what felt like a long time. I was terrified they'd react badly. I was scared shitless, to be honest. But it worked out. My parents have never treated me differently from the way they always have. They love me regardless . . . it really bothers me that you didn't get that."

I can't help but feel a twinge of jealousy, wishing that I had what he has. How easy it must be, but in a way, he's right. Although I have Candace, I still feel very much alone.

"Well, since I can't introduce you to my family, you want to try and get together with me and meet Candace and her roommate, Kimber? They are pretty much who I spend most of my time with."

He smiles, big, and it's perfect. "I'd love to."

I smile back and can't really understand why he's being so nice after what I did, but I'll take whatever he gives me, and right now, it's more than I deserve. "Okay. I'm going to see Candace later today, so I'll find out when she's free. Sometime this weekend?"

"Yeah, I have nothing going on. Just planning on taking it easy before classes start back up on Monday."

When we finish our coffee, I look over at him and ask, "You wanna come over to my place for a while?"

"Yeah, where do you live?"

I laugh as I say, "Right here. I live in this building."

"That's convenient," he says with a knowing smirk as we head out.

When we get off the elevator and head into my apartment, we make ourselves comfortable on the couch and flip on the TV, although we don't watch it because it doesn't take but a second for Mark to distract me. He reaches over and threads his fingers with mine. Staring at me with his deep green eyes, I slowly move in and brush my lips against his. I tug him in closer to me and press my lips more firmly onto his. He didn't shave this morning, and the roughness of his kisses do nothing but turn me on. I hate that I had to hurt him to be able to be with him like this. I should have just been honest. I should have trusted him. Pushing those thoughts away, wanting to be here with him and not in my scattered head, I loop my arms around his waist and pull him down on top of me as I lie on my back.

He hovers over me, running his hand down my cheek to my neck and wraps it around the back of my head, lifting me closer to him as he slips his tongue in my mouth. I run my hand up his smooth back, underneath his shirt, and when he grinds himself against me, I can feel what I'm doing to him. I tug at the hem of his shirt and peel it off. Wrapping my arms back around him, I hold him against me.

Moving the way we are together ignites more than just lust inside of me, but feelings I never knew were there. The connection that I feel with him, even though I still really don't know him, is intense. I know Mark isn't into anything casual—he's told me this—and that makes this even better because for once, I don't want to walk away.

He moves his lips from mine, and when he asks, "Same page?" I know he wants the confirmation for this same question he asked me a couple weeks ago. The question I was too afraid to acknowledge.

Looking up at his flushed face—able to respond this time—I nod and affirm, "Same page," and my anxiety about this starts to dissolve into the happiness that is swarming through me when he looks at me like he is.

I watch his muscles flex as he slowly lowers himself onto me and reaches down, slipping his hand under the waistband of my gym shorts. When he wraps his hand around me, I let out a low growl with the pleasure that pulses through me as I harden under his touch. His grip is strong as I fist my hands in his hair and slam my mouth over his. Not holding back, I possess his mouth with my tongue as his hand continues to work me.

Fumbling with his belt, I manage to unclasp it and pop the buttons open on his pants. I yank them down enough to be able to freely give him back what he's giving me. He's hot to my touch, and just the feel of him is enough to keep me from holding on any longer. I thrust myself into his hand, burying my head in his neck, and moan in intense pleasure as he makes me come. He doesn't let go of me as I begin to pump him in my hand, gripping tight.

He lets his body fall onto mine, and we shift to our sides. He takes my lips with his, and I move with him in a way I haven't with anyone else. I go slow and take my time, not wanting to take my hands off of him anytime soon.

Heading over to your place.

Okay. Just let yourself in.

I walk through the parking garage to my spot and click the locks open. Mark wound up staying over for most of the morning. I feel good about where we stand at this point. Allowing myself to open up to him and lay it all out there for him to know, freed some of the fear inside of me.

When I pull up to Candace's house, only her white Acura is here. I go ahead and let myself in. Kimber isn't home, so I go straight to Candace's room. She's sitting at her desk doing something on her laptop as I walk in.

"Hey, sweetie."

"Hey," she says as she closes the lid, and I lie down on her bed as she gets up from her chair and walks over to lie next to me. I was worried that Mark would have an issue with Candace. I think he will have a better understanding of us when he meets her. She lays her head on the pillow next to me, and I shift to face her.

"I need to talk to you about something," I say, still a little nervous. Not nervous about her reaction—it's me. It's taking another step towards cementing the fact that this is truly me.

Turning towards me, she says, "Okay, talk."

"I haven't been completely open with you about some stuff that's been going on, and I need to talk to you about it and tell you everything."

She pinches her brows together and says, "Okay," slowly with worry.

"I should have told to you about this from the start, but I was embarrassed."

"Jase, you can tell me anything," she assures me.

"I know, and that's why I feel so awful," I say and then I just let everything out. "I ran into Mark last night when I left the club. He was the reason

I went home and came out to my parents. I really like him. I mean . . . I like him more than I have ever liked anyone. You know how I am with guys, but with him, it's different, and it started stirring up a lot of stuff I thought I had gotten past."

"I don't understand."

"I told you what it was like for me in high school. Well, I thought I was over that. When I met Mark and started spending time with him, I had feelings for him in a way I hadn't ever felt towards another guy. It made me scared. When he told me that he wasn't interested in anything casual, I freaked out."

She interrupts me and says, "Like, the idea of having a real relationship with a guy would solidify that you're gay?"

God, she completely gets it. "Yeah," I say, and then tell her, "So I went to his house when his roommate was there, knowing that Mark would be home soon, and made out with him just so that Mark could catch us. I felt like shit, but I was too much of a coward to just be honest with him. I still feel like shit."

She shifts herself closer to me and drapes her arm around my waist. "That's awful. What did he say?"

"Nothing really. I knew I'd hurt him. I was such a shit; I didn't even say anything to him. I just grabbed my keys and walked out."

"So you went home to tell your parents because you thought that it would be easier for you to accept you were gay if you came out?"

"Do you know how much I love you?" She smiles up at me as I brush her hair back. "I knew you would understand. I shouldn't have kept this from you."

"It's okay. I understand why you did. But I hate that you were going through this and I wasn't there for you."

"I'm sorry."

"So, you talked to him last night? What did you say?"

"I was just honest. I apologized and explained everything. I even told him about my parents."

"How did it go?"

"He told me that, despite what I did, he still has feelings for me, and I told him that I do too. So he asked if we could just start over. He came over for coffee this morning and we talked more about my family and stuff."

She pulls back to look me in the eyes. "So, you two are seeing each other? I mean . . . exclusively?"

"Yeah."

"How are you feeling about it now?"

"Nervous," I admit. "Mostly because I have never done this, but I love the way he makes me feel when we're together."

She tilts her head up, pecks me on the lips, and then gives me her beautiful smile. "I'm really happy for you, you know? I hope he can see how special you are."

I kiss the top of her head and tuck her under my chin. I don't know what I ever did to deserve such an amazing friend. I love how she just gets me. She doesn't even have to try. Telling her about Mark feels so good. Hell, everything about today feels good. I just hope he will be patient enough with me so that I can figure this all out and get to a place where I can be free of the shame.

chapter nine

AFTER MY TALK with Candace yesterday, I totally forgot to ask her what her plans were this weekend and if she'd be up to meeting Mark. I've been calling and texting her for the past couple of hours, but I can't get ahold of her.

I spot her car when I pull in front of Common Grounds, the coffee shop that she works at. When I walk inside, I spot Roxy, her boss, behind the counter.

"Hey, Jase."

"Roxy, how've you been?" I ask and lean over the counter to give her a hug.

"Good. You looking for Candace?"

"Yeah. Is she busy?"

"She's in the back; it's been pretty slow," she says before yelling over her shoulder, "Candace!"

"Hey, Candace," I say as she walks up to the counter. I lean in to give her a kiss. "I've been trying to call you."

"Oh, sorry. I was at the studio this morning and let the battery drain on my cell, and I never remembered to plug it in to recharge," she says. "I'll go do that now before I forget again." She seems a little spastic when she runs to the back and then quickly returns with her cell and charger.

When she plugs it in, I ask, "So, I wanted to see if you and Kimber could get together with Mark and I later tonight?"

"I'd love to, but I'm working late tonight. How about tomorrow afternoon? We can do a cookout at our house."

"That sounds great. I really fucked up with him, and I want to make it right. Plus, I want you guys to meet him."

She leans down on her elbows and looks up at me. "Of course, Jase."

"Great, I'll call him and let him know," I say, and then quickly kiss her forehead. I catch her smile as I turn to leave.

Walking back out to my car, I call Mark.

"Hey, Jase. What's up?"

"Not much. Do you wanna get together at Candace's place tomorrow afternoon?"

"Um, yeah. That works for me."

"Great. I think we will just hang out back and cook out since the weather is supposed to be decent for a change."

"That sounds good. Are you doing anything tonight?"

"Nothing set in stone. Why?"

"I'm heading out to go for a run, but I was just gonna chill and watch the football game later if you wanted to come over."

"Oh, umm . . ." is all I can say. No way in hell do I wanna run into Kyle, not after that crap I pulled. But Mark interrupts my thoughts and says, "Kyle doesn't live here anymore."

"God, I feel like a dick," I say as the guilt returns.

"Don't. We never got along that well anyway." He tries brushing it off, as if it isn't the big deal that it actually is.

"Still, I feel like shit about everything."

"Are you coming over or what?" he interjects, and I can't help but laugh.

"Yeah. Just text me after your run."

"Okay, I'll talk to you later.

"Later."

When I got to Mark's house later that day, we spent the evening drinking beer and watching the game. It was nice to spend that time with him, just taking it easy. We didn't do anything more than just hold hands and be close to one another. The more time I spend with him, the more I find myself falling for him.

Now here we are, driving together to Candace's house. It's important to me that he likes her because she's such a big part of my life. But at the same time, I really hope she likes him because her opinion is important to me.

When I park the car, I look over at Mark, and he gives me a smile before he steps out. I take his hand and hold it as we walk up to the house. Opening the front door, I call out, "We're here."

As I start leading Mark through the living room, Candace walks in from the kitchen and gives me a warm hug.

When I back away, I introduce the two of them. "Mark, this is Candace."

She smiles big when she turns to Mark. "Hey! It's great to meet you. Come on in. We're in the kitchen getting the food ready."

Walking into the kitchen, Kimber is chowing down on a mouthful of chips when she says, "Hey, Jase."

Shaking my head, I look at Mark then back at Kimber. "And this crazy girl is Kimber."

"Nice to meet you guys," Mark says with a grin.

The girls move around the kitchen and Kimber asks if one of us will start the grill for her.

"Yeah, I can do that," Mark replies, and Kimber leads him out back as I stay inside with Candace, helping her get all the food to carry out.

"This is a nice place you have," I hear Mark say to the girls as we walk outside.

Kimber flops down in a chair. "I suppose," she says with a sigh.

"Please, just ignore her dramatics," Candace tells Mark as Kimber just laughs. I know she loves trying to get reactions from people, and she is constantly cracking me up. If there is one thing about Kimber, she doesn't give a shit what people think about her. I love her freedom. I'm jealous of it in a way.

"Hey, Jase, will you run inside and grab the case of beer that's in the fridge and bring it out? There's a cooler next to the door that already has ice in it," Candace says.

"Sure." I go into the kitchen to get the beers and when I walk back outside, Candace and Mark are chatting about school.

"What are you studying?" I hear her ask him.

Mark takes a swig of his beer and responds, "Same as Jase—Architecture." She looks over at me and Mark adds, "That's how we know each other."

I smile at Mark as he continues to talk with Candace. I get up and walk over to the grill to cook the burgers. I keep turning my head to the two of them and love that they are having an easy time talking to one another.

"He's really hot," Kimber says as she steps next to me, nudging her arm against mine.

"Yeah, I know."

I start taking the meat off the grill and then get a beer before sitting next to Kimber at the fire pit. I leave Mark with Candace since they seem pretty inseparable at the moment. Mark says something to her and she laughs out loud, tossing her head back as he starts to crack up as well. I have no idea what they are talking about, but seeing the two of them laughing like they are, makes me laugh too.

The afternoon passes quickly, and I spend most of it with Kimber, drinking and bullshitting around, all the while, watching Mark and Candace from across the backyard. They've been talking and laughing non-stop.

"Help me clean up?" I ask Kimber, and she rolls her eyes at me. "You are such a spoiled brat. Get off your lazy ass, and help me out."

Sighing in exasperation, she says, "Fine."

Candace and Mark join us in the kitchen after a while and we decide to call it a night.

Walking us to the door, she says, "It was so good to meet you, Mark."

"Same here," he responds.

She pulls him in for a hug and tells him, "You're welcome anytime, and you don't need Jase with you to stop by."

I laugh and shake my head at her when she says this.

"Thanks," he says.

Kimber yells her "goodbye" from the kitchen and we yell it right back. I grab Candace and give her a tight hug. She whispers softly in my ear, "He's perfect."

"I know," I mumble quietly. I give her a chaste kiss and then head out. Walking to my car with Mark, he takes ahold of my hand and gives my neck a few pecks. We stop at the car and I kiss him. Seeing him so comfortable with my best friend, my only family, makes me happy, and I smile against his lips as we continue to share our slow kiss.

Mark whispers over my lips, "What's so funny?"

I move back and look at him. "Nothing's funny. I'm just happy."

He wraps his arms around my waist and says, "Me too. I see why you love her so much. She's great."

"Yeah, she is. So are you."

The smile that grows on his face is beautiful, so I take one last kiss before we get in the car and start driving back to my place. Since neither one of us has an early class tomorrow, Mark decides to stay the night.

After changing clothes and sliding into bed, Mark wraps his arm around me as I ask into the darkness, "Did you have fun today?"

"Yeah, I did," he responds softly. "Thanks for introducing me to your friends. Did you know them before coming to Seattle?"

"No. I met Candace the first quarter I was here. We had a Gen. Ed. class together. I also had a Communications class with Kimber, but I never spoke to her until I found out she was Candace's dorm mate."

"So what's her story?" he questions. "She seems so different from you and Candace."

Letting out a laugh, I tell him, "I don't know where to begin with that chick. I've always found it odd that Candace is such good friends with her because they are so opposite." I start laughing harder when I think back to our Communications class we had together freshman year. "Oh my God. You wouldn't believe this speech she gave in that class we shared."

"What?" Mark chuckles as I try to control my own laughter.

"We were assigned an informational presentation. We were free to choose our own topic, but we had to perform a demonstration. So she walks to the front of the class with a blow-up sex doll. No. Shit. Mark. Mouth open for a blowjob, big tits, sex doll!"

He's now laughing just as hard as I am. "Are you serious?"

"No joke. She tried going for a sense of modesty by throwing one of her t-shirts over it. I swear, I was about to piss my pants when she laid that thing face down on the demonstration table and began giving that doll, with its ass all exposed, a thorough body massage. Everyone was cracking up, but she kept a straight face and proceeded as if she was giving some political speech."

"What did your professor say?"

"Nothing. He just let her do her thing as if what she was doing was completely normal."

"Oh my God," he says as we both lie there in my dark room and laugh together.

"But that's Kimber. She doesn't care what people think about her, and she is totally unpredictable, whereas Candace is reserved, quiet for the most part, and extremely focused. The two of them are an odd combo."

"So how do you fit in to that?"

Laughter aside, I roll over and lay my head on his chest. "I hang out with Kimber a lot, only because Candace rarely goes out, but we don't have a deep friendship at all; more like buddies. It's nothing close to what I have with Candace."

"I don't think many people have that. You're lucky."

"Yeah," I whisper. "It's a lot like what I had with my sister, well, except the physical stuff," I joke. "But she gives me what Jace used to when I had her."

I pull my head back and look Mark in the eyes when he says, "Tell me something about her."

It's always hard for me to talk about my sister, but I want to share her with him, so I take a hard swallow before I open up. "We were best friends. It was always like that with us. We did everything together. There was this one time, we were young, maybe ten or eleven," I say and then pause when I feel the sadness well up in me along with the happiness. It's a strange conflict of emotions that causes my throat to slightly constrict.

Shifting and tucking my bent arm under the side of my head, I continue, "We had dug up a pail of mud down at the creek that ran through the back of our neighborhood. Jace thought it would be funny to make mud pies and blow them up with firecrackers on one of our neighbor's front porch. The lady that lived there was always crabby, so needless to say, we didn't like her that much. Jace found one of the leftover boxes of Black Cats from the Fourth of July, and we set those suckers off." I start laughing at the memory. "That shit was so loud, and there was mud flying everywhere. That crotchety, old woman opened her front door and Jace and I ran as fast as we could, laughing our asses off."

"You guys sound like trouble," Mark softly chuckles.

"We really were."

"Did you guys get caught?"

"Yeah. Our mom made us go over and clean up the mess. We had to use toothpicks to poke out the mud that slung into the window screen. It was a bitch of mess, but so worth it." My smile fades when the sadness takes over. I hate that memories are all that I am left with. "I miss her," I breathe out.

Mark doesn't speak, he just holds me tighter in his arms. I lie quiet for a while until I finally say, "But when I'm with Candace . . . she just makes it easier."

"I wish I could have met your sister."

Mark doesn't say anything else and neither do I as we lie there holding each other. Sharing this part of myself with him is hard. It's hard when I share it with Candace too. But it's also nice, being able to talk about her. I don't do it often, but she's a big part of me, so giving that to Mark makes me feel closer to him. And I want that—the closeness.

We spent the night wrapped up in each other's arms, and it was the most intimate thing I have ever done with someone. I know I'm completely falling for this guy.

Looking at him now, sleeping next to me, I lean over to kiss his bare shoulder. When I do, he begins to stir and wake up. I tangle my legs with his and pull him in tight.

"Morning," he grumbles with his eyes closed.

I laugh and ask, "Coffee?"

"Please."

I can tell this guy is not a morning person, so I give him time to wake up. I slip out of bed and go into the kitchen to start a pot of coffee. While it's brewing I pick up my phone that's lying on the counter and see I have a missed text from Candace.

Had fun last night. The three of us should hang out soon.

I start typing out a response when I hear, "God, who are you texting this early?"

I look up to see Mark as he strolls lazily into the kitchen and straight to me. "Just Candace," I say as he wraps his arms around me. When he nips my jaw, I tell him, "Coffee's ready."

"Oh, good." He grabs one of the mugs I've already gotten down and pours his cup, drinking it black. "I've got to head out soon. There are some errands I need to run before my eleven o'clock class."

"Yeah, I have a ten o'clock Structures class."

We go sit on the couch, and I drape my arm over him as he leans into me, kicking his feet up on the coffee table. I love that he feels relaxed with being here.

"So I was going to run by the Athletic Club to pay my deposit, if that's cool with you."

"Yeah, that'll work. We should meet up Wednesday morning. It's my long workout, so I'm there for a couple of hours and then run after."

"Perfect. I don't have any classes on Wednesdays, so I'm free."

We spend the next half hour lying around and finishing off the pot of coffee before Mark heads out. I have a full load of classes today, so I quickly take a shower and get cleaned up before driving up to campus.

Walking into Candace's bedroom, I hear the shower in the bathroom. Sitting at her desk, I decide to check my bank account to make sure the money from the bursar has been deposited. I've been able to get through college without help from my parents. I came here on an academic scholarship and have been able to qualify for several grants along the way.

"What are you doing?" I hear Candace ask from behind me.

Staring at the screen, I say, "Nothing really, just messing around. I just finished my last class and thought I'd come chill with you."

I turn around and see her putting on her underwear and bra. "You going somewhere?"

"Yeah, there's a party at Jack's fraternity tonight, and he asked me to go."

I can see that there isn't an ounce of happiness behind her words. "You sound thrilled."

"It's just . . . I'm not into him aside from kissing. We have nothing in common, and I feel nothing towards him."

I can't help the smirk that crosses my face. This is just like Candace.

"This should not be a surprise to you, Jase," she says with an eye roll.

"Nope, no surprise at all. Typical Candace, devoid of all things emotional. Well, except for me." I flash her a big smile and then turn back to the computer as she turns on her hair dryer. I shut the lid to the laptop when I finish up and walk over and sit on the edge of her bed. I watch her as she gets ready and when she turns to me, she questions, "What?"

"Stay with me tonight. I can tell you don't want to go out, so come to my place."

"I can't. He'll be here any second. Plus, I need to talk to him."

"About what?"

"I just need to let him know that I don't have time for dating or anything."

I laugh at her, and she smacks me on my arm. "I'm sorry, girl. You know I love you and all, but I don't know why you even bothered with this one."

She sits down next to me and resigns, "God, I have no idea either."

"Call me when you get home."

chapter ten

THE RINGING OF my phone wakes me up. I roll over, pluck it from my nightstand, and answer it, trying not to open my eyes in the process.

"God, Candace. What time is it?" I complain.

"Is this Jase Kenrick?" a woman, who's clearly not Candace, asks. I hold the phone out for a second to see that it's almost one in the morning.

"Um, yeah. I'm Jase," I say as I sit up.

"My name is Allie Thompson. I'm a nurse here at Harborview Medical Center. Your name was given to me by Candace Parker."

Now, I'm awake. Wide awake. "God, is she okay?"

"She arrived here by ambulance a little while ago and asked that I call you. She's requested for you to come up here to be with her."

"What happened? Is she okay?" I ask again. My mind is racing with the worst, and I'm already out of bed grabbing my clothes.

"They are about to take her to run some tests. Will you be able to bring her a change of clothes? If not, we have some scrubs she can change into."

What the fuck? "No, I'll bring her clothes." I don't waste any more time and toss the phone on the bed, hanging up on the call. My heart is pounding. I have no clue what the hell is going on, but I throw on a pair of gym shorts and a t-shirt. My hands are shaking as I'm fumbling to tie the laces to my running shoes.

I find my backpack, dumping out my notebooks, and rush over to my dresser. Candace has clothes that have accumulated here over the past few years, so I grab a pair of her jeans and a shirt, along with some underwear.

Slinging the backpack over my shoulder, I get my keys and don't even bother with the elevator. I bolt down the stairs to the parking garage and jump into my SUV. I know I'm driving like a maniac, but I can't get to the hospital fast enough. My mind is in overdrive, wondering if she got into a car wreck or something.

When I finally make it to the hospital, I rush through the sliding doors into the ER. I don't even wait for the lady sitting behind the desk to look up at me when I frantically ramble, "My friend, Candace . . . she's here. Umm . . . Candace Parker. I got a call. A nurse called me a few minutes ago."

"Okay, hold on, sir. Let me call back there to see if they are ready for you."

I'm trying to control my breathing, but the pressure in my chest is making it nearly impossible. Time seems to stand still as I wait. I just want her to be okay. I need her to be okay.

"Sir, Allie, one of her nurses, is on her way up to get you."

"Okay, thanks," I say as I back away from the desk. I don't sit down. I can't. I'm too anxious, so I just stand and stare at the locked wooden doors that lead back to where I know she is.

When the doors open, I see a nurse with short, blonde hair, wearing green scrubs. She talks to the lady at the desk then turns around and begins walking towards me, in what feels like slow motion, and the weight at the pit of my stomach becomes painful.

"Are you Jase Kenrick?"

"Yes. Please tell me what's going on. What happened?"

"Let's go sit down, okay? She asked that I speak with you first."

I don't respond; I just follow behind her as she walks me back into the ER and takes me to a small room with a couch and a couple of chairs.

"Please, have a seat," she says as she closes the door behind her. *Fuck.* Whatever this is, it has to be bad if I'm in here and not with her. *God, I just want to be with her.* I can't even swallow; my throat has tightened so much.

Sitting down next to me on the couch, she lays her hand on my knee, and I can't do anything but stare into her green eyes that are filled with sadness. I know she's trying to hide it, to be professional, but I can see it.

"Your friend was brought here by ambulance," she says softly. "There was an altercation. She's fine. We haven't found any major injuries at this time. She is pretty banged up though." She takes a moment before continuing, "But . . . she was raped."

Everything tunnels: my hearing, my vision. My heart thuds. Hard. I drop my head in my hands, and the tears just spill out. Allie continues to talk, but I've already heard all my soul can handle at this point. This girl is my fuckin' heart, and I'm terrified to see what's left of it.

I turn to look at the nurse when she hands me a tissue, but I don't reach out to take it. I just look at her with no words.

"I'm so sorry. You can utilize this room for as long as you need, but it's not going to be good for her to see you so upset. You need to be strong for her right now."

I nod my head. She's right. I've got to pull my shit together. I finally take the tissue from her hand. I could sit here and cry for the rest of my life if I allowed myself, but I need to see her. So that's what I tell the nurse. "I need to see her."

"Okay then." She stands up and leads me out of the room and down a corridor that is lined with private patient rooms. When we stop outside one of the rooms, she opens the door. I walk in to see my girl's bloody, swollen face. I know I can't hide my horror, and she falls apart, sobbing. Rushing over to her, I wrap my arms around her head as much as I can since she's wearing a neck brace. I can't stop kissing the top of her head and telling her that I love her. My tears fall effortlessly from my eyes and into her hair. I just keep repeating it over and over as her body jerks with her wails.

She cries for a long time, but I never loosen my hold on her. I've never been so scared for anyone in my life. Candace is so strong and always keeps her emotions held tight. Hearing the pain that's coming out of her is killing me.

Her body begins to shudder as she starts to quiet down. I loosen my grip on her and scan her face. It's covered in scratches, and the whole right side is swollen with a black eye. *God, what happened?*

I pull a chair up next to the bed and sit down. Finally noticing that there's another nurse in the room, I turn to her and ask, "What's going on? Is she okay?" I hold Candace's hand tightly in mine and when I shift my eyes to it, I'm nauseated when I see her brittle nails. It's as if someone has been sawing at them. They are covered in dried, cracked blood and worn down. There are chunks of flesh under what's left of a couple of her nails. I jerk my head back to the nurse, not able to look any longer.

She asks Candace if she would be willing to go through a rape kit exam and she freaks out, snapping her head to me, saying, "No."

"Candace, I really think you should do it. I get that you're scared right now, but maybe in a few days you might feel differently about this." I turn to the nurse and ask, "If she does this exam, then what?"

"If she decides to press charges, we will hand over the kit to the police. If not, we keep the kit here. If she changes her mind about prosecuting, then at that time, we will hand the kit over to the criminal lab."

I squeeze her hand and assure her, "I'm right here. I think you should do this, sweetie."

I watch as her eyes well with tears and then she slowly nods her head. I know she's scared, but she's strong.

The doctor comes in, and they take her for a couple of scans and x-rays while I wait in the room for her to return. When she leaves, I let go and cry. I try to get as much of it out as I can before she comes back and I have to shove all this pain back down. But I'm scared. I'm scared to know what this has done to her spirit. How will she ever heal from this?

When she is brought back into the room, I am by her side and holding her hand that I still can't look at. I can't even imagine how hard she must have fought for her hands to look the way they do.

The nurse talks to Candace about starting the rape kit then goes into the bathroom for a minute. When she returns, she looks at Candace and instructs, "Candace, I need for you to carefully remove all of your clothing, including your jewelry. I have laid down a large sheet of paper that is there to collect any evidence that may fall off of your clothes or body. Just stand on the paper while you undress, hand me each article of clothing as you remove it, and I will place each piece in a separate evidence bag. There is a hospital gown hanging on the door that you can change into."

I look down at her and ask, "Do you want me to leave?"

"No. I don't want to be alone." She clings to me, and I see the fear and despondence in her eyes. I want to take it away, but I feel so helpless. I don't know what to say to her, so I just help her off of the bed and walk her to the bathroom. She's clutching a blanket to her and when she holds it out to hand to the nurse, I see she's nearly naked. Her body is bloody and badly bruised. She begins to cry, and in a panic, turns around and asks where her pants are.

"The EMTs collected them. We already have them," the nurse tells her.

Candace looks up at me, her whole body shaking, and I can barely get my voice out when I try to calm her and say, "It's okay."

She slowly starts taking off the remnants of her ripped up clothing, which isn't much. Candace is such a small girl—tiny—and although she's strong as hell, there would have been no way she could've fought off the guy who did this. *Fuck, who did this?*

Slipping on the hospital gown, she walks straight into my arms, and I hold her; I cling so tightly to her.

"Candace, whenever you are ready, I need you to have a seat on the exam table behind the curtain," the nurse instructs.

Looking up at me, her dirty face soaked in tears, she says, "I don't have anything to wear."

"When the nurse called me, she told me to bring clothes with me. They're in my backpack."

She nods and we walk over to the exam table. She steps up to sit down on it, never letting go of my hand. I hate that she is so scared. She's never scared.

I concentrate on her face as the nurse starts collecting the evidence from underneath her nails. I watch as the life leaves her eyes and she completely zones out. It kills me to see her so void and incoherent right now. That her pain is so wrenching that she has to escape somewhere deep inside her head.

When she lies down, the nurse explains the internal exam that she's about to do. I hear every word, but I know Candace isn't hearing a thing. She just stares at my t-shirt as tears run freely down the side of her face.

My mind is consumed with a million questions, and I know that I will probably never get any answers. I don't see Candace talking about this. Ever. I want to murder the piece of shit who did this to her.

I snap out of my internal rage when Candace screams, "Enough!" She's freaking out and shrieks, "Get out!" Scrambling back on the table, trying to get away, she keeps screaming, "Stop touching me, and get the hell out!"

"Candace, calm down, sweetie." I try to say this as calmly as I can, but seeing her reaction is throwing me into a panic as she yells at the nurse, who quickly collects everything and leaves the room.

Curling into a ball, she cries, "I want to go home."

"What happened?" I ask, wondering what triggered her outburst.

Glaring at me, she says in a slow, stern voice, "I want my clothes, Jase."

I don't say anything because I don't want to upset her any more, so I pick up my backpack, and when I turn around, the door opens and the nurse who spoke to me when I first got here steps in.

"Candace, Detective Patterson needs to ask you a few questions," she says. "Can I send him in?"

Knowing that Candace needs space, I ask, "Can she at least get dressed first?"

"Of course," she says, and then leaves the room.

I hand Candace the bag and watch as she drags herself to the bathroom. While she's in there, someone knocks on the door. I open it to see an older man with a badge clipped to his belt standing there.

"Hi, I'm the detective that's been assigned to this case."

"She's in the bathroom," I say before Candace walks out.

"Ms. Parker," he says. "I'm Detective Patterson. Do you mind if I ask you some questions?"

"Right now?"

"Yes, ma'am."

"I've already told the nurse everything. Why can't you just ask her?" I can tell she's at her end, and I just want to get her out of here. She shakes her head, and says, "Look, I don't want to press charges or anything like that, so . . ."

Fuck. I knew she would do this. She avoids everything, but her words feel like a goddamn stab to my lungs.

"Ma'am, I know this is difficult, but there's a good chance we can catch this guy, and the fact that we have a witness—"

She hangs her head and completely shuts down as he continues to talk. When he hands her his card, she shoves it in her pocket. I shake the detective's hand as he walks out, and as soon as he leaves, another nurse walks back in. *Christ, it's never-ending.*

"I'm just going to clean up and bandage these cuts for you, okay?"

I take a seat in one of the chairs across from Candace. The nurse is cleaning up her face when I hear her ask Candace if she needs the morning after pill. My head snaps up, and I stare at Candace as she sits there for a second, revulsion plastered all over her face. "I think so," she whispers.

"Fucker," I mutter and drop my head in my hands, trying my hardest to control my anger and not start throwing my fist into the walls. I have *never*—not in my whole life—felt the wrath that I feel right now.

The nurse keeps talking, but I don't hear what she's telling Candace. I'm too focused on settling myself down, trying to weaken the erratic pounding of my heart. Once all the discharge papers are signed, I can't hold

Candace tight enough to me as I walk her out to my car. She cringes in pain as I help her up into her seat. I reach over her and strap the seatbelt across her lap. Tears flood her eyes when I reach out to touch her face, wincing when I make contact, and then letting her head fall into my hand. She begins weeping, and I just stare at her—desolate. I wish I could do something to help her. I wish she would've come to my place tonight like I had asked her to. I could throw a thousand worthless wishes into the air, but none of them would change this nightmare, so I quit tormenting myself. I kiss her shoulder before closing the door.

She's silent as she stares out the window while I drive her back to my place. The misery is palpable; the way life can change in a matter of a moment. I look over at her as she sits there—lifeless—and I desperately want to make it all disappear.

I help her out of the car and hold her hand as we walk into the building. She keeps a death grip on my hand but doesn't speak. When I unlock the door to my apartment, she lets go of me and heads straight to my bathroom, closing the door behind her. It feels like there are bricks in the pit of my stomach, razor sharp. The past few hours are a complete haze. I hear the water to the shower turn on as I sit down on the couch. I wish I knew what to say, what to do, but I feel so helpless.

Laying my head back, I hear her start to cry. Dropping my head in my hands, I can't stop my own tears from falling. *Fuck.* When her cries turn into howling sobs, I leap off the couch and rush into the bathroom.

I look at her through the steamed glass, on her knees, at the bottom of the shower. I feel like all the air is sucked out of my lungs. Seeing her like this is almost unbearable, so I quickly kick off my shoes and socks, open the shower door, and wrap my arms around her from behind as she breaks. I don't know what else to do, so I just cover her bruised and cut body with mine.

I have no clue what the hell really happened, and knowing Candace, she will never say. He beat the shit out of her, that much is evident. Rage roils in my gut when I think about what he did to her. I know I have to keep it together though, 'cause she's going to need me.

Listening to her wails is excruciating. I love this girl more than anything, and to see her in this much pain kills me. I'm so scared for her; I'm afraid of what this has done to her. I know there is nothing I could possibly say, so I just cling to her as she falls apart in my arms.

When she exhausts herself and quiets down, she remains frozen in my hold. I don't think twice when I stand to get my body wash. Still in my gym shorts and t-shirt, I begin to clean her as she sits there, vacant, on the bottom of my shower. When I finish washing her hair, she finally looks up at me, and I see it. Desperation.

I shut the water off, strip out of my wet clothes, and grab some towels. Drying her off, I help her change. She just cries and apologizes as if she's a burden. I pick her up and carry her to my bed. Tucking her into me, I wrap myself around her and never loosen my grip.

chapter eleven

I DON'T EVEN question skipping my classes today. We didn't get home from the hospital until close to six o'clock this morning, and Candace has been waking from nightmares all day. When she's up, she sobs, and when she sleeps, she thrashes around and screams herself awake. I don't know what to do for her, so I just hold her.

I just finished up cleaning the cuts on her face, and she's asleep again. My phone vibrates from the nightstand and when I pick it up, I see the time is almost five p.m. I swipe my screen to see that I have several missed calls and texts from Mark and Kimber. I read a missed text from Mark first.

Why aren't you at studio?

I scroll down to the next text.

Tried calling you. Where have you been all day?

I'm not sure what to say to him. I hate that we have only been back together for a week and I feel like I have to hide things from him. I need to show him that he can trust me, but I know I can't say anything until Candace tells me what she wants.

I open up the text from Kimber next.

Freaking out. Is Candace with you? She never came home last night.

I don't respond. Candace didn't want to go home and face Kimber, so she asked to stay with me. I know she doesn't want to deal with Kimber. She's pushy and aggressive and Candace clearly wants to be left alone. She won't even talk to me.

I ignore the texts and don't even bother listening to the voicemails. I have hardly slept and I'm exhausted. Rolling over, I hold Candace and try to get in some sleep before she wakes again.

The sounds of Candace crying and vomiting in the bathroom wake me up. The apartment is dark as I rip the covers off of me, rush into the bathroom, and flip on the light. She's huddled over the toilet and begins screaming and crawling back into the corner. She's panicking, and I can't tell if she's still dreaming or not. I drop down on my knees in front of her. Gripping her wrists, I freak out when I see her glazed over eyes.

"It's okay, Candace. I'm here," I say as calmly as I possibly can.

Her eyes shift to mine, and I keep repeating, "It's okay," to her. When her screams turn to cries, I pull her into my arms and slowly rock her. I don't know what the fuck to do. I have no clue what just happened.

She clings to me and her cries start to soften, sniffing between shallow breaths. Scooping her up off the floor, I carry her to the living room and set her down on the couch. She hasn't eaten or had anything to drink since we came home, so I get a box of crackers and some bottles of water.

Handing her one of the bottles, I tell her to drink.

I sit down next to her and ask, completely confused, "What just happened?"

"I don't know. It felt like a nightmare, but I was awake," she says and then takes a drink of water.

I let out a sigh and lean over, resting my elbows on my knees. "You scared the hell out me. I know you don't want to talk, but maybe . . ." I trail off when I hear her cell ring.

"You have my phone?"

Standing up, I walk over to the kitchen bar to grab it for her. "Yeah, the nurse at the hospital gave me your purse."

When I sit back down and open the box of crackers, I ask, "Who was it?"

"Kimber."

"You should call her, she's probably freaking out and wondering where you are."

"Maybe later." She sets her phone down and leans her head back on the couch, staring up at the ceiling.

"She probably knows you're with me. She sent me a text earlier asking if I knew where you were. I figured you didn't want her to know just yet, so I didn't respond."

When she rolls her head to the side to look at me, I hold a cracker up to her mouth and feed it to her.

After she swallows, she says, "I don't want anyone to know."

I knew she would react this way. I knew she'd shut herself off, and I hate that. "I know, but she's going to know that something happened. She's going to want to know how you got all these bruises."

"I don't know what to say."

"Why can't you tell her? You know she wouldn't say a word to anyone." I'm trying to support Candace, but I shouldn't have just said that. Truth is, Kimber is unreliable and unpredictable.

"I just can't. Even the way you look at me now is different."

Her words make me feel horrible. I don't want to hurt her, and I don't want to make her feel uncomfortable, but I'm worried.

She continues, "It makes me feel weird. It just reminds me that it happened when all I want to do is forget."

"You know you can't do that. It did happen."

She begins to quietly weep when she questions, "But why? I don't understand what I did that was so wrong."

"You didn't do anything wrong," I say as I run my thumbs under her eyes

"Then why did this happen to me?"

I shake my head. Her voice is so desperate. Desperate for answers I can't give her. My chest tightens, and I can't control the tears that start running down my face. "I don't know, sweetie. But I do know that you didn't do shit to deserve this. This isn't your fault."

"But maybe it is. I mean, I really led him on when I had no intentions of . . ."

"You mean Jack did this?!" I snap. *Holy shit.* "Christ, Candace. I thought it was just some random asshole. Why didn't you tell the police? Why didn't you say anything?" My mind is racing, and I have to fight the urge to grab my keys to go find that dipshit and kick his ass.

"Because I can't. Everyone would know. Everyone, including my parents."

I'm on fuckin' fire, and I swear to God, if he were here right now, I would murder him.

"Fuck," I spit out. I turn to look her dead on, and say, "I'm gonna kill that fucker."

"Jase!"

"What the hell happened?" I need to know what he did to her.

"Don't."

"Candace, you have to tell me."

"Please, don't," she cries, and I know I'm scaring her, but I'm losing control.

I stand up and walk out to the balcony, slamming the door hard behind me. Rage is cutting through my veins, and I can feel it seeping through every inch of my body. Leaning my elbows on the railing, I let my head fall, and I focus on taking deep breaths as I cry. I need to calm the hell down because the look in her eyes, the fear that's there . . . I can't fuckin' do that to her. As much as I hate it, I know I have to put it aside and be exactly what she needs me to be. I'm all she has and the only one she isn't hiding from.

When my head starts to clear, I sit back in one of the chairs and watch the sun begin to rise. My eyes sting, and I can't stop crying. I know I can't go back in there until I have myself in check. I try to keep my focus on Candace instead of Jack because just the slightest thought of him makes my skin burn with disgust. What kind of sick fuck would do this to someone?

When I finally walk inside, Candace is curled into a little ball on my bed. She looks so broken. I slide behind her, and wrap her up in my hold, whispering in her ear how much I love her and how sorry I am for scaring her. I know she can't hear me, but I don't have it in me to wake her up, so I just let her sleep.

Waking up, I notice Candace isn't in bed with me. I blink a few times and can feel that my eyes are swollen from how upset I was earlier this morning. When I walk into the kitchen, I see Candace standing there watching the coffee pot percolate. I walk straight to her and cup her head in my hands. Looking down at her, all I say is, "I'm sorry."

She nods her head, and I draw her in and just hold her. When the coffee is done brewing, we break our hold on one another and pour our mugs of coffee and sit on the couch.

"I didn't mean to push you earlier this morning. I just don't know what to do here."

Cradling the mug in her hands, she whispers, "I know."

She doesn't look at me; she just stares down at the ribbons of steam drifting off of her coffee. I watch her for a minute before breaking the silence. "I think you should stay here until you're ready to go back home." I want her here more for my own peace of mind. I'm worried about her nightmares, and I want to make sure I'm with her when she sleeps.

As she takes a sip from her mug, she finally looks up at me. "All my stuff is at home. What if Kimber's there?"

"How about we just drive over there, and you can get your car and come back here while I pack a bag for you? Just tell me what all you need, and I'll get it."

Letting out a sigh, she says, "Thanks. I think she might be in class this morning, so . . ."

"Go throw on some clothes and let's just go then."

I can tell she's nervous when we start driving down her street, so I reach over and hold her hand, which is cold and clammy. She stares out the window, not looking at me, and quietly says, "He knows where I live, Jase."

I turn to look at her, but she's looking away. If I could keep her with me forever, I would, but I know I can't. "He won't hurt you," I say, but I don't even believe my own words. Will he? Would he be stupid enough to come to her house? My gut tells me that he will stay away, but what if he doesn't? She doesn't say anything, and I don't either.

Candace is already on her way back to my apartment, and when I'm done packing her bags and leaving her house, I shoot her a text.

Got everything you asked for and more. On my way home.

Thank you so much. See you in a bit.

Walking into the apartment, I see Candace in the bathroom as I start unpacking her bags. When she comes into the room, she starts putting her things away and I sit on the bed and, watching her as she moves around. She seems so hollow when she used to be all smiles and laughs, so full of life. She has a pained look on her face, like she's using all her strength not to cry. I wish she would; I wish I could make her—drain her of her misery—but I can't. She's so closed off.

"Stop," she says, and I snap out of my thoughts.

"What?"

She comes over and sits down next to me on the bed. "Stop looking at me like that."

I deflect her thoughts when I say, "You know Kimber's going to flip when she comes home and sees that a bunch of your things are gone."

"I know. What am I going to tell her?" she asks as she lies back on the bed.

I lie down with her and say, "We'll figure it out."

When the tears fall from her eyes, I reach down and hold her hand, squeezing tightly as I stare into her eyes. They are so swollen and bloodshot; I know they have to burn.

She curls up and rests her head on my chest. It isn't long before I feel myself falling asleep.

"Oh my God," I hear a man say, and I'm slowly pulled out of my sleep.

"What the hell happened to your face, honey?" I roll over at the sound of Mark's voice. When I open my eyes and see him looking at us, I shoot up next to Candace, who is already sitting up and hiding her face in her hands.

Needing to get him out of the room, I say, "Um, hey. I'm sorry, but could you give us just a minute?"

Mark is staring, almost in horror, at Candace then turns to me. I know he can see the panic in my face because I feel it all throughout my body. "Yeah, man. Sure. I'll just be in the other room."

Mark turns and closes the door behind him.

"Shit. I'm so sorry," she says as she hangs her head down.

"What for?"

"I don't know. For having your boyfriend see us in bed together."

"Don't worry about it. I talk about you all the time. He knows how we are; it doesn't bother him," I tell her, trying to reassure her, but I'm freaking out because now I don't know what to say to Mark. Come to think of it, I haven't spoken to him since she's been here. I haven't even thought about it because I've been so consumed with her. But Mark and I are trying to make whatever we have going on right. "Candace, I don't know what to do here. I just got back together with Mark, and I can't lie to him."

She looks up at me, and I see the worry etched across her face. She doesn't speak; she just stares at me. I can tell she's confused, but she eventually nods her head. I feel like I just asked too much of her, but I need her to do this for me, as selfish as it is. I need her to allow me to tell Mark the truth.

Lifting her chin with my finger, I assure her, "Mark would never say anything. He isn't like that."

She nods her head again as her face scrunches up in pain and she starts crying.

"Don't cry," I whisper as I wipe her tears, but they're falling too fast for me.

"I'm so embarrassed."

I band my arms around her. "I know you are, sweetie, but you shouldn't be."

I continue to hold her as her cries turn into wails. I rock her back and forth in an attempt to soothe her as she buries her head in my neck. The sounds coming out of her are so hard for me to hear, and I can't keep the pain bottled up, so I cry as quietly as I can. I've haven't cried like this—so painfully—since I lost Jace.

I manage to get myself under control as she continues to sob in my arms. She's so loud. I can only imagine what Mark must be thinking. She's been crying for nearly an hour when I look up and see Mark quietly walking across my room. My eyes follow him as he sits down next to Candace on the bed. Her arms tighten around me when Mark puts his hand on her back. I know she's embarrassed, and I fuckin' hate that. She clings to me and continues to cry as Mark and I stare at each other. He looks at me with questions written all over his face as I lay my cheek on top of her head.

When I feel Candace's body going limp in my arms, I loosen my hold and look at her. She's completely worn herself out. Mark slides off the bed and onto the floor in front of her, and she turns to look down at him. I watch him take her hand before he gently asks, "Who did this?"

I know she won't speak. I know I'll have to be the one to say it. *Fuck. I don't want to say it.* It's gonna kill her.

Mark's eyes stay locked on her when I clear my throat to try and speak around the lump that's lodged in it. "Um . . . Candace was attacked Monday night."

When I say that, she lowers her elbows to her knees, hiding her face in her hands. I keep my hand on her back, and see Mark wrap his hands around her knees.

"What happened?" Mark asks.

Staring down at Candace, she starts shaking her head. I know I just need to say it. I shift my eyes to Mark, and he looks up at me with his brows knitted together. My face heats with tears, and I hate that Mark is seeing me like this, so I just say it.

I grip her shoulder tightly and let it out. "She was raped."

Mark's eyes close, and he huffs out a pained breath, dropping his head onto her lap as a new slew of sobs rip through Candace.

The three of us sit there and cling to each other. I hate seeing her so broken and wonder what the hell must be going through Mark's head right now. I hate feeling so powerless. I hate everything about this.

Candace begins to quiet down, and she lifts her head, wiping her face with her hands.

"I won't say anything, if you were worried about that," Mark assures her.

"I'm so tired," she responds.

"I told her she could stay here for a few days. She doesn't want anyone to know, and if Kimber saw her face, she would question her."

"I think that's a good idea," Mark tells me, then looks at Candace and says, "I know we don't know each other that well, but I'm here if you ever need me. I feel like I know you by how much Jase speaks of you. The both of us are always here for you."

God, I can't even describe what his words do to me. That he doesn't even hesitate for a second. I didn't realize how much I might actually need him because just having him here in the same room as me right now makes me feel like I have the support I've been missing to keep it together. I don't know how this guy can do that for me, but he does.

chapter twelve

SLINGING MY BACKPACK on, I hate that I'm leaving her. I look at Candace curled up on my couch, wrapped in a blanket.

"I'm fine," she tries to convince me as I walk over and kiss her head.

I can't miss any more classes this week. It's the first week of the quarter and it's the week where we pick our projects for graduation, so I have to go.

"I have a break in between my classes, so I'll come back here, okay?"

She nods her head at me as I turn to leave.

When I get to class, I see Mark sitting at a drafting table next to a window. I grab a stool and slide it beside him.

"Hey, how are you?" he asks as I sit down.

I still hate that Mark saw me crying yesterday; maybe it shouldn't bother me, but it does. No one has ever seen me like that except for Candace, but now I feel like I have to hide everything I'm feeling from her. The last thing she needs is to worry about me, but I'm having reservations about letting Mark in.

"I'm good," I lie, not knowing what else to say.

Cocking his head, I'm worried that he's going to call my bullshit, but he doesn't. "How's Candace?"

"Not good," I say. I keep my own feelings to myself and just talk to him about her. "She's having these freaky nightmares at night, and I'm really worried about her."

"What do you mean?"

"It's weird, man. It's like she's still dreaming, but her eyes are open. She says she feels like she's hallucinating. She screams and cries and gets so worked up that she begins throwing up. It's really bad."

"What does she say?" he asks me.

"Not much. She doesn't like to talk about it. She doesn't talk about anything."

Leaning his elbows on the drafting table, he looks over and says, "Maybe you could talk to her about getting on a sleeping aid or something. It might help relax her enough to get her into a deeper sleep so her dreams aren't so vivid."

I look at him and wonder how he knows about this.

Reading the curiosity on my face, he explains, "I used to have nightmares when I was in high school. I took Prazosin to help me sleep."

I don't question him about why he had nightmares; I just nod my head and say, "Yeah. I'll try talking to her."

He gives me a smile and opens his notebook when our professor walks in. It feels a little strange to be here, away from her, but it also feels nice to get a break and to see Mark. We spend the next ninety minutes discussing our final capstone projects for graduation. After class, I tell Mark that I need to go home and check on Candace before my next class.

"You mind if I tag along? I'm done for the day, so I can hang out with her while you're in your next class."

"You don't have to."

Looking over at me while we make our way through the quad, he says, "I know I don't have to, but I want to."

I nod my head and say, "Okay, I'll drop you off at your car then."

I am suddenly feeling a little self-conscious when he reaches down and takes my hand. I haven't felt this way since I first came here three years ago and started being with guys, but that never felt like this. Serious. Intimate. Something about this makes me feel very aware of the people around me. My body tenses up, but Mark never says anything. He switches the subject, and I try to focus more on what he's saying rather than what I'm feeling.

"So, the guys and I got booked to play a gig this Saturday," he says.

"Oh yeah? Where at?"

"Blur. It's a bar right off campus."

"Yeah, I've been there a couple times. Nice place," I say as we walk through the parking lot towards my car.

"I know you'll say no, but I wanted you to know that I want you to come."

When we get to my car, I unlock the doors, and he drops my hand to walk around and get in. I've only seen Mark play that one time, and that image passes through my mind. How hot he looked while playing his guitar and sweating through his shirt. Yeah, I want to see him play again, but he's right, I'm gonna say no. I just can't leave Candace for the night.

"I'm sorry," I say and he interrupts.

"Don't be. I know you need to be with Candace, I just wanted you to know."

"Thanks for understanding, man."

I turn into the lot where Mark's Range Rover is and drop him off.

"Go ahead and go on up to the apartment, I'm gonna stop by Peet's and pick up some food for Candace," I tell him as I take the key off my key ring and hand it to him.

"Okay, grab me a coffee while you're there, will ya?" Mark asks, and I nod my head before he slides out of my car.

When I arrive at Peet's, I place my order and take a seat while I wait. I watch the rain collecting on the window and allow a moment of peace among all the strain from these past few days, but that peace is short-lived when I hear that all too familiar accent.

"You look like shit."

I don't even want to look at him. He's a sick reminder of what I've been trying to escape. Mark makes me wish I could just forget about all the crap I used to do, and having Preston here just fills me with guilt. Fills me with the thought that I don't deserve someone as good as Mark.

"What do you want?" I ask with a fleeting moment of eye contact.

Dropping his head slightly to the side, he says with a cheap grin, "Pathetic," but it comes out more taunting than anything as he walks away towards the pick-up counter.

I hear my order being called, and I pick up the food and drinks that are sitting next to him. He looks over at me, and again, with the same mocking tone, tells me, "See ya around, mate."

When I walk into my apartment, I'm happy to see Mark sitting on my couch watching ESPN.

"Where's Candace?" I ask as I hand him his coffee and set the bag of food on the coffee table.

"She's sleeping. When I got here, I checked in your room, and she was passed out, so I shut the door so I wouldn't wake her."

"She's got to be tired as hell. She hardly sleeps." I sit down next to Mark and lean back into the couch, kicking my feet up on the table.

When I let out a deep breath, Mark pulls me into his arms, and I let him. I can hear his heart thudding in his chest, and I wrap my arms around him and just lie there. I'm tired as hell too. Candace keeps me up most of the night, and I feel like I haven't slept in weeks. Mark doesn't say anything. He doesn't really need to, so I shut my eyes while he holds me and watches TV. His is the only touch that has ever comforted me like this. It's so different coming from him, and I try to shut out that awkward run-in with my past. There is too much other stuff going on right now to let crap like that get to me.

Mark's arms squeeze tight around me, and the pressure wakes me up.

"Hey, you need to get back to campus for your class," he says softly, but being here, wrapped up in him, I couldn't care less about school.

"Don't look at me like that," he teases, and I know he can tell what I want, so I pull him down to me and kiss him. I keep my lips on his, needing to feel his touch. These past few days have drained me, and having this quiet time with him, although short, has given me solid ground to land on, and I needed it.

Removing my lips from his, but not wanting to, I whisper, "Thanks."

"For what?"

"This," I say, and he drops his mouth to mine but removes it too fast. "You need to go."

I nod my head and push myself off the couch. "You gonna stay?"

"Yeah. I'll stay."

I grab my bag and lean down to give him another quick kiss, just needing one last taste before I leave.

The next couple of days are pretty much the same. Candace is still at my place, taking the week off from school and work. She emailed her professors to tell them she was out sick, and Roxy didn't question her when she called to tell her the same thing earlier this week.

I spoke to Candace last night about calling the doctor to see about getting something to help her sleep. I thought she'd put up a fight, but she didn't. I think she's just so sleep-deprived that she would do anything to get some rest. Last night, I woke up to see her still awake; I know she was fighting sleep. She told me she was scared to dream. I hurt so much for her, but have been keeping everything bottled up. I feel like I'm at my breaking point.

I'm driving home from my last class before the weekend starts. Candace mentioned going home on Monday, but I wish she would stay with me. She says that she needs to get back to her normal life. I know it's her way of avoiding, and I didn't question her. She still hasn't talked about that night, and she refuses to see a therapist. I wish she would talk, but she doesn't.

When I walk in my living room, I'm shocked to see Mark sitting on the couch with Candace.

"What are you doing here?"

"Just hanging out," he says as if this is a normal thing for him to be here while I'm out.

"Oh, I didn't know you were going to be here."

"Is that a problem?" he asks, concerned.

I smile as I walk over to Candace, kiss her head, and then look to Mark, saying, "It's never a problem. I'll be right back; I'm gonna go change."

I toss my bag in my closet and grab some clothes to go for a quick run when Candace walks in.

"How was your afternoon?" I ask her.

"It was okay. Mark's been here to keep me company."

Walking over to her as she's sitting on my bed, I look at her cuts then kiss her cheek, "Your face is looking better."

She nods and runs her hand down the side of her cheek when I continue, "Well, I'm glad he had time to stop by."

"Me too. He came by a couple of times yesterday when he was in between classes as well."

I turn around and slip my shirt on when she says this. "What?"

"What?" she questions in confusion.

"He was here yesterday too?"

"Yeah, I thought you knew. I thought maybe you told him to check in on me."

"No." I can't believe he's been coming over here to spend time with her. The fact that he would do that, on his own because he wanted to and not because I asked him to, surprises me. It's apparent that he cares for her, and knowing that she has him, the only other person who knows what she's going through, gives me reassurance that he's different—he's special. I've always known he is, but realizing he cares that much about me, to care that much for her, fills something inside of me I wasn't aware was empty.

"He really likes you, you know?"

Lacing up my shoes, I say, "I really like him too."

When I stand up and look at her, she's just staring at me.

"What?" I ask.

"If you feel that way, then why did you kiss me and not him?"

"When?"

"Just a minute ago when you walked in."

I drop my head before I look up at her. "It's not that easy for me."

"What's not easy?"

"Having people see me this way. Having *you* see me this way."

She shakes her head at me. "How do you think I see you?" When I don't respond, she says, "You don't have to hide from me. I love you."

I go ahead and take this moment to open up to her a bit more about this and confess, "He held my hand when we were walking through the quad the other day, and I froze up. I've never done that before with a guy, but now that I think about it, I've never really held hands with a guy."

"I don't understand."

"What I have with him is so different than what I'm used to. It's one thing for me to screw around with guys, but to be with Mark the way I want to be, like holding his hand, in front of others . . . it just makes me uncomfortable to know what people might be thinking."

She stands up and walks towards me. "It doesn't matter what people think. You should be able to hold your boyfriend's hand without having to worry about what other people are thinking. Mark is great. Don't let that stuff get in the way of you guys."

Taking her hands, I draw her into me and hug her. "I know. I'm trying to get past it."

"It's another reason why I should go back home. I feel like I'm intruding on your time together."

Looking down at her, I insist, "You will never be an intrusion. I want you here," before kissing her forehead.

chapter thirteen

"WHY ARE YOU wanting to eat so late?"
"Because today was the first day that Candace went back to work. I just wanted to have something to distract her when she gets home in case it didn't go so well," I tell Mark as he walks through the apartment. Candace has been at work all evening, and I have a feeling that what she was hoping for by getting out and going back to work is not what happened. I know she expects everything to go back to the way it was by going back to her normal routines. I tried talking to her about it last night, but she's determined and completely shut me out.

"When is she supposed to be getting off?" Mark asks, coming into the kitchen and leaning up against the counter as I finish chopping the tomatoes for the bruschetta.

"A little after eleven."

"Can I help?"

Looking at him, I smile and say, "Yeah, could you turn the heat down on the sauce and stir it?"

I watch him as he walks over to the stove and fiddles with the knob. I laugh to myself because I can see that he isn't comfortable in the kitchen.

Adding the oil to the tomatoes and onions, I look over at Mark and ask, "Will you go turn up the music?"

"Yeah, sure," he says, and then comes back to the stove to stir the sauce again. I know he hasn't a clue what the hell he is supposed to be doing, but I find it sweet that he's trying to be helpful. I come up behind him and start nipping along his neck. When he turns in my arms, he looks over my shoulder and says, "Hey!"

I turn to see Candace standing in the middle of the living room and the look on her face tells me everything that I feared. She looks upset and starts walking to my bedroom. Leaning my hands against the counter, Mark slides his hand over my shoulder and says, "I'll go talk to her."

I want to say something, but it's taking everything in me to keep myself in check. I hate seeing that look on her face. She tries to be so strong, and I could see that she was fighting hard not to cry.

I nod my head and Mark kisses the center of my neck before heading back to my room, and I try to keep myself busy by finishing up dinner.

They are back there for quite a while, but when they return, Candace is smiling. I walk straight to her and bring her in for a hug before kissing her. "Hey, sweetie. How was work?"

"Weird at first, but it wound up being a busy night, which was good," she says as she picks out a bottle of wine and starts to open it.

I quickly slice up the baguette and set it on the bar with the bruschetta. Candace and Mark sit and eat while talking. It's great that they have become friends. It makes me feel more content, knowing that Candace has him to lean on as well as me.

"Hey, didn't your band have a show last night?" Candace asks Mark.

"Yeah, we played at Blur. It was a great gig; the place was packed."

"I've never been there before."

Looking over at her, I tease, "Candace, you haven't been anywhere." She scrunches her face at me, which causes me to laugh. "You should really hear them play sometime. You'd like their sound."

There's a knock at the door, and Mark hops off the barstool to go answer it. I rush to Candace's side when I see Kimber walk in. *Crap.* Both Candace and I have been avoiding her calls and texts, and she looks pissed.

"What the hell is going on?" she barks. *Fuck, she's mad.* "You two have been avoiding me all week, and I have no clue what I did to piss you guys off!"

"We're not pissed at you," I try and convince her. I know she doesn't believe me, so I try to cover for Candace because I know she's freaking out by the shock on her face. "Candace just wanted a little time away, that's all."

"From me? I'm supposed to be your best friend!" she says, looking at Candace. "Why won't you talk to me?" she demands.

"I'm sorry," Candace says, and Mark walks back into the kitchen. Candace looks scared as shit, and I would say just about anything to get Kimber to leave her alone, but when Candace sits on the couch, she starts talking. "Jack and I got into an argument at the party. I was upset, he was drunk, so I called Jase to come pick me up."

I help her out by adding, "I suggested she stay here in case he showed up at your house. That's all."

"So why couldn't you just call me and tell me?"

"I didn't want you getting involved. You can sometimes overreact, and I just wanted everything to die down without any drama. It's no big deal, and I haven't heard from him. It's over, so can we just drop it?" Candace says, and when I look down at her hands, I see that she's shaking.

"Bullshit!" Kimber snaps and starts walking out.

"Kimber, wait. Please don't be mad at me. I'm coming back home this week. It's not a big deal, please don't make it into one."

She walks up to Candace, and I am back at her side, holding her hand when Kimber says, "You're the one who made it such a big deal when you decided to avoid me all week. We have always been honest with each other, but if you really want me to believe your story, then fine. I believe you."

Candace drops back down to the couch when the door slams shut and begins to cry.

"I don't know what to do." She looks up at me and pleads. "What do I do?"

Sitting down next to her, she falls into my arms and cries. Mark comes in and sits opposite her and rubs her back, trying to calm her down.

"She's so mad at me. She's never been mad at me."

"Just give her some time," I tell her. "We've both been avoiding her, so you can't blame her for being upset."

"It's all my fault."

"It's not your fault, Candace," Mark assures her, and I listen as he continues. "It's just the shit situation you were dealt, but it's not your fault. You can't blame yourself for this, for any of this."

She pulls back from me and turns to face Mark.

"What do I do?" she asks him.

Wiping his thumbs across her cheeks, he tells her, "You do whatever you need to do to get through the day. You do what you need to do to protect yourself. That's all you can do."

"Even if it hurts her?"

"I don't think you can do anything else, sweetheart, when you're trying so hard to just hang on."

Hearing them talk, hearing his words to her . . . it's near perfect.

I'm supposed to take her back home tomorrow morning before her classes, but I can't have her leave with Kimber so mad. "I want you to stay," I tell her.

She leans back on the couch, Mark and I on either side of her. "I can't stay."

"You can. Give Kimber a few days to cool down at least."

"But I feel like I'm just interfering with you guys."

Letting out a sigh of irritation, I tell her, "You're not. I already told you this the other day."

She turns to look at Mark and eyes him for his input.

"Jase is right. You should give her a little time to calm down."

You home?

Yeah. AutoCAD is going to be the death of my laptop.

I've been trying to get some work done on my project while Candace is in class. It's her first day back, and I've been worried about her all day. My

phone chimes again with another text from Mark.
Mind if I stop by?

Never.

Mark and I haven't spent a whole lot of time together, just being alone, so I shut down my computer and pour a cup of coffee. I don't have to wait very long before he gets here.

"Hey, what have you been up to?" he says as he walks up to me and gives me a hug.

I pull him in for a quick kiss before I respond. "Just trying to get some work done, but my computer is running slow as shit today."

Mark seems a bit distracted as he nods and takes a seat on the couch. I walk over and sit next to him when he says, "Can we talk for a second?"

"Yeah, what's up?"

Shifting to face me he asks, "Have you heard from Candace today?"

"No. She has her two-hour studio today and a lecture. But she should be back soon."

"You worried?"

"Always," I say as I kick my feet up on the coffee table and lean back into the couch. I watch Mark, and I can tell he wants to say something, and now I'm not worrying about Candace so much. "What's up with you?" I ask him and when he looks at me, I can definitely tell he's nervous.

"Look, I know you love Candace, and I need you to know that I do too. She's amazing. But I think her staying here is hurting her more than it's helping."

I let out a deep breath and look straight forward as he continues. "I think her going back home will help her. She's so dependent on you right now, and I worry that she's going to fall into a rut."

I turn back to him and defend, "She has really bad nights."

"I know this isn't easy on you. I get it. And I know you want her here, but I think her standing on her own will maybe force her to deal with this more."

What he's saying makes sense. Of course I want her here. All I want to do is protect her. Looking down at the cup of coffee, I nod my head, and Mark takes it from my hands and sets it on the table.

"You two are so close, and I understand why, but I think her going back home might be the best thing you can do for her." He takes my hand in his and says, "You can't keep her here forever, you know?"

But I want to.

Mark and I both turn around when the door opens and we see Candace walking in. She quickly glances our way while walking straight to the bathroom. I look at Mark and sigh when I hear her turn on the shower.

"You know her better than I do. I just wanted to be honest with you and tell you my thoughts." Mark looks down and shakes his head before looking back up. "I'm sorry if I—"

Cutting him off, I tell him, "Don't be sorry. It's fine. And maybe you're right. I just feel helpless, and I don't know what else to do."

He lies back next to me and we just sit there. Mark is right; I can't hide her away forever. She has to be able to deal with this on her own, but I hate the thought of not being there for her because I know that right now, she's crying in the shower. I could see it all over her face when she walked through the door. Guilt is a bitch, and it's consuming me as I sit here with Mark.

I look over at him with defeat written all over my face. He reaches out and runs his hand down my neck before I just can't take it anymore. I hop off the couch and walk into the bathroom.

Sure enough, she's sitting in the corner of the shower with her head in her hands. I open the door and shut off the water, handing her a towel. When she looks up at me with bloodshot eyes, I reach for her hand and help her up. Wrapping the towel around her, we walk into my bedroom.

"Talk to me, sweetie."

She heads over to the closet and tells me, "Give me a second and I'll come out, okay?"

"Okay."

When I return to Mark, he stands up and places his hands on either side of my face. "She will be okay," he tries to assure me, and all I can do is nod.

When she comes out into the living room she scrunches in between the two of us.

"What happened?" I ask as I lace my fingers with hers.

"Nothing happened. I just . . . I didn't think I'd be so scared."

"Scared of what?"

She looks at me with tears rimming her eyes and says, "Of *him*."

When I shake my head, she continues, "What if I see him? I was so paranoid all day. I kept thinking I would turn a corner and he would be there. It was awful."

"Have you ever seen him on campus before?" Mark questions, and she shakes her head. "Do you want me to try and meet you when your classes get out so you don't have to walk across campus alone?"

I snap my head to look at Mark when he says this. I can't believe how genuine this guy is. Even though I don't want Candace to leave, I know that Mark's heart is in the right place with what he said to me. He's probably seeing things more clearly than I am. But before I can even mention anything, she says, "I'll be fine. I just need to keep going about my days like I used to." Looking up at me, she asks, "Can you come home with me on Wednesday. I don't want to go alone in case Kimber is there."

"What?"

"I need to go back home. I just want you to come with me."

I'm caught off guard when she says this, and when I look across at Mark, he gives me an encouraging nod.

"Yeah, of course. But—"

"Jase. I'll be fine."

I don't believe her lie for one second, but I don't say anything because I know she doesn't want me to. Nothing about this feels good to me.

chapter fourteen

I GRAB CANDACE'S bags and follow her down to the parking garage. I hate that she's going home. I hate this feeling in the pit of my stomach. I just hate this whole situation. She tried convincing me that she would be okay when we woke up this morning. She finally got her sleeping pills and the past two nights she's been getting more rest. She still wakes throughout the night, but she hasn't had a nightmare. I still worry though; I can't help it.

"I'll follow you," I tell her as I toss her bags in her trunk.

"Okay."

When we drive up to her house, Kimber's car is gone. Candace has been uneasy about seeing her again, and I don't blame her.

When I get out of my car, I get her bags and carry them in for her.

"Are you sure everything is all right?" I ask as I start helping her unpack.

"Yeah, Jase. I can't stay with you forever, and you and Mark don't need me around all of the time."

It upsets me that she feels this way, but I can also tell that Mark has been feeling the same thing as well. We barely get to spend any alone time together and I know it bothers him, but he would never come out and say anything. He's too nice.

I watch Candace, and I know she's upset. The thought of her sleeping alone tonight bothers me, but Mark is right, this is probably the best thing for her, so I need to put my feelings aside and just let her be.

"What time do you get off work tonight? Do you want me to meet you afterward?" I ask.

"I close tonight, so I'll leave around eleven, but you don't have to meet me there. I'm working with Roxy, so I won't be alone."

She grabs her laundry basket and starts heading toward the laundry room as I follow. When we walk into the living room, I pick up my backpack and Candace walks me to the door.

"Thank you," she says, and I turn to face her.

"For what?"

"Everything." When her brows pinch together, I know she is trying not to cry.

"Sweetie, I feel like I haven't done nearly enough."

I know she doesn't like to talk when she gets like this, so she shakes her head and the tears spill over. I pull her into me and brace my arms tightly around her, combing my fingers through her hair until she settles down.

"You keep the key to my place, okay? Come over anytime you need, even if it's the middle of the night."

Nodding her head, she finally speaks. "I love you."

"I love you too. Text me tonight when you get home."

"Okay," she says, and I give her a kiss before turning to walk to my car.

I told Mark I would come over to his place after I dropped Candace off, so I start driving that way. I take this time to relieve myself of everything I have been keeping bottled up this past week. The tears come effortlessly. The pain that I feel for Candace is unreal. I want to turn my car around and go pick her up. I feel guilty that I'm going to spend my day with Mark and not her.

Turning into his driveway, I wipe the tears with the back of my hand before getting out of the car. I know I look like shit, and I know Mark will be able to tell how upset I am, but for once, I don't let it bother me. The way he has been there for me and for Candace this past week has revealed a side of him that I find myself falling for.

As I walk to his front door, I know I am walking towards a person who has proven to be dependable for me. So when I knock and he answers, I don't hide my pain. It's written all over me.

He wraps his arms around me, and I finally let my walls down and cry. He pulls me inside, and I grab onto him as I let out everything I've been keeping in. Mark doesn't say a word; he just holds me tight and allows me to accept the comfort that only he can give me. I can't do this with Candace because I need to be her anchor, but I've finally found a person that I *can* do this with. I'm finally allowing myself to be open enough to have this release, and to have it with Mark is more than what I deserve.

Shifting back from me, he braces his hands on the sides of my face and looks into my eyes. I don't hide from him. I don't want to. He leans in and presses his lips onto mine. This kiss is different. I feel like I need it. Like I couldn't breathe without it. So I don't move as we linger in this moment for a little longer.

We finally drag our lips from each other, and I rest my forehead against his as I take in a deep breath. Mark holds my hand and walks me over to the couch to sit down. Leaning back in his arms, I say, "Sorry."

"Don't be."

"I just don't know what to do," I admit.

"You're doing everything you can do, babe. Was she okay when you left?"

"She was crying. I hate seeing her like that. She never used to cry. Ever.

And now, it's all she seems to do."

Mark tightens his grip around me, and when he does, I feel a need for closeness consume me, so I decide to talk for a while. "She's just broken, and I don't know how to fix her. And now I feel guilty that I'm here with you and not there with her. But at the same time, I feel like an ass because I want to be here with you . . . alone. I know you want to have time with me, and I want to give you that, but I'm torn in a way, and no matter what, I feel guilty."

"Jase, you're not doing anything wrong, and neither Candace nor I feel that you are. That's only in *your* head." He takes a moment before he continues. "And yes, of course I want time alone with you. But I need you to want that too. Same page, right?"

"I do want that but not with the guilt."

He shifts so that he is looking at me when he says, "Knowing that you want it, guilt or not, is all I need. I hate that you feel guilty, but I know it's only because you love so much. I promise you, you're not doing anything wrong, so you shouldn't hold your choices against yourself."

When I see the sincerity in his eyes, I try to convince myself of his words. I sit up and lean my elbows on my knees, and when I feel the touch of Mark's hand on my back, I drop my head and blink out the tears that have been rimming my eyes. Thoughts of Jack start to pierce into my thoughts, and I grow angry as I think about how much this has changed her. When I think about what that piece of shit did to her, I feel my blood heat in my veins. Resting my head in my hands, I seethe, "I want to kill him."

"Who?"

"Jack. The asshole that did this to her." I stand up, not able to sit still with the bitter fury that is starting to overtake me.

As I pace back and forth, Mark scoots to the edge of the couch and says, "I know you do."

My gut roils with anxiety and rage. Raking my hand through my hair, I turn to Mark and tell him, "She begged me to not do anything, but I have to. Fuck!"

"You are doing something. You're giving her what she needs from you." He says this so calmly, but I feel myself starting to lose it.

"It's not enough when that son of a bitch isn't paying for this shit!" I spit out and take my car keys out of my pocket. "Fuck it!" I rush to the door, but Mark lurches over the back of the couch and is there before me. "Get the fuck outta my way, man."

"You need to calm your shit down," he says in an even, stern tone.

Reaching out to force him to move, he takes one quick step to the side, banding his arms around my sternum and pinning my arms to my sides.

"Get the fuck off me!" I bend my arms and try thrashing my elbows into him, but I can't get any movement.

"Not until you calm down."

Adrenaline is pumping through me, but his hold is too strong for me to break. "You didn't fuckin' see her, Mark! You didn't see what that fucker did to her!"

"I saw enough, man! I get it."

"He fuckin' destroyed her!" This time, when I jerk my body, I break his hold on me.

When I get to the door, he yells, "You're the only one she trusts!" His words stop me from turning the knob. "If you leave, you'll fuck that up for her."

Everything tunnels, and all I can see is *her* on the bottom of my shower. My heart is heavy, and it beats hard against my chest. I feel so goddamn worthless. I don't move as I speak into the door, breathless. "She's never going to do anything about this. She's just gonna pretend it never happened, and he's never pay for what he did." I choke back a breath as tears fall down my face and then turn to look at him. "So tell me . . . what the hell do I do?" I beg and when he steps to me, I drop my head into the curve of his neck and break.

Mark wraps himself around me and doesn't loosen his grip. I feel myself start to calm down and try and force myself to relax. "I feel worthless knowing who did this and where to find him but not doing anything."

"I know you do, but you have to get your head around reality." When he says this, I pull back and look at him dead on. He wipes my cheeks with his knuckles and says, "Reality is, if you beat the shit out of him, then what? You break your promise to Candace and wind up hurting her more."

"So I just do nothing and let him get away with this?" I ask, not sure if I can do that.

"If that's what she wants, then, yes. But that's her cross to bear, not yours." When I drop my head, he tells me, "You have to stop beating yourself up. You aren't doing anything wrong, Jase."

I let out a deep sigh, feeling defeat wash over me. "She's all I've had for a long time."

"I know."

"I can't lose her."

"I know, but you can only do so much."

"But I feel like I'm not doing enough."

"You don't even have to do anything . . . it's enough because you're enough."

His words hit deep. I suddenly think back to how I hurt him. How could I be so scared of someone that's so sweet? I take his hand in mine and offer another apology for my actions. "I'm so sorry that I hurt you before."

Giving me a hint of a smile, he says, "It's done with."

"It doesn't make it right."

"I know, but I also understand why you did it, and I hate that you ever felt that way." Tugging on my hand, he says, "Come on. You look exhausted, and I have no intentions of going to class today."

He leads me to his room, and we kick off our shoes before lying down in bed. Mark pulls the covers over us, and I draw him in close to me, grazing my jaw along his neck. I've never lost my cool like that in front of anyone, but having him see me so stripped makes me feel a new level of closeness with him.

"I have an idea," he mumbles close to my ear.

"What's that?"

"Why don't we have a night in with Candace? Try and take her mind off of everything. Just have fun."

Tilting my chin up, I kiss him. I wrap my hand around the back of his neck and grip tight.

"So that's a yes?" he laughs when I pull back.

"Thanks," I whisper against his skin, and he presses his lips to mine as I breathe, "No one has ever given me what you do."

He runs his hand down my cheek and looks me in the eyes when he tells me, "I want to give you everything." Those words are the only affirmation I need to know how he feels about me—about us—and I feel it too.

Mark and I spent most of the day in bed together. We really needed this time, so we took it. Having him like this . . . it feels right. For once, it finally feels right. In the midst of this chaos that surrounds me, he has a way about him that brings me back to solid ground. I know I need him. I need him in a way I haven't needed anyone in the past.

We go back to my place after running out for a quick dinner. I told Mark that I gave Candace a key to my apartment, and that I wanted to be there in case she came over in the middle of the night. He agreed that was probably the best thing to do.

Both of us get ready for bed, and I'm happy that we don't have to be apart, especially after today. A big piece of me needs him close right now. I lie down and Mark slides in behind me, wrapping his body around mine. I reach for my phone when it chimes. "It's Candace," I say as I open the text to read. She texted me when we were at dinner to let me know she had gotten off work and was heading home.

Goodnight. I miss u.

I hold the phone out so that Mark can read what she sent and what I type back to her.

Miss u too. Did u see Kimber?

Yeah. Didn't really say much. It's awkward.

I'm sorry, sweetie. Hopefully it will get better and things will get less weird for you guys.

Maybe. Is Mark with you?

Yeah.

Tell him I said HI. Love you guys.

We love you too.

I set the phone down next to my pillow, and Mark nestles his head in the crook of my neck, giving it a couple pecks before asking, "Are you okay?"

I shake my head no.

"Talk to me?"

"It doesn't feel right," I say as I roll over in his arms and face him. "Neither one of us wants to be alone, but I'm here with you, and she's all by herself."

His eyebrows knit together, and he lets out a sigh. He doesn't say anything, but really, what can he say? He just kisses me and holds me, and for some reason, it's enough.

The heat from the sun feels good on my face. The mixture of sand and salt on my skin and in the air I breathe is comforting, and I need it so badly—the comfort. How did I get here? How did life get so fucked up? I stare out at the sun as its first drop of fire hits the water and soaks it up.

"This is my favorite part, you know? Fire and water."

"Yeah," I whisper.

"The way they melt together flawlessly. You wouldn't think that two things that should never unite would be so perfect for each other, but they are. It's beautiful."

Her voice echoes in my head as I see the reflection of fire scatter across the choppy water. She's right. It's beautiful.

"I miss you." The words hurt coming out of me. My throat constricts in pain, and my voice trembles. But I have to say it.

"I've never left you."

"I've needed you so many times, but you're never there," I choke out around the tears that run down my face.

"I'm here, Jase."

Peeling my eyes away from the blue ocean, I meet gold. She still looks the same. Eighteen years old and soft golden eyes. I age, and she remains.

You would think she would be cold, but when I reach over and take her hand in mine, she's so warm. She's gorgeous but painful to look at.

She smiles—happy and peaceful.

"I'm so alone, Jace."

As she shifts to face me, she says, "No, you're not."

I don't respond. I simply stare at her, etching every detail into my memory because I know this won't last. It can't. Life is just cruel like that.

"She's going to be okay."

Denying her words, I say, "I don't think so. She's so lost."

"You're her home. You can't be lost if you're home," she assures me.

"But you're *my* home. So where does that leave me?"

She shakes her head slightly when she questions, "What about Mark? What is he to you?"

"I don't really know. God, Jace, I've done horrible things," I confess as I continue to cry. "Mom and Dad won't even talk to me."

"You couldn't keep lying to them though. And Mark loves you. You can't be afraid for the world to see you."

"I'm afraid they won't understand."

"Maybe they won't, but the Jase I know wouldn't care what others think. You're gay . . . so what?"

Her words make me laugh, and I've needed to hear them for so long.

"You're so much stronger than this. Don't let life stand in the way of what you want—what you deserve." She grips my shoulders under her hands and tells me, "Life isn't gonna be here forever. It passes by quickly and the time is lost, so don't waste it." When she lets go of me, she turns to stare out at the water. "Jase, you have everything that was stolen from me. I lost it all and you're wasting it. And for what? Because you're scared?"

Taking her words, I admit, "I think I might love him." I meet her eyes and continue, "I know I hardly know him, but I think I could really love him."

Her smile is perfect and everything I need to see right now. We turn our attention back to watch the last of the sun before it's completely submerged in the water. A union that should never be but always is. Day after day. A cycle that never ends.

I'm content. In this moment, I'm happy. I feel like I have everything until I look to my side and find myself staring down an endless path of sand.

My eyes flood, and I let them fall shut.

When I open my eyes again, I stare out the rain-covered window in my room. Even though Mark's arms are wrapped around me, I want to leave him and go back. Just like that—she's gone, and I am here, under the gray-covered sky, far from our beach.

Sitting up, I turn and shift to the edge of the bed and lower my head in my hands. I replay her words; I try not to lose the sound of her voice, but my focus is interrupted when I hear, "Are you okay?"

I hate that dreams have to end, but they do, and reality ensues.

I turn and fall back down on the bed. Mark doesn't say anything else, he just watches me as I lie here. My chest hurts. It aches. I'm sure the pain is written on my face. Rolling on my side, towards Mark, I tell him, "I miss her."

"Who?"

"My sister."

He reaches over and pulls me close to him. I can see the question in his eyes, and I know he doesn't know what to say, so I fill in the blanks for him. "She was in my dream." I pause before revealing, "I know it isn't real, but it feels like it is."

"I don't know what to say," he admits, but I move past his words and continue.

"She knew everything; I didn't even have to tell her." I watch as Mark's eyes begin to rim with tears that he never allows to fall. I'm pretty sure I know what he's thinking: *You're crazy. Of course she knows everything; she's just a figment of your imagination. It's all in your head.* I know that's logic, but I choose not to believe it.

I lie there in his arms as I allow my mind to drift back to the beach, not wanting to lose her just yet. Pretending that the warmth of Mark's body is the warmth of the sun. I know it's desperate, but I do it anyway.

chapter fifteen

"WHAT THE HELL is all this?" I ask as I dig through the black and white Sephora bag that Mark tossed on the coffee table.

"I told you, we're gonna make her smile tonight."

Taking out a small tub, I read the label, "Glam Glow? Tingling and exfoliating mud mask." I start laughing and shake my head.

"Dude, girls like this shit."

"Really?" I say with a tilt of my head. "How do you know?"

"'Cause my sisters are into this junk."

I tease Mark, but I love that he has gone to this length to give my girl a fun night. I watch him as he walks into my kitchen, takes a bottle of beer from the fridge, and returns to his bag of nail polish, pore strips, and a couple more things I can't recognize. He makes me laugh, and I intend on thoroughly enjoying watching him emasculate himself tonight.

I take advantage of the alone time we have before Candace gets here and all but devour him on the couch. I'm surprised that we haven't had sex yet. Normally that's the first thing I do with guys. Hell, that's the only thing I have ever really done with guys. But with Mark, it doesn't bother me to move slowly.

We scramble off the couch when we hear the door open. Candace steps in and gives both of us a knowing look, but Mark grabs her hand and starts talking to her before she can say anything.

After a few beers, I sit back in my chair and watch Candace and Mark apply mud to each other's faces.

Laughing, I say to Mark, "You know how ridiculous you look with that shit on you?"

"Shut up," Candace teases. "Your face could benefit from a good cleansing if your panties weren't wadded up so tight."

Mark and I both laugh, and it's nice to see her in a more lighthearted mood. Candace sips her wine as she questions Mark about everything from his band to his family. She props her feet on his lap and Mark proceeds to paint her toenails. I watch him with her. He sits there, wearing nothing but a pair of gym shorts, with mud on his face, trying to cheer up the only other girl I have ever loved aside from my sister. It's in this moment that I know I'm starting to fall in love. The fact that he is doing this, and I know it's more for me than it is for her, makes me see how much he really does care.

When Mark finishes, he hops off the couch and heads into the kitchen.

"Grab me a water while you're in there," Candace hollers to Mark as he's rummaging around.

When he starts sauntering back into the living room, water in hand, with his face covered in a brown facial mask, I notice the smile that finally appears on Candace's face. I laugh at how ridiculous Mark looks right now.

Handing Candace the bottle of water, he says, "Here you go, sweetheart."

"Thanks." She shakes her head at him and grins.

I hear her let out a small giggle and then she turns to look at me. I feel less weight in my chest knowing that Mark just gave her this. If only for a moment, he gave her a piece of her old self back.

I give her a wink before Mark falls across my lap and pulls me in for a kiss, getting mud all over my face. "Dude, that shit is everywhere!" I try to say with force, but it's betrayed by my laughter.

"Come on. Kiss me, Jase," he teases, and I try pushing him away, but he fights to stay on top of me, smearing that crap all over me. Mark and I both stop wrestling when we hear Candace laughing loudly at us. The three of us stare at each other, all knowing each other's thoughts without even speaking. We know what just happened was big, so we just absorb the moment.

When it starts getting late, Mark and Candace go to the bathroom to clean their faces off, and I get ready for bed. I can hear the two of them laughing quietly over the running water. It's the best damn sound in the world to me right now, and he gave it to me.

When they walk into the room, Candace slips under the covers, and I wrap myself around her as Mark slides in behind me and wraps himself around me. I love that the three of us can be here. These are the two people I love the most, and knowing they love each other too is near perfect.

Candace lets out a deep breath and says, "Thanks guys."

I kiss the top of her head when Mark says, "Anytime," and then presses his lips to the back of my neck.

Candace wound up spending most of the day with me. Mark had to get some stuff done before his show tonight. It's been a while since I've heard him play, but tonight I'm going with him to Blur to hang out.

I shrug on my shirt and throw some gel in my hair when I hear my cell ring.

"You here?"

"Yeah. I'm around the corner by Peet's," Mark says.

Walking out of my building, I round the corner and see Mark's white Range Rover parked by the curb. When I hop in, I lean over and give him a quick kiss before he starts making the short drive to the bar. He parks in the back lot and grabs his guitar from the backseat.

"So, Ryan, the guy that owns this place, wants us to start playing every Saturday," he says as we start walking through the lot to the back door.

"Yeah? You guys gonna commit to that?"

"I think so. The money is really good and saves us the headache of trying to find gigs around the city."

Opening the door, we walk through the back and into the bar. The place is packed, but then again, it's after nine o'clock on a Saturday night.

"Hey, man."

"Hey," Mark says to a guy whose arms are covered in tattoos. "Chas, this is Jase." Looking over at me, he says, "Chasten plays drums."

Nodding my head, I say, "Yeah, I think we've met before."

We shake hands and then he tells Mark, "Everyone's ready, so we should—"

"Hey, guys, can you get the others and meet me in my office real quick."

"Yeah, no problem," Mark says to the guy that is approaching us. "Ryan, this is Jase, the guy I was telling you about."

Ryan reaches out his hand, and I shake it as he says, "Jase, man. Good to meet you."

"Yeah, same here," I respond, and I wonder what Mark has told him. I start to feel a little insecure being with Mark like this around these guys. I wish I didn't. I wish I could be as comfortable as Mark is, but I'm not. Not yet.

Chasten follows Ryan to the back and Mark tells me, "I gotta go with them. I'll catch up with you later though." I nod my head, and I tense up when he kisses me. I know he senses my reaction by the look on his face.

"I'm gonna go get a beer. I'll see you later," I say before Mark turns away.

I walk over to the large bar and have to wait a while before one of the girls comes over.

"Hey, sorry about the wait. I'm Mel. What can I get you?"

"You have Full Sail? Amber?"

"Yeah. In the bottle," she replies as I nod my head.

"Jase." I turn to see Ryan standing beside me, leaning his elbows on the bar top. "You ever been here before?"

"Yeah. This crowd is a bit insane though," I say when Mel hands me the beer.

"Here you are."

"Don't bother with a tab, Mel," Ryan tells her.

"Thanks, man."

"No problem," he says when I hear Mark's band starting to play.

The music is loud and blasts through the bar. I take a seat on the stool that opens up next to me and drink my beer. Leaning my back against the bar, I watch Mark as he plays. He looks hot with his guitar slung low on his body. Muscles flexing in his arms and shoulders as he plays.

"Your guy's band is fuckin' popular. They brought in a huge crowd last time they played here as well."

Having him refer to Mark as *my guy* makes me uncomfortable. The fact that he knows I'm gay and that Mark is my boyfriend, embarrasses me. Not because of Mark. It's me, and I know this. Ryan doesn't seem to be phased by it at all, which surprises me. To look at him, you can tell he is all man.

"You go to school together?" he asks when I don't respond to his last statement.

"Yeah," I holler over the music. "We're in the same major."

"And what's that?"

"Architecture."

He turns around and yells for Mel to grab him a beer when a guy approaches him from behind and claps his shoulder.

"Ryan! Fuck, man!"

He turns around and questions, "What?"

"That chick you flung on me last night was a fuckin' psycho."

Ryan shakes his head and introduces us. "Jase, this is my dick of a friend, Gavin."

"What the fuck ever," Gavin says as he laughs at Ryan. Looking at me, he says, "Watch out for this dipshit, and don't let him hook you up with anyone. His matchmaking skills suck balls."

"Find your own ass, Gav. I'm not your fuckin' hookup."

"Not anymore. What the hell has happened to you lately?"

"Nothing," Ryan tells him. "Just sick of wasting my time."

Turning to me, Gavin says, "Ryan's been a bit of a pussy lately."

I laugh at him and take a swig of my beer.

"Don't waste your time buddying up with Jase," Ryan tells him.

"Sad. I guess it's just me trying to get laid, huh?"

"Sorry. Looks like it," I say.

"Are these the same guys that played here last week?" he asks Ryan.

"Yeah, they're gonna be playing here every Saturday now. They just signed a contract earlier."

"They looking for a label?"

"Ask this guy. I have no clue," Ryan responds as he tips the neck of his bottle towards me.

"You know them?"

"Yeah," I say. "But I dunno. I only know Mark and just met the drummer."

"This is Mark's guy," Ryan tells him, and fuck if that doesn't make me want to leave this bar. But Gavin doesn't even blink when he says, "Yeah,

I met Mark the other day. Cool guy. Well, if they are, I work for Sub Pop Records. I'd be interested in talking with them."

I nod my head, still feeling awkward, and turn to holler for another beer. Ryan wanders off while I wait for Mel to get my drink. Sitting down next to me, Gavin says, "How long have you known Ryan?"

"Just met him tonight," I say as Mel hands me the beer. I turn back around and watch Mark while listening to Gavin talk about some of his history with Ryan. From what I'm hearing, Ryan doesn't seem too far off from me. Well, from who I used to be before I started seeing Mark. I don't judge him 'cause I have to wonder what demons he must be trying to cover up. I can tell Gavin fucks around for the sake of fucking around. This kid is obnoxious, but he's hot; I'll give him that much credit.

I look over and spot a tall blonde running her hands down Ryan's stomach, but he clutches her wrist before she can slip them in his pants. Whatever he's saying to her is pissing her off. He lets go and starts walking back toward the bar.

"What the hell is up with you? That chick was all over your nuts," Gavin says.

Ryan ignores him and leans over the bar to holler at Mel. "Mel, I'll be up in my office. I'll come down later, okay?"

"Yeah, no problem, Ry," she says as she's mixing a drink.

Gavin catches Ryan's arm and questions, "Dude, seriously? What the hell is going on with you?"

Jerking his arm back, he says, "Not in the mood."

"You haven't been for a couple weeks."

As he shakes his head, looking frustrated as hell, he says, "You wouldn't get it, man," before turning and walking away.

"That guy used to be so much fun. Used to bang anything that stepped in front of him. Dude's been in a fucked up mood lately."

"Maybe he just got tired of using people," I say, and he looks over at me, eyebrows raised.

"It's not using when they willingly give."

I don't expect him to understand, so I don't bother saying anything else, and luckily I don't have to when that same blonde approaches him and diverts his attention away from me. I just sit back, drink my beer, and watch the one guy I know I would never use the way I did so many before him.

I spend the next hour drinking and getting to know Mel a little better. She's a pretty cool chick. Her husband is a drummer in a local band. We talk off and on while she works, and eventually Ryan returns. Sitting next to me, he looks worn out. Mel sets down a cup of coffee in front of him and after he thanks her, he turns to look at me.

"Did Gav leave?"

I look over my shoulder when the band stops playing. Mark slings his guitar over his head, and I turn back to Ryan.

"I don't know. He ran off with some girl over an hour ago, so probably."

Shaking his head, he says, "Sorry about earlier. He's a lot to take at times."

I turn around when I feel Mark's hand on my shoulder. He looks hot as hell. His sweaty shirt clings to him and my conflicting feelings start colliding.

"Hey, you bored yet?" he asks.

"No. I had the pleasure of hanging out with Gavin for a while," I joke and hear Ryan laughing.

"That guy's crazy, but funny as hell," Mark says as he wraps his arm around me. I move back slightly when he starts to pull me closer to him. "You okay?"

"Yeah, just tired." I lie to him. I hate that. I'm not okay. Fuck. I wish I was, but I'm not. I hear my sister's words replay in my head: *"The Jase I know wouldn't care what others think."* But to not care takes more strength than I think I have. Mark has never done anything wrong; he's perfect. He deserves to be with someone like him. Someone sure of himself and not so damn awkward and scared for people to see him for what he is.

I know Mark senses my hesitation because he quickly removes his arm, grabs the beer that Mel set down for him, and walks towards Chasten, who is still on stage working on his drum kit.

"You guys okay?" Ryan asks as he sips his coffee.

I try blowing it off and respond with, "Yeah. It's been a crazy couple of weeks."

"You have no idea, man," he says and then lets out a sigh. Clearly this guy has a lot on his mind, but I don't say anything as we sit there and drink.

For the next half hour, Mark's band finishes their last set. A couple of girls approach Ryan, and he pushes them away without giving them a glance. Mel walks over to him and whispers, "Why don't you head home? Max and I can close everything up."

He doesn't speak when he pushes his coffee mug towards her and stands up. Giving me a nod, he turns and walks away. Mel takes the mug, and when I look at her, she just shakes her head and quietly says, "Don't ask."

When the night winds down, Mark packs up his stuff, and I follow him out to his car. He seems irritated from earlier, so the drive back to my place is silent. When we get close, I say, "Park in the garage," because I don't want him to go to home. I need to talk to him. I need to figure out how to move past this, and I need to be honest with him.

He doesn't respond; he just turns the corner and drives down into the underground lot. When we walk inside my place, he heads to the kitchen and grabs a bottle of water.

"You mind if I take a quick shower?"

"No," I say as he is already walking to my bathroom.

When he turns the water on, I text Candace to check in.

Just got home. Interesting evening.

I go to my room, strip out of my clothes, and throw on a pair of gym shorts. My phone chimes as I slide into bed.

Is that good or bad?

Bad. Everything was weird.

With Mark?

It's me with Mark. I was really cold to him because I was embarrassed.

You have nothing to be ashamed or embarrassed of.

But I am, and Mark knows it.

What did he say?

Nothing. He's in the shower now. How are you?

You need to talk to him, and I'm fine. About to go to bed. Just been studying.

I'm gonna talk to him. I love you, sweetie.

I love you too. Tell Mark the same.

I hear the water turn off and I shoot one last text.

I will. Call me tomorrow, okay?

Mark walks into the room with a towel slung low on his hips and water still beaded on his smooth skin. *Fuck he's hot.* He looks over at me when my phone chimes again. I pick it up to read the text as Mark opens my dresser to get a pair of my shorts.

I have to work early. I'll text when I'm off. Night.

Night.

"Candace says she loves you."

He doesn't say anything when he slips under the covers with me. I turn to face him and tell him, "I'm sorry. I know I shouldn't feel this way, but I don't know how to let it go."

Mark just lays there, his hair still wet, and looks in my eyes. I let down my walls and open up. "I don't want to hide parts of me from you, but I don't know how to do that. I get scared. I'm afraid people are judging me." I close my eyes for a second before looking back at him. "You seem so sure of yourself, and I'm so far from that. I want to give that to you. I don't want to mess this up, and I don't want you to change the way you are with me because everything you do, you do it perfectly."

When he reaches his hand around the back of my neck, he shifts closer to me. He barely presses his lips to mine when he whispers, "It's not always that easy for me either."

I look into his eyes and can see the honesty there. Having him give me those words takes some pressure off. I wrap my arms around him and kiss him. When I seal my lips with his, he slides his tongue along mine, feeling me, and I roll on top of him. I drag my mouth down and along his jaw as he tangles his fingers in my hair. Running my hand down his cut stomach, I softly bite the curve of his neck when I slip my hand down his shorts and grip him firmly in my hand. He throbs against my hold, and it intensifies my desire to have him. As I let out a deep moan, I inch myself down the length of his body and between his legs. Slipping his shorts off, I toss them aside before lowering myself and taking him in my mouth, tasting him.

"Uhh, fuck," he moans out and tugs my hair.

This isn't something I've ever done with guys; they've always done this to me. The shame that has always come along with me giving a man anything like this would dredge up all of my feelings about how uncomfortable I am with being gay. Like the idea of me giving another guy head would somehow take me to a new level of gay. It's stupid; it's my own fucked up way of trying to rationalize things. But I want to give this to him. I want to leave those screwed up thoughts behind because I love him, even though I'm not quite ready to say it. I'm scared, and I know it. I feel closer to him than anyone else, but I still need more, and this is the only way I know how right now.

I take my time and focus on making him feel as good as I can. I give, not wanting anything from him in return. My mouth is clenched firmly around him as I use my hand to add more pressure, and when I squeeze tighter, his moan is deep. "Oh God, Jase."

Hearing him say my name like that does me in, and I quicken my pace and suck harder. I know he's close when I feel him swell even more. He bucks his hips, and I grip him with my free hand as he begins to come.

"Oh God, don't stop," he pants, and I don't. I let him ride it out for as long as he can hold on, and when he relaxes underneath me, he reaches down and pulls me up to him. I hover over him as he stares up in my eyes, his face flushed. He gives me a sexy grin before he lowers me down to him and kisses me. There's something about this kiss that's more intimate than any of our others.

Giving Mark this, something I have never given anyone else, makes me want to give him even more. There's no shame, no regret; there's only love for the man that is showing me that it's okay to be me. I rest my body on top of his, and we wrap each other up in our arms as we continue to slowly move our lips together. It's all we do for a while. It's all I want to do; getting lost in him is peaceful in a way I can't describe. He calms me when we are together like this, and I don't want this with anyone but him.

Not wanting to stop, I mumble against his lips, "I just want you."

He pulls back and places his hands along my jaw. "You have me."

chapter sixteen

"WHAT ARE YOU doing?"

"I don't know," Mark says in frustration as he stares at the smoke rising from the pan.

I laugh and nudge him away from the stove. Flipping the bread over, it's charred black. "You are completely helpless in the kitchen, you know that?"

"I told you; it's pointless trying to teach me how to cook."

"Dude! It's grilled cheese," I say as I toss it in the trashcan. "Any child could make that, but you, you turn that shit on high and scorch it."

Mark laughs as he says, "Babe, can we just order a pizza? I'm done trying to cook."

Rinsing out the pan, I look up at him and smile while shaking my head. "Hopeless."

"We're eating pizza," he asserts as he plucks his cell from the counter.

"Hey, can you plug in my laptop? I think my battery is about to die."

Nodding his head, he gets my computer from my backpack and plugs it in as he's ordering us dinner. The past couple of weeks at school have been busy with our project's initial presentations to our professors. I've fallen a little behind with everything, so although Mark insisted on coming over and hanging out tonight, he promised to help me with some of the drafting I need to get done.

"Okay, pizza is on its way."

I wipe down the counter and walk over to the couch where my laptop is plugged in and open it up.

"Do you have any heat packs here?" Mark asks. "My shoulder's been killing me ever since we left the gym this morning."

"Yeah, I have some in my bag in the closet."

When he comes back out of my room, he takes his shirt off and sits down next to me, holding the pack against his shoulder. I never knew that Ryan worked out at our gym, but last week Mark had run into him, so we've been meeting up a couple times a week to lift weights. Ryan is pretty quiet for the most part, but despite what Gavin had told me, he seems like a good guy.

"I think Candace left some Tiger's Balm over here if you want to use it," I tell him.

"She's crazy with that stuff," he laughs out. "She is the only person I know who smears that crap on and then wraps her legs up in Saran Wrap."

I bust out laughing at all the times I have seen her do that. "She swears it works better that way. She's been doing it for years."

Shaking his head, he says, "That girl cracks me up with how serious she is."

"Yeah," I sigh out as he props his feet on the coffee table and leans into me. He grabs the remote and turns it to SportsCenter as I get some AutoCAD work done while we wait for dinner to get here.

When a commercial comes on, Mark asks, "Has Ryan said anything about Gavin? I haven't been seeing him around lately."

Continuing to work on my project, I keep my eyes fixed on the screen, when I tell him, "Ryan isn't much of a talker, but I could tell that Gavin was starting to piss him off the other week."

"Huh."

"Why?"

"No reason. Just wondering," he says.

I chuckle at him, and tease, "You're nosey."

"I'm not nosey."

"It kills you that you can't know everything that goes on outside of your presence."

He starts laughing because he knows it's true. We both do. Mark loves gossip, and is always filling me in on crap I couldn't care less about, but I don't ever say anything. It's just one of his quirks that I get a kick out of.

"Dude, I just want to know what the hell happened. Gavin said they used to be really close."

"Okay, fine. All I know is that Gavin had said that Ryan has started acting weird in the past few weeks. He told me that Ryan used to spend his time doing not much more than hooking up with chicks, and then suddenly he stopped. That's all I know. Is that enough gossip to satisfy you?"

"Did you ask anything?"

"What? No, man. I don't really care."

"Hmm."

I just laugh at him as I continue to work. When the pizza comes, I take a break and eat before getting back to my project. Rolling out my blueprints, he helps me mark them up. I hear my phone ring from the kitchen, and when I walk over and pick it up, my stomach clenches with anxiety.

Looking up at Mark, I say, "It's my mom," before I answer it and walk to my bedroom.

"Mom, hi."

"Jason," she sighs out, and I can tell that she's crying. I walk around my bed and sit on the edge.

"Is everything all right?" I ask her. Despite everything, I still love my parents. Flaws and all. They are the only family I have.

"I haven't been okay since you left. I've been praying for you every day. I miss you."

"I miss you too." I grasp on to the hope that she's had a change of heart about me.

I hear her cries thicken as she continues to talk. "I'm worried about you, dear."

"Mom, don't cry. I'm fine. You don't need to worry about me," I try to assure her.

"But I am. I want you to come home."

"I can't come home right now. I'm in the middle of the quarter."

"No, I think you should move back here."

Lowering my elbows to my knees, I ask, "What are you talking about?" as hope slowly starts to fade.

"Ever since you left, you've been a completely different person. I talked to Pastor Richardson, and he agreed to see you for counseling to try and help you work through whatever is going on."

"Mom," I breathe out, and I hear the desperation in her voice when she pleads, "Please, Jason. You're the only child I have left."

She's crying, and I take a moment before I speak as disappointment overtakes my wasted optimism. "There isn't anything to fix. And this didn't happen when I moved away, Mom. I've been this way my whole life."

"I know that's not true. God didn't make you this way. You can't live like this; it's wrong."

Hearing her voice and hearing her pain, I feel so guilty. I listen to her cry when she says, "This is a choice, Jason, and you're choosing wrong."

I feel the bed dip down behind me, and Mark rests his forehead against my back as I defend, "There's no choice to make. It is what it is, Mom."

"At least come home for a few days so we can talk about this."

"I don't think that's a good idea."

"Please let me try and help you. Please."

Holding my head in my hand, I swallow hard against the disappointment and hurt building up inside of me. "I don't need help. I need you to love me enough to accept me." I don't wait for her to say anything before I hang up and toss the phone on the bed. Cradling my head in my hands, Mark plants a kiss on my back through my shirt.

He doesn't say anything, and I take my time before speaking. "She's so upset."

"I'm sorry."

"She's so upset, and it's all my fault." I shift to the side and lie back on the bed, draping my arm across my forehead.

Lying down next to me, Mark props himself on his side and says,

"You're not the cause of her pain."

When I don't say anything, he grabs my arm and moves it away from my face. "Look at me," he says and then repeats, "You aren't the cause of her pain."

"I am," I say when I look up at him. "She wouldn't feel this way if it weren't for me. Because of me, there's this rip in my family."

"You're not responsible for that though. They are. They're the ones that pushed you out."

"Because of me."

As he rakes his hand through my hair, he says, "Because of *them*, Jase. It isn't you. You're not doing anything wrong."

"What if I am? I mean . . . maybe that's why I can't get past this shit."

"What shit?"

I shift over so that I can lie on my side and face him. "For the most part, I'm fine. With you, I'm fine, but I can't help the times when it feels wrong to be myself."

"There is nothing about you, that I can see, that's wrong," he says softly.

"But that's you. She thinks I'm a sin. That I'm going to hell." I pause before asking, "Am I?"

He closes his eyes and leans his forehead against mine. "I don't believe that." When he pulls back, I look into his eyes when he tells me, "It doesn't make sense to me if that were true; why God would do this and then force us to deny it. That's fucked up. You know this isn't a choice. So how can it be a sin if God created us this way?"

His words hit where they always do, straight through my heart. I've always had these thoughts, but have never said them to anyone. Getting this out, and having Mark be the one to do this with, makes me trust him. How can this be wrong? To love someone. How can love be a sin? Whether it's right or wrong, all I know is, Mark is the one person I need.

"Don't walk away from me if I push you. I know how I get sometimes, but I'm trying to get past it," I confess.

Running his hand down my cheek he says, "I'm not walking away, and I'm not gonna let you screw this up."

I know what I feel for Mark. So I don't even give it a second thought when I finally tell him what I've already been feeling.

"I'm falling in love with you."

That sexy smile I love so much creeps across his face and then he tells me, "Good, 'cause I've been in love with you for a while. I just didn't want to say anything until you were ready."

I don't deserve to have this man who puts my feelings above his own, but I won't deny him. Wanting to put an end to this war I've been battling inside of myself, I surrender my heart and trade it for his.

I press my lips against his and move slowly as I graze my teeth along his bottom lip. Mark pulls me flush against him, and I wrap my arms around him, feeling the muscles flex in his back as he moves against me. I want him so bad, and I have to force myself not to rip his shorts off and bury myself inside him.

I reach my arm back and tug my shirt off over my head. Rolling on top of him, I run my mouth down his neck, nipping along the way to his chest. His skin is hot on my lips, and when I hit the waistband of his shorts, I shift them down and peel them off. But before I can do anything, Mark has me flipped on my back.

He crushes his mouth with mine and possesses me with his tongue. My emotions are running on high, and I've never wanted anyone like I want him. All of him. Grinding himself against me, I grow harder for him. He tugs my shorts off and fists me in his hand, stroking me slowly. Closing my eyes, I roll my head back into the pillow and feel the intense pleasure when Mark takes me in his hot mouth.

"Jesus," I nearly growl out when he brushes his tongue over me.

Mark slows his movements and switches our pace. He begins to trail kisses up my abs and then straddles my hips, settling himself on top of me. I cup my hands on his face and bring him down to me. His head rests against mine, and I feel the need to assure him of my feelings. "I really do love you."

"I know you do," he whispers.

"You're the only one." And he is.

Nodding his head, he kisses me but doesn't move his lips. We're just still for a while. It's only when I reach over to the nightstand and open the drawer that he finally drags his lips from mine. When Mark makes sure we're ready and protected, he reaches behind and guides me inside of him.

With his legs spread across my lap, he takes his time taking me in before he starts to move, and when he does, it feels so fuckin' good. I've never had emotions tied to sex, and the closeness I feel with Mark right now is more than what I thought could be possible.

Running my hands up his thighs, he rolls his hips over me. I slide one of my hands behind his neck and bring him down to me, needing to be closer to him. He kisses me, and I can't control myself when I groan into his mouth. We continue to take our time with our kisses as I begin to stroke him. He wraps his hand around my hand, and we work together as we both start to increase our movements.

When Mark whispers in my ear, "God, I love you," I find it hard to control myself, and I thrust myself deep inside of him. His hand tightens around mine, and I quicken my pace slightly as I pump the length of him. Everything about this feels so good, and I'm on the verge of losing it.

Dropping his forehead to mine, Mark grinds himself down on me as I feel the heat of him when he starts to come in my hand. His body jerks, and seeing him like this, on top of me, throws me over. I bury myself deep inside of him as my body explodes beneath his. I grip his hips and dig my fingers into his skin as I thrust up into him a couple more times.

He looks down at me, grinning, with a sheen of sweat covering his neck. "Come here," I breathe. And when he leans back down to me, I kiss him, licking him deep and taking all that he's willing to give. He shifts off of me and reaches over to grab my shirt. After he cleans us up, he tosses the shirt to the floor, and I draw him in close to me.

Lying face to face, he says, "Thanks."

I run my fingers along his face and softly ask, "For what?"

"Giving me something new."

"What do you mean?" I ask.

"That's not normally my thing, but I know it isn't yours either," he admits, and suddenly I feel like a dick.

"Shit, I'm sorry."

"No, I mean, I've bottomed before, but it's never been like that." He kisses me before continuing. "I've never felt for anyone the way I do you, so I don't mind."

"You should've said something."

"I love you, so it doesn't matter. I just wanted you to know."

We shift and get comfortable in each other's arms. We don't talk. We don't need to. He knows where my heart is at as we simply lie together in the aftermath of making love and wrap ourselves up in each other.

chapter seventeen

THE PAST COUPLE weeks have been busy with school. My professors didn't like my initial design, so I have been busting my ass trying to come up with a new concept. I've fallen even further behind, and Mark has been helping me with the tedious renderings and mark-ups to help me catch up.

My mom called again last week in another attempt to get me to come back home. Hearing the pain in her voice is hard on me. I hate it. I love her so much, but her unwillingness to accept me tears me apart. Mark is right though; I'm not the cause of her sadness.

A text from Mark brings me out of my thoughts.

On my way. Got hung up with practice.

It's cool. I'll go ahead and get your drink.

I grab Mark a coffee and wait for him to meet me. He's been having more band rehearsals, because they've been busy writing some new material since they play every week at Ryan's bar.

When he finally walks into the coffee shop, he looks pissed. He spots me and makes his way back to where I am. Sitting down, he grabs his coffee and takes a sip.

"What's wrong?" I ask.

Setting his cup down, he lets out a deep breath. "Aiden is just pissing me off. He keeps fuckin' around with my music and changing it up. I don't have time to be learning all these new songs to have him go right back and change them."

"What does everyone else say?"

"Everyone is pissed at this point, so today was nothing but a bitch session, wasting my time." Leaning back in his chair, he continues, "He wants to play some of the new stuff tomorrow night, but it isn't ready."

"That sucks."

"Yeah, I know. Anyway, enough of my bitching. Did you show Gibson your new design?"

"Uh huh. He really liked it, so hopefully I won't have to go back and change anything, and I can start to catch up," I say. I have been so stressed out lately with this project.

"That's good. Well, I'm about to submit my stuff for presentation, so when I do, I'll have some more free time if you need any help."

His eyes shift over my shoulder as I say, "Thanks."

When Mark gives a slight nod, I turn to see who he's looking at. *Shit!* When I see Preston walking over, I turn to stone as panic courses through me. *How the hell does Mark know him?*

"Hey, what's going on?" he says as Mark stands to give him a friendly clap on the shoulder before sitting back down.

"Not much. Was actually just with Aiden."

I shift uncomfortably in my seat and then Mark looks at me, saying, "Jase, this is Preston. He's a friend of Aiden's."

"I already know Jase," Preston butts in with a snide smirk on his face, and I quickly stammer and tell Mark, "Yeah, we've run into each other a few times."

Suddenly, what I felt was nothing more than an irrelevant hookup, just like all the others, seems more like a lie of omission from Mark, and I'm caught in the confines of remorse and anxiety. Distraction saves me when I hear my phone ring. When I take it out of my pocket, I look to Mark and say, "It's Candace."

As soon as I answer it, I can hear her crying. And the bullshit happening in front of me vanishes in an instant.

"Sweetie, are you okay?"

She can hardly get her words out through her breaths. "No. I need you. Please."

"What happened?" I ask and immediately stand up, shrugging on my jacket, needing to get to her. Mark stands up and starts following me out the door as I walk away from one of the many regrets of my past.

"I can't breathe." Her voice is strained as she speaks through heavy gasps.

"I'm on my way, just try to relax," I tell her.

She hangs up the phone, and I rush to my car.

"What's going on?" Mark asks.

"I have no clue, but she's crying and freaking out. I gotta go. Sorry. I'll call you, okay?" I say as I hop into my car.

"Yeah, go. Let me know what's going on."

I don't even respond when I peel out of my parking spot and start speeding to her house. Everything from that exchange back there seems so trivial compared to what Candace is going through, and right now, she needs me. My heart beats hard as I try to get to her. Running through stop signs and honking at the slow-ass people driving on the road, I finally rip into her driveway. Fiddling with my keys, I find the one for her door. When I walk in, I can hear her faint cries. Going into her room, I open her closet door and see her lying on the floor covered in vomit.

"Shit. What happened?" I say as I rush to her and scoop her up in my arms.

She clings to me as I carry her into her bathroom and start stripping off her soiled clothes. She's vacant as she sits on the edge of the tub, crying and shaking, and my heart breaks for her. Never have I seen a person so broken, but to have Candace be this person debilitates me in a way I wish I'd never have to feel.

I toss her shorts and shirt into the tub and kneel down between her legs. Holding onto her knees, I whisper, "What happened, sweetie?"

She just shakes her head and covers her face with her hands as she cries. I wrap her up in my arms and hold her. I hold her for what feels like a long time until she softens in my arms. When I look at her, she's exhausted. I don't say anything. I know she hates talking when she's this upset. I walk over to the shower and turn the water on. I return to her and pull her up.

"You need me to help you clean up?" I ask.

She shakes her head and takes off her underwear before stepping into the water. I give her space and leave her alone while I go to the laundry room and grab some towels to clean her closet floor. I don't know what the hell happened, but I'm pretty sure she had another one of her nightmares. This is the stuff that makes me feel so guilty for not being around more.

After cleaning everything up, I go back into her bathroom to grab her clothes, and I see her arms braced on the tile wall as she stands under the showerhead. Her head is hanging down, and I just want to grab her and take it all away, but I can't. I can't do anything to make this stop hurting her. I walk back to the laundry room and toss everything in the washer and start it.

When I return to her room, the water is still running, so I call Mark.

"Hey, babe. How is she?" he asks.

"Not good. I hate this," I say, defeated. Like somehow I've let her down.

"What happened?"

Letting out a sigh, I tell him, "When I got here she was in her closet crying. She had thrown up and was lying in it."

"Oh my God." He's worried; I can hear it in his voice.

"She hasn't said anything yet. She's in the shower now, but I know she had another nightmare. She doesn't take her sleeping pill when she takes naps in the middle of the day."

"You need me to come over there?" he asks, and I love that he does.

"No, it's fine. I'm gonna stay here for a while though." There is no way I can leave her like this. I don't want to.

"Maybe you should talk to her about seeing a therapist or something."

"Yeah, I'll try, but I know she'll just shut me down," I say and then hear the shower turn off.

"God, I feel so bad for her," he says in a soft breath, and I am right there with him, feeling the pain.

"I know. She's getting out of the shower, so I need to let you go."

"Okay. I love you."

"I love you too. I'll call you later."

I go ahead and grab Candace some clothes from her dresser and take them to her in the bathroom. She gets dressed and throws her hair up on top of her head. I take her hand and pull her into bed with me and hold onto her. She clings to me and buries her head in my chest.

Whispering, I ask, "Another nightmare?"

"Yeah," she breathes out.

"Wanna talk about it?"

"No."

Pulling her hairband out, I start combing my fingers through the wet strands.

"I really think you should talk to someone about this."

"Jase. Please don't."

"I know you don't want to, but it's been a couple of months and I feel like you're just sinking further away. I'm worried."

"It's fine. I just need a little more time to pass," she says, and I kiss the top of her head.

Time. She believes time is all she needs and everything will just fade away. She's living in denial, and I don't know how to get through to her. I have tried so many times in my own way, but she avoids the conversations every time. I just need her to be okay, and she is so far from it. She's just deteriorating into a shadow of what she used to be. My heart has never ached as much as it does for her.

"You don't have to stay here," she mumbles against my chest, and she's crazy if she thinks I'm leaving her here alone after what I just saw.

"I'm not leaving you."

It takes a while, but eventually she falls into a fit of restless sleep. I check the time on my phone and see that it's nearing seven o'clock. I hate to wake her, but I do anyway.

"Candace," I whisper, not wanting to startle her out of her sleep. "Candace, wake up."

"Mmm," she moans in response.

"It's almost seven. Why don't you go ahead and take your pill for the night since you're so tired."

She nudges her head against me before lifting it up to look at me.

"Where are they?" I ask.

"In the bathroom in the second drawer."

I slide out from underneath her and grab a pill from the bottle. When I walk back to her, I hand her the half bottle of water already on her nightstand along with the pill.

She sits up on the edge of the bed and when she sets the water down, she looks up at me and says, "I'm sorry."

I sit next to her and hold her hand. "Never be sorry for needing me." I lean in and give her a kiss. "I will always be here for you."

I stayed with Candace all night last night. We barely got any sleep 'cause she kept having night terrors. Although I'm tired, I'm going to go hang out at Blur while Mark's band plays tonight. He already left to go meet the guys to run through some new songs they'll be playing tonight, so I text Ryan to let him know I'm on my way there.

Ryan and I have been hanging out a bit more lately. He's a cool guy to chill with, so he stops by every now and then to have a beer and watch TV. And whatever funk he was in when I first met him seems to have dissipated a bit and he has become a little less intense and moody.

I pull around to the back lot of Blur and park my car. When I go in, I head up to Ryan's office to hang out for a bit.

When I walk in, he is sitting behind his desk drinking a beer and flipping through a pile of papers.

"Hey, man," I say before walking over to the small steel fridge that sits on the floor behind his desk.

As I grab a beer, he says, "Can you toss me another one of those?"

I pop the caps and hand him a bottle before I sit down. "So, you been up here all day?"

"Pretty much. You know how Saturdays are—crazy as hell all day." He takes a long swig of his beer and then says, "Missed you last night. Mark said you got hung-up with a friend."

"Yeah, sorry about that. She's been going through a rough time, so I decided to stay with her last night." I was supposed to go out to a private concert to hear one of the bands that Gavin had just signed. I told Mark to go ahead and go when I decided to stay the night with Candace.

"You missed a pretty good show."

"That's what Mark said."

Ryan laughs and says, "Your guy's a little crazy when he drinks."

"I'm not even gonna ask, but he was in a piss-ass mood when I saw him earlier," I say through my laughter as I shake my head.

"Ha! I bet. He drank a shitload, probably hungover as fuck."

We both laugh when the door opens and Mark walks through. "What's so funny?" he asks as he stands there.

"You, man," Ryan says.

"If this is about last night, I don't even wanna know what the hell I did. My head has been pounding all damn day, and now I have to play for the next two hours."

"Go find Max. He always has earplugs," Ryan tells him.

"Not a bad idea." Looking at me, he asks, "Can I stay with you tonight? My new roommate just decided to tell me that he's throwing a party tonight."

"Yeah, no problem."

"Well, I gotta run. I just wanted to catch you," he says and then turns to leave.

Mark has been keeping more distance between us when we are out, knowing that it still makes me uncomfortable. I hate that he feels like he has to do that for me. I know I need to get over it and try to force myself to show more affection with him when we are around others. I just need to push myself to take that step. But now I need to be honest and tell him about Preston. I never even felt like it was something I ever had to disclose to him, but now, knowing that they know each other, makes what happened relevant.

When Ryan and I walk down, I head over to the bar to say hi to Mel. We talk off and on, like we usually do, while I sip my beer.

"What's up with Mark?" she asks as she nods her head towards the stage.

Turning to look at him, I laugh at the crap mood you can tell he's in and the neon orange earplugs he's wearing. I look back at Mel, and say, "He's hungover."

"That sucks."

I look over to see Ryan being mauled by some redhead. He normally pushes off every girl that comes his way, so I'm a bit shocked, and just laugh as I turn back to Mel.

"Looks like he's back to his old self," she says with a smirk before walking away to help some customers.

After some time has passed, I watch Ryan take that chick out the back by her hand.

"Hey, Mel," I holler down the bar. When she looks up at me, I say, "You think I could get a bottle of water when you get a chance?"

"Sure, hun."

I overhear the two girls next to me talking about Mark and how the one girl plans to slip him her number. This isn't the first time I've heard this. Girls are all over his junk, and lately it's been making me feel more possessive of him. Everyone assumes he's single *and straight* because I'm so self-conscious of what people will think of me if they saw us simply holding hands.

I continue to eavesdrop as they start downing shots and getting drunk. The band takes a break between sets and Mark approaches me as he lifts up the hem of his shirt to wipe the sweat off his forehead, exposing his abs, which the drunken girls thoroughly enjoy. Sitting next to me, his elbows propped up on the bar, I take a big push and lay my arm up on the bar and hold his hand, lacing my fingers with his. He looks over at me and into my eyes as he smiles. I know this gesture means a lot to him, and all that really matters is that this makes him happy.

Chasten comes over to grab a beer, standing next to us.

"Oh my God!" one of the girls yells out, drunk off her ass, and the three of us look over at her. She's laughing and shaking her head as she looks at Mark before slurring, "You're a fag?"

I jerk my hand away from his, and my neck heats from fear and embarrassment.

"You're fucking wasted and need to watch the shit you say," Chasten barks at her.

I stand up and start walking away, needing to get out of this situation when I hear her continue, "I would have never guessed he was queer."

When I look back, I see Mark following me and Chasten grabbing the girl's elbow, dragging her out. I walk through the back door and out into the parking lot, welcoming the cool mist that's falling.

"Jase, wait!" Mark shouts from behind me, pleading me to stop, but I don't want to.

Walking to my car, I say over my shoulder, "I just need space, man." But I need so much more than space.

"That girl was drunk and a total bitch. Don't let her upset you."

When I reach my car, I turn around to him and say, "I'm not upset." Embarrassed. Ashamed. Humiliated.

Walking up to me, he backs me up against the side of the car. "Well you're something and you shouldn't be. I don't want you to be."

I hang my head down before looking back up at him. "I'm irritated." I then admit, "The thing is . . . you get a lot of attention from girls, and I feel invisible when what I really want is for people to know that you're mine. But I don't know how to do that."

"You don't have to do anything. You know I'm yours. I don't see anyone else but you." He reaches down and holds my hand. "People will always say shit, but you need to let it go."

"I'm trying."

"I know you are," he says as he slides his free hand around my waist and kisses me. "Come on. Let's go," he says and then walks around to the passenger door.

"What are you doing? You still have another set to play."

"I'm done. My head is pounding, and I feel like shit." He opens the door and hops in.

When I slide into the driver's seat, Mark pulls out his cell. "I'll text Chasten and have him tell the guys."

"Are they gonna be pissed?"

Reaching over and grabbing my hand, he says, "I don't care. I just want to go home and lie down."

I begin to stir and slowly wake up. When I roll over, Mark isn't there. I lie there for a bit when I hear soft voices coming from the living room. Walking out, I'm surprised to see Candace in Mark's arms, crying quietly on the couch. Her head is buried in his chest, so she doesn't see me, and I don't say anything. Mark looks at me with a slight shake of his head, so I just sit in the chair and stay quiet.

I hurt for her. Seeing her broken and hopeless tears me up inside. I hate the thought that she was so scared or upset that she had to drive here in the middle of the night. I want to hold her, but I let Mark take care of her.

"Wanna talk about it?" he quietly asks her, and when she lifts her splotchy, tear-stained face, she looks over at me.

I give her a reassuring nod, and she looks back at Mark and whispers, "I'm sorry. I . . . I just didn't want to be alone, but . . . I guess I just didn't think you'd be here. I'm not used to Jase having a boyfriend." She stumbles over her words and closes her eyes when she continues. "I'm just so tired."

"I know," Mark says as he brushes her hair behind her ear. He tucks her head under his chin, and she clings to him. Mark and I stare at each other across the dark room as he holds her, and I know I'm in deep with him. I love him so much.

Mark has completely been there for me in the past couple months, giving me strength and a shoulder to lean on. I've never had that before. I never knew I needed that until him.

Standing up, I walk over and pull Candace up off the couch, and hug her. When Mark starts heading back to the bedroom, I take her hand and follow. She slides into bed with Mark and I on either side. Facing her, I wipe her cheeks with my thumbs and give her a kiss.

"I'm sorry I barged in."

"You didn't. I'd rather you be here with us than alone and scared."

"I just don't know how much longer I can do this," she says. "He's always there at night, and it's so hard lying in the dark, waiting to fall asleep. But I never know if he's gonna be there too—in my dreams."

Mark curls in around her from behind and tells her, "You need to talk to someone."

I watch as her face scrunches up and she begins to cry again. Leaning my head against hers, she weeps, "I can't."

"You can. I know you're scared, but you can," Mark tries to convince her.

I look into Mark's eyes and see the concern. I know Candace wants to ignore and forget. I don't push it because she doesn't need to hear it again. "You'll get past this. There will be a time when it'll begin to fade," I tell her.

"But how long will that take?" she whimpers.

Mark wraps his arm over and around her waist, and wedges it in between Candace and me. "However long it takes, you have us, but Jase is right, it will eventually become easier."

She closes her eyes and lets the tears seep out onto the pillow as I tighten my hold on her.

Even though I know she's hurting, even though I know her pain is nearly unbearable, this is one of my most favorite places. Next to being in Mark's arms, being with the two of them, like this, is a close second.

chapter eighteen

WHEN I WALK into the gym, I spot Ryan over by the free weights. I make my way back there and when he finishes his set of squats, he looks over and says, "Hey, man. I didn't expect to see you here."

"One of my classes was cancelled, so I wanted to come since I figured the afternoon would be dead."

I walk over and start sliding the weights onto the barbell, securing them with clamps. Pumping out my sets of bench presses, Ryan stands above and spots me. "Got any plans this weekend?" he asks as he grabs the bar from my hands and sets it in the rack.

"No. Isn't it Mark's off weekend?" The band gets one Saturday off a month.

"Yeah."

"We don't normally do anything. Just hang out at home," I tell him as I lie back down to start another set.

Ryan lifts the bar and places it in my hands. Pushing out my reps, he says, "I've got some extra tickets for a small concert at Spines if you guys are interested."

Taking my time to finish my set, I don't respond until he grabs the bar back out of my hands. "Who's playing?"

"The xx."

"No shit? How did you score something like that?" I ask as we switch places, and he lies down on the bench.

He grabs the bar, and I help lift it out of the cradle for him. Before he lowers it down to his chest, he says, "Gavin."

The xx is Candace's favorite band. She is constantly playing their music when she studies. The last few weeks, we have been trying to get her out of the house to go out with us, but she refuses. If I tell her about this, I am almost positive she wouldn't turn it down.

Knowing she's really freaked out with crowds, I ask, "How many people do you think are going?"

As I take the bar from him, he sits up and says, "Small, man. Hundred or so. You coming?"

"Yeah. You have three? A good friend of mine is a huge fan, but she doesn't do well with a lot of people, you know?"

When he lies back down for another set, he asks, "Why's that?"

"Paranoid, I guess," I say, and then catch myself. I shouldn't have said anything, knowing that she will most likely be meeting him.

He gives me a strange look and then says, "Yeah, I've got three," before finishing his last set.

We continue lifting, working on arms, chest, and back for the next hour. When we finish up, I grab my bag and take out my cell to text Mark about Saturday. He's spending the day with Candace, so I make sure to tell him to keep his mouth shut until I can talk to her.

"You ready? I've got the tickets in my car," Ryan says as he grabs his bag.

"Yeah, let me get out this last text to Mark."

When I shove the phone into my bag, we start walking out and Ryan states, "So, you guys seem to be doing better."

"Yeah. I mean, we weren't ever not good. I was just . . ." I trail off, not really wanting to tell him too much, but when he prompts, "Just what?" I decide to tell him.

"I used to screw around a lot, so I wasn't too quick on letting Mark in."

Ryan nods and says, "I get that. I never get involved."

I know why I never got involved, so I wonder what his reason could be. I go ahead and reveal, "I don't like people judging me, so I used to put a lot distance between us when we'd go out together."

When we get to his black Rubicon, he tosses his bag in the back seat and shuts the door, saying, "People who would judge are fuckin' assholes. And I can assure you that no one that works for me would."

"Thanks, but it's my hang-up, and I know it."

Opening up the driver's side door, he reaches over to the center console and pulls out the tickets. He hands them to me and says, "Well, at least you're working it out. So, I'll see you guys Saturday?"

"Yeah. Thanks for these, man."

"No problem. I gotta run, but I'll catch up with you later," he says as he hops up into his Jeep.

"Later," I say and then turn towards my SUV.

I take the rest of the afternoon to study and finish writing a paper for one of my classes. Candace picked Mark up earlier today, so I'm about to head over to her house to get him. I grab the tickets that Ryan gave me, hoping that it will be enough to pull her out of her funk and go out with us.

I make the short drive through Fremont and into her neighborhood. The night is cold and misty, and when I get to her place, I let myself in. The house is dark and quiet. Walking into the kitchen, I see the two of them sitting around the fire pit in the backyard.

When I open the door and walk out, they both turn to look at me. "Hey, guys," I say while I walk over to Mark to give him a kiss and then turn to kiss Candace. "What are you guys doing out here? It's cold."

"I'm fattening up your rail-thin girl over there," he says as he holds up a nearly empty bag of marshmallows. He then turns to Candace to give her a wink.

She just laughs and says, "Good luck, fatty."

I'm relieved to see that she is in a playful mood, so I don't waste any time when I sit opposite her and say, "So, I want you to come out with Mark and I Saturday night."

"Jase." She shakes her head and suddenly that grin that Mark had just put on her face is gone.

I start to explain before she completely shuts me down. "It'll be low key, promise. Spines is closing early to have a private concert, and I was able to snag three tickets for us."

"You want me to go to a concert?"

"Candace, seriously? It's at a book and music store. It's a private show, but forget about that. You won't turn me down when I tell you who's playing." I know she's gonna be excited, so I can't help the smile that crosses my face as I reach into my pocket and pull out the tickets. I hand her the solid black ticket with two white X's on it.

Her eyes grow wide and she all but snatches it out of my hand when she says, "Are you serious? How did you get these?"

"A friend of Mark's."

"Who?" Mark asks.

"Ryan. I ran into him at the gym earlier today. We got to talking about music, and he mentioned the show. When I told him my best friend is a huge fan of The xx, he gave me a few extra tickets that he wasn't using."

"Who's Ryan?" Candace asks as she looks over at me.

Mark speaks up and tells her, "He owns the bar that my band has been playing at."

She sits back, and I can tell she's hesitant and debating on what she should do as she stares into the bright fire. I really want her to do this. I want to show her that she doesn't always need to be scared. That she can be out, be around people, and realize that she's fine. I reach over and take her hand and try to reassure her. "I really want you to go. You'll be with the two of us. Nothing will happen."

"I don't know. It makes me nervous."

"I know," I whisper. "But nothing will happen. You have to start trying."

Mark gives her an encouraging nod when she turns to look at him. She turns back to me, letting out a slow breath, and I know I got this.

Her voice trembles slightly when she says, "Okay."

I know she hates it when people fuss over her, so I simply sit back and say, "Thank you."

"I need more marshmallows," she says.

I laugh when Mark tosses her the bag, and she starts stabbing them onto her skewer.

"Did you finish your paper?" Mark asks as he picks up the bottle of wine that is sitting next to his chair.

"Yeah. I'm pretty much caught up with everything at this point. I am *so* ready for Thanksgiving break."

"I could pass on that," Candace says as she eats her charred marshmallow.

"When was the last time you spoke with your parents?" I ask her.

She tosses her skewer down and tightens the blanket that's wrapped around her. "About three weeks ago. Last time my mother called, I hung up on her and we haven't spoken since."

"What happened?" Mark asks her as he continues to drink his wine.

"Same thing that always does. She tells me how I'm not good enough, I'm not measuring up, I disrespect family commitments. Honestly, I'm used to it and normally just deal with it, but I don't have the energy right now."

"Are you gonna go home then?" I ask.

"Yeah. It's not worth the backlash if I don't. I mean, it's Thanksgiving. I can't *not* go home."

We hang out for another half hour. Mark finishes off the bottle of wine, and he is definitely feeling the effects. I decide it's time to head out before he turns obnoxious.

As we're driving back to my place, Mark leans over the console and starts biting along my neck, and by the laughing that accompanies it, I know he's had too much wine. I laugh at him, but quickly stop when he reaches down and starts rubbing me from outside my jeans.

My grip on the steering wheel is firm, and I try to focus on the road so I don't get into a wreck.

"We're almost home. I can't concentrate with your hand on my dick."

Mark laughs, and it only encourages him to not let up. Unbuttoning my pants, he grazes his nose up my neck, and then bites my ear. Hard.

"Christ," I say as I jerk my head away and slightly swerve the car into the other lane.

Mark starts cracking up and begins tugging down my pants. He slips his hand beneath my boxers, and I'm already hard when he starts stroking me.

"You are so fuckin' hot," he nearly growls in my ear, and I could almost come from the sound alone.

I grip his wrist and force him to stop. "I'm gonna drive us off the road if you don't quit."

He doesn't let go of me, and I don't loosen my hold on his wrist either as he begins ravaging my neck. Everything about this car ride home is making me lose control, and I throb in his hand.

I pop the curb as I speed around the corner to get into the parking garage. Mark laughs, and I don't even give a shit when I turn to park, taking up two spots. I shut the car off, slam the seat back, and let go of his wrist. I practically pull him on top of me, claiming his mouth with my tongue as he jerks me off.

After the fun we just had in my car, I say to Mark, "Hey, I need to talk to you about something," as we step into the elevator.

"Yeah, I want to talk to you about something too," he says, and even though I need to tell him about Preston, my curiosity piques.

"Yeah, what's up?" I ask him.

The doors slide open and we walk up to my apartment door as he says, "It's about Thanksgiving."

Opening the door, we head over to the couch to sit down. I normally go home for Thanksgiving, but given the last couple of phone calls with my mother, that's really not a good idea right now.

Propping my feet on the coffee table, I slouch back as he continues, "Why don't you come home with me?"

My head snaps up to look at him. I'm caught off guard. "What?"

"Don't freak out on me, Jase," he says as he cocks his head to the side. I'm sure he can see the hesitation all over my face.

Trying to keep my cool, I tell him, "Thanks, but I'm gonna stay here."

"And do what?"

"Look, it would be one thing if your parents lived here and I stopped by for the day, but—"

"I get it. But they don't live here, and I want them to meet you. So if that's ever gonna happen, then you're gonna have to come to Ohio with me."

It's not so much the meeting them; it's not knowing what their reaction will be. Shit, I barely even talk to my parents at this point. Even though he tells me they are cool with everything, I'm not about to put myself in a situation that could backfire on Mark's intentions. How will they look at me? At us? Us as a couple?

"Are you gonna say anything?" he asks.

I don't want to hurt him, but I can't go. I can't chance the rejection. I'm not ready, not yet. "I love that you want me to meet your family, but I don't think it's the right time."

Shifting to face me, he says, "You know I love you, and you need to know that I would never ask you to put yourself in a situation that would hurt you."

I know that he wouldn't, but I also know that people are unpredictable, and flying across the country to meet my boyfriend's parents after almost four months is a bit terrifying.

"Yeah, I know," I sigh, and he returns with, "Don't say no. Just think about it."

"Do your parents know about me?" That's probably a stupid question, but I'm curious about what he has told them.

"Yeah. They were the ones that wanted you to come out." When I lay my head back on the couch and stare up at the ceiling, he says, "They're totally cool with everything."

Rolling my head to the side to look at him, I say, "I don't know, but I'll think about it."

He grins as he leans over to kiss me, and the knots in my stomach begin to loosen.

"So, what was it that you needed to tell me?" he asks, and the knots—they're back.

"We can talk about it later."

chapter nineteen

RYAN HAS SCHEDULED the band to play a short set for the Thursday night crowd. I told Mark that I wasn't going to go. I've been trying to finish up the requirements for my design before the quarter ends, but I'm worn out and need a break. When I check the time and see that I can probably catch Mark before the end of their gig, I decide to go ahead and go up to the bar for a little bit. I toss on a loose-fitting t-shirt hoodie and run a little gel through my hair before heading out.

When I arrive at Blur, the band is still playing. The place is busy, as expected for a Thursday night in a college town. Thursday's are always big nights around here.

"Jase!" I hear Mel holler at me when I walk in.

Leaning against the bar, I tease, "Do you ever get a night off?"

"No, never," she laughs out and when the seat next to me becomes vacant, I get comfortable and order a beer.

I listen to the band play from behind me, and find myself zoning out. I'm not sure how much time passes when I hear Aiden telling the crowd goodnight. When I turn around, I catch Mark's eye as he steps off the stage. His half-smirk brings me out of my seat and has me wanting to be near him.

"What are you doing here?" he asks, surprised, as he draws close.

"Just wanted to see you."

"How long have you been here?"

"Not long. Wanna head back to my place?"

Giving me a smile, he says, "Yeah. Let me go pack up my stuff."

I follow him when he heads back to the stage. Watching him pull the cords from the amp, I turn my head and spot Aiden and Preston. *God, this guy just won't disappear.*

Not wanting another awkward exchange, I rush and ask, "You almost ready?"

"Yeah," he says as he zips up his guitar case and stands to sling it over his shoulder, across his chest.

"Aiden, I'll catch you later, okay?" Mark says as he jumps off the stage.

I look over at Aiden as he gives Mark a nod, then cringe at that fuckin' accent that keeps tormenting me.

"It was good seeing you again," Preston says to Mark as he takes a couple of steps closer. "You should come out with Aiden and me on Saturday," he adds without taking his eyes off of Mark, and I swear he's doing this shit just to piss me off.

Things have been so crazy lately that I haven't found the right time to tell Mark, and now the guilt floods me, along with irritation at this whole scenario, and I snap. "What the fuck is your problem?"

"Jase?" Mark questions sharply.

"What the fuck is *your* problem?" he throws back at me. "If you have something to say, then say it."

"What's going on?" Aiden asks as he approaches, and I look over at Mark, whose expression I can't quite read.

Shifting my attention back to Preston, I want to knock the shit out of him. But instead, I grit through my teeth, "Nothing," and then walk away, heading straight out the doors and to my SUV. I'm beyond pissed. Pissed at myself for more reasons than I'm probably willing to admit.

"Jase."

Mark is right behind me when I reach my car, and I turn and just spit out what I should have told him as soon as I knew his connection to Preston. "Preston and I hooked up. A couple of times."

"Hell, Jase." His two words are soaked in disappointment, and it's enough to send me to a place filled with self-afflicting regret.

"I should have told you when I found out that you knew him, but . . . everything has just been so upside down lately."

Shaking his head, he asks, "So what was that about back in there?"

I lean against my car, and explain, "The last time we hooked up ended badly. I was messed up and upset with what happened with Kyle and hurting you. I was lost—"

"You fucked that guy after that?" he throws at me, pissed now.

Words escape me as I stand there and drop my head, feeling completely embarrassed.

"What's wrong with you? Why do you use people like that?"

"Because I don't know what the fuck I'm doing!" I yell at him. "Because I've never done this before and I'm fuckin' confused!"

"*You're* confused? Really, Jase?"

Backing up my words, I'm so goddamn frustrated with myself as I continue to yell, "No! I was. I'm not now. I'm not confused with how I feel about you."

"Why couldn't you just tell me? When you knew that I knew him . . . you should have told me."

"I know," I say in a mass of failure.

"I feel like an idiot. Oblivious that you fucked both of us, and the two of you knew that I was clueless."

His words sting. They burn deep when I realize that I've hurt him a lot more than I thought. In ways I didn't even consider. I want to tell him I'm sorry, that I love him and nothing about this was done out of malice, but looking at the pain in his eyes, I know my words would be nothing more than cheap.

When I don't speak, he turns and starts walking away.

"Mark," I plead, not wanting him to go.

He looks back at me and says, "Go home, Jase," in a soft voice filled with disappointment before turning his back and leaving me to stand alone, the one thing I was hoping I wouldn't have to do again.

Lying in bed, listening to the rain fall, I wonder what he's doing. I've sent him several texts since I got back to my place, but it's been hours, and nothing. I feel like I was just playing a losing game with him. There was no way to win him with all my issues. I never deserved what he gave me. I pulled back from so many of his touches because of my own baggage. Baggage that didn't deserve to be unloaded on him.

He took it all and never made me feel like I wasn't giving him enough. I gave him all that I could, but truth is, it wasn't nearly enough. He needs more than I can give.

I tried. But I keep making mistakes. Mistakes I can't take back. I wonder if—for me—there's more than this, if I'll ever be more than this. For once in my life, I really tried letting go. Tried letting go of the fears I held inside and gave it a chance. I don't think I'll ever be the same after him. If this is all we were ever supposed to be, at least I loved enough to hurt. The hurt isn't enough though; it needs to be more than this, but I know it won't be.

Turning my head, I look at the large rain-covered window as the drops twitch down, colliding with other drops, gathering, until the weight takes over and they quickly fall the rest of the way down. Desperate, I reach for my phone. It's almost three in the morning, but I'm selfish and don't want to be alone. Walking out of my room, I take my keys, and before I make it to my door, there's a light knock. Letting out a deep breath, I find it ironic that she needs me at the same time I need her, although for much different reasons.

My heart skips a beat when I open the door to find Mark. *What is he doing here?* He looks at me, taking his time. Time is my affliction. I deserve it, but I don't want it. It stands still and pangs inside of me as I wait for him to speak, to tell me he can't do this, to tell me it's done with. But I also don't want time to continue ticking because I want this, even if it's just a look—I'll take it forever.

He moves past me and steps inside. Shutting the door, I lean against it when he turns to face me. Time begins to move when he finally speaks.

"What you did carries no weight on what we are; I know that. But you not telling me hurts. I don't expect for you to tell me about your past, but when that past is part of *our* present—"

"I know," I interject.

"You really let me down."

"I'm sorry. I honestly wasn't trying to hide it from you, I just . . ." I let my words trail when I start struggling to speak around the lump in my throat.

"I know, but I still can't help feeling disappointed in you." He takes a moment as he leans against the wall next to me. "I want more from you. I need you to not hold back from me. It's only fair, Jase."

I don't know how to respond because his words are coming out of left field for me. How is he not pissed? How does he see value in this?

"Look . . . I don't want to pretend that knowing how you used to be with guys doesn't bother me . . . it does. And running into your past may or may not happen again, and I hate that. But it's only because I love you. If I didn't, then I wouldn't care."

"I feel like I keep hurting you."

Releasing a deep sigh, he tells me, "Just be upfront with me. Talk to me; that's all I ask. I get that this is new for you, but in a way, it's new for me too. I've never felt so strongly for someone like I do you." He takes a moment before saying, "I'm not mad."

"I *need* you to be mad."

Taking a step toward me, he asks, "Why?"

I walk over and sit on the arm of the chair before admitting, "Because I need to feel it. So that I know that you can see this for what it is."

"And what's that?"

"Imperfect. Unequal." Dropping my head, I release a deep breath before looking back up at him. "I'm undeserving and selfish. You're worth so much more than what I'm capable of giving you."

He moves to stand in front of me and takes my face in his hands as he questions me intently. "You don't think you give me what I need? You think I'd stick around if you didn't fill up pieces inside of me that only *you've* been able to?"

As he moves his hands to my shoulders, I drop my eyes when I tell him, "My pieces feel stripped bare." I catch his eyes when I look back up and tell him, "I'm not sure I even have enough of them."

"Maybe I have what you're missing. But if you keep holding back, you'll never find out. You'll never know how well we can fit together unless you try." I grip his shirt in my hands, almost pained by my confessions when he affirms, "I need you to try."

"So that's it?"

"It's really all it needs to be. There's no point in making this into anything bigger than what it is. I'm not that guy. You didn't tell me about Preston; I get it. I'm not blind to everything going on in your life right now. But

I told you how I feel and what I need from you. What else is there?"

When I shake my head, not sure how he can be so understanding, Mark clips the thoughts that are already starting to invade when he says, "Don't tell yourself that you don't deserve it. You do."

Standing up, I wrap my arms around his waist and bring him to me. "No. I don't. All I know is that I love you. And I'm sorry. You'll never know how much, but I am."

He moves to kiss me, and I take it, lingering in it until he pulls back and says, "You can't be scared to talk to me," before pressing his lips to cover mine.

I run my hand behind his neck and hold him close, not sure who to thank for bringing this man into my life, but there's no doubt in my mind that someone—someone who knew everything I was needing—sent him to me.

We find ourselves in my bed. Although exhausted as the sky takes on a lighter hue with morning starting to filter through, I hold Mark in my arms, connected in a way I never knew was possible, feeling his heart beating against my chest. We quietly make love, moving together, giving exactly what we know the other needs.

In our own way, we release everything from earlier and move forward. That's all we can do because it's just us here. And when Mark runs his lips up my neck and breathes his words, "I love you," into me, I know I'm his.

chapter twenty

"I DON'T KNOW about this," Candace says from the backseat as we turn into the parking lot at Spines.

She's been a bit nervous ever since we picked her up. Getting out of the car, Mark opens her door and takes her hand. "No worries, okay?" he tells her.

I smile over at him. We've spent the past couple of days together, feeling like we just needed the time to feel settled with what happened the other night. Mark is right though, nothing needs to be bigger than what it really is. And me not telling him about Preston doesn't even really measure up to what Mark and I have. We're bigger than that, and I'm glad we're both on the same page about it.

I follow the two of them as we walk in. Ryan was right; there are only about a hundred or so people here, and the lights are low with candles all around. I spot the bar and leave Candace with Mark while I go get us drinks. When I grab the beers, I turn to see her holding Mark's hand while they're flipping through the vinyls.

I look over and see the band step up onto the platform stage and head over towards the two of them.

Handing them each a beer, I say, "Come on, they're about to start playing."

We find a spot behind one of the low bookshelves, and when the band starts playing, Candace leans into me—her way of saying thank you. I wrap my arm around her and pull her into me. I'm so proud of her for stepping out of her comfort zone tonight.

We listen to a few songs, and when we finish our beers, Candace and I go to grab another round.

"You having fun?" I ask as we wait for our drinks.

With a slight grin, she says, "I am. Thanks for this."

The bartender hands over the bottles and we begin to walk back over to Mark. Ryan is with him, and Candace nearly chokes on her beer. I can tell they recognize each other by the looks on both of their faces.

"You again," she says to Ryan and he doesn't speak. He watches her with the strangest look, but snaps out of it when Mark asks, "You two know each other?"

"Not really," he says as he finally breaks his stare.

"He's come into Common Grounds a couple times to get coffee. How do you guys know each other?" she asks Mark.

"He owns Blur, where the band has been playing lately."

"And the guy who gave me the tickets," I add. "Thanks, man."

"No problem at all."

Candace turns to listen to the band while Mark and Ryan make plans to go shoot pool next week. After a while, I grab Candace and the four of us find a table to sit down. I listen to her as she starts to talk to Ryan, and I can't help notice the way he is staring at her. Ryan normally ignores women; he definitely never looks at them like he's looking at her. I glance over at Mark to see if he's seeing it too and when I do, Candace places her hand on my thigh under the table. I look at her while she's listening to Ryan talk, and I can tell that she's panicking. I hold her hand and give it a light squeeze, reassuring her that she's fine.

I'm sure that having Ryan here is maybe pushing her a bit more than she's comfortable with. But I want to push her, and knowing that Ryan is a pretty trustworthy guy, I back off a little and go sit next to Mark, leaving the two of them to chat.

I lean into him while Ryan and Candace talk and say, "Are you seeing the way he's looking at her?"

"Who?"

"Ryan," I say a little irritated at his distraction.

He looks over and then back at me. "Sorry, I wasn't paying that much attention, but the fact that he's talking to her is unusual for him."

We both turn our heads to look at them, and then Mark, being nosey, butts in. "What are you two talking about?"

"New York City," Ryan says as Candace excuses herself to go listen to the next song.

When I get up to follow her, Mark and Ryan do too. I stand beside her as she leans her elbows on the bookcase, and Ryan comes to stand on the opposite side, leaning down next to her. I watch her turn her head and stare at him. Candace never showed any interest in guys before what happened to her, and ever since, she's been so closed off to everything. I'm taken aback when I see her looking at him the way that she is.

Wanting to push her, I lean over and say, "Mark and I will be right back."

She eyes me with curiosity, asking, "Where are you going?"

"Don't worry about it. We'll be back in a second." I kiss the side of her head and then grab Mark's arm, leading him over to the bar.

"What's going on with you?" he asks.

"Look at her," I say as I nod my head toward Candace from across the room. "She's never looked at a guy like that before."

"Really?"

"She's always been closed off, even before what happened," I tell him.

"You think we should tell her about Ryan?"

Turning my head to look at Mark, I ask, "What do you mean?"

"I don't know, but it's Candace, and Ryan is known for screwing around with anything that walks past him."

"That's what Gavin says, but I've only seen him with one chick."

"Still."

Stepping in front of him, I say, "I really like Ryan despite what we've heard. Don't forget, I did my fair share of that crap too before I met you, but this guy seems pretty straightforward and honest. At least that's the impression I get. I just want her to start living again."

"I know you do. Come on. Let's go back before she gets mad at you for ditching her."

When we walk back over to the two of them, Candace seems on edge, and I can tell something has switched inside of her because she wants to leave immediately.

Telling Ryan bye, Candace rushes out the door, and Mark and I follow closely behind. We all get into the car, and when Candace slides into the back seat, I turn and ask, "What was that all about?"

"You tell me. Where the hell did you two run off to?"

Shit. She's clearly upset, but I go with honesty and say, "Just thought you two should talk without Mark and me around."

Shaking her head in annoyance, she asks, "Why?"

"Just got that feeling. You two kept staring at each other with that look."

"And what look would that be?"

"Candace, the guy is hot. You know what look he's talking about," Mark adds.

Slouching back in the seat, she says with a defeated sigh, "Doesn't matter."

"What do you mean it doesn't matter?" I ask, but she avoids looking at me.

Ignoring me, I can see her chin quivering, but I want her to talk to me.

"Candace?" I say, trying to get her to focus.

"It just doesn't matter, Jase. It's wrong," she says as she stares out the window.

"It's not wrong for you to find someone attractive."

"Yes, it is."

I hate that she feels this way, and I know Mark does too. He turns off into an empty parking lot, parks the car, and gets out. When he opens Candace's door, he slides in next to her and firmly says. "Stop punishing yourself."

Before she can deny his words, he says it again. "Stop punishing yourself."

Shifting in my seat to look back at her, I tell her, "Nobody says that you can't enjoy life. You can. You should. You just won't allow yourself."

"How can I feel like that after what happened? It feels wrong."

"It's not wrong," Mark says. "You need to let yourself feel happiness and not run away from every good feeling that comes over you."

"It doesn't feel right."

"Why?" I ask.

"Because . . . it makes me feel cheap—dirty." Fuck, I hate that son of a bitch for leaving her so broken that this is how she feels about herself.

"You aren't either of those things, not even close," Mark tells her. "What happened doesn't make you cheap or dirty or whatever else you're thinking. It happened, and you have been punishing yourself ever since."

"He's right," I add. "You can't keep doing this to yourself. You can't keep taking this wound and ripping it further open beyond repair. You have to try and leave it be, and allow it to heal."

"I don't know," she says and I can tell she's about to cry, so I drop it and change the subject.

"I'm proud of you," I tell her "I honestly didn't think you would come out with us tonight. Thought you might back out." I give her a smile and she leans forward, between the seats, and gives me a hug.

"I'm glad I came," she whispers in my ear.

Mark gives her a kiss and then gets back behind the wheel. When we get to her house I offer to come in, but she assures me that she's fine. Once, she's inside, I grab Mark's hand and admit, "I hate this."

Looking over at me, he asks, "Hate what?"

"The way she feels about herself. It pisses me off because it's so messed up."

"I know, but it makes sense that she would think that way, as crazy as it sounds," he says as he drives us back to my place.

"I just want her to be happy."

Mark squeezes my hand. "I know you do. She will be. It just might not be for a while."

Lying down in bed, Mark rolls on his side and says, "I don't want to pressure you, but Thanksgiving is in a few weeks. I just was wondering where your head is at with it all."

I fold my hands behind my head and sigh. "I don't know." A part of me is still surprised that he hasn't wavered on me.

"What are you so worried about?"

Everything. Meeting his family, their reaction to me, their reaction to us, taking our relationship further. "I just don't know what to expect."

"Jase, you have nothing to worry about. I swear. Whatever you're thinking, it's only in your head."

I get so much from Mark, and I know it isn't fair. He gives and I take. I think about how much I want Candace to push herself, but in a way, I'm holding back just like she is. Scared of the unknown. I know I need to trust that Mark has my back, but more than that, I need to show him that I have his. That I am in this. Because I am.

"If the answer is no, that's fine, babe. Just say the word, and I won't bring it up again."

"I'll go," I say as I roll on my side to face him straight on.

Shaking his head, he questions, "Are you sure?"

"I'm sure. And I'm sorry. I don't want to hold back with you anymore. It isn't fair."

Looking deep into my eyes, he says softly, "It's not about being fair. I love you, Jase. I'm not going anywhere, so I'll give you whatever you need."

When I wrap my arm around his waist, I tell him, "I've been taking too much though."

He brushes his lips over mine before kissing me. As he trails his lips down my neck, he breathes on my skin, "I don't care how much you take."

I grab his hair and guide him back up to my mouth. Mark slides his tongue along my lower lip and nips it. His chest is hot against my skin, and I cling to him, pulling him flush against me. We tangle our legs, and I just can't seem to get close enough to him. I want him. All of him. And I want to give him back everything I've taken.

I shift on top of him and take my time as I graze my mouth across his chest, flicking my tongue over his nipple, and kissing my way down his taut abs. Hooking my fingers around the waistband of his boxers, I slide them down and toss them on the floor. I look down at him, and everything is near perfection for me.

Settling myself between his legs, I trail my tongue up the length of him before sucking him into my mouth. His hands are twisted in my hair, gripping tightly as he guides me at his own pace, and I let him take control.

I know that Mark has gone out of his comfort zone with me to give me what I want, and I want to be able to do the same for him.

When Mark's breathing grows heavy, I drag my mouth off of him and grip him in my hand as I shift to his side. He kisses me slowly, dipping his tongue in my mouth. We move lazily together, not wanting to rush while I continue to stroke him in my hand.

I'm so turned on and hard right now, and I have to resist the urge to bury myself deep inside of him, because for once, I want to give him the satisfaction he's been denying himself. For me.

Mumbling over his lips, I hesitantly whisper, "You can have me." Never have I been the bottom, but I know it isn't Mark's thing either. He's let me take control all the times we've had sex in the past, but I'm done being selfish with him.

As he shifts back slightly to look in my eyes, he takes a moment before asking, "Are you sure?"

I nod my head, and he begins to question, "You've never . . . ?"

"No."

"Jase—"

"Don't," I cut him off. "I love you. I really fuckin' love you. And I—"

He doesn't let me finish when he covers my mouth with his. He moves on top of me and breaks our kiss only long enough for him to remove my shorts and sling them aside. He lies between my legs and returns his lips to mine as I band my arms around him, pulling his weight on top of me. I'm nervous about doing this, but there isn't anyone else I would do this for, and I know it. I trust Mark, and I love him. That's enough.

He leans over and opens the drawer to my nightstand. I watch him as he moves slowly and takes his time getting me ready for him. Reaching down, he braces himself over me with his one arm.

"Just relax, okay?" he breathes out as he slowly pushes himself inside of me. My breathing begins to stagger at the unfamiliar and uncomfortable feeling. My body instinctively tenses up around him, and he repeats, "Relax, babe."

And when I do, he continues to ease himself the rest of the way in. We lie there for a while, kissing slowly, as he lets me get used to him and not feel so tense.

"You okay?"

"Yeah," I say as I nod my head, and when I do, he begins to move. I hold him close to me as his body lies on top of mine. And the closeness alone overwhelms me. Having him inside of me is intense. There is no give and take right now. We just are.

We take our time and never move too fast. Eventually the uncomfortable feeling passes and my body heats up with the pleasure that begins to overtake me. Closing my eyes, I moan out, "Oh, God," as he pushes himself inside of me.

Dropping his head in the crook of my neck, he breathes hard, "You feel so good."

His words burn through me, and I reach down and start stroking myself, needing more of this feeling that's shooting through me. I stare up into Mark's green eyes as he looks into mine. Neither of us speaks through our labored breaths. I take my free hand and wrap it behind his neck, and he drops his damp forehead to mine.

I lift my chin and kiss him as I feel myself getting close. I know Mark is with me when he grows harder, swelling inside of me, and the pressure building is more intense than I have ever felt before. I can't hold back when I start to come. Violent euphoria rips through me, and I can't even keep my eyes open as I roll my head back into the pillow. My abs constrict as the pulses of pleasure take me over. I hear Mark groan as he begins to lose himself, grinding himself into me. The longer he moves inside of me, the more he prolongs my release, and like a greedy bastard, I don't want him to stop. And he doesn't, knowing what he's doing to me.

When he collapses on top of me, I wrap my arms around him. I can feel the thudding of his heart through his chest, and I know I am with exactly who I should be. No doubts. No questions. He's freed me in a way I didn't think was possible. I didn't know I could open myself up this way to another man and be so exposed. But he doesn't judge. He has only ever given me the benefit of the doubt, letting me stumble at my own pace. And even though I am scared shitless about meeting his family, I want to because there isn't anyone else I want to be with.

He's it.

chapter twenty-one

"HEY, MAN," RYAN says as he's walking into my apartment. "You guys ready?"

"Mark is still at Aiden's place going over some of the new songs."

Sitting down on the couch, he asks, "How's that been going? Those two have been at each other's throats for a while now."

"You wanna beer?" I ask from the kitchen before answering him.

"Yeah."

Grabbing a couple of beers from the fridge, I hear the door open, and when I look up, I see Candace walking in, looking like a mess, startled, staring at Ryan.

"Hey, is everything all right?" I ask as I start walking into the living room.

I hand a bottle to Ryan and look at her with her wet hair like she just got out of the shower.

"Umm, yeah . . . I mean, no." She's stumbling over her words, and I know I'm not gonna figure out what has her on edge with Ryan here. But I ask anyway. "What's that mean?"

"Nothing, never mind," she sighs as she flops down in the chair. "I didn't know you would have company, or I would've called or something."

I laugh and tell her, "Candace, I gave you a key so you wouldn't have to call. You can come over whenever."

As she turns to watch the TV, I look over at Ryan, who's staring intently at her. He's leaning forward with his elbows on his knees, gripping the neck of the bottle with his hand. There is no doubt he's interested. I suddenly feel very protective of her, knowing that he has no clue how fucked up she is right now. I like Ryan; he's a nice guy and all, but I'm wary about whatever intentions might be running through his head. Candace never dealt well with guys even before the attack. Now . . . well . . . now she's just barely staying afloat.

"You okay?" Ryan asks her.

She looks at him and then over at me. "I don't want to talk about it," she says as she focuses back on the TV. "Where's Mark?"

"He's finishing up rehearsals with the band. He should be here shortly, then we are heading out to Malone's to shoot some pool and chill," I say as my cell starts ringing. When I pull it out of my pocket, I see it's Mark. Knowing he's probably going to be in an irritated mood, I grab my jacket and head out to the balcony to talk to him.

"Hey, where are you?" I ask.

"I'm heading over now. Sorry I'm running late. Is Ryan there?"

"Yeah. So is Candace."

"Is everything okay?" he asks.

Leaning against the railing, I watch the rain fall from the dark sky. "Yeah. Something's going on, but whatever it is doesn't seem to be bothering her too much. I didn't pry 'cause Ryan is here."

"Okay, well, I'm about ten minutes away."

"How did everything go with the guys?"

"Not as bad as I thought. Aiden is just on a different page with this whole music thing. He's a lot more serious about it than the rest of us. He's pissed, but he's been easier to handle."

"Is he looking to push this into something bigger?"

"Yeah, but I'm not looking to get signed or anything. This is just a hobby for me," he says.

I turn, looking into the apartment, and see that Candace and Ryan are talking. "I'll see you in a bit. I'm gonna head back inside."

"Okay, see ya."

"Who was that?" Candace asks when I walk back in.

"Just Mark. He's on his way."

"Hey, did you get a chance to think about Saturday?" Ryan asks her, and I am caught off guard.

When the hell did they talk about making plans on Saturday? "Saturday?" I ask.

"Yeah, I asked her to come hiking with us."

Instead of questioning when this conversation happened, I take the bait to try and get Candace to step out of her comfort zone a little more and go with us. I never asked her before 'cause I figured she'd shoot me down, but since apparently Ryan has invited her, I add, "Oh yeah? You coming?"

She lies to me when she says, "I have a lot of studying to do before finals."

I'm not gonna let her avoid this, so I don't let up. "Please, we both know you are way ahead in all your classes. You should come. We are hiking up to the Tolmie Peak Lookout."

She looks over at Ryan, and I am sure she doesn't want to fight in front of him when she lets out a sigh, saying, "Fine."

She shakes her head at me when I smile in satisfaction.

"Hey, sorry I'm late," Mark says as he barges through the door with his guitar case slung across his chest. "Let me put this up, and I'll be ready to go."

Candace stands when Ryan and I get up to toss our bottles in the trash. She walks over to Mark when he heads to the door, and we join them as I hear her ask him if she can stay over. He tells her it's cool and draws her in for a hug as she looks over his shoulder at Ryan, and he's staring back at her.

Not too comfortable with what's happening, I say, "Okay, I'm ready. Let's go," and open the door. I give Candace a kiss before the three of us head out.

I've been uneasy since we left my place, so after Ryan racks the balls on the pool table, I ask, "So when did you see Candace?"

Chalking his cue, he says, "What?"

"When you mentioned our hike."

"This morning." He lines up the cue ball and breaks. "She left her scarf at the concert. I stopped by her work to drop it off."

He looks at me while I stand there, and I'm curious about how she handled that.

"You're up," he says.

Lining up my shot, I hit the five into the side pocket.

"You guys want another bucket of beers?" Mark asks us, and when I look up at him and nod, he heads over to the bar.

"So, what's her story?" he asks, as I line up my next shot.

Being cautious and territorial, I leave it at, "No story." Distracted, I miss my shot and watch Ryan as he walks around the table. I wanna know where his head is at and what he's thinking when it comes to Candace. I'm not nervous about him as a person; he's a good guy. I'm nervous about what his intentions might be.

He continues and asks, "You've known her a long time?"

He's obviously interested, so I just come right out and let him know, "She's not like that, man. Not even close."

Leaning over the table about to take his shot, he peers up at me, and I tell him, "She's like a sister to me."

Mark walks over, setting our drinks down on the table, and Ryan takes his shot, knocking his ball into the corner pocket. He doesn't ask any more questions, and I'm relieved. I like Ryan, but he's older and used to getting what he wants out of women, at least from what I've heard, so I wonder if he is looking for something quick and easy with Candace. I hate having the feeling that I would need to protect her from a guy who has become a pretty good friend.

We hang out for several hours, drinking and playing pool, but we decide to call it a night when Ryan gets a call from his bar, and has to run up there. Mark and I leave, and instead of dropping him off at his car, I ask him to come home with me.

"I told Candace that I wasn't going to stay and that she could," he says.

"I think we should tell her about Ryan. He was asking a lot of questions about her earlier tonight, and I'm just worried."

"You weren't the other day. What happened?"

Turning into the parking garage, I tell him, "I don't know, but I can tell he's into her. He stopped by to see her at work this morning."

"How do you know that?"

"He told me. He invited her to go hiking with us on Saturday."

When I park the car, he questions, "Is she going?"

"Yeah."

Shifting in his seat, he asks, "I thought you liked Ryan?"

"It isn't that, but I know how Candace is with guys. Hell, man, she's practically a virgin. I don't want her to get hurt, and after everything that's happened, I just—"

"I think you need to relax. If she's as closed off as you say, then I wouldn't worry. I mean, the girl never goes anywhere aside from school and work. I think you're stressing over nothing, but if you want to talk to her, then you should."

I lean over and kiss him before getting out of the car and heading upstairs. When we walk in, we make our way into my room to see Candace curled in a ball in the center of the bed. Stripping down to my boxers, I lean over and whisper, "Hey, sweetie, Mark's staying the night with us."

Keeping her eyes closed, she nods her head.

"I just didn't want you to wake up and be scared," I say, and I slide into bed at the same time Mark does.

The following morning, we sit around and drink coffee before we have to get ready for class.

"You guys have fun last night?" Candace asks from the kitchen as she's refilling her mug.

"Yeah. Why didn't you tell me that Ryan came to see you at work?" I question as she walks back into the living room and sits at the corner of the couch.

"I don't know."

"Well, what happened?" I pry, wanting the answers I didn't feel like I could get from Ryan last night.

Taking a sip of her coffee, she says, "He had my scarf that I had left at the concert. He just returned it, and then Roxy, being Roxy, told him that I would have a drink with him when he asked me."

"So you guys hung out?"

"Yeah. It was fine though. We just talked about school, and then he invited me to go hiking with you guys." Staring between Mark and I, she shakes her head and asks, "What?"

"Jase is just being protective," Mark answers.

"I thought you'd be happy that I agreed to go with you guys," she says, a little confused.

"I am," I try to convince her and then Mark takes over. "Jase is just worried about some stuff we heard about Ryan."

"What stuff?"

"He has a reputation for sleeping with a lot of women. But ever since I've known him, I have never seen him be that way. At all. So, I'm not sure how much truth there is to it," Mark tells her.

"You don't need to tell me this. I have no interest in him. In anyone. Why would you even think that?" she states, clearly bothered with what we are insinuating.

I don't tell her that I think Ryan feels differently because it might freak her out, so I just let it go for now. "I don't. It's just me feeling like I need to protect you."

She looks at Mark and he tells her, "Ryan's a good guy. Jase is just worried, that's all."

I reach over and pull her down on the couch with me as I lean into Mark behind me. Wrapping her arms around me, she says, "I don't know if I'll ever be able to have that."

"Have what?" I say and then kiss the top of her head.

"Feelings like that."

Letting out a deep breath, I tell her, "You will. One day, you'll get everything you deserve."

chapter twenty-two

"I FEEL WEIRD about leaving Candace all week," I tell Mark as I pull a few t-shirts from my closet to throw into my suitcase.

"Isn't she going home tomorrow?"

"Yeah, but that's what I'm worried about. They have a horrible relationship."

"Jase—"

"I know," I say when I turn to face him. Mark has been pushing me to take a step back. He thinks she depends on me too much, and I know she does, but I like being that for her.

"She'll be okay. I mean, she was completely fine getting out with us on Saturday and being around Ryan," he says, and it's true. "Hell, I think she actually enjoyed herself for a change."

Mark made sure that I gave her space when we went hiking. When I wanted to stay with her, he dragged me ahead, leaving Candace to spend most of the time with Ryan. And he's right; she was fine. Spending the whole day together, seeing Ryan with Candace, actually settled some of the feelings I was having about wanting to protect her from him. I don't really think there is much to protect her from. If anything, I like the fact that she could possibly see Ryan as another friend, or at least open herself up to that idea.

"Did you talk to your mom?"

"Yeah, I feel bad that I waited so long to tell her I wasn't coming home, but she had to know that it probably wasn't going to happen anyway," I say as I toss the last of my things in my bag and zip it shut. Mark grabs it off of the bed and takes it into the living room while I finish shutting everything off before we leave.

"What did she say?"

"Not much. She's upset, but she's always upset. A part of me feels guilty that they will be alone for the first time this year, but if I went home, it would just be a disaster."

Turning off the lights, Mark steps in front of me and says, "I'm sorry," as he wraps his arms around my waist.

"Don't be. Honestly, I don't see them moving past this, and I just have nothing left to say."

I cup his jaw in my hands when he kisses me. This fracture in my family would hurt a lot worse than it does if it weren't for the solidity Mark gives me. Somehow, it makes up for all the other crap going on.

"You ready?" he asks when he pulls away.

"Yeah."

Grabbing my things, I lock up and we head down to Mark's car. I'm nervous, and this drive to the airport is becoming unsettling. A thousand different scenarios are running through my head, and none of them are good. As he reaches over to hold my hand, I continue to stare out the side window.

When Mark turns into the parking garage and parks, I turn to look at him as he shuts off the car. He's staring at me, still holding my hand.

"Tell me what you're so scared of," he demands softly.

"What do you mean?"

Shaking his head, he sounds irritated when he says, "You don't think I know you well enough by now to read you? Just be honest. What are you scared of?"

I lean my head back on the seat and exhale before admitting, "Everything. Everything but you."

"Then trust me enough to know that I would never put you in a situation with my family if it weren't anything but safe. So whatever has been consuming you since you got into this car, let it go."

Eight and a half hours later, we land in Cleveland, Ohio. I know that Mark's mom will be the only one meeting us here at the airport. He called her to tell her a bit about my family, and that it would be best if everyone wasn't here to meet us.

We make our way down to baggage claim, and my heart is racing with nerves. I don't know what to expect, and I shove my hands in my pockets to keep myself from fidgeting too much. When a woman with shoulder-length, dark brown hair walks towards us, he quickly pulls her into his arms.

"Hey, Mom."

"I'm so glad you're here," she says as they hug. "I've missed you so much, sweetheart."

"I've missed you too," he says as he steps back to introduce us. "Mom, this is Jase."

"Please, call me Andrea." She walks straight to me and gives me big hug.

I laugh lightly at her affectionate demeanor when I say, "It's great to meet you."

Loosening her grip, she looks at me with a big smile. "Well, I am so glad that you came. Mark has told me a lot about you. How was the flight?"

"Long," I say as she hooks her arm through mine, and we head to the carousel to get our bags. I instantly feel my nerves calm with Andrea's relaxed nature. Mark walks ahead of us, as she continues, "Have you ever been to Ohio before?"

"No, I've always stuck to the west coast. I grew up in California," I tell her.

"Are you boys hungry? We had lasagna for dinner, and there are plenty of leftovers. Or we can stop and pick something up."

Mark grabs the last piece of luggage off of the tether and says to his mom, "We can eat leftovers."

I take my bag from him as we walk out into the dark, snowy night. The chill hits me hard, and Mark turns and laughs at me.

"It's freakin' cold," I chatter out.

Andrea shoots me a smile, and we load our things into her SUV. Mark hops in the back, and I sit up front with his mom. I look at her in surprise when she turns the car on and 'Neon Lights' by Demi Lovato blasts through the speakers.

"Good Lord, Mom!" Mark shouts over the music from the back seat.

She quickly turns it down, and I start laughing as she claims, "Your sisters were using the car earlier."

Calling her out, Mark says, "That explains earlier, but *you* drove here—alone."

"So what?" she teases and turns it back up, but not nearly as loud as what it was. "Jase, Mark tells me you like to cook."

"Yeah, I've tried teaching him a couple times, but all he seems to be good at is setting off my smoke detector."

"All my kids are worthless in the kitchen, so I hope you don't mind, but you are stuck with me cooking on Thursday."

"Not at all," I say with a smile. I only hope that the rest of his family is as laidback as she is.

It's a little before eleven o'clock when we pull into the driveway of a large two-story home. Everything is covered in snow, but you can see the lights are on through the big windows. Suddenly those nerves that Andrea had so easily erased are back.

Walking in, the house is quiet. I follow Mark as he leaves his bag at the foot of the stairs, and I toss mine next to his. Rounding the corner, his father walks up. My chest tightens but only for a second before he says, "Son, come here," and gives Mark a quick hug.

"It's good to see you, Dad."

"Same here. Your mother and I have missed you," he says, and then turns to me. "And you must be Jase?" He reaches out and shakes my hand, "I'm Ben. Glad to have you."

He catches me off guard. My father is a stern, quiet man, so to see Mark's dad come across so opposite, takes me a second before saying, "It's good to meet you, Ben."

"I'm going to go heat you boys up some dinner," Andrea tells us as she walks down the hall.

"Well, come in. You want anything to drink?" Ben asks as we follow him and Andrea back to the kitchen.

"Just some water," I reply.

Closing the fridge, Mark's mother says, "The cups are in that cabinet over there," as she nods her head towards the sink.

Mark takes a seat at the table as I get my drink. I like that his mom didn't get it for me, that she would treat me as if I've been in this house a hundred times before. She turns and smiles at me as I walk over to the table and sit with Mark and his father.

"The weather is supposed to turn bad this weekend, so your mom is insisting that the Christmas lights go up tomorrow."

"Great, I'm back for all of five minutes, and you're telling me I have to freeze my ass off all day tomorrow?" Mark says as he laughs.

"Blame that woman over there," he says as he points to his wife, who is taking a plate of food out of the microwave. "I have to freeze my ass off too."

"Oh, please. You men are pathetic." She sets down a plate of lasagna and salad in front of me as she adds, "There are three of you; there is no way it will take you all day."

She hands me a fork, and I thank her when Mark looks at her and says, "Then I demand steaks for dinner."

I laugh and shake my head when Ben slaps his shoulder in approval, and clarifies, "Ribeyes."

"Fine. No more complaining," she tells the two of them and hands Mark his plate.

The both of us eat as Ben starts talking and asking Mark and I about school. My father and I haven't spoken since I told him I was gay, and I can only imagine how skittish he would be around me, now that he knows. Although I'm feeling comfortable hanging out here with Mark and his parents, the idea of Mark touching me in front of them makes me anxious. It's almost like I'm a college buddy of his spending the holiday with his family, not his boyfriend. I guess I'm waiting for the *look*. The freak-out. The 'oh my God, he's gay' reaction.

We finish eating and clean up our mess before saying good night to Mark's parents. Grabbing our bags, we head upstairs to Mark's room.

"Come on," he says. "I'll introduce you to my sisters. Fair warning, they have no filter."

We walk down the hall, and when Mark opens the door, the first thing I hear is a high-pitched, "God, Mark! Knock much?"

I can't help the burst of laughter that comes out of me as I step into the room. The two girls are lying on the bed, huddled over a laptop, looking at us.

"Whatever. Jase, this is Emily and Erin."

I knew that Mark's sisters were twins, but they seriously look just alike. Both with long, straight brown hair and the same bright, green eyes that Mark has.

They clamber out of bed and not only give Mark hugs, but me as well. Mark has told me that he's really close with his sisters, but seeing them now, I can't help the twinge of jealousy that creeps in, only wishing it was my own sister I was hugging. He's lucky to have them.

"When did you get here?" he asks them.

"After finals last week. The dorms emptied out, so we went ahead and came home a couple days early."

"So . . . Jase . . ." Erin says as she shoots me a flirty wink.

When I cock my head at her, slightly amused, her eyes begin to pan down the length of me in a dramatic fashion. I laugh at her blatant nature as Mark says with annoyance to Erin, "You're seriously messed up."

"This is almost too much," I chuckle out when Emily breaks out into a fit of laughter as well.

"Yeah, I agree. We'll see you two in the morning," Mark tells them, and when we walk out, the two of them burst out laughing. I can't help but do the same as Mark looks at me with an apologetic look on his face.

We head back to his room, unpack, and get ready for bed. It's a bit odd to be sleeping in the same room as him in his parents' home, but I try to shake off my insecure feelings for the sake of Mark. Sliding into bed, it feels so good to finally be lying down. It's been a long day, and I huddle down under the blankets, wrapping myself around Mark.

I close my eyes, and I'm about to fall asleep when we hear squealing from the next room where his sisters are. Mark sits up and looks down at me for a second before shifting to his knees and placing his ear on the wall.

"What the hell are you doing?" I ask.

"Shhh." He stays there, eavesdropping for a moment, when he whispers, "I can't make out what they're saying."

"Oh my God, you are just as crazy as they are."

We hear another squeal, and Mark jumps out of bed.

"What are you doing?"

As he slips on a pair of pajama pants, he says, "I'm gonna see what they're up to."

As tired as I am, I am getting a major kick out of seeing this new side of Mark. He quietly walks across the room and slowly opens the door, trying hard to not make any noise. He looks back at me, and nods his head for me to follow. Sighing, I get out of bed and follow him to his sisters' door. With his hand on the handle, he quickly opens the door, barging in. One of the girls is sitting at the desk, on the computer and the other one is standing on top of the bed.

"What's going on in here?" Mark asks, and Erin jumps off the bed, runs over to us, and drags us in, shutting the door quietly behind us.

"Jesus, you're loud. You're gonna wake up Mom and Dad," she snaps at him before glancing at me, or rather, my bare chest. "God, you're hot."

"What?" I say at the same time Marks asks, "What the hell's the matter with you?"

"Geez, nothing!"

"Em, dish it. What has the two of you acting so secretive?" Mark asks as I walk over and sit on the edge of the bed.

"You have to promise to not say anything to Mom and Dad."

"Yeah, sure."

"Okay, so there's this guy, Travis, that is totally hot and all. I mean, seriously. This guy is like—"

"Get to the point," Mark interrupts.

"Anyway. Erin is like madly in love with this guy—"

"No, I'm not!"

"Okay, I'm out," Mark tells them as he starts heading for the door.

"Fine. Jase will help us," Emily says.

"I don't even know what's going on here," I say in complete confusion.

When Erin finally stops molesting my chest with her eyes, she looks up at me and pleads, "You have to take us to this party tomorrow night."

"What?" Mark asks.

"Umm, excuse me. I'm talking to Jase."

"Why do you need us to take you to a party? Just go," he tells her.

Getting up from the computer, Emily walks over and sits down on the bed with Erin and me. "Because, there is no way that Mom will let us go to a party the night before Thanksgiving. But if we say that the four of us are going out together, you know, like a brother-sister type thing, then I know they won't question it."

Laughing at their scheming, I say, "I'm in."

Erin wraps her arms around me when Mark glares at me with a look of complete betrayal, and I laugh at him. "It sounds completely harmless," I tell him.

"I already love you," Emily tells me as I hear Mark let out a deep breath. "Oh, come on, Mark. Even Jase is cool with it."

"How old is this guy?" he asks.

"I don't know. He's in his third year," Erin says when she finally lets go of me. "What does it matter?"

"Because you're nineteen and my sister. It matters."

Suddenly thinking about Candace, I stand up, taking Mark's side, and tell them, "We'll go, but we're staying with you."

"Yeah, I agree," Mark says, probably understanding my change of tone.

"Are you serious?" Emily questions, clearly not liking that her older brother is, in a sense, chaperoning them.

"Em, who cares?" Erin says. "Maybe Travis will get jealous when he sees me with Jase."

Tilting my head at her in disbelief, she defends, "What? I get that you're gay and all, but who knew my brother would snag a hottie? So yeah, I plan on using you."

With mild laughter, I say, "This is slightly uncomfortable."

"No shit," Mark says as he turns to walk out, and I follow.

When we get back into bed, I replay the last ten minutes and begin to laugh.

"What's so funny?" Mark asks.

"You weren't kidding around about them."

"No, man. They're crazy as hell. All the women in this family are."

I'm glad that they are because it takes my mind off of the nerves of being here. I like Mark's family, and his sisters make it all that much better, because even though they are completely different than Jace, they kinda remind me of her.

Mark runs his hand behind my neck and asks, "What are you thinking about?"

I tug him close to me, when I say, "I'm glad I came."

"Me too."

We lay there for a moment, silent, before I say, "Your dad seems really great." I just wish my own could be as understanding as his.

"It's not easy on him, you know?"

"What do you mean?"

He shifts slightly before continuing. "He had a really difficult time with it at first. It's just been hard on him. He's a work in progress."

I nod my head, not really knowing how to respond. I'd like to think maybe my father could come around as well, but I think that's a far cry from my reality.

Interrupting my thoughts, he adds, "I don't want you to think my family's perfect. Things weren't always like they are now, but they've known for a few years. It wasn't just me coming to terms with it; they had to as well."

"I don't see that happening for me, for my parents, I mean," I tell him. I can hope, but what's hope? My hopes are rarely ever fulfilled.

Mark pulls me in closer, his body warm against mine. "Maybe it's just another piece I can fill for you."

I smile and remember our conversation from the other week. Not wanting to deny his words, I simply whisper in response, "Yeah, maybe," before I cover his lips with mine.

Although the both of us are exhausted from the day of traveling, we spend a good amount of time quietly kissing before falling asleep.

chapter twenty-three

THERE'S A KNOCK on the door as I'm slipping on one of my old UW hooded sweatshirts. I open the door to Erin standing there, still in her pajamas. Walking into the room, she jumps onto the bed and asks, "Where's Mark?"

"Taking a shower."

"Is he gonna talk to Mom about tonight?"

"He didn't say," I answer as I sit next to her.

"Say what?" I turn to see Mark as he's walking out of the bathroom.

"Are you going to talk to Mom about tonight?"

"Yeah, I'll talk to her," he says as he grabs his clothes and heads back into the bathroom.

I turn to look at Erin, and she has a huge smile on her face.

"Who's going to this party anyway?" I ask.

"People from Kent State that live around here."

"That's where you go?"

"Yeah. Em and I are freshmen," she tells me. "So, you're an Architect major with Mark?"

"Yeah."

"You've known him this whole time?" she asks as she leans against the headboard, getting comfortable.

"Sort of. We never really spoke until this summer."

"Well, for what it's worth, he seems really happy," she says with a grin right before Mark comes back out. "Why are you guys dressed so early?" she asks as she looks between the two of us.

"It's not *that* early, but Mom wants the lights up today, so we're gonna be stuck on the roof for the next several hours."

Hopping off the bed, she prances out of the room, calling, "Have fun with that!"

Mark closes the door and locks it before walking toward me and hovering his body over mine, pushing me back onto the bed.

"What are you doing?" I barely get out when Mark starts kissing me. Mumbling over the skin on my neck as he moves his lips down, he says, "Not being able to touch you is going to drive me crazy today."

His words unintentionally make me feel guilty. He knows I'm not comfortable with anything physical in front of his family, and I hate that I'm still holding back with him. I don't want to. I don't want to pretend to be something we're not. And we are *not* distant.

When he drags his lips back to mine, he pushes back off of me and smiles. "I need coffee."

Sitting up, I hold his face and pull him down to me once more, kissing him slowly, allowing myself to taste him. He moans as I lean back and stare up at him.

"I love you," I say with all seriousness.

Running his fingers through my hair, he confirms, "Not even close to how much I do."

And I don't need to hear anymore as I smile up at him.

I follow as he walks to the door and unlocks it. Heading down the stairs, I take his hand, and when he looks at me, surprised, I just give him a slight grin. No more pretending. No more wavering.

We walk into the kitchen where his mom and dad are sitting at the table and drinking coffee. They look up at us, and for a moment my stomach knots when his mother looks down at our hands. She stands and walks over to us, smiling, and says, "Good morning. You boys want anything to eat?"

Returning the smile, knots vanishing, I say, "Just coffee."

Mark and I fix our coffee and join his parents at the table.

"Mom, would it be a problem if we went out with Em and Erin tonight for a bit?" Mark asks.

"What are you guys gonna do?"

"Not sure, but we thought it would be fun for the four of us to hang out."

"Yeah, sure. Just try to not be out too late," she tells him as she picks up her coffee to take a sip.

Mark looks over at me and shakes his head, not excited about having to follow his sisters around tonight.

"You boys ready to get out there and get this over with?" his dad says.

We take a few minutes and drink our coffee before heading out into the snow.

Several hours later, Mark has gone to the store to pick up some things for dinner tonight, and Ben and I are sitting on the roof, drinking a couple of beers Andrea tossed up to us. The snow keeps falling, but after three hours, I'm completely numb.

"So, Jase, Mark tells me that the two of you have some classes together."

"Yeah. We share the same studio this year and one of our lectures."

He takes a swig of his beer and then asks, "How has this year been treating you?"

"It's been a little challenging," I say quietly, knowing it's been probably one of the most difficult years of my life.

"Why's that?" he asks as he looks over at me, curious to know.

Talking to Mark's father like this is far from what I'm used to with my own father. He's a quiet guy and was never too involved in my life. With Ben, however, it doesn't feel forced.

"There's just been a lot going on, and I fell behind in some of my classes," I tell him and then take another sip of my beer.

"You able to catch up?"

"Yeah. Luckily, Mark worked ahead and was able to help me with a few things. I just had to refocus for a moment."

Staring straight ahead, looking out over the street, he says, "Mark seems really happy."

I look at him when he says this, and he turns to me. Feeling a little nervous about where this could go, I don't respond.

"He said you don't really talk to your parents."

"No," I breathe out, disappointed that it even has to be this way with them.

"That's too bad," he says as he grips my shoulder. "You seem like a stand-up guy."

I shift my attention down to see Mark pulling into the driveway, I respond to Ben's statement, as I watch Mark getting out of the car. "I really appreciate that."

When Mark walks into the house, Ben claps his hand on my shoulder, saying, "Let's finish this up, son. I'm starving and ready to get out of this snow."

He stands and tosses his bottle down onto the snow-covered front yard. Hearing him call me son was all I needed. Whether it's just a figure of speech he uses freely, or it was meant with more intent, it felt accepting. No shame. No embarrassment. No fear. No opposition. He gets it.

"You coming?" he says, and I nod before tossing my bottle down as well.

After watching a movie huddled under blankets with Mark and his sisters, I helped Andrea out in the kitchen, getting dinner together. I took care of the steaks and the scalloped potatoes while she made a salad and also worked on a couple of piecrusts for Thanksgiving. I feel as if I have been coming over to this house for years. Comfortable.

Finishing dinner, Mark and I decide to go lie down before we head out for the night. The quietness is short-lived when his sisters barge in and are ready to go.

As we walk through the living room, Andrea says, "Seriously, don't stay out all night," as the four of us leave.

"Trust me, we won't," Mark tells her. He and I are completely worn out from getting all the lights on the house earlier today.

Sliding into the front seat with Mark, his sisters pile into the back, both buried in their cell phones.

"How long are you guys wanting to stay?" Mark asks as he drives down the slick road.

"Long enough for Erin to suck on Travis' face," Emily laughs out.

"I don't need to hear that crap," Mark says in clear disgust.

"Oh, whatever," Erin says.

The three of them continue to bicker until we finally pull up to the large, two-story house with a wrap-around drive. Cars flood the street, and when Mark parks, he turns around and says, "Two hours."

Rolling their eyes at him, Emily tells him, "You're such a pussy," as both girls laugh.

When they get out of the car, he looks at me while I try not to laugh. "I'm not a pussy," he tells me as if he needs to convince me of this fact.

Now I'm laughing at him when I hear my phone chime. I pull it out of my pocket and tell Mark, "It's Candace."

How's your trip so far?

"What's it say?" Mark asks, and I read it to him before typing out my response.

Good. Mark's family is oddly great.

LOL! What's that like? :)

Take it you're not having a good time.

It actually hasn't been too bad. Went shopping with mom, all the while bragging about how great her friend's children are doing. As if I'm slumming it at UW.

"Is everything going okay?" Mark asks.

"I think so," I mumble as I continue to text her.

Sorry. Just a couple more days.

I really miss you. I'm so happy for you though!

Thanks. I miss you too. Text if you need me.

I will. Love you!

Love you too.

"I think she's just lonely," I tell him as I shove my phone back into my pocket.

Smiling at me, he gives me a quick kiss before opening his door.

We walk into the crowded house and immediately spot his sisters, already drinking from their red plastic cups.

"They don't waste any time," I joke, and when I look over at Mark, he's staring at me in disbelief.

"Dude, they're only nineteen," he says.

"Right. So you mean to tell me that you never had a drink your freshman year or sooner?"

"I just don't want anything to happen," he tells me.

It's evident that he's a bit protective over them. "Nothing's gonna happen," I assure him.

"Come on. If I'm stuck here with your broody ass, I'm drinking too."

Walking back to the kitchen, I fill a couple of cups from the keg. I hand one over to Mark, and we walk back into the main room to keep an eye on the girls. Finding space on one of the couches, we take a seat and watch his sisters being loud and obnoxious, but clearly they're the most entertaining thing at this party.

The music is loud and everyone screaming over it to hear each other speak is even louder.

Leaning back, I notice a guy across the room eying Mark. I don't say anything when Mark leans over and asks, "So how are you feeling about everything now?"

I take a sip of the cheap beer and tell him, "You were right. I shouldn't have been so worried." He smiles at me, and I continue, "I'm just not used to this, that's all."

"Even before they knew?"

"Ever since Jace died, really. My family is just very different, but your parents are cool as hell. Your father surprised me."

"How's that?" he asks and then takes a drink from his cup.

"Just didn't expect him to be so easy to talk to."

He grins and slips his hand into mine, and I don't even give a second thought to what anyone else in the room might think if they saw. I grip his hand tightly as I smile back at him. We make ourselves content, sitting there, watching his sisters every now and then.

I let my beer grow warm; I'm tired and not in the mood to drink. Scanning the room, I notice that same guy from earlier looking over at Mark and me.

Leaning in, I ask him, "Do you know that guy standing by the stairs?

He keeps looking at you."

"Shit," he says under his breath when he spots the guy I'm talking about.

"What?"

Mark looks away from him and leans his head down, seeming annoyed. "I knew him back in high school."

"And?" I prompt, wondering why he's having a strong reaction to seeing him.

"I'll tell you later, okay? Just not here," he says, almost pleading in a way, which only sparks my curiosity. "I'm gonna go get another beer. You want one?"

"No, I'm good."

Mark stands to head back into the kitchen, and I follow, needing to move around since I'm starting to get tired. He fills up his cup and when we turn to walk back out, we run into that same guy.

"Mark, hey," he says hesitantly.

"What's up, Carter?" Mark's voice is drenched with irritation.

"Not much. Just home visiting my parents."

Mark takes a sip of his beer and doesn't respond. When a cute blonde hooks her arm through Carter's, he looks down at her before looking back at Mark. "Oh, um, this is Valerie."

"Val," she clarifies as she reaches out to shake Mark's hand.

When he doesn't take it, I reach out my hand and say, "I'm Jase."

Shifting her eyes to me, she says, "Oh, nice to meet you," with a soft smile, probably sensing the same tension that I do.

I nod my head and notice Mark walking out of the room. "You too," I tell her as I turn around to follow him. "What was that all about?" I ask, and when he turns to me he quietly says, "Don't ask."

I don't. Whatever it is, it's really bothering him, so I leave it alone.

"You're fuckin' kidding me," he sighs out, and when I spot Erin dancing on top of a chair with a beer funnel in hand, I know it's time to leave.

"I'll go grab her, and you look for Emily," I tell him.

Walking over to Erin, I stand next to the chair she's on top of and when she looks down at me, she clutches my hands and squeals, "Jase!"

"Come on. It's time to go."

"What? Hell no!"

"It's late, and you're wasted. Come on. Your brother is already flipping from seeing you over here. Be lucky it's me dragging you out and not him."

Without any warning, she jumps onto me, wrapping her legs around my waist, almost knocking me over.

"Shit." I peel her off of me, and she stumbles over onto the floor. "How much did you drink?" I ask as I pick her up.

"I dunno."

"Come on." I hold her up and lead her to the front door. I turn to scan the room to see where Mark is, and I spot him holding Emily, who seems to be in the same drunken condition as Erin.

Walking up to me, he shakes his head, and tosses me the keys. "You're driving," he demands, and when the two girls see each other, they practically leap into each other's arms, giggling uncontrollably. "This shit's obnoxious."

We practically have to carry them out to the car. Crawling on their knees, they both pile carelessly into the back seat. I hop into the front, and when Mark gets in, I hear a loud thud followed by laughing. Looking back behind my seat, Erin has fallen onto the floorboard.

"You're a sexy bitch," Emily slurs as Erin climbs back onto the seat.

"Mark, you need to get their seatbelts on."

He sighs at me when he gets back out of the car to open the back door and helps them out. Their laughing is so distracting, and it takes all the concentration I have to drive on these slick roads and get us home without wrecking.

Pulling into the driveway, the girls are still loud as hell.

"How are we going to get them inside without waking up your parents?" I ask Mark as he looks at me and then back at the circus in the back seat.

"You guys have to shut up if you don't want to get busted by Mom and Dad," he tells them, and they burst out into an even louder fit of laughter.

Turning around, I say, "Seriously. You two have to calm down so we can get you upstairs."

"You're so serious," Emily says in mock sternness, and I shake my head as I open the door to get out.

We help the girls out of the car, and Erin clings herself to me. Walking up the driveway, we hit a patch of ice and Erin goes down, taking me with her as we hit the pavement hard. On my back, I look up to see Mark joining in with his sisters as they all laugh. Picking myself up, and grabbing Erin, we manage to make it inside and up the stairs with minimal noise. Mark finds a bottle of aspirin and says, "I'll be right back," as he walks out of the room and down the hall.

I take a quick shower, more for the warmth than anything, and when I walk out of the bathroom, Mark is already in bed. I slip under the covers next to him and he pulls me in close, facing him. "I'm beat," he breathes out, and I nod my head. "Sorry about being in such a crap mood tonight."

I wrap my legs around his and ask, "You wanna talk about it?"

He takes his time and then says, "That guy is the reason I moved to Seattle."

"What happened?"

"We used to see each other during our senior year in high school. I wasn't out yet, and by the looks of him tonight with that chick, he still isn't." He shifts his eyes down when he continues. "He was the first guy I ever got involved with, and at the time, I thought I was in love. But his older brother walked in on us and caught us kissing. That was it. He totally flipped, calling me a faggot and threatening to tell everyone that I was gay if I even looked at him the wrong way."

"God," I sigh, wanting to kick the crap out of that guy, but in a way, I also understand him.

"I backed off, but he wound up telling some guys at school right before graduation. They made my life hell, taunting me and shit. Word started spreading, and I knew my sisters would hear about it soon. I was scared my parents would hear it too. It was a really fucked up time, and that's when I started having trouble sleeping and having nightmares. I was forced into telling them. I was so worried that my secret would ruin the relationship with my family."

"Why? I mean, they seem so down to earth," I say.

"Yeah, but I had no idea how they would react to having a gay son. My sisters were mad at me for a while. After that summer, everyone knew. I was already gone to Seattle, but my sisters were here, dealing with everything I had escaped from. When school started back up, they were just known as the sisters of the gay guy that just graduated. They didn't talk to me for months. It killed me 'cause I love them so much, and I felt like their being bullied was all my fault, and I just left—I ran away."

"That's so messed up."

"It was a rough time all around," he says. "But it worked out for me, for all of us. Before I told them though, I honestly thought that they wouldn't take it well. That it would be done; I'd be out."

He looks up at me when I infer, "Like me?"

Nodding his head, he admits, "It kills me to know that my fear is your reality." He rests his forehead against mine and says, "That's why I wanted you to come here with me. I felt like I needed to give you this."

Keeping my eyes closed, I ask, "But why me? After what I did with Kyle . . . well, it just doesn't seem too far off from Carter."

He doesn't respond for a while, so when I open my eyes and look into his, he finally tells me, "Because when I ran into you that night at Remedy and you were so honest, the guilt was written all over you, I just knew that I would wind up falling in love with you."

"I don't want to imagine not being with you," I whisper as I lean in and seal my lips with his.

I hold him close, and don't even question the love I feel for him. I can't. It's heavy and palpable. It's everything I have been missing and makes up for all the time I had been avoiding what was in me. What I was. What I am.

chapter twenty-four

EVERYONE IS IN the living room while Andrea and I have spent the majority of the morning in the kitchen. We just cracked a bottle of wine and are making a few things for the family to snack on while we finish up everything for Thanksgiving dinner.

Taking the wrapped Brie out of the oven, I set it on the platter that Andrea has already set out and layered crackers on.

She takes the platter and says, "I'll be right back," as she heads to the other room.

I've missed having this. I used to have this with my own family, but that feels like forever ago. When she returns, she asks, "Could you get the bag of potatoes out of the fridge for me?"

"Yeah."

"So who taught you how to cook?" she asks as I hand her the bag, and she dumps them into the sink to wash them.

"My mom. It was something we always did together since I was little." I step next to her and start chopping the potatoes after she scrubs them.

"Well, I'm impressed," she says as she hands me another potato. "I hope I'm not intruding, but Mark told me that you haven't been talking to them much lately." Looking over at her, she turns to face me. "I'm sorry, I—"

"Don't be," I assure her. "Honestly, we haven't spoken much since my sister died."

"Oh, God. I'm sorry. I didn't know," she gasps with concern flushed across her face.

"It's okay. It was a while ago. We were both in high school."

She turns, leans her hip against the sink, and says, "Can I ask what happened?"

I set the knife down, and turn to face her as well. I've never spoken about this to anyone besides Candace. I just briefly told Mark, but I want his mother to know me, to know where I'm coming from, because I love her son, and I want this family to accept me. All of me.

"She was in a car crash with her boyfriend. She was about to graduate.

My parents fell apart, and in a way, disappeared. They pretty much stopped talking, and it's been that way ever since."

"That's awful," she mumbles as she looks down. When her eyes meet mine, she asks, "Have you called them today?"

I shake my head.

"Do you want to?"

I look away because looking into her eyes makes me miss what I used to have with my mom. "I don't know. Things have gotten worse since . . ." Shifting my eyes back to her, I continue honestly, " . . . since I told them I was gay."

She rests her hand on top of mine that's gripping the edge of the sink, and when she does, I tell her, "They threw me out."

Not saying a word, she wraps her arms around me, and for a moment, I pretend they're my mother's. I wonder if she'll ever hold me like this again, like she used to so many times in my life. My mind creeps back to reality, and I wonder, through all the hurt I've caused people, what I ever did that was so right to deserve this. This right here.

I have to swallow hard against my tightened throat as I try to control the mixture of pain and happiness that wells up inside of my chest. When Andrea pulls back, her eyes are rimmed with tears, and a part of me is comforted by the fact that she cares enough to feel this way.

"You're amazingly strong," she says softly, and when I shake my head, she affirms, "You are. I see why my son loves you the way that he does."

"I don't deserve him," I admit.

"It isn't about deserving; it's about accepting. None of us deserve anything. Everything we have is a gift, and you have to learn to simply accept what God gives you."

"Is that what you believe?" I ask her. Her words are such a contrast to everything I've ever been told.

She nods her head, and says, "I do."

And I do too.

"You guys look serious," Mark says as he walks into the kitchen.

He grabs a beer out of the fridge and his mother says, "Come here."

He eyes me as he walks towards her, and she gives him a tight hug. Keeping his eyes on me, he chuckles out, "She's not getting all sappy on you, is she?"

I laugh at him, lightening the mood, and shake my head. When he steps back from her, he looks between the both of us, and I don't hold back in front of his mom when I tell him, "I love you."

His smile is big, and he doesn't skip a beat when he cups his hands along my jaw and kisses me. I take it. I don't even try to shy away from it. This is what I've been needing; what I've been missing. Acceptance. And coming from these people, in this house, I know I'm exactly who I'm meant to be. I just needed Mark to show me.

Spending this time with Mark and his family has been great. The past few days have gone by fast, and I finish packing up my bag while Mark gets his things together as well. Everything I worried about before getting on that plane with Mark was immediately negated when I met his family.

Mark smiles at me when he grabs his bag, and I zip up mine. We head downstairs to say goodbye before Mark's dad drives us to the airport. It feels good knowing it won't be long until I get to see everyone again. Andrea insisted that I come back for Christmas. She even booked my ticket last night after I had a long talk with her and Mark about my parents. She told me to not give up on them, so I gave them a call when Mark and I went to bed. We didn't talk long, but it was still nice to hear my mother's voice. I'm not sure how often we will talk, but I'll never stop loving them, and I never want to turn away from them no matter how they feel about me.

Loading everything into the car, Ben starts driving toward the airport. When he pulls up to departures, we all hop out and get our things. After Mark says his goodbye, he takes my bag and heads inside to check them while he leaves me with his father.

"I don't know everything that's going on with your parents, but I just wanted to let you know that we're here if you need us."

Reaching out to shake his hand, I say, "Thanks," when he gives my hand a tug and brings me in for a hug.

When I take a step back, he smiles and nods before saying, "Give us a call when you guys land, okay?"

"Will do," I tell him as he gets into the car and drives away.

I make my way inside to find Mark and we get everything checked in and head to our gate. About an hour later, we are in the air, flying back to Seattle. It's crazy to think about how my whole frame of mind has taken a shift from when I flew out here just a few days ago.

I never should have doubted coming out here to meet Mark's family. I should have trusted him enough to know that he would have never asked me to come with him if he wasn't certain that it would be a safe thing for me to do. But he's always been ahead of me. Confident. He accepted being gay years ago. I've been struggling to figure it out for a while when Mark has already known for himself, before ever getting involved with me. He was already there. He's just been waiting for me to get there as well—and I think I am. I know I am.

I look over at him and take his hand, holding it, lacing my fingers with his. He's beautiful and perfect and all I'll ever want. He has no idea what he's given me. He'll never understand no matter how much I tell him. Everything I've been searching for from the time I realized I was gay, he's given me: my realization, my understanding, my accepting. He makes it okay for me to be who I was always meant to be.

Before him, I was afraid. Always in denial. I thought that finally coming out to my parents would free me. But it didn't. It was Mark. It was him that opened me up, that freed me of everything I was so scared of. He will always have everything that's inside of me that I have to give.

For years I've been trying to free myself of these fears, free myself from my tormenting thoughts, free myself from the walls that have kept me trapped in a hole of self-loathing. Since I met Mark, I've been fighting. Fighting to be free. But now I realize, it isn't about fighting. It's letting go of the fight to see that what I've been searching for is within him. Mark is my freeing.

epilogue

Six Months Later . . .

"DID YOU GET your cap and gown today?"

"Yeah. I went with Candace earlier," I respond as I kick my feet up on the coffee table and lean back into the couch.

Sitting next to me, he asks, "How's she doing?"

"She seems to be doing a little better. I think her finally seeing a therapist is helping the most."

Nodding his head, he says, "You're probably right." He wraps his arms around me, and I rest my head on his shoulder. "So I wanted to talk to you about something."

"What's up?"

"My roommate is moving out after graduation, and I was thinking . . . maybe you would want to make it our place."

Turning to look at him straight on, I clarify, "You mean move in?"

He nods and says, "Yeah."

"Are you sure?" Mark and I spend most nights together anyway, but it's the knowing. Knowing that he's serious and in this as much as I am to want to live with me.

"You're it for me, Jase. I want to be with you. Only you. And I want to make my home with you."

I smile big. This past year with Mark has been nothing short of perfect. Even with the downs, they have been what has bonded us so tightly together. I've never been so connected with another person.

I lean over and kiss him, grazing my teeth along his lower lip and sliding my tongue along his as he fists the hair on the back of my head. I climb over him, lowering him on his back as we continue to kiss.

Everything is changing, but having this makes it more bearable. When Candace told me she accepted a job dancing in New York City, I couldn't have been more happy for her, but inside, my stomach was in knots. It had been a long time since I cried, but when I went to Mark's place to tell him, I lost it. I hate the thought of not having her with me. She's been my heart for so many years. She still is, but now she shares it with Mark, and having him to lean on when I'm losing a big part of me, makes the change seem okay.

Dragging his lips off of mine, he insists, "Be with me. Tell me you're mine and that this is it for you."

Looking down at him, into those green eyes I have fallen so in love with, I give him my affirmation. "I've only ever been yours." When he runs his hand around the back of my neck, I vow, "You're it for me," before lowering myself, pressing my lips softly against his, and I'm here—I'm home.

Struggling with your sexual identity? There is support out there. The GLBT National Help Center provides several support programs along with two national hotlines.
http://www.glbtnationalhelpcenter.org

GLBT National Hotline supports callers of all ages with concerns/questions about coming-out issues, relationship concerns, HIV/AIDS, anxiety, safer-sex information, and lots more.
Toll-free 1–888–THE-GLNH (1–888–843–4564)

GLBY National Youth Hotline is comprised of volunteers that are in their teens and early twenties and speak with teens and young adults up to age 25 about coming-out issues, relationship concerns, parent issues, school problems, HIV/AIDS, anxiety, safer-sex information, and lots more.
Toll-free 1–800–246–PRIDE (1–800–246–7743)
Hotline Hours: Monday thru Friday from 1pm to 9pm, pacific time; Saturday from 9am to 2pm, pacific time

BONUS MATERIAL

HOPING

a short story

(Erin, Mark's sister)

I WATCH MY big brother as he plops his duffle bag down on the floor. He's wearing the vintage Mudhoney shirt I got him for his birthday a couple years ago. I love that he still wears it, but it's grown smaller on him since he's been hitting the gym more often.

"I'm gonna miss you."

He looks over and starts walking toward me. "I'll be back in a few months for Thanksgiving break."

I love my brother. We're close; we've always been that way, but this summer we really grew tight. I was worried about him right around his high school graduation a couple months ago. He became distant from my twin sister, Emily and me. He isolated himself from everyone, and it wasn't long after when I overheard him telling our parents that he was gay.

Sitting at the top of the stairs, I listened to him cry while he told them. I was shocked, but more than anything, I was sad. He's always been my strong, big brother. The one I go to with all my problems, knowing he will help me fix them. He's always been protective over me and my sister, so when I heard the pain coming out of him, it killed me. I could tell he was scared. I was too. Afraid my parents would reject him and make him feel worse. I was terrified I would lose him if they did. I wanted to run down there and give him a hug, give him what little strength I felt like I had in me.

He mentioned a few guys at school knew and had been tormenting him toward the end of the semester. I'm glad he graduated and no longer has to deal with their bullshit. But now he's leaving me to go across the country to The University of Washington. My heart feels like it's too big for my chest as the sadness swells in me. I'm losing a big part of myself, but he seems happy to be going, so I try and suck it up for his sake.

"Are you ready, sweetheart?" my mother asks as she walks into the living room where Mark and I stand.

"Yeah, I think so," he tells her before reaching down to hold my hand.

I can't even keep my sadness in. I try, but my quivering chin is my tell, and he sees it. He pulls me in, folding me up in his arms as I let the tears fall.

"Don't cry. I promise I'll call you as soon as my plane lands," he assures me, but it isn't enough to calm me.

"I want you to stay," I choke out around my tears.

He pulls away and looks down at me, pretending to be unaffected, and says, "I know, but I can't."

He's running. I can feel it. He would never admit to it, but I know he's scared to stay here. This summer was rough on him when nearly all his friends turned their backs on him. Word spread fast that he was gay. I try and remind myself that leaving is probably the best thing for him, even though it hurts me.

I nod my head and sling my arms back around him.

"Where's Emily?" my mom asks.

"She went over to a friend's house," Mark tells her. "We said our good-byes earlier."

"We should get going," she says, and Mark loosens his hold on me.

"It's gonna be weird not having you here," I murmur.

"Just don't take over my room with all of your crap. I'll be back in a few months, and I want it untouched," he jokes with me.

"Promise," I say before he kisses my forehead.

(3 weeks later)

Mark has been gone for almost a month now, but he calls and texts often. He's settled and started classes at U-Dub last week. He seems happy, so I'm trying to be as well.

"Em! Hurry up. We're gonna be late!"

"I'm coming!" she snaps. "And we're not gonna be late."

Emily is feisty as hell. We are alike in that respect, but I tend to wear my emotions on my sleeve where she has a toughness that I admire.

When Em comes down the stairs, I grab the car keys and head out. As she hops into the passenger seat, she starts, "I wonder if Gabe ever broke it off with that sophomore?"

"Why would he?" I question, and when I do, I see a huge grin spread across her face. "Oh, God. What did you do?"

"Nothing," she says in a singsong voice that tells me she's been up to no good.

"Spill it."

"You can't say a word. Promise."

Watching the road ahead, I respond, "Promise."

"So that party I went to Saturday night that you were too tired to go to . . . well, apparently his girlfriend was tired too and wasn't there."

"Cut to the point," I tell her, not needing all the chitchat.

"He kissed me."

"Em!"

"What?"

"He has a girlfriend!"

"Sooo?" she says as if she hasn't a clue to how inappropriate it is. "We're in high school," she defends. "It isn't like they're getting married or anything."

"You are unbelievable. Breaking up a relationship is not the way you want to start your junior year."

"Oh, God," she moans at me as I pull into the parking lot behind our high school.

Familiar faces are all around and everyone is happy, meeting up with their friends they haven't seen all summer. I find our assigned spot and park the car.

"Well, as fun as this car ride has been, I'm gonna go see if I can find Gabe before the first bell rings," she says before grabbing her backpack and hopping out of the car.

"Em."

"Yeah?"

"That girl is gonna be hurt when she finds out. Just . . . don't rub it in and make it worse on her," I tell her.

She releases a deep sigh and nods her head. "Fine," she reluctantly agrees and then walks away.

I reach in the back for my bag before heading in too. Walking through the busy halls, I find a few of my friends gathered around a locker.

"Hey guys," I announce when I walk up to them.

Turning to look at me, Jenn closes her locker and walks away after giving me a snide look. I wonder what the hell I could've possibly done to piss her off. We haven't spoke in about a month, but during the summer, that isn't too uncommon.

Adjusting my backpack higher on my shoulder, I make my way to my first class. Already wanting to ditch, I pull out my phone and text Mark.

First day sux.

Switching my cell to silent, I walk into my English Comp. class and find a desk to situate myself at. I sit here, feeling uncomfortable when I notice the whispering going on around me. I wish my phone would buzz with Mark's reply. Anything to distract me from my self-conscious thoughts.

I sit through class, anxious for it to end. Fifty minutes pass and I never feel my phone vibrate, but then the time difference dawns on me. It's not even 6am in Seattle.

When the bell rings, I shove my book into my bag and try finding Em in the hall while I make my way to second period. Instead, I see Jenn, and I call out to her. Her friends walk away when I approach.

"What's going on?" I ask.

She sighs, saying, "Come with me."

I follow her as she leads me into the girl's bathroom. She looks around to make sure we're the only ones in here before speaking. "Everyone is talking about you and your sister."

"What? Why?" I ask, completely confused.

"Erin . . . everyone knows about your brother. It's all over school that he's a fag."

Emotions flood. A whole multitude of them. Worried. Embarrassed. Defensive. Angry. Sad.

"Don't call him that," I tell her, hating that term.

"Well, he is, isn't he?" she whispers, like the words are infectious.

"No," I snap. "He's not a fag; he's gay."

"Don't get all bitchy with me," she snaps right back. "I just thought you should know what people are saying."

"So they're calling him a fag?"

She nods her head, adding, "They're calling you things too."

"Are you serious? Like what?" Oh my God. I can't believe this. Panic shoots through me and I wanna run, but I stay to hear what I'm almost afraid to hear.

"That you're a dyke."

"What?!" I nearly shriek in disbelief. "Why would they say that?"

"I don't know, but they are."

"You told them I'm not, right?"

When her eyes shift down, I see it. Shaking my head at her, I plead, "Please tell me you said something."

She doesn't look at me, and my face heats as the tears begin to stain them. Jenn and I have been friends since elementary school, but I suddenly feel like I don't even know her. How could she not defend me, but instead, betray me?

"Jenn?"

She meets my eyes when she looks up, and her words are drenched in annoyance when she defends, "Look, it's bad enough that they're saying that stuff about you, but I don't want them saying it about me too."

"So you'll let them make fun of me as long as your name isn't mentioned? I thought you were my friend."

"I am," she says softly. "But . . ."

"But what?"

She takes a moment before admitting, " I don't wanna be part of the gossip."

I hear it. I hear the beating around the bush. I'm not stupid. "No. You'd rather be spreading the gossip than *be* the gossip," I sneer before storming out the door, pissed that my friend would be so self-centered, worried about her own reputation than to stand up for me.

I rush through the halls, looking for Em, and when I spot her, she's yelling at Gabe.

"What the fuck is your problem? You think you're so goddamn perfect, huh?"

"Em!" I holler, trying to get her attention, but she keeps on, not even acknowledging me.

When I get close enough, I see Gabe laughing at her, and she loses it, fisting her hand and punching him right in the junk.

"Bitch!" he squeals out, clutching himself and falling to his knees.

"Em!" I shout, but before she can answer me, the principal is there.

"Office. Now."

"Please explain to me how you manage to get suspended on the first day of school!"

"Mom, don't yell at her," I say, trying to defend Emily.

"No, really. Ms. Childers said that you punched a boy in the crotch? I mean . . . what in God's name were you thinking?" she questions as I bust out laughing at the image of Emily socking that jerk in the nuts and his beet red face as he fell to the ground.

"This isn't funny," she scolds, and I immediately straighten up.

"Mom, everyone was calling Mark a faggot," Emily tells her, and my mom leans back into the chair. Sadness washes over her face.

Em and I sit together on the couch, watching her try to hold it together. It takes her a moment when she finally speaks.

"They're calling him that?" she questions in disbelief.

"Yeah, Mom," Emily says softly, as if her words were spoken too loudly, could hurt our mother.

"Jenn pulled me aside and told me that they're saying I like girls. That I'm a dyke," I add.

"Well, did you tell the principal that?"

"Yeah, but she didn't want to hear it. She was more concerned about the fight," I explain.

"I want you to go talk to her tomorrow and tell her what those kids are saying."

"I'm staying home." Emily was the one who got suspended, not me, but I'm not going there without her.

"You can't just stay home. You need to go and stand up for yourself. Don't let them make you feel like you can't go to school."

"Mom, it doesn't work that way. You don't understand," I tell her and then I feel my phone buzz from inside my pocket. I pull it out to see that Mark has finally responded to my text from earlier, but honestly, it's too late. I don't even read it when I shove it back into my pocket.

"I'll go up there with you."

"What? That's even worse. You can't come with me to school, Mom."

"Just let her stay home tomorrow," Emily chimes in.

Not wanting to argue, she surrenders, "Fine. One day. That's all you get," before standing up and walking out of the room.

I turn to look at Emily. "Thanks."

She gives me a faint smile and says, "Yeah, sure," in an almost defeated tone and then heads upstairs.

When I finally drag myself out of bed, it's almost noon. No one has bothered me all morning. No one bothered me last night either, not even my dad. I know he's been having a difficult time accepting that Mark is gay. He loves him, there's never been any doubt about that, but he hasn't been dealing with it well. I'm sure when Mom told him about what happened at school yesterday, he went into shutdown mode. He's good at that when something is bothering him.

I go downstairs to grab a soda, and when I return to my room, I see the screen on my phone is lit up. It's a missed text from Mark.

Never heard back from you yesterday. How did the rest of your day go?

Tossing the phone on the bed, I sit down and take a long drink. For the first time, I don't wanna talk to him. Honestly, I'm mad at him. Mad that he created this storm that's been slowly brewing. A storm that landed right on top of me. But he's the lucky one. He had the ability to run away, and the first chance he got, he did. Ran straight to Seattle, leaving Emily and me to deal with the backlash. He's a coward.

"Come in," I say when there's a knock on my bedroom door.

Emily opens it slowly, saying, "Hey," as she walks in. "Mark just texted. Said he hasn't heard from you in a couple days."

"Yeah, I know."

She cocks her head at me, asking, "What's going on?"

"Aren't you mad?"

"About yesterday?"

"About Mark. How he conveniently moved away and left us to deal with this crap," I say.

As she takes a seat on the bed next to me, she admits, "In a way . . . yeah. I feel bad for saying it though."

"It's not fair. He's off, having fun, while we're stuck here." I pause for a moment before adding, "Jenn didn't even defend me when she heard what people were saying about me."

"She's a twat," Emily says, and I burst out in laughter at her choice of words. And for a moment, as brief as it is, I feel the weight being lifted.

"Yeah, she is," I agree through my now light chuckles. "But still. How shallow can a person be?"

"She's pathetic and clearly not worth your time. Let her be a bitch to someone else."

"But she's being a bitch to *me*. She was actually pissed at me when I got upset when she told me she didn't stop them from saying those things," I say.

"People are stupid; you know that."

"Yeah."

"Call Mark so he doesn't worry, okay?" she tells me and I nod. "I'm gonna go fix some Ramen for lunch. Want any?"

"Gross. No."

"Oh, I'm so sorry," she teasingly mocks. "I forgot how refined your palette is."

"Well, it's better than having it tainted by Gabe's tongue like yours is," I shoot back at her.

"Ugh. Don't remind me," she says in disgust as she leaves my room.

Picking up my phone, I scroll through and bring up Mark's cell number. I really don't want to talk to him right now, but I suck it up and call him anyway.

"Hey," he says when he answers.

"Hey, what's up?"

"Just got out of class. About to head back to the dorms. What about you? You at school?"

"No. Home," I clip out, growing more irritated that he seems so happy.

"Why are you at home?"

"Em got suspended."

"Wait. What?"

"Em. Got. Suspended." I say this slow and condescendingly.

"Why?"

"Oh, I don't know, Mark. Could it be the fact that everyone knows you're gay and you couldn't stick around here long enough to take some of the heat that's now our burden to bear?"

Silence. He doesn't respond.

"Are you gonna say anything?" I push.

"I'm sorry."

"Sorry that you ran away?"

"Erin . . ."

"No one will even talk to me, Mark. They're calling me a dyke. Em wound up getting into a fight and now she's suspended for the rest of the week."

"Who's saying this?"

"The whole school!"

"Tell me what I can do 'cause I'll do anything," he says to me.

"Nothing. There's nothing you can do, so just have fun and enjoy your year so at least someone in this family is happy." I sling my words at him and then hang up.

My phone immediately starts ringing, and when I see it's Mark, I decline the call and switch my phone off. I'm so mad at him. I know what the kids at school are saying isn't his fault, but I need to blame someone and he's the obvious choice, so I unload my anger onto him.

"Erin!" I hear Em shout front downstairs.

Opening my door, I walk and lean over the banister. "What?"

"Jenn just posted some shit about you on Facebook."

I run back to my room and flip open my laptop. Once logged on, I type in Jenn's name and go straight to read her status update.

Jennifer Carmichael

Erin, that nasty lezbo, tried coming on to me in the bathroom yesterday. That family is nothing but disgusting homos.

"Oh my God," I whisper. There are eighteen comments and over seventy 'likes' and it was only posted ten minutes ago.

"Have you seen it?" Em asks as she walks into my room.

My heart pounds with anxiety and humiliation for something that isn't even true.

"What do I do?" I ask as the tears rim my eyes.

Em sets her bowl down and moves to squeeze in and sit next to me on my desk chair. She wraps her arms around me, and I let the tears fall.

"Did you read the comments? People actually believe her," I say.

"People are stupid."

"It doesn't matter. They still believe her." I pull back and wipe the tears from my cheeks. "Why are you not more pissed?"

"I am. Trust me."

"So what do I do?" I ask again.

"Honestly? I wouldn't do anything. Don't even feed into it."

I took Emily's advice, but the kids at school aren't letting up. I only have a couple of friends that talk to me at this point. I just have to wonder when this will all die down and people will lose interest.

For the past few weeks, I have been forced to walk these halls that are constantly filled with sneers and whispers. Jenn has completely turned her back on me. Tonight is our school's first football game. The one thing I refused to do was quit the cheer squad. I've been on it since freshman year.

"Hey, is it all right if I just drop you off tonight?" Em asks as she stands in the doorway to my room.

Lacing my shoe, I look up and ask, "Why?"

"'Cause I don't wanna sit around with a bunch of people I can't stand to watch a game I couldn't care less about."

Em is taking a lighter load of the bullying than I am, but I know it affects her all the same. For some reason, I'm the bigger target with people. Probably because I'm quiet where she has a loud bark. She's more intimidating.

"Yeah, that's fine. I'll just text you as soon as the game ends," I tell her as I tighten my ponytail and grab my cheer bag.

When she drops me off, I keep my head down as I make my way out to the field. I don't worry too much about anyone teasing me since the stands are loaded with parents and faculty.

The game passes slowly, and we are finally nearing the end of the forth quarter. I step away from the cheer line to quickly grab my cell out of my bag to text Emily. When I swipe the screen, I notice a text waiting on me from Mark. I don't read it. Instead, I shoot out my text to Em and rejoin the girls.

Once the game is over, I gather all my belongings and head out to the parking lot. I stand and wait on Emily to get here, which is taking her longer than it should. I hear a few kids laughing at me when they pass, and I pull out my phone to distract me. I open up the text from Mark and read it.

I miss talking to you. I never meant to bail the way I did.

I'm surprised when I notice Ashton step up next to me. He plays cornerback and we have known each other since he moved here in the middle of our freshman year. He gives me a slight nod of his head, acknowledging me, and I turn my focus back to my brother's text.

I haven't spoken with him since I yelled at him on the phone a few weeks ago after that crappy first day of school. He calls and texts often, but I haven't ever responded. I miss him, but I'm mad at him too.

When I lean over to shove the phone back into my bag, a group of girls pass me as I am bent down and purposely bump into me, knocking me off balance. I catch myself with my hand, and when I look up, I see Jenn.

"Hey, freak," she says, and her friends bust out laughing at me.

"Don't be a bitch," I hear Ashton snap at her.

Standing up, I watch the girls walk away, and I turn to him, saying, "Thanks," in a quiet voice. I wonder why he, let alone anyone, would stick up for the school leper.

"She's turned into such a snob this year," he says, and when I look back at him, I shyly agree.

"Sorry I'm late," Em shouts out the driver's side window when she pulls up.

Taking my eyes off of Ashton, I grab my bag and tell her, "It's okay," and then slide into the car.

Before she puts the car in drive, Ashton says, "See you Monday."

I don't say anything, and Emily gives me a knowing look. Turning my attention away from her, I notice he isn't standing on the sidewalk anymore. I scan and spot him walking to a white jeep with keys in his hand. I allow happiness to creep inside when I realize that he wasn't waiting for a ride like I was. He has his own car, but he stood with me anyway.

"So, Ashton, huh?" Emily teases.

"Just drive," I tell her and keep quiet as we head home.

When we arrive, I go up to my room to shower and work on my homework. After a while, I notice it's almost midnight and close my books to call it a night. Slipping into bed, I shut off the lamp and pull out my phone to read before I fall asleep. Before opening my iBooks app, I open up the text that my brother sent earlier. No matter what, I miss him. As mad as I am about how this year is turning out, I still want him here. I type out my text, my first in weeks.

I miss you too. Goodnight.

Closing my texts, I open up Facebook really quick, not really sure why since all it seems to be is another outlet for people to make my life hell. I clear my notifications and notice a *Friend Request* alert come through. I click on it and can't control the smile that grows.

Maybe this could be one of the few good things this year.

Here's to hoping.

I click *Accept,* and immediately get a *Private Message.*

Ashton Yates:

You're up late. :-)

FALLING

a novel by
New York Times Bestselling Author
e.k. blair

For my husband
No fall could ever compare to the one I had with you.

"Your flaws are perfect for the heart that is meant to love you."

~Ash Sweeney

prologue

TWO PILLS. TWO fuckin' blue pills. I swore I'd stop this shit, but I can't stand the pain that still radiates in the back of my head where he shattered his beer bottle the other night. I hate that I'm just like him—dependent on this shit. *Fuck it.*

Tossing them into my mouth, I pour the cheap tequila down my throat and relish the burn that singes in my chest. My body falls lifelessly back onto the bed while the muffled music pounds through the walls.

"Give me some," Rene says. Or is it Rachel? Who the hell cares? She pulls the bottle out of my hand and takes a draw of the amber liquid.

Handing it back to me, all I see is a hazy shadow as I feel her crawl on top of me. This chick leeched herself to me when I walked into this party earlier. I knew she'd be an easy lay, and when she shoves her hand down my pants and grabs my dick, she proves me right.

I don't even try to focus as my body starts to weigh down from the effects of the pills. I love this feeling. Numb. Heavy. Warm. Hazy. It takes me over, and I don't even realize that this girl is now fucking me until I look up. Closing my eyes, I begin to drift. Drift from the hell that consumes me. It's Saturday night. The night he stays out late drinking just to come home and impale everything he hates about his life into me.

Waking up, head still heavy, vision clearer, I sit on the edge of the bed. I look over my shoulder and see some redhead, naked, sleeping. *Who is she?* I don't remember what happened, but I know we screwed because my pants are flung across the room, and I see the used condom on the floor.

My watch says it's after one in the morning, and I need to get home. Pulling on my pants, I stumble slightly as I make my way through the house filled with people I barely know, drinking, dancing, making out.

When I start my car, I know I shouldn't be driving, but I also know that I need to go because my dad normally drags his drunk-ass in around this time. I hate knowing that my mom will be there alone with him.

Pulling up to the dark grey, two-story house I have always lived in, I can't help but think about how the impeccably manicured structure is simply a mask for the madness that lives within. My stomach clenches when I see his truck in the driveway. I shut the car off and rush inside, but I know I'm too late when I hear my mother crying. Bolting through the house and into the kitchen, I get there just in time to see my dad swinging his arm around and smashing a coffee mug into the side of her head. Turning to face me, her face is void as she falls to the floor, blood everywhere.

"What are you looking at, you piece of shit?" he spits at me, and I fuckin' lose it.

My body roils with vengeance when I charge at him, and we tumble, crashing to the floor. Rage takes over as I begin to pound my fists into his face relentlessly. Over and over. Skin splitting. Blood gushing. The sounds of my mom screaming and the grunts I force out with every blow to his face are a distant echo in my head.

He thrashes beneath me, but I don't stop. I know I'm gonna kill him, and I hope I do. My teeth snap shut when he drives his palm into my jaw, causing me to bite my tongue. He continues to fight his way out from under me, flailing his arms, and dumping shit everywhere when he yanks one of the kitchen drawers out of its tracks.

My mouth fills with blood, and just when I spit it into his face, I fall over onto the floor.

"Fuck!" I scream through gritted teeth as I grab my side. I hear the clatter of metal falling to the ground and watch my father's black boots stumbling away from me.

Cold shivers prick at my body, and my vision fades as my breathing becomes more and more shallow. My mother's warm arms scoop my shoulders onto her lap as she cries, and I let my head fall to the side. When I see the bloody butcher's knife, I lift my shaking hand that's clutched to my side and raise it in front of my face. All I see is red.

I wake up the next morning, body sore and twenty-seven stitches in my side, along my ribs, where that son of a bitch stabbed me last night. Sitting up, I flinch against the stinging flesh. My mom is still asleep. I made her stay in my bed last night in case my father came back home, which he didn't.

I quietly make my way downstairs and feel the guilt from everything that happened last night flood through my veins. If I'd never gone out, my mother probably wouldn't be sleeping in my bed with a concussion and stitches in her head.

I've been so selfish lately and getting too fucked up on ecstasy and alcohol to protect my mom. The drinking, the drugs, the rage that fired through me last night—I'm him. He's a part of me. He runs through my blood. I hate him. I don't want to be him, but I am.

Having him consume me like this makes me sick to my stomach, and

I swear to God, I will do everything I can to avoid what I fear is destined to be my future. I've gotta stop the fuckin' pills. I've gotta . . .

A loud knocking on the door pulls me out of my thoughts, and when I make my way to the front of the house and open the door, two cops are standing there, staring at me with a look I can't quite make out.

Taking off his hat, one cop asks, "Is this the home of Richard Campbell?"

chapter one

"HEY, BOSS. THAT clown you call your friend is asking for you."

"I'm finishing up," I tell Max as I sign off on a few orders. "How long has he been here?"

Standing in the doorway to my office, he answers, "Not long. Half an hour or so."

I don't say anything as I finish up my paperwork and toss my pen on the desk, leaning back in my chair with a deep sigh.

"Everything okay?"

"Tired," I say as I look up at my friend. Max has worked for me for a few years now. He serves as security ever since business picked up at the bar after I bought it out from its previous owner. He's a good guy and extremely loyal, which makes him a commodity I can't afford to lose. Beneath his shaved head and insane build that intimidates most people that walk through the doors here, he's got a big heart.

"Call it a night, man. It's late, and you've been up here all day."

"Yeah." I push back from my desk and stand up, making my way out of the office. When I pass Max, I clap his back, saying, "I'm gonna go talk to Gav then head out."

Max follows as we walk down the stairs and into the bar that I've owned since I graduated from the University of Washington. This place has become a second home to me. It's where I spend most of my time.

Bumping shoulders through the crowd of people, I spot my old college buddy, Gavin, tossing back a bottle of beer.

"Ryan, dude? Where the hell have you been?"

"Working."

"Mel!" he shouts over to one of the bar girls. "Get this old man a beer."

"No, Mel. I'm good," I tell her, and she just shakes her head at Gavin, knowing what a partier he is.

"What's up with you tonight?"

"Tired, man."

"You not staying?"

Before I can answer, a tall blonde catches my eye as she starts making her way through the crowd and up to the bar. She steps next to me and leans over the bar top to get Mel's attention, and when I eye her, Gavin mumbles, "Yeah, you're staying," all too knowingly.

"Ryan, right?" the blonde asks as she turns to look at me, and when I nod my head, she introduces herself with a slow, "I'm Gina," trying to sound sexy, but it's lost on me 'cause I couldn't give a shit what her name is. Girls like her are an almost daily occurrence.

"Have we met before or something?" I ask since she already knows who I am.

"Not officially. I've seen you around though." She grins at me as she says this, but her fake tits are too distracting for me to focus on her face. It's when she giggles that I snap my attention up. "You own this place, right?"

I nod my head again. One thing about me, I'm not much of a talker. I'm a pretty quiet guy for the most part, but with chicks especially, I don't talk. There's no need to. I don't care to delay the inevitable. I'm a straight shooter, and being as tired as I am, I cut the shit and say, "Wanna get to know me better in my office?"

Her smile grows, and I take her hand, leading her to the back stairs. I spot Gavin trying to nail his own bait, and he gives me a cocky grin when he sees me pass by.

We walk into my office, and I close the door, pinning her up against it, clasping her wrists in my hand above her head while I run my other hand up her skirt and between her legs. Letting go of her wrists, she works with my pants, anxious to get them off.

I fumble in my back pocket, and when I retrieve the condom, I quickly rip it open with my teeth, spitting out the shredded foil as she tugs my pants down. I waste no time. Closing my eyes, I shove her panties to the side and take her against the door.

I never care to look too much at the girls I bang. Honestly, I don't want to connect in any way.

This is me—disconnecting.

Screwing chicks as they come along. I don't talk. I don't watch. My escape lasts for as long as it takes for me to get off, then I move on. I've been this way my whole life, from a fifteen-year-old freshman in high school to a now twenty-eight-year-old man. I'm emotionally messed up, and I don't even try to hide it.

Clinging herself to me, legs wrapped around my waist, I bury my head in her neck, and the thick perfume she's wearing makes me screw her harder, wanting to finish up so I can go home and wash this shit off of me.

Pouring another cup of coffee, trying to wake up before heading out to the gym, my phone starts to ring. I know it's my mom before I even look. She always calls first thing Sunday morning—predictable.

"Hey, Mom."

"Hi, honey. How're you doing?"

Taking my coffee, I walk over and plop down on my couch as I say, "Good. Nothing new."

"What time do you think you'll be here tomorrow?" she asks.

"Around two," I tell her. My mom still lives in Oregon at the same beach house that I grew up in down on Cannon Beach. After high school, I moved here, to Seattle, to go to college, but I still go back home often to visit. "Tori's gonna come too. Sorry I didn't tell you earlier. Is that cool?"

"Of course. Is she bringing the kids?"

Taking a sip of my coffee, I laugh and say, "No. She's going crazy. That's why I invited her to hang with me for a few days. She's desperate to escape. She said that Connor has been a nightmare lately, throwing crazy temper tantrums. So she's going to leave the kids home with Trevor."

"Oh, dear. Four is such a rough age. I remember when you were four. You were always embarrassing me. You hated wearing pants, so it didn't matter where we were, you would just strip down bottomless in public for all to see." She starts laughing, and I can't help joining in with her when she continues through her chuckles, "I would be so embarrassed, but when I tried getting you to pull up your underwear, you just screamed and drew even more attention."

"I don't remember that," I laugh.

"Well, I do. Eventually, I had to tell you that it was against the law and the police were gonna come get you and throw you in jail if you did it again."

"Great parenting, Mom!" I say as I shake my head in pure humor. I love hearing these funny stories of my past since most of my memories are ones I wish I could forget.

"Well . . ." she squeaks out. "I didn't know what else to say, so I went with scare tactics."

"Did it work?"

"No," she says with a soft giggle. "Well, it'll be great to see the both of you."

"You too. I'm gonna go hit the gym, but I'll call you when I'm on my way tomorrow, okay?"

"Okay, dear. Drive safe, and I love you."

"Love you too, Mom"

I go upstairs to change before I head out to the gym to meet up with Max. We've always worked out at the same gym; that's how we first met. Making sure everything is locked up, I hop into my jeep and make the short drive to the Athletic Club. Max's car is already in the parking lot when I pull up.

"Hey, boss," Max shouts through the empty gym. Nobody is ever here on Sunday mornings, so we make it a point to get together at this time.

"What's up?" I say as I walk over to him. "You been here long?"

"Nah."

We head towards the indoor track to do a quick run before lifting.

"Oh, I forgot to tell you, but I'm going out of town for a few days, so Michael will be at the bar all week."

"Going to see your mom?"

"Yeah. Mostly plan on surfing with my cousin," I say as we make our laps.

"Well, when you get back, I need your help."

"With what?"

"Traci is moving in, so I need you to help me with her furniture."

Looking over at him, I question, "She's moving in?"

Laughing at me, he says, "Ryan, don't act so surprised. We're almost thirty. Don't you think you should slow it down a bit yourself? Find a girl?"

"Nope. You know I don't do the whole girlfriend thing. Never have. I like being alone."

"No one likes being alone."

"I like being alone," I repeat, but it's a lie. Truth is, I've always been too scared to have a girlfriend. Too scared to allow myself to even have feelings towards someone else. Too scared of putting myself in a situation only to discover the person I believe lives inside of me. A person just like my father.

"Whatever you say," he teases as we continue our run. "My buddy, Chase, was wondering if we needed his help when classes start up in a few weeks."

"Working the door?"

"Yeah. He's a good kid. He's in school full-time but said he's free to work evenings."

Rounding another lap, I tell him, "Yeah. That'll work. Have him call Michael." Michael has been managing the bar for the most part lately. Knowing that the bar is in good hands and is running smoothly has allowed me more freedom with my schedule, and the income has been nothing but generous.

After a long workout with Max, I decide to stop by the office and take care of a few things before heading out of town.

"Hey, Mel," I say as I make my way past the bar to the stairs, and she gives me a flirty wink laced with mockery. Shaking my head at her, I go up to Michael's office.

"Hey, I thought you were out of town," he says from behind his desk. Michael started working here at the beginning of the summer. He's in his mid-thirties with a wife and kids. Dependent on the paycheck I write him, he's proven to be dependable.

"Tomorrow." Taking a seat in one of the chairs, I tell him, "Max has a friend that's gonna be calling you about a job. Check him out, and if he doesn't work, I need you to find someone who does. We need another guy to work the door. Summer has been a little slow, but shit always kicks up when classes at the university start."

"Got it," he says as he files through a stack of orders. "Anything else?"

"Yeah, I need you to start booking out the bands for at least six weeks. I'd really like to find a few we can book steady, so see what you can come up with. You can always call Gavin to see if he has any leads as well."

"Sure thing. When are you gonna be back?"

"Few days or so," I respond as I stand up to leave. "You got everything under control?"

"Yeah, man. Don't worry about things here. I'll catch you when you get back."

chapter two

"IT'S ABOUT TIME you got here."

"Sorry. Got tied up this morning," I say when I walk through the front door.

"Spare me the details," Tori teases as she shakes her head before giving me a hug.

Walking into the kitchen, I ask, "Where's Mom?"

"You just missed her. She ran to the store to get stuff for dinner."

"Wanna head out so when we get back you women have enough time to cook for me?" I joke while she gives me a jab to my ribs.

Tori is only three years older than me. Our moms are sisters, so we spent a lot of time together growing up. I have three cousins, all girls, but Tori is the closest in age to me and the only one that surfs, so we were pretty inseparable when our families would get together. We've always been good friends. She married Trevor in her early twenties and now has two kids. Seeing her as a wife and mother never deters me from giving her shit the same way I did when we were younger.

"You know Indian Beach is going to be insanely busy today," she tells me.

"Yeah," I sigh and look out the windows onto Cannon Beach. The waves aren't hitting as hard here, but they're big enough. "Let's stay here then."

"You sure?"

"We can wake up early and hit Indian tomorrow before the crowds get there."

Nice weather is short-lived around here. Once the grey skies clear and the rain slows, everyone swarms to the Oregon coast, and Indian Beach is the spot that draws in the most people.

Hopping off the couch, she says, "Sounds good. I'll go grab my wetsuit."

We spend the next hour in the water until I hear my mother calling my name up on the beach. Paddling in, I walk out of the water, and my mother knows me too well when she starts taking a couple steps back, but I rush in and wrap my arms around her, soaking her clothes.

She laughs, and when I let go of her, she grumbles, "Now I have to go in and change. Thanks!"

"You're welcome," I tease.

Shaking off the mock irritation, she says, "It's good to see you, honey."

"You too."

She tucks a lock of her short blonde hair behind her ear and asks, "How much longer are you guys going to be out here?"

"Not too long."

She gives me a smile. "Okay. Well, I'll be inside whenever you two are done," and turns to go back in.

When I paddle back out, Tori is sitting on her board, and I join her as we bob up and down in the choppy water.

"What're you doing?" I ask.

"Taking a break," she responds as she looks out to the setting sun.

I can tell something is bothering her, so I come out and say, "Talk to me, Tor. What's up?"

She looks over at me, annoyed that I can read her like I do. Letting out a big sigh, she questions, "You ever wonder what it is we're doing?"

"Meaning?"

"Life," she says, taking a pause before continuing, "I guess I just thought I would feel more content than I do. Truth is . . . sometimes I feel like I'm too settled. Kids. Husband. Like I'm stuck."

When she looks over at me, I grab her board, steadying it next to me. "You're not happy?"

She doesn't respond.

"No," I answer for her.

"I didn't say that."

"You didn't have to. You're thinking too much."

"Are *you* happy?" she asks.

It's a loaded question. I'm numb most of the time. Friends are dropping off the scene, settling down with girls, and I'm still doing the same old shit. But the fear outweighs the jealousy, so I don't get too hung up on the fact that I'm emotionally incapable of having that. I never have had that. Never allowed myself the opportunity. All I know how to do is care for myself. I'm selfish just like he was. I'm not a provider the way a man should be; I'm a taker. I stay disconnected—and take.

"I'm as happy as I can be, I guess."

Tori never knew about my father, that he was a dick who used to pound his fists into his wife and son. Black eyes, broken ribs, bruises, and concussions. We kept it hidden well, my mother and I. They knew he drank, maybe not as heavily as he did, but that much they knew. Everything else, we never spoke about. Once he died, Mom was determined to start a new life. A life that had nothing to do with our past.

"Do you ever think about settling down?" she asks.

"No," I respond with forced ease.

"So you're happy? Having a different girl in your bed every night?"

I laugh. "Every night is an exaggeration, and those chicks aren't in my bed either. They stay downstairs."

"How is it that you haven't gotten the shit beat out of you yet?" she jokes in disgust.

My laughter grows as I say, "Lucky, I guess."

We sit for a minute or two when I finally ask the kicker, "Are you not happy with Trevor?"

It doesn't take but a second for her eyes to gloss over as she admits, "I don't know." When the tears fall, she reveals, "Maybe it's supposed to be this way. Maybe what I was expecting just isn't reality. My reality is . . . I've lost myself along the way somehow. Between two kids and not working, I'm just lost. I don't know of any other word to describe what I feel."

"What does Trevor say? Does he even know?"

"He doesn't want to hear me complain after he's been at work all day."

"Talk to him, Tor. Whatever is going on with you, he loves you and the kids. Maybe it's time for you to get out of the house. Go back to work."

She wipes her face and laughs softly. "The thought of not being with my kids kills me. I know you're right, but mommy guilt is a bitch."

"Yeah, I wouldn't know about that," I chuckle. Shifting, I lie down on my board and say, "Come on. Let's drink," before paddling back in.

After dinner, I walk into the kitchen to grab a beer and check my phone while Tori and my mom talk in the living room. Popping the cap off the bottle, I take a long sip before picking up my phone. I scan through some new emails that have come through and forward a couple to Michael.

Setting my phone back down, I lean against the counter and take another swig when my eye catches the cracked wood in the corner of the kitchen island.

"What the hell is your problem, kid?"

"I'm sorry. It was an accident."

Quickly grabbing a towel to clean up the juice I spilled that is now pooling under his briefcase, large hands grab my neck and shoulder. He abruptly throws me onto the floor, and the force of his strength sends me flying into the center island. The sharp corner pierces my back and sends a fire of pain up my spine as my head ricochets hard against the wood. I hear the crack and start crying. I'm scared he's gonna get more upset with me if he sees the damage.

I lie on the floor, avoiding eye contact, and grip the back of my head. I can already feel the bump growing.

"I'm sorry. It was an accident," he sneers, throwing my words back at me as he slings a dishtowel at me. *"Clean this shit up."*

That crack has been there since I was seven years old. It's such a faint line that I doubt my mother has ever noticed it.

"I'm calling it a night," Tori announces as she walks in and gives me a hug, pulling me out of my past.

"Early morning. Let's try and head out around seven."

"Sounds good," she says before she turns back to the living room to tell my mother goodnight and then heads upstairs.

My eyes shift back to the crack briefly as I turn to go into the other room. I walk over and sit down with my mom on the couch.

"How are you doing, darling?" she asks, patting my knee as I get comfortable.

Thinking back to my conversation with Tori in the water, I ask, "Are you happy, Mom?"

"Where is this coming from?" she questions, and I mindlessly find myself rubbing the back of my head where that bump from twenty-one years ago doesn't exist anymore, but the memory still does.

"You're all alone here in this house. I worry."

"I've always been alone in this house."

She never remarried after my dad died. I haven't even known her to date. We've never talked about it, but I just figured she was too scared.

"Can I ask you something?" I say as I turn to her.

"Anything."

"How come you never sold this house?" I wonder if the past still haunts her like it does me.

"What do you mean?"

"It's filled with so many bad memories."

"But it's filled with so many good ones too, dear." She smiles when she continues, "I remember holding you in my arms when I brought you home from the hospital. This is our home. It always has been. The one thing that bastardized this place is gone." She pats my knee as she says this. Nervous reflex. She isn't convinced of her own words. I'm good at reading people, especially her. "What about you?"

"Me?"

"Are you happy?"

I dig my thumbnail under the damp label on my beer bottle. Nervous reflex. I'm sure she sees it too. We are good at reading each other like that.

"I worry about you," she says softly.

"You don't need to worry about me. I'm good. Business is good," I assure her.

She leans back on the couch and lets out a sigh as she says, "I don't doubt that work is good, but I wonder how much longer you plan on keeping up like you are. I wonder when you'll decide to slow down and settle."

"You know why I don't settle, Mom." This is no secret between us. She has always known why I've never gotten involved with anyone. She knows my fears. I tell my mother nearly everything.

"You're nothing like him," she affirms sternly, and when I look at her, I deny her words.

"I'm a lot like him."

She doesn't respond, and I feel bad for cheapening her words. "Sorry."

"It hurts me to know this is how you think of yourself. I don't want you to be alone. I want you to find someone that you can be happy with."

"I want the same for you," I tell her.

"I know you do, but you're young. You have time on your side."

I can't help but laugh. "God, Mom, you act like you're a blue-haired lady at the bingo hall."

She laughs with me and says, "You know what I mean."

"I know." Letting out a deep yawn, I take the last swallow of my beer and lean in to kiss her on the cheek. "I'm gonna hit the sack. Tor and I are headed to Indian in the morning."

"What time will you guys be back?"

"Around ten or so."

"I'll cook you kids breakfast."

I smile at her referring to us as kids and say, "I love you, Mom," as I stand up and look down at her.

"Love you, too."

chapter three

BEFORE THE WATER gets too busy, Tori and I decide to call it and head back to shore. Tossing our boards aside, we sit and take a breather. The morning is cool, and the sun rising behind us casts a glow across the water. People filter in, trying to get as much of the sun as they can before the season changes and the rain and grey haze finds its home for the rest of the year. Personally, I love the darkness.

"I gotta head back tomorrow," Tori tells me as she unzips her wetsuit and tugs her arms out of it.

I start doing the same, saying, "I thought you were gonna stay for a few days."

"I was, but Trevor called late last night, and he just got a big case, so he has to go in this weekend." She digs her feet into the packed sand and shrugs, "Life of an attorney."

"You gonna talk to him?" I question.

She looks over at me and nods. "I'll talk to him."

"Good."

"So when are you coming back home?"

"I don't really know. Whenever. For sure Thanksgiving though."

"Connor was asking if you were going to take him trick-or-treating this year."

I love her kids. Although they are my cousin's children, we've always just referred to them as my nieces and nephews. I have a lot; three nieces and four nephews. Being an uncle is great, and I take pride in spoiling them rotten despite their parents. "You know it's always a busy night at the bar, but I'll see what I can do. Don't say anything to him though because if I can't make it back here, I don't want him to be let down."

She smiles and says, "I won't."

"How is Bailey doing?" I ask about her one-year-old daughter.

"Crazy," she laughs. "She's a tiny diva. I look at her, and I know I'm in for trouble in about fourteen years."

"Well, if she's anything like you were . . ."

"God, don't even say it!" she whines.

We both laugh, knowing all too well how much of a partier she used to be when we were in high school.

Recalling a memory, I mention, "I will never forget seeing you hanging over the docks and puking into the water."

"Ugh! That was awful. I was trying to be cool in front of that guy, Shawn, so that he would notice me."

"Oh, he noticed you," I joke, laughing harder. We used to get together in Astoria, where she's from. We'd meet up with friends late at night and drink on the docks. Every now and then we'd get busted, but it never stopped us from going back.

"You ready?" she asks.

"Yeah, I'm starved," I respond as I stand up and grab my board. We head up the stairs, off the beach, and to my jeep. Loading everything up, we make the drive out of Ecola Park and back home.

The smell of coffee and bacon fills the house as we walk through the front door. We toss our gear into the laundry room then head into the kitchen where my mom is scrambling eggs.

"How was the beach?" she asks as I pour a mug of coffee.

"Good," Tori answers.

"Well, it's a good thing you guys went when you did. It's supposed to rain this afternoon."

"You know rain doesn't stop us," I say as I walk by and kiss her cheek.

She plates our food, and we all sit to eat.

"Tori has to bail tomorrow," I tell my mom.

"Oh, no. Everything okay with the kids?" she asks.

"Yeah, the kids are good. Trevor has to go into the office, that's all."

"When are you heading back?" she asks me before taking a sip of her coffee.

"I'll probably stay here for a couple of days. I'm in no rush to get back. Michael should have everything under control."

Finishing breakfast, I help my mom clean the kitchen before heading to my room to get cleaned up.

After my shower, I lie down on my bed and call Gavin.

"Hey, man. How's the beach?" he says when he answers.

"Good. Anything going on Tuesday?" Too many serious conversations yesterday and my head needs an escape when I get back home.

"Whatever you want to go on," he responds.

Gav and I have been friends for nearly ten years now. Through the years, I feel like our friendship, although it remains constant, has grown a bit superficial. He still parties the way we used to in college. We go out a lot, and he's into the chicks as much as I am. He's loud and obnoxious, where I'm more laidback, but he's my one friend that isn't tied down.

"Monkey Pub?" I suggest.

"Yeah, that works."

"I'll text you later then."

"All right, man. I'll catch you when you get back."

I spent the rest of my time with my mom, hanging out and taking it easy. It's always good to see her and catch up, although we talk on the phone often. She's always sad to see me leave. I know she was hoping I would move back to Oregon after I graduated college, but Seattle is my home. I love it.

When I get back in town, I head to Monkey Pub to meet Gavin. The lot is packed as I pull in to park. Walking in, the crowd is thick, and there are a few drunken college girls on stage, murdering a song in karaoke.

"Ryan," I hear Gavin holler, and when I spot him by the bar, I make my way over.

"Mel, what are you doing here?" I ask, but before she can answer, I catch her husband, Zane. "Shit, man. I haven't seen you in forever," I say to him as I clap his shoulder.

"Busy with the band. Things are finally starting to take off."

"God, don't get him started," Mel complains before she downs a shot.

"Fill me in," I encourage, and he proceeds to tell me that his band has been offered a contract for a recording deal.

"No shit? That's great," I tell him.

"Thanks. We're pretty stoked."

When I see the irritation in Mel's eyes, I question, "What's got you so pissy?"

"Zane forgot to mention that he would have to move to L.A."

"You'd think she'd be happy, but I can't get my woman on board to go to California," he tells me as he wraps his arm around her.

"I love Seattle. All my family is here," she responds.

"You guys will work it out. For better or worse, or some shit like that, right?" I laugh.

"Right," she sighs, not happy about the situation.

Turning around, I shout down the bar for a beer, and when the bartender gives me a nod, I take a seat next to Gavin.

"What did you do today?" I ask as he drinks his beer.

"Just work. Shit never ends."

"Dude, you love work. Don't give me that crap," I joke.

He laughs and says, "Not gonna lie, it's a good gig. I'm gonna go check out a new band the label is showing interest in on Thursday. Wanna tag along?"

"Yeah," I say as the bartender hands me my beer. Gavin has been working for Sub Pop Records for the past few years, so we hit up a lot of concerts.

He turns to a couple of girls that walk up and stand next to him as they wait to order drinks. Taking a quick look back at me, he shoots me a wink, and I laugh at him. When he turns back to them, he says, in tacky Gavin form, "Hey, ladies."

I sit back and drink my beer. Mel and Zane are off talking to friends, but when Gavin nudges me and says, "I got one for you," I turn around to see a tall, curvy redhead smiling at me.

Giving a slight nod, I say, "You go to college here?" Small talk—it's almost annoying to me because if I do too much of it, it makes me feel like a dick for possibly giving girls the impression that I'm interested in more than just a fleeting hook-up.

"Uh huh. Education major," she tells me with a thick Southern accent, and I can't control the chuckle that slips out. "What about you?"

Is she kidding? "College was a few years back for me."

As she nods her head, she says, "Oh." Naïve. "So, what do you do . . . ?" she trails off, not knowing my name.

"Ryan."

"Right."

God, this is painful. "I run a bar off campus," I tell her.

"Cool."

Looking over at Gavin, he's staring at the redhead and shaking his head. Yeah, I got the ditz outta the two, that's for sure.

"You need a drink?" I offer, and when she smiles and nods, I turn to get the bartender's attention. "What do you like?"

"Vodka."

"Shots?" I ask.

"Mmm hmm."

I shoot her a smile, and I know I'm in when she smiles back, biting her lower lip. I order four shots, and we waste little time knocking them back. We sit there as time passes, and she talks my ear off about school and moving up here from Oklahoma. I half pay attention but make sure I nod to give her the impression that I'm keeping up.

Her hand grips my knee when she leans in and begins talking closely into my ear as the bar grows louder the later it gets. Brushing her hair behind her shoulder, I let my fingers graze along her neck, and she shifts to look at me, no longer talking, just staring. When her hand tightens on my knee, I lean in and kiss her, tasting the alcohol and willingness as she moves her lips with mine.

She's not hesitant, but eager, so when I tug her hair, she moans into my mouth. Dragging her lips to my ear, she whispers, "Wanna get outta here?"

This one seems like she could be clingy. Not wanting to go to my place, and being tired after the drive back from Oregon, I lay it out there for her. "Car?"

She pulls back, looking at me with question in her eyes, and I explain, "I just got back in from being out of town. I'm tired."

When she doesn't respond, I ask, "That a problem?"

It takes a second, but eventually she shakes her head, and when I stand up, I see Gavin.

"You heading out?" he asks.

"Yeah, I'm gonna walk . . . umm . . ."

I look at the girl when she says, "Mary."

"Huh?" I question.

"My name. It's Mary."

I'm an ass. I turn back to Gavin and quickly tell him, "I'm gonna walk Mary out."

I take her hand and lead her out into the rainy night to my jeep. Not wanting to get my ass arrested, I go for the back seat, and she hops in behind me. She's on me quick, kissing me and running her hands up my shirt. I return the gesture and grab her large tits when she begins undoing my pants. Tugging them down, she leans over and takes me in her mouth.

"Shit," I exhale as I fist her hair and take control over her. Selfish? Yeah, I'm selfish. Escaping for my moment, not thinking. Enjoying. All thoughts vanishing from my mind. This is my vice. It used to be drugs. I rolled on X when I was in high school, but *this,* well this is just my version of a healthier release.

Zipping up my pants, she runs her fingers through my hair. This is the part I hate. I turn cold to make it clear that this wasn't anything more than what it just was.

"Thanks."

"Thanks?"

Opening the door, I step out and hold my hand out for her. "Like I said, I'm tired."

She hops down and hesitantly says, "You wanna call me sometime?"

"I don't do the whole girlfriend thing."

She nods her head, and my guilt appears as she turns to walk back into the bar without saying anything else. I take a moment and enjoy the rain that's falling, but when I hear my name being called, I turn around to see a familiar blonde walking my way from across the lot.

"Gina," she says, answering my unspoken question, and I suddenly remember the girl I had in my office a few days ago. "What are you doing out here in the rain?" she asks as she leans up against my car.

"Nothing. About to head home."

"Alone?"

"Alone."

She takes me by surprise when she shoves her hand in my back pocket and finds my cell, pulling it out.

"What're you doing?" I ask when she starts punching something into my phone.

"Storing my number," she explains. She hands it to me when she's done and says, "For when you don't want to be alone," before heading inside.

chapter four

"DUDE! YOU SAID help with *some* furniture, not a whole house full," I complain to Max as we stand inside Traci's home.

"You have something else going on today?"

"If I said yes, would you let me off?"

He looks over at me with a straight face and admonishes, "You want me kicking your ass?"

Shaking my head, I laugh and say, "That's what I figured."

Walking over to her large sectional couch, he starts pulling off the cushions. "Come on."

We begin to load the furniture into the U-Haul when Max asks, "What are you doing later tonight?"

"No plans. I need to run up to the bar to see if Michael was able to get any bands booked," I say as I jump down from the truck to go inside for another load.

"You wanna stop by later? We're having a few friends over."

"*We're?*" I question.

Max just looks over at me and laughs. Although he and Traci have been together for a while, I know I'll be seeing much less of him now that they're living together. But hanging out with a house full of domesticated bliss isn't my idea of fun, so I tell him, "I'm probably gonna call it an early night."

"You sure?"

"Yeah."

We spend the next two hours loading everything up in the truck before driving it over to Max's house. Once everything is moved, I head into the office to get some work done and to talk with Michael. He was able to book a few bands and hire Chase, Max's buddy, to work the door. Since it looks like he has everything under control, I call it a night and go home.

Hopping out of the shower, I throw on a pair of pajama bottoms before going downstairs to watch some TV. I settle myself on the couch and flip on an old movie, one that I've seen countless times, but I watch it anyway.

An email notification lights up my phone, and I pick it up to see that it's work stuff that Michael sent. Not wanting to hack into it tonight, I start mindlessly going through my phone, opening apps, and wasting time. I begin scrolling through my contacts and stop when I see Gina's info scan by. I tap on her name and stare at her number.

"For when you don't want to be alone."

She's one chick that didn't make me feel bad after we hooked up. She got it. She accepted it for what it was, and clearly she's on the same page as me.

Before I know it, the phone is ringing, and when she answers, I say, "Hey. It's Ryan."

"Hi. What's going on?"

"Nothing. You busy?" I ask, keeping the chitchat to a minimum.

"Not anymore."

"Gotta pen?"

I give her my address, and when there's a knock on my door about thirty minutes later, I drag myself off the couch to see her standing on my doorstep.

Long blonde hair, tall, and wearing clothes that makes her look like she's trying a bit too hard for something that's a guaranteed giveaway.

Her heels click against my hardwood floors when she walks in, smile-clad face as she gives me the lookover. *At least I won't feel guilty with her.* I tell myself this a couple times before I take her hand and kiss her. She doesn't stop me or even slow me down as we stumble across the room.

It isn't long before she's bent over my couch, ditching her self-respect just to moan my name in what is nothing more than another throw of diversion. But I'm no better. I'm far from respectable. So the both of us use each other for the mere minutes that we're able to hold on before lust takes over, and we lose control of ourselves.

As I yank up my pants, she rights herself and turns to face me, sated.

"I'm glad you called."

I nod my head and start walking over to my kitchen to grab a drink. "You thirsty?" I offer.

"Yeah. Umm, where's your bathroom?" she asks, and I point down the hall.

"It's on the right."

"Thanks."

When she returns, she situates herself close to me on the couch, getting more comfortable than she should, but I don't say anything.

As she picks up her glass of water, she says, "So you have the night off?" before taking a sip.

"I don't keep a schedule," I tell her, and when she doesn't respond, I clarify, "It's my bar. I own it."

"That's right. I remember hearing that from Gavin."

"How do you know Gavin?" I ask.

"He stops by my place every now and then."

Giving her a confused look, she assures, "Not to see me. My roommate, Ashley, and him have known each other for a while."

Nodding my head, she continues, "Bar must do pretty well."

"Why do you say that?"

"This is a big space you have. It's nice." She takes another sip of water and sets the glass down on the coffee table.

I bought this loft with the money my father left behind. When he died, everything stayed locked up in an account, untouched for years. My mother wanted nothing to do with it for the longest time. She lived off of the interest, which was more than enough to support us.

My father dealt in acquisitions, making a name for himself until he no longer had a name to make. I was still living with Gavin in an apartment after I graduated college when I fell into my business deal with the bar. I had been wanting a place of my own, but with the money I was sinking into the buyout, I couldn't afford anything. When I stumbled upon this place, it was perfect. The previous owner had done a full remodel, so it was turnkey ready. I couldn't turn it down, especially with the housing market in the shitter. I tapped into my father's money, bought it, and never looked back.

"It's getting late," I tell her.

"You don't talk much, do you?" Her inquiry is laced with curiosity to get to know me.

"No."

"Yeah," she sighs. "I'll see you later?"

Knowing that her offer is probably the one with the least repercussions, I say, "I'll call you." This chick is a no strings girl. Perfect.

She stands up, and I walk her to the door, giving her a chaste kiss before she leaves.

It wasn't but a few days after I had Gina over that she called me. We've been getting together for the past couple of weeks. It beats having to go out all the time only to wind up back at square one. But the last time she came over, she wasn't so quick to leave. I know my reputation; girls know it too. But if this one thinks that she's gonna be the one to tie me down, she's got it all wrong.

I know I'm only making it worse as I lie here, watching her pad out of the room to go grab me a bottle of water. But what she gives me is what I need. So I take.

When she walks back into the room, holding my camera, she says in a flirty voice, "What kind of pictures do you have stored on this?" She slips back into bed, still naked, and I take the camera from her that I left out earlier today when I was taking pictures of one of Mel's friends. "You photograph people?"

"Mainly."

"Really?" she responds with a hint of excitement.

"Really," I say.

I've always loved art, and photography is something I started tinkering with while I was in college. I don't do a whole lot of it, but what little I do, I enjoy. It's nice to have something to focus on every now and then.

Rolling onto her stomach, she peers up at me and whispers, "Photograph me."

I step out of the bed and find my boxers slung across the room. Pulling them on, I walk back to where she's lying and focus on her back. She has a curvy figure, which enhances the sway of her spine. I zoom in and start shooting. She has no idea what I'm photographing when I stop snapping and look up to see her giving seductive looks into the camera. I don't want her face, just the line of her back.

After I get my shots, I instruct, "Sit up and face away from me."

She does, swinging her legs over the edge of the bed. I swipe the hair off of her shoulder and bring it around to her other shoulder. I then get a few shots of the contour of her neck. I'm close, and when I move to the side of her, she shifts to kiss me. There's something to it. Something I'm not feeling.

Quickly pulling back, I say, "You shouldn't do that."

"Why?"

"Because I'm not that guy."

"I don't believe that," she whispers, and it's now that I see the shift. I see the strings. "You've had me in your bed for weeks now," she says.

I don't want to make her feel like crap, but I don't want to lie either. "This isn't my bed."

When she shakes her head, confused, I clarify, "My bed is upstairs."

"Oh." Her brows dip slightly, and I can see the letdown.

Gavin warned me about Gina, but I blew it off. He found out from her friend, Ashley, that we were getting together regularly. He told me that Ashley said that she wasn't interested in anything casual with me. I blew it off 'cause Gina has never led me to believe otherwise. Until right now.

"I thought we were on the same page here," I say.

"No. We are."

"You sure? I'm not into hurting people, but I'm not into feeling either. So if that's what you're—"

"No," she says, cutting me off. "I just misread you for a second, that's all. No strings."

Her words aren't the least bit convincing. I see right through her, and wonder why she would put up with me for a hopeless shot at something more.

"I should probably go," she says as she starts putting her clothes back on.

When she's dressed, she makes her way out of the room, down the hall, and to the front door. Grabbing on to her arm, I turn her to face me. "Hey. I just need to be clear with you that this is all it will ever be."

"It's clear," she responds.

"Good."

After she leaves, I start to grow more uncomfortable with the situation. I shouldn't have kept calling her. I thought I was upfront but wonder if I was just leading her on. I stew around, thinking about how to remedy this situation, when my phone buzzes with a text.

Can I see you tomorrow?

Shit. She couldn't even wait an hour. Yeah, I've gotta cut this off. Looking at the time, I can't believe it's still so early. Not that our escapades last any longer than they have to. She likes it fast and rough, which works perfectly for me since that's all I like. But shit has to come to a stop. Sooner than later. The last thing I need is a clinger.

It's been a few days since Gina was here last, but tonight she stopped by unannounced, saying she had a stressful day at work and just wanted to vent. She spent the whole time bitching about some chick she works with that's friends with some other chick Gina used to be friends with. Shallow shit. Shit I couldn't care less about. But the fact that she thinks coming over here and talking to me about this crap is okay is all I need to know. She's getting attached, and it's time to cut it off. The calls, the texting—it has to stop.

I grab my keys and decide to head up to the bar to get some work done and to get my mind off of the situation I've created with Gina. When I walk in, it's packed. A good thing for a Monday night. Today was the first day of classes at UW, so business will pick up as it usually does after the summer. I look over to Mel, but she's too tied up with customers to notice me. I make my way through the crowd to the back stairs.

I stop in Michael's office to pick up some paperwork from him. When I go into my office, I look at the schedule he set up and start working on inventory orders. Time passes, and I'm deep into paperwork. We're closed, and I can hear the bar girls downstairs, laughing loudly as they clean up.

"Bad news, man," Max says as he walks into my office.

Looking up from my desk, I lean back in my chair, tired, and ask, "What is it?"

"The band that was scheduled for this Saturday night cancelled."

Throwing my pen across the desk, irritated, I gripe, "What do you mean they cancelled? They've been on the books for weeks."

"I don't know. I didn't take the call, but we've gotta fill that slot in the next couple of days. Classes at U-Dub started today, so this weekend is gonna be busy as hell."

"Shit!" I pause for a second, frustrated as fuck. "It's too late to do anything about it tonight. I'll make some calls tomorrow and try to get another band booked. Oh, hey, if those fuckers call back, tell them to find another bar to play."

"Right, boss. You heading out soon? It's past midnight already."

"Yeah, in a little bit. I need to finish this paperwork and I'll be gone. Go ahead and go."

"See you tomorrow, man."

"See ya."

Time passes as I try working on the inventory supply sheet that I need to get in to our liquor distributor, but my mind is elsewhere. I really need to call Gina and tell her it's over.

A clatter outside snaps me out of my thoughts. I look down at my watch to see it's nearing one in the morning. *Shit.* When I start packing my things up to head home, I hear more commotion from outside. I shake my head, knowing it's probably just some drunk guys heading back home from a party. People are always cutting through the back alley.

I start locking everything up and make my way downstairs to the back door. "Crap," I mutter to myself, realizing I left my cell in my office. Walking back up the stairs to my office, I grab my phone off my desk.

I hear screaming.

A girl screaming.

chapter five

"FUCK!"

Bolting out of my office, I haul ass downstairs to the back door and out to the small employee parking lot in the alley.

"God, please! Stop!" a girl shrieks.

Before my mind can process what I'm seeing—naked girl, guy's hand between her legs, girl thrashing, screaming—the bastard smashes his fist into her face.

Adrenaline fires through my body, and I run. Yanking the guy off her, I start slamming my fist into his face over and over. I completely lose control of myself and relentlessly whale on him. I'm gone. My knuckles start to burn as the flesh begins to split open. He manages to get a few swift hits to my jaw and ribs, which allows him a quick moment to work out of my grip and flee.

Before I can charge after the guy, I catch a glimpse of the girl. It doesn't take but a second for me to refocus. She lies there, unconscious, bare, with her clothes ripped off of her. My stomach convulses at the image before me. I slowly approach her—scared—and kneel down next to her. Terrified to touch her, I take off my shirt and cover her naked, battered body. Her face is covered in blood and dirt, skin scraped off on one side and the other is already swelling from where the fucker's fist landed. Her knees are ripped open and covered in gravel. The blood between her thighs tells me exactly what that piece of shit did to her. My heart thuds hard in my chest, and my gut is in knots.

I pat my pockets for my cell, but it's not on me. I must have dropped it as I ran out here. Not wanting to leave her, I look around and spot her purse. I lean over and grab it in search of her phone. When I find it, I swipe the screen and dial 911.

My voice is shaky as I try to talk to the dispatcher. My thoughts are all over the place, and I stumble as I try to answer all of her questions. When she tells me that the police and EMTs are on their way, we disconnect. I slip the phone back into her gold purse and slowly zip it up as I stare at her. I don't want to look, but I can't stop.

As I sit next to her, she lies there, breathing peacefully. Whatever is running through her head right now has to be a million times better than the hell she's going to wake up to.

What the fuck just happened? I watch her. I don't know what else to do. She is so small, and when I look at her tiny hands, her nails are shredded. *Shit.* She fought. She had to have fought hard. The thought nearly makes me vomit, and when I shift my eyes away from her hands, I notice a little tattoo. An outline of a heart—simple black ink—on her lower hip that's still exposed. Sliding the shirt over a little to cover it, I finally hear the sirens in the distance.

"Thank God," I whisper.

The sound grows louder the closer they get, and when the red and blue lights strobe across the parking lot, I reluctantly stand to my feet, but don't move away from her until the EMTs approach.

"Sir, can you step over here?" an officer asks.

We walk over to the rear of his vehicle. He pulls out a clipboard from the car and opens the top of it, retrieving a few forms.

"I need to get your statement," he says while he organizes the papers under the clip. "You're the one that called 911, correct?"

"Yes, sir," I answer before turning my head to see them sliding the girl onto a backboard, strapping her down. She's now covered in a large blanket, and it's at this moment that I feel. Pain. Sadness. Anguish. It wells up and floods my eyes. I don't even know this girl, but I hurt for her.

"Where are they taking her?" I ask the officer.

"You know her?"

"No." I turn back and watch as they slide her into the back of the ambulance. Another EMT is collecting the scraps of her clothes that remain on the ground.

"Can you tell me what happened?" the officer asks.

"I don't know," I mumble. I can't seem to get my head straight. *What just happened?*

"Take your time. It's important that we get a detailed account of everything that occurred. Everything you saw."

"Is she gonna be okay?" I ask as the ambulance drives off.

"Do you need to sit down, sir?" I faintly hear the officer as he speaks. Pressure on my arm shifts my focus when I realize he has his hand on me, guiding me to sit in the front passenger seat of his vehicle. The door shuts, and I lean my head back against the seat. I watch him walk in slow motion around the front of the car. He sits in the driver's seat next to me.

"Start from the beginning."

"He raped her," I choke out.

"My God."

"He beat the shit out of her, Mom. I can't close my eyes without seeing it," I tell her. "I couldn't sleep at all last night. I just laid in my bed, replaying it over and over."

"Is she okay?"

"I don't know. They wouldn't tell me anything. It feels weird . . . to see that and not know."

"Are *you* okay?"

"How am I supposed to answer that? What do I say?"

"Say how you feel," she tells me with worry and concern.

"I feel sick. What he did to her . . . what I saw . . ."

"I hate that I'm not there."

"It's okay, Mom. I don't really wanna talk anymore; I just needed to tell you. I needed to tell someone."

"I'm so sorry that you had to see something like that," she says.

I've seen so much shit in my life. Too much to ever forget. You can't rid your mind of images that burn themselves into who you are. I've had to watch my mother getting the life knocked out of her at the hands of my father more times than I ever want to remember. But I also have her sounds etched in me. Her painful, pleading screams.

And now . . . now I have this girl. This unknown. A Jane Doe. Blanks that will never be filled.

"I'm so sorry I couldn't protect you better," I confess.

Guilt.

"Ryan, don't."

The knot in my throat makes my words painful to say, but I force them out. My confession. "I was right there. I heard the noise out back. If only I would have gone out there. Fuck, why didn't I go out there sooner?"

"How could you have known?"

"I could have stopped it. Prevented it. But instead, I ignored it." The whole time I knew there was someone back there, and I ignored it. I sat in my office while that girl fought so hard she had no nails left. "What have I done?" I breathe out, suddenly feeling the weight of the responsibility I now hold.

"You didn't do anything," she tries assuring me.

She's right. I didn't do anything. Nothing. I close my eyes, and I see it. The blood between her legs. The image I know will forever be with me. I toss the phone aside and rush to the bathroom, vomiting. Expelling the toxins, but not the images. Those remain.

Needing to move, needing to get out of the house, I drive up to work. I park out front and head straight to my office, shutting the door behind me. *Fuck. Why am I here?*

There's a knock on the door, and when I say, "Come in," Max walks in.

"Everything all right, boss?"

"Shut the door," I tell him, and he does.

"What's going on?"

I didn't get any sleep last night, and I feel like shit. I know I look it, and by the expression on his face, I know he sees it.

Folding my hands, I lean forward on my desk. "Something really fucked up happened here last night after you left."

He walks over and takes a seat in the chair.

"A girl was raped out back," I tell him.

"Christ," he breathes as he drops his head.

I don't say anything else. I'm not sure I can. We both sit there in silence as seconds pass by.

I finally speak the words that have me so fucked up. "I saw her."

"The girl?"

"I heard her screaming, and when I went out there, he was on her." I spin around in my chair and stare out the window that overlooks the street in front of the bar as it rains.

"I want cameras installed back there," I tell him.

"I'm on it," he responds. "You okay?"

Still facing the window, I admit, "I don't know, man. That shit was fucked up."

"Did the police come?"

When I turn back around to face him, I answer, "Yeah. I gave my statement, and they took her to the hospital."

"Was she okay?"

"I don't know. He beat her pretty badly. She was unconscious."

"And the guy?"

"Don't know. I had him for a moment, but I couldn't keep him in my grip. I couldn't leave the girl though, so he fled." I take a minute before telling him, "I don't want the girls walking to their cars alone. You and Chase need to be with them when they leave. Got it?"

"Of course." He takes a moment before asking, "You sure you want to be up here?"

Looking up at him, I let him know, "I can't be home. I need a distraction."

"I hear ya," he says then switches the topic, which I'm thankful for. "I talked with Chase earlier today, and he says he knows of a band that's gotten pretty popular lately. If you're tied up, I can get Michael to see about getting them booked for Saturday."

"Nah, I'll take care of it. Is he here?"

"Yeah, I'll send him up," he says as he stands and starts walking out. When he gets to the door, he turns back and says, "I'm here, man. If you ever . . ."

"Thanks." His friendship is genuine. It always has been. I might not be a man of many words, but I stop him before he walks out and tell him, "I really appreciate it," because I feel like he should know.

He gives a nod, accepting my words, and turns to head downstairs.

I spend the next few hours reviewing the financials and going over payroll. It's Michael's responsibility, but I absorb myself in it for the distraction. I speak with Chase, and I am able to contact one of the guys from the band he suggested and get them booked.

Filing some papers away, I notice the sky darkening. Somehow the day has passed, and I still feel like I'm on autopilot.

"God, please! Stop!"

I shake my head, trying to wash out the shrill of her voice. The panic.

There's a soft knock on the door, and before I can say anything, it slowly opens.

"What are you doing here?" I ask when I see Gina step in and close the door behind her.

This is the last thing I need to deal with right now.

"I never heard from you last night."

"I wasn't feeling well," I tell her. "Look, things are getting a little weird, and honestly, I'm just not feeling right about what we have going on." I should have told her this the other day, but I know that I can't keep having her come around, thinking that this has any value in it.

She sits down and questions, "What do you mean?"

Getting up from my chair, I walk around to the front of my desk and lean back against it in front of her. I need to lay it out there honestly for her so that there isn't any confusion.

"I'm starting to feel like what's going on between us is exactly what I try to avoid. It isn't working for me, and I'd feel like an ass if I led you to think otherwise."

She looks hurt. Proof that she's feeling too much. She plays it off well though when she says, "Well, it was fun while it lasted, right?"

I don't respond as I watch her stand up.

"Keep my number though," she says before turning her back to me and walking out.

I release a deep breath. A failed attempt to make me feel better. Truth is, I'm in a haze. A cloud. My mind is elsewhere—it's back in the alley. But that girl's cloud is no doubt thicker and darker than mine right now. *Why didn't I go out there sooner? What if I had?*

"Fuck!" I grit out, slamming the door shut, knowing I'm at fault, that I could have done a lot more if only . . .

chapter six

WALKING THROUGH THE back stockroom, I ask Mel, "Hey, have you seen Max or Michael?"

"Michael left a couple hours ago, and last I saw, Max was out back talking to Traci," she tells me as she loads her arms with a case of beer, almost dropping it.

"Here. Give that to me," I say, taking the heavy case from her. She follows me as I walk out and set the beer on the bar top. The place is starting to fill up. The band that Chase had recommended played here last week and really drew in a crowd. I went ahead and booked them again for tonight, and he wasn't kidding when he said they were well-known around here.

I help Mel behind the bar, stocking the beer while she serves customers. When I catch Max heading to the front door, I shout, "Hey, Max!"

"What's up?"

"You seen the guys yet?" I ask.

"Chasten is here, but I'm not sure about the others. Everything cool?"

"Yeah, if you see them before I do, tell them I need to talk with them before they go on tonight."

"Got it," he responds as he turns to head out to work the door.

I need to snag this band while I can. Getting them in a contract will alleviate the hassle of trying to book bands week after week. The guys seem pretty cool from what I got to know of them last week, which wasn't a whole lot aside from the guitarist, Mark. He stayed late that night, drinking and bullshitting with me and Gavin after he was done playing.

Gavin tried leeching some chick on him but got a good laugh when he found out that his hard work with the girl went down the shitter when Mark told him he was gay. The look of disappointment, that he wouldn't have another wingman, was something I selfishly took pleasure in.

He's been on my case lately since I ditched him a couple of times this week. I haven't been in the mood to go out just to find someone to use simply to make myself feel better. Ever since I saw that girl being attacked a couple weeks ago, it feels wrong.

"You got everything covered, Mel?"

"Yeah, Ry. I'm good," she says, and I start making my way to the back.

I spot Chasten and Mark talking and announce, "Hey, guys, can you get the others and meet me in my office real quick?"

"Yeah, no problem," Mark says and then introduces me, "Ryan, this is Jase, the guy I was telling you about."

"Jase, man, good to meet you," I say as I reach out to shake his hand.

"Yeah, same here," he responds with a note of hesitation, but I don't stick around 'cause I've gotta get up to my office to talk with everyone. "I'll catch up with you later, man."

"Sounds good," he says.

Once all the guys are in my office, I offer, "What do you guys think about making this gig a steady one?"

"You serious?" Aiden, the front vocalist, says.

"Yeah. I'm not gonna bullshit you guys. Finding bands is a bitch, so if you're in at a ten percent pay increase, all you have to do is sign this simple contract and we're good."

I take the contract and hand it over to Aiden, who reads through it first and confirms, "I'm in," before handing it over for the rest of the guys to read. When they are all on the same page with the agreement, they sign and call it a deal. Adding them to the payroll takes a load of stress off my back and simplifies my job even more.

When they leave to head down, I stay a little while to enter their info into our database. I write a note to Michael about the new payroll and employee additions and toss it on his desk before heading down. The band is just about to start playing when I make my way over to the bar and see Jase.

"Jase." I move to stand next to him, leaning my elbows on the bar top. "You ever been here before?"

"Yeah. This crowd is a bit insane though," he replies.

Watching Mel hand him his beer, I tell her, "Don't bother with a tab, Mel."

"Thanks, man," he says as he turns to me.

"No problem."

The music starts blasting through the bar when I say, "Your guy's band is fuckin' popular. They brought in a huge crowd last time they played here as well."

He keeps his focus on the stage, not responding, so I leave it and ask, "You go to school together?"

"Yeah," he hollers over the music. "We're in the same major."

"And what's that?"

"Architecture."

"That's cool," I say and then turn to yell for Mel to grab me a beer.

"Ryan! Fuck, man!" I hear Gavin shout with irritation from behind me. I turn and question, "What?"

"That chick you flung on me last night was a fuckin' psycho."

Ignoring his complaint, I turn to Jase and say, "Jase, this is my dick of a friend, Gavin."

"What the fuck ever," Gavin says as he laughs. He looks to Jase and warns, "Watch out for this dipshit, and don't let him hook you up with anyone. His matchmaking skills suck balls."

"Find your own ass, Gav. I'm not your fuckin' hookup," I let him know because I'm not into his game tonight.

"Not anymore. What the hell has happened to you lately?"

"Nothing. Just sick of wasting my time."

I take a swig of my beer while Gavin tells Jase that I've been acting like a pussy, so I clip him and say, "Don't waste your time buddying up with Jase."

"Sad. I guess it's just me trying to get laid, huh?"

"Sorry. Looks like it," Jase tells him, laughing.

"Are these the same guys that played here last week?" Gavin questions.

"Yeah, they're gonna be playing here every Saturday now. They just signed a contract earlier."

"They looking for a label?"

"Ask this guy. I have no clue," I say as I tip the neck of my bottle towards Jase.

"You know them?" he asks Jase.

"Yeah, but I dunno," Jase responds. "I only know Mark and just met the drummer."

"This is Mark's guy," I tell Gavin.

He gives me a nod then says to Jase, "Yeah, I met Mark the other day. Cool guy."

I turn away from them and spot annoyance. Gina. She's here. I don't even say anything when I walk away and head toward her to see why she's here. She texted me the other day, but I ignored it. So seeing her here, when she knows this is my bar, winds me up a bit.

Weaving through all the people, I see her turn and spot me. Her smile grows along with my irritation.

"Hey, you," she says as she slides herself up next to me.

"What are you doing here, Gina?"

"Just wanted to see what you were up to," she flirts as she runs her hand down my stomach, straight towards my pants.

I grab her wrist and stop her, snapping, "If I were up to anything that had to do with you, you would know about it. You being here is just desperate." I suddenly feel like crap for my harsh words. But part of me, the big part of me that used to use people like I used her, pangs with regret.

She doesn't respond, and I know I just humiliated her, so I let go of her wrist and say, "Look, I'm sorry. I'm a dick, I know. But I need you to leave," before walking away and back to the bar.

"What the hell is up with you? That chick was all over your nuts,"

Gavin says when I approach, knowing damn well who Gina is.

Ignoring him, I lean over the bar and holler, "Mel, I'll be up in my office. I'll come down later, okay?"

"Yeah, no problem, Ry," she says as she's mixing a drink.

Gavin catches my arm and questions, "Dude, seriously? What the hell is going on with you?"

Jerking out of his grip, I tell him, "Not in the mood."

"You haven't been for a couple weeks."

"You wouldn't get it, man," I exhaust and then walk up to my office.

Shutting the door behind me, I flop down in the chair, and close my eyes.

"You're the one that called 911, correct?"

"Where are they taking her?"

"You know her?"

"Is she gonna be okay?"

"Take your time. It's important that we get a detailed account of everything that occurred. Everything you saw."

My eyes pop open, wanting to escape the scene that keeps creeping in. The rouse of my stomach weighs heavy when realization hits. My actions, though acted out on a totally different scope, are the same as that fucker who raped that girl. We both used someone to satisfy some twisted piece of our self with completely selfish intent. I've used so many people just to numb the ache I feel. *Fuck.*

I wonder how many girls I've hurt. I know of one for sure. She's downstairs, and I just made it worse after throwing my words at her. *What's wrong with me?*

I'm restless. It doesn't matter where I am, it follows me. But I need to move, so I head back down, not knowing what else to do with myself. Mel can see right through me, telling me to go home. I say a few quick words to Jase and then do as Mel says and go home.

chapter seven

IT'S BEEN ALMOST two months since I last saw Gina when she came by the bar. It's been longer than that since I've been with a girl. Ever since that night in the alley, my mind hasn't been in the same place. The images have started to fade, but I just can't continue to use people like I used to. When I think about going out to find a hook-up, all I think about is that fucker I let get away.

I never heard anything regarding my statement that the police collected, so I have to assume no charges were ever pressed or else I'm sure I would've been contacted by now. I've only ever mentioned that night to my mom and Max. I never told Gavin about what I saw. He's still running his game and has been hanging out with a couple of his buddies more often, now that I've been lying low. It doesn't bother me because I've been spending more time with Mark and Jase.

The two of them are pretty solid guys. Although they're a few years younger and still in college, I feel like we're on more of the same level than Gav and I are. We've been hanging out and hitting the gym on a pretty consistent basis. That, along with seeing them every Saturday night at the bar, we've gotten to know each other pretty well.

I ran into Gavin the other day, and he gave me some extra tickets to check out a band that Sub Pop is considering signing, so I invited Jase and Mark to meet me at The Crocodile where this band is going to be playing.

I throw on a black v-neck t-shirt, a pair of dark-wash jeans, and black boots. Running my fingers through my long hair that is due for a trim now that it's hit my ears, I grab my keys and head out to my jeep. When I drive past, there is a huge crowd gathered where the legendary club is located. I park down the street and walk. Once inside, I make my way backstage where Gavin told me to meet him.

"Ryan, you made it," he says when he spots me.

"I told you I would."

"Just didn't know if you were gonna bail." He gives me a friendly clap on the shoulder and then introduces me to the band before we head out to the bar to get a drink.

Mark is already there waiting on the bartender to take his order when we approach.

"Hey, man," I say to him. "When did you get here?"

"Just now. I ran into Mel's husband a second ago."

"Zane's here?" I ask.

"Yeah. He's around somewhere."

"Mel here?"

"I don't think so. Haven't see her," he responds.

"Mark, good to see ya," Gavin says after he's done putting in our drink order.

"You too. Thanks for the tickets."

"Have you ever played here?" he asks Mark.

"Shit, I wish," he laughs. "No, man. Before our gig at Ryan's bar, we were just taking anything we could get."

"I hear that a lot. Well, I gotta go meet a couple guys from work. I'll see you all in a bit," Gavin says as he grabs his beer and walks off.

I pick up the bottle that's on the bar for me and take a long pull when I notice Jase isn't around.

"Where's Jase?"

"Got tied up with a friend. He's not gonna make it," he tells me.

"Tied up all night?"

He nods his head and explains, "Yeah. She's going though some heavy stuff, so Jase is staying the night with her." He takes a sip of his beer, and then adds, "He'll be at the bar tomorrow though."

We sit and talk for a while as we continue to drink. The place is packed tight with people, and when the band takes the stage, the music blasts through the place, and there's no more talking.

When Zane finds us, he orders a round of Jack and Cokes, and it isn't long before Mark orders his second. He isn't paying attention when I hear a woman's voice in my ear.

"Did you need anything?" she asks as she sets Mark's drink down. She's hot. Deep tan, long brown hair, tall, and wearing a short black skirt that raises the question of what's underneath.

I shoot her a smile and nod my head for another Jack and Coke. She turns to make my drink, and maybe it's the alcohol that's already flowing through my veins, or maybe it's the fact that I haven't gotten laid in months, but lust takes over.

My indecent thoughts are interrupted when Mark stumbles into me, laughing uncontrollably. As soon as he opens his mouth to slur out his words, it's clear he's wasted.

"How many of these have you had?" I say as I point to his drink in hand.

"Check this shit out," he nearly shouts as he shoves his phone in my hand, and before I get a full view of what that chick is doing with a glow stick, I shove it back to him, saying, "Dude, that's fucked up."

Mark can hardly catch his breath, he's laughing so hard, and I'm getting a kick out of the show he's giving me, so I sit back on my barstool and laugh right along with him. Mark is a cool guy, much more outgoing and funny than Jase is. Jase tends to be more on the serious, calm side.

"I bet you'd like to be that glow stick, huh?"

"That's sick," I cringe. "Plus, you're the one that has that crap stored on your phone. Does Jase know that you get off on that?" I tease.

"You wanna see what I get off to?" he says as he starts scrolling through his phone.

"No. Love ya, man, but I don't wanna see what you're about to show me," I say as he starts pushing his phone towards me.

"Oh, come on," he taunts while I continue to laugh at him. "I know you think Jase is hot."

"What?"

"He's totally hot. Admit it! HOT!"

Holy shit this guy is far gone.

"I'm not saying a word," I tell him.

"That's a yes," he says in a singsong voice followed by an evil smirk. He's trying to get a rise out of me, and I find it pretty hilarious.

"It's not a yes."

"The dude is sexy as hell and you know it."

He's not gonna stop, so I just give him what he wants, and for the hell of it, I say, "Yeah, man. He's hot."

"I knew it!" he shouts through his laughter as I shake my head at all the attention he's drawing to himself. He takes a moment and then, with a straight face, sets his phone on the bar next to me and says, "Here, you enjoy glow stick girl. I gotta take a piss," before stumbling off.

I turn around in my seat and don't touch the phone. The girl behind the bar looks over at me and gives me a small grin. When she walks over, she looks at my glass and asks, "More?"

"I'm good."

"Your friend's pretty funny."

"My friend is pretty drunk," I tell her, and when she rests her forearms on the bar top and leans forward, she asks, "And what about you?"

"I'm in total control," I say in a low voice, and when I do, I get the look I was hoping for.

"We'll see about that," she says as she pulls back and walks away to continue helping customers.

I sit there for a while and nurse my drink. When I realize how much time has passed and Mark hasn't returned, I grab his phone to go look for him. I spot him towards the back of the club, talking with Gavin. When I step up to them, I hand Mark his phone and tell Gavin, "Call this guy a cab, will ya?"

"Yeah, man," he responds. "You heading out?"

"Not yet," I say, heading back towards the bar, but before I can get there, I run into the bartender as she's about to turn down a hall that looks like it leads to an office.

"You leaving?" she asks.

Wanting to know if this is worth wasting my time, I cut to the chase. "Not if you don't want me to."

An all-too-transparent grin spreads across her face before she says, "Come here."

She takes my hand and starts leading me down the hall. Opening a door to a small closet, she pulls me in and shuts the door. I can't see shit; it's so dark, and the smells of bleach and booze fill the room.

Her body presses up against mine, and I begin running my hands up underneath her top, grabbing her tits. She starts kissing my neck while fumbling with my pants, and the heat takes over. We begin moving at a frantic pace. I yank her top up and pull her bra down as she shoves her hand down my pants, fisting me tightly.

I throw my head back and hear the *thunk* as it hits the wall.

"Are you okay?"

"Is she gonna be okay?"

Suddenly, I'm back in the alley as my words play back in my head. This chick is all over me, but in an instant, my mind is somewhere else completely. Somewhere it hasn't been in a long time. I try to shake it off, but it's so dark in here that my eyes have nothing to focus on.

"God, please! Stop!"

"Stop."

"What's wrong?" she pants.

"Stop," I repeat and move her away from me. Buttoning up my pants, I know I can't do this. I know that she isn't, but all that floods my head is that this girl could be *that* girl. And what the hell am I doing with her anyway? Using her for a quick fuck to satisfy some sick need I have that I can't seem to get rid of? *Fuck.*

"Did I do something?" she questions, and the last thing I wanna do is make her feel like shit.

"Pull your shirt down," I tell her before opening the door. When I do, I look at her and say, "You didn't do anything. I'm just . . . I just can't do this. Sorry." I turn to walk out and back into the club. I don't even look for the guys; I just head straight out the door and continue to my jeep, to head home and jerk off.

I sit in my office at the bar, drinking beer and not getting much work done at all. Last night was messed up, and I know I can't be doing that shit again. I need something else to focus on, so I spent the morning clearing the images off of my camera and loading them onto my computer to start editing and enhancing. I figure I can work on those to suck up all the free time I seem to have on my hands at night now.

When the door to my office opens, Jase walks in.

"Hey, man," he says as he walks straight to the little fridge that's behind my desk that I keep stocked with beer.

"Can you toss me another one of those?" I ask as I throw my empty bottle into the trash.

Handing me the beer, he asks, "So, you been up here all day?"

"Pretty much. You know how Saturdays are—crazy as hell all day." I take a drink and then add, "Missed you last night. Mark said you got hung-up with a friend."

"Yeah, sorry about that. She's been going through a rough time, so I decided to stay with her last night."

"You missed a pretty good show," I tell him, referring more to his boyfriend than the band.

"That's what Mark said."

I can't help but laugh at the thought of him last night. "Your guy's a little crazy when he drinks."

"I'm not even gonna ask, but he was in a piss-ass mood when I saw him earlier."

"Ha! I bet. He drank a shitload, probably hungover as fuck."

We both laugh when the door opens and Mark walks through. "What's so funny?" he asks as he stands there.

"You, man," I chuckle.

"If this is about last night, I don't even wanna know what the hell I did. My head has been pounding all damn day, and now I have to play for the next two hours."

"Go find Max. He always has earplugs," I tell him.

"Not a bad idea." Turning to Jase he asks, "Can I stay with you tonight? My new roommate just decided to tell me that he's throwing a party tonight."

"Yeah, no problem."

"Well, I gotta run. I just wanted to catch you," he says before he heads back down to the bar.

I start to shut down my computer when I ask, "So, is she okay?"

"Who?"

"Your friend. The one you were with last night," I say.

Standing up, I grab my beer and start to head out when Jase stands to follow me, saying, "She's getting there."

chapter eight

SINCE THAT NIGHT at The Crocodile a few weeks ago, I've been out of touch with Gavin and spending more time with Jase and Mark. I hit the coast the other week to get a break and do some surfing. I've finished working on several of the photos that were stored on my camera and picked up the mattings from the framer yesterday. I don't know what I plan on doing with them, but I spent so much time working on them, that I felt like I needed to finish them off by getting them matted.

I had to call Tori to let her know I wouldn't be making it back home for Halloween. I know she was disappointed, but Michael has had some things come up at home and hasn't been at the bar very much. Not sure what's going on with him, but I've had to be at work more than usual, covering for him.

Pulling out my phone, I open up my video chat and connect to Tori. I promised her I would call to say hi to Connor and Bailey before they leave to go trick-or-treating.

The call connects, and I see Tori when she answers.

"Hey, Ryan," she says, and I can tell she's flustered. The background is filled with the kids laughing and being loud as usual.

"You look rough," I tease.

"Connor had a Halloween party at a play date we went to earlier, so the kid is hopped up on sugar," she explains.

"Put him on. I wanna see him."

"Connor, Uncle Ry is on the phone," she hollers over her shoulder, and I see a miniature Superman with not-so-miniature padded muscles.

"Buddy! When have you been hitting the gym?" I ask.

"I have muscles," he says and then crooks his arm up with an intense face and growls, "Arrrr."

I laugh at his mock intensity and say, "Dude, you're getting bigger than me."

"Show me yours, Uncle Ryan," he requests.

Crooking my arm in the same way he did, and giving him the intensity right back, I flex and growl, "Arrrr."

His eyes grow big, in the way only an innocent four-year-old's can, and he says, excitedly, "Wow!"

"Yeah, man. Keep lifting those weights, and you'll get big guns like me."

"You're ridiculous," Tori teases as she pops her head back on to the screen.

"Hey, Connor. Don't let your mommy make fun of me, okay?"

"Mommy, be nice," he scolds her, and I let out a laugh.

"Where's your sister, little man?"

I watch as he runs off, red cape flying behind him. These kids have a way, in a matter of only seconds, of putting me on top of the world. I doubt I'll ever have any of my own, so I try to get the most out of my cousins' children.

"Here she is," I hear Tori say as she hoists Bailey onto her lap.

She's the sweetest little poodle I have ever seen. "My little angel's a poodle," I say, not able to wipe the smile off my face. The cuteness is too much.

"Say hi," Tori encourages, as Bailey raises her chubby arm and waves at me before pointing, pressing her finger against the screen and saying, "Wy-Wy."

"That's right. It's Ry-Ry," she says to Bailey.

"Give Ry-Ry kisses," I tell her.

Perking her lips, she gives me an exaggerated, "Muah."

"Muah," I give her back in return.

"Are you coming for Thanksgiving?" Connor asks when he walks up, standing next to Tori and Bailey.

"Yeah, buddy, I am. Promise! I miss you guys so much, you know that?"

"I miss you too," he says.

"Well, I'm gonna let you guys go. Make sure you get a ton of candy. Be good for your mommy and daddy, okay?"

"Yay! Can we go trick-or-treating now, Mommy?" Connor asks with way too much energy, and I have no clue how Tori and Trevor are gonna get through Halloween without the aid of alcohol.

"Yes, we can go. Say bye to your uncle."

"Bye, Uncle Ryan," he shouts before running off.

"Say bye-bye," Tori tells Bailey.

Waving her hand again, she says, "Bye-bye."

"Bye, sweetie," I tell her.

"We gotta go before Connor drives me crazy," I hear Trevor, Tori's husband, say as he walks up.

"Okay," she responds.

"Hey, Ryan. What's up?" Trevor says into the phone.

"Not much. Looks like you have your hands full."

"You have no idea. Get your ass here and help us out," he jokes.

"Soon, man. You guys have fun tonight."

"Same to you. Bye."

"Bye," Tori adds.

"Take it easy, guys," I say before disconnecting the call.

I take the next half hour to call my other two cousins and check in with their kids. Envy starts to move slowly inside of me, and before I let the feeling take over, I go upstairs to my room, blast some music, and hop in the shower. It's gonna be a busy night at work, and I don't need to be in a funk. I love my family, but the idea of having my own worries me. What I grew up with was far from perfect. I've never had to take care of anyone other than myself, aside from my mom. But she's a strong woman, always has been. I don't really know what it means to provide for someone else emotionally. Even if I did, I doubt I would be capable of it. I live a selfish life. I only take care of myself, and at times, I feel like I do a shitty job of it.

After my shower, I grab a bite to eat and watch a little TV. I find myself focusing on the rain outside rather than the show that's playing. It's pouring as I stare out the solid wall of windows. I've always loved the weather here, never getting tired of the constant rain.

My phone rings, and when I look at the screen, I see Max's name.

"What's up?" I say when I answer.

"When are you getting here?"

"What time is it?"

"Almost ten. We're already at capacity, and I feel like shit," he complains.

"I'm leaving now," I tell him as I drag myself off the couch and start heading out.

I walk out to my black Rubicon and decide to grab a coffee before I go to the bar. It's gonna be a late night, and Mel sucks at making coffee. I drive around the corner and spot a coffee shop right off campus. Not that hard to do since there are coffee shops on every street corner.

Throwing the car in park, I step out into the heavy rain. I keep my head down as I walk to the door, getting soaked. When I go inside, my phone buzzes with a text from Jase. He's asking when I'm heading in, and I'm distracted when I walk up to the counter.

I briefly notice a girl sitting on a stool behind the register, reading a textbook, studying. She sees me and hops up as I turn my attention to the drink menu on the wall.

"Hey, what can I get for you?" she asks softly.

Still looking at the drinks, I settle on my usual. "Uh, just a twenty coffee. Black," I tell her when I start typing my text back to Jase.

"Easy enough."

On my way now. Give me 15min. Busy?

Insane.

"That's one ninety-three," she says as I shove my cell into my pocket.

Pulling out my wallet, I hand over a five. Finally, not distracted, I look at her. I think I know this girl 'cause something about her seems familiar. I stare, trying to pinpoint who she is, but she's so different from any girl I would ever go for, so I'm just confused. She has a small frame, can't be much taller than five feet. Her hair is a deep brown like mine, and it's pulled up, messy, on top of her head.

"Everything okay?" she asks, catching me staring, as she hands me my change. This girl has me so caught off guard that I don't even realize I haven't responded when she questions, "Anything else?"

The small features of her face, aside from her large hazel eyes, seem more delicate with her fair, almost porcelain-like skin. Not my usual type, but God she's pretty.

"Um, no. No, that's all," I say like an idiot, and I can tell I'm freaking her out when she nervously takes a step back and stumbles into her stool.

I turn to leave before I say anything else that makes me look any more like a moron, but dammit if I can't help turning to look at her a couple more times before I leave. As soon as I step out in the rain, it hits me.

"God, please! Stop!"

Snapping my head back to get another look at her through the rain-covered window, I feel my heart begin to pound. Her back is to me, so I can't see her face. *No. It can't possibly be her. What are the chances? There's no way.* Fuck, my head is really playing with me tonight. I get into my jeep and start driving. My mind is consumed with crazy thoughts that I need to dispel because none of them make sense to me.

She's tiny . . . just like the girl from that night. But her face . . . there's no way I could even make a comparison because that girl's face was so badly beaten and covered in blood. There's no way to know what she really looked like.

All I can think about is that night in the very alley I just pulled into and parked. I get out of my car and walk over to the dumpster, to the spot I found her. I rack my brain, but there are no real details I have to link these two girls.

The images flood through me. My stomach knots up, and I feel sick. That was a fucked up night that I wish I never had to witness. I wish I could forget. I wish my head would stop messing with me. *Give it up, man. Let it go. Just forget about it.*

When I head inside, I go straight to my office. Sitting down at my desk, I pick up my desk phone and call downstairs to the bar.

"Blur," I hear Mel answer.

"Mel, it's Ryan. I just got here. Can you send Max up to my office?"

"Sure thing."

Hanging up, I sit there, anxious for some reason, but need to talk, and Max is the only one who knows about that night.

"Hey, boss."

I look up at Max as he walks in, and when he sees me sitting there, soaking wet, he questions, "You okay?"

"Do you think it's possible . . . to connect two strangers . . . I mean . . ." I trail off, not able to get my thoughts together to form a coherent sentence.

He takes a seat and says, "What are you talking about?"

I breathe in a deep breath and let it out slowly when I tell him, "I went to grab a coffee before coming here, and the girl working there . . . well, when I saw her, my mind went straight to the girl from the alley. The girl who was attacked here a few months ago."

"You think it's the same person?"

Raking my hand through my wet hair, I fist a lock of it in frustration before saying, "I don't know. I mean, I guess for a second I did, but really, the chances would be next to nothing, right?"

He doesn't respond. I know I must sound crazy, but I continue anyway, "It's probably not. That girl was unrecognizable. I don't even know why my mind even took me there."

"I think it makes sense."

"You do?"

"Yeah. After it happened, it really bothered you that you didn't ever know what happened to her. If she was even okay. So it makes sense that your mind would still need closure and that it would come out at random times trying to make that connection." He takes a moment in thought, and then adds, "I dunno. Just my thought."

"No, you're right. I'm probably subconsciously trying to put an end to that situation. But that's not gonna happen. I just need to let it go."

"Yeah, 'cause you're gonna do nothing but drive yourself crazy," he says.

"That chick probably thought I *was* crazy. I couldn't stop staring at her, like some sick perv or something," I joke, trying to lighten the mood.

"She wouldn't be too off base," he throws back at me, and I laugh with him. "I gotta get back to the door. You gonna come down soon? Jase is here with Zane."

"Yeah, I'm gonna try and dry off, and I'll be down."

He turns back before walking out of my office and says, "That girl, whoever she is, I'm sure she's okay. It's been almost three months since it happened."

"Yeah. You're probably right," I reluctantly agree.

"Like you said, just let it go."

chapter nine

I COULDN'T LET it go like Max told me, like I told myself even. I went back to Common Grounds a few days later. Back to the coffee shop and she was there. I just had to see her again. Had to get the confirmation that there wasn't a connection. The only similarity I could see was that the two girls are petite. That's all. No other connection. So now . . . now I let it go.

Before I hit the gym today, I need to stop by the bar to pick up a few files that I have to drop off to my accountant. It's early in the morning, so when I get there, I'm surprised to see Mel's car in the back lot. Walking in, it's dark. None of the lights are on, and the sun hasn't started to rise under the cloud-covered sky.

When I walk out from the back, I see Mel sitting on top of the bar with her legs crossed, nursing a cup of coffee.

"Hey," I say softly as I approach her.

She looks up and that's when I see the tears streaming down her cheeks.

"He's gone," is her only response, and I know she means her husband. Zane, back when he was her boyfriend, played gigs here every now and then. They would hang out here a lot, and when Mel needed a job, I brought her on.

I sit on one of the stools in front of her, and when she looks down at me, she explains, "They signed the deal, and he left."

"Why aren't you with him?"

As she lets her head fall, she says, "Because he didn't want me to be."

I clasp my hands together, not knowing what the hell is wrong with Zane. "I don't understand."

She wipes the tears from her eyes and sits up a little straighter. "He said he was tired of hearing me bitch about something he'd been working towards for years. He knew I didn't want to move to L.A. My life is here. My whole family is here. I didn't want to leave all that, but it was pissing him off. He feels like I'm not supporting him."

"Do you support him?"

"I don't know, Ry. Honestly, between you and me, even though I don't want to be alone, I'm kinda glad for the break. We haven't been on the same page for a while." After she says this, she hops down behind the bar and walks over to refill her cup of coffee. "Want some?" she asks.

"Yeah."

She pours it black, like I always take it, and sets it in front of me as she stands on the opposite side of the bar top.

Taking a slow sip, I then ask, "So, why are you here?"

"I just had to get out of the house, and I knew nobody would be here. That is, until you decided to crash my pity party," she jokes, laughing at herself. "What are *you* doing here at six a.m.?"

"I'm on my way to the Athletic Club. I needed to pick up some paperwork to drop off to my accountant later today."

"You coming back?"

"Nah. I'm gonna take the day off."

"That sucks," she complains.

"Why?"

"'Cause Michael is boring as hell, and he's been in a shit-ass mood the past few days," she tells me.

"You know why?"

"Not for sure, but I overheard him on his cell the other day."

"Eavesdropping?"

She starts laughing, and says, "You know it! But anyway, from what I heard, I think . . . and don't say shit about this, Ryan. Got it?" she warns.

"Yeah, whatever. Just say it."

"I think his wife is having an affair."

"That fuckin' sucks."

"I know. But you didn't hear that from me, and I'm not saying it's true. It's just what I pieced together from what I heard," she defends.

"Well, for his sake, let's hope you're full of shit and your eavesdropping skills suck."

The ringing of my phone interrupts us. I look to see that it's Gavin before I answer.

"Hey, what's up?" I say.

"You at home?"

"No. I'm at the bar."

"Even better. I wanted to drop off some tickets that I can't use for a concert this Saturday."

"Dude, I'm not in the mood to hit up another club."

"No club, man. It's a private concert over at Spines."

"The book store?" I ask.

"Yeah. My boss gave me a few tickets, but I had another work thing come up, and I have to bail. You want 'em? It's for The xx. They're in town for a couple days before their overseas tour," he explains.

"Yeah, definitely, man," I respond. That's one band I've been dying to see, but never had the chance before now.

"Great. Don't go anywhere. I'm about five minutes away."

"Later," I say before hanging up.

After Gavin dropped off the tickets the other day, I wound up running into Jase when I made it to the gym. We spent a couple hours lifting, and he took a few of the tickets off my hands, saying that he would go with Mark and bring along one of his friends, who I assume is the same person that Mark was telling me about a while back. We also made plans for the three of us to head down to Mount Rainier to go hiking next weekend.

After talking to my mom, I'm now running a bit late. I take a quick shower, fix my hair, and throw on my typical dark jeans, grey shirt, and black boots. I make my way downstairs and grab my jacket before I head out. The night is misty as I drive across town to Spines, a local book and music shop that has managed to stay open and alive while most of the others have closed.

I swing by one of the many espresso stands in this town and grab a cup of coffee. I don't plan on drinking tonight, so I need the buzz of caffeine to keep me going since I was up so early this morning.

I pull into Spines and park my jeep. When I walk in, the place is dimly lit, with people everywhere. The store is small, so even though there aren't too many people here, it feels like there are. The band is already playing, and I leave my jacket on one of the coat racks before spotting Mark.

He's by himself, hanging out next to a low bookcase, and I make my way over.

"Hey, Mark."

He turns around and claps my arm. "Hey. You just get here?"

"Yeah. Where's Jase?" I ask.

"He's grabbing a few beers," he responds. "There he is," he says as he looks over my shoulder.

When I turn around, I'm taken by surprise when I see that Jase's friend is *her*. Her eyes catch mine, and she coughs against the sip of beer she just took, looking shocked to see me just as I am her.

She's dressed casually in a long-sleeved, white v-neck shirt, jeans, and worn, brown leather boots that run up to just below her knees. She stands small next to Jase when she speaks, "You again."

"You two know each other?" Mark asks.

"Not really," I answer, finally breaking my eyes away from her.

"He's come into Common Grounds a couple times to get coffee. How do you guys know each other?" she asks Mark.

"He owns Blur, where the band has been playing lately."

"And the guy who gave me the tickets," Jase says and then turns to me and adds, "Thanks, man."

"No problem at all," I tell him and flick my eyes over to the girl, only to see she now has her back to me as she listens to the band play.

Mark and I go find a table to sit down while Jase stays back for a moment with his friend. *I still don't know her name.* I sit down and look over at them. She looks upset when Jase reaches down and holds her hand. I immediately wonder if her mood has something to do with me being here. *God, why am I feeling so self-conscious?*

They start heading over, and she sits down across from me, slipping her leopard scarf off her neck and laying it on the table. The two times I've seen her, her hair has been pulled up, messy, but for some reason, it looked good on her. Tonight it's down, thick and layered. She pulls my focus when she says, "I'm sorry, but I never caught your name."

I smile. I don't know why, but something about her is intriguing, so I let it linger on my lips when I tell her, "Ryan. Ryan Campbell."

"I'm Candace." She looks at my cup of coffee, and teases, "Ever drink anything besides coffee?"

"I work a lot of late nights."

"So, Ryan," Jase starts, "Candace will be graduating this year as well. She's a dance major."

I notice Candace looking annoyed at Jase for saying that, but I shrug it off and ask her, "Dance. What kind?"

"Ballet," she tells me and then takes a sip of her beer.

"Can't say I know anything about that," I say with light laughter.

"It's okay. Nobody ever does."

This chick seems way out of the realm of the girls I normally talk to. *A ballerina?* I find myself wanting to keep her talking because I like the sound of her soft voice. "So, I take it you're the best friend who loves this band?" I question, nodding my head toward the stage.

She shifts, almost nervously, in her seat. "Yeah."

She looks over at Jase, who is sitting next to her, and I watch their silent exchange, unsure of what's going on. I think back to what I've heard Mark say about this girl.

"She's going through some heavy stuff. . . . Jase is staying the night with her."

Watching her peel off the label on her beer bottle, I try to push whatever is bothering her away, and ask, "So, Candace, what do you plan on doing when you finish school?"

When she looks up at me, I notice the coloring of her eyes. They're a light gold that almost flake into a deep emerald green.

"I hope to dance professionally while time allows. Not sure where that will happen. New York was always the plan, but I'm not so sure now." She looks over to Jase again, but he's engrossed in a conversation with Mark. I notice one of her brows twitch up. Nervous tick. I wonder if she's even aware that she has one.

Man, this girl is easily distracted. I bring her back in when I say, "I love

New York. You ever been?"

"Yeah, several times. It's a great city. I actually lived there the summer before my senior year of high school. I had a scholarship to one of the conservatories in the city."

"So, your parents just let you live there alone for the summer?" I ask, surprised that a parent would let their teenage daughter run off to New York City all by herself.

"Umm, yeah. My parents are . . . well, not your typical involved parents," she tries to explain.

Moving past it, I continue, "So, that's where you'd like to wind up then?"

"That's the plan," she says with a hint of a smile, which also reveals a hint of a dimple in her right cheek.

Damn, I feel like a deprived puppy, infatuated over details of a chick I don't even know.

"What are you two talking about?" Mark asks, and I take the distraction, answering, "New York City."

The band starts in on another song, and I know it well—'Infinity.' I watch Candace stand and walk back to the bookcase Mark was at earlier. The three of us get up and follow her over, and I step next to her, resting my elbows on the bookcase as I lean forward.

I listen to the music, all the while feeling her eyes on me. I know I shouldn't look, but I do anyway, catching her. She gives me a soft grin and turns her attention back to the band.

Mark and Jase head to the bar, and I notice Candace taking a step back. I don't look at her. I don't want her to know that I want to. I'm not even sure I know why I want to—but I do. I keep my eyes forward, and when I can't help myself, I turn my head back to see her eyes locked on me. She's flustered as she stumbles around and runs smack into Mark, whispering something in his ear. Mark turns to Jase, and when he does, Jase steps over and asks her, "You ready to go?"

Mark looks to me and says, "Hey, man. It was good seeing ya. We'll catch up later this week."

"Yeah, catch you later," I tell him and then hold my hand out to Candace. "I'm glad I ran into you again."

Hesitantly, she slips her hand into mine, and I like the way it feels.

"Yeah, it was nice," she says, quickly pulling her hand back and turning to leave.

Interactions with this girl are weird. Jase told me, when I gave him the tickets, that the friend he wanted to bring didn't do well with crowds. Maybe the small space was making her uncomfortable.

Looking over, I spot her leopard scarf still lying on the table. I go over and pick it up. The greedy man in me is happy that she left this behind, giving me an excuse to see her again. The pull of this girl has me confounded, and I know I should make the smart move and stay away.

chapter ten

COMING BACK FROM the gym, I finally make the decision to just go and see her. I could just as easily give the scarf she left behind the other day to Mark, but I keep holding on to it. I've never chased a girl. It's always been the opposite. But I'm curious to get to know her and that curiosity surprises me, but I decide to go with it.

I take my time getting cleaned up. I'm not even sure if she's gonna be at work, but I'll take the chance and stop by before I head into the bar for a few hours. When I walk downstairs, I look out the large windows to see that it's another rainy day. Grey and cold.

Shrugging on my jacket, I walk over to the coffee table to grab her scarf. Her scent is encased in the fabric. Light and floral. I laugh at myself for being so shot with this girl that I actually smelled it the other night.

When I pull up to the coffee shop, I park my jeep and pick up the scarf. *Why am I nervous?* Walking through the door, I immediately spot her and happiness swarms, thankful that she's here and I didn't miss an opportunity to see her again.

She's talking to a chick with crazy hair and wiping down the counter. She doesn't see me, but her friend does and gives me a smirk as she continues to talk to Candace. Finally, looking over her shoulder, she spots me as I make my way to the counter.

"You're gonna get an ulcer," she teases, and it's cute as hell.

I laugh and say, "I didn't come for coffee," as I hold out the scarf.

"Oh, I thought I had lost this," she says as she takes it from my hand. "Thank you."

"No, you left it on the table, but you rushed out so fast, I didn't have a chance to catch you."

Her head lowers, embarrassed I'm guessing, before quietly saying, "Sorry."

"No need to apologize."

She takes her apron and sets it on the counter when I ask, "Are you taking a break?"

"Um, no. My shift is over."

"Perfect timing." I smile and take this opportunity to spend a little time with her. "Want to have a quick drink?"

"She'd love to," her friend says over Candace's shoulder, and when Candace shoots her an irritated look, she starts to stumble over her words.

"Actually, I . . ." she starts, but never catches her sentence when she finally gives up. "Sure," she resolves. "Let me go grab my bag."

I watch as she walks away, and her friend steps up with her tattoo-covered arms and asks, "What can I get you?"

"Coffee. Black."

She gives me a wink as she turns to get my drink, and when she returns to me, she sets down two cups. "Candace likes hot tea," she says with a smirk, and I wonder why she's so eager.

When I pull out my wallet, she tells me it's on the house, and I go to find an empty table by the front window. Sitting down, I look up to see Candace walking towards me. She eyes the drink that's on the table, and I tell her, "Your co-worker said you like hot tea."

"Oh, thanks," she says as she takes a seat. "She's actually my boss. Roxy." She seems nervous, just like the other night. She takes a sip of her tea and focuses her attention out the window.

"Did Mark tell you we are heading down to Mount Rainier on Saturday?" I ask to try and draw her attention back to me.

"Yeah, Jase mentioned something like that to me."

"You should come with us."

"I don't know . . . I have a lot of studying I need to get done."

I can tell she's avoiding me. I'm not used to girls not being interested in me, but this one . . . she hardly seems to notice me.

"Well, if you change your mind, we are heading out in the morning around eight."

"How did you know I would be here today?" she asks, changing the subject on me.

"I didn't," I say, trying not to be too transparent. "I just thought I would stop by, and if you weren't here, I was just going to leave your scarf with whoever was working," I tell her, not needing her to know that I'd been hanging on to that scarf for days, hoping when I did stop by that she would be here.

"I didn't mean for that to come out rude."

"It didn't."

Watching her small hands clutch her cup of tea, I shift my eyes up and ask, "So, what are your plans for the rest of the day?"

"I have class in a couple hours, then I go to studio until five o'clock."

"Studio?"

"It's dance class."

Nodding, I question, "You do that every day?"

"Yep. Two hours a day except for Tuesdays and Thursdays, which are three hours. But I tend to go in on the weekends as well for extra practice."

"That's a lot. When do you have time for anything else?"

"I don't," she says with a shake of her head.

"That bother you?" I ask, wondering if she does anything besides school.

"No . . . Why?"

"I don't know. When do you ever get down time?"

"I don't. But I love dance, so I consider that my down time. It relaxes me."

"So school and work, huh?"

She grins and responds, "Pretty much."

"That doesn't sound like very much fun," I joke.

Shifting her eyes down to her hands, she doesn't respond. She's difficult to read, so I back pedal, and say, "I didn't mean for that to come out like it did."

Her eyes catch mine when she looks up. "I just like to stay busy."

I back off the questions and offer her another tea, but she says she has to get going.

"I'll walk you out," I tell her. We slip on our coats, and she gathers her things before we head out into the rain. She nods her head to a sporty, white Acura, and we start walking that way.

"Thanks for the tea," she tells me as she opens her door and slides into her seat.

Gripping the frame of her car, I lean in slightly and say, "Think about Rainier."

"I will," she tells me with fake intent, but I laugh it off and shut her door before she pulls away.

I hop into my car and head to the bar. When I get there, I go upstairs to my office and run into Max in the hall.

"Hey, boss. I didn't know you were coming in today."

"Yeah, I need to get a few things done. I'm not staying tonight though." I had made plans with Mark and Jase to go shoot pool, so when I leave here I'm gonna hang out with Jase at his place before we head out.

"You seem upbeat," he remarks as he follows me into my office.

Shutting the door, I walk over to my desk and take a seat. "So you know that girl from the coffee shop I told you about the other week?"

"Yeah."

"I had coffee with her this morning," I tell him.

"What? Why?"

"Turns out, she's friends with Jase and Mark. I ran into them a few nights ago, and she was with them."

He looks at me with a curious tilt of his head, and I admit, "It's weird."

"What's weird?"

"Her. I mean . . ." I can't seem to find the words to explain what I'm trying to say, but he jumps in and asks, "You like her?"

"I don't know her," I immediately defend, knowing that the first word that came to my mind was yes.

"You don't have to know her."

Sitting back in my chair, I tell him, "There's this pull she has that no one has ever had on me before. But she's not like any of the girls I've ever been with."

He laughs at me and says, "That's probably a good thing."

I laugh with him for a second. "She's a ballerina."

"No shit? So why is she hanging out with you?" he teases.

"That's the thing . . . I don't know. She's really standoffish, and I can't figure out why."

"Maybe she's just not into you. That is possible, you know?" he jokes with a knowing grin on his face.

"Yeah, man. I know," I give him right back. "But it isn't that obvious. More like she's got thick boundaries. I dunno."

"You gonna see her again?"

"I have no idea. She's very evasive."

"I think I like this one," he says with a cocky smile.

"Oh yeah. Why's that?"

"She doesn't stroke your ego like most chicks do. She's gotten under your skin."

"She's not under my skin," I refute. But is she? Maybe he's right.

"Whatever you say," he sighs as he stands up and starts walking to the door.

Taking a swig of beer, I mindlessly watch Mark and Jase finish up their round of pool. My head is back at Jase's apartment where she is. She stopped by unexpectedly while Jase and I were hanging out. Flustered. Something had upset her from the time I saw her earlier today at the coffee shop. She didn't say anything, but I overheard her asking Mark if she could stay the night with Jase, which I find a little odd.

"So when did you see Candace?" Jase asks me, knocking me out of my thoughts.

"What?" I say as I grab my cue and chalk it.

"When you mentioned our hike."

"This morning. She left her scarf at the concert. I stopped by her work to drop it off," I explain right before I break.

Jase is protective over her. I see how he acts with her; I saw it the night of the concert. Holding her hand, touching her back—almost assuring her. Of what? I don't know. But I see it with Mark too. These guys care deeply for her, there's no question about that.

When I look up at Jase, he's staring at me, almost zoned out. "You're up," I say.

He moves to make his shot, sinking his ball into the side pocket.

"You guys want another bucket of beers?" Mark asks.

"Yeah," Jase tells him before Mark heads over to the bar.

I take this time to try and get a little more info on this girl, so when he lines up his next shot, I ask, "So, what's her story?"

"No story," is all he says and then misses his shot.

I walk around the table, looking for my play, when I try to casually ask, "You've known her a long time?"

"She's not like that, man. Not even close," he quickly responds, and I suddenly feel like I'm way out of my league. Jase doesn't know me like that, but knowing Gavin, I'm sure he's told Jase stories. By the time I met Jase, and even Mark, I had pretty much stopped fucking around.

I lean over the table, ready to take my shot, when I peek up at Jase, who's staring. "She's like a sister to me," he adds, and I know he knows I'm interested in her. And I also know that he doesn't think I'm good enough. *Maybe he's right.*

chapter eleven

CALL ME WHEN you get a chance.

I read the text from Jase while I'm working from home today. Our conversation a couple nights ago was a little awkward, so I'm curious as to why he wants me to call him. I don't waste any time thinking too much about it when I tap his name and it begins to ring.

"Hey, what's up?" he says when he answers.

"Not much. Just getting some work done. You?"

"Heading home from class," he says before adding, "Look, I'm sorry if I came across short with you the other night. I wasn't trying to make you feel like you couldn't hang out with Candace. I just get a little protective of her at times."

"No worries. I know the two of you are close, so I wouldn't ever . . ." I trail off, not even sure of where I'm going with this statement, but he cuts the silence and says, "Yeah, I know. But, hey, if you wanna come over tonight, Candace and Mark will be here. We're just gonna lay low and hang out."

"Yeah, man. I've got some things to take care of, but I'll stop by later."

"See ya."

"Later," I say and then hang up.

I spend the day taking care of a few work things. I'm trying to lessen the time that I have to spend up at the bar, so I've been getting most of my work done from home. Michael has been putting in the hours, and I feel I'm at a point where the bar is running smoothly without me having to be around all too often.

It's a little after eight when I head over to Jase's apartment building. When I get there, Mark lets me in, and I look over to see Candace wrapped up in Jase's arms on the couch. My head takes me to wishing it was my arms wrapped around her. I shut that thought down fast, but it lingers in the back of my mind. Truth is, I've never been that way with a girl in my whole life, so to see Jase have that with someone who's only a friend makes me a little envious.

He looks up at me when I walk by and says, "Hey, there's beer in the fridge. Help yourself."

Giving him a nod, I head straight into the kitchen to grab one. When I turn around to get the bottle opener, Candace walks in, holding an empty wine glass.

"Could you hand me a bottle of water?" she asks, and I open the fridge to grab one.

Handing it to her, I take the wine glass out of her hand, and with a smirk, I say lightly, "I thought you never did anything fun."

When I walk over to the sink to set her glass down, I hear her respond, "I never said that. I said I like to keep busy."

I turn around to face her and lean back against the counter. She stands there in what looks to be a pair of Jase's boxers and a UW t-shirt. Her hair is piled on top of her head again, and I don't think she could look any more attractive than she does right now—relaxed.

"Did you have a better day today?" I ask, knowing that the last time I saw her something had clearly upset her.

"It was okay. How about you?"

"Hung around my place for the most part."

"Candace," Jase calls from the other room, "It's back on."

She doesn't say anything else to me, she just turns to go sit next to Jase on the couch, pulling her legs up as he wraps his arm back around her. I sit on the other end of the couch while Mark is comfortable in a chair.

I turn to the TV to see some drunk jackass climbing his kitchen cabinet just to have the whole structure rip off the wall and fall of top of him, dishes and all. When I hear Candace laughing, I turn to her and ask, "What the hell are we watching?"

"'Ridiculousness,'" she answers, keeping her eyes fixed on the TV.

Jase looks over her to me, and says, "For such a refined girl, she loves this show."

"You're the one who first told me about it," she accuses him.

"Just ignore their banter," Mark says to me. "They both love trash TV."

I listen to the three of them go back and forth and their connection seems strong with one another. I know that Mark just recently started dating Jase, so to see them interact like this, like they've known each other for years, makes me realize just how alone I am. The deepest friendship I feel like I have, outside of my mom and Tori, is Max. But it's nothing like these people have. So I sit here, drink my beer, and enjoy the company.

Before I call it a night, I catch Candace quietly sneaking off to go to bed in Jase's room. My curiosity grows as to why she's staying here, but I don't ask. Mark tells me to meet him at his place in the morning to pack up for our hike as I head out.

After about three hours of hiking, we start making our way down Tolmie

Peak. It's been raining for the better part of the hike and the four of us are cold and drenched, and when I hear, "Crap!" I look back to see that Candace has fallen in the mud.

Jase and Mark are further down the trail, so I go back and hold out my hands for her to grab on to, pulling her out of the mud.

"You're a complete mess," I tease.

"Yeah, I know," she says, almost unfazed that she's covered in mud.

She keeps her hold on my hand, and I like it, as we make our way down to the bottom. Once there, she lets go as we continue our trek back to the car. Jase and Mark are several steps in front of us, lost in their own conversation, and it's not long before Candace starts talking. She seems more comfortable around me, but we did just spend most of the last three hours hiking without the company of Jase and Mark. They've been keeping their distance from us.

"So, how did you come about owning a bar?" she asks me.

"Just kind of fell into it. When I graduated college, the economy was starting to decline, and I couldn't find a job. So, when I found out that the previous owner of that bar was about to shut the place down, I worked out a deal with him and was able to do a slow buyout."

"You went to U-Dub?"

"Yeah, I graduated back in 2007."

"So, that makes you . . . ?" she pries.

Laughing at her, I answer, "Twenty-eight."

"What did you study?" she continues, and I like that. For once, I'm not having to struggle to get her to talk.

"Business Finance. So, it wasn't too far out of reach that I would come to own my own business."

"You enjoy it?"

"I do. When I did the buyout, I changed the whole place out and created a new vibe for it. It wasn't before long that the business was taking off quicker than I expected. At this point, the staff pretty much runs the place, and I have a trustworthy manager, so my schedule is very flexible."

"Sounds like the perfect job."

"You ever been there?" I question.

"No. I don't really ever go out." She smiles and adds, "I'm sort of a workaholic. Jase is always nagging me about that."

"Well, you should stop by sometime."

"Yeah. Maybe," she says, but I know she doesn't mean it.

Laughing, I joke, "You're full of shit, aren't you?"

"Yeah. Maybe," she repeats as she laughs with me. Her smile is perfect and that shallow dimple makes it hard to not lean over and kiss her, but this girl has walls—unbreakable ones—that I'm determined to start chipping away at.

Getting back to Mark's house, we each take our time showering and cleaning up.

Mark and I tune in to the Washington vs. Colorado football game. Mark throws a couple of logs onto the fire, and when I pull out my cell to order some pizzas, I see Candace walking through the room and straight into the kitchen. I'm distracted when the line is answered and I'm putting in the order.

"What kind of pizza do you want, Candace?" I holler into the kitchen.

"I don't care. I'll eat anything at this point," she tells me as I order the pizza.

She walks back into the room carrying a bottle of wine to share with Mark. Those two have proven to be the wine drinkers of the group while Jase and I watch the game and toss back a couple beers, but apparently I haven't kept that good a count 'cause Jase has definitely had more than a couple when he starts screaming at the penalty that was just called.

We all laugh at him when he runs into the kitchen to answer Candace's phone that starts to go off.

He walks back in, total mood shift, mouthing 'I'm sorry' as he hands Candace the phone.

"Who is it?" she asks quietly.

"Your mother."

She looks irritated when she heads outside to the patio to take the call.

"What's that all about?" I ask Jase.

"Her parents are assholes to her," he blurts out and Mark butts in, almost scolding when he calls his name, "Jase."

He looks to Mark and says, "What? They are. They treat her like shit and she doesn't deserve it."

Getting up from the couch, I head into the other room where I watch her through the glass French doors. I can hear her yelling, "Of course this is my fault, right? You are unbelievable, Mother!"

"It's not my fault. I swear."

I watch my father's glare as he spits out, "It's never your fault, you piece of shit," before grabbing the broom and whacking the wooden handle into my back. I hear the wood splinter and crack when it slaps across my skin, sending shards of heated pain up my spine.

"Get your ass up and walk to school. Don't ask me to drive you again. You miss the bus, you walk."

Coming out of my thoughts, I fight the urge to storm out there and take the phone from her so she doesn't have to listen to whatever her mother is saying to her that's making her so upset. Instead, I stand here and watch her. When she hangs up and shoves the phone in her pocket, she sits back in one of the chairs and stares up into the sky. She's sad. And it's not just tonight. Underneath the few conversations that we've had, I can see it buried in her. On the drive to Mount Rainier this morning, she must have had a nightmare or something when she fell asleep in the back seat of the car while Mark and I were up front. I didn't want to give it too much attention because I didn't want to embarrass her, but she was scared. She was in Jase's arms in a matter of seconds, and now, watching her staring into the blackness, I feel there's more to her than she lets on.

When she stands and turns, she catches me watching her, but I don't even care. I open the door and ask, "You okay?" because I really need to know.

But when she blows it off and says with mock humor, "My mother's lost her mind, that's all," I see her walls.

"Wanna talk about it?" I keep on, trying to chip as she walks past me.

Turning to face me, she casually says, "Nothing to really talk about."

I want to touch her, just brush her cheek, something, but I don't. Being with her today, talking with her, laughing with her—she's different. Sweet, funny, athletic, and soft. God, she's soft. But it's more than that; she has depth to her. A depth I've never seen with the girls I've been with. Not that I've been with them in a way to even notice if they did, but they all seemed so shallow. Even though she doesn't mean to let on, I can tell there's a lot going on under her exterior, and I feel this eagerness to explore.

When she walks back to Jase and lies down with her head in his lap, he asks, "What did she want?"

"She wanted to know when I would be home for Thanksgiving."

"When are you going to leave?" Mark asks.

"I told her I would be there Wednesday night. I'll probably leave Saturday morning," she answers as I walk across the room and take a seat on the stoop of the fireplace.

"When are you and Mark heading out?" she questions Jase.

"Our flight leaves around noon on Tuesday," he tells her.

"When do you guys get back?"

"Late Sunday afternoon."

"What about you?" she asks me as she rolls onto her side to look at me.

"I'm going to go spend a few days with my family down in Cannon Beach in Oregon. My aunts and uncles always come to my mother's house with my cousins for a big dinner."

"Will you be there for the weekend?"

"Nah," I tell her. "I'll come back home that night. My mom and her sisters spend the day plotting for Black Friday, so I always come back home and just lay low."

"Sounds like you have a big family," Jase says.

"Yeah, man, three cousins and between them they have seven little kids. I love them, but shit they're loud," I say as I laugh.

"Must be nice though. I'm an only child with no cousins. Small family," she tells me.

"So, it's just you and your parents?"

"Mmm hmm."

"They live very far?" I ask her.

"No. They still live in Shoreline where I grew up."

Knowing that Jase is going home with Mark to Ohio for the holiday, I offer, "Well, I'll be around."

When I see a hint of a smile, I feel like maybe I've finally made a nick in her exterior.

chapter twelve

WHEN I PULL into my mom's driveway, I see my family's cars littering the street. I'm the last one to get here, and when I walk in, the noise confirms it. I make my way through the foyer to the back of the house, and the scene looks the same as always. The guys are drinking beer and watching football while the kids run around and play. The girls are all in the kitchen with the babies, laughing and gossiping.

"Sweetheart!" my mom squeals when she notices me walking into the kitchen. She gives me a big hug, and I wrap my arms around her. I feel like a lot has changed since I last saw her, so I take the embrace I feel like I've been missing for these past few months.

We exchange our 'I love you's' and 'I've missed you's' before I say hi to everyone else. The kids are running wild, excited to see me, as I hand Tori the keys to my jeep so she can go bring in the bags of gifts that I always have every time I see the kids. I love spoiling them, but it's also my method of distracting them, and giving them new shit to play with keeps them occupied and out of their parents' hair for a while.

When Tori walks back in, arms full of gifts, she mouths 'thank you,' desperate for the reprieve. I laugh and follow her into the living room where all the kids are. I sit on the floor with them as they rip through the paper, finding puzzles, toy cars, dolls, and a small bubble machine that is sure to keep these kids entertained by the hour.

"And where did you plan on the kids playing with that?" my mother gently nags, in only the way a mom can do.

"In the playroom upstairs."

"Can I send you the bill for the carpet cleaning?"

Rolling my eyes at her, I say, "It's bubble solution, Mom, not a turd."

"What's a turd, Uncle Ryan?" Madison, my three-year-old niece, asks.

Smiling at her, I say, "It's poo poo."

"Ewwww!" she squeals through her fit of laughter, and her mom, Katie, scolds me with a simple, "Ryan!"

I love getting a rise out of my cousins when it comes to their kids. I swear they can take the most harmless thing and make a big issue about it.

"Katie, they know what poop is. Relax."

"Connor, you're a turd head," we overhear Madison say, and then I get *the look* from Katie as I start laughing.

"Hey, Tor. Can you grab me a beer?" I holler over to her while I sit next to her husband, Trevor.

"All these men are helpless," I hear her tell my aunts.

My mother gathers the older kids and takes them up to the playroom, and when Tori hands me my beer, she sits on the floor between her husband's legs.

After taking a long swig, Trevor asks, "So, man, how's life in Seattle?"

"Good. Can't really complain."

"I need to get some free time to get up there and run around with you for a few days," he tells me.

"You should. I haven't been going out as much as I used to though."

"Oh yeah?" he questions before Tori butts in and adds, "Why's that? You seeing someone?"

Shit. This girl sees right through me, so I quickly defend, not wanting to reveal my personal shit to anyone, "What? No. Just been busy and haven't had much time."

Narrowing her eyes at me, she says, "You lie. You told me last week that the new manager is freeing up your time and you haven't been going into the office as much."

"Dude, who is she?" Trevor pipes in with a nudge to my arm.

"Who's who?" my mother says as she walks down the stairs.

God, my family is nosey as hell.

"Nothing, Mom. They're just giving me crap."

My mom walks into the kitchen to join her sisters.

"Seriously, Ryan," Tori pries.

Looking down at her, I say, "Seriously," in an attempt to clip her curiosity.

"Don't listen to her," Ethan, Katie's husband, tells me. "Enjoy the freedom."

I give him a nod and take another sip of my beer, while Tori teases him, "That's nice, Ethan. Does my sister know that you miss your freedom?"

"Every. Single. Day," he jokes right back with her, and the three of them start laughing.

"I can't lie, I miss it too," Tori admits through her chuckles.

I listen to them while they complain, wishing I knew what it felt like to have what they do. Someone to share their bed with, kids, a family to make a home with. I've been alone my whole life. I feel like I don't have a choice. I see what my cousins have, and it seems happy. But what I had, what I *know*, is a stark difference. It was pure chaos and dysfunction. Misery. I fear I'll wind up just like my dad. I don't know what it takes to be functional with anyone. I was never exposed to what a healthy relationship looks like. But when I think about where I'd like to wind up in life, it isn't alone.

I head upstairs to my room to grab a coat and then make my way out to the back patio that overlooks Cannon Beach. It's cold and windy with a faint mist under the grey sky. I love it out here, so I sit and kick my feet up onto the wooden railing in front of me.

I hear the door open, and when I look back, I watch my mom join me as she sits in the chair next to me.

"What are you doing out here in the cold?" she asks as she ties her leopard scarf around her neck, and my mind goes to Candace for a second before I answer, "Just thinking."

"About?"

"I don't know. I guess nothing, really."

She shifts to face me, and I don't even hesitate when I open up to her. "I met someone."

"Really?" she says, completely surprised.

I laugh at her enthusiasm and shake my head. "Don't get too excited, Mom. I'm not even sure she notices me."

"Why's that?"

"I don't really know. She's hard to figure out."

"You meet her at the bar?" she questions.

"No. She isn't that type of girl," I say before taking a draw from my beer. "She's quiet. Reserved. She's studying dance at U-Dub." Looking over at my mom, she's smiling at me. "What?"

"Nothing. You've just never talked about a girl before."

"No girl has ever given me a reason to."

"So, have the two of you gone out yet?"

"No. Like I said, she's hard to read," I tell her as I look out over the water. "She's different than the chicks I normally go for."

"In what way?"

I turn back to my mom and respond, "In every way."

She sits back in her chair and asks, "What's her name?"

"Candace."

"Pretty name."

"She has these ticks though," I reveal.

"Like what?"

"She's awkward around crowds. She's close friends with a couple of guys I know, and they're really protective of her. I notice she stays the night with one of them a lot."

"Is she seeing him?" she asks, and I laugh.

"No."

"Why are you laughing?"

"'Cause they're gay, Mom."

"Hmm," is all she responds.

"I dunno. There're just these things I pick up on that she does, but she's so standoffish with me, and it's hard trying to get her to talk."

"Sometimes the things worth keeping are the things we have to work for," she tells me.

"Maybe," I sigh. "We'll see. I don't even really know her. It's just . . . I want to."

She reaches out and takes my hand as I look over at her and smile.

The house has been noisy and busy for the past couple of days. Every room is filled, and having the whole family here is always something I enjoy. I went for a run along the beach this morning, and when I came back, my mom and her sisters were already in the kitchen, preparing food for Thanksgiving dinner.

After getting cleaned up and heading downstairs, the kids are still lying on the floor, watching the Thanksgiving parade while my aunts are scouring the Black Friday ads with my mom. I swear, it's the highlight of the year for them. They take their middle of the night shopping seriously and always have a mission plan before heading out. I look over at the three of them, huddled over the paper, and laugh as I walk into the kitchen to make a pot of coffee.

"What's so funny?" my Aunt Carol asks.

Pulling a mug down, I say, "The three of you—plotting."

"Wanna be our driver?" she jokes.

"Sorry, ladies. You're on your own."

"Are you still heading out this evening?" my mom asks.

"Yeah. Even though the bar's gonna be dead, I let most of the staff take time off, so I need to be around."

I take my coffee and go sit with the kids as they watch with excitement when they see a cartoon character they know float by. I sit back on the couch and wonder about *her*, remembering what Jase told me the other day before I saw how upset she was after talking with her mom.

"Her parents are assholes to her. They treat her like shit and she doesn't deserve it."

I wonder how she's doing. I wonder how bad her parents really are. I wonder if they're the reason why she's so closed off. I wonder why I'm wondering so much, but I can't shake the fact that I need to know. For some reason, it bothers me, and I can't let it go.

I pull out my cell and go back and forth on whether or not I should take this jump. I don't know what I'm doing. I've never done this before. I've never wanted to. But now . . . *Fuck it, I'm jumping.*

Punching out a text, I send it to Mark.

Can you send me Candace's number?

I sit and wait. No response. I'm hoping he's busy with his family, and not asking Jase what they should do to keep me away from her. *Fuck.*

My phone starts vibrating with an incoming call, and when I pick it up, I see it's Mark. I answer the phone as I step outside.

"Hey."

"Hey, man. How's everything going?" he asks.

"Good. You?"

"Really good. Jase is with my mom, cooking, so I wanted to give you a quick call."

"Okay," I respond, waiting anxiously for what he has to say.

"I just wanted to lay it out there for you. Jase loves Candace in a way that's hard to explain. He worries. I do too. She's had a hard time this school year, and I don't want to see her get hurt."

"I'm sure you've heard things about me—"

"So you know where I'm coming from," he interrupts.

"It isn't like that," I tell him.

"Good."

Before we hang up, I get her number and store it into my phone. When I go back inside, I don't text her. I hold off. Instead I distract myself with the kids. I spend most of the day putting together puzzles and playing dolls with Maddie and Bailey.

After we all eat and I'm lying in my bed, trying to nap off my food coma, I stare at my phone. Looking at the numbers that are my connection with her. It's a little after six o'clock. The day is nearly over, so I fight against my apprehension and type out my text.

Got your number from Mark. Wanted to see how your Thanksgiving went.–Ryan

Lying there, I stare at the screen, waiting. I start questioning if that move was too bold for this girl. It's a move I've never had to question in the past. My moves have always been pretty blunt, so the fact that I'm worried about a text is unnerving. And then my phone buzzes with her reply.

I think we managed to fall into the universal tradition of holiday drama. :)

That bad?

I respond, naturally wondering what happened.

Kinda. Now I'm home with no food.

She's already back at her house. She wasn't supposed to be back for a couple more days, so whatever happened was bad enough that she bailed out early.

"Ryan!" I hear my mom call from downstairs. Setting the phone down, I go to the top of the stairs to see what she wants.

"What's up?" I call down.

"I need to run out and get some Pepto tablets for Connor. When are you planning on leaving?"

"I'll just head out now, if that's okay?"

"It's never okay," she teases.

I grab my phone and make my way downstairs. I feel like I'm rushing, saying goodbye to everyone, just so I can text Candace back. But once hugs are exchanged, I walk out with my mom.

"What are the plans for Christmas?" she asks.

"Same as always. I'll be here on the twenty-third."

"You drive safe, you hear," she tells me.

"I hear."

"Call me so I know you made it okay."

Nodding my head, I tell her I love her before hopping in my car and pulling out of the driveway. Before I'm even at the main street, I have my phone out and text her back while I sit at the red light.

Sorry, saying bye to everyone. About to head home myself.

Did you have a good time with your family?

Yeah, I did. Ate way too much. Feel like I need to hibernate.

LOL. Drive safe. Is it pouring where you are?

Not too bad. Try and have a good night.

Thanks.

I toss the phone onto the passenger street and drive the four hours that it takes to get home, all the while thinking about her.

chapter thirteen

I'M UP EARLY and just got off the phone with my mother. They haven't even made it home yet. They've been out shopping all night. It's almost embarrassing. I find myself rummaging through my kitchen, and something about eating so much yesterday has me craving another heavy meal.

I jump into the shower to get ready and remember what Candace texted me last night.

I'm home with no food.

When I get out of the shower, I take a shot and send her a text.

I am heading out for breakfast. Wanna join?

I pull some clothes out of my closet and get dressed when I hear my phone buzzing.

Sure. Where?

I'm a little shocked that she so easily agreed, but I go with it and don't even question her.

The Dish Café. 9:00?

See you then.

After another cup of coffee, I head out and make my way to the local dive. I'm there first, so I go ahead and order her a tea while I wait. I pick up the menu to give it a lookover, and when I shift my eyes up, I see her walking in. I notice her leopard rain boots peeking out underneath her jeans, and laugh to myself. This chick obviously has a thing for leopard.

"Hey," I say as she shrugs off her coat and sits down.

"Hi, thanks for inviting me. I literally have no food at the house."

"So, what did you wind up doing last night?" I ask.

Slumping back in her chair, she says, "I ate an old bag of popcorn and passed out on the couch."

"That's pathetic," I laugh.

Widening her eyes, she agrees, "My thoughts exactly."

When the waiter stops by and brings us our drinks, she eyes the tea he sets down in front of her and I say, "I ordered you a hot tea."

She looks a bit surprised when she replies, "Oh, thanks," before picking up her menu. I watch her and notice her eyebrow give a slight twitch, but she distracts me when she suddenly asks, "So, how was your Thanksgiving?"

"It was good. We did the typical family thing like we do every year. Mom and her sisters being loud and gossipy, cooking all day. I hung out with the guys and watched football while the kids ran around screaming and playing. My head was pounding by the end of the night."

She keeps a serious face when she says, "That actually sounds nice."

"Yeah, it is," I agree. "It's not too often that everyone can get together, so when it does happen, it's fun. Crazy, but fun."

"What can I get you guys this morning?" the waiter asks when he drops by again.

"Um, I'll have the two blueberry pancakes," she tells him as she hands him the menu, and then I place my order.

She takes a sip of her tea and then asks, "So how many nieces and nephews do you have?"

Setting down my coffee, I say, "Three nieces and four nephews all under the age of five." I smile when I add, "I'm not lying when I say it's loud and crazy."

When she doesn't say anything in response, I ask, "So, you're an only child?"

"Yeah. I have a pretty small family. My grandparents on my father's side died when I was in high school, and I have never met my mother's parents or her sister. My father is an only child as well, so it's just the three of us."

"Quiet."

"Hmmm . . ." is all she replies before switching the topic back to me. "Is your mother out with the crazy Black Friday crowd today?"

"God, you have no idea. She and my aunts go bat-shit over the sales."

When the waiter stops by and drops off our food, Candace lets out a satisfied sigh that I find humorous as she inspects her pancakes. She picks up her fork, and she must be hungry by the look on her face.

"That's a shitload of food. You gonna be able to eat all that?" I ask.

Eying me, she cuts a huge piece off and for such a sophisticated looking girl, she shoves it in her mouth, giving me a gratified nod, and I literally laugh out loud at the scene she's putting on.

"So, is all of your family in Oregon?" she asks while she eats.

"Yeah. I grew up there."

"Why didn't you ever go back after you graduated?"

"Because I bought out the bar. It was too good an opportunity to pass up. But honestly, Cannon Beach is a small town. I love Seattle and had already been here for four years and felt pretty settled. So I stayed," I explain. "My mom had a hard time though. She had hoped that I would eventually move back, but it's been ten years since I've been here, so she's accepted that this is my home."

"You two sound close," she says before taking another bite.

"Yeah," is all I respond when I take a sip of my coffee and continue to eat.

When Candace tosses down her fork and leans back, almost painfully, in her seat, she closes her eyes and lets out a groan that I laugh at.

"I can't believe you ate all that. You sound like you're about to die," I tease.

"You have no idea," she says as she opens her eyes.

"You gonna be able to walk, or will I have to carry you?"

Shifting around in her seat, she tells me, "Honestly, I really need to walk this off."

"Come on, let's get outta here," I say as I stand up, not wanting to become a victim of a missed opportunity. I toss some cash onto the table and reach my hand out for her to take, and she does.

Walking her out into the rain, I nod my head over to where I'm parked for her to follow.

She stops in her steps and asks, "What?"

"I know you don't have shit to do today, so come on," I say as I walk over to my Rubicon. When I look back at her, she's still standing there. "Come on," I repeat.

"Where are we going?"

"I'll figure that shit out when you get in."

Wanting to keep Candace around for most of the day, I took her to the aquarium. I knew we could easily burn a few hours there, and I was right. She seemed relaxed and had fun, but now I'm sensing tension from her. We just left her house after grabbing a few groceries from the store. I could tell she was uncomfortable with me being there.

As I'm driving her back to her car that's still at the restaurant, she watches the rain out the window and quietly says, "Thanks."

"For what?"

"Today. I had fun hanging out," she responds as she looks over at me.

"You should say yes when I ask you to go running with me tomorrow morning."

"Is that you asking me or telling me?"

When I look over at her and give her a smirk, she starts to giggle as she says, "Okay then."

Satisfied with her answer, I repeat her words, "Okay then."

Feeling a little more comfortable talking with her after spending the day together, I decide to ask her about what happened with her parents. So when I turn into the parking lot, I put the jeep in park and sit for a moment. The rain is coming down hard, beating against the steel. Turning to face her, she looks at me when I say, "I didn't want to say anything earlier, but I can't help but wonder about what made you come home yesterday."

She shifts to face me and lets out a sigh, leaning her head against the headrest. "I got into a fight with my parents. Some pretty nasty things were said, so I just left."

"You guys fight a lot?"

"My whole life," she tells me. "My mother is a difficult woman to be around. She doesn't approve of the way I want to live."

"What do you mean?" I can't imagine what this girl could possibly be doing wrong to earn her parents' disapproval.

"My parents are more concerned about their social standing than my happiness. So, having a daughter who wants to be a dancer and isn't engaged to be married is not a good look for them."

"That's pretty shitty."

"I'm used to it," she mumbles, and I hate the fact that this has been going on so long that she expects it.

"No one should be used to that," I tell her softly. "They should be proud of you. I've only just met you, but you're pretty great from what I know so far."

She fidgets with her hands, seeming uncomfortable with my words, but I needed to say them.

She keeps her focus on her hands when she speaks again. "I had always hoped that somewhere beneath their hard exterior that they would be proud of me, but after last night, I now know that they aren't." When she looks back up at me, she looks abashed as she tells me, "My mother actually said she was embarrassed by me."

Jase was right; her parents are pieces of shit. I can't even help myself when I lean into her, and slide my hand over hers. I want to do so much more, but I leave it at this. She stares at our hands, and I can sense her tensing up at the contact.

She sits up and pulls her hand out from under mine—flustered—she grabs for the door handle, but it's locked. I hit the switch when I see her panic.

"Thanks," she whispers before abruptly getting out of my car.

I watch her and wonder what's causing her to flip moods in a mere instant. Fumbling with her keys, she finally gets in the car and starts it up. She quickly glances over at me, embarrassed, and I hate that. All I can manage to make sense of is that her parents have fucked with her head so much that she's become removed from feeling emotions. I get it. That's been me my whole life, but now, with her, I find myself wanting to feel instead of running away from it.

I was nervous about meeting up with Candace this morning to go running. I was a little unsure of how she would react to me after what happened yesterday in my car, but she didn't seemed fazed by it, so I moved past it, and we spent a good hour running around campus and her neighborhood. She kept up with my pace, and I really enjoyed working out with her. I don't even think she noticed how distracted I was though, trying to sneak a peek at her whenever I could. She's small but there's no doubt that this chick is in extreme shape. Her legs are insane, and in her tight running pants, I couldn't keep my eyes off of her.

And now, sitting up here in my office, I can't keep my mind off of her. I start packing my things up to head out early. It's Saturday night, but being the holiday weekend, the place is dead.

"Hey, man," Gavin says when he bursts into my office. "You leaving?"

"Yep."

"We going out?"

Standing up, I start heading out when I tell him, "No. I'm gonna go home and just chill."

"Are you serious? Dude, you avoiding me?" he asks as I make my way downstairs.

"No. I just have other shit going on, that's all," I explain. He wouldn't get it if I told him, so I don't.

He continues to follow me to the back door, but before I can open it, he steps in front of me and snaps, "Seriously. What the fuck is going on?"

"Nothing, man. Don't take it personally."

"Kinda hard when I'm the one you're avoiding," he says.

Taking a moment, I explain without telling him too much. "Gav, I'm almost thirty. I'm sick of going out all the time to just fuck random chicks. I'm tired."

He doesn't say anything. He's the same age as me, and I know he's perfectly happy doing the shit that he does, but it doesn't make me happy anymore. It never did make me happy; it only made me numb. Stepping to the side, he walks away, throwing a, "See ya," over his shoulder before I walk out to the parking lot.

Heading home, I decide to stop and grab a pizza and some beer to take back to my place. When I get back into my jeep, I start driving home, but quickly find myself taking a few new turns. I'm not ready to go home just yet as the urge to see her again takes over, and I wind up pulling into her driveway behind her car.

I wonder if she's gonna be irritated that I'm just dropping by unannounced, but it's too late now that I've rung her doorbell. She appeared to be less skittish about having me in her house when she invited me in after our run this morning, so I try and let that worry go.

"What are you doing here?" she asks, completely taken off guard.

I don't even let her see an ounce of my uncertainty when I give her a playful grin and step inside. "I ran out to grab some dinner and knew you weren't doing anything tonight, so I drove here instead of back to my place."

"Oh . . ."

"That a problem?" I ask as I head into her kitchen.

"Ummm . . . no. I just . . ." she mumbles.

"Just what?" I ask, looking at her, cute as hell in her pajamas.

"Just surprised that's all. Why didn't you just text me?"

"Because I figured you would probably tell me you were studying." I start rummaging around, opening drawers, until I find a bottle opener. Popping the caps off the beer, I hand her one as she nods, agreeing with my last statement, and I shoot her a wink before taking a sip.

"So, how was the rest of your day?" I ask as I move around her kitchen, grabbing plates and a few napkins.

"Good. I got a lot done actually," she says as she watches me.

"Great, let's eat then. Do you mind grabbing the beer?"

"No problem."

Walking into her living room, we set everything down on the coffee table and make ourselves comfortable on the couch.

She opens the pizza box to grab a slice, and then turns to me, asking, "How did you know I like pineapple on my pizza?"

"I didn't. Like I said, I got this for me before deciding to come over."

"Oh."

Leaning forward I take a slice and sit back to eat as I watch her do the same. The thought of being out with Gavin right now just doesn't even compare to this—sitting here, with this girl I'm getting know. I'm enjoying it. It satisfies me in a way I never would have expected.

"So, you know what I did with my day. What about you?" she asks.

She told me this morning that she was spending the day studying then going to the studio to rehearse. "After our run, I went to the gym to do some lifting. Then later, I went to the bar to work. Had to sign off on a bunch of paperwork and inventory orders. That's pretty much it," I tell her.

Nodding her head, we continue to eat our dinner when I suggest, "Wanna watch something on TV?"

She picks up the remote and hands it to me. Flipping through the channels, I already know she's a fan of MTV, so I decide to go for one of my channels. When I land on TCM and they're playing one of my favorite movies, I set the remote down, get comfortable, and wait for it. Knowing she's gonna tease me, I find myself already enjoying her reaction when she says, "What the heck is this?"

"You don't know this movie?" I ask, mocking a serious tone, playing right into her.

"Does anyone know this movie?"

Smiling, I say, "Candace, it's a classic." Seeing the blank look on her face, I continue, "It's 'Double Indemnity' from the 1940's. It's a great movie."

"You watch a lot of these movies?"

Shaking my head, I tell her, "Sit back and just watch. You'll like it."

When she sits back with me, I start to explain the movie. "See that girl? Her name is Phyllis and that guy is an insurance agent that she is trying to seduce."

"Why?"

"Because she wants him to murder her husband so she can collect the money from his policy."

"Oooh, I like her already," she playfully says, and gets me laughing.

"Just watch."

Kicking our feet up on the coffee table, we lean back and watch the movie. After a while I feel her head drop onto my shoulder. Looking down, her eyes are closed. I don't move for a while, scared of how she'll react. After what happened in my car yesterday, I make sure she's sound asleep before I slip my hand under her head and lower her onto my lap.

She curls up into a ball, and I take this moment to really look at her. Her skin is light and flawless. I gently run the back of my hand down her cheek and along her jaw. She's soft. I knew she would be. My heart begins to beat faster at the subtle contact.

I sink down into the couch, getting comfortable, and observe the stark contrast of her dark, thick lashes as they fan across the tops of her cheekbones. Leaning my head back, I relax with finally having her close to me. The warmth of her against me is something I've been craving. Even though she isn't giving this to me—I'm taking it right now—it appeases me for the time being, hoping that one day she'll want to give this to me. That simple thought alone is enough for me to know that I'm falling hard for this girl, and that worries me, because I know better than to allow myself to feel like this. But with her, all my logic seems to dissipate.

I let her sleep for a while, but when I begin to grow tired myself, I know I need to wake her. She's out cold when I lean over and whisper, "Candace."

When I run my hand down her arm, she starts to stir. "Candace . . . Candace, wake up."

Her eyes slowly flutter open and when she looks up at me, she locks them to mine. I can tell she isn't fully awake as she continues to stare. Out of nowhere, she startles me when she lurches off of the couch, finally coherent and free from her haze.

"Are you okay?" I ask when I stand up, and as soon as I step towards her, she shoots her hands out, wanting me to stay away. She's scared of me, and I hate that. Whatever it is she's dealing with, whatever is causing her to react this way, I just want to comfort her, but there's no way she'd let me if I tried.

"I'm sorry," I say as calmly as I can, not wanting to freak her out any more than she is. "I didn't want to leave you without you locking the door behind me. You fell asleep, and I didn't want to wake you, so I let you sleep for a while."

"I'm sorry," she breathes out.

"For what?"

Lowering her hands, she looks a little mortified when she explains, "Startling easily. I didn't know I fell asleep. I'm just . . . I was just disoriented."

"Candace," I quietly say, not wanting her to feel uncomfortable with me. I step toward her, and when she doesn't move away, I take my hand and brush aside a lock of her hair that's fallen across her forehead. I feel her stiffen, and I quickly pull back.

"I'll lock the door behind you," she says.

"Let me help you clean this up."

She looks at the mess and tells me, "I'll do it. It's all trash anyway."

"You sure?"

"Yeah."

She follows me as I walk to the door. Before I leave, I turn back and she's right next to me. She has to tilt her head to look up at me, and when I see her from this angle, she looks so fragile. When her eyes shift up to meet mine, I softly tell her, in all seriousness, "I want you to feel comfortable with me."

I notice her shallow breaths when she whispers, "I know."

"Okay. So, we'll talk later?"

When she softens her face and says, "Yeah," I feel better about leaving.

chapter fourteen

WHEN I PULL into the parking lot of the gym, I spot Jase's 4Runner already here. He got back in town a couple days ago, and the three of them have been busy with school as the quarter is coming to an end, so the two of us arranged to get together to do some lifting.

"Jase, hey," I say as I walk in and see him mixing his Gatorade.

"Hey, man," he says as he turns around. "You ready?"

"Yeah."

We head over to the free weights and pick up our dumbbells to start our bicep workout.

"So, how was Ohio?" I ask him, knowing it was the first time he met Mark's family.

"Better than I anticipated. Never had to meet parents in the past, so I was uneasy going there."

Jase told me that before Mark, he was a lot like me. Random hook-ups. But he seems to really love Mark, so I'm glad everything is working out for them.

"His family cool?"

"His sisters are a little wild," he laughs. "But yeah, his parents are great. Much different than mine."

"How so?" I question.

Taking his weights over to the bench, he sits down and says, "I'm pretty nonexistent to them. And when I told them I was gay . . . they were done."

"That's fucked up."

"Before Mark came along, all I really had was Candace. She's been my family since I moved here."

"You guys seem really tight," I respond as I set down the dumbbells and start racking the weights on a barbell to do some bench presses.

"We've always been that way," he tells me, walking over to spot.

As I lift the bar out of the rack, he stands over me, saying, "Thanks for checking in on her. I didn't even know she had that blowup with her parents until I got back home."

Pushing out the last of my reps, he grabs the bar from me as I sit up.

"Yeah, well, I was home with nothing to do, so it was nice to have someone around to hang out with," I say, downplaying the whole situation. I'm not sure how Jase would react if he knew how I'm starting to feel about his best friend.

"Well, for what it's worth, it's good to see her hanging out with someone else besides me and Mark."

"Is she really that closed off?" I ask. I know what I've seen, but it isn't much.

"Lately? Yeah."

That's all he says when I lie back down to pump out another set, and I wonder what he means by 'lately.' Was she not always like this? Then I make the connect—I wasn't always like this either. Never really. Not until her. But it was before that—it was that night that got me thinking so differently. That night that messed with my head so much that I started drifting away from old habits, old friends.

My mind goes back to the alley, and I get a flash of Candace on that rainy night in the coffee shop. *Fuck.* Why am I thinking about that? I thought I let it go, but it's back—the question. Ripping through my reps, I force that sick thought out of my head.

There's no connection there. It's just your mind trying to put an end to what was left unresolved. I repeat this silently to myself a few times, knowing that my subconscious is just screwing with me. *There's no connection . . . is there?*

I spend the next hour distracting myself, talking with Jase about football and how the season is going so far for the Huskies. Anything to keep my mind away from that night. After we finish up and say our goodbyes, I head out.

When I'm not around her, my mind seems to drift, so I selfishly pull out my phone and text her, knowing when we hang out, I'm too consumed with her to think about the other shit that tends to creep up in my head.

You hungry?

I start driving home, which is only about ten minutes from the gym, and it takes about that long for her to reply.

Can't eat. Have a 2-hour dance studio today.

Well shouldn't you fuel up?

Not if you want me to barf. :-)

I laugh at her text as I sit in my jeep that's now parked in my driveway.

I'd love to see that.

That's disgusting.

More for having something to tease you about and less for the actual barf.

Can we stop talking about barf? LOL

You free for a run tomorrow morning?

Yeah.

Happy to spend more time with her, I type out my last text. **Be at your place around 7.**

"You sure you wanna go?" I ask as we walk out to her front porch. She looks exhausted, and by her bloodshot eyes, I can tell she didn't get any sleep last night.

"I'm sure," she says with her head down as she walks past me.

We start with a light jog through the mist that fills the chilly morning. I look over at her as she stares straight ahead.

"Bad night?"

"What?" she questions when she looks over at me, and then responds, "I was up late catching up on school work. It's the end of the quarter."

I don't buy her lie. I know this chick wouldn't be behind in school, but I don't push it 'cause if she's choosing to give me an excuse, then she doesn't want me to know what really kept her up last night.

Going along with her, I ask, "You ready for the break?"

"Mmm hmm," she hums, and we're back to closed-off Candace.

I pick up the pace when we get close to campus, and she strides along with no problem right beside me. I wish she would talk to me, but even if I'm with her in silence, it's better than not being with her at all.

"I'm sorry," I hear her say softly, and when I look over at her, I ask, "For what?"

"I'm just tired, that's all," she explains.

"Candace," I say, and when she turns her head and catches my eye, I continue, "You don't need to be sorry."

I see the corner of her mouth turn up before she looks away.

"So what did you do yesterday?" she asks, and I'm glad she's talking now.

"Not much. Hit the gym with Jase and that's about all."

"I think he mentioned that to me," she mumbles.

"What about you?"

"After studio, I had to work. Jase came up there and hung out for a little while," she tells me. "It was pretty dead, and Roxy left early."

Because the curiosity is killing me, I go ahead and bring up Jase. "You guys seem really close."

She looks over at me and narrows her eyes, like she's questioning what the real meaning is to that statement, but she goes ahead and gives me a response. "We've always been close. He's like my family."

"It's good that you have someone like that."

She doesn't speak as we continue to make our way through campus, jogging up the stairs as we leave the quad. We take the rest of the run through the surrounding neighborhoods with nothing more than random small talk before I drop her off back at her house and head home.

Something was clearly bothering Candace yesterday when we met up for our morning run, so when I call to see if she wants to grab a bite to eat before I head into work tonight, I'm surprised when she easily agrees.

I meet up with her at the sushi-go-round restaurant close to my loft. She looks a lot better than she did yesterday morning, and I smile as we sit down.

"You ever been here before?" I ask when we start picking our plates off of the carousel.

"A couple times. Mark likes this place."

"You coming to see him tonight?" I ask, knowing that she's never come to the bar to hear his band play.

She shakes her head as she plucks her sushi up with her chopsticks and takes a bite. When she's done, she says, "I'll see him after."

"After?"

"I'm staying with Jase tonight. So I'll see Mark for a little while before he goes home."

"You spend a lot of nights with him?" I ask, and when she looks up at me, she defends, "It's not weird or anything."

"I didn't say it was."

"We've always been this way," she tells me.

"What way's that?"

"Close."

I'm a little confused as to why she spends nights with him, but I don't push the subject anymore. It's not my place to question, so I drop it.

Changing the subject, I ask, "Are you free tomorrow?"

"Why?"

Grabbing another plate of sushi before it passes, I tell her, "Didn't know if you wanted to get in another run."

She doesn't say anything as she turns her attention to her food and starts eating. She's uncomfortable, so I add, "Wanna?"

"I have to work in the morning."

"After?"

Looking over at me, she nods and says, "Yeah. I'd like that."

Satisfied with her response, we grab a few more plates and finish up our dinner.

"Sorry I've gotta run, but I haven't been working much lately, and I need to get a few things done," I explain as we head outside, and I walk her to her car.

"It's okay," she says as she unlocks her door and then turns to face me.

I want to touch her, hug her, anything, but nothing about her is telling me that it's okay as she turns back around to open her door, and before I can even try to do anything, she's in her seat.

"I'll see you tomorrow," she says, and I wonder if I'm ever gonna get her to let me in.

When I walk into Common Grounds, I don't see Candace, but quickly notice her boss eying me. She's obvious and doesn't even try and hide it. I walk over to the counter where she's standing with her indigo hair, and for some reason, it totally works on her.

"Candace here?" I ask.

"Mmm hmm," she playfully hums as she turns away from me and walks into the back.

She pops back out after a couple minutes and says, "She said to give her ten minutes and she'll be out."

I nod my head and scan the tats on her arm, asking, "Who does your work?"

"Place next door. My boyfriend works over there."

"That's convenient," I tease.

"My thoughts exactly," she says with a hint of indecency, and I have to laugh at her vibrant personality. "You got any?"

"Yeah," I say as I lift the sleeve of my t-shirt to show her the half-sleeve I got a few years back. My mother's favorite flower is the peony, so I have an almost cryptic interpretation of one surrounded by shaded water with the words, 'Struggles are not identities,' woven through the art.

"Nice," she says as she moves her eyes over it, noting the details. "Any others?"

"No," I lie. I have another, but I keep it private and don't ever mention it to people if they ask. "How long did it take you to get all those?" I ask about the full colorful sleeves that run down the length of her arms.

"Here and there for a few years," she says when I notice Candace out of the corner of my eye.

"Hey."

"What are you guys talking about?" she asks as she walks over to me.

"Your friend, Ryan, was asking about my tattoos," Roxy tells her.

Walking towards Candace, who is already in her running gear, I ask, "You ready?"

"Yeah, I just need to put my bag in my car."

I take the bag out of her hand, and she turns to Roxy to say bye as I start heading out.

Candace is quiet while she listens to me talk about work. She asks a few questions along the way, and I end up venting about some of my aggravation with a couple of the staff that I had to get rid of the other night. But when the conversation shifts to Mark and his band, we start talking about music. When I ask her what some of her favorite bands are, I'm surprised to hear that they sync right up with mine.

We eventually weave into my neighborhood, which is only a couple blocks from her house. We both live right outside Fremont, which Jase's apartment is in the heart of. Candace stops talking for a while, and when I look down at her, I can see she's struggling a bit with her breathing.

"You okay?" I ask.

"I'm thirsty. We forgot water."

"No worries," I tell her, knowing that my loft is at the end of the street we're on. When we get close, I slow down and start walking up my drive.

"What are you doing?" she asks, and when I look back, she's standing in the middle of my drive—anxious.

"Getting you some water. Come on," I say, trying to act like her being here shouldn't be a big deal, but by the way she's hesitantly walking towards me, I can tell that it is for her.

Pulling out my keys, I click the fob and open the garage.

"Do you own this building or something?" she asks, not registering that this is my place, and I guess I can't blame her because it's a three-story loft—much bigger than one person should need.

"This is my loft. I live here," I say with a grin.

"Oh," she breathes and then stops in her tracks, no longer following me. She doesn't want to be here, but I want her here. She shifts uncomfortably before walking into my garage and following me up the stairs to the door.

When we walk inside, she stays in the living room while I head straight to the kitchen to grab a couple bottles of water.

"Here you go," I say as I walk back to her and hand her one.

She takes a big gulp before saying, "This is a great place. How long have you lived here?"

"About five years." I watch as she moves her eyes around my space, taking it in.

My phone begins to ring, and when I see it's Max, I answer.

"Hey."

"Ryan, Michael's a no-show. Said he has shit going on at home."

"Hold on a sec," I tell him and look over to Candace. "Make yourself comfortable. I need to take this call really quick. I'll only be a few minutes, okay?"

She smiles at me, and I head back to my office, closing the door behind me.

"Okay, I'm back," I tell him.

"Where are you at?"

"My place. Why?"

"Who are you telling to get comfortable?" he inquires, implying I'm trying to get laid.

"Candace," I tell him honestly.

"Who?"

"That girl I told you about," I explain.

"What's going on with you?" he asks, knowing damn well that I don't ever hang out with girls and that I have never even been interested in anything more than a passing screw.

"Nothing," I shrug off, not wanting to leave her in the other room alone for too long. "I'll be there in a few hours, okay?"

"Sounds good," he says before hanging up.

Walking back out into the living room, I find Candace kneeling down, looking at some of my mattes that are stacked against the wall. Stepping next to her, she looks up at me.

"I'm sorry," she says as she puts the mattes down and stands up.

"For what?"

"I wasn't snooping or anything, I just noticed these and was curious," she nervously explains.

"Candace, I have nothing to hide. I told you to make yourself comfortable, and I meant it." I take a seat in one of the overstuffed leather chairs and drink my water.

"Where did you get those?"

"They're mine," I tell her.

"Yours?"

"Yeah. Sometimes I get bored and like to mess around with my camera."

"That's pretty amazing for just messing around," she says as she continues to stand against the large panoramic window. "You only shoot people?"

"For the most part, yeah." I get up and walk over to the photos and pick up the one lying on the top. It's the shot I took of Gina. It's a nice photo, but makes me almost feel guilty for having it. For spending so much time working on it, only to have Candace admire it.

"She a model?" she asks as she looks at the photo with me.

"No, just some chick I used to know." I toss the matte down and motion for her to sit with me on the couch, and when she does, she continues, "So, when did you get into photography?"

"When I was in college I took some art classes. So, one day I just decided to buy a camera and started taking pictures. Like I said, I pretty much have no clue what I'm doing. Just a little hobby of mine I mess around with every now and then."

"You ever do anything with them?" she asks.

"No."

I watch her as she begins to relax, getting more comfortable the longer she's here. Having her here in my space—I like it.

"Maybe you should," she encourages, and when I look into her eyes, I'm at a loss for words, so I simply repeat hers, "Maybe I should."

We sit here for a few moments without speaking. I don't pull my eyes away from hers, and when I see the nervous shift in her, I cut the intensity and ask, "You sure you don't want to come out to the bar tonight to see Mark play?"

Taking a deep breath and looking down, she says, "I told you, I have to work."

"I just picked you up from work."

"I know, but I have to go back. One of the girls quit and Roxy hasn't hired anyone to replace her, so I've been picking up extra shifts," she explains. "Plus, I'd probably be tired and no fun to be around."

"I can't imagine it not being fun to be around you," I admit much too honestly, and when she shifts her eyes to look out the window, I take her cue and ask, "You ready to finish the run?"

Standing up, I reach out for her hand. She doesn't take it at first, but when I smile down at her, she slips her hand into mine. I keep a strong hold on it as I lock up and we head out.

When we get outside and to the end of my driveway, I still have her hand. This is the longest she's ever let me touch her.

"Wanna make it a long run, or are you ready to head back?" I ask.

She takes a moment, and then looks up at me, saying, "Long."

I give her hand a soft squeeze before letting it go, and something about the way she's looking at me right now makes me feel like I'm finally having an effect on her.

chapter fifteen

LEAVING NOW. SEE you in two hours?

I read Candace's text as I'm working in my office at home. She's been really busy this past week, but we managed to grab another run a few days ago. We decided to meet up after her dance practice today before I have to go into work.

I'll meet you in the parking lot.

OK, catch you later.

Before I can type another response I get an incoming call from my mom.

"Hey."

"Hi. What are you up to this weekend?" she asks.

"Not much," I tell her as I stand up to go get a drink from the kitchen. "I'm supposed to meet up with Candace in a few hours then go to work."

"Really?"

She's surprised, knowing that I have never shown interest in a girl before.

"So . . . you really like her?" she asks, not even skating around the subject.

I grab a water and flop down on a chair in the living room. "Yeah," I sigh as I lean back and stare up at the exposed beams.

"Have you told her?"

"It isn't like that," I tell her. "She's slow to warm up to people. Well . . . at least with me."

"But you've known her for over a month. Seems like enough time."

"Not with her."

"So what are the two of you going to do later?" she asks.

"She's at the dance studio now, so we're just gonna grab a coffee afterward."

"And how's work been going?"

"Same as usual. What about you?"

When she starts talking about some fundraiser that she went to with her sister, I lose focus as my eyes shift to the stack of mattes that are still lying on my floor. The photos that Candace had been looking at last week.

"Well, I better let you go. I just wanted to check in," she says as she pulls my attention back to her.

"I love you, Mom. I'll talk to you soon."

"Love you too, dear."

Shoving my phone into my pocket, I walk over to the photos and grab them. It seems like forever ago when I shot these when really it was only four months back. I was so distracted then, but now . . . now I feel focused. I'm not quite sure if anything will ever happen with Candace, but I love spending time with her regardless. But, God, I do hope that something will happen. I've never had to fight for a girl's attention or affection, but this one . . . she makes me work, and I find myself liking it.

I take the photos back to my office and shove them inside my credenza, not wanting to think about that time—about all those women. Sliding the door shut, I turn to get some work done—anything to kill time while I wait to see Candace.

Pulling into the studio lot, I park next to Candace's car. Stepping out, I take a moment to enjoy the chill in the December air. The dark clouds roll through the misty sky.

My eyes dart to the doors when I hear them bang open and see her storming out. She's upset—frustrated—and when she looks at me, she freezes, startled to see me, with tears streaming down her cheeks. When I rush over to her, she quickly wipes her face with her hands, trying to hide what she knows I already see.

She drops her head, but I catch it with my hands, cupping her cheeks as I tilt it up for her to look at me. "What happened?"

"Nothing, honestly. Just a tough rehearsal." Her voice trembles as she speaks, and seeing her this upset has something panging inside of me that I'm not used to—protectiveness.

I look down at her as a few tears seep out of her eyes, and I wipe them away with my thumbs. When I do this, I feel her tension melt, and she falls into my chest, wrapping her arms around my waist. This unexpected affection is like a reward I've been waiting so patiently for. And here it is. Sliding my arms around her, I hold her close, and she doesn't flinch away from me. I can feel her body relax, and when this happens, I lean down and rest my cheek on top of her head.

She sniffs and I know she's crying. Having her like this, in my arms, is an intimacy that's completely foreign but comfortable. I'm sure she can hear my heart pounding, but I need her to hear it. I need her to feel it as it thuds in my chest because I need her to hear me falling for her, 'cause that's what's happening here—I'm falling. I never wanted to before, but with her, all I want to do is fall. Fall into her. Fall so deep inside of her heart so that

I never have to be without her. That's what this girl does to me. That's how powerful she is even when she thinks she's at her weakest. She's broken. I see it clearly, but whatever it is that's haunting her, I wanna make it fade. I wanna make it fade and make her fall too—with me.

When she begins to pull away from me, I selfishly want to tighten my hold on her and keep her like this for a little longer. I worry this was just a random need for comfort from her, that I won't get this again, that she doesn't feel what I know I'm starting to. *Fuck, this hurts.*

She looks up at me, and I ask again because I need to. "Are you sure you're okay?"

With no words, she simply nods. Unwilling to take my hands off of her, I step to her side with my arm around her shoulders and lead her to my car. She doesn't question me as I help her up into the seat. When I get in, her eyes are closed, so I don't turn on the stereo. I let her relax and drive her to my place, wanting her in my space. I watch her at every red light I hit. I turn on the heater because I know she has to be freezing, wearing nothing but long, baggy black pants with her pale pink leotard. Her hair is pulled into a tight bun and everything about her is screaming that she's way out of my league. Way too refined for me.

Her eyes open when I pull into my drive. She rolls her head towards me, and we watch each other for a moment before I get out of the car and open her door.

When we go upstairs, she gets comfortable on my couch as I grab a water for her from the kitchen. Walking back, I sit close to her while she gulps the water down.

"Feeling better?" I ask as I take the bottle from her and set it on the coffee table.

"Yeah, I'm sorry. After being yelled at for two hours, I just . . ."

Needing that affection back, I wrap my arm around her and pull her in tightly next to me, and again, she allows it. "Don't worry," I tell her because I want her to show me this side of her—a side I know she hides.

"No . . . It's embarrassing."

"Don't let it be."

As she shifts forward, she turns to look at me. "Can I ask you a huge favor?"

"Anything."

"Do you have a dry shirt I can change into?" she asks with a coy smile. "I've been dancing for the past few hours, and I'm sweaty and stinky."

I laugh and say, "You don't stink at all actually."

"Liar." I catch her dimple when she says this with a slight grin.

"I'll be right back," I respond and then head upstairs to my bedroom. I pull out a pair of my long pajama pants and an old UW shirt.

"You need socks?" I holler down to her.

"Please. It's cold."

When I walk back downstairs, I hand her the clothes and show her to the guest bathroom.

"Thanks. Just give me a few minutes."

"Take your time," I say as I close the door and return to the living room.

Sitting back on the couch, I turn on the TV and start flipping through the channels. When I hear the bathroom door open, I watch her walk towards me. She's gripping the fabric of the pants, trying to keep them from dragging on the floor. My pants and t-shirt swallow her up and hang on her, but she's adorable as hell.

Seeing her in my clothes—I like it. And in this moment, I pretend that she's mine because I want her to be. I can't figure out why. Why this girl? All I know is, when I'm not with her, I want to be.

She sits down on the couch with me, but not close enough. Her hair is still in a bun, and I grab it, wanting to make her laugh, and tease, "This is cute."

Ducking her head, she says, "Whatever," as she swats at my hand, and gives me what I want—her smile.

"Come here," I say as I lean back into the couch and she follows, settling herself in my arms when I wrap them around her. "So, what happened?" I ask, wanting to know what made her so upset earlier.

"I have this tough piece of music," she starts to explain. "I'm having a hard time connecting with it. My instructor keeps telling me what I need to fix, but I don't really know how. It's frustrating. I can perfect my moves, but I don't know how to get into this piece."

"So she just bashed you the whole time?"

"It's how she is. But the fact that she even came in to work with me is unheard of. She's extremely stern, but she's only trying to help me."

"I didn't like seeing you upset," I admit to her.

When she looks up at me, she says, "It's not a big deal, really."

"I didn't like it," I repeat, wanting her to know that I feel for her in a way that seeing her like that bothered me. I keep my eyes on her, and when I sense her feeling uncomfortable, she looks away from me and I ask, "You want that cup of coffee?"

"That'd be great; I'm still really cold."

"There are some blankets in the trunk by the fireplace," I tell her as I walk into the kitchen. I watch her move around the room as I quickly brew her a cup of coffee. "How do you take it?" I ask as she wraps herself up in one of my blankets and sits back down on the couch.

"One sugar and really blond," she responds from across the room.

"You getting warm?" I ask when I walk back in and hand her the cup of coffee.

"Trying too." She cradles the mug in her hands and takes a slow sip. When she turns to see what's playing on the TV, she laughs softly under her breath.

"What's so funny?" I question.

"You." She looks at me when she continues. "I don't know anyone who watches the classic movie channel, aside from you."

"You want me to change it?"

"No, it's fine," she says as she shifts back on the couch, allowing me to drape my arm around her. "I'm only teasing you."

Kicking my feet up onto the coffee table, we watch 'The Blue Dahlia' with her head resting on my chest.

She's still in my clothes when I drive her to her car that's back at the dance studio. As I pull up next to her car, I ask, "Why don't you come up to the bar and hang out with us tonight?"

"I can't."

I nod my head at her response, which never changes every time I invite her to Blur.

"I'm sorry," she tells me. "But I'm just really tired and will probably go to bed early. Plus, I have the early shift at work tomorrow."

"Your boss doesn't strike me as the type who would mind if you came into work a little hungover," I joke.

"You're probably right about that," she says with grin. "But I've never drunk enough to have ever been hungover."

"Never?" I question, shocked that this girl is so innocent that she's never been drunk.

"Don't act surprised," she defends.

"I'm more relieved." I love that she's pure in a way. That she's good and not tarnished like me—like all the others.

"I'm not even going to ask why," she laughs as she shakes her head. "But thanks for today."

"Anytime."

"Tell Mark and Jase I said hi when you see them tonight, okay?" she says as she opens the door and gets out. When she turns to look back at me, she adds, "Thanks again for being there today. It probably would have ended up being a crappy day if I just went home."

"Thanks for letting me be there."

I watch as she gets into her car and drives off before backing out and heading to work. When I walk in, I make my way over to the bar and spot everyone hanging out while Mel works the bar. I'm a little surprised to see Gavin since our last run-in wasn't all that pleasant.

None of them see me as I watch them interact. I look at Jase and Mark and see how they're so happy. They have a direction in life that I've been missing. They have a close relationship with each other and even with Candace, something I've spent my whole life avoiding. I shift my focus over to Gavin who's putting the moves on some random chick and I see me. I see the person I've been for so many years, and from this angle, it doesn't look good. Drifting. That's all I've been doing.

My life has been empty, but I never really saw it so clearly until seeing Candace, Mark, and Jase. I see their connection, their focus, and it makes me realize how unfulfilling my life has been up to this point. Up until her. The draw is there; it always has been, but it's beyond the pull. She's filling me with an awareness I never saw before. She's made me take a step back to see my life for what it is—disconnected and stagnant.

Before any of them sees me, I turn and walk up to my office. Pulling out my phone, I call Tori. I need assurance, and I know she'll help me.

"Ryan, hey."

Sitting at my desk, I ask, "You busy?"

"Not at all. Trevor's putting the kids to bed. What's up?"

"Are you happy?" I ask, remembering the flipside of this conversation when we had it back in the summer at my mom's house.

"What's going on?" she asks, picking up on the seriousness in my tone.

"Just tell me. You and Trevor, are you happy?"

"Yeah," she breathes. "I'm happy. We have our issues. Everyone does, but I'm happy."

I'm scared to fall any more than I already have for Candace, but I want to. God, I want to so bad. I want to connect. I want everything that I've been too afraid of.

My mom and dad used to be happy. There was a time when they really loved each other. She's told me about it, but it didn't matter. It wasn't enough, and that love transformed into a living hell. The hell is all I remember. The screaming, the fighting, the beatings, the constant turmoil and fear. Then I see Tori and her family. They're happy. They're okay.

I'm still scared though, but the thought of walking away scares me more.

"Ryan, you there?" she asks.

"Yeah. Sorry."

"So are you gonna tell me what's going on?"

I've always been honest with Tori, so I go ahead and tell her, knowing my words are safe with her, "I met someone."

"Is this *that someone* you denied back at Thanksgiving?"

"Yeah."

"So what's bothering you about it?" she questions.

"I have a seedy past, and I've never done this. I've never wanted to. But she's nothing like anyone I have ever known, and she makes me nervous."

"You think she'll judge you for the choices you've made?"

"She's nothing like me. She's so green, and I've been fucking chick after chick since I was fifteen." Just saying the words is almost mortifying. Sickening. And what was once something I couldn't care less about is now something that I'm embarrassed about. Ashamed.

"I don't have a picture perfect record either. You know that. But Trevor loves me regardless of who I was before him," she tells me. "That's the thing about love . . . it's a pretty powerful force that can show a side of you that you never knew existed. Show you that you're capable of becoming someone you never thought you could be, and you do it for the other person because you love them, because you want to put them before yourself."

I don't say anything. I just let her words soak in. I don't know what the fuck I'm doing. All I know is, I want to—for her.

"Just a piece of advice," she adds. "Don't ever lie to her about who you are. If she ever asks, be honest."

"Yeah." When she says this, I begin to have doubts that it will ever get to that point. I don't even know where this girl's head is at. Just because I want her doesn't mean anything. What if I'm just wasting my time? *Shit.* I see how she is with Jase. What if that's just how she is with her friends? I even see it when she's with Mark. All she has given me is exactly what I see her giving to the two of them.

Suddenly, I'm questioning everything.

chapter sixteen

I'VE BEEN TRYING to shake my self-doubts about Candace for the past few days. We continue to chat on the phone and text back and forth, but I can't help wondering if any of this is different with me than it is with Jase and Mark.

Needing a distraction, I decide to get my Christmas shopping done for the kids today. I thought hitting the gym would help, but here I am, still doubting. My cell starts ringing as I'm grabbing my coat to head out.

It's her.

"Hey."

"Hi. You busy?" she asks, and something about the sound of her voice erases my questioning thoughts.

"No," I lie as I toss my leather coat onto the couch. "What's up?"

"Nothing. Jase and Mark left early this morning for Ohio, and I've just been sitting around the house. I didn't know if you wanted to hang out."

"Oh, I see. Second best since the boys aren't there to keep you entertained," I tease with a laugh.

"No," she drags out in feigned annoyance at my joke. "And you're not second best," she adds, and I'm happy she does because I like hearing it.

"What did you have in mind?"

"Anything. I just want to get out of my house," she says in a way that makes me think of her non-existent roommate. I know she lives with a girl, but in the past couple of months I've been hanging out with Candace, I've never seen or heard her talk about her roommate, but if she needs to get away, I'll take her away.

"You up for shopping?"

"Shopping?" she questions.

"Yeah, I need to do some Christmas shopping for my nieces and nephews. You in?"

"Um, yeah. That sounds good."

"I'll come pick you up," I tell her before we hang up, and just like that, my day got better.

When I pull into her drive, I see her walking down the steps of her front porch. She looks perfect with her leopard scarf wrapped around her neck and her hair down. When she gets into my car, she looks at me staring at her and asks, "What?"

Being honest, I tell her, "I like your hair down." She usually has it in a piled mess on top of her head, which always looks sexy on her, but I have to admit that it's cutest when she's in school, and it's almost always in a tight bun since she dances every day. But I rarely ever see her with her hair down like it is now.

She looks uncomfortable with the compliment and doesn't respond to it, instead asking, "Can we stop by Peet's and grab something to drink?"

Laughing at her deflection, I say, "Sure," before backing out and heading over to Fremont. As I'm driving, I notice that she seems a little absent as she stares out the window.

"Is everything okay?" I ask, and when she faces me, she questions, "Why?"

"You seem distracted."

"Sorry," she says and I can tell she's abashed. "Thanks for picking me up."

Not sure what's causing her mood, I intend to dispel it. Smiling over at her, I say, "Anytime."

We luck out, finding a parking spot right in front of Peet's, and the place is crowded when we walk in. Candace stands close to me while we wait in line. She's fidgety, absentmindedly wringing her hands together.

A burst of cold air floods in, and when the chime from the door goes off, Candace startles and turns to see an older couple walking in. Her face is nearly stone when I look down at her.

"Hey," I say as gently as I can, and when she turns around, I ask, "You sure you're okay?"

Fixing a smile on her face, she looks up at me and assures, "Yeah. Maybe I should just get a decaf tea or something," with humor I'm not buying, but I'm not questioning it either. I reach down and when I take her hand in mine, she grips me tightly as if she needs the comfort of my touch.

After we order our drinks, we walk out into the brisk air, and she finally seems to breathe easy. Crowds. I forgot for a moment that she doesn't like them, and Peet's was packed with people needing a hot drink to warm up.

Opening the car door for her, I help her up and then walk around to get in. We drive across town to a massive toy store that's my go-to spot for the kids. We listen to an old David O'Dowda album as we fight the holiday traffic, and when we pull up, we grab our drinks and head inside.

"So, what are you looking for?" she asks as she gets a cart and starts following me down one of the aisles.

"Don't know. These kids aren't too hard to please though," I tell her as I stop and flip through a few board puzzles.

"How old are they again?"

"Young. All under five," I say as I start wandering around. "Honestly, they'd be happy with a box of tissues and a stick."

She laughs at my words, and I turn back to her to get a glimpse. "That's nice," she says, teasingly.

"It's true."

When we turn down the next aisle, filled with pink . . . *everything*, Candace stops to admire a collection of dolls. I step up behind her and quip, "You want one?"

She looks at me over her shoulder, and mocks, "No, I don't want one," before looking back at them. "They're pretty."

"Grab a couple," I tell her and watch as she picks out two of the dolls and puts them in the cart.

We take our time, slowly strolling, grabbing toys here and there as she continues to ask about my family.

"So, seven nieces and nephews . . ."

"Yep."

"All cousins' kids?" she asks.

"I'm an only child, remember?"

Nodding her head, she says, "That's right. I forgot. You all sound close."

"I'm closest to my cousin, Tori. We spent a lot of time together while we were in high school. We lived in different towns, but would always get together on the weekends. Partying and surfing."

"You surf?" she asks as she looks over at me.

"I grew up on the beach."

"Jase surfs," she tells me.

"Yeah, he's mentioned that to me. Grew up in San Diego, right?"

"Uh huh. He goes to Westport every now and then."

"I've been there a few times, but I go back to Cannon Beach frequently, so I normally get my fill when I'm there," I tell her and catch her staring down the next aisle. "What are you looking at?"

"I always wanted one of those," she whines with excitement as she starts walking towards a huge wire bin filled with inflated Hop N Bounce balls. I laugh while I watch her grab one out of the bin and turn to me. "My friend had one of these when we were little, but she would never let me play with it."

"Why didn't you ask your parents for one?"

"I did, but . . ." she trails off, and when she does, I encourage, "Take it for a spin."

She completely surprises me when she doesn't even hesitate. Holding the ball by the handle, she walks over to me and hands me her drink. "Here.

Hold this."

Taking her tea, I question, "You serious? That's a toy for an eight-year-old," I poke.

She sets the large ball on the ground and sits on top of it, saying with a huge smile, "In case you haven't noticed, I'm about the same size as an eight-year-old," before spinning around and bouncing away from me down the aisle.

I watch her, laughing as she bobs up and down, enjoying seeing her let go for a moment. She isn't worried about how she looks; she never has been. Not embarrassed in the slightest and I revel in this moment.

When she turns to bounce back towards me, I start cracking up at the laughter coming out of her. I've never seen her like this—so carefree. It's beautiful, and I just want to grab her off that stupid ball and kiss her. Just take her and make her mine, so I can touch her whenever I want—to have her.

She finally stops bouncing and stands up, still holding the ball in her hands. She continues to giggle while telling me, "Totally worth the wait."

"Must have been a good ride," I say. "I think the whole store heard you laughing."

She tosses the ball into the cart, and as I cock my head in question, she clarifies, "You have to buy that for the kids."

She takes her tea out of my hand, and I'm lost in her. Everything about her. I follow her lead as we continue to make our way through the rest of the store, thankful that she doesn't skip a single aisle because I need all the time I can get with her.

"Michael here?" I ask Mel when I walk into the bar.

"Yeah," she hollers over to me. "Upstairs."

The place is busy tonight as I head up to Michael's office. It's been a good day, although dropping Candace off at her house to come up here was the last thing I wanted to do, but I need to sit down with Michael. He's been dropping the ball on a few things, and shit needs to get back on track.

His door is open, so I go ahead and walk in.

"Ryan, hey, man," he says from behind his desk, which is a mess of papers.

I cut to the chase and say, "Talk to me."

While he sorts and stacks a few files, he asks, "About what?"

"Not showing up. Supply orders going in late. Schedules not getting out on time."

He drops the files onto his desk and leans back in his chair. "Fuck, man," he sighs.

"You know I can't have this, so either we figure it out or I'm gonna have to let you go," I tell him honestly. No need to bullshit when it comes to my business.

"No, I'm getting everything in order. Things have been a little crazy at home, and I let it filter into work," he explains.

"Kids okay?"

"It's not the kids," he says and takes a pause before revealing, "I found out that Amber's been fucking around on me."

Seems Mel's eavesdropping skills don't suck.

"Shit, man."

"Yeah. It's fucked up," he tells me. "Don't worry about things up here though. I've got it under control."

Not too comfortable with chatting about this guy's issues, I leave it as is and let him get back to work, trusting that he's gonna get his crap together.

I make my way back down to check in with Mel, and as I pass along the edge of the bar, someone grabs on to my arm. Turning around, I'm face to face with my past.

"What are you doing here?" I ask, and when her hand lingers on me, I take a step back and out of her grip.

"Having a drink. Waiting for a friend, but he's running late."

"You should pick a different bar next time," I tell her, turning to leave and spot Gavin walking in.

"M.I.A.," he calls out to me while shaking his head.

I've found myself drifting from Gavin as well as most of my bad habits, so seeing him is a little awkward, but not as awkward as him walking past me and straight to Gina, kissing her.

Irritation causes my shoulders to tighten, and when Mel appears from behind the bar, I snap, "Back room."

She follows behind me as I head into the back stockroom, closing the door behind her.

"What the fuck did I just see?"

"He brought her in here the other day," she tells me. "Said he's been hooking up with her for a couple months now."

The door opens, and Gavin walks in, thankfully alone.

"You mad?"

"Mad? No. Disturbed? Kinda," I respond. "Dude, weren't you screwing her roommate?"

He gives me an almost proud smirk and boasts, "Yeah, man."

"Have fun with that one," I tell him.

"So we're cool?"

"I don't care who you're hooking up with, but that girl seems like trouble," I tell him.

"Maybe so, but she's good in bed, you know?" He laughs and then adds, "Yeah, *you* know."

Regretfully, I do know. I wanna forget, but that isn't gonna happen. It's my past, and unfortunately, you can't escape your past. I've dealt with that little piece of knowledge my whole life. But I do what I can to shut it out and tell him, "Don't bring her back up here again."

When he turns to walk out, not responding to me, I face Mel and say, "I'm serious. You see her in here, I want her out."

"Yeah, no problem," she says. "You okay?"

Switching the subject, not wanting to discuss it any further, I tell her, "Let me know if anything starts to fall through the cracks up here."

"Did you talk to Michael?"

Being irritated as shit, I don't want to go into this with her, so I leave it with, "Just let me know," before walking out and calling it a night.

chapter seventeen

CAN YOU HELP me run an errand?
Yeah. What do you need?
I want to go pick up some firewood but I want enough to last and it won't fit in my trunk. Can you take me since you have the space in your jeep?
At gym now. Will you be ready in a couple of hours?
Yes. THANKS!!!

After I finish my workout with Max, I head home to grab a quick shower and a bite to eat before I leave to pick up Candace.

The night is colder than usual as I walk out to my jeep. I make the short drive through the neighborhood, and when I get to Candace's house, I run up to her door to get her. She's shrugging on her grey, wool coat when she answers.

"Hey," she says with a smile when she sees me.

"You ready?"

"Yeah." I watch her slip on her black gloves as we walk out.

As I pull away from her house, she tells me, "There's a tree lot on Holman, up from eighty-fifth street."

"How much are we getting?"

"I dunno. Probably just a fourth of a cord," she answers as she adjusts the vent on the dash.

"You cold?"

"Yeah," she says, and when I laugh, she turns and asks, "What's so funny?"

"Nothing. You just have no meat on you to keep you warm," I say teasingly. She's lean with defined muscles, but nothing that takes away from her femininity.

"Yeah, well, I can't do much about that," she shoots back at me.

When we get to the tree lot, Candace places her order with one of the attendants. After paying for the firewood, we find ourselves strolling the lot, looking at the Christmas trees as the guys load up the wood.

She stops in front of one of the trees and looks up at it, shivering. Reaching down, I take her hands and rub mine over hers, trying to warm her up. She seems a little apprehensive as she looks up at me, but she doesn't back away. When she starts to drop her arms, I reach down and hold her hand. It isn't the first time I've made a subtle move like this, and I hate the uncertainty of it all. Not knowing how she's feeling about this—about us.

"I miss Jase," she quietly says out of nowhere as she looks at the tree. She turns to me, and with an almost apologetic look, she explains with a shrug of her shoulders, "I'm not used to him being gone."

"Have you talked to him?"

"This morning," she says and then turns back to the tree. "We should buy this."

I look down at her, and even though she didn't mean it literally, I like that she said 'we.'

As she helps me unload the firewood and stack it in her garage, I ask, "What are you going to do for the next few weeks?"

"I don't know. This is the first year that Jase isn't here with me. We normally spend most of the break together when I'm not at my parents.'"

"How's that going?" I ask, knowing that the last time she saw them it ended badly.

"It's not, really," she tells me. "I spoke with my father for the first time since Thanksgiving a few days ago, and he wants me to come over for dinner Christmas Eve."

"You haven't spoken with them for all this time?"

"No," she says as we walk back out to grab some more logs.

"So, you're going over to see them then?" I ask, already feeling like I want to keep her from going. I know I have no right to say anything, but I can't stand the thought of her being here alone if she winds up in another fight with them.

"Well, yeah, I don't really want to, but it's Christmas and all. I'm just a little scared about how it will all go. The last time I saw them, we said some pretty nasty things to each other, and I have never gone this long without talking to them."

"What are they so upset about?" I ask, confused by what this girl could possibly be doing that they don't approve of.

"Everything," she says as we walk into her house and into the kitchen. She grabs a bottle of wine that has already been opened and starts pouring a glass, adding, "Turns out I've been nothing but an embarrassing disappointment to them all along."

Taking a beer out of the fridge, I can't help the sigh of irritation that comes out of me. I follow her into the living room, and when we sit down on the couch, I wrap my arm around her, just wanting her to be close to me any way I can get it.

"I'm sorry, babe," I say softly and immediately catch the slip and hope she isn't freaked out by what I just said. But when she continues talking, I wonder if she even noticed that I called her 'babe' or if she did notice and is okay with it. *Shit, I really hate this grey area.*

"Honestly, it's nothing that I didn't already know deep down, but it was the first time that it actually hit me that these were their true feelings toward me."

I feel it. It's strong and causes a reaction I can't control, and I act on it, demanding, "I don't want you going over there." She looks up at me, and there isn't a hint on my face that I'm anything less than serious about what I just said.

"Ryan, I have to," she defends. "They're my parents."

"I don't care. I don't want you going over there for them to treat you like shit." My words are hard, but they come out before I can even think to soften them up for her.

She sighs and leans back into me, resting her head on my chest, and I enjoy the contact.

"I have to go," she whispers. "It's Christmas, and I really should be there. I'm only going for dinner. That's all."

"Then I'm going with you."

"What?" she says as she pulls away and sits up.

"I don't want you going alone, Candace," I tell her. "I'll go with you."

"I don't think that's a good idea," she says, but I'm not letting up on this.

"Well, I don't think it's a good idea that you're going. So we can argue about this, or you can just say okay."

Her eyes are locked on mine, stunned by my tone, but the feeling that I have to shield her from getting hurt again is powerful, almost uncontrollable. It takes her a moment, and I watch her brow twitch right before she turns and slowly leans back.

"Okay," she resolves with uncertainty.

Certain or not, I don't care. She said 'okay,' and I take it a step further, pushing her when I add, "And I don't want you spending Christmas alone either, so why don't you come home with me. I could use the distraction at the madhouse."

"What?! No. Thanks, but I'll be fine," she says in a high-pitched voice.

"I'm sure you will be fine, but I don't like the thought of you sitting here alone, so you're coming with me." I need her to come with me. I just need her . . . with me.

"Ryan, it feels weird," she argues.

"Why?"

"Because. It just does. I know you have a big family, and I just don't want to intrude."

"It's not an intrusion," I assure her as I move to face her. "My family isn't like that."

She drops her head and takes her time contemplating. Questioning. *Shit, did I go too far? Did I scare her?* As soon as I start to regret my words, she speaks.

"Okay, but no gifts. It makes me uncomfortable."

"Why's that?"

"I don't know. It just always has. Please," she says, almost begging, and I don't push it any further.

Excitement rushes through me, a feeling that's all too new for me. But I can't help it, knowing that I get to have her with me for a solid chunk of time.

"Okay. No gifts," I say with a smile.

We both sit back, and when she gets comfortable in my arms, she asks, "So when did you start making all the rules?"

"When you started making me worry about you," I respond, completely transparent.

Sitting there, I continue to hold her. We don't talk at all. It's quiet and peaceful, and having her warm body tucked in close with mine gets my heart racing. All I can think about is how I want to kiss her, touch her. Pick her up and make good use of her bed. But I know once that happens, I'll never want to leave that bed. The thoughts alone turn me on, and I need to get control of myself.

"Hey," I whisper, looking down at her. When she tilts her head and peers up at me, she's close. So close, that if I lean down slightly, I could kiss her. Maybe I should. But I know myself. I won't want to stop. I don't think I could with her, so instead, I say, "I should get going."

She nods her head, and feeling the movement against my jaw makes leaving so difficult, but that's what I do. I stand, and she walks me to the door.

"Thanks for helping me out tonight."

"You don't need to thank me," I tell her and then walk out to my car after she gives me another nod.

The drive home is almost painful because all I want to do is turn around and take her, claim her as mine, but nothing about this girl is telling me that I should handle her in that way. I'm holding back, and I've never had to do that before. The anticipation drives me crazy, wondering when I'll get to see her again, hear her voice when she calls, or read her words when she texts me.

I need to talk to her. Be honest and tell her how I'm feeling. But I just got her to agree to spend the holidays with me, so I'll selfishly take the time and won't mention anything right now. God, this is killing me.

When I wake up, I fix myself a cup of coffee before calling my mom to tell her about the change of plans.

Taking my coffee over to the couch, I kick my feet up and call her.

"Hi, dear," she says when she answers the phone.

"Hey. You busy?"

"No. How are you?" she asks.

"Good. Um, I have a minor change of plans for Christmas," I tell her. "I'm gonna bring Candace with me." I say this, almost cringing at what her reaction is going to be. I've never brought a girl home with me—ever.

She's surprisingly understated when she says, "That doesn't sound like something minor. So what's going on with you two?"

"Nothing's going on."

"But you're bringing her here. Home. With the whole family. And nothing's going on?" she pries.

"She's alone, and I don't want her to be. That's all," I explain, but we both know that's not all.

"Alone? Where's her family?"

I take a long sip of my coffee before explaining, "She doesn't have a good relationship with her parents. The last time she saw them, they wound up in a huge fight and they said some pretty bad things to her. She's going back to see them for dinner on Christmas Eve, and I told her that I would go with her."

"Oh. So, when are you coming home?"

"We're gonna drive down on Christmas, so I won't be there in the morning with the kids," I tell her, feeling a little guilty that I won't be there when they wake up.

"They'll understand. I'll talk to them," she assures me. "I'm glad I finally get to meet this girl," she says with excitement.

"Mom, she can be really shy," I warn. "I know she's gonna be overwhelmed with everyone at the house, and I don't want to make it any more awkward for her if anything was to be insinuated. It's just not that way with us."

"I'll be on my best behavior," she teases, and I know she will be. "Well, I should run out and get her a little something."

"No gifts."

"It's Christmas, Ryan," she says, annoyed by my demand.

"She made me promise. Told me that gifts make her uncomfortable."

"Ryan, how much do you know about this girl?" I can hear the uncertainty about Candace in her voice.

"Why?"

She lets out a heavy breath before saying, "It just sounds like she has some issues going on, and I wonder what you really know about her."

I take a moment because all I want to do is defend this girl. Truth is, I know she has issues. I'm not blind to the odd behavior I catch glimpses of and the couple of things that Jase and Mark have said about her. But whatever is going on, I don't think it could ever be enough to keep me away. So,

I bypass my mom's concerns and leave it at, "She's special. I don't know what's going on with us, but she's important to me."

I can almost hear my mother's smile when she says, "Well, then she's important to me too."

"She's a good girl, but her walls aren't that easy to break down."

"Sometimes it isn't about breaking walls, dear. Sometimes it's simply about proving yourself to the other person that they're willing to just let them down."

My mom's support is a constant in my life, and I'm grateful that I can depend on that from her.

"Thanks, Mom."

chapter eighteen

THERE'S NO DOUBT she's nervous when she gets into my car and I start driving up to Shoreline to her parents' house. She doesn't speak as she sits there, looking all proper in her plum, knee-length dress and black high heels. She hardly ever wears jewelry or makeup, she doesn't need to—she's perfect. But I don't like seeing her so worried.

"Relax," I tell her.

"Ryan. You need to know that—"

"Candace, relax."

"They're just very judgmental people," she warns.

"There is nothing that they can say that I haven't heard before," I tell her. If anyone can deal with people who degrade you, it's me. I spent my whole childhood listening to a father telling me, every way he could, what a piece of shit I was. I'm sure I can handle whatever it is I'm about to walk into. But it isn't me I'm worried about, it's her.

When I pull into the gates of The Highlands, an upscale affluent community, I look over at Candace and lay my hand over the two of hers that are clenched tightly together. I weave through the neighborhood and when she points to the house, I pull into the drive and shut the car off. She doesn't open the door or move in any way. She sits, and I let her take her time.

After a few moments pass, I ask, "You ready?"

"Yeah," she sighs and then opens the door.

Walking up to the large, two-story home that overlooks the Sound, she takes a deep breath before opening the front door. We walk in, and I take in my surroundings. I knew that she came from money—I do too—but there's a big difference between affluent and wealthy. This is wealth.

"Bunny," her father beams as he walks through the foyer with his arms out to pull her into a hug. From his demeanor, you would never expect the family drama that lies underneath the surface. My father was the same way. No one would ever suspect the violent man that he was behind closed doors.

He takes a step back from Candace and turns to me. He wears a tailored charcoal suit and has almost polished, silver hair. "And you must be Ryan. Thanks for joining us," he says to me, shaking my hand.

"Good to meet you, sir."

"Come in," he says as he leads us back through the formal living room and into the kitchen. He turns to Candace, and tells her, "Your mother is finishing getting ready. She should be out shortly."

She only smiles up at him.

"What can I get you two to drink?" he asks.

"A beer is good, Mr. Parker," I say to him.

"Please, call me Charles."

With drinks in hand we make our way back to their library that spans the two stories of the house with a large walk-in fireplace.

I sit next to Candace on the tucked leather couch as her father asks, "So, Ryan, what is it that you do?"

"I own a bar right off campus," I tell him as Candace shifts nervously at my side.

"Oh, how did you get into that type of work?"

I briefly explain how I acquired the business after I graduated from UW, and he follows along, nodding his head.

"What did you study in college?" he asks before taking a sip of his scotch.

"Finance."

"Now that's a respectable degree," I hear, and when I turn my head, I see a petite woman with shoulder-length, brown hair, wearing a dress similar to Candace's, only in navy. But where Candace is more reserved, there isn't a question about her mother's social standing by the way she carries herself in a much too proud manner as she walks across the room, almost demanding attention.

Candace stands to give her mom a stiff hug.

"Hi, Mom."

"Good to see you, darling," she drawls before turning to me. "And Ryan, welcome."

I step closer and take her hand, saying, "Thank you for having me."

"Of course. It isn't every day that our daughter brings a man home," she says in a patronizing tone, and I look over to see Candace rolling her eyes as we sit down.

"Ryan was just telling me about the bar he owns," her father announces.

"A bar?" she questions as if the words have a bad taste to them. She has no idea that the bar I own has afforded me an extremely comfortable lifestyle.

Before she can continue, Candace jumps in and changes the subject, asking about her parents' upcoming trip to Aspen.

Candace and I sit back and listen to their plans before her father excuses himself and Candace takes me to show me around the house.

We walk outside to the backyard and look at the view of the Sound.

"I'm sorry about that," Candace says softly as we take a seat on one of the benches.

"About what?"

She looks at me with apology. "They can be a lot. They're pretty pretentious."

"Candace, no one has perfect parents. Everyone's flawed in some way."

I slip my arm over her shoulders as she tightens the scarf around her neck.

"So, you grew up here in Shoreline?" I ask.

"Yeah. In this very house. The Kelleys, who live across the street, have a daughter that's the same age as me. We used to be best friends when we were growing up."

"And now?"

"And now all I really have is Jase, Mark . . . and you," she tells me and knowing that she sees me as someone she can at least group with Jase and Mark gives me a little relief.

"What about your roommate?"

"Kimber? We used to be really close, but not so much anymore."

"So what happened to all your friends from high school?" I ask, curious as to why she secludes herself in a manner that prevents her from having more people in her life.

"They've moved on. Applying to grad schools, getting married, making a life for themselves. Most of the kids here wind up becoming people like my parents. More concerned about their image and what social circle they're in. It's not me, so I never cared enough to stay in touch with anyone."

I see how her parents could be upset that she doesn't seem to follow suit with their expectations. That Candace would be driven enough to step out of that life to create a new one, a more comfortable one, for herself. She's ambitious in a way that's unique from her parents. Following a passion—dance—to build a life that she can find pleasure in.

"We should go back inside," she tells me, and when we walk in, her father calls from the other room, "Candace, could you come in here?"

"Yeah, just a second." She looks at me and says, "I'll be right back. Make yourself at home."

"Do you want me to come with you?"

"No, it's okay," she assures before heading back to the library.

I take this time to stroll aimlessly through the house. Walking into the formal living room, I scan the framed photos that are displayed on the black grand piano. Family portraits through the years. Candace as a young girl, wearing a frilly white dress with white gloves, searching for Easter eggs on the greens of a golf course. A picture-perfect family, but from what little I have picked up from Jase, she was miserable. But out of all the photos, none of her dancing.

I'm curious to know what she would look like dancing. She's so poised as it is, but to see how she would move intrigues me.

My attention shifts to the library when I hear Candace yelling. I don't miss a beat when I start walking through the house to where she is, concerned about what they're talking about and what has Candace raising her voice when she's always so quiet. I can draw my own conclusions about what kind of relationship she has with her parents and wonder if they are the ones she needs to be protected from.

When I step to the closed double doors, I hear her father bark, "You have a name to uphold!"

"I just don't understand you," her mother snaps. "You should be thanking your father, not pouting," and the sound of her condescending voice irks the hell out of me.

"You are unbelievable, Mother! I'm not a child!" Candace's voice is strained as she yells, and I can't bear the pain in her words. I barge in and see the annoyance on her mother's face, so I lock my eyes on Candace, but she doesn't notice as she continues shouting at her mom. "You can't just step in and take away everything I have worked so hard for during these past four years! How can you call yourself a mother? You're nothing! You say you're embarrassed by me, well, it goes both ways."

I rush across the room to her side, and when she finally stops to catch her breath, she sees me.

"We're leaving. Now," I demand as I take in her tear-stained face.

"Excuse me, but this is a private matter," I hear her mother say, but I don't take my eyes off of Candace as she continues to cry, staring at me in shock. I'm pissed, and she sees it.

Holding out my hand for her, her mother doesn't stop when she threatens, "Candace, if you walk out, it's over. Don't come back. We refuse to sit back and watch you ruin your life."

When her mother says this, anger roils inside of me, and I want to slap the fuck out of her lily-white ass for threatening her own daughter.

"Daddy?" Candace says as she looks to her father, pleading, and it hurts to hear her so desperate.

"We're done letting you play games, bunny. No more."

She stands there, tears falling from her eyes while she looks at her parents. All I want to do is take her away. Comfort her and get her out of here. And when she slides her hand in mine, that's exactly what I do. I grip her tightly and get her out of this house as fast as I can. I snatch up our coats and walk her out to my car.

When I open the door for her, she reaches out to grip the side of the seat, and I know she's about to break, so I grab her and pull her into me. Clutching my arms around her, I hear it. Painful sobs start to break through, and she clings to me, crying.

The tension in my body is heady with the urge to put her in the car and go inside to knock the shit out of her parents. I'm fueled by disgust for these people. That they would lash those words at Candace, leaving her broken in their driveway, falling apart in my arms. But at least they're my arms that are attempting to comfort her, because even though she doesn't know it, I don't think anyone could give her what I want to give her. I'd give her the fuckin' world if I could.

After a while, her body begins to shiver with chills as she starts to quiet down. She keeps her head tucked against me, and I feel her fingertips pressed into my back. Her breathing is staggered, and when she pulls back, she keeps her head down, not looking at me—embarrassed. I lean down and kiss the top of her head before helping her up into the car.

The drive back is somber. I look over to her as she stares out the window. She's sad, and my need to comfort her is overwhelming. She must sense me watching her when she turns her head to me. Her chin quivers, and she shrugs her shoulders, defeated, as fresh tears fall down her cheeks. I reach over and take her hand, pulling it onto my lap. I keep it there all the way back to her house.

Once we're inside, I go to the kitchen to get her a glass of wine, figuring she could use one. As I walk into the living room, she's curled on the couch with her heels kicked off on the floor. I hand her the glass and she swallows it fast before handing it back to me. Setting it on the end table, I sit down, leaning into the corner of the couch and pull her between my legs and on top of me. She lies there and doesn't move as I thread my fingers through her soft, thick hair.

"You okay?" I ask.

She doesn't answer, she just shakes her head and after a second begins crying again, wetting my shirt as she nuzzles into my chest. I strengthen my arms around her and let her cry without saying anything.

The hurt coming out of her is hard to listen to, but I do, and it breaks me. Breaks me in a way that even though I hate it, I find myself savoring it. The connection. Her need for me right now and the contentment I find in being the one to give it to her.

Time passes and she's fallen asleep on me. I can feel her steady breaths against me, and I'd hold on to her all night, just like this, if I knew she'd be okay with it. I want to be selfish and take it, but I know she wouldn't be comfortable with it. So as much as I don't want to feel her move off of me, I comb her hair with my fingers, and whisper, "Candace."

"Hmm," she softly hums as she stirs awake.

"It's getting late. You should go sleep in your bed."

Placing her hands on my chest, she pushes herself up, and I notice her bloodshot eyes.

"Are you gonna be okay if I leave?" I ask, hoping she'll want me to stay, but knowing that it's just a hope.

She nods her head and sits up. I move to stand and turn to take her hand, pulling her off of the couch and into a hug. She bands her arms around me, and I tell her, "We can stay here tomorrow. We don't have to go to my mom's."

Leaning her head back to look up at me, she says, "It's okay."

"Candace . . ."

"I could use the distraction. I'll be okay," she tries assuring me.

"Call me when you wake up. You might feel differently in the morning."

She walks me to the door and before I leave, she stops me, saying, "Ryan . . ." I look back at her, and she takes a pause before continuing, "I'm sorry . . . tonight just . . ."

"Don't worry about it. Honestly."

"Thanks," she says softly before I walk out.

Candace called me when she woke up this morning, assuring me that she still wanted to go to Oregon. I offered to stay here with her, but she told me that she really did want the distraction, so I didn't question her any more about it.

I finish packing my bag, and I think about how things with the two of us have shifted in the past couple of weeks. I'm falling for this girl hard, and I know I'm not gonna be able to keep this from her for very much longer, but I'm nervous that I might ruin what we have. Honestly, even though it isn't enough for me, I'll take it if this is all she wants to give.

I carry my bag downstairs, and decide to call Jase. I don't know if Candace has spoken with him this morning, but I call him anyway to let him know what happened last night.

"Hey, Ryan."

"Jase, hey. You have a minute?" I ask as I start making myself a coffee for the road.

"Yeah. What's up?"

"Have you talked to Candace this morning?"

"No, why? Did something happen with her parents?" he asks, sounding worried.

"It wasn't good, man."

"Tell me."

"Her parents are a piece of work. Pretentious dicks. I don't know the whole argument 'cause I was in the other room, but there was a lot of yelling, and when I went in there to get her, her parents threatened to cut her off. Told her they were done with her—threw her out."

"Shit," he sighs out. "How is she?"

"She didn't talk, but I didn't ask either. She was just really upset. I stayed with her for a while last night, but I wasn't sure if she had called you, so I wanted to let you know," I tell him as I screw the lid on to my travel mug and walk over to sit down on the couch.

"Thanks. I'll try giving her a call. I hate that she's stuck there."

"She's not. I'm about to go pick her up."

"Where are you guys going?" he asks, and I'm surprised that he doesn't already know.

"Has she not told you?"

"Told me what?" he questions.

"She's coming home with me to my mom's for a few days."

"What?" Yeah, he had no clue by the shock in his tone. "I can't believe she didn't say anything to me."

"Sorry. I figured you knew."

"No."

All of a sudden, I feel the need to talk to him about Candace. Knowing that the two of them are like family and that he's really protective of her, I need to know if I should be pursuing her. As awkward as this is, I go ahead and lay it out there.

"I need to tell you something."

"Yeah . . . ?" he responds.

"Look, I know the two of you are really close, so I feel like I should let you know that . . ." I pause briefly before admitting, "I really like her."

"I figured as much," he lets out with a chuckle under his breath. "Have you told her?"

I'm relieved that he's being so relaxed about what I just said.

"No. I don't know where her head is at. I'm not sure if she'd even be interested in anything."

"I think she is," he says, giving me hope, and then adds, "Look, I get that she's closed off, but she wouldn't be hanging out with you like she has been if she didn't trust you."

"She's the hardest person I've ever had to read," I admit with a laugh.

"I probably shouldn't say this, but you need to know that she's been going through a lot this year. It's been rough, and I'm just gonna leave it at that. So if you're anything less than serious about her, then don't go there."

He tells me this, and I try not to wonder too much about what's going on with her, though I'm beginning to think that there could be a lot more to her parents than what I've seen.

"I hear you," I tell him.

"I'm serious. She isn't like most girls. She's really innocent, so don't push her," he warns.

"It's not like that with her."

"I don't mean to sound like an ass or anything."

"Jase, man. It's fine. I get it," I tell him, and a part of me is glad that he's being this way about her, that she has someone like him there for her.

"Mark and I are hanging out with his family, so I've gotta run. I'll try giving her a call though."

"Okay. Thanks, man. I'll talk to you later."

Hearing him assure me that I'm not wasting my time soothes some of the anxiety I've been having about Candace. This girl has woven herself into my life, and for a change, I want to keep her there.

chapter nineteen

CANDACE WAS A little antsy when I picked her up this morning. We're running later than what I told my mom because I didn't want to rush her. She didn't get much sleep last night, so she just wasn't herself, worrying about how she looked and wondering if my family would think she was rude since she tends to be quiet. I've never seen her so uptight, so I let her move at her own pace.

She fell asleep about halfway into the drive, and as I look over at her, she's still sound asleep, sitting there in her modest black dress. She looks beautiful as she sleeps, but it bothers me to think that at this moment, she's probably happier in her dreams than she is when she's awake.

When we start getting closer to the coast, I decide to go ahead and wake her up. Trying not to startle her, I run my knuckles up and down her arm until I see her eyes start to blink open.

"How long have I been asleep?" she murmurs.

"A couple of hours."

"Really?"

I smile over at her. "Really."

She adjusts the seat and sits up to look out the window. The canopy of trees that hide the sky on the winding road through the mountains makes it dark.

"How much longer do we have to go?" she asks.

"About twenty minutes. Are you feeling better?"

"Yeah. I was really tired."

"Music?" I ask and when she agrees, I tell her, "You pick."

She takes my cell phone since she likes all my music and syncs it up with the stereo, selecting 'Ride' by Lana Del Rey. She sets my phone down and sits back as the music fills the car, and I enjoy the doleful, limpid melody of the song.

"You're quiet over there," I say after a while.

"Just a little nervous," she tells me as she continues to watch the mist collecting on the window.

I give her knee a squeeze and say, "Don't be."

Seeing the unconvincing grin on her face, I decide to just let her be for the rest of the drive. When we arrive, I park the car and walk around to open her door. She's not quick to get out, so I take her hands to help her down, encouraging, "Don't be so nervous. Just relax."

I laugh under my breath as I watch her fidgeting with the skirt of her dress, smoothing it down.

"Why are you laughing at me?"

"Because I've never seen you so wound up before."

I take her hand and start walking her to the front door, but when she tugs back and stops, I turn to hear her say, "Ryan . . . I don't do well around a lot of people."

I try to coax her with my words, telling her, "My family will love you, but if you feel that uncomfortable, we can go. Just say the word."

"No, I want to meet them, I'm just . . ."

"Hey, I'm right here. No worries, okay?"

"Okay."

Holding her hand, I lead her inside as two of my nephews run through the entryway, chasing each other. I laugh and walk her back to the kitchen.

"Finally, you made it," my mom says excitedly and rushes over to hug me, but I keep my grip on Candace.

"Mom, this is Candace," I introduce, and my mom pulls her in for a hug as well.

"I'm so glad to finally meet you, dear," my mom tells her, and she's not even trying to hide that she's thrilled with the fact that I brought a girl home and she isn't some barfly.

My Aunt Carol brings me in for a hug, excited to see me, and before I know it, the kids all start flooding into the kitchen, screaming my name. I spot Sophie, one of my nieces, and pick her up as Tori and my other cousins' husbands come in to say hi. Tori and my other cousin, Jenna, give me curious looks, and I try to ignore them, knowing they are just waiting to start digging into my business about Candace. I told my mom to discreetly tell my cousins to keep a tight lip so they don't embarrass Candace, but I know Jenna and Katie, and those chicks are nosey.

When Sophie starts poking her finger in my ear, I catch Bailey, toddling over to me. Bending down, I scoop her up in my other arm, ravishing her neck with playful kisses as she squeals and giggles.

"You weren't kidding," Tori whispers to me as my cousin, Jenna, comes over to take Sophie out of my arms.

"What?" I question, trying to keep my voice under my breath.

She laughs, "She's *way* out of your league."

"Thanks," I say with mockery.

"You know I'm teasing. She's just . . . polished."

"Tell the girls not to interrogate her."

"Donna already said something, but you know how Katie is."

"Where is she by the way?" I ask.

"Upstairs with Maddie. She had an upset stomach earlier."

"My room?"

"Yeah."

"Why is my room always the hot spot for everyone's spawn when they get sick?" I joke and then turn to look at Candace, but she's no longer in the kitchen, and I quickly realize, that in the madness of saying hi, I left her alone.

"Mom, where's Candace?" I ask.

'Ladies' room,' she mouths to me, and I walk down the hall to wait for her, feeling bad, and wondering if all that was too much for her. Who am I kidding? Of course it was. My family is big and loud, and Candace doesn't even like being in a crowded coffee shop.

When she doesn't come out after a few minutes, I gently knock on the door.

"Everything okay?" I ask as she opens the door. "When I looked up you were gone."

"Yeah, just needed a moment to myself."

"Sorry about that."

"It's okay. I'm just not used to . . ."

"I know." I see that she's a bit rattled, so I step closer to her and run my hands down her arms. "Do you need a few more minutes?"

"No, I'm fine."

When we walk back into the kitchen, the kids are watching their movie, and the chaos has dissipated. I pour her a glass of wine, and hand it to her, whispering, "Come on," in her ear. I lead her through the house, showing her around as I take her to one of the back rooms that looks out over the water.

We're alone, and it's quiet as we stand in front of the large picture window.

"Better?" I ask, and she smiles as she looks at me.

"I guess I didn't realize how big your family actually is. I mean, you've told me, but . . ."

"It can be a lot," I tell her. Having twenty of us here can be overwhelming. It's more the women and kids. The guys are always laying low, trying to dodge the madness.

"This is a great view," she says. "Have you always lived here?"

"Yeah."

"Small town."

"You have no idea," I say with a hint of humor. "I used to spend most of my time in Seaside or Astoria. That's where Tori's from."

"Is there even a school here?" she asks with a huge smile, finding it funny. Not a whole lot of people are permanent residents of this area. It's mostly vacation rentals, but we're one of the few that actually call it home.

"No," I tell her. "The schools are in Seaside, but I went to private school."

"Me too."

We chat for a few more minutes, and when she seems more at ease, we head back. Tori and Jenna are sitting in the dining room when we pass through.

"Candace, come join us," Tori offers, and when Candace hesitates, I tell her it's fine, letting her know that I'll be in the other room with my mom. I know Tori is curious about her, and I also trust her enough to know Candace will be fine.

I find my mom in the kitchen, working on dinner. It's just the two of us, and she stops what she's doing as we lean against the counter and talk.

"How did this morning go with the kids?" I ask, a little bummed that I wasn't here.

"Anarchic," she laughs.

"I bet."

"They missed you."

"I have all their presents outside," I tell her. "We can open them later."

She takes a sip from her glass of water, and then asks, "Where's Candace?"

"Dining room with Tor and Jenna."

She nods her head with a smile, and I know she's biting her tongue, so I tell her, "Just say it."

"What?"

"Whatever it is that has you looking at me like that, Mom."

When she sets her glass down on the counter, she reveals, "She's different than I was expecting."

"How so?"

"Just . . . different." When I narrow my eyes at her, she grins and assures, "It's a good thing, dear. Relax," before patting my arm a couple of times and walking away.

"Where are you going?"

"Dining room to visit with the girls."

I let her have her time with Candace, even though I feel like I want to go in there and check on her. But I don't. Instead I busy myself with Connor, helping him out with a puzzle on the floor. When I look up, I see my mom and Candace passing through the kitchen. She catches my eye, and I give her a small half grin as they walk through, heading to the study. I like seeing her here, with my mom, in my familiar surroundings, mixed in with my family.

Candace is now in the kitchen, helping Mom cook while I drink a beer and hang out with the guys. I can't keep my eyes off of her as I watch her laughing with my mom while they get everything ready for dinner, and I know instantly that I want to see this again. Have her here again.

She makes me nervous because she has this power about her that is dragging emotions out of me when no one in the past has been able to. She has no clue what she's doing to me, and that's a scary thing when I think about admitting how I'm feeling about her.

After a while, I unload the gifts and let the kids open everything. My mom was right—they're much crazier than they were last year, but they're another year older, and I'm sure next year will be even wilder. Candace sits on the couch with Tori while they laugh at me being overtaken by the little ones.

When dinner is done, Candace excuses herself to go upstairs to relieve Katie from mommy duties. Her daughter, Maddie, hasn't been feeling well all day, and Candace told me that she needed some quiet time, so she's up in my room with Maddie, and Katie is finally getting to eat dinner.

My aunts are cleaning up, Jenna and the guys are getting all the kids ready for bed, and Tori and I band off into the study to talk.

"I got a job," she tells me as we sit down.

"What made you decide to go back to work?"

"After you and I talked this summer, I decided to just be honest with Trevor. Told him pretty much what I told you," she says. "He suggested the same thing. Thought I should get out of the house, get back into a routine. So I called my old boss, and it was as easy as that."

"When do you start?" I ask.

"Second week in January," she says with a little uncertainty.

"You ready to leave Connor and Bailey?"

"Yes and no." Tori is a great mom and is very attached to her kids, so it makes sense that this transition would be hard for her since she's been a stay-at-home mom for the past four years.

"It'll be fine," I say. "So you and Trevor are on the same page?"

"He never got off track. It was me. I think I've been miserable because I've been lost. I wasn't doing anything about it, and it made me start questioning everything. But he's supportive. Always has been. He just had no clue how I was feeling. Once I was honest with him, things started to change. So yeah, we're good."

"Good."

"What about you?" she questions.

"What do you mean?" I ask, not understanding what she's asking.

"Being honest," she starts, "Candace told me that she thinks you brought her here because you feel sorry for her."

"She said that?" I feel horrible that she would even think that.

Tori nods her head and then questions, "How long do you plan on avoiding telling her how you feel?"

Letting out a deep breath, I tell her, "She makes me nervous." When

Tori smiles, I say, "I'm glad you're enjoying my discomfort."

"I'm just enjoying seeing a girl have this effect on you," she admits before she stands up. "I'm heading to bed, but for what it's worth, I really like her."

I follow her out, and the house is quiet. I see my mom in the kitchen, turning everything off.

"You going to bed?" I ask her.

"Yes. It's getting late. Is Candace still upstairs?"

"Yeah, I'm gonna go up there and get her. I think we'll just crash down here and let Maddie take my bed."

"Well, tell her that I'll see her in the morning, will you?"

"Okay, Mom."

We say good night, and I go to the hall closet to pull out some blankets and pillows. I toss everything on the floor, making a makeshift bed for me to sleep on and lay out a blanket and pillow on the couch for Candace. We had planned on her taking my room, but since Maddie is sick, I figure this is a fair alternative.

I pick up Candace's bag and head upstairs to my room. Quietly, I open the door to see Maddie passed out, lying on top of Candace. When she rolls her head to the side and looks at me, I walk in and laugh. "Are you stuck under Maddie?"

"I didn't want to move and wake her up. What time is it?" she asks.

"Past eleven. Everyone has gone to bed. I told Katie that I would check on you and Maddie."

"I wanted to thank your mother before she went to bed."

"Don't worry about it. Here's your bag," I tell her as I set it next to the bed. "I made a big pallet of blankets and pillows downstairs in the living room. Since Maddie is in my room, we're just going to sleep down there. We can watch a movie or something if you want."

"Oh . . . umm . . ." she stutters, and I know she's uncomfortable with the change in plans.

"Don't worry. I'll take the floor, and you can have the couch." I walk over to my dresser to pull out a pair of pajama pants for myself and let her know, "I'll be downstairs. You can use my bathroom to change," before walking out and heading back down.

It doesn't take too long before Candace is walking down in a black sleeveless top and a pair of pajama pants. She has no clue how sexy she looks right now, and I have to look away. I open the fridge to grab a bottle of water.

"You mind if I take the floor?" she asks.

"You sure?"

"Yeah. It looks more comfortable anyway."

"Okay."

She sits down and slides herself under the pile of blankets as I walk over and sit next to her. The thought of sleeping, even in the same room as her, has me on edge. It's like dangling a piece of meat in front of a starved animal. It's life's sick revenge for taking things way too easily and now making me restrain myself in the worst way possible because I've never wanted anything more.

"TCM?" I ask as I flick on the TV.

"It's all we ever watch," she teases, and I like it. "Why switch now?"

"I think you're starting to like my movies."

"Maybe."

We sit back and start watching a movie before I ask her, "Were you okay today?"

"I was. You're really lucky; you have a great family."

"Well, everyone really likes you, especially my mom."

"She's really nice. We had some time to visit earlier."

She starts to grow tired as she inches herself under the covers and lays her head on the pillow by my side. When I look down at her, she has her eyes closed. Knowing she's still awake, I don't let that stop me from running my fingers through her hair.

I continue to do this as I zone out on the TV. My mind can't even focus, and when I hear her breathing steady, I slip my hand under her head and gently move her to my lap. When I do this, she unconsciously wraps her one arm around my waist, and with greed, I savor the contact.

She seemed to enjoy herself today, and I'm grateful that I was able to give this to her since yesterday went horribly wrong, having to walk away from the only blood family she knows. The reactions she sparks in me are intense, and I know I need to heed Tori's advice and be honest with her—soon. But I take this moment and just relish her being so close to me.

I don't want to fall asleep, but when my eyes grow too heavy for me to fight, I reluctantly slip myself out from underneath her, laying her head back down on the pillow, and find myself alone on the couch. I lie there, across the room, the only hint of light coming from the last sparks of fire in the fireplace. It's enough of a glow that I can still watch her, so that's what I do—I watch her as she sleeps until I finally drift off.

chapter twenty

MY EYES SHOOT open when I hear a hard gasp of air. Candace is panicked, trying to catch her breath as her body thrashes awake. I lurch off of the couch, and I'm by her side in an instant, pulling her into my arms.

"You okay?"

Her body is stiff with tension as she shakes under my hold.

"What happened, babe?"

"Bad dream," she quietly whispers through her erratic breaths.

"Slow your breathing down, okay?" I tell her as I hold her against my chest. I'm slightly disoriented, still in a haze as my head catches up to my body's sudden alertness. When she wraps her arms around my waist, I begin to rub her back, trying to soothe her from her nightmare. She scared the shit out of me, yanking me out of a deep sleep.

I can start to feel her breathing slow down, and when it does, I ask, "Wanna talk about it?" curious as to what she was dreaming about that caused her that much panic.

She shakes her head no against me, and I keep her folded in my arms as I lower us down and pull the blankets over us. Face to face, her eyes shift up to mine. I have her tucked tightly to me as she begins to get her breathing under control and relaxes. I don't want to think about what's in her head that's clearly tormenting her because looking at her as she peers up at me with her hazel eyes is all I want to focus on. I can't read her expression, but right now, I try not to decode her. I just take her in. I feel the build-up beating inside of me, and I can't keep it in any longer.

I want her.

I run my hand over her forehead and down to her cheek where I keep it. I study every detail about her, and her breathing increases slightly along with mine. I know she feels it. Feels what I want. I don't even need to say anything because the attraction is *that* palpable. Her brow twitches when she slides her small hand over my cheek and rests it there. Wrapped up in each other—close—I scan her face for a sign. Permission. For anything that tells me this is okay.

I can tell she's scared. I can tell she doesn't know if she wants this—wants me. God, I just want to kiss her. But more than that, I want her to kiss me. I want her to want it as badly as I do, and when my eyes find hers again, she gives me the slightest nod of her head, and I've never felt so relieved in my life.

She wants me.

Knowing that I'll want more than she'll give me, I move slow, needing this to last for as long as she'll let it. Her eyes fall shut and she begins to tremble. I hate that she's scared of this when it feels so right to me, but I'm determined to take her apprehension about this away as I softly press my lips to hers.

I'm gone. I knew I would be.

My heart thuds hard as I tighten my grip on her, needing her as close to me as I can get her. I kiss her slowly, and when she finally relaxes and begins to move her lips with mine, I take more. I can't help myself. I drag my tongue across her lip, smooth, soft. She's the sweetest thing I've ever tasted. Threading my hand in her hair, pressing her body into mine, she wraps her hands up from underneath my arms and braces them tightly on my shoulders.

A soft whimper breaks from her, but she never takes her lips from mine. She has me, and I'm fuckin' lost in her right now. I've never had the ties of emotion with a girl, so to say this one has me bound would be an understatement. What she gives me is something I never even knew I needed, so I never even looked for it.

Moving us off of our sides, I roll on top of her, and I feel her soften beneath me. She runs her hands down my shoulders and grips my forearms tightly as I gently nip her lip before she allows me to dip my tongue inside of her mouth. I linger, moving slowly, needing to feel as much of her as I can. She caresses my tongue with hers, and having her like this, giving this to me like she is, I know I have to make her mine because I'm never gonna want to let her go.

But when she pushes her hands against my arms, everything is questionable again as she pulls away from me.

"I'm sorry," she whispers, eyes still closed.

Tucking my arm underneath her, I speak quietly. "Look at me, Candace." I brush the back of my fingers along the soft skin of her face. When she finally opens her eyes and looks up at me, I say, "I don't want you to feel sorry for that."

She lets out a small hum as she slowly nods her head, but it's when she slides her arms around my back, holding on to me, that I begin to calm. I rest my forehead on hers and breathe her in, taking all I can. I feel her head shift as she tilts her chin up, and this time, I don't have to take. She lifts up and melds her lips with mine, and I slowly fall into her touch as she holds my face in her warm hands, keeping me close to her.

When I finally drag my lips off of hers, she stays close, and I keep her that way until she falls asleep. I watch her; I can't help myself. I have her arms around me and spend a lengthy amount of time stroking her back, touching the bare skin along her neck, her arms, her jaw, before falling asleep with her.

I'm awake. She's doesn't know it because I'm greedy and don't want to move away from her. She woke up a few minutes ago, but I lie here with my eyes closed, arm around her, legs tangled with hers. It feels too good to disrupt, so I don't.

I wonder how she's feeling after last night. A thousand questions start to rack my brain, and now I fear that I'll never get that again. So for now, I pretend to sleep.

"Night night over," I hear Bailey's voice declare, and I know the pretending is done.

"It's not over, Bailey," I mumble, just wanting a few more minutes with Candace. I feel her shift, but I keep my eyes shut, and I know I'm busted. I don't care though.

"I eat bweakfast. Night night over."

"Okay," Candace whispers and begins to slip out from my hold, but I tighten my arm around her and pull her back to me.

"Where are you going?" I ask, finally opening my eyes.

"To go get her something to eat."

She slides out of the blankets, and I can only hope that I'll be able to get her in my sheets again. That I can continue to have her like I did last night.

I roll over and watch as she settles Bailey with a bowl of cereal. Getting up, I make my way into the kitchen to start a pot of coffee while Candace busies herself with Bailey, peeling a banana for her.

"Want some?" I ask as she walks back into the kitchen.

She keeps her eyes down and gives me a nod. *Fuck.* She doesn't want to look at me. She's embarrassed. Nervous. Not what I was wanting.

"Umm, I'm gonna sneak upstairs and get cleaned up," she says as I rip open a packet of sugar for her coffee.

After I stir in the cream, I hand the mug to her, and she finally meets my eyes. Timid. She quietly thanks me and stands there for a moment, staring at the steam floating off of the coffee. I'm scared to know what she's thinking so intently about, but I ask anyway.

"Hey. You okay?"

"Yeah, I'm fine. I just want to get ready before everyone wakes up."

"Okay."

I know she just really needs to get space from me, and I have no choice but to accept it as I watch her head upstairs to my room.

I wander over and sit down next to Bailey at the table as she smacks on her cereal. Nursing my cup of coffee, I decide that I'm not gonna let her shut down. I don't want her feeling uncomfortable, so I'll get her out of the house and take her to one of my favorite places. I need to talk with her. Be honest. Let her know where how I'm feeling because if I don't, then she's just gonna continue to feel awkward for the next couple of days that we're here. I try to not think about what she's going to say. None of this is in my control and not having that power is unsettling.

Looking up, I see Tori walking in.

"What are you guys doing up?" she asks as she pulls down a mug.

"Your little rugrat was hungry and snuck downstairs," I tell her as I give Bailey a wink before I stand up. "I'm gonna go get ready."

When I walk upstairs, Maddie is still asleep, and I can hear the shower running as I grab some clothes out of the dresser and closet and then go to one of the downstairs guest bathrooms to shower.

She still isn't downstairs when I'm ready. I pass by the kitchen, which is loud as everyone is making breakfast and visiting. When I spot Maddie, I decide to go up and check on Candace.

The bathroom door is closed and the smell of her shower fills the room, intoxicating me, making this more agonizing. But I suck it up because I don't want to make her uncomfortable with how strongly I'm feeling about all of this.

When I knock on the door, she says, "Come in."

She stands there in a pair of jeans and one of her college sweatshirts, hair stacked on top of her head, applying her lipgloss. I slide up next to her, leaning back against the counter, and watch. *Grab her. Touch her. Kiss her.* I shake my scrambling thoughts as she tosses her things into her small bag, and avoids acknowledging me. But when she moves to walk past me, I grab her by the waist and pull her to me, asking, "What's wrong?"

"Nothing. Really," she lies, shutting me out.

Looking at her, watching that tick of her brow, I ask, "You wanna get out of here for a while?"

She doesn't miss a second when she nods her head. Relief. She doesn't want to stay away from me.

I slide my hand down her wrist and hold her hand, but this time, I lace my fingers with hers, holding her differently—needing to—and head out.

It's rainy this morning as I drive through the narrow, winding road in Ecola Park. I've always loved this area, dense with lush, tall trees and deep cliffs. I try to focus on the surroundings, but I can't escape my nerves. This is all new to me. I've never done this before, and I don't know what the fuck I'm gonna say. All I know is that I want her.

I park the jeep and grab one of my raincoats from the back seat for her to put on.

"Here, wear this," I tell her as she takes it from me, and starts slipping it on.

We get out, and I hold her hand again as I walk her down the old wooden stairs that lead down to Indian Beach. The wind is hitting hard as it mixes with the rain. It's cold, but I love this type of weather. Walking along the packed, wet sand of the beach, I hold on to her as we step over the piles of smooth, black rocks to some logs of driftwood that sit back from the water. We sit down on one of the logs, and I watch Candace as she takes in the view. She has the hood popped up over her head. I like seeing her in my clothes, even if it's an oversized raincoat.

I wrap my arm around her, and when I do, she speaks.

"This is amazing."

"Yeah, I love it out here. I used to surf here a lot growing up."

She looks out at the hard-hitting waves, her cheeks already pink from the chill. My heart is racing, and I know it won't stop until I talk to her.

"Candace," I say as I turn, kicking my leg over the log to face her straight on. "What's bothering you? And don't say 'nothing' because I know something is."

She looks away, back out at the water. Her hands fidget, and I know she's deep in her head, but I need her here with me.

"Candace," I urge, bringing her focus back.

She faces me, brows pinched together, worried. "I just don't really know what we're doing."

"Tell me what you want." *Tell me that's it me. That you want me. So I don't have to keep pretending.*

"I'm not good at this stuff, Ryan."

Neither am I.

"Come here," I say as I grab her leg and move her to face me.

Time to get honest.

"I've wanted to kiss you since the night of the concert," I confess. "I don't know where your head is at, but whenever I'm not with you, I want to be."

I watch as she drops her eyes. Shy.

"Talk to me, babe." *Tell me you feel it too.*

"I just . . ." she starts, trying to find her words and settling back on, "I don't do this well."

"Do what?"

"This . . ."

I can't take her shyness, so I hold her head in my hands, angling her to look at me when I finally admit, "Whatever *this* is, I want it. I just need to know if you do."

My tone is intent because I know what I want here. Her eyes don't move from mine, and I wait for her response. For anything. I put it out there, and now my heart is racing with nerves, uncertain of her response. Then finally, she gives it to me, and I wanna fuckin' cling to her when she nods her head yes.

Keeping my hands on her, I guide her to me and kiss her. I've never wanted anything as much as I want her, and when she slides her arms under my coat and around my waist, my heart finally starts to settle. I have her.

Her lips are cold and wet with rain, and I squeeze her to me. I move slowly because the thought of rushing anything with her, to quicken the pace of her touch, would be stupid. So I take my time as I graze my tongue along her soft lips, and when she relaxes, allowing me to take more, I pass her lips and taste the warmth of her mouth.

I'm relieved that she's giving me this, that she wants what I want, but I'm anxious because I've never done this before. Never have I had feelings like this for anyone. Not even close to thinking that I could.

She presses her fingers into me, tightening her hold, and I keep my hands on her jaw, marking her as mine like some pathetic puppy, but I do it anyway.

She moves with me, sliding her tongue along mine—gently—without any sign of urgency, and I love that about her. That she would want the time the same way I do.

When I feel her move her hands out from under my coat and wrap around my wrists, I pull back and ask, "Should we get out of here?"

"Let's stay."

"Come here," I say as I slide her on top of my lap, and she slips her arm around my neck, steadying herself on me.

"Can I ask you something?" she says quietly.

"Anything."

"I never asked before because I didn't want to intrude, but . . . where's your father?" she asks with a hint of trepidation.

I don't talk to anyone about my dad. Never have. I hide it, bury it, and mask it with vices that make it easier to deal with. But I know she's hiding something too. I wish I knew what it was, so I go ahead and break off a piece of me and give it to her. "He died about ten years ago."

"I'm sorry," she says and drops her head away from me—abashed. "I shouldn't have asked."

"Candace, you can ask me anything," I tell her as I lift her chin up. "I don't want you to feel like you can't, okay?" I don't know what else to say, but I do know I want her to start opening up to me.

"Yeah," she breathes softly.

"My dad was an asshole," I tell her, wanting to be honest with her. "He drank way too much and was never around, but when he was, he was a total dick. So, don't feel bad for asking, because I don't feel bad that he's dead." I know my words come out hard, but they come out in truth.

She scans my face for a moment. She knows there's more behind my words, but I don't elaborate because what I just gave her is more than I've given anyone. So I leave it.

I clutch her waist and hold on to her when she looks over my shoulder and asks, "Is there a trail up there?"

"Yeah, it's a pretty decent path if you want to go up there."

"Yeah, let's go," she suggests, and I eye her leopard rain boots, asking, "Those have enough traction?"

Laughing, she says, "We'll see."

Stealing another kiss from her, enjoying the freedom of being able to, I stand and smile down at her before scooping her up and over my shoulder. This chick weighs nothing, and she begins to laugh as I haul her up the stairs. The giggles and squeals coming out of her are beautiful, and she never complains. I adore this side of her.

chapter twenty-one

AFTER HIKING IN the rain for over an hour, I didn't let the fact that we were rain-soaked stop me from taking Candace into Seaside to the Broadway Strip. We took our time, walking in and out of the shops and grabbing lunch.

We came home and had an early dinner before everyone said goodbye and headed back home. It's just the two of us and my mom, so we've made no plans for the night. After Candace gets cleaned up, she makes herself comfortable on the couch downstairs, reading a book, while I take a quick shower.

I was surprised with how easygoing she was after our talk on the beach. We fell into the laidback feeling we have built up to in our friendship, but now there's no more grey.

Toweling off, I throw on a pair of pajama pants and dry my hair. I hear my mom's voice when I walk out of the room, and I start making my way down the stairs, spotting Candace and my mom sitting on the couch.

"No child should ever have to hear that," I overhear my mom telling Candace and I ask, "Hear what?" curious as to what they're chatting about.

As I walk across the room, I notice Candace's splotchy face, and I know she's been crying. She keeps from looking at me as she faces my mother, so I take a seat next to her on the couch and slip my arm around her when my mom answers me.

"Candace is telling me about what happened the other night."

"Mom." I've been avoiding asking Candace how she's been feeling about the whole situation to keep from upsetting her.

"It's fine," Candace assures me, so I stay quiet and listen as they continue to talk.

I watch my mom take ahold of Candace's hand when she asks, "Do you have any other family at all?"

"No. It's only ever been the three of us since my father's parents passed away."

"What about your mother's family?"

"I've never met them," Candace tells her. "I have never known them to speak. I'm not even sure they know about me." Her voice trembles as she says this, and I run my hand up her back, wondering why she would have a side of her family that she's being kept away from. But before I can question it too much, my mother leans in and takes Candace in her arms, hugging her. We both have her in our hold when she begins weeping.

I feel horrible, but glad that she's here with me and that she would open up to my mother, who's nearly a stranger to her. I think of how long it took Candace to show me even a hint of this side of herself, but I know my mom has a way about her that can make anyone want to open up. She's always been that person for me, so seeing her provide Candace a little of that when I know she's probably never gotten it from her own parents is a good thing.

My mom pulls back, telling Candace exactly what I'm feeling as she wipes the tears from Candace's cheeks.

"I'm glad you're here with us." Candace only nods when my mom says, "I'll let the two of you be," before walking out of the room.

I pull Candace to me, resting her back onto my chest as I lean against the armrest. She continues to let out soft whimpers.

"Don't cry, babe," I say quietly.

"I'm tired," she tells me. "I don't want to talk anymore."

So I don't say anything else. Taking her hand, I lead her upstairs so that she can lie down. It's late, and I'm sure she's exhausted from our busy day.

I let go of her hand when we hit the doorway and watch as she walks into the bathroom. I wait, listening to the faucet run, and when she returns, she doesn't say anything as she looks at me and gets into my bed.

Her back is facing me, and I'm not sure what she wants me to do. I know what I want to do, so I swallow the questioning thoughts and decide to not leave her in here alone. I walk over to the edge of the bed, pull back the covers, and slide in behind her. She's curled into a ball, so I wrap myself around her, tucking her into me, when she wedges her hand underneath mine for me to hold. This small move is all I need to assure me that she wants me with her tonight, so I stay.

Waking up with Candace is something that I can get used to, and I want to. So much so, that when I dropped her off at her house after we drove back to Seattle today, I asked her to stay at my loft tonight. She didn't want to at first, hell, even after trying to talk to her about why she's so apprehensive about it, I still don't think she wants to, but she wound up agreeing anyway.

I know that Jase told me that she was inexperienced, but I'm not quite sure *how* inexperienced he meant. After seeing how shy she was when I told her I wanted her here tonight, I'm pretty sure this girl is more innocent than I thought. But I want her here, and I want her in my bed. I've never wanted anyone in my bed. I avoid it. Always have. Always keeping everyone I've ever brought here downstairs. But her . . . I want it with her.

Getting a drink of water, I see headlights shine through the windows as her car pulls into my drive. She had to work the closing shift tonight, so it's a little past midnight as I watch her get out of her car. I head over to the door and wait for her to knock, but when I hear nothing, I wonder if she's having second thoughts. Hell, I'm surprised she came in the first place with how hesitant she was earlier. I startle her when I open the door.

"What are you doing out here?" I question with a tilt of my head, knowing all too well what she was doing—worrying.

"Umm, nothing. I was just about to knock." A clear lie, but I find myself liking it.

I take her bag as she walks in, setting it at the foot of the stairs. When I turn, I see her fidgeting her hands as she stands awkwardly in my living room. Needing her to relax and not feel this way when she's with me, I go over and take her in my arms. She accepts the touch willingly and clasps her hands behind my back, leaning her forehead against my chest. When she lets go of a deep breath, I give her head a kiss, asking, "Better?"

Her hum is soft when she says, "Mmm hmm."

"Good. I'm wiped. What about you?"

"Yeah," she breathes.

I take her hand, leading her upstairs. Walking her into my room, I aim her past the large closet, saying, "The bathroom is right over there."

She looks up at me, smiling, before taking her bag out of my hand and closing the bathroom door behind her.

I change clothes while I hear her taking a shower, and just knowing that she's naked in there—in my shower—starts a swarm of thoughts I know I need to get under control before I get her in my bed. Heading back downstairs to grab a bottle of water for her, I hang out in my kitchen, giving myself a few minutes before I go back up.

She's stepping out of the bathroom when I return, wearing a similar tank and pajama pants as she has the past couple of nights. I watch her hop up onto the tall bed, and I have to laugh at her as she slides under the covers. Sitting next to her, back against the cool leather headboard, she settles herself into my hold. When I look down at her, she's looking at the tattoo that's inked on the side of my ribs. I know she's gonna ask me about it when she lays her hand on top of it, so I decide, on the fly, to just tell her. She was so scared to be here with me earlier. I told her she could trust me, but I know my words aren't enough, so I'll give her a reason to try.

"What's this for?"

"A reminder," I say as I take her hand off the tattoo that covers my scar and hold it to my chest. "Like I said, my dad was an asshole." Her eyes shift up and meet mine when I continue, "He was a drunk and liked to take his anger out on me and my mom. I took more of it than she did. The drunker he was, the worse it would get. He was like that for as far back as I can remember. It was all I knew. Then one night, I beat the shit out of him when he was wasted, and when he got in his car and left, he never came back. His car was found wrapped around a tree, and that was it. He was dead."

The look on her face is beyond disbelief, so I pull her in tighter, knowing that was probably the last thing she expected me to say. It was a couple months after the funeral that I didn't attend when I got the words *Pain is a reminder you're still alive* tattooed over the scar that he gave me. But after all the hell he inflicted on me, I'm the one that's still breathing.

I don't know how else to show this girl that she can trust me and not be so closed off like she's always been with me. I need her to know that I trust her, so I let her know, "You're the only one who knows that, outside of my mom and me."

"I feel really stupid," she mumbles as she closes her eyes. "I'm so sorry about complaining about my parents."

"Candace, you're far from stupid," I say when I run my hand along her jaw to urge her to look at me. "Your parents treated you like shit. They filled you full of misconceptions of yourself and fucked with your head. Anyone would be devastated. Don't dismiss your pain because you don't think it's worthy. It is."

She takes a moment after I tell her this and looks at me. I know she acknowledges my words when she reaches up and threads her hands in my hair, drawing me in to kiss her. I slide down to meet her face to face, and I take her lips with mine. Bracing my body over hers, I soak in the heat of her as I run my mouth down her smooth neck, taking my time, nipping her gently along the way. When I start taking little sucks across her collarbone, she uses her hands to guide my face back up to her lips.

I know she's scared to move fast, she told me this earlier, so I go at her pace. Taking one of her hands off my cheek, I slide my fingers between hers and hold her hand as I move past her lips and explore her mouth. I grip her hand tightly, pressing it into the mattress, and I'm finding it hard to not want to take her, feel her breasts, run my hands up her thighs. My thoughts intensify, and I slow down, pulling back. Her face is slightly flushed, and I finally notice how strong her hold is on my hand.

"I could do this all night." I lean my forehead against hers, and she closes her eyes, keeping them shut until I say, "Look at me, Candace."

It takes her a second before she opens her eyes and peers up at me.

"Tell me why you're nervous with me."

"Ryan," she whispers and turns her head to the side to break the contact.

"Tell me," I say, needing her to just give me a small piece of what's going on inside of her head.

She moves to look at me again and starts, "Because . . ."

"Because why?"

"Because this is new for me," she finally reveals.

I don't respond, I simply smile down at her, and I can feel her start to relax.

The smile on her face is perfect, and when I catch her dimple, I finally take what I've been wanting and lean down to kiss it before I lie next to her and band my arms around her.

I watch as she begins to wake up. She clutches the blankets around her, eyes still closed and shimmies herself further down into the bed. She did the same thing yesterday morning at my mom's house. I reach down and pull her back up to me, and she starts blinking her eyes open when I begin to run my hands up and down her back, attempting to warm her up.

"Hey," she mumbles as she scoots in closer to me.

"Why don't you wear something warmer if you're always so cold?"

"I've tried, but it's hard for me to sleep when I wear heavy clothes," she says.

"I'm not gonna lie," I tell her. "I think I would prefer you cuddling into me like this every morning."

Tilting her head away from my chest, she questions, "Every morning?"

"You know I'm gonna want you back here."

When she leans her forehead against my chin, she begins to nervously mutter, "I'm not . . . I mean, I don't know if . . ."

"Candace," I say to get her to stop. "I like having you next to me at night. I won't push, if that's worrying you."

She doesn't move her head away from me when she says, "I'm not sure what you're used to, but—"

"Just give me a couple days a week," I tell her to calm her nerves about moving too fast.

She nods her head, and I don't say anything else. We lie together with no words, and I enjoy the touch of her body against mine until we finally decide to crawl out of bed.

We spend a slow morning downstairs, drinking coffee and hanging out. I want to ask her about how she's feeling with her parents, but I decide to hold off because I don't want to upset her. So instead, I flip on the TV and we kick back on the couch. Just another excuse to have my arms around her.

chapter twenty-two

CANDACE STAYED OVER with me a couple more times this past week. Jase is back in town, so she's been spending time with him and a lot of time at the dance studio to get in some solo rehearsals before classes start back up next week. Work has been a little busier with the quarter break ending and students coming back into town, so Candace and I have been snagging time together for a few morning runs. Jase picked her up earlier today to hang out, so I'll stop by his apartment to pick her up after I get off work tonight.

When I walk into the bar, I spot Mel and Max and head over. The other bartenders have everything under control, so I take a seat next to Max to catch up since he took the past week off.

"Good to see you back up here," I tell him. "How was your Christmas?"

"I got to meet all of Traci's family."

"Yeah? How'd that go?"

"Cut the small talk and just tell him," Mel pipes in as she leans her elbows on the bar.

"Tell me what?" I ask.

"She's pregnant," he says to me with a straight face, and I can't tell if he's happy about this or not.

"Is this good news or bad news?" I ask him.

Setting his drink down, he admits, "I don't know. It's shocking news."

"How does she feel about it?"

"Scared. It wasn't something we had even talked about, and now here we are, not sure what this means for us."

"You two just need to talk and be honest with each other," Mel tells him.

"Like you talk to Zane?" he responds with a chuckle.

She smiles and holds her hands up, surrendering, "Hey, I never take my own advice, I just dish it out."

"Have you heard from him?" I ask her.

"He came home for a couple of days, but it was awkward. All he can talk about is how happy he is in L.A. How happy he is to finally be recording an album. He's my husband, and I'm clueless to what his life is like out there."

"You're choosing to be clueless," Max tells her. "You could easily pack your shit up and be with him."

"He doesn't want me to be. He told me that before he moved there."

Max looks over to me, surprised about that little fact that Mel had told me about when it happened. I haven't talked to Zane since he left, so I don't have any idea what's going on with him.

"Enough of our shit. How did everything with Candace go?" Max asks and immediately Mel's eyes widen. I've never mentioned anything about this to her.

"Who's Candace?"

"A friend," I cautiously tell her, but my words are deceived when I see the look Max is giving me.

"You lie," she says to me. "I'm your only female friend. Have been for the past four years."

I keep a straight face, not sure what to say about Candace, and she picks up on my seriousness when she says, "I knew something was going on."

"What do you mean?"

"Just been noticing your moods these past few months. You're quiet. Well, more than usual," she laughs softly. "Your distance with Gavin, girls . . ." she shrugs her shoulders and adds, "Everything really. So who is this chick?"

"A friend of Jase and Mark's," I tell her and then turn to Max to answer his original question. He knew I was taking her home with me for Christmas, so I tell him, "It went better than expected."

"It wasn't too awkward?"

"What are we talking about?" Mel questions.

"I took her to Oregon."

"What the hell have I missed? You took her to meet your family?" she nearly squeals.

"And no," I say as I turn back to Max. "It wasn't awkward."

"So things are good with you two?" he asks.

"Yeah, man. Things are perfect."

Laughing, Mel says, "How ironic, out of the three of us, Ryan is the one without any hang-ups." She turns to grab a bottle of beer and then says, "I need a drink," before walking away.

I spend most of the night in my office going over supply orders and inventory, double-checking Michael's work to make sure he's handling his shit. I'm not seeing anything out of place, so I call it a night around ten o'clock and head over to Jase's.

When he opens the door, I see Candace lying on his couch.

"She's passed out," Jase tells me. "She's been tired all night."

"What did you guys do?"

"Mark came over for a while and we had dinner. Just hung out though," he says as I walk around the couch to see her sleeping under a blanket.

Sitting down next to her, I lift her head into my lap and run my hand through her hair, telling Jase, "I haven't seen him since you guys got back from Ohio."

He sits down in the chair and watches my hand in her hair before shifting his eyes to me, explaining, "He's been working on some new songs, so he's been busy. Why don't you meet up with us tomorrow before we head up to the bar?"

"I can't. I've got to be there early, but I'll catch up with you guys later," I say as Candace begins to stir and wake up.

Her eyes open as she rolls her head to look up at me. "What's going on?" she mumbles as she sits up.

"Nothing. Just got here."

She lets out a yawn and lazily leans into me, asking Jase, "What're you guys talking about?"

"Mark's gig at the bar tomorrow."

Giving her arm a soft squeeze, I suggest, "You should come."

"Umm . . ."

Jase laughs at her and says, "Just come. You still have never heard Mark play. It'll be fun."

"I don't know."

"We'll all be there," he says, trying to convince her.

She keeps her eyes on Jase, and when he gives her a nod and says, "Come on. One night," she gives in to him.

"Okay. Fine," she sighs, and I watch as Jase gets an almost victorious smile on his face, not understanding why it's such a big deal for her to go out.

"Wipe that smile off your face, Jase," she scolds with humor. "You're embarrassing me."

Before their banter can continue, I say, "Come on, babe. Let's go. It's getting late," as I stand up and take her hand.

"I'll pick you up tomorrow," Jase tells her and she walks over to hug him goodbye. "I'll call you."

"Night, Jase," she says.

"Bye, guys."

We take the elevator down and she asks, "Why is Jase picking me up and not you?"

"I have to be there early to get some work done so I can take the night off and not have to worry about going in too much this next week. But I'll be there when you and Jase get there."

When the elevator opens, we step out to go back to my place for the night.

"Ryan, how've you been?" Mark says when he walks in with Chasten, the drummer of the band.

"Good, man. How was Ohio?"

"Great. We got a ton of snow, so we were stuck at the house for a couple of days, but we survived," he chuckles.

"Survived?"

"If you knew the women in my family, you'd be scared to be cooped up with them during a snow storm. Luckily, my sisters are like a fresh new toy for Jase, so he just sits back and laughs at their shit while I try and find a way to escape it."

"So I take it you're glad to be back then," I tease.

"Yeah. Oh, hey, Jase said Candace was coming up here tonight. Is that true?"

"Is there something I should know about Candace that I'm not getting?" I ask as I follow him over to the stage so he can start setting up with the guys.

"What do you mean?"

"Why don't you tell me why you're so surprised by the fact that she's coming here?" I question. Maybe I shouldn't, but curiosity gets me.

He sets his guitar down and then turns to me. "Candace likes to avoid crowded places."

"I get that. I just can't figure out why," I tell him, hoping he'll throw me a clue, but he doesn't.

"She's slow to open up, but I'm sure I don't have to tell you that," he says.

"Yeah, I know."

"Just be patient with her." He leaves it at that, and I accept the advice because that's all I can do. I wanna get into my girl's head and unfold everything inside. Patience isn't my strong suit, but it's the only hand I have to play with her.

I go upstairs to get a few files from Michael's desk, and when I walk in, I look out his large window that overlooks the back lot and see Jase's SUV as he turns in. I find the files I need and then watch as Candace steps out of the car. God, I'm falling for this girl. I'm wound up just thinking about getting to spend time with her tonight.

Her back is to the building, so I can't see her face, and I wonder what she's staring at as she stands there. Jase says something to her but she remains standing next to the dumpsters. When she finally moves, her heel catches on the pavement, and she takes a hard fall onto her bottom. As soon as she hits the ground, I watch, numb, trying to make sense of what I'm seeing. She's freaking out, frantically stumbling back on her hands. Jase rushes over and huddles down in front of her, picking her up, and I can faintly hear her screaming.

I snap out of my trance. Tossing the files, I run down the stairs and fly out the back door to see the both of them back in Jase's car. Candace is crying and screaming, and I stand there in near shock, confused as hell by what just happened. As her eyes find mine, she throws her hands against the dash and yells at him hysterically as he peels out of the parking lot.

"Candace!" I yell after her as the car pops the curb when Jase hits the main street.

She's gone, and I don't have a clue what the hell is going on, but I'm freaked out at what I just saw. I don't even think about going back in, I just take the keys that are in my pocket to go to the one place I know she'll be.

While I drive to Jase's apartment building, hitting every damn red light, I replay what happened and try to figure out what she saw that triggered her like that. I pull up to the building and throw my car in park when it hits me.

Holy shit.

Chills prick my arms, and I swear my gut hollows out when the memory of that night floods me.

Oh my God.

She was standing right there. She's small. She's timid. Scared.

No. Get your shit together. It's not her.

My mind is racing faster than I'm able to keep up with. I feel like I'm out of my body and can't decipher reality from my fucked up head-trips. If Candace was *her*, I would know.

I would know, right?

I sit in my car as I feel my emotions swarm into a rotation of visions I wish I could just forget. All I can see is that girl. Her beaten face, her naked, bloody body.

"Fuck!" I slam my fists into the steering wheel, desperately trying to rid the memories, but they're too vivid. I don't even want to think about that girl being Candace. It's too fucked up. Pressing my palms against my forehead, I attempt to pull myself together. I know Candace is with Jase, and I just want her to be with me.

Pressing my head back against the seat, I squeeze my eyes shut and attempt to refocus on the fact that Candace is upset and that I need to get my shit together and quick. I take a few moments and sit here in silence before I finally get out of my car.

On the elevator ride up, I take some deep breaths, and calm myself before I knock on the door. When Jase opens it, he immediately tells me, "Man, it's not a good time."

But I don't care. I just want her. "Where is she?" I ask as I move past him and start walking to his bedroom when I see she isn't in his living room.

"Ryan, just give her space," he yells out to me, but I don't even acknowledge him when I open the door to his room and see my girl sitting on the edge of the bed sobbing.

The sight of her slows me down—stops me. She looks up, and her face is soaked with tears. I feel like the slightest move on my part could snap her, so I gently shut the door behind me and walk over, kneeling on the ground in front of her. I brace my hands on her knees, and I'm at a loss with her. Confused. But she doesn't let me dwell on it when she opens her mouth and begins to cry out, "I'm sorry. I'm sorry, Ryan. I'm . . ."

I reach my arm behind her back and drag her off of the bed and onto my lap. "What happened, babe?"

"I'm so sorry," she continues to say with her hands masking her face.

I hold on to her while she cries, and I'm desperate for answers. Wrapping my hands around her wrists, I move her hands from her face so I can see her. I hate that she's hiding from me. "I need you to talk to me."

She avoids my eyes when she tries explaining, "I just . . . I got myself too worked up and had a panic attack. I know you wanted me there tonight, but I couldn't."

She's still hiding from me, and I'm unsure of how much I should push the issue, so I simply ask, "Why couldn't you just tell me?"

"I was embarrassed," she says when she finally looks at me. "This has happened a few times in the past, but only Jase knows that I have these."

My gut is telling me not to believe her. That she's lying to me. But hearing the pain in her words makes the lie okay in a way. She's not opening up to me, and I need her to so badly. Have her trust me. Have her run to me instead of Jase. So I tell her that because I don't know what else to say to her.

"You could've come to me. Jase isn't the only one you have, you know? I need you to trust me enough to talk to me. I understand you and Jase, but I know how I feel about you." I tell her this because watching her run away from me like she did hurt. Like I'm not enough for her to want me like that, and I need her to, for me.

"I want you to need me more than him," I finally tell her, hoping I didn't just sound like an ass for saying it, but I have to say it.

"He's all I've ever had."

When she says this, I know I have a lot to prove to this girl who clearly doesn't trust so easily. I take her hand and press it against my chest, needing her to know how serious I am when I say, "You have me now too."

I know my words get through to her when she fists my shirt in her hand and slings her other arm around my neck, hugging me close. I feel her tears running down my neck as I hold on to her, so I sit here with her on the floor until she calms down and relaxes under my arms.

Brushing her hair behind her shoulder, I kiss her below her ear before whispering, "Let's go home."

She pulls back and looks up at me. I wipe her cheeks and cup her face in my hands when she says, "I don't want to hurt you."

Hearing those selfless words does something to me. And I'm becoming more aware, every day that I have with her, just how much I'm feeling for her.

I press my lips against hers because I don't know how to respond to her words. So I kiss her, but I don't move, I just take in the warmth of her lips against mine, and it's all I need right now. This is enough.

chapter twenty-three

COMING BACK TO my place, Candace is still being very quiet, but I'm not saying much either. I watch as she walks up to my room, and I give her some space while I grab a beer from the fridge. When I do head upstairs, she's in the bathroom with the door shut, taking a shower. I'm noticing that she takes a lot of those, but figure that right now, she probably wants to be left alone.

I go back downstairs and flop down on the couch, mindlessly flipping through the channels before stopping on ESPN. I can't even focus because my head is still upstairs with Candace. I keep replaying what I saw from Michael's office over and over until I hear the creak of the wooden floor. Turning around, I see her standing at the foot of the stairs. As I walk over to her, I can see she's tired.

"You need anything?" I ask, and she shakes her head.

We walk over to the couch, and she lays her head against me as we sit here. Neither one of us says anything. I know she's embarrassed about what I saw, so I don't mention another word about it.

After watching the football highlights and catching the score updates, I say, "Let's go lie down."

Shutting everything off, we head upstairs and crawl into bed. I pull her onto her side, facing me, and hold her close. Her eyes are closed, and I'm sure she's tired, but I lean down anyway and brush my lips across hers, wanting to be close to her. She reaches up and runs her hand along my jaw as she moves with me. We lie there, no words, in the darkness, as we continue to kiss, and after a while, she shifts down on me, resting her head on my chest and falls asleep.

She keeps me up though. Her sleep grows restless, and I watch her as she begins to tremble. I rub her back, wondering, yet again, what's running through her head. She had a night like this just the other day, but I didn't say anything to her about it when she woke up. My need to comfort her overwhelms me, and I want to take her out of the dream that's haunting her.

I add pressure as I continue to rub her back, trying to wake her subtly, but she startles me when she springs out of her sleep, choking in a hard gasp as she abruptly sits up. I'm up next to her, holding on to her shoulders while her whole body shakes.

"Hey," I whisper. "Are you okay?"

Nodding her head, she takes in a deep breath and holds it for a second before slowly releasing it.

"Come here," I urge as I lay her back down with me, and she snuggles in close. Smoothing her hair back, I kiss her forehead. "Talk to me," I say on a hush.

"I'm okay," she tries to assure me.

"Babe . . ."

"I think I'm just stressed. That's' all."

"About what?" I ask.

"School. Dance," she says. Those seem to always be her go-to excuses for a lot of things, and I know she hides behind them. Uses them to distract her.

"You wanna talk about it?"

"Not really," she responds as she weaves her legs with mine.

Looking into her eyes, I encourage, "I want you to talk to me. I know something is bothering you, and I want you to talk to me about it."

She doesn't speak. I can tell that she's trying to think of something to say, but nothing comes, so I give her an out and tell her, "I just want you to try."

Nodding her head, she closes her eyes and after a while, she falls into another fit of sleep, keeping me up most of the night.

When I wake up, Candace is sound asleep, so I slip out of bed and let her rest since I know she didn't get much sleep last night. Looking down at her, she finally looks peaceful. Everything about her is soft and relaxed.

I head downstairs to grab a cup of coffee as my phone begins to ring. It's Sunday morning, so I know it's my mom. We talk for a while until I hear Candace walking down the stairs.

"Hey, Mom. Candace just woke up, so I'm gonna let you go."

"Let me say a quick hi," she says, and I know she's wanting to try to get to know her.

"Hold on," I tell her and then look up at Candace as I hold the phone out to her, mouthing, 'My mom.'

Probably feeling a little awkward, she takes the phone anyway, saying, "Hi, Donna."

I listen to Candace talking with my mom while I make her a cup of coffee. She talks about the solo that she's been piecing together for her audition next month. Walking over to her sitting on my couch, I hand her the coffee. She seems comfortable talking with my mom, and I like that she can have this with her, even if it is a random phone call. Both of these women are important to me, and to see Candace laughing at something my mom must have just said makes me feel like whatever it is that Candace and I are moving towards could be something special.

"What did she have to say?" I ask when she hangs up and hands me the phone.

"Just wanted to know what I had been up to," she says and then takes a sip of her coffee. "She's really nice."

We sit back and get comfortable when she starts, "Ryan . . ."

"Yeah?" I say as I slide my arm around her.

"Nothing," she mumbles, dismissing whatever was running through her head.

"Don't say 'nothing,'" I tell her, and when I do, she wraps her hand behind my neck and moves me in for a kiss before she nuzzles her head under my chin. Her instinct to avoid is strong, and I try not to question it because I've spent my whole life avoiding. I think about what my mom told me about not trying to break down her walls. Taking her advice, I don't pry. I'm gonna be what I think she needs so that she'll want to open up to me. I need her to want to do that for me.

Got out of class early. You home?

Yeah. Door is unlocked.

Classes at the university started back up this week, and I'm getting to see how busy Candace actually is with her dancing. She wasn't kidding when she told me that she lives in the studio. With her busy schedule, I've been trying to get most of my work done while she's in class so I can free up my time at night when she's typically not busy, unless she's working.

"Ryan?" I hear Candace call out when she gets here.

"Back in my office."

She taps on the door before walking in.

"Hey, babe. Come here."

She walks around my desk, and I reach out to pull her onto my lap. Brushing the hair off her shoulder, I ask, "How were your classes today?"

"Uneventful, but it's only the first week," she tells me. "Nothing but going over the syllabus for the most part."

"I'm glad you're here. I've missed you," I say and then bring her head down so I can kiss her. She looks good in her jeans and fitted sweater. She's always so pulled together, even when she wears her old college t-shirts. She always has a polished look about her that I find really attractive.

"So, don't be mad, but . . ."

"Oh, God," I interrupt because it sounds like she's up to something that I *would* be mad at.

"Just listen," she says as she pokes me in the ribs. "When I was on campus today I ran into Stacy Keets who works at the Henry Art Gallery.

She was telling me that one of her pieces got picked up for a gallery show next month."

"So, you want to go?"

"Yes, but I was thinking that you could submit one of your photos."

There's the kicker. "Babe," I say as I shake my head. "Those are just a hobby that I hardly even take seriously. I'm far from having them displayed in a gallery of all places."

She rolls her eyes at me, dismissing my words when she says, "Well, I happen to love the few photos I've seen. They're a lot better than you think they are."

"You're cute," I tease. The fact that she can view those pictures as something worthy of being displayed as art is a bit far-fetched for me.

"I'm serious, I think that you should at least submit something and see if it gets accepted. If not, nothing lost, right?"

"And if they are?"

A smile crosses her face as she says, "Then you can take me as your date for the showing."

"If I say I'll think about it, will that suffice?" I ask, but truth is, I'd take this girl anywhere for a date, so if that means submitting a few pictures, I'll do it.

"Yep." She looks like a kid who just convinced her parents to buy her an ice cream, and I can't help myself when I bury my head in her neck and start playfully ravishing it, knowing how ticklish she is in the spot I'm nipping. She squirms, laughing hysterically as she tries to wriggle her way off of my lap, and when she finally manages, she catches her breath and says, "Show me all your photos so I can pick out the ones for you to consider submitting."

Clearly I don't get any input in her little mission. Sliding the door to my credenza open, I pull out the stack of mattes and hand them to her.

"Here, boss," I say with a wink.

When she turns to head out into the living room, I follow and offer, "Want something to drink?"

"Yeah, anything hot."

I begin to heat up some water and pull down the tea she likes. She's been spending more time here, so we took a trip to the store, that way I could have some of her staples here at the loft. I love seeing pieces of her in my home, even if it's as simple as a canister of her Harrods Ceylon tea that she brought over the other day. As I dip the tea bag in the mug, I look up, and she has the mattes lying facedown on the coffee table.

"I'll be right back," she mumbles before rushing off to the bathroom.

Shit. She hadn't seen all the photos before, and I can only assume that she didn't like what she saw. They're mostly nudes, but she had to have known that by the few she had already seen.

I give her a few minutes, but when she doesn't come back out, I give the door a light knock.

"What are you doing?" I ask suspiciously, even though I have a pretty solid idea as I step into the bathroom with her. When I take a step toward her, she takes a step back, keeping the distance, and the gesture irritates me. "Babe, what's wrong?"

"Nothing." She's being evasive, and I wish she would just be honest with me.

I drop my head and let out a deep breath, trying to control my frustration with her.

"Is it the photos?" I ask, already knowing the answer, but I feel like I need to spell it out for her because I know how much she likes to avoid talking when she's uncomfortable.

She doesn't answer, but her brows are scrunched with worry, and it's all the confirmation I need.

"Candace, you asked to see them. You knew what they would be of."

"I know," she admits as she lowers her head and looks at the floor. "I'm sorry. I didn't think they would all be like that."

Leaning against the sink, I cross my arms around my chest. I hate that I feel like I have to explain myself when I've been nothing but open with her, but I do it anyway. "They're just pictures, that's all."

She takes a seat on top of the toilet lid and says, "But . . . they just seem so intimate."

"Babe, don't." I drop my arms, hating that she feels this way because she's got it reversed. There was nothing intimate when I took those photos. I have no connection to them.

She looks up at me, and I see the hesitation in her eyes when she quietly asks, "Did you sleep with them?"

"Yes." I respond immediately, not wanting to bullshit her. Wanting to be completely transparent with her the way I wish she would be with me.

"How many have you . . . ?"

"A lot."

"And you photograph them?" Her words are laced with disbelief, and she's got it all wrong, so I try to explain it to her.

"No. I've only photographed a couple of women. Most of those photos are the same person."

"Oh." Dropping her head, she tries hiding her insecurities that I can see right through. She's so opposite of what I know she is comparing herself to. She's modest and private. It's been three weeks since Christmas and she's never let me touch her, see her, anything.

Kneeling down in front of her, I grip her thighs and speak firmly when I say, "I know what you're doing, and you can stop. None of them meant what you mean to me. I never had or wanted a relationship with them."

"Then why?" she tries to argue, and I can't stand seeing her doubt herself, doubt me.

I take her hands in mine, holding them, when I look into her eyes and give her another piece of me that only she gets to have. "Because for most of my life I've been lost," I confess. "I dealt with a lot of shit growing up, and I used women as a way to escape. But when I met you . . . you're just different. I wanted to know you, really know you. You're nothing like those women. Nothing. I've never looked at them or wanted them the way I do you."

"I don't know what I'm doing," she says, unsure of herself, but I feel the same way, so I tell her.

"I don't either."

"I mean . . . I haven't . . ."

"Been with anyone?" I ask, my words slipping out, wondering if that's why she's moving so slowly with me.

I know I've embarrassed her when she covers her face and doesn't say anything, but I'm not appeasing her this time by letting her avoid me. I need her to start talking and stop being afraid that I'm gonna judge her.

Grabbing on to her hips, I pull her down onto my lap, taking her hands away from her face.

"Talk to me."

She takes a moment before she finally exposes a part of herself to me. "Only once, but he was really drunk and it . . . well, it was pretty much over before it began."

God, this chick is practically a virgin, and the thought of some guy using her gets under my skin. Shit, just the thought of any guy, other than me, touching her makes me jealous as hell.

"Sounds like an asshole."

"He was," she responds. "But it kept my parents off my back. They really liked him and his family, so we would go out every now and then, but that was about it. So, I can't help but sometimes wonder what you're doing with me."

"Look at me," I demand because I hate that she would belittle herself for even a second. "I don't give a shit how inexperienced you are. In fact, I prefer that because the thought of another guy touching you pisses me off. That guy was a dick for treating you like you were disposable. But don't devalue yourself because of that. I won't rush you into anything. You know that, right?"

When she nods her head, I try to make it even clearer when I add, "You're what I want. No one else, okay?"

"I just get scared, and I feel like you might start thinking you're wasting your time with me. I know you'd prefer that I stay here with you every night, but that's what scares me. I just need to move slow with this."

"You're not a waste of my time. You're worth every second."

If she only knew how I take in every moment with her, she wouldn't have to even question this. So when I see her nodding and letting out a sigh, almost in relief at my words, I take her face in my hands and kiss her. Slow. Because time doesn't matter to me with her. I don't even move; I just rest my lips on hers. It's only when she slips out a giggle that I pull back, and with a smirk, ask, "What?"

"Can we get off your bathroom floor now?" she says with a smile, and I have to laugh at her, happy to see that she's feeling better about this situation. At least I hope she is.

"Let's get out of here," I suggest and stand to help her up off the floor.

"Where are we going?"

"Let's go hang out at Zoca's and get some coffee."

"Perfect."

chapter twenty-four

YESTERDAY, AFTER CANDACE got upset about seeing the photos, I took her to a local coffee shop where we ran into Gavin. I was nervous having Candace meet him, someone who knows way too much of my past, after she had just gotten a glimpse of it. Oddly, he wasn't as brash as he normally is, and the two of them seemed to get along for what small talk they wound up having, which wasn't much.

I've definitely put space between us, but I've known him for nearly ten years, and it's strange not having him be more of a presence. He stops by the bar on occasion to listen to bands and grab a drink, but it's not like it used to be.

I turn around from my desk, sliding the credenza open to take out a few files that I need to run up to the bar, when I see the mattes that I had thrown in here last night. I hate that Candace had to see those. I didn't consider her reaction then, but now, I regret ever showing her. I don't blame her for being so upset, having to see images of women from my past, knowing that I had slept with them. It's something we haven't done with each other, haven't even come close, and I tossed those images out there for her without thinking about how hard it would be for her to see.

I don't even want to think about her kissing another guy, touching another guy, but to see images like that . . . I know I would have lost my shit, so I can't hold her reaction against her. She has every right.

These photos are my past, a past where I never considered meeting a girl like Candace. A past full of masks, trying to hide from the person I was scared to be. A person that I am now realizing I might be able to be—because of her. Because she is the one I want to take care of—protect. No girl has ever made me feel that way, but she does, and wanting to love her is so much more powerful than my fear of loving her.

Grabbing the mattes, I head downstairs to my garage and don't give it a second thought when I toss them in the trash. They have no meaning to me, and she doesn't need reminders of my past lying around my home. I don't need the reminders either.

When I go back upstairs, I grab the files and my keys and head over to the bar. When I get there, I run into Max out in the parking lot, and he follows me up to my office.

"How's everything with Traci?" I ask as he shuts the door, and I sit down at my desk.

"I'm freaking the hell out, man," he says, running his hand over his head.

I chuckle under my breath. I've never seen him this tense. "You've gotta relax."

"Relax? Dude, we're talking about a fuckin' baby."

"You asked her to move in with you. You were all ready to have her there to share your life with, so what the hell?"

"Yeah, we shared all of, what, five months?" he says.

"But you guys have been together longer than that."

"Yeah, but I never really considered the whole kid thing," he says and pauses before adding, "We went to a doctor's appointment this morning."

"How'd that go?" I ask as I watch him lean back into the chair, fully stressed.

"She's fourteen weeks pregnant."

"I don't know what the hell that means."

"Don't you have like twenty nieces and nephews?" he overstates, and I laugh at this guy's jest.

"Dude, that doesn't mean I know shit about pregnancy."

He sits up and rests his elbows on his knees when he states, "Baby will be here in June."

"It's so weird to think about," I say. "You with a baby. You spend your days barking and intimidating people." We both laugh, and I know he sees the same image I see in my head.

"Ugh," he groans. "Can we talk about something else, like you and your very unpregnant girlfriend?"

I shake my head when he continues, and asks, "When am I ever gonna meet this chick? You should bring her up here."

"I tried."

"What does that mean, 'I tried'?"

I've always been honest with Max about Candace, but I also know how private she is, so I just tell him what she's told me, which isn't much. "She has a thing with crowds. They make her uncomfortable. She tried coming, but it was too much for her."

"What's up with the crowds?"

Shrugging my shoulders, I admit, "I don't know. She doesn't say anything beyond the fact that she doesn't like them."

"Have you asked?"

"I don't feel like I can."

"I don't get it," he says, but I feel like I'm saying too much at this point, so I cut it off.

"She's doesn't like crowds; it's probably as simple as that."

He catches my intent and backs off, not saying anything else about it.

Hey! You home?

On way now. Leaving gym.

Mind if I stop by?

Not at all. Be there in 10.

See ya!

After I left work the other night, Candace came over and she spent yesterday here as well. I didn't want her to leave my bed this morning, but she had to go into work since one of the guys quit unexpectedly, so I decided to hit the gym with Jase and Mark to kill some time.

I leave the door unlocked when I get home and run upstairs to grab a quick shower. After throwing on some clothes, I leave my hair wet when I think I hear Candace downstairs.

"Hey, babe," I say while I walk down the stairs and see her riffling through the drawer in one of the end tables in the living room.

"Hey."

Walking over to her, I cradle her face and give her a kiss before asking, "What are you scrounging around for?"

"Your mattes. I can't find them."

"That's because they're not here," I tell her and then claim her mouth with mine again, taking my time and not backing away, but that doesn't stop her from mumbling over my lips.

"Where are they?"

"I tossed them."

She pulls back and breaks the kiss when she questions surprisingly, "What?! Why?"

"Because they made you uncomfortable."

"But I was looking for the photo of the woman's back so I could submit it to the gallery."

She looks disappointed when she says this, and I tell her, "I don't have it. I threw them all away."

She's frustrated when she falls back into the large chair. I move to sit on the edge of the coffee table in front of her and lean forward, asking, "What's wrong?"

"Nothing, I was just excited to submit that photo." She leans her head back and looks up at the ceiling, saying, "Maybe it was a stupid idea."

"Is it that important to you?"

"I just thought if you saw one of your pieces in a showing, that you would see the art in it."

Thinking about how I could just photograph her, I smile when I say, "It wasn't difficult to capture or enhance. I can recreate it if you want."

"We don't have time for you to find someone to pose. It needs to be submitted tomorrow by the end of the day."

"We don't need to find anyone," I tell her, already excited about being able to get photos of her. "Let's go upstairs. I'll shoot *your* back."

She immediately blushes. "No."

"No, what?"

"I'm not taking my top off for you to photograph me."

"You don't have to take anything off, promise. It's an extreme close-up; you only need to hike it up a little," I try to assure her. Her inhibition is nothing that I'm not aware of, but I also want her to be comfortable enough with me so that we can start to move forward.

"What?" she questions when I stand up and take her hand.

"We're going upstairs."

"Ryan, no."

She tugs her hand out of mine, and I ask, "What's wrong?"

"It feels weird to me."

"Don't let it."

"You just can't say that and expect me to be okay. I'm not like the girls you took those pictures of. I'm . . ."

"No, you're not. You're nothing like them, which is why I threw them in the garbage." I move to kiss her, needing her to just relax, knowing it's just the two of us and no one is judging. When I pull back, I look at her and affirm, "I only want you. No one else. The only photos I want are ones of you."

She hesitates, but then she nods. I want her to do this, so I don't say anything else as I walk her upstairs. Letting go of her hand, I leave her in the center of my room as I go into the closet to get my camera, and when I return, she's still in the same spot. I let her be while I pull the drapes shut, blacking out the room before taking her hand and leading her to the bed.

"Just lie on your stomach," I gently instruct and watch as she climbs up and lies down, folding her arms underneath her head.

Her eyes stay on me as I crawl onto the bed next to her. Her body flinches when I take the hem of her shirt between my fingers.

"I'm just going to lift it up a little."

It's just her back, but she always keeps herself covered up, and I can't help myself when I drag my knuckles along her spine as I lift her shirt up and then tuck it under the strap of her bra. Her skin is milky and flawless. Perfect.

She takes a deep breath and I ask, "You okay?"

"Mmm hmm."

I notice her eyes are closed when I get off of the bed to kneel beside it. Picking up my camera that I haven't used in months, I begin to adjust the settings for the lack of light in the room. I shift my eyes to see she's watching me, and I give her a small smile then bring the camera up to my eye to set the flash.

"I'm gonna take some test shots to get the shutter speed right, okay?"

Resting my elbows on the mattress, I move in close to her back and capture a few images to make sure the lighting isn't distorting her lines. When I look at the shot, I notice that there isn't much curve to her back, so I take a pillow from the bed.

"Here, lean up." She pushes her chest up from the mattress, and I wedge the pillow under her as I explain, "I just need a little more curve to your spine. Just lie down and relax."

Kneeling back down, I aim the camera close to her back and softly murmur, "That's perfect," and I begin to shoot. I only take about ten quick shots when I set the camera down because everything about this is turning me on.

I've never felt anything when taking pictures in the past, but this . . . this feels intimate. Looking at her lying on my bed. I know she feels exposed, and I can see how tense her body is. But for the first time, I feel like we're connecting in a way that we haven't before. That she's starting to trust me.

I pull her shirt out from her bra and lower it back down, covering her again before I lean over her, bracing my hands on the bed.

"Thanks," I whisper, and she rolls to her side as I lower myself next to her.

I move in and lightly graze my lips across hers, just wanting the feel of her before I cover her mouth with mine. She tangles her hands in my hair, and everything about her touch makes me want her. And even if this is all she'll give me right now, it's more than the meaningless sex I've had with all of those other women. Everything is so much more with her, and I can't help but think about what it will be like when we finally get there. If just kissing her feels like this, I can't even imagine what I'm in for.

I roll her onto her back, finding it hard to control myself. I run my kisses down her neck and across her collarbone. She grips my arms, and her hold is tight on me when I reach down and grab on to her thigh, needing more of her as I run my hand slowly up her leg. Burying my head in her neck, she clamps her hand around my wrist, stopping my hand from moving between her legs.

Pulling back, I look over her face, but she keeps her eyes down and then whispers, "Sorry." But there is nothing about this that she needs to be sorry for because I can feel her trying, and that's all I need from her.

"You don't ever have to be sorry," I tell her as she looks up at me. "God, you're beautiful."

She doesn't respond when I tell her this, but it's okay. I've never ached for anyone like this. I've never ached to touch someone so badly before. So to hold back with her hurts because it's the last thing I want to do. But I know I'm falling in love, so I do it.

Taking her hand in mine, I hold it as I run my other hand through her hair.

"Stay with me," I tell her, not wanting to spend the night without her.

"I told you, I can't."

"You mean you won't," I respond. She's spent the past two nights here with me and told me this morning that she was going to go home tonight. I get that she doesn't feel comfortable being here every night, but I don't want her to go either.

"Ryan," she breathes out. "Don't make me feel bad."

"I don't want to make you feel bad; I just want to keep you in my bed," I say with a sly grin to lighten the mood because I really don't want to make her feel bad for wanting a night in her own bed.

She shakes her head at me, then pulls me down to her and kisses me, holding me close. We continue like this for a while and it makes the anticipation so much worse when I keep thinking about what it would be like if she would just let me touch her. So when she finally does leave, I take that anticipation to the shower.

Turning the water on hot, I let it wash over me as I allow my mind to run free. God, I want her, and the more time I have with her, the harder it is to control myself. Having her stop me when all I wanted was to keep running my hand up her thigh. To know what she feels like. To let myself go with her.

I can't hold back when I fist myself in my hand, imagining her soft skin against me. Fantasizing about having her naked in my bed and how she would look. My mind begins to lose itself in a myriad of thoughts when I finally zone in and see her so clearly.

She lies underneath me, running her hands along my chest, with a sated look on her face while I move inside of her.

The intense vision causes me to catch my breath, and I have to brace my hand on the tile wall, dropping my head.

Her legs wrap around my hips, pulling me in deeper, gripping my hair in her hands. Her body is warm against mine while she moves with me. She's into it, losing herself.

The hot water runs down my back, and my shoulders tense as I begin stroking myself faster.

I drag my tongue over her nipple and suck it into my mouth, making her breathe my name for more.

Tightening my grip, I work myself through my heady breaths.

Sitting back on my knees, she rocks her hips into me, bowing her back off the bed as I run my hands up her torso and between her breasts. She's completely exposed to me. Her naked flesh, smooth, damp with sweat.

My muscles tighten, and I feel myself swell as I'm about to go.

She's moaning.

I'm panting.

Running my hands inside of her thighs, I slide my thumb over her wet core as she throws her head back into the pillow.

"Uhh, fuck," I moan out when I finally feel the pulses of release I've been needing from the eagerness that's been building up inside of me. I let it go as my head falls back while I ride out the images that are still reeling in my mind. The air is thick with steam, and when I'm able to stand without the support of the wall, I turn the heat down on the water to cool off before I get out.

After my shower, I get ready for bed and slide under the covers, replaying our evening together. Thinking about how she looked when I was photographing her. Realizing, that in her own way, she was finally opening herself up to me with her trust. It wasn't obvious, but I saw it anyway.

I grab a pillow from her side of the bed, and smile at the thought that I've allowed a girl to claim a side of my bed. But I have and I like it. Rolling onto my side, I wrap my arm around her pillow and can smell her on the fabric. She smells so good; I know I'll never grow tired of it, so I lie there as she finds a way to flood my mind again.

Fuck, I need another shower.

chapter twenty-five

CANDACE STOPPED BY a few days ago to pick up the photo after I finished enhancing it. I think she was surprised to see herself like that. Even if it was just the sway of her back, the photo was beyond sensual. For some reason, she's really uncomfortable with exposing herself. She's confident in her body—it would be odd if she wasn't, being a dancer and all—but being comfortable with herself in a sexual way doesn't seem to come easily for her. It could just be that she's never been that way with a man, but I see her starting to try with me.

The whole thing got me thinking about how I spend my time. Candace keeps herself busy with work and school, but mostly with dance. She loves it; it's her passion in life, and I admire her focus. I don't have a focus like that in my life, and although she takes it a step beyond most people, I feel like I need to find something outside of work and Candace to do with my time. I talked to her about this yesterday on the phone, and she encouraged me to spend more of my time working on my photography.

I've always enjoyed the editing aspect of it, but never took a whole lot of pleasure in the actual shoots until last weekend when she let me shoot her. She made me a very loose promise that she would let me photograph her again, and I plan on holding her to her word.

I hear my phone chime in the next room, and I'm surprised to see Gavin's name when I open his text.

You at work?
Home. What's up?
In the area. Mind if I stop by for a while?
Come on over.

After the random run-in that Candace and I had with him the other week, I didn't think I would actually hear from him when he said he would be in touch. But when he gets here, he says he just wanted to stop by and catch up. So we crack open a couple of beers and flip on ESPN, hanging out like we used to do, simply killing time.

"So I ran into Max and his girlfriend the other night," he tells me.
"Oh yeah, where at?"

"Lakeside," he says and then takes a pull of his beer before adding, "Did you know she's pregnant?"

"Yeah, man. I knew."

Shaking his head, he says, "I couldn't believe it when he told me that shit. We used to have so much fun before he got tied down with that chick. Speaking of chicks, who was that girl you were with the other day?"

Looking over at him, I don't even know why I'm even gonna waste my time telling him, but I do. "We've been seeing each other."

He gives me a smirk and says, "Nice, man," mistaking my word *seeing* for *hooking up with*.

"No, I mean we're together," I clarify.

Giving his head a questioning tilt, he says, "She doesn't seem your type."

"She's exactly my type."

"You sure about that?"

"Yeah, man. I'm sure about that," I tell him, annoyed with his almost condescending tone.

He takes my hint and changes the subject, asking, "You gonna be at the bar tonight?"

"Yeah. I've been going in on Friday nights to free up my weekends lately."

"A few buddies of mine were gonna hit up Monkey Pub, but we'll stop by to hang out if you have time for a drink."

"Yeah, come by. I think Mark and a couple guys from the band are gonna be there too," I say when there's a knock on the door.

I'm surprised when I open it to see Candace standing there. "Hey, babe! What are you doing here?"

"I wanted to see you before you left for work," she says with a smile before I pick her up off the ground in my arms and give her a kiss, appreciating the unexpected visit.

"I've missed you this week," I tell her when I set her down.

"Sorry. Auditions are in a few weeks, and then I won't be living in the studio."

"Candace!" Gavin says from behind me.

"Hey, Gavin. What are you doing here?"

"Just stopped by to bullshit with Ryan."

She looks up at me, saying, "I'm sorry, I should have called before stopping by."

Before I can respond, Gavin takes her hand and pulls her inside. "Wanna beer?"

"Um, no."

"I'll get you a water," I tell her as I walk by, knowing she just got out of a two-hour studio.

"Thanks."

She takes off her coat, and the two of them sit on the couch. When I return with her water, I hear Gavin making fun of her bun, saying, "What's with the hair, grandma?"

"Don't be a dick," I tell him when I sit down, pulling her to my side.

"I was in the dance studio all day," she says and then takes a long drink of water.

"How'd that go?" I ask.

"It actually went pretty well. My instructor complimented me on my solo."

"Really? That's great, babe."

Candace's instructor has been continuing to ride her ass a lot, so I'm glad today was a good day for her because she's been really upset about it.

"Well, actually all she said was 'That's better,' but coming from her, that's huge."

"You coming out with us tonight?" Gavin asks her.

"Umm . . ." She turns to look at me, and I explain, "Gavin's just coming by the bar tonight with some friends, that's all."

"Oh. No, I've got plans," she tells him.

"What are you doing?" I ask, not remembering her telling me of any plans for tonight.

"I'm going to Jase's to hang out. We haven't had a lot of time to see each other lately."

Wanting to be alone with her for a moment because I need more than the short kiss I got when she walked in, I stand and say, "Come with me to my office before you go."

We start walking down the hall when Gavin snarks, "If you guys are gonna fuck, I'm out."

"Dude!" I snap, pissed that he would say shit like that in front of my girl who already has enough insecurity about this shit.

Shrugging his shoulders, he says, "What? It wouldn't be the first time."

I see the way Candace is looking at him. She's embarrassed when he adds, "Just sayin.'"

Taking her back to my office, I know she's upset when I close the door and brace my hands on either side of her, caging her against the door, and I see it. It's all over her face. The doubt.

"Sorry about that. The guy has no filter," I tell her lightly. But she isn't looking at me, and she isn't talking.

"Candace," I quietly say as she lowers her eyes to the floor, and I hate that she has to know that side of me. A side I'm ashamed of because I want to give her so much more than what I am. I'm embarrassed that she knows how much I used to use people.

"I'm sorry," I breathe out.

"Did you really do that?" she asks with a shaky voice when she looks at me.

Mortified to have to admit this to her, I nod my head and answer, "Yes."

I watch as her eyes begin to fill with tears, and I instantly hate all my choices before her. She blinks and the tears roll down her cheeks.

"Is that what you want?"

Taking her head and cradling it in my hands, I try to assure her with everything I have when I say, "No. I was miserable then. None of them ever gave me what you give me."

"That's the problem, though. I can't give you what they could."

"You give me everything," I say, trying to convince her of the raw truth as I use my thumbs to wipe the tears from under her eyes. I feel my chest constrict when I try to make her believe my words. "You have more of me than any of them ever had. And when you're ready to move forward, I can promise you that it won't be like what I had with them. It was just empty with them."

I rest my head against hers, wishing I could take back all those times I gave myself away to women I never even cared about. Wishing that it could have always been her because she's all I want. She's all I have ever wanted, and she doesn't deserve to feel like shit because of my past choices.

"I shouldn't be upset. I didn't know you then," she rationalizes.

"You have every right to be upset."

Her next move is much too forgiving, more than I deserve, and I'm not sure how she can be so understanding about all this when she wraps her hands around the back of my neck and draws me down to her lips. I feel like I don't deserve all of the good that's inside of her, and I let out a sigh as she moves her lips over mine and holds me close. Gripping her waist in my hands, I keep my lips on her when I say, "I've missed you."

She seals her lips with mine, kissing me intently as we both cling to one another. The taste of her on my tongue is intoxicating and there's no doubt. There's no question. She has a part of me that I never knew was up for grabs, but she has it.

Parting our lips, I ask, "Stay with me tonight?"

"I can't."

"Why not?"

"I promised Jase I'd stay with him."

I haven't had her in my bed since last Sunday, and it frustrates me to know that she'll be in Jase's tonight and not mine. That she'll be in his arms and not mine. I respect Jase, and I understand their relationship, but I want to be the only man that she shares a bed with.

"You have to work anyway," she says.

"I want you in my bed when I get home."

"Ryan . . ." she whispers, and I know she doesn't want me to push it, so I drop it—for now.

She cups my jaw in her hands and kisses me slowly before saying, "I should go."

After I walk her out and say goodbye for the night, I close the door and turn back to Gavin. "Don't ever say shit like that around her again."

"You really like her, don't you?" he asks, taking in my severity about the matter.

"Yeah, man. I do. And that shit just hurt her. She knows about my past, but she doesn't need you throwing it in her face."

"Dude, I'm sorry. I didn't know you were that serious about her," he says as I walk over and sit down in a chair next to him. "I'm just a little shocked. I've known you for years and never thought I'd see you like this."

"Me neither, but shit changes, Gav."

When I got home from work last night, I found it hard to sleep, thinking about Candace over at Jase's when I just wanted her with me. But it's more than that. She runs to him for everything, she always has, and until I came along, he's all she ever had. But I don't like the feeling that I have to compete, that I have to convince her to let me be that guy for her when she should *want* me to be that guy.

She needs to realize that she can trust me enough to come to me for anything. That she doesn't have to hold back from me. But I also know how I feel about her, and I don't think any guy would like the idea of their girlfriend sharing a bed with another man, gay or not. Having her in my arms at night is special, and I want her to only share that with me.

I don't know how she's gonna react, but I need to tell her how I feel about this because I don't like losing sleep over it. So I don't even call her to let her know I'm stopping by her house. She's happy when she opens the door and sees me, giving me a hug before taking me back to her room. She's got books everywhere and she gathers them up and shuts down her laptop before joining me on her bed. When she sits down, I decide to go ahead and cut to it.

"I need to talk to you about something."

"Okay," she says curiously as she folds her legs in front of her.

"Look, I get your relationship with Jase, and I haven't ever had any issues with it, but I don't like that you guys still sleep together," I tell her honestly, laying it out there.

"But, it's not like that."

"I know," I tell her, completely understanding their relationship. "But I still don't like it."

"But . . ."

I turn to face her straight on, placing my hands on her knees when I explain, "I know it isn't like that with you two. I get it. But I don't like the thought of you in bed with another man holding you. I want to be that guy. I want you to want me to be that guy, not Jase." My voice cracks when I say that last part because it hurts me to even have to ask her to want me like that.

"I want you to be that guy, but I don't know how," she tells me, and I'm glad she isn't shutting down, but instead, opening up. "Jase is so unthreatening to me because he's just my friend."

"Why do you think I'm threatening?" I ask, bothered that after all this time together, she's still scared of me.

I notice her nerves hitting her when she begins squeezing her hands together, but she continues to talk when she admits, "Because you could easily walk away from me."

"You think it would be easy for me to walk away?" I ask, dumbfounded that she can't see right through me to know how I feel about her. "It wouldn't be easy, babe. And I doubt there is anything you could say, or do, that would make me want to walk away. It kills me that you're so scared of me."

She takes a moment before she locks her eyes with mine, and finally gives me a piece of her that I've been dying for when she reveals, "You're the only person I've ever felt this way about, and I don't want to lose you."

Her words hit hard, and I just need to be close to her when I shift to my knees and lower her onto the bed, kissing her. Slowly. I hold her head in my hands, and I can't go another day without exposing my feelings to her, so when I break away, I give it to her.

"You're not gonna lose me, babe. I love you too much to let you go."

She's doesn't even need to say it back to me. I don't need the verbal affirmation because the tears that spill out of her eyes and down her temples are all I need to know that she loves me too. She nods her head, telling me in her own way before I lean down and cover her sweet lips with mine. She opens her mouth and I take more of her, caressing her tongue with mine. When I do this, she grabs my hair and pulls my weight on top of her.

Shifting slightly to the side, I drag my knuckles along her bare skin between her shirt and pants. Her muscles tremble under my touch, but she does nothing to slow me down. I pay attention to her cues, cautious to not push her too far when I slowly slip my hand under the hem of her top and begin running it up the span of her stomach. Her breathing grows heavy, and her grip on me tightens when I hit the bottom of her bra. I stop my hand, waiting for her permission, and it's in this moment that I realize she has her head buried in the crook of my neck.

"It's okay," she breathes against my skin, and suddenly, I feel too much.

Dropping my mouth onto her shoulder, I kiss and gently suck along the curve of her neck. When I slide my hand over her breast, she lets out a soft whimper, and I hold her in my hand, feeling the lace against my skin.

"God, you're perfect," I whisper against her lips.

When I graze my thumb over her hardened nipple, she pushes her head harder into my shoulder, and I need to see her.

Pulling my head away from her, I say, "Don't hide from me, babe."

She's timid when she lowers her head onto the pillow and opens her eyes. I watch her as I run my fingers along the edge of the lace, touching the smooth skin of her chest. I can see the tension in the crease between her eyes as her brows pinch together. She's in her head and not here with me. Wanting her to stop thinking so much, I gently squeeze her small breast in my hand, and when I do, she grabs my face and pulls me down, kissing me.

Her legs tangle with mine, but her body is stiff as she keeps still beneath me. Hearing the way she's breathing though is hot as hell, and I want to feel more of her. So I hook my fingers under the seam of her bra and tug the fabric down, but when I do, her whole body instantly locks up.

"Please, don't." Her words come out quick, and I immediately slide my hand out from under her top, and move it to her head, threading my fingers in her hair. "I'm sorry."

I hate hearing those words from her. I hate that she feels like she's doing something wrong.

"Look at me," I say, and the words come out strong. "When we're together like this, I don't ever want you to be sorry for anything, okay?"

She nods her head, and I soften my tone with a kiss before telling her again, "I love you, babe."

I never thought I would say those words to a girl. Never thought I would be able to open myself to being vulnerable enough to feel those emotions, but with her, it comes so easily. I realize now that the hard part was keeping myself so far removed, seeking the disconnect, but with her, I crave the connection. It's all I want with her.

chapter twenty-six

"WHAT ARE YOU doing?" I ask when I see Candace walking down the stairs still in her pajamas. "Get that cute, little ass of yours upstairs and change into your running gear. It's already after seven."

She walks into the kitchen to where I am and says, "I'm gonna pass," as she pulls down a coffee mug from the cabinet.

"You passed a couple days ago too. What's going on?" I ask. Candace loves running, so I don't get the sudden aversion.

"Nothing," she says while she stirs the sugar into her coffee and takes it to the living room.

"Not buying it," I call her out. "What's up?"

"I can't tell you," she says coyly when I sit down next to her as she leans back, propping her legs across my lap.

"You can tell me anything. Now spill it," I say while I run my hand up her calf and behind her knee. I love these legs.

"Uh uh," she says with a shake of her head. "You'll make fun of me."

"Now I've *got* to know," I respond with a much too curious grin.

"You can't tease me. I get enough of that from Mark and Jase."

"I can't promise you that, babe. Come on. Out with it. Why won't you run with me anymore?" I question.

"Because I'm scared," she says and then quickly takes a conveniently long sip of her coffee.

"Scared of what?"

"We're almost out of creamer."

"That's because you use a crap-load of it. Stop trying to distract me. Scared of what?" I ask again.

She takes a moment, and I can tell she's trying to hide her grin when she admits, "I'm scared I'm gonna break my leg or something."

"From running?" I ask as a chuckle slips out under my breath.

Nudging me with her foot, she says, trying to defend, "Yes, from running. It could happen."

"From running?" I repeat. "Candace, you're not gonna break your leg. That's ridiculous."

"Okay, maybe not a break," she says when she sets her mug down on the table. "But something could happen. Pulled muscle, strained ligament. That would ruin everything. My audition is in a few weeks, and getting this solo could be the difference between having a job after graduation or not." Although I find her seriousness amusing, she is, in fact, completely serious.

"Okay, so no running. Well, I'm proud of you for walking down the stairs this morning without any assistance. That was a big risk," I joke with complete mockery, and this time, when she nudges me, I grab her ankle and shift to move between her legs. "You're putting your tiny feet in a dangerous situation when you nudge me like that," I say and then kiss her along the ticklish spot on her neck.

She begins to giggle and squirm underneath me when she tries to throw out a firm tone as she says, "Are you threatening me, Ryan Campbell?"

"You're cute," I continue to tease as I devour her neck with my mouth, and she can't seem to manage to get any words out around her fit of laughter. When I pull away, she has a wide smile, but it fades with her laughter. She stares up at me and doesn't say anything.

"What is it, babe?"

"Nothing," she says softly.

"Tell me."

"It's just . . . You give me butterflies. That's all."

Looking down at that pretty face of hers, I tell her, "Fuck butterflies. I feel it all when I'm with you," before kissing her. She grips my shirt in her hands, and I decide to forego the run to spend the morning making out with her.

I haven't seen Candace much in the past couple of days now that I'm losing out on my morning runs with her. So when she texts me that one of her lectures got cancelled, I jump on the opportunity to snag some time with her even though I'm hanging out with Gavin.

In Fremont. Do you have enough time to meet me?

Yeah. Where are you?

The Barrel Thief.

In the middle of the day?

The Barrel Thief is a well-known wine and whiskey lounge that works with one of the distributors that Blur deals with. The owner called me this afternoon to swing by and sample some of the new ales he got in, and when Gavin called to hang out, I invited him along.

Think of it as a work thing. ;) I'm here with Gav.

I'll be there in 10.

When she walks in and takes off her raincoat, she slides into the booth next to me with a big smile on her face.

"What's that smile all about?" I ask.

"You two are the only ones in here. Are they even open?"

"Ryan has good connections," Gavin says, and when I kiss her temple, I tell her, "The owner is a friend of mine. Wanted to show me what one of his distributors was able to get him."

"Where's he at?"

"Had to take a call. Here, try this," I say as I slide the glass over to her.

She takes a sip and says, "That's surprisingly good. What is it?"

"Maudite. It's from Chambly. Good, huh?"

"Yeah."

"Figures she would like it," Gavin says with a smile.

"Why's that?" Candace asks him, and he responds with, "'Cause it's the most expensive."

She laughs at him, saying, "You're cheap."

"With girls? I tend to be," he jokes with her.

"I feel bad for them," she shoots back, and he agrees with a chuckle, "Me too."

I watch their banter, and I'm relieved that what happened at my loft last week isn't playing into Candace's attitude towards him.

"Are you drinking your water?" she asks me, and I hand it to her.

"So how long do you have?" I ask.

"About an hour before my studio begins. It's my three-hour day and then I have to work the late shift tonight, so I won't be over till after eleven."

"Okay," I say as I reach over to hold her hand.

"Hey, Candace," Gavin says, and the next words out of his mouth come as a shock to me when he tells her, "Look, I feel bad for the shit I said the other day. I'm sorry if I embarrassed you."

Never have I seen Gavin own up and apologize to anyone. It's out of character for him, and I appreciate that he would do that.

"Thanks, Gavin," she says to him, and I can see that she appreciates the gesture as well.

"It was a dick thing to do."

"Don't worry about it. Really," she tells him.

We spend the rest of our time chatting about nothing in particular, and then head out after making plans to stop by Gav's place in a few days.

When I pull up to Candace's house to pick her up, I see her roommate's car sitting in the drive. Candace has been trying to avoid her for the past couple of days after Kimber upset Candace when she told her that she wanted her to move out after graduation. I couldn't get a clear answer when I asked about the rift between them, but I hated seeing her so upset when she told me about the conversation.

"Hey, babe. You ready?" I ask when she opens the door and steps out into the cold mist.

"Yeah."

I help her into the car, and when I get in and start driving to Gavin's place for the party he's throwing, I ask, "How's everything with Kimber?"

"She's been in her room all evening. There's just nothing to say."

"You could at least try talking to her," I suggest, but it doesn't surprise me when she shuts down the idea.

"It wouldn't do any good," she says softly as she looks out the side window. I reach over and pull her hand into my lap, deciding not to mention it anymore.

Pulling up to Gavin's house, I park along the curb that's lined with cars. It's been a while since I've been over to his place, but the past couple times we've hung out since that awkward day at my loft with Candace, it seems that he's been trying to make an effort, so I'm here, reciprocating.

I take Candace's hand in mine as we walk inside. There aren't a ton of people here yet, and she doesn't seem to be affected as I start introducing her to a few buddies of mine. I think I'm more uncomfortable than she is, but I know what they're thinking about her—about what I'm doing with her—and I'm already regretting bringing her here. These people know my past all too well, but for them, my past is still my present because I don't talk to them all that often, aside from the infrequent run-ins when they drop by the bar.

"It's about time you guys showed up," Gavin says when he walks over to us. "Help yourself to whatever is in the kitchen."

"Hey, Gav," Candace says.

"Hey, gorgeous. I can't believe you haven't left this ass-hat for me yet."

Smiling at him, she pokes, "If it weren't for your delicate language, I might consider it."

"Leave her alone," I tell him, feigning irritation, before taking her to the kitchen to get a couple beers. But as soon as we walk in there, my gut confirms that this was a bad idea. Gina is standing with a group of women, and the wink she shoots me makes me very nervous. I hand Candace her beer and send Gina a message when I lean down and give Candace a kiss before taking her back into the living room.

I don't want to say anything because I don't want to draw any attention and embarrass Candace. Plus, last I heard, Gavin was still fucking her, so I'm just hoping that for Gavin's sake, she'll stay away from me.

We take a seat on the couch with one of my old college buddies, and after introducing him to Candace, we begin catching up. I keep my hand on her knee while I talk to my friend, but my mind is elsewhere. Bringing Candace here was more for her than for me. She had expressed to me that she was curious to get to know my friends since I'm now a part of her small circle with Jase and Mark, already knowing so much about the three of them. But these friendships here are superficial. None of them have a clue about Candace, and probably just assume she's a random chick I'm banging.

There was a time that I would hang out with these people on a regular basis, but it's been a while.

The evening wears on, and eventually Candace leans into me, saying, "I'm gonna go get another drink. Want one?"

"Yeah, babe. Thanks."

When she heads into the kitchen, Gavin flops down next to me.

"What the fuck is Gina doing here?" I ask under my breath.

"Dude, relax. She's chill."

"You still seeing her?"

Cocking his brow at me, he says, "First off, you know I don't *see* anyone. But I haven't hooked up with her in a while. Between you and me," he says when he shifts himself on the couch, "she was only fuckin' me to get to you."

"What?"

"Yep. Her roommate told me, and that's when I backed away from that crazy bitch," he says with an exaggerated shudder.

"That's sick," I tell him and then add, "And you're trying to tell me she's chill?"

Gavin starts to respond, but I'm no longer listening when Candace walks back into the room, fuming mad. She doesn't even stop when she passes me and snaps, "Take me home," and then heads out the door.

Grabbing her coat, I don't say shit to Gavin or even look back when I go outside.

"Candace," I call out, and when she gets to my jeep, she turns, and I see the humiliation all over her face as she yells at me, "Did you sleep with that girl in there? Gina?"

I release a hard breath, hating that I have to do this to her, but she cuts me off before I can even open my mouth.

"Forget it. Just take me home."

She opens the door and hops in. She's pissed and rightfully so. I knew it was a mistake to bring her to Gavin's. Why the hell would she want to see what I'm trying to forget? I don't know what the fuck Gina said to her, but I hope I never run into her again.

As I start driving back across town, Candace is silent, staring out of her window.

"I didn't know she was going to be there," I start to tell her, needing to clear the air because I can't stand her being upset like this. "When I saw her, I didn't want to say anything to draw attention."

She doesn't speak. She only pulls her one knee up to her chest and turns to face out the window, giving me nothing but the back of her head. I don't know if she's crying or not, but the fact that she won't talk to me hurts.

"Candace, say something."

But she doesn't. I know she wants to go home, but I'm selfish and don't want her to run from me, so I take her to my place. Pulling up to my loft, she quietly says, "Ryan, I really just want to go home."

I don't respond when I get out of the car and walk around to open her door. Holding out my hand for her, she doesn't protest when she takes it and follows me inside and up to my room.

"Ryan, what are you doing?" she finally asks when I drop her hand to grab her some clothes from my dresser.

"You're not going home. Here," I tell her when I hand her a pair of my boxers and a t-shirt.

She takes them and makes her way into my bathroom, closing the door behind her. I quickly change, not enjoying a second of this tension, but I'm not letting it go unresolved.

"Ryan," she calls to me when she cracks the door open. "Can you bring me my purse?"

Picking it up off the bed, I go hand it to her before she shuts the door again. It bothers me that I've never seen her undressed. That she always hides herself in my bathroom to change. I've never been so in the dark with a girl before, and I don't know what to make of it.

I turn the lights off but leave the shades on the panoramic windows open so that I can watch the rain that is now falling hard. The moon must be full with the glow of the clouds that casts a faint bluish hue throughout the room.

When she finally comes out of the bathroom, I watch her as she pads across the wooden floor and climbs up onto the bed. I never get tired of seeing her in my clothes, and when she slides in, I instinctively pull her into me, face to face.

"Talk to me," I tell her softly.

She lets out a slow breath and is so forthcoming with me when she says, "I'm sorry. I'm not mad at you, and I shouldn't have snapped at you. I just . . . I don't like feeling the way she made me feel. It's embarrassing."

"She was nothing to me."

Looking down, she hesitantly asks, "When did you . . . I mean . . . How long ago?"

"August or so," I give her honestly. I brush her hair back when she closes her eyes and quietly say, "They were only there to distract me, but when I saw you, you faded everything I needed distracting from."

"Did you love any of them?" she asks when she opens her eyes and looks at me.

"No."

"Do you love me?"

"I've only ever loved you," I assure her, not even wanting to think about the absurdity of her question.

When I roll myself on top of her, she doesn't miss a beat when she pulls me down and kisses me. It's strong and sure. It's the first time she has ever kissed me this way, and I feel like I need it right now. The confirmation that we're okay. I return her intensity when I dip my tongue inside of her mouth and start running my hand down her neck, over her shirt, and between her breasts. She fists my hair, and I'm gone.

My desire for closeness takes over, and I need to feel her skin against mine. Slipping my hand under her shirt, I notice she's still wearing her bra when I take her in my hand. Her nipple hardens as I slide it between my two fingers, and when I press them together gently, her body arches up into mine, and I can't control the moan that comes out of me.

"God, I want you," I whisper when I sit back on my heels and pull her up to me. I can see it in her eyes, the want, so I don't ask as I slowly start peeling her shirt off when she lifts her arms up.

Tossing the shirt aside, I look at her as I gradually run my hands down her sides. She's perfect in her purple lace bra. She doesn't have large breasts, but fuck, she's sexy as hell, and I just want my hands all over her.

I peer into her eyes when she cups my face in her hands, and my heart starts beating in a way it never has before. "Babe . . ."

As I lay her back down, I drag my lips along her neck as she holds on to the sides of my head while I keep trailing down. I suck her nipple into my mouth, dragging my tongue over the swollen bud. Heat courses through me, and I need to feel more of her when I begin to run my fingers along the underside of her waistband. Hooking them under the fabric, I sit back, and when I slightly tug down, I see it.

No.

Suddenly, reality stabs into my chest, and I feel everything I never wanted to be true pour out of me. Time freezes. I can't breathe, and the panging inside of me is unbearable. I know I can't deny what I see, but I want to. Because it can't be. It just can't.

God, don't let it be.

Slow motion. Everything moves in slow motion as I bring my hand to her hip, and with a trembling thumb, I drag it across what I can no longer blame on head-trips. I brush it again, not wanting to believe what my eyes see. A thin black outline of a tiny heart. *That* tiny heart from *that* night.

The thudding of my chest is painful; it's the most painful thing I've ever felt in my entire life, and before I know it, she slings hers arms around me, but I'm in shock. I can't fuckin' move. I'm too scared.

It can't be her.

Not her.

Not that girl.

Not *my* girl.

Squeezing my eyes shut, it's all I see now. Her bloody thighs. Her beaten face. Her shredded nails.

"God, please! Stop!"

I hear it. Her voice. Her shrieking, desperate voice. Opening my eyes, I'm jittery. She has to feel it. Her body is clung tightly to mine, and I realize that I'm not touching her. I feel like I can't touch her. Like I don't know how, but I force myself to. And when I cautiously wrap my arms around her, I feel her shaking too. And now everything is clear. I can't pretend that I don't know exactly why she's shaking. I'm such a fuckin' dick, rubbing up on this girl because I can't fuckin' control myself around her.

God, what the hell is wrong with me?

Her body begins to soften into mine, and I don't know what to say. How do I tell her? Do I tell her? Do I say something?

Say something.

"Candace."

"Please, don't say anything."

Her voice is pleading, so I don't. And now, I'm scared to take my hands away from her. Like she would break if it weren't for my arms. I keep her close when I lie us down and pull the sheets over us.

She's doesn't say anything else, and the silence rings in my ears. My head is loud. It's a maniacal filtering of memories, flashes weaving together to form a solid image that's undeniable. But I denied it. How could I have done that when it all makes sense now? Every panic, every startle, her fear of crowds, her night terrors, her constant hesitation with intimacy. And fuck. That dumpster. How stupid could I be? She stood *right there*. She panicked . . . in my parking lot. My bar. That's why she's never come back.

I can't be with her.

I have to be with her.

God, I love this girl so much. I can't let her go even though I know I should. But with me, I have the guarantee that she's safe. And I need her. Because it's only with her that I'm finally realizing that I can be the man I never thought I could be, and I don't think I could be this way with anyone else but her.

Lifting up, I scoot back so that I can lean against the headboard, bringing Candace with me and tucking her head under my chin. I don't want to lie to her, but do I tell her who I am? Does she even know that someone was there? This girl has been hurt so much, and by too many people, that I can't have my name added to that list. I can't do that to her. And for what? What difference would it make, if any at all? For this, I resolve to not say anything. I just can't do that to her.

This shit hurts. Bad. And now, every time I close my eyes, I see her lying there naked, raped in the alley of my bar. It's like someone's slowly gutting me. And for the first time in years, I let myself break. Candace has long fallen asleep in my arms when I feel the first of many tears roll down my cheeks and into her hair.

When I release the pain, I see that I hold so much of the blame. I heard her from inside. I heard the banging around, and I ignored it. If I would have just gone out there, I could have saved her. I could have done so much more than I did because I dismissed the ruckus for a couple of drunken guys. She was being raped when nothing but a brick wall separated us. How could I be so irresponsible?

We've taken our slow time getting to know each other, but now I feel like she's different, and I don't know what to do with that feeling. I always knew she was hiding something. Jase even told me that she was going through some tough shit, but *this?* I don't know what to do with this. I feel like an ass for all the times I've tried to touch her in ways that were too much for her and she had to stop me.

I'll never be able to tell her how sorry I am. There aren't enough words. There isn't enough in this world that I could give her to show her how truly fuckin' sorry I am. So I sit here and cry for her because I don't know what else to do. I love this girl beyond anything. Love her from a place in my heart I never knew I had.

So now . . . now she sleeps in my arms while I stay up, because sleep isn't strong enough to take me out of my head tonight. When I close my eyes, it's August, and I'm hovering over my Jane Doe. The girl I spent weeks wondering about. The girl that kept finding her way back into my head, only to realize that I've had her in my arms for months now.

chapter twenty-seven

MY HEAD IS pounding, and I'm tired as hell. Now that she's awake and moving around my loft, I suddenly don't know how to act. I don't know what to say. This realization has flipped a switch for me, and I don't know how to respond, so I stay quiet.

I'm in the kitchen, fixing her a cup of coffee when she walks over to me and asks, "Did you not sleep last night?"

Screwing on the lid to her mug, I'm evasive when I tell her, "Not much," before handing her the cup and walking into the other room to grab our coats so that I can take her home. I feel like I can't touch her. Like I can't be the same with her. I want to scream and punch my fuckin' fist through the wall. Why did it have to be her? And what piece of shit would do that to her? She's the sweetest thing I've ever known.

Handing her the coat, I ask, "You ready?"

"Yeah," she says shyly as she keeps her eyes down.

She slips it on, and I know that my attitude is making her uncomfortable, so I take her hand in mine as we head outside into the bitter cold.

It only takes a couple of minutes to drive to her house, and when I pull up and park the car, she turns to me and says, "I'm sorry about last night, and I get that you're mad, but—"

"What?" I interrupt, not understanding what she did that she would need to be sorry for. "Why would I be mad?"

She shakes her head, unsure of herself when she tells me, "Because I keep pushing you away. You've hardly said two words to me this morning. So, I just figured . . ."

Fuck. I've been so wrapped up in myself that I didn't realize I've been a total dick to her this morning. Getting out of the car, I walk over to her side, open her door, and unclick her seatbelt, grabbing on to her hips to face me. I don't know what I'm doing, but seeing the look on her face snaps me out of my fears immediately. I feel like I can't be the same with her, but I have to be. I want to be, because I love what we are together.

I'm firm when I declare, "Everything you give me is perfect. You have to stop feeling like this. I'm here with you, and I'm not going anywhere."

Needing her to believe me, I don't hesitate when I take her lips with mine. It bothers me that she doubts herself so much with me. My thoughts are all over the map, but one thing is certain, as hard as this is, I know I can't let it change us. I can't allow it to filter in and affect me because I can't give her any reasons to doubt that I love her from the purest part of me there is.

When I break our kiss, I softly tell her, "I'm sorry if I've been a dick, I just didn't get much sleep."

"It's okay. I overreacted."

But she isn't overreacting because her observations are astute and this is my fault. Taking her hand, I help her out of the car and shut the door, leaning her back against it when I take her face in my hands and look into her eyes, trying to connect in a way so that there is no doubt within her when I tell her, "I never thought I needed anything in this life until I met you. Everything you give me is exactly what I have always needed, and you do it perfectly."

I don't give her a chance to respond when I pull her into me, pressing my lips into hers. Her hands around my back are firm as she holds me close, and I wish she didn't have to go to school because I want to keep her wrapped up in me like this all day.

We say goodbye, and when she's inside, I start driving to work. When I pull into the lot and park, my phone buzzes with a text from Candace.

Can I stay with you?

I've never been so sure of anything when I type out my response.

Of course, babe.

I don't know what happened in the past ten minutes since I dropped her off, but if she needs me, she has me. Sitting in my jeep, I go ahead and call her so that I can make sure everything is all right.

"Hey," she answers apprehensively.

"Did something happen?"

"I'm sorry. I don't want to impose, but I just . . ." she trails off when I assure her, "You're nothing close to an imposition, babe."

"Kimber is here, and it's not good. I just think I should give her some space."

The comfort of knowing that she ran to me, and not Jase, shows me that she's in this, and I love her even more for that. "When do you get out of class?"

"I'm going straight to work after I get out of school, so I won't be home till a little after seven tonight."

"I'll meet you at your place and help you get a couple bags together, okay?"

I hear her release a sigh before she says, "Thank you, Ryan. Really."

We hang up, and when I get out of the car, I can't help myself when I turn to the back of the alley. I walk over towards the dumpster and can see that son of a bitch on top of her again. Shoving his hand between her legs.

Slamming his fist into the side of her head. The images unleash a rage inside of me when I think about what happened to her, and the guilt that I was right fuckin' here and didn't protect her from it.

Questions storm inside. Is she a different person now because of it? What did she go through after it happened? What is she going through now? I know she has to be masking the pain because I'm pretty certain that I now know what it is that's constantly causing all of her restless sleep at night. Is that what she dreams about? Fuck! Is that the shit that fills her head when she's in bed with me?

Raking my hands through my hair, I drop my head and spot a small crate of empty bottles. When I can no longer stand the rapid banging of my heart against my chest, I fume as I pick up the whole crate, smashing it violently against the side of the dumpster. Screams grit through my lungs, and the explosion of glass shattering echoes in the quiet morning air.

"What the hell are you doing?" Max yells out from behind me, but I keep my eyes on the shards of glass that are scattered on the ground. The same ground where some fucker . . .

"Ryan, man," Max says and knocks me out of my thoughts when I turn to face him, and the anger inside of me is blatant. It's a force that I can't push down when I yell, "It was her!"

"What are you talking about?" he questions as he moves closer to me, glass crunching under his boots with each step.

"The girl that was raped . . . It's her."

He shakes his head, not piecing it together while my muscles tense up in frustration with everything.

"It's Candace," I breathe out because the constricting of my throat makes it painful to speak.

His face drops, stunned when he asks, "How do you know?"

"Because that girl, she has the same tattoo that I saw on Candace *last fuckin' night!*" Those last words seethe out of me as I pick up a bottle from another crate and barrel it into the dumpster, creating another spray of glass after it smashes into a splattering of pieces. My breathing is heavy as I press my palms to my forehead and admit, barely holding myself together, "I don't want it to be her, man." I can barely choke out the words, but I had to hold my shit together quietly last night and now . . . now it bleeds out.

"Fuck," I hear him mumble before he asks, "What did she say?"

Looking up at him, I tell him, "She doesn't know. I couldn't tell her." When I see the way he's looking at me, like I'm an idiot for not telling her, I shout at him, pleading, "What would I fuckin' say, Max?! What should I have said to her?!" I pause, catching my breath before I continue in a calmer tone. "I love her," I tell him with a defeated shrug of my shoulders. "I can't hurt her like that."

"Has she even told you that she was . . . you know?"

"No," I respond. "I don't think she ever intends to either." I start walking away, not wanting to talk about this shit anymore, and when I pass him, I stop and look over at him. "We're never gonna mention this again. Got it?"

"Yeah, man," he whispers to me. "Got it."

I'm not talking about this shit with anyone. Max knows and that's where it stays. It won't come up again. I won't talk about her like that. Whatever happens, it's private and stays between Candace and me.

Candace's roommate wasn't home when I went over to help her get a few bags packed. Most of her belonging were all ready to go by the time I got there, so it didn't take us too long before we left, which was good because she was really upset about the whole thing.

We spent a while moving things around in my room to make space for her. She didn't want to go through the hassle, but I wanted to make sure that she was comfortable and that all her things had a place in my home. She didn't say how long she was staying, and I told her to play it by ear. I'm just happy that I don't have to say goodbye to her at night anymore. That she will be here every day with me.

Getting into bed, I sit back against the headboard and watch her as she ties her hair up on top of her head.

"Come over here," I tell her as I wrap my arms around her.

She slips her arm around my waist as we lie here. It feels good to have her close after the shit day I've had. She's always has this effect on me, and I've never needed it more than I do now.

When I kiss the top of her head, she runs her fingers along my scar, asking, "How did you get this?"

"My dad."

"Sorry," she says as she looks up at me.

"Why?"

"Because I don't want to bring it up if you aren't comfortable talking about it."

"Babe, I'd tell you anything." She keeps her eyes on me when I open up to her and show her the side of me that no one else gets to see. "I came home from a party one night and walked in on my father beating the shit out of my mom in our kitchen. He smashed a coffee mug into the back of her head, and I lost it. I started whaling on him. Eventually, he managed to get his hands on a butcher's knife."

"Oh my God," she whispers. I know it can't be easy to hear, but I give her this, knowing that I hold what is probably her darkest secret.

"That's the night he died. He left, and my mom called 911, so we were taken to the hospital by ambulance. The next morning, we were back home, and two cops showed up at the front door to tell me about the car crash."

"I don't know what to say," she quietly admits.

Running my fingers up and down her arm, I tell her, "There's really nothing to say. I hated him. He had beaten the shit out of me my whole life. He didn't even need a reason. Sometimes he would just come home from work and knock me around for the hell of it."

"But why?" she asks, and when she looks up at me, her eyes are rimmed with tears.

"I don't know," I admit. "But I do know that he couldn't stand me. He hated me just as much as I hated him."

"What could anyone possibly hate about you?"

Her words are sweet, and I lean down to give her lips a quick kiss before she continues, "So . . . nobody knew?"

I shake my head.

"How did you deal with all of that alone?"

"Vices. In high school I used to do a lot of drugs, but I stopped shortly after my dad died. I felt like what happened to my mom that night was my fault. I was wasted and passed out at a party when I should have been at home with her."

"That wasn't your fault though," she tells me.

"I know that now. But it got me to give up popping so many pills. In turn, I just traded one vice for another. I was searching for a way to numb myself. I'd been doing it since I was a little kid, and by the time he was dead, it was all I knew to do. So I kept looking for ways to escape."

"I can see that," she responds. "The need to hide."

I shift us down so that we're lying on our sides. She hides behind her dance and school. She busies herself when there isn't anything to really keep her busy. She's an overachiever, but I don't point out her vice, instead I reveal, "I don't want to hide from you though. You're the only one I can say that about." She runs her hand along my cheek, when I go on, "I've always been scared to connect with women."

"Why?"

Giving her my fear, I let it all out there. "Because I'm afraid I'll wind up just like him."

Keeping her hand on my face, she whispers softly, "That won't happen."

"How can you be so sure?"

"Because you're the kindest person I know. Because you've never put yourself before me. You're a genuine guy, Ryan."

"You're probably the only woman who would say that about me."

"But how well did they know you?"

"They didn't. Nobody does except you."

"Can I ask you something?" she says coyly.

"Anything."

Closing her eyes, she lets out a slow breath and then asks, "If you never wanted to connect with those girls, then why sleep with them?"

"Because they offered me an escape. If even for a few minutes, it was my way of disconnecting." Tucking a loose piece of hair behind her ear, I lean my forehead against hers and tell her, "I was too scared to feel because I hadn't ever done that before. I don't know what it's like to care more about someone other than myself."

"But why me?" she breathes.

"You've always intrigued me. You aren't like any girl I've ever known. Without even trying, you get me thinking about myself and what I want out of life. You're everything I never thought I wanted, but when I met you, you were everything I needed."

She rests her hand on my jaw, and slowly runs her thumb along my lips when she says, "Somehow, you make up for everything I was missing before you. I have a hard time opening up to people; I know that. But I don't want you to doubt that you have me, because you do."

I know she struggles, and I'm still waiting for the day she will drop that wall with me to feel safe enough to tell me she loves me, but this . . . this lets me know that she's trying.

"God, you are so much more than I deserve," I breathe against her mouth before I kiss her.

I take what I learned last night and refuse to let it stand in the way of what we have together. I'm not gonna beat myself up because I want to touch her, because I know that each touch I want is because I love her. And that's the only reason. I simply love her.

chapter twenty-eight

"WHAT ARE YOU doing?" I ask when I walk through the front door and see Candace bent over in my kitchen, wrapping her thighs in Saran Wrap.

Peeking her head up, she tells me, "Helping my muscles recover," as if this image isn't anything out of the realm of normal.

I start laughing at her while she continues to wrap her legs. "Explain this to me because I'm dying to know."

She rips the plastic from the roll and sets it on the counter before defending, "I swear it works. I've been doing it for years."

"Wrapping yourself up like leftovers?" I tease.

"No," she drags out. "You see, I use Tiger Balm," she says as she hands me a tiny brown jar that can't hold any more than an ounce. "Then, I seal it in with plastic wrap. It traps in the vapors, which allows for maximum absorption, bringing more relief to my muscles."

Setting the jar down, I say, "Are you not worried about a chemical burn or some shit like that?"

"It's never happened before," she says as she walks out of the kitchen and into the living room.

Watching her, I laugh at the image . . . and the sound.

"Candace, this is some crazy shit you do, you know that right?"

She takes a seat on the couch as I move to join her.

"Yes, I know, but I swear it helps. Look, I have my audition in two days, and I'm freaking out because I keep getting these cramps in my legs. I've upped my calcium and potassium, but it's still bothering me."

"Give me your legs," I tell her and she shifts to lie on her back, kicking her feet onto my lap.

"What are you doing?" she asks when I turn to the side to face her.

"I'm gonna give your calves a solid rubdown."

She smiles as I start to knead my fingers into her muscles. I can't get enough of her legs, even wrapped up like she has them. They are solid and sexy, and I take my time, thoroughly enjoying myself, as I give her calves a deep massage. She closes her eyes and relaxes while I make good use of the next thirty minutes.

When I'm done, I take her up to my bathroom where she begins to unwrap her legs.

"God, that shit stinks," I complain as she wads up the wrap and tosses it to me.

"Be nice," she scolds playfully. "I'm gonna take a quick shower. I'll come to bed in a few minutes."

"Okay," I say when I lean down to peck her lips before I leave and close the door behind me.

I run downstairs to plug my cell into its charger in my office before locking up. Candace has her dance bag by the front door with her toe shoes lying on top of a towel. Walking over, I kneel down and run my finger over the dirty, torn pink satin. You can see the burn marks on the ribbon where I can tell she has used a lighter to stop them from fraying.

It's ironic how these shoes mirror Candace. On the verge of falling apart. Barely holding together. Yet they do. She's strong even though she's breaking. I don't see her doing anything to heal; she's hiding and masking what I know is eating away at her. And these shoes, as worn as they are, they're still strong and beautiful.

Turning off the lights, I head back upstairs and lie down. When Candace is done drying her hair, she crawls in next me, and I curl myself around her. We don't talk as we both drift off to sleep.

When I stir awake, I'm alone in bed. Sitting up, I lean over to her nightstand to check the time on her phone. It's after two in the morning. I roll out of bed and walk out to the top of the stairs and see her. She's downstairs, sitting on the couch in the dark, watching the rain fall. The past couple nights since she's been staying here, she hasn't slept well. I haven't said anything to her, but she spends most of her nights in a fit of restless sleep, keeping me awake while I hold her and just watch.

Quietly, I walk down the stairs and across the room. As I round the couch, I see her wrapped up in a blanket, and she's crying. My heart is so heavy, and I don't know what to do. All I want is to take it all away, but I don't know how to do that.

She senses me and turns to look. I see it all over her face—the pain. She's so tired. Without any words spoken, I sit down next to her and wipe the tears that stain her cheeks.

"I can't sleep," she whispers to me.

I look over her face, searching for words, but my own sadness wells up inside of my chest, and I can see the pleading in her eyes. She doesn't want me to question why she's crying, so I don't. I already know. Pulling her closer to me, I hold on to her as she draws her legs up to her chest, cuddling into me. She turns her head and continues to watch the rain while I sit here in a painful silence. All that fills my head is the sound of her shrieking cries from that night, and I do everything I can to keep my emotions intact. Eventually, she dozes off and I scoop her up, carrying her back to bed.

I've been sitting here, anxiously waiting for Candace to get back. She left a couple hours ago for her audition at Meany Theater. I wanted to go with her, but she made me stay, saying that she didn't want anything to distract her. I wouldn't have been able to go into the theater to watch, but I wanted to at least be there to support her, but I understand.

She was a jittery mess all morning, and I did what I could to relax her, but she was too distracted to focus on anything, including me. Her determination and the neurotic behavior that comes along with it make me smile. She even broke out the Saran Wrap again when she woke up.

As soon as I hear the front door open, I walk out of my office to see Candace running down the hall. She jumps into my arms, wrapping her legs around my waist, and I've never seen a more perfect smile. She's elated, and her joy is infectious, making me laugh, saying, "I take it you kicked ass?"

"I totally kicked ass. It was amazing!"

Her legs are clutched so tightly around me that I don't even have to hold on to her, so I take my hands from her hips, move them to her face, and kiss her smile. She crashes her mouth with mine, enthusiasm controlling her. Taking her, I press her back up against the hallway wall, and before I can go in deeper with our kiss, she pulls away and starts laughing, telling me all about her audition. She spews out a bunch of French ballet shit, and I have no clue what she's talking about, but she's excited and happy, and that's all I need to know. My smile is big as I stand here and watch her.

"I'm so proud of you, babe. I wish I could have seen you."

"I know. I'm sorry," she says as she combs her fingers through my hair. "Auditions are always closed."

"When will you find out?"

"March first."

"Next week?"

"Yeah, Friday," she answers excitedly before pulling my head back to hers to kiss me, but I've got something to tell her as well.

Mumbling over her mouth, I say, "I've got news too."

Not willing to take her lips from mine, she mutters, "What's that?"

"Thinkspace Gallery called."

Her head pops back. "And . . . ?"

"They accepted your photo."

"Your photo?!"

"No, *your* photo, babe."

She smiles. She knows that picture is all her, and I refuse to take the credit for it.

"Congratulations," she tells me, and I slow her down, wanting to really feel her against me.

I kiss her softly, gently sucking on her bottom lip as I graze my tongue along it. She tangles her hands in my hair when I band my arms around her. We move like this, taking our time, and when she pulls back, she peers into my eyes. There's a look in her eyes that I can't peg, so I ask, "What is it, babe?"

She takes her hand and runs it slowly down the side of my face, and I see the wall crumbling.

"I love you."

Every part of me awakens, and I've never felt so alive. I didn't think I needed to hear those words as much I did, but the trust that comes with them was what I craved the most.

"You'll never know what those words just did to me," I tell her and then carry her over to the couch so that I can show her, in our own way, how much I love her.

I lie on top of her, and she begins to lift up my shirt, so I reach over my head and pull it off. Sliding my hand down her leg, I lift it and wrap it around my hip.

"I'm sorry you had to wait so long," she breathes.

"Don't be," I tell her. "You don't even know how much you have already given me. When I met you, I found me."

She smiles, saying again, "I love you."

"I love you too, babe."

We move slowly and spend the next hour making out the way we tend to do. I want more with her. I'll always want more, but for now, I enjoy taking my time with her and savor every piece as she gives it to me.

"Ryan?"

Her soft voice pulls me from my sleep as I roll over and drape my arm around her from behind.

"Yeah, babe?" I whisper with my eyes still closed, but she doesn't answer, so I let myself begin to drift back to sleep.

"Ryan?"

She calls my name louder, almost panicky, and when I open my eyes to look over at her, she's still sleeping. I watch her for a second and then she screams, "Ryan!" as she flips onto her back, her hands clenched into fists.

"Baby, wake up," I say as I hover over her, scared to touch her.

She begins trembling, pleading in a strained voice, "Please, not again."

Fuck. Knowing exactly what her dream is, I panic. "Candace, babe. Wake up."

"Get off of me!" she yells, frantically kicking her legs.

Quickly straddling them, I grip her upper arms as she thrashes herself against my hold.

"Get the fuck off of me!" she shrieks, and when she opens her eyes, tears fall freely down the sides of her face. She looks at me, but there's nothing there. No focus. Her eyes are completely glazed over, scaring the shit out of me. "God, please stop!"

"Candace, wake up!" I bark at her, desperate for her to snap out of her nightmare.

She's in a frenzy, screaming hysterically. Crying. I let go of her, and when I do, she desperately shuffles back and away from me, falling off the bed and hard onto her hip. I hop off the bed and kneel down in front of her as she's huddled in a ball against the wall, sobbing.

"Don't fuckin' touch me!" she screams when I hold her shoulders with my hands, but I don't take them off of her.

"Candace, open your eyes," I beg as she covers her face with her hands. She's so loud, and my mind is overwhelmed with anxiety.

Her breathing is rapid and she's terrified, but I need her to know she's safe.

"Candace, please. Look at me. It's only me here with you."

I take her wrists to move her hands from her face, and she turns her head to the wall as she cries.

"Babe, please don't hide from me."

She struggles to breathe through her tears, and when she begins to gasp, I tug her between my legs and her body gives in, falling limp into my arms. I hold her tight. Tighter than I have ever held anyone. She has to get this secret out of her. It's agonizing to see how this is tormenting her. I just need her to get it out.

I rub her back while she has her head tucked into my chest. She's no longer screaming, but the crying continues.

I don't want her to hide from me, so I tell her, "You have to look at me. Please." With my hands, I move her head up to face me. She opens her eyes, and I hate the fear and embarrassment I see in them.

"You okay?"

She simply nods.

"What happened?"

Lowering her head, she takes a couple deep breaths before asking, "Can you please call Jase?"

"What?" I hate this shit. That she would run to him in a heartbeat like I don't exist. Like I'm not enough for her, but he is. "Shit, Candace, no," I tell her, refusing to allow her to run from me. She told me she loves me, I just need her to trust me enough to be here for her.

"Please." She begins to cry again.

"Candace, no. You can't always run to him. Need me for a change," I beg. "Talk to me."

"I can't."

"Yes, you can," I urge. *God, just talk to me. Tell me. Get this out of you so that you can start dealing with it.*

"No, I can't. Please. I just can't," she strains through her sobs.

"But you can with Jase?" I question in disbelief. I thought we were past this.

"I want you to need me," I plead, tightening my hold around her. I feel desperate.

"I do."

"You don't," I say. "You cling to him for everything. Look at me," I demand and then hold her hands, pressing them hard against my chest, and beg, "Cling to *me*. Love me enough to *need me*."

"I can't . . . I . . ."

"Why?"

"Because . . . you'd leave me."

"Not happening, babe."

"Ryan, please."

"I'm not leaving you," I assure her. She can tell me this; I know she can, and I need her to. "Nothing you could say would make me want to leave you."

"I'm just too fucked up." Her face is covered in tears that I just want to kiss away. I wanna take all of her pain away, but I resist the urge to give in to her. So I keep encouraging, knowing that I'm guiding her to a painful place.

"We're all fucked up," I tell her. "I want you to let me in."

Her body is shuddering as the sobs wrack her. I'm powerless, and it fuckin' sucks.

"I can't! You'll never look at me the same. You'll run away."

She says this and I want to cry for her. Take her pain and shove it deep inside of me. I'd take her misery as my own in a second.

Wrapping my hand behind her head, I hold it close to my heart when I vow, "I promise you, nothing will change the way I look at you. Nothing will change what you do to me when you're next to me. You make my heart beat in a completely different way—nothing will ever change that."

"I'm so embarrassed," she cries into my chest as she slips her arms around me, clinging to me like she's about to fall—maybe she is, but I need her to.

"God, babe." I'm fighting my own tears so hard. "Please, don't be."

I strengthen my hold on her, and when I do, she falters with a whimper when she releases it.

"I was raped."

Those words. I already knew it. I even saw her body afterwards. But hearing those words. I can't take the pain and guilt any longer. It's like a knife to my lungs, and I can barely breathe. I take a hard breath in when the tears slip out and fall.

I'm helpless. I don't know what to say to her, but I knew that she had to tell me. To stop hiding it away, but what have I done to her? She's broken in my arms right now, sobbing, and I don't know what to do to help.

We sit, clinging to one another as we both cry. Time passes and she begins to tire, now softly weeping as I continue rocking her and planting kisses on top of her head.

"I've been lying to you," she mutters quietly.

"I don't care. It doesn't matter."

"I feel horrible."

"Candace, don't do this," I tell her. "You have every right to lie."

"I can't go to see you at work because . . ."

"Shhh . . ." I want her to stop because she doesn't need to apologize for shit. She shouldn't feel bad for trying to cover this up. I get it. Understand it.

"Because it happened in your parking lot. By the dumpster," she tells me, and I figure she simply needs to get it off her chest, so I don't say anything. I just listen as she relieves herself of whatever guilt is weighing on her as she continues. "That's why I freaked out. I didn't know where I was until I saw the dumpster."

Hearing her say this to me is hard. It's hurts to think about her trying so hard to hide this from me and what that was doing to her. My breath catches, and when a small noise cracks, she pulls back to see my tears falling. Her face scrunches up as she begins to cry again.

"I'm so sorry," she chokes out, and I've had enough of her apologizing for shit that doesn't matter.

"Don't ever fuckin' say that again," I tell her when I cradle her cheeks in my hand. "Don't ever be sorry for anything again."

"I'm just so far from what you thought."

"You're not."

"I am. Every day is a struggle. Everything. I'm scared every day," she admits as she drops her head from my hands.

I've always wanted to know what she was hiding, but I couldn't have imagined this. And that she lives with this every day. Terrified. The fact that she has held herself together around me so well is shocking.

Candace finally looks back up at me, pained when she tells me, "I'm fading." I shake my head at her, hardly able to stand the misery in her voice. "He took all my light, and I've been fading ever since."

Giving her nothing but the core of my intentions, I tell her, "You're not fading. I won't let you."

Her words beat at me. In disbelief because she's brought so much to my life in such a short amount of time. The mere idea that she would see her life in such shambles that she would fear fading ignites a fight in me to do everything I can to pull her out of this darkness. To show her just how bright she is. How amazing and powerful she is. She's nothing but heart, and I'm going to make sure she sees every bit of it. That there's no way for her to fade in my eyes.

She tucks her head down and leans into me as I fold her securely in my arms, vowing to myself that I will do everything I can to show this girl how strong she really is.

"That's why Kimber is mad," she says as she continues to talk. "I didn't go home after it happened. I stayed with Jase and never told her why. She knows I'm lying."

I listen. That's all she wants from me, so that's what I give her.

"I've been taking sleeping pills, but I stopped last week. That's why I haven't been sleeping." She pauses before revealing, "I dream about that night—about him. All I see are his eyes. He made me watch him."

A new bout of sobs courses through her, and anger courses through me, but I keep my cool for her. I take myself out of this and focus on her when she adds, "So, I take pills to keep him away."

"Babe, why did you stop taking them?"

"Because every night when I take them, it's only a reminder of what happened. I just want to forget, but I can't."

"Have you told anyone?" I ask as I brush her hair behind her shoulder.

"No. Only Jase and Mark. Jase was with me in the hospital. Mark only knows because he walked in and saw my face. I was pretty banged up."

"Your parents?"

"God, no. It was because of them that I went out with that guy at all."

"You knew him?" I ask, not expecting that she knew the fucker. "But you didn't do anything?"

"No."

"I wanna fucking kill him," I spit out, anger swelling inside of me. I swear to God, I'm gonna kill that piece of shit. My body tenses up, and I do everything I can to bring myself back down—for her. It takes a while, but I begin to focus on Candace and what she needs out of me. I know she's afraid I'm gonna run, but she's wrong.

Looking at her straight on, I assure her, "This changes nothing for me. Okay? Nothing. No one will ever love you like I do." I kiss her. I feel it's all I can do right now to show her that I'm here and I'm not leaving her. When I do finally drag my lips away, I give her more of me when I say, "You are the only reason there's light in my life. Before you, there was nothing but darkness."

As the tears linger on her cheeks, I lean in and kiss them, tasting the salt of her secret that's been eating her up. But now it's out there, and she doesn't have to find ways to hide from me anymore. She trusts me enough to allow me to see the darkest side of her, and I love her for that.

chapter twenty-nine

I DIDN'T WANT to leave Candace the day following her nightmare. I felt like being close to her, but she told me that it would have made her feel uncomfortable if I cancelled work to stay with her, and even though I didn't like it, I understood it. She's afraid things have changed between us, and just because I assured her that they haven't, I need to show her. So I went into work, and she went to Jase's where she managed to drink way too much wine, and for the first time in her life, got wasted.

Candace is still sleeping when I finish my shower and get dressed. Bringing her home last night was an adventure. She's gonna feel like shit when she wakes up today, but seeing her drunk was about the cutest thing I've ever seen.

I woke up in the middle of the night to find her fighting sleep. She said she was scared of having another nightmare, and it was tearing me up inside, so I stayed up and talked to her so that she could fall asleep. After she was out, I found myself wanting to stay awake to watch her, make sure she slept peacefully. Her nightmare scared the crap out of me, so I can't imagine how scary it was for her.

The past few weeks have drained me emotionally, so while she sleeps, I decide to head up to the bar before anyone gets there to get a little space from everything. I write Candace a note before I leave, letting her know where I went and to call when she gets up.

Walking into Blur, I leave the front door unlocked while I busy myself filling bottles behind the bar. I spend a good amount of time staying occupied, but my mind is elsewhere. It's in that alley, and my stomach won't seem to unknot itself to buy me any relief. I grab a bottle of scotch and take a seat at the bar, filling my glass.

I don't take a sip; I just sit and stare at the burnished liquid. It's placid, and I get lost as I zone out in the glass. I'm so deep in my head that I don't even hear the door open, but when someone takes a seat next to me, I turn to see Jase. His expression tells me that he knows I know. Candace must have told him last night. I focus back on my glass that's still sitting on the bar, cradled in my hands.

"I'm sorry," he says.

I can barely move my head up and down to acknowledge his words that take me out of my daze and bring me back to the mass of emotions.

Without looking at him, I talk. "I always knew she was hiding something, I just . . ."

"I know."

"She has these moments in her sleep . . . almost nightly . . ."

"It's a lot better now," he says, and I turn to look at him.

"Better?" He nods and I ask, because I want to know, "How bad was she?"

His head drops to the side, not wanting to tell me when I ask again. "How bad?"

"Don't do this."

"How bad?"

He takes a pause before he tells me, "Bad. It was like suddenly the Candace I had always known was gone."

I turn back to my glass and take a drink before setting it back down, relishing the burn in my chest. Warmth.

"So she was different?" I ask, wondering what she would have been like if only I'd met her before that night.

"Yeah, but like I said, she's better."

"Better," I repeat, not knowing what else to say, trying hard to keep the pain at bay. "How?"

"She used to have these hallucinations. It freaked me out. They were intense, and I'd always find her vomiting in my bathroom."

His words punch me in the gut. Thinking about her like that is almost too much, and I feel the tears return, but I fight to hold them back.

"She said she knew him." My words crack as they find their way out past the lump in my throat.

"Yeah."

I turn back to him and ask, "You know him too?"

Shaking his head, he tells me, "I met him once."

"Who is he?"

He releases a hard sigh when I press, "Who is he?"

He still doesn't respond when I question, "Did you ever do anything?"

"I wanted to. I still do." His breathing staggers as his eyes redden and gloss over. "But I can't. Candace made me promise, and I just can't break that promise. It would hurt her too much."

"Why didn't she do anything?"

"She was scared. Embarrassed. I tried talking to her, but she'd rather bury it, so that's what she did."

I shake my head, and when I do, he speaks up, "Look, man, I wanna kill that bastard. I do. I saw what he did to her, and he fucked her up . . . bad. But I love her. And as much as I hate that all she wants to do is hide this shit, I don't fight it because I don't want to hurt her." I watch his tears fall as he adds, "I know what you two have is completely different than what I have with her, but she's my fuckin' heart, man. I hate her choices, but I also know how fragile she is right now, so I let it be. Right or wrong, I just give her what she wants."

I can't speak even if I wanted to because the pain in my chest is nearly unbearable at this point. All I can do is give him a nod, and I know he sees the emotion on my face. How could a person hide it?

He stands up and grips my shoulder, saying, "I couldn't deal with this shit if it weren't for Mark. If you ever need to talk . . ."

"Yeah. Thanks," I respond on a breath before he turns to walk out the door.

When he's out of my vision, I drop my head in my hands and let it out. It's a haze of unrecognizable emotions beating through me. To look past this and let her continue to sit and do nothing is something that I don't think I'm capable of. But Jase is right. My girl is so damn fragile even though she's so damn strong. It's a paradox that's hard to deal with. She's gonna break one way or another.

Irritation boils inside, and the longer I sit here it starts to eat away at me until it takes over and I stand up, kicking over the stool, screaming, and smashing my glass against the brick wall behind the bar followed next by the bottle. The blast of glass shattering and sprinkling to the floor is all I hear through the ringing in my head. I grab my keys, leaving the mess, and head to my jeep.

I drive. Making my way back to my loft and upstairs to find Candace standing in my closet, slipping on a sweater.

"Why didn't you do anything?" I ask, unable to control my frustration.

She turns to look at me, confused, when she asks, "What are you talking about?"

"Don't make me say it."

"Ryan, please. Don't," she says and then walks past me to sit on the edge of the bed.

"Who is he?" I press, emotions getting the best of me.

She keeps her chin tucked down. Avoiding.

"Candace, tell me his fuckin' name!" I belt out because sitting around and not doing shit isn't gonna work for me.

"Please don't do this," she chokes out as she begins to cry.

"Why aren't you more pissed?"

"I am."

"You're not," I tell her as I stand in front of her. "I don't see it."

She doesn't respond, and I plead with her, needing to make sense of all of this. "Tell me why I don't see it. Make me understand because this shit is killing me."

"Because I don't know how to show it," she weeps as she looks up at me.

My heart is hammering hard in my chest. She's so locked up, and I don't know how to help her.

"I need you to show it. I need to see it," I tell her as I kneel down in front of her, gripping her legs.

"Don't."

"I wanna see you fighting. I wanna see you doing something since you won't let me do shit."

"Why? For what?"

"For you, Candace! It's for you," I say in a hard voice. "Show me that you're mad because my anger is beyond what I think I can handle right now."

Her breathing picks up as she cries harder.

"Show me," I push.

"I can't."

"You can. Use me," I urge. "Yell at me. Scream. Hit me. Punch me. Something! Just do something!" I shout as she sobs. "Stop crying and do something! Hit me!"

"Ryan, stop!" she screams, and when she tries to move away from me, I grab on to her wrists and she kneels down next to me, bracing her hands on the floor as she cries.

"I want you to fight. I want you to fight because I'm so fuckin' mad and you won't let me fight for you."

"You wanna fight?" I stand in the doorway and listen to my dad. "Come here," he says to my mom with a crooked finger, and she steps towards him. "Hit me."

"No."

"Hit me, you little bitch!"

She stands there crying when he pulls his clenched fist back and punches her in the stomach, forcing out a gush of air as she heaves and doubles over.

"Daddy, stop!"

He looks at me. "You want me to stop?" he asks before impaling her ribs with his boot.

Her screams are strained as I start to cry.

"Stop!"

He kicks her again as she lies there, lifeless.

"Tell me to stop again, you sack of shit."

I look at Candace doubled over on the floor—crying—and it hits me.

"God, baby. I'm sorry," I say, reaching out to touch her, but she coils back from me.

"It wouldn't even do anything," she snaps. "You want me to fight? Why? It's not going to change anything. It's not going to make it better. It's not going to take it away."

Realizing that I pushed her way too far, that I scared her by yelling at her, I reach out, and again, she resists my touch. "I'm sorry."

She doesn't hear me, she just continues, "I just wanna forget. I just want it to go away. But me fighting isn't gonna make that happen. The damage is done, and I can't go back."

"Baby," I say as gently as I can. "You can't pretend it didn't happen."

"Why not?" her voice a mere whimper. So desperate. "What's so bad about pretending?"

This time when I reach for her, she doesn't flinch, and I fold her up in my arms. "Because it *did* happen."

"Why?" she cries into my chest. "Tell me why this happened. Why me? What did I do to deserve this?"

There are no answers as she completely breaks and continues crying, collapsed in my lap. I feel like absolute shit for pushing her to this point, and all my fears are brought back to the forefront. I can't deny for one second that I don't resemble my father in frightening ways. That I could be so selfish to be screaming at my girlfriend as she's crumpled on the floor crying. I don't know what the hell is wrong with me, but I can't do that shit to her. Fuck, why did I just do that to her?

"I'm so sorry." I'm desperate as my voice cracks.

She grips her arms around me while I rest my cheek on top of her head. I can't believe I let my anger take control of me. Just knowing the thoughts of what I would do to that guy if I ever saw him scares the shit out of me. I can't let this happen again with her; I just can't because I know myself well enough to know that I'll never walk away from her, so I have to get my shit under control.

I rub her back until eventually she quiets down, taking in hiccups of breaths. She has the sleeves of my t-shirt fisted in her hands, and when she lifts her head up, she keeps her eyes closed. I kiss her forehead, and she presses her weight into my lips. She's exhausted.

"Hey," I say lightly, and when she hums in response, I encourage, "Can you look at me?"

She does, and when I see how red her eyes are, I feel disgusted with myself.

"I'm so sorry. I should have never raised my voice like that. I just feel so helpless, but how I feel isn't your fault. I don't want you to think that it is."

"You can say that, but the thing is, it's because of me that you feel this way."

I don't know how to respond to her words, but she doesn't give me time when she says, "I just . . . I don't want to lose you. I don't have very many people that . . . I mean . . . I don't even have a home anymore."

When she looks up at me and into my eyes I tell her, "You *are* home."

"Am I?"

Wiping under her eyes with my thumbs, I ask, "Is this what you want?"

Nodding her head, she whispers, "Yes."

"Then you're home," I give her and wrap her back up in my arms.

Candace wound up getting a bad headache and is sleeping again. Not only is she worn out from what happened earlier, she's also not feeling well after drinking so much with Jase last night.

I leave her be as I head down to my office. Despite the shit day, I need to call my mom because in Candace's drunken state last night, she revealed that her birthday is in a few days, and I want to surprise her by having my mom here. They have been talking more and more on the phone, and I know Candace would like to see her. Hell, after this month, it'll be nice to have her here for a few days.

"Hi, dear," she says when she answers my call.

"Hey, Mom. I have a favor to ask."

"Sure. What is it?"

"It's Candace's birthday on Thursday, and I was wondering if you can manage to get away for a few days and come stay here with us?" I ask.

"*This* Thursday?"

"Yeah."

"Ryan, that's in five days. Why didn't you tell me about this sooner?" she nags.

"Because I just found out last night. This was sprung on me too, Mom."

"Why did she wait so long to tell you?"

"I don't know, but it slipped out last night. I know she'd love to see you, so I was hoping . . ."

"I'll be there."

"Thanks. I'm not gonna tell her, so if you two talk before then, don't mention anything. I want her to be surprised."

"Lips are sealed."

"And no gifts," I remind her.

"Ryan."

"I have no problem with it, but I know how she is, so . . ."

"Fine. No gifts," she says with a faint laugh. "How has everything else been? I haven't talked to Candace in a few days; how did her audition go?"

"It seemed to go really well. She was insanely happy afterward. She should know if she got the solo on Friday."

"That's great. Is she around to talk to?"

"She's sleeping."

"Oh, okay. Well, tell her to call me when she has time."

"Yeah, I will."

"Everything else okay?" she asks, and although I've always been open with my mom, I know this thing with Candace will forever remain private, so I simply tell her, "Yeah, Mom. Everything's great."

We continue to chat for a few more minutes before we say goodbye. When I walk upstairs, I see Candace curled into a small ball in the center of my bed. Shrugging off my shirt, I crawl in to take a nap with her. I slide in behind her, and as I pull her into me, she rolls over to face me, eyes still closed. Draping my arm around her, she nuzzles her head in the curve of my neck, and finally, after all the tension of the day, I relax in the warmth of her.

chapter thirty

"WHAT DO YOU want to do for your birthday, babe?" I ask as she stretches before heading to the studio for rehearsals. I always enjoy seeing her like this—poised, hair up tight in a bun, leotard with an old pair of torn, baggy sweats. There's no doubt she was made to dance because she completely looks the part, and that look is doing things to me that I need to get under control.

"Nothing. I told Jase that the four of us could just grab dinner."

"We do that all the time."

She sits on the ground to roll her ankles when she says, "Please don't get any ideas. I really don't like doing anything for my birthday."

"Why?" I ask when I sit in front of her and take her leg in my hand to rub out her muscles.

"My mom would always throw me these over-the-top parties when I was little. Well, she threw them for her and her friends. It was all show with the moms, everyone trying to one-up the others. It was never what I wanted, and I would spend the whole day upset but forced to pretend to be their perfect daughter and behave as etiquette told me I should."

"So let me do something nice for you," I suggest.

"It makes me uncomfortable. It always has. I'm a year older; I just don't see the big deal in making a fuss over it."

"Candace."

Her only response is a shrug of her shoulders.

"So tell me then, what was it that you really wanted when you were a kid?" I ask when I move to massage her other leg.

Her hands rest in her lap as she sits on the floor and tells me, "Simple. It sounds trite, but what I really wanted was my friends to come over and play with me. Have a cheap cake from the grocery store instead of the fondant covered ones my mom would order from the bakery in town. That fondant tastes like crap, you know?" she says with her brows raised with exaggeration, and I laugh at her.

"I don't even know what that is," I admit with a smile.

"Well, it's gross. And I hated—*hated*—being forced to open all the gifts in front of everyone. I never got toys, but instead little trinkets and things. Like that bouncy ball," she exclaims. "I never got stuff like that."

"So that's why you hate getting presents?"

"It's just awkward for me, so I'd rather not deal with it."

"I'll call Jase. Why don't we just hang out here? Eat pizza, watch TV," I suggest.

She smiles, agreeing, "Sounds perfect."

She's simple in ways that I like, but for reasons that shouldn't be. I'll give Candace her *non-birthday* birthday party, but I can't *not* get her something to make it special. Because it is. So I'll find a way to do that for her without making her feel uncomfortable. My girl can be a challenge, but I like that about her.

While Candace is busy on campus all day, I head over to Fremont to stop by a couple vintage antique shops. Jase and Candace are always hanging out here, and I know Candace well enough that she doesn't buy most of her things from mass marketed retail shops. Yeah, she's simple, but she likes nice things.

I spend a couple hours roaming around, but nothing catches my eye, so I decide to walk down to Peet's and grab a coffee. When I pass by one of the little shops, the name stops me because Candace came home the other day with some shaving lather for me from here.

Stepping into Essenza, the place is filled with fine European perfumes, soaps, clothes, and jewelry. This looks like a place that she would shop. I'm the only one here and the lady behind the counter steps out and walks over to me, saying, "You look lost," with a friendly smile.

"That obvious?"

Her smile is warm and even though she screams elegance, she's quite relaxed when she offers me a glass of wine.

"I'm good."

"So what are we shopping for?"

"A girl. I know she's been here before, so I thought I would stop in," I tell her.

"What's her name?"

"Candace."

"The ballerina?" she squeals.

I nod my head when she adds, "She's been shopping here for years. We're the only boutique in the state that carries the perfume she wears, so she's pretty loyal."

"Why does that not surprise me? That she would've picked a perfume that was exclusive to one store in the whole state of Washington," I laugh as she joins in.

"You must be the guy she was shopping for last time she was in a couple weeks back."

I nod and introduce myself, "I'm Ryan."

I give her a friendly handshake as she says, "Well, I'll let you be. Please, I'm Viv, let me know if I can help you or if you change your mind about the wine."

Joking, I ask, "Does your boss know you drink on the job?"

"Please," she drawls and winks at me, adding, "It's a requirement."

I wander over to check out the perfumes, and sure enough, I spot her bottle of Flou. Next to the display there is an old antique wrought-iron table with a locked glass case that serves as the round table top. Looking down through the glass, there are a few pieces of handcrafted jewelry, most of them rings. There are a couple hand stamped pieces with various quotes. I eye one of the necklaces. It's the only one with a flat, rectangular bar at the drop that connects the thin, delicate chain. I stop looking at the rest of the jewelry when I read words that couldn't be more true, and I know I have to get this for her because *this*—these words—is exactly how I see her and how I need her to see herself.

Looking up to Viv, who is sipping her wine, I ask, "Can you show me a piece from this case?"

She hops up and comes over to unlock the glass, and I show her the one I'm looking at. She pulls it out and hands it to me.

"It's perfect," I murmur as I look it over. The stamped letters are rugged and uneven, a contrast to the polished silver bar and fragile chain.

"A Midsummer Night's Dream."

I look up and she clarifies, "The quote. It's from 'A Midsummer Night's Dream.'"

I run my thumb over the jagged impressions of the words, *And though she be but little, she is fierce.* "Was this here the last time she was in?"

"No."

"I'll take it."

When I hand her the necklace, I follow her over to the counter. "A gift?" she asks.

"It's her birthday."

"Shall I wrap it?"

"No," I say, and when she looks up at me, I add with a smirk, "She hates gifts."

She smiles as she takes my credit card. "Ryan, Ryan, Ryan," she tsks and then swipes my card before handing it back to me. "I like you."

"Not gonna lie, Viv, I like you too," I respond with a light chuckle before she hands me the bag.

I head out to my car, having one more errand to run, because I'm not quite satisfied yet.

When I get home later, I hear Candace in the shower, so I go ahead and stash my purchases. I walk into my closet, shoving them into one of the drawers and cover them up with a couple sweaters. My camera sits on the tabletop of the drawers, and I grab it, taking it with me as I flop on the bed and wait for Candace to come out. I scroll through the only pictures that are stored—the ones of Candace's back. I click on each one, zooming in on the preview screen to get a closer look.

The bathroom door opens, and I look up to see her walking out, towel drying her hair, wearing a t-shirt and a pair of my boxers. God, she's hot.

"I didn't know you were home," she says as she stands at the foot of the bed.

Ignoring her statement, I let her know, "I like it when you wear my underwear."

"Stop," she says in a nagging voice as I pop up to my knees.

"I'm serious. It's hot as shit."

When she laughs at me, I hold my hand out to her and pull her on top of the bed with me, twisting around and laying her on her back. Her skin is still damp from her shower, and I weave my fingers into her wet hair as I begin to plant slow kisses down her neck. She smells insanely good, and when I pull back to look down at her, I'm taken by how beautiful she looks right now.

Leaning over, I pick up my camera, and as soon as I bring it up to my eye, she covers her face, complaining, "No."

"What?"

"You can't just take my picture."

I laugh at her. "Don't be shy with me," I tell her and then sit back on my heels. "Let me see you."

She removes her hands from her face, and when she does, I say, "Let me photograph you."

Lying there, she doesn't respond one way or the other, so I bring the camera back up to my eye and snap a few quick shots of her. Hair splayed around her face, flushed cheeks, and a soft expression on her face.

"Thanks," I say when I'm done capturing her face and then shift to the side of her, holding the camera back to my face.

"What are you doing?"

"Giving myself something to work on," I mutter before adding, "Bend your legs up, babe."

She does without question, and I use my hand to maneuver them to my liking until they are at the perfect angle. The clicks of the shutter are the only sounds that fill the room as she lies there, watching me intently every time I shift my eyes to hers. I'm glad she's comfortable with this and not so tense like she was the last time we did this.

I move to set the camera on the nightstand and then back to her, easing my weight on top of her. She runs her hands along my face, drawing me down to kiss her. We let ourselves get lost in one another, moving in a way I have only done with her, and when her shirt hits the floor with mine, I drop my head to her chest. Her arms encircle my head as I cover her in my mouth, finding that the feel of her lace bras are a turn-on I never expected.

Her skin is soft beneath my hand as I run it down her side and to her leg as I tighten my grip because she feels that damn good. When she grazes her lips up my neck, she sends chills down my arms. Our breaths begin to run deep, and my need for her strengthens as I slide my hand in from her hips, over the waistband of her boxers, and down between her legs, cupping the heat of her.

"Stop," she snaps and jerks my hand away, startling me.

"Babe?"

"Just . . . don't," she whispers.

I accept all of her hesitations, but it still hurts when she rejects my touches. Her eyes are closed when I lie down beside her, pulling her hip over so that she's facing me.

"Please look at me," I urge in a hushed voice, and when she does, I go with transparent honesty and say, "I want to touch you."

"I know. I just . . ." I see the worry in her eyes and the lines in her forehead.

"You can tell me anything, babe. I'll never judge you."

She takes her time as I run my hand up her arm and into her hair. When she does speak, it's strained as she confesses, "He's the only one that's touched me there."

I work hard to not get upset. To stay calm so that I can talk to her about this because we can't keep avoiding it. I know this is the last thing she probably wants to discuss, but it has to be done, so I choose my words carefully, telling her, "You know that I would never hurt you."

"I know. It isn't that."

"Then tell me what it is. I need to understand."

She tucks her chin down, and when I lift it back up with my fingers, I explain, "I need you to talk to me about this because I need to know."

"It's embarrassing," she admits quietly.

"There is nothing for you to be embarrassed about, babe. But I'm gonna be honest with you—it hurts when you push me away because I don't want you to be scared of me."

"I'm not scared of you."

"Then what?"

After she lets out a slow sigh, she finally reveals, "It makes me feel dirty."

My forehead gently falls against hers, and I close my eyes, shaking my head. With my hands on her back, I feel the soft heaves, letting me know she's crying. It infuriates me that he did this to her. That this is how she views intimacy. The last thing I would ever expect or want her to feel when she's with me like this is dirty. Knowing that makes me sick to my stomach.

"Listen to me," I say when I pull my head back to look at her. "That guy was a piece of shit, we both know that. He's a sick fuck, and yeah, what he did and how he touched you was dirty. The disgust is beyond that. But that isn't what this is. That isn't us," I try to explain to her. I pull her in tight, continuing, "I want to touch you and feel you. He made that something ugly for you, and I hate him for that. That he could take that away from us."

"I'm sorry," she cries.

"You have nothing—*nothing*—to be sorry for," I scold. "He did this, not you. The way I want to touch you is nothing like that. I love you, and I want to touch you like this because it's a way for me to feel close to you. It's a way for me to love you and to make you feel that too."

The tears run down the side of her face as she responds, "I want to give that to you. I do. I feel awful that I can't, but I'm trying. I need you to know that I *am* trying."

Wiping her face, I say, "I know you are. I see it. I'm not blaming you, but we need to talk about this so that I can understand."

"I hate this," she confesses and then buries her head in my chest.

"I know you do, and if I could do something I would. I just don't know what that would be. But I love you, even the parts of you that you think are ugly. I love it all."

chapter thirty-one

"WHAT THE HELL is this, Mark?" I call out from the kitchen when I open the box with the cake.

He's on the couch, drinking a beer with Jase, and responds nonchalantly, "You put me in charge of the cake, so I got her a cake."

"She's turning twenty-three, man."

"Yeah, I know. Trust me, she'll like it," he tells me with an exaggerated wink.

"There are fuckin' rats in tutus."

"They're mice," he corrects as I look back down at the cake that's fit for a five-year-old. "It came with a free 'Angelina the Ballerina' ring," he laughs as he holds up his hand to show me the pink plastic ring he's wearing on his pinky.

I shake my head and laugh with them as I grab a beer and join them in the living room.

"You gonna give that to her?"

He smirks, saying, "No way, man. This is mine."

We hang out and watch TV for a few minutes until Candace walks through the door. She gives Mark and Jase each a hug and kiss before I call her over and pull her onto my lap.

"I missed you," I whisper as I run my nose up her neck and then tease, "Mmmm . . . coffee."

She always smells like she's bathed in a latte when she gets off work.

"I'm gonna take a quick shower. I'll be back," she says as she hops off of my lap.

I watch as she goes up the stairs, and as if we had planned it, my phone buzzes with a text from my mom letting me know she's about fifteen minutes out.

"Did Candace find out about her audition yet?" Mark asks.

"Not yet. She should know tomorrow."

"So what are you guys gonna do this weekend?" Jase asks as he takes a sip of his beer.

"My mom is only able to stay through tomorrow afternoon, so we will probably just lay low."

We continue to talk about nothing in particular for a while when the doorbell rings.

"Hey, Mom," I greet as I open the door.

She steps in and gives me a big hug, saying, "It's good to see you, dear."

"Donna?" I hear Candace call out from behind me, and when I turn to see her walking down the stairs, the surprised look on her face makes me smile.

"Candace," Mom says, excited to see her.

"What are you doing here?" She is completely caught off guard, wearing her pajamas with her hair pulled on top of her head, as she gives my mom an excited hug.

"I wasn't going to miss your birthday. But I'm a little disappointed that I had to hear about it from Ryan when you and I talk every week."

I step beside Candace, shoot her a wink, and kiss her on the cheek.

"Sorry, I . . . I don't normally do anything for my birthday, but I'm so happy you're here," she says and then hugs Mom again. "I can't believe you drove all this way."

"It's a few hours, dear. Hardly a chore." I watch as my mom takes Candace's hand and walks over to Mark and Jase.

Candace introduces them, and I make my way into the kitchen.

"Mom, what do you want to drink?"

"A glass of wine will be good."

"Me too," Candace tells me, and I laugh at the memory of her drunk the last time she had wine with Jase, so I just have to tease her, asking, "You're not gonna get drunk, slap my ass, and tell me how sexy I am, are you?"

"Ryan!" she scolds, completely embarrassed, and shoots a look towards my mom.

I laugh at her, knowing that she has nothing to be concerned about when it comes to my mom. She adores Candace, and the two of them have become quite close in the past couple of months.

I take a seat on the couch next to Candace as the three of us chat. I wanted to do something more for tonight, but this was probably the best idea. As we spend the evening relaxing and visiting over pizza, wine, and beer, I take in the fact that I have never had this before. At least not here in Seattle. I'm close with my family back home, but never felt that connection here, until now—until her. I've always known from the start that Jase, Candace, and Mark were tight. Just the three of them. And before I realized it, I'd become a part of that.

I've never had friendships and connections like I have with these people. I never wanted to. Even though they are all younger than me, when I saw the level of closeness and trust between the three of them, I saw what I had been missing. Candace made me want that—the connect. The commonality between us was something that was lacking in my previous friendships. For the first time since I moved here, the first time in the past ten years, I have people that I trust and care about.

It's unfortunate when I think about it, but in a way, it's Candace's trauma that has bonded the four of us. I know we all love her in our own unique way, and at the root, there's never been jealousy. Only three men that love this girl. And knowing that she has all of us gives me a level of security that I never expected to feel.

So we take this night, and like any family would, we laugh and eat cheap birthday cake straight from the box. Mom helps me clean up in the kitchen while Candace sits on the floor, cuddled into Jase, bantering back and forth with Mark, determined to get that plastic ring from him.

"I love her."

I look at my mom when she says this to me as we load the dishwasher.

"She's really something special," she adds.

"Yeah, she is," I agree as I watch her from across the room.

We finish up and wipe the counters down, and Candace asks as we walk back in, "Hey, you guys wanna watch a movie?"

"You all go ahead. I'm going to get some sleep so I'm rested for tomorrow," my mom says.

Candace walks over and gives her a hug, saying, "Thanks again for coming, Donna."

"How about we spend a little girl time tomorrow, just the two of us?"

"That sounds perfect."

"I love being ditched by the women in my life," I tease as I step behind Candace and wrap my arms around her shoulders.

"I'm sure you can find something to busy yourself with," my mom shoots back at me. "Good night, you two."

"Let me help you get settled in," I offer when she starts to head back to the guest bedroom. I stand there for a moment with Candace in my arms and then turn her around to face me. Tilting her head back to look up at me, I kiss her before saying, "Give me a couple of minutes."

When I return, the lights are off, and the three of them have made a pile of pillows and blankets in the middle of the living room with the fireplace going.

"You guys work fast," I murmur as I lie down next to Candace and tuck her into me.

We watch 'The Breakfast Club,' and about halfway through, Jase and Mark call it a night and head out, leaving Candace and I alone for the first time tonight.

She rolls over in my arms and weaves her legs with mine.

"Thank you," she says softly.

"For?"

"Your mom and the cake."

I kiss her nose, and she smiles as I say, "Anytime."

"I love you," she says before she kisses me.

When our kisses turn into more, I stop and sit up. "Come on." I grab her hand and tell her, "I want you in my bed, under my sheets," before taking her upstairs.

As expected, the girls woke up this morning and went out for breakfast and shopping. I decided to take the time and work on the photos of Candace's legs that I took the other day. I spent most of the morning in my office, working on the computer before going to the gym to grab a quick workout.

It's a little after noon by the time they get back. When they walk through the door, their hands are full of shopping bags.

"Damn, that was a long breakfast," I joke as I help them with their bags.

"Sorry, time got away from us. If I didn't have to go home, I would have spent the whole day with her," Mom says.

"Well, thanks for bringing her back. I'm sick of sharing her," I tease as I wrap my arm around Candace.

Nudging me in the gut, she playfully scolds, "Ryan!"

"Sorry, babe, but it's the truth," I remark and then go in for a nibble on her neck.

"Okay, kids. I've seen enough. I'm going to go pack," my mom says, heading down the hall.

"Ryan, that tickles," she laughs, trying to squirm out of my arms. Picking her up, I haul her over to the couch where I lay her down and start planting soft kisses on her. "Did you have a good time this morning?" I ask between my nips and then lick the hollow of her neck.

"Uh huh."

I continue to kiss her like this until she says, "Ryan, we should stop."

"Why?"

"Because your mom is about to leave, and you should go spend a little time with her before she goes."

Not wanting to stop, I let out a groan and tell her, "Okay, but I'm not done with you."

Candace takes her shopping bags and goes upstairs while I check in with my mom.

"Did you two have fun?" I ask, sitting on the edge of the bed as she gets her things together to leave.

"We did. She took me over to the coffee shop where she works."

"What did you guys talk about?"

"You're nosey," she quips, and I laugh at her, but she quickly straightens her face and comes to sit next to me on the bed. "She's worried."

"About what?" I ask.

"Have you given any thought to what's going to happen after she graduates?"

"Yeah, Mom, I have. Is that what's bothering her?"

"It would be odd if it weren't. Isn't it bothering you?" she questions.

"I try not to let it. But whatever happens, I'd never leave her."

"Sometimes girls need a little extra reassurance," she offers as she pats my knee and smiles.

I help my mom with her bag as I walk her out.

"Candace," I call to her upstairs.

"Coming," she responds, and as she's walking down, I see the sadness creep across her face. She doesn't say anything, going over to hug my mom. I feel bad as she starts to cry, knowing she wants to spend more time with her.

I reach out and place my hand on her back when she pulls away from the hug, and my mom says, "Come see me, okay?"

Candace nods her head, and I know that she hates the sound of her voice when she's this upset, so she stays quiet as I wrap my arms around her from behind.

"When is your next break?"

"She has the last two weeks of this month off before her last quarter," I answer for her so she doesn't have to speak.

"You and Ryan come visit, okay?" she offers as she looks at her.

We say our goodbyes, and she leaves to drive back home. Turning Candace around, I hold her in my arms and give her a few minutes to just be sad. I'm grateful for the bond the two of them have forged, but I don't like seeing my girl upset like this.

"You okay, babe?"

"I hate that she lives so far away," she says as I wipe her face. "I really like having her around."

"I know you do. We'll go visit her when you're on your break."

She rests her head on my chest and sighs before saying, "My parents never even called me." I grip the back of her head and hold her tight as she adds, "I mean . . . I knew they wouldn't, but it still hurts."

"I know it does."

And this is the shit I hate. Thinking about her mom and dad, wondering how they could turn away from their daughter so easily. I know it's possible because of my own dad, but thinking about everything Candace has gone through in the past several months cuts me deep, and all I want to do is protect her from anything that could hurt her.

"Come on, let's go grab something to eat before we go to the campus," I tell her and just hope to God that she got this solo because I don't want to see how upset she'll be if she didn't.

Seeing the look on her face was priceless. She was shocked and giddy and couldn't control her enthusiasm when she jumped into my arms, squealing. She got her solo, and I couldn't have been more proud. This girl works her ass off, but it got me thinking more about what my mom said. I'm not ignorant of the fact that Candace will probably get a job that requires her to move. I've been taking a lot of time away from the bar these past few weeks, and I need to start considering what her moving means for me and my business.

When I walk into the bedroom, I notice that the door to the bathroom is cracked open. Slowly opening the door wider, I see her standing there in my boxers and a tank top, finishing up brushing her teeth. It's been a long day, and she's been through a string of emotions since this morning. I walk up from behind and slip my arms around her as I drop a few kisses along the curve of her bare shoulder. She holds on to my arms with her hands as we watch each other in the mirror.

She turns around, and I lift her up onto the edge of the sink and look down at her; she has a peaceful look about her tonight.

"You're fuckin' gorgeous," I tell her, and my words make her laugh as I lower my mouth to hers.

Sliding my tongue past her lips, she hooks her ankles behind my waist, burying her hands in my hair. Her touch excites me but in a soothing way. I pick her up, walk her across the room, and fall into bed with her. I stare down, and I know, that no matter what happens, she has me. I don't want to belong to anyone but her.

She runs her hands up my chest and around to the back of my neck, pulling me down, and we kiss. We kiss in a way that's different than all the times before. I can't explain it, but it takes over me, holding a new level of passion. I press her firmly to me, tasting the mint that still lingers in her mouth.

Lifting her back off the bed, I sit her up and watch her as she removes her top. I get caught up in her and press her back down onto the bed, situating my hips between her legs. She's so warm against me, and my chest begins to tighten with the effect this girl has on me.

I never gave my heart to anyone before. I never wanted to. I was scared. But maybe I was just saving it for her. And now, I want to give this girl more than my heart. I want to give her everything.

Realizing that I'm getting too carried away with myself, I pull back, nearly panting, "We should stop," as I rest my forehead on her sternum.

She runs her hands through my hair, whispering, "Don't."

Her words are unexpected, so I pull up to look over her face, to try and read what she's thinking.

"Babe," I breathe out, heavy.

She looks me straight in the eyes and tells me, "I don't want you to stop."

"I need you to talk to me," I respond with nerves coursing through me, unsure of what to do here.

"I don't want to stop tonight."

Fear. That's what comes over me when I hear her words. Closing my eyes, I drop my head to hers. My heart is racing when I urge, "Please tell me this is okay," because the thought of this scares me.

She nods her head against mine, but it isn't enough. "I need to hear you say it, babe."

I finally open my eyes when she cups my face and assures me, "It's okay. I want this, with you, I just . . . I don't know if I can."

But suddenly, I don't know if *I* can. I want to. I've wanted to since I met her, but now . . . now I'm afraid, and I don't know what to do with her. I'm not sure if she sees my panic when she takes my hand in hers and places it over her breast, urging quietly, "Just touch me."

Her hand trembles against mine, and if this does happen, I can't have her feeling like this. So I do everything I can to push my anxiety away to focus on making sure she's relaxed. She's been taken advantage of by the two people before me, and I want to make this perfect for her.

I lower myself and kiss her. I take my time and *really* kiss her. Pressing my lips slowly into hers, grazing my tongue along her lip, and sealing my mouth with hers. My hand slides up from her breast and underneath the strap on her shoulder. As I move my hand down her arm, I take the strap with it, slipping it off, feeling the tension in the elastic releasing.

She's never let me see her naked. The closest, a bra and my boxers. So when I begin to reach around her, my anticipation is overwhelming. But then, in a moment, she nervously mutters, "I'm scared. I've never . . ."

"It's just you and me," I tell her. "You're all I'll ever want."

She faintly nods, and when I unclasp the hooks behind her back, she crosses her arm over her chest. Laying my hand over hers, I lift it up and drop her bra to the floor. I look at her. I've always wanted to but she's always been too shy. Then my eyes stop on a serrated, crescent scar on her left breast, and what I think it might be is confirmed when she shamefully bares, "He bit me."

I won't let that piece of shit filter into this moment. She's embarrassed, and there's no fuckin' way I'm gonna let that bastard claim another piece of her. Even with this scar, he can't take away from how gorgeous she is.

Leaning down, I kiss her scar and breathe into her skin, "God, you're perfect."

I take my kisses and drop them down her stomach before sitting back on my heels to remind her that she isn't alone. I bring her hand to my ribs and over my scar. We don't speak. There's no need. She gets it when she brushes her thumb across the jagged line and then pulls me down to her, hands trussed in my hair.

The feel of her naked body against my chest is gratifying beyond words. With no barriers, I run my tongue up the smooth skin of her breast and slowly across her pert nipple before taking her into my mouth. The pressure of her fingertips pressing into my shoulders strengthens when my hands find themselves at the band of her shorts. She lifts her hips when I begin to remove her boxers and panties at the same time. God, every inch of her is stunning, and I suddenly feel undeserving to have this girl who is far above what I could have ever imagined for myself.

She watches as I slip off my pants and then lower myself back to her, grabbing the sheets and covering us up. I lie here naked with her and have never felt so connected. She's warm against me, but as I trail my hands slowly along her soft skin, I can feel her trembling.

"Babe, you're shaking."

"What if I can't do this?" she says with an uneven voice, worry etched in the lines of her face.

"Then we stop."

Her eyes fall shut, and I assure her, "We'll move as slow as you need. You just tell me when to stop."

"I don't want you to stop," she says, opening her eyes.

She slides her arms around me and draws my body back to hers as she kisses me, caressing her lips with mine, taking her time as she runs her hands along my chest and down my abdomen, making my muscles cinch at the touch. Her lips drag along my neck and down my shoulder while I gently knead her supple breast in my hand and kiss her exposed neck. When my mouth finds her hardened nipple again, I roll my tongue over it and begin to gently suck, her body writhing in response.

"Ryan." The sound of my name on her lips is sexy as hell, and I need her to tell me again before we move any further, so I ask, "You sure?"

"Yes."

My anxiety is back. The rush of emotions swarms in my chest as I try to stay calm for her, but I just need to hear it. "Tell me that you want this, that you want me."

"I want you to make love to me," she says with her eyes pinned to mine.

I take a moment to slip on protection before I reach down and slowly begin to guide myself inside of her, but as soon as I touch her, she locks up on me. Pulling myself back, I look down to see the rapid rise and fall of her chest.

"Are you okay?"

Holding on to my shoulders, she nods. "Yeah."

I've never been so scared to have sex, but I know with her, that's not what this is. I've never been with a woman like this before. I know I'm gonna make love with her, and I want to do everything possible to make this perfect. 'Cause for the first time in my life, this isn't about me—it's about her. So when I continue to push myself inside of her, I can feel every bit of how tense she is. It takes me a while, but when I'm finally inside of her, the feeling is almost too much for me. My head drops to her neck as I moan, "Fuck, you feel so good, babe," unable to keep it in.

I hold myself still while her thighs tremble as she clenches them against my hips. I wrap my hands around her head and give her time to relax. When I pull my head back, I immediately feel like shit when I see her eyes clamped shut with tears falling down her temples.

"Open your eyes, Candace. Look at me," I tell her, concerned about what she's seeing if she isn't seeing me.

"Don't make me look," she pleads, but I need her to. I need her to not be scared of this. To not let her mind drift to that alley. To show her that this can be something amazing.

"Baby, please open your eyes. I need you here with *me*. It's only me."

It takes her a second, but she eventually opens them and focuses on me. When I feel her body soften against mine, I gradually begin to move. Being this close with her—inside of her—I never want this to end. I can't even imagine wanting to be selfish with her, so I move slowly, needing this closeness to last. To make her see this for what it is—love.

Banding my arms around her, she clings to me, and the sounds of pleasure coming out of her are all I hear. Sighs, breaths, quiet moans. They turn me on even more as our bodies begin to work together, moving in a way I know I'll always want with her.

"God, I love you," I release on a ragged exhale and slide deeper inside of her.

Moving to kiss me, she mumbles over my lips, "I love you."

I notice her hands are still clenching my shoulders, so I reach up and take one of her hands in mine, lacing my fingers with hers, pressing our hands into the mattress. She begins to sway her hips up to mine as she starts moving with me. Her body is so tight around me that it takes a lot for me to hang on and not let go. I watch her beneath me, her body against mine, completely exposed to me, and I don't think I could fall any more deeply in love with her. I'm not sure how that would even be possible.

We take our time with each other, making love, lingering in the moment. When she closes her eyes, she constricts her legs to my hips, and I know she's close. I also know that she's never had this before.

"Relax, babe," I tell her because I want her to feel every piece of what I'm about to give her.

She has her hand braced tightly around the back of my neck when her breathing falters. I kiss her, simply resting my lips on hers, as I continue to ease myself in and out of her, feeling every part of her around me. Her hand jerks in mine, and I lift my head to tell her, "Open your eyes. Stay with me," wanting to be sure that I'm all she sees.

Locking her eyes with mine, her body is damp with a sheen of sweat, and I give in to the intensity that has been building inside of me when I hear her let out a whimper. It doesn't take me long to get to where she is, so when I say, "Baby, let go for me," her hips buckle, and she clamps her hand strongly around mine as I watch her lose herself, face flushed, panting out soft moans. I can't hold on when I feel her walls tighten and spasm around me. Dropping my head onto hers, I moan her name as I come hard, feeling the impassioned throbs with my release, giving myself in a way I didn't know was possible for me.

We lie here, bodies pressed together, breathing labored, as we both come down. When I finally lift my heavy head to look at her, the tears are back. Afraid that this has had some negative effect on her, I ask in utter worry, "God, baby, what's wrong?" as I wipe her tears.

She takes a slow moment before giving me words that almost break me.

"Being with you . . . that's all I want."

This is a lot. My emotions are all over the place, but they all lie within her heart. I keep myself inside of her, never wanting to leave, and when I lay my head against hers, I quietly confess, "You're the only one I've ever done that with. You're the only one I've ever made love to."

I didn't think there was anything I could give her that would be new, untouched, and only hers—until now. She's the only one that will ever have me like this. And finally experiencing sex in this way, I'll never want it any other way.

chapter thirty-two

WATCHING HER SLEEP right now, hair draped over the pillow, face soft, lips slightly parted—she's beautiful. I could stare at her for hours when she's this peaceful, but I know she's going to wake soon, so I go ahead and slip quietly out of bed and head into the closet. I knew I wouldn't give her the necklace on her birthday. She probably would have resisted, so that's why I held off. But we're alone now, and it's not her birthday anymore.

I take the necklace out of its box and go into the bathroom, shutting the door behind me. I set it in between the two sinks and then brush my teeth before I get back into bed. Wrapping myself around her, my movements start to wake her, so I feign sleep as she begins to stir awake. I lie there, still, as she slides out from under my arm, and I can hear her close the bathroom door a few seconds later. I roll over and wait for her to come out. Listening to the water run, I wonder if the gift is going to irritate her when she made it perfectly clear she didn't want me to get her anything.

The door opens, and Candace walks out with a sly grin, holding the necklace up in front of her.

"What's this?" she questions, knowing very well what it is, but I play into her and say, "Well, it's definitely not a birthday gift, because that was two days ago."

Her laughter is a relief when she hops up into bed and hands me the necklace to put on her.

"I love it," she says as I clasp it on, and she doesn't need to say anything else about it. She's read the scribed words. She's accepted it without hesitation. That's all I wanted.

Crawling over her as she lies on her back, I drop kisses along the chain. "Do you know how beautiful you are?"

"Mmmm," she hums.

"You were amazing last night," I tell her when I start removing her clothes because I need her again. We were both so cautious last night, and now, seeing her naked and having her calm, I want to give this to her again, and she lets me.

As we remain wrapped up in each other after making love, I stroke my hand through her hair lazily, enjoying her as our breathing slows back down.

"How are you feeling?"

She's in a tranquil state when she responds with a simple, "Happy."

That one word makes me smile. That's all I ever want her to be—happy. I begin to laugh when I think about the other surprise I have for her.

"What's so funny?" she asks with a grin of her own.

"I have something else for you."

"Besides the necklace?"

"Besides the necklace," I say.

She squints her eyes at me, and I defend, "I promise, you're gonna like this better. It's not a trinket."

That smile of hers grows and she sits up, clutching the sheet to keep herself covered, and her modesty is adorable. Leaning over, I open the drawer to my nightstand and then hand it over to her.

"I don't know what to say," she says as she keeps her eyes on the Hop N Bounce box, which holds the deflated ball.

"I have a pump out in the garage if you wanna take it for a spin around the living room," I tease.

Setting the box down on the bed, she crawls to me, sheet still clung around her, and gives me a kiss.

"You'll never know how much I love you."

After spending most of the morning in bed with Candace, I decided to run into work so that I can take the night off. Candace called Jase and went to spend the afternoon with him and Mark. I told her I'd be back at the loft around six tonight, but that quickly changed when one of our vendors stopped by today with a shipment only to inform me that the bar is now on COD with them. When I started digging through the backlogged bills, I discovered that Michael has been missing payments.

This is the second time this guy has fucked up, and I'm done. Walking into his office, the place is a disorganized disaster. Digging through his files, I find the ones that I need, and I spend the next few hours scouring through all of our various vendors' invoices, checking them against the bank statements, and then having Mel double-check the inventory.

I can't be having things fall through the cracks like this. I need to seriously start thinking about what's gonna happen to this bar if I wind up moving after Candace is done with school, but leaving it in Michael's hands isn't gonna happen. I need someone I can trust.

"Max," I call out while Mel and I are buried behind the bar as I help her check the last shipment.

"Yeah, boss."

"Get Michael on the phone. Tell him to get his ass up here," I shout over the band. I've been so busy, I didn't even realize how late it is or that

Mark is here with the guys, but they're already on stage playing.

"Ryan!" Max shouts, and the chaos around me right now is giving me a headache.

"Did you get ahold of him?"

"Yeah, he's on his way, but Candace is on the phone. Line two," he says.

Making my way through the crowd, I run upstairs to take the call in my office where it's quiet.

"Babe, hey."

"Hey, I didn't think you were going to be working this late," she says, and I feel bad that I'm still stuck up here when all I want is to be home.

I explain everything to her, stressed about the whole situation, as she listens and then let her know that I'll be heading home in a bit. Hanging up the phone, I start getting my things together, and about five minutes later, Michael walks into my office.

"Shit, that was fast," I say.

"I was on my way up here when Max called. What's up? You leaving?" he asks as he stands there watching me.

"Yeah, but we need to talk," I say as I take a seat, and he follows suit. "I found out today that invoices haven't been getting paid. Never, in the six years I've owned this place, have we missed a payment, and now we're on COD with one of our vendors."

"Ryan—"

"Look," I say, interrupting him. "I'm gonna cut to the chase. This bar is my livelihood, and when shit starts going wrong, then that livelihood is compromised. Feelings aside, I gotta let you go, man. I can't trust you to handle things up here when I'm not around, and that's a problem for me."

"Ryan, man. Come on."

"Look, my ass is tired. Been up here all day trying to fix your mistakes, and I'm ready to go home," I tell him as I grab my coat and leave. My stress is through the roof, and I don't have time to dick around with this guy.

I find Max when I get downstairs.

"Hey, I need to talk to you."

"What's going on?" he questions as we step into the back storage room.

"I just fired Michael, so I want you to go up there and oversee him as he packs his shit up. Make sure we get his keys and everything—"

"Hey, I got it covered. No worries."

"Thanks. I'm getting the hell out of here. I'll be back in the morning. There's a stack of papers on top of my filing cabinet. Make sure he signs them before he leaves."

"Got it."

I don't waste any more time, knowing that Max will handle the Michael situation, and I head home to my girl.

Candace and I camped out downstairs with some wine and an old movie when I got home last night. We hadn't done that in a while, so it was a perfect way to end the stressful day. I did manage to talk to her about trying to come to the bar again. I wasn't sure if I was pushing too much, but I figured this morning would be a good time since it would only be the two of us. She took me by surprise when she said she would try. I know this isn't easy for her, and while I'm in the kitchen fixing her a coffee to take with us, I watch her sitting on the couch, wringing her hands together. She's a nervous wreck. I walk over and hand her the coffee, telling her, "Babe, you don't have to do this if it's causing you this much stress."

"I told you that I would try, so . . . I'll try."

Holding my hand out, she takes it and we head to the bar. The morning is cold and the sky is dark with cloud cover. Candace is silent, and I keep my hand on her knee as I pull up and park along the curb in front of the building like I promised her.

When I open her door, she finally snaps out of her zoned-out state and holds my hand as I help her out. We walk inside, and I show her around before I take her back to the stairs.

"My office is up here," I tell her as I lead her up.

I keep my hold on her hand when I walk into Michael's office to grab the papers I need. Taking a few steps into his office, she jerks around, stumbling over her feet and into me.

"Babe?"

"I want to go," she says with her head down, and as I reach around her to quickly grab the file, I see what she saw and kick myself for not thinking beforehand that Michael's office overlooks the back lot.

I tuck her under my arm as I quickly pull her out and walk her down the hall to my office, tossing the file on my desk, and turning to hold her.

"I'm sorry, I didn't think," I say as she shakes under my arms—panicked.

I back us up to the desk and lean against it as I pull her between my legs. She keeps her head on my chest, and I continue rubbing her back, trying to calm her down. She isn't speaking. I know she's trying hard to keep herself together, and all of a sudden, being here with her isn't something I want to be doing anymore. I hate that this was the first place I ever saw her. I hate the visions that are starting to play back through my head.

I hold her, but all I can see is her covered in blood and dirt, lying naked on the ground. My heart rate picks up as the guilt returns. I could have done so many things differently that night. If I would have just gone out there sooner . . .

I focus back on Candace when she lifts her head. Keeping my focus on her before I get too consumed, I ask, "You okay?"

She nods, placing her head back on my chest, saying, "I hate seeing that dumpster." I hold her closer when she says this because I hate it too. I hate everything about that goddamn night. "It's weird because I also love it in a messed up way. It's all I had to focus on."

"I'm so sorry." I think about what must have been going through her head, the sheer terror she must have felt, and my stomach begins to knot up.

"When I dream about that night, it's always taken away from me. There's nothing to distract me."

"I wish I knew his name." I would find him and destroy him if given the chance. I would kill him for everything he took away from her.

She looks up at me and cups my clenched jaw, lifting onto her toes, and planting a kiss on my lips. I pull her into me and take a deep breath, letting it out slowly. Being here with her, I'm starting to feel like I'm lying, and the guilt is eating at me the longer we are here. I never thought that deciding not to tell her about who I am would make me feel like it is right now. Deceitful.

I'm trying to keep the memories out of my head, but I can't help the constant flashes I'm getting each time I close my eyes. I'm not sure I'll ever stop hearing her pleading screams from that night. It's a part of her that I'll always have to bear, but it'll never even come close to all that she has had to endure.

I shift my thoughts because this is huge for her, and I need her to know that. I tell her how proud I am that she came up here with me, but I can tell she wants to leave, and honestly, so do I.

chapter thirty-three

I CALL MAX as I drive to see if he can meet me at the bar after my workout. I've been giving a lot of thought to getting things settled at work since I fired Michael a couple weeks ago, and the one person who knows that place inside and out, the one person I trust completely, is Max. It only makes sense to me that he would be someone that I could have complete confidence in, and knowing that he has a baby on the way, he'd be an idiot to not take the opportunity I'm about to offer him.

After a couple hours of lifting and running, I head up to Blur to meet with Max. He's sitting at the bar, chatting with Mel when I walk in.

"Hey, man. Let's go to my office," I say, and he follows me up the stairs.

"So, what's on your mind?" he asks as we sit down.

"I'm gonna be honest with you here," I start. "Candace is graduating in a couple of months, and I doubt that she's gonna be staying here in Seattle."

"You think you'll go with her?" he asks.

"I can't let her go without me, but I can't let this place fold either," I tell him. "I know you have a lot going on with Traci, but . . ."

"Look, you know I'll help out in any way I can."

"I was hoping you could help run this place," I say. "You know everything about the job, and you've always been loyal to me. Shit's been crazy since I let Michael go, but I'd like to bring you on as his permanent replacement, which means a sizable salary increase."

"Are you serious?" he says as he leans forward, resting his elbows on his knees.

"Completely. It's yours."

He stands up and I follow as he walks towards me and claps his hand in mine for a solid shake as he grips my shoulder with his other hand.

"So, you're in?" I ask.

"I'm in, boss."

"Great," I sigh in relief as I sit back down. "You know the drill, man, so let's get this going in the next couple days if you can manage on short notice?"

"Yeah. No problem. You still going out of town this weekend?"

"Yep. I'm not sure how long I'll be gone. A week, give or take a few days. It's Candace's last break before graduation, and I know she wants to spend time with my mom."

"You need an extra guy for the door?" he asks.

"I don't think so. Chase has been doing a good job at keeping everything under control in that department. Plus people are used to seeing you down there, so I think if you can keep that gig going when you have extra time, that would be great."

We finish up, filling out a few forms and going over some stuff I need him to take care of while I'm in Oregon next week. Having this situation settled takes a lot of stress off my shoulders, and even though Candace has yet to bring up school coming to an end, she has nothing to worry about.

When I'm all done, I head back to the loft, but Candace's car is still gone as I pull into the driveway. I grab a quick shower and get cleaned up. When she gets home a little while later we spend the afternoon listening to a few demos from local bands. Mark is graduating with most of the guys in the band, so I need to go ahead and find alternatives for when their gig is up with me in June.

I watch Candace in the kitchen, and when she walks back into the room, I tell her, "Something's been bothering me today." As she moves past me, I grab her and pull her onto my lap. "I've never seen you dance."

"Oh . . . yeah, I guess not," she says and then adds, "But you will in May when we have our production. You'll see me a lot. I have three ensembles plus my solo."

"It just bothers me that there is a huge part of your life that I've never seen." I see her nearly every day wearing her leotards, warm-up pants, and leg-warmers. I even watch her stretch and do her ankle exercises every chance I get. But I have yet to see my girl dance.

"Well, I can grab some videos at the studio of past performances," she offers. "They have also recorded some of our studios this year. Would that suffice for you, watching me on video?"

I grab her, flipping her down on the couch onto her back, and nip her neck before letting her know, "Nothing about you will ever suffice for me. I'm always gonna want more."

She laughs as we continue to kiss, and when she begins tugging my shirt up, I reach back and pull it over my head, tossing it onto the floor. Her smile is big and she keeps it on her face when I take her ankle and begin kissing and sucking my way up her leg. I love these legs.

I grip her behind her knees and go in for a slow kiss. The taste of her in my mouth is something I'll never tire of, so I take it as she runs her hands up my arms, my neck, and into my hair, fisting it in her hands.

She's playful with me as we take our time removing each other's clothing. My need to touch her is strong, but I know she's still really hesitant about being touched in that way, so I don't even try. Her light-heartedness right now is charming, and when she giggles and admits, "This tattoo is hot," as she grazes my shoulder with her hand, I smile down at her and laugh.

"Why's that?"

Pressing her lips together, she shakes her head, too shy to say what she's thinking, and I tease, "Don't let it fool you. I'm a private school prep just like you."

She laughs at me, responding with, "Your small town private school?" poking fun.

I run my hands down her small shoulders and take both of her breasts in my hands as I say with a smirk, "That small town has a lot of money running through it, and you love it there."

"I do love it there," she agrees and then runs her hand down the center of my chest, before adding in a more serious tone, "But I love it here—with you—more."

After I put on some protection, I make my way to the place I love the most—inside of her. She wraps her arms around my neck as we make love on my couch while the rain pours outside the windows. The beating of the rain mixed with our breaths fills the room as we take our time with each other, her eyes never straying from mine as I give myself to her.

I roll to the side, bringing her with me as I grab her thigh and drape it over my hip. Taking her bottom in my hand, I rock her into me as our heads are pressed together. Her eyes fully sated, green with golden flakes, her hands on my cheeks, sweet breath brushing my lips. Fuck, she's amazing at this.

Running my hand lazily up and down her bare back, we lie on the floor, wrapped up in a blanket together. With her head on my chest, she's been really quiet ever since we made love earlier.

"What are you thinking about, babe?"

"Hmm," she hums softly.

Laughing under my breath, I say, "That's a pathetic answer," and then feel her chest as she silently laughs.

"Seriously though. What's on your mind? You've been really quiet."

"I ran into Kimber today. She was leaving Jase's when I walked into his building."

"Did you guys talk?"

"She just asked where I've been, and I could tell she was hurt. Jase told me she reached out to him and that she's really upset."

"I'm sorry, babe. I know how much this bothers you. Have you thought anymore about talking to her?"

Now that I know what the issue is between them, I tried talking to

Candace about reaching out to her roommate the other week, but she shut it down, telling me that the only way Kimber would talk to her is if she told her the truth, and she didn't want to do that. I know that she doesn't want to say the words. She told me that she never even said them to Jase; she made a nurse tell him at the hospital, and that I'm the only one she's spoken them to. When she explained this to me, I dropped it.

"I just can't. I don't trust her enough to not do something."

"I don't know what to tell you to do. Just try talking to her and see if you guys can move past this," I offer weakly.

She closes her eyes before saying, "I think it would help if I went back home."

"Candace . . ."

"Ryan, I was only supposed to be here for a week or two. I never intended on moving in like this," she tells me. "But, we are about to graduate, and I'd like to see if this is fixable. I can't do that if I'm not there."

"I still want you here," I let her know, not wanting her to leave.

"And I'll still be here. Just not *every* night."

Candace has been staying with me for a little over a month, and I love that she's here and that I get to come home to her every night. But I also know that this is important to her, and even though I don't like the idea of her no longer staying here, I won't be anything other than completely supportive of her.

"Okay," I respond. "We can go tomorrow and take some of your things back."

She smiles and says, "Thanks for understanding," and then gives me a kiss as I press her naked body against mine, fully savoring the rest of our night.

"Babe, you don't have to pack everything," I complain as I watch her pulling her clothes out of my closet. Truth is, I don't like this feeling in my stomach right now as she packs her stuff up. I like seeing her things in my space.

Getting off the bed, I walk inside the closet to where she is and say, "Just leave a few things."

With an armful of clothes, she turns to me and says, "Ryan, I live less than five minutes away from you. I'll still be here."

I know I'm being a pussy about this, but I don't give a shit. I like her with me, here in my home, in my bed. So I repeat, "Just leave a few things."

She steps to me and looks up as I fold her in my arms. "I love you," she whispers, and I give her back the same words.

I carry her bags downstairs and out to the car before I drive her back to her house. Kimber's car is there when we pull up, and Candace lets out a deep breath.

"You okay?"

"I know I need to be here, but it's just so hard."

I get out of the car and walk around to her side, opening the door. "Call me or come over whenever. You don't even have to ask. You have the keys—use them."

She turns in her seat as I move between her legs, grabbing on to her behind her hips, and she takes my face in her hands and kisses me. I don't let up. I keep kissing her, taking in the feel of her soft lips as she melds them with mine. She has no idea what she's doing to me, and I have to pull back.

"Come on," I say. "I'll go in with you."

When we walk in, I take her bags back to her room and am helping her unpack her things when her roommate, whom I've never met, steps in the doorway and asks, "You're back?"

"Um . . . yeah," I watch Candace tell her nervously.

When Kimber doesn't respond, I try breaking some of the tension and introduce myself. "I'm Ryan, by the way."

She nods her head, saying, "I'm Kimber."

That's it for our exchange as she stands there. She's tall with platinum blonde hair and has a look about her that's very different from Candace's.

"Well, Seth's on his way over, so I'll be in my room," she says before walking out.

Candace goes over and closes the door, keeping her hands on it as she drops her head. I step next to her and see she's crying.

"Babe," I whisper as I hold her face.

"I don't know what to do," she says as she hugs me.

There's nothing I can say because I honestly think there isn't much of a friendship to be mended at this point. Candace chose to keep this secret from Kimber, and I don't blame her. From what little I have heard about this chick, she's seems like a spitfire who would probably run her mouth. But regardless, Kimber's been out of the loop while Candace has been dealing with some heavy shit, and even Jase told me that she's a completely different person now. Kimber's missed all of that, so it's not so far-fetched to safely assume that what once bonded them is no longer there.

We lie down on her bed for a while, not ready to leave just yet. She's no longer crying, but I know she's still upset about the whole situation, so I tell her, "I don't want you thinking that you're the one to blame for what's happened with you and Kimber. This isn't your fault. You made the best decision that you could at the time when you chose to not tell her about what happened. Nobody holds that against you, and I don't want you too either."

"It's easy to say, but . . ."

"You haven't done anything wrong here. Sometimes life just sucks, and things fall apart. Not all friendships can last forever. People change, and whether you want to admit it or not, you've changed. And I don't want you thinking shit about yourself because I love every single piece of who you are—right now."

I watch as her face scrunches up and she begins to cry. "Baby, don't."

Looking up at me through her tears, she reveals, "I wish every day that you knew me before. That you didn't have to deal with this baggage. I think about how everything could have been so different than it is now. Better."

"Who says it would be better?" I question as I smooth her hair back.

"Because it never would have happened."

I shift to my side to face her, saying, "I wish, more than you will ever know, that this never happened to you. But there isn't one single part of you that I would change. That night is a piece of you, but it doesn't tarnish you. Not for me. I love us. I love what we have together and what you give me. Somehow you got inside me. No one has been able to do that before, but you did. You've seen shit that I've never let anyone see. Shit that I've masked for years, but with you . . . you made me want to take the mask off and in the process I fell in love with you. So I don't know how you think we could be any better than we are because I think we're pretty perfect." I run my thumb across her cheek, wiping her tears.

"I don't . . . I don't even know what to say."

"You don't need to say anything. Just know that you have me. I'm here because of you. I'm yours because I don't want to give myself to anyone else. No one could ever compare to you."

chapter thirty-four

I CAN BARELY focus on the road as I drive to Thinkspace for the gallery showing tonight. Candace looks amazing in the lace dress she's wearing. I never thought pencil skirts were sexy until I saw them on her. Most of her dressier outfits are of the same style and tonight, I would have rather stayed in with the dress tossed to the floor, but I have every intention of ending the night that way.

Candace hasn't stayed over with me since she went back home, and I've missed not having her there with me. I also worry. There is rarely a night when she doesn't have problems sleeping. Ever since that one horrifying nightmare, she's been back on her sleeping pill, but she says they only help control the really vivid dreams. She still wakes often from night terrors, and I don't like the idea of her dealing with that alone, but she insists that she's fine.

When we arrive, I help Candace down from her seat and lead her inside. She's been so excited for tonight, inviting Jase, Mark, and Gavin. I never took my photography that seriously until lately. I've been spending more time shooting, mostly Candace, and editing. I like the focus of having a hobby, and knowing that I can share that with her is a bonus.

"I'm really proud of you, you know?" she says as we walk inside.

"Babe, the only reason that photo is on display is because you're in it. You're perfect."

I take her coat and check it when I hear a lady call, "Candace!"

"Stacy, hi," Candace says and hugs a tall, slender woman who looks close to my age with short, raven hair.

"That dress is amazing," she says to Candace.

"Thank you."

"And this is . . . ?" she asks as she looks at me.

"Ryan," Candace introduces.

"Ahh, 'Nubile.' Beautiful photograph," she says as I reach out to take her hand. "I'm Stacy Keets. I work at the Henry Gallery."

"Ryan Campbell," I say.

"Well, your piece is great. I saw a couple eying it a minute ago. Do you have more pieces?"

"A few," I tell her. "It wasn't ever something I intended to show anyone or have displayed, but Candace insisted," I add with a smile as I wrap my hand around her waist.

"I'm glad she did. I'd love to see more of your work," she tells me before looking at Candace and asking, "Do you still have my number?"

"Yes, I do."

"Give me a call," she says to me. "We have some wall space opening up soon, so if you're interested, we can discuss the possibility of displaying some of your pieces."

"Will do. I'll have Candace give me your number."

She turns back to Candace, telling her, "And I owe you a congratulations. I heard about your audition from Sergej."

"I hope it was all good."

She softens her voice when she says, "He thinks people will be fighting for you to sign with their companies."

"I can only hope," Candace responds with her modesty that I love so much. She's humble and gracious. She knows she's amazing but would never say it out loud.

"No hoping. I'm looking forward to seeing you perform in May."

"Thank you. I'll be sure Ryan calls you," she tells Stacy.

"Enjoy your night."

"You too, Stacy," I say and then head over to the bar where we spot Jase and Mark.

"Hey, man," Mark says when we approach.

We visit for a few minutes when Candace excuses herself to roam around the gallery with Jase. Art showings really aren't my thing, so I grab a beer and chat with Mark. I don't wait too long before I make my way over to the registrar.

Walking up to the desk, there's an elderly woman in a black cocktail dress who greets me. "Sir, how can I help you?"

Leaning my elbows on the counter, I say, "I'd like to inquire about one of the pieces being shown."

"Title?"

"'Nubile.'"

After a few clicks on the computer, she says, "It's been flagged by three interests, but no purchases yet."

"I'd like to purchase it then."

"Great! I have it marked for twelve hundred."

Shit. I had no idea my work would be worth that much. I had the photo canvassed in a large 24x40 wrap after it was accepted.

When I hand her my credit card, she begins to explain, "The piece is scheduled to remain on display until mid-April. At that time, preparatory will wrap it and have the piece delivered, unless you would like to pick it up yourself."

"Delivery is fine."

"Name?"

"Ryan Campbell."

She types it into her system and then looks up at me. "Ryan Campbell?"

"Yes."

She grins, asking, "Mr. Campbell, is this *your* piece?"

I respond with a mere wink as she continues to enter my information. There is no way in hell I'd let that photo of my girl hang in anyone's home but my own. Taking that photo was a huge deal for her, and I wasn't lying when I told her it was hers. She doesn't know I'm buying it. She'd probably be mad if she knew, but that's a memory I refuse to let someone else enjoy.

Once I finish with the purchase, I walk around and find Candace sitting on a bench with Jase.

"There you are," I say as I walk over to them. Jase stands and excuses himself, giving me and Candace time alone. "Where have you been?"

"Just walking around with Jase," she says as she leans into me.

"I heard someone bought your photo."

"Really?" she questions excitedly, and I get a kick out of her enthusiasm. But I'm done here tonight. I just want to be alone with her, away from everyone, because I've missed her.

I stand up and take her hand. "Walk with me."

When she slides her hand in mine, I lead her through to the back of the gallery, hoping I can come across a private area so that I can get my hands and mouth on her in a way that just wouldn't be appropriate in front of all these people.

"What are we doing back here? We're gonna get in trouble," she says nervously.

I laugh at her. "You're so cute."

We turn to go behind a wall, far from everyone else. I back her up against it, caging her in with my hands braced on either side of her. She knows what I want and gives it to me when she takes my face in her hands and draws me in, kissing me. I take over, eager for her. I want her right here, but I know my girl, and she's a private person. I'm shocked she's even doing this with me right now.

"We should go," she mumbles between kisses.

Pressing my hips against her, she grabs on to me, whispering my name.

I don't waste a second, taking her hand and leading her out the back, avoiding the time it would take to say goodbye to everyone. I just want to have her. Alone with me. In my bed.

Pulling up the driveway, I open her door, scoop her into my arms, and carry her up the stairs to the front door and then up to my room. I lay her on the bed and stand to look down at her. The light from the moon filtering through the clouds drapes a muted silvery hue on her fair skin.

I take my hands and run them down the length of her body, needing to feel the lace under my hands and the curve of her body beneath it. When I get to her legs, I wrap my grip behind her knees and trail them over her calves and down to her ankles, slipping off her heels, letting them fall to the floor. I toss my jacket over the chair and remove my shoes and socks before I climb into bed and back over her.

"I love you so fuckin' much."

"I love you, too."

I need her. The desire to have her is powerful. She looks incredible tonight, and I want her to give me another piece of her, so I make my request, saying, "Make love to me, babe."

By the look in her eyes, I know she understands what I mean. She's a little apprehensive every time we've had sex, so I have always taken the lead. But I need this from her—the certainty. I know she'd never do anything she didn't want to, but I also know that there is a level of fear about sex with her, and I want to give the control over to her.

She nods her head, and we pull up to our knees. As my lips land on hers, I fix my hands on her hips and slowly drag them up her lace-covered body before finding the zipper and sliding it down. She begins to unbutton my shirt, grazing the tips of her fingers against my chest while she works her way down. After she removes my shirt, she adjusts her shoulders, allowing the dress to slip off of her and pool at her knees.

She hangs on to my neck when I lower her down to the mattress and then pull the dress over her legs, tossing it on the floor with the rest of our clothes. My lips trail up her legs as I nip gently on her sensitive flesh, making her sigh, but she grips the sides of my head when I start planting soft kisses along her inner thigh. She clamps her hands on me, pushing me away before my mouth can reach her panties.

Patience is hard when I want her in ways I know she isn't ready for, but I move at her pace and allow her to lead me when she pulls my head up to her stomach. I kiss her heated skin as I start to shift her underwear down her legs. Sitting up on my knees, between her parted thighs, I run my eyes over her bare skin before she hitches her legs around my waist and pulls me down to her. But I pull back so that I can unhook my pants and kick them off.

Before I return to her, I slip on a condom and then reach around her back, shifting her on top of my lap as I sit with my legs in front of me. With her straddling me, I unhook her bra, slipping it down her arms. She rests her hands on my shoulders, staring into my eyes, when I move my hands to her hips. Lifting up on her knees, I reach down and help guide myself inside of her as she lowers herself on top of me.

Her head falls onto the curve of my neck when she slides over me slowly, and I let my head drop against her as pleasure radiates through my body. Her frame is so small, and she's so tight around me. My arms slide around her waist, and I hold on to her tightly when she finally lifts her head and looks into my eyes, foreheads pressed together. She rises up and takes her time as her body slowly falls back down over me.

"God, I love you," I breathe out.

Our bodies are pressed together, her arms wrapped around my neck, my head dropped to her chest. I needed her to give this to me, and hearing the soft moans coming out of her, I know I'm gonna need her like this again and again. Watching her take this pleasure from me is intoxicating as I begin to lose myself in her. The way she's moving, the way her skin smells with the light scent of her perfume, the way her hair feels as it brushes along the skin of my arms—it's a heady combination of elements that consumes my senses, but I still crave more.

Kissing her breasts, enjoying the feel of her soft skin against my lips, her body shudders as she rocks her hips into me. She's clinging tightly to me, and I can hear her unsteady breathing picking up. I'm able to read her body after all the times we've been together, so when her thighs tighten on me and her body grows more rigid, I know she's getting close, and knowing that she's giving herself this makes it all the better for me.

"Look at me, baby. I want to watch you come," I tell her as she leans her damp forehead against mine and opens her eyes.

She grips my hair in her hands, and I begin to feel her pulse around me.

"God, Candace," I moan, unable to hold on anymore, and she's right here with me as she rides out her pleasure, all the while giving me an intense release. Heat explodes throughout my body as she continues to move over me. I run my hand up her back and catch the sweat rolling down her spine. She lets go of a heavy breath, laced with a whimper, as she draws out the last of her orgasm with me.

My heart is pounding, and I can barely keep myself upright, so I hold her close and lie us down. Candace brushes the hair off of my forehead, and when she does, I tell her, "'I love you' will never be enough for what I feel for you."

She smiles, planting her lips on mine, and I keep myself inside of her as I pull the sheets over us and band my arms around her. This is the part I love. Having her completely content in my arms. Eyes closed and peaceful.

Candace scares me out of a deep sleep when she violently thrashes up, gasping for air. Her breaths hit hard as she fists the sheets, knuckles white, completely shaken.

"Babe, are you okay?" I ask as I pull the sheet up to cover her bare chest, knowing how modest she is. She clutches the sheet and begins to cry as she brings her knees up to her chest.

"Baby, it's just us," I assure as I pull her into my arms.

She's tucked in a ball as I move her between my legs and cuddle her against my chest. She hasn't scared me like this in a while, and I can tell that she's completely overwhelmed right now, so I keep her close, stroking her back as I soothe her.

"I'm sorry," she mutters when her cries weaken.

"There's nothing to be sorry for."

Taking in a deep breath, she lets it out slowly while I ask again, "Are you okay?"

She nods her head and sits up in my arms as I run my fingers under her eyes.

"I forgot to take my pill," she says to me.

"Shit, babe. I'm sorry," I tell her, feeling guilty that I didn't ask her before we fell sleep. I brought her home and never gave her a moment before we made love and went to bed.

"It's not your fault."

"Where are they?"

"In my purse, but it's too late to take it now," she says, and when I grab my phone and touch the screen, it reads a quarter past three.

She's right. If she took her pill now, she'd sleep most of the day.

"What do you wanna do?" I ask.

"Nothing. It's fine," she tries telling me, but I know it isn't. I remember her last nightmare, and I worry if she falls asleep that it could happen again. "Ryan, I promise," she says, sensing my concern. "Let's go back to sleep."

I lay her down, but keep her tucked into me and wrap my body around her from behind. We spend the rest of the night in a state of restless sleep because she continues to toss and turn, and I find myself awake and watching her as she drifts in and out.

chapter thirty-five

WHEN WE ARRIVE at my mom's the following day, it's late, and Candace is overly exhausted with a bad headache, so she goes to bed early while my mom and I stay up visiting. By the time I wake up the next morning, Candace is already out of bed and downstairs with my mom. While drinking our coffee, Mom mentions that she has to drive out to Portland for the day to take care of few things, leaving the day open for me and Candace.

While Candace is in the shower, I check the weather report, figuring I'll take her to Indian Beach to try and get her up on a board. When the bathroom door opens, she's wearing nothing but a towel and leftover drops of water, and suddenly, she has my full attention.

"Fuck, babe," I say as I walk towards her.

Holding her hand out to my chest to keep me from coming any closer, she says, "Don't start. Your mother is downstairs."

"I don't care who the fuck is downstairs when the only thing covering your wet body is that towel."

"That's why I'm getting my clothes," she says with a smile before running back to the bathroom, shutting the door behind her.

Once she's dressed and comes back into the bedroom, I start getting my things together and tell her, "Tori has an extra wetsuit in my closet that should fit you okay."

"What?"

"Surfing. You and me."

"I'm fine with trying anything new, but that water is freezing," she says.

"I promise, when you're in that wetsuit, you'll be fine. Tori loves to surf, so she has her wetsuit here and some swimsuits in my closet."

Grabbing Tori's wetsuit, Candace finishes getting ready before we hop into my Rubicon and head to Indian Beach.

Candace is such a sport about being outdoors, and it's great that we share that. The running, the hiking, and now, getting her up on a board—she's a natural and is taking her first wave in on her second try. I knew she'd be great at it, and she didn't let me down. We spend the morning hanging out in the water and having fun with each other. When we aren't surfing, she's fighting me when I try getting frisky with her.

After a few hours, we decide to call it and head back. She's freezing and wrapped up in blankets that I packed in the car. When we get back, she heads upstairs to take a hot shower and warm up. I unload the jeep, giving her just enough time before I go up to join her. I made a bet with her on the beach that if I got her up on the board, I would get a little action from her. I know she thought I was just kidding around, but when I strip off my clothes and walk into the bathroom, I take a moment to look at her through the fogged glass of the large walk-in shower before opening the door.

"What are you doing?!" she startles as I close the door behind me and wrap my arms around her.

"It's time to ante up, babe," I tease as I duck my head under the water and then push her against the glass wall. She gasps as the cold surface meets her skin, arching into me in response.

She doesn't push me away or make light in this moment. She stays quiet as I dip my head to kiss her. Gripping my hands behind her thighs, I easily lift her off her feet as she wraps her legs around my waist. My mouth runs down her wet neck, licking and sucking as she holds on to me, breathing heavily at my touch.

The water cascades down her naked body, between her breasts where my hand finds her, squeezing her soft flesh. When I press myself against her, she breathes hard, "I want you."

"I don't have anything with me in here," I tell her, but before I can set her down so that we can move this to the bed, she says, "It's okay. I've been on the pill for a while. I trust you."

"When did you get on the pill, babe?" I ask in shock, never knowing that she did this.

"I've been on it. I got it . . ." She hesitates before finishing, "I got on it after what happened."

Leaning my head on her shoulder, I sigh as she assures me, "It's okay. I just want you."

"I've never . . . I promise you I've always been safe," I tell her. "I've never been with anyone without a condom."

"You don't have to explain. I know you'd never do anything to hurt me."

She holds my face when I kiss her, water seaming between our lips as it falls over us. I focus on her mouth, exploring it with my tongue, tasting her slow and deep. Her arms stay slung around my neck, hands trussed in my hair as I begin to drag my kisses along her neck and down to her chest. Lowering my head, I circle her nipple with my tongue before gently sucking it into my mouth, pressing my tongue against the hardened bud.

Her body writhes in my arms, and I pull back to look at her when I move my hands under her bottom and lift her up, reaching down to hold myself for her. Slowly, with her head rested on mine, I lower her down. We take each other completely as our bare flesh meets, and I slide myself inside of her. She's so warm; she always has been, but to feel her like this, to have her give me this, I know it comes solely from our love for each other.

The air is heavy with steam, making my breaths ragged as I hold on to her. She clings her arms tightly around my shoulders, hugging me as I listen to her soft panting in my ear. I pull her off the wall and simply hold her. Feeling her naked body with mine. Savoring having her this close to me. Bared to each other with nothing but trust.

She draws her head back to look at me, and when she does, she brushes her lips across mine, breathing into me, "I love you."

With those words, I use my hands to move her, and when I do, I find it hard to stand with the pleasure that courses through me. Being inside of her like this, nothing separating us, it's an intensity that takes over my body. I turn so I can rest my back against the glass as I lift her back up and let her descend slowly down on me. Her legs are tight around my hips as I steadily maneuver her up and down.

It's hard to hold on to everything I'm feeling in this moment, and the pleasure moves us to the floor of the shower. I sit back against the wall as she keeps her legs wrapped around my body. The air is thick and she's all around me as I watch her. She's stunning with her soft eyes on me, her labored breaths escaping her lips, fingertips pressing into my back as we move together. Never in a rush, because I need this. Every piece of this.

"God, I want you," I say on a heavy breath, and she braces her arms around my neck, using the leverage as she sways her hips into me.

"You have me."

When her body begins to respond, she drops her eyes to mine. I don't even have to tell her, she just knows. It's my security of knowing that she's always with me in this moment. Never wanting her mind to drift. It shouldn't be the reason, but it is, and it's something that, even though it originates from such an ugly place, has become something I can redeem with her, because she's so beautiful when she comes.

My muscles tense up when I feel her spasm around me, moaning my name in the heat of the air as we both lose ourselves to each other. The pleasure she gives me radiates through my entire being, and I clutch my hands to her hips when our movements begin to falter as passion takes over.

She's incredible. She doesn't know it, and if I told her, she'd deny my words, so I don't speak. We just remain like this, together, on the bottom of the shower as our tired bodies collapse against one another.

We decide to stay the week here, so after Candace spends a couple of days with my mom, shopping and dining out, leaving me to fend for myself, I choose to steal her for the day.

We went to Astoria this morning for a late breakfast with Tori and the kids, and now I'm driving her up to Washington to take her to Long Beach to drive her along the water and spend the rest of the day together.

When we get there, I pull off the road and onto the sand, and she asks, "Are you sure this is okay?"

Laughing at her, I say, "Yes. Everyone does it." When I pass a sign that states the driving dates for the beach, I point, and tell her, "See. There's the proof," with a smile.

It's still cold this time of year, and today can't be any higher than fifty degrees, so aside from a group of guys hanging out, the place is pretty empty. We drive along the water, and I get a kick out of her laughing the whole time. The simple fact that driving on sand can make this girl so giddy is a trip, and I'm enjoying every giggle coming out of her.

Pulling away from the water, I find a spot back by the sea oats that's already set up for a fire. I pull the jeep up the beach and park.

"You wanna grab the blankets?" I ask as we get out of the car.

I open the back hatch and pull out the firewood to start a fire while Candace bundles up. Once I have the fire going, I sit next to her, wrapping the blankets around the both of us as she cuddles into me.

"I had fun at Tori's this morning," she says as she clutches the blanket to her. "She's really nice."

"Yeah, she is."

"So her mom is Donna's sister?"

"Uh huh."

She laughs quietly, saying, "It's hard to keep it straight."

"It's my mom and her two sisters. And then all my cousins are girls as well," I explain. "Tori and I always linked up because of our age, and she's really into surfing too, so we get together a lot to hit the beach."

When the wind kicks up, she turns her head and rests it on my chest. "I was wondering something."

"What's that?"

"If that's the house you grew up in, why does your mom still live there?"

"I don't know. I asked her that not too long ago," I tell her. "She told me that she loves the house and that she chooses to remember all the good memories we had there."

"What about you?" she asks as she looks up at me.

Adjusting to pull her between my legs, I lean back against the log lying behind me before answering her. "It's hard for me to remember anything good. Being in that house is sometimes hard on me. I'll see things that remind me of a particular beating and stuff like that, and it dredges up a lot of shit for me."

She lets go of the blanket and wraps her arms around me, asking, "Why did she stay?"

"Honestly . . . I never asked her. Now that I'm older, I would just assume that she was scared. Worried about how she would support the two of us if she did leave."

She doesn't say anything, just leans into me as we hold on to each other. I stare into the fire when I continue to talk and explain, "My dad was a frightening man. I was terrified of him. Scared he was going to kill my mom one day. He would drink heavily and lose control. You never knew how far he would go. I used to sit and watch him beat her, scared if I left that he might go too far and I wouldn't be able to help her."

"So you watched?" she asks, horrified.

"I couldn't say anything because every time I would scream for him to stop, he would just go harder on her, making it worse."

"I can't even imagine. But what about you?"

"He hated me, Candace. At least with my mom, he had once loved her. But never me. He didn't give a shit what he did to me. I was always walking around in pain. Broken ribs, concussions. That's mostly why I started using X. It just felt good."

She looks at me, and I watch her eyes puddle with tears that don't fall.

"And nobody ever knew? Nobody helped you?" she questions.

"The only other person who knows, beside me and my mom, is you."

"No one in your family?"

"Only you," I tell her.

"Does Donna know that I know?"

"No."

She shifts to her knees and faces me. I know she doesn't know how to respond to everything I just laid on her, so I take away the pressure when I hold her face and kiss her. She grips my wrists with her hands, and I keep my eyes open as I watch her tears finally fall.

I pull back and wipe her cheeks before I lie us down on the pile of blankets in the sand, the only heat from her and the fire. I've never unloaded this weight that I've been carrying for years the way she allows me to.

"You're the strongest person I know," she whispers against my neck.

"I'm not."

"You are."

"Before I met you, I hid everything. I was selfish and used people. I was weak."

"But you're not now. I don't see any of that in you," she says, and I know the only reason for that is her.

chapter thirty-six

AFTER A FEW more days, it's time to head back to Seattle. I'm finishing packing our bags while Candace gets ready in the bathroom. Having this week away has been good for us. And having her here with my mom makes this connection that we have so much stronger.

Needing to grab a few things out of the bathroom, I don't knock when I see she has left the door cracked. When I open it, she startles as she pulls down on her sweatshirt.

"What are you doing?"

"Nothing," she says as she still has her top clutched in her hands.

I walk over to her and take her hand, lifting it up along with the shirt, and when I do, she says, "I don't like it," referring to her tattoo that is peeking over her pants that she has tugged down.

I lower her shirt and ask, "Why?"

"Because it's not me," she admits. "I was trying to be someone different, and it only led to bad things."

"What do you mean?"

"I got it in a moment of rebellion, I guess. It was stupid, really. I got it and started acting foolishly, which led to . . . umm . . ." her words stammer off as she drops her head away from me. I know what she's trying to say, and it's insane to think getting a tattoo would result in her getting raped.

"I get it. But, babe, nothing you did led to that."

When she doesn't say anything and refrains from looking at me as she starts walking out of the bathroom, I grab ahold of her because I need to know that she agrees with me.

"Wait. You know that, right?"

God. She doesn't agree with me. I can see the guilt in her eyes. How could she possibly think this?

"Come here," I tell her as I sit on the bed, taking her hand and pulling her towards me. "Tell me you don't think that."

When she doesn't respond, I say, "Babe, there is nothing you could have possibly done to deserve that."

She turns away from me as I say this, and when I tug her back to me, she's crying.

Fuck.

How did I not know that she blames herself for this?

"Shit, babe. I had no idea this is how you feel."

"Please, don't," she says in a broken voice.

"I need you to talk to me about this. You have it all wrong. What that guy did was fucked up, babe, and you didn't do shit to deserve what he did to you."

She looks up at me and pulls her hands out of mine when she gets mad and yells, "You don't get it, Ryan! What I did was stupid, and I completely led him on. It wasn't right, and I knew it, but I did it anyway."

Infuriated that she feels this way when her logic is so fucked up, I raise my voice at her, saying, "What the fuck could you have possibly done? Because I know you, Candace, and I know you couldn't have led him on that much. But that shit doesn't even matter because you could've stripped down in front of him, and you still didn't deserve to be raped."

"Don't say that fucking word, Ryan!" she snaps and then begins to fall apart, sobbing.

Banding my arms around her, I hold her close. "Babe, I'm sorry. I just had no idea that this is how you think."

"I didn't even really like him," she begins to stammer out between her cries. "But I was stupid and lonely, so I would let him kiss me, knowing that I didn't like him. And I fucking hate my mother for this, because if it wasn't for her being such a bitch, I never would have gone out with him."

"Candace, please don't do this."

"You just don't get it. I did lead him on, and I pissed him off. I never should've acted like that. I should've just been honest."

"This isn't your fault." I tell her in a hard voice.

"Yes, it is!"

"It isn't your fault, Candace."

Facing me, she takes my shirt in her hands, fisting the fabric when she yells, "But it is!" and then falls into my chest. Her cries are loud, staggered, and strained. It's hard to listen to, but I do because I love her. I don't say anything else because I'm only upsetting her worse.

I can't argue her irrational thinking because she isn't seeing it with clear eyes. This guy screwed with her head so badly that she's been carrying the weight of the responsibility on her own shoulders. And here I am, blind to this fact. My girl has been holding fault when that son of a bitch is the only one to blame.

Moving her with me as I lie down on the bed, she tucks her head under my chin and continues to cry for a while. She's in so much pain, and I don't know how to make it any better for her. I've always questioned her choices for how she's been dealing with this, but now, knowing this piece of the puzzle, it's clear that she needs to do something.

We're face to face when she finally speaks. "It's been seven months, Ryan."

"I know, babe."

"I just want it to go away."

"I know. But it's never going to get easier if you keep blaming yourself. It kills me that you feel this way. It fuckin' kills me that I can't take this away from you."

Knowing that there isn't a goddamn thing I can do to lessen her misery frustrates me beyond anything I have ever dealt with. I want to take care of her, to be the person that makes this better for her, but that's what's so fucked up about this situation—that's what's so scary—because it all lies within her. She's the only one who can make this better, but she refuses to help herself. She figures if she just ignores it for long enough then it will fade away and everything will go back to normal. It's not a sane way to deal with this. In fact, I think it's just making it worse for her with every day that passes. The avoiding is catching up with her, and I'm afraid she's just going to—one day—crumble.

When her breathing begins to even out, she asks, "Can't we stay another night?"

"Anything you want," I tell her.

I lie here, and I can't shake my own guilt about this whole situation. I've always had it. I've always asked all the what-ifs, but the fact remains, this girl was outside fighting for her life while I was mere feet away. If only I would have gone out there, I wouldn't be lying here with my girl falling apart on me. She wouldn't be carrying this around with her every day. I was the only other person there, and I did nothing.

Noticing that her body has gone limp, I remember that she hasn't taken her sleeping pill. Slipping out of bed, I go to her purse to grab the bottle. I take out a pill and fill up a glass of water from the bathroom before waking her.

"Baby," I urge as she slowly opens her eyes. "Here, take this."

She does and then hands the glass back to me. I crawl back into bed and hold her until she falls back asleep. The whole time, my mind is just eating away at me. At everything. When she's finally asleep, I quietly head downstairs because I need a little space to get my thoughts together, but shit is just spinning more and more the longer I sit at the dining room table.

"Hey, dear," I hear my mom say softly when she crosses the room to sit with me.

"Hey," I sigh.

"Where's Candace?"

"She's sleeping. We're just gonna head back tomorrow," I tell her as I look at her from across the table.

"Are you okay?" she asks. "I heard you two fighting earlier."

Leaning forward in my seat, I rest my forearms on the table, saying,

"We weren't fighting, Mom."

She shakes her head at me and questions, "Well, is everything all right?"

I normally tell my mother everything, but when I found out about Candace, I held it secret. But I feel like I'm in so deep with this girl, and the stuff I'm dealing with is some of the heaviest shit I've ever dealt with. I haven't had anyone to really talk to about it, and knowing how much my mother loves her, I trust her enough to make this confession that I have had locked up inside of me.

"No." I drop my head when I say this because I already feel the remorse building inside for betraying Candace by telling her secret, but it's breaking me, and I don't know where else to turn.

She places her hand over mine as she says, "Talk to me, sweetheart."

Staring at our hands, I take in a deep breath and begin, "There's something I've never told you about Candace."

"Okay."

"Remember the attack I told you about that happened this past summer at the bar?"

When she nods, I swallow hard and reveal, "It was her, Mom. That girl was Candace."

"Oh my God," she whispers as she removes her hand from mine to cover her mouth. She's in complete shock when she asks, "How did you . . . ?"

"She doesn't know," I confess. "I didn't even know it was her for a while. I thought it could be, but I wasn't sure. I was so confused, thinking my head was just trying to make something out of nothing with her weird behavior. But I honestly didn't know."

"I don't understand. Where did you meet her?"

"I grabbed a coffee from where she works. And then I kept seeing her because she's friends with a couple buddies of mine. But there's this tattoo," I say as I fight to hold back the tears that threaten. "I saw it on that girl, and then after I had already fallen for Candace, I saw that same tattoo on her. I was scared, so I never told her."

"Ryan . . ."

"We weren't fighting earlier. She told me that what happened to her was her fault. I was trying to talk to her about it, and she got really upset." Pressing my palms to my forehead, I tell her, "God, Mom, you have no idea what that fucker did to her. What she looked like when I found her."

It's when I drop my hands that I see the tears running down my mom's face and that's what sends me over. I don't cry, but I feel it stabbing inside of me.

"Honey, you have to tell her."

"It felt like the right thing to do at the time. That I was keeping it from her for all the right reasons," I try to explain. "I didn't want to hurt her, but now . . . now it feels like a lie, and I'm scared. I'm scared I'm gonna lose her."

"But now things are different with you two, and she needs to know."

I can feel the heat of the tears welling in my eyes when I ask, feeling desperate, "Do you think she'll understand?"

She takes her time before responding with, "I think you have a girl that's been shown, in the most horrendous way a person can be shown, just how gruesome life can be. She's been stripped of her security and faith in people. It's awful, and people like that don't trust easily."

Dropping my head in my hands, I nearly beg, "What do I do? I love her."

She takes my hand and pulls it down when she looks at me and tells me to do what I'm terrified of doing.

"You have to tell her . . . You just have to."

But I don't want to. I can't risk losing her. All I want to do is keep her forever, so I selfishly go back upstairs, crawl under the sheets next to her, and hang on to the one good thing that finally came into my life and changed everything about me. I can't lose her.

Waking up with Candace just didn't feel right with the dread that has made its home in the pit of my stomach. And seeing how clingy she's been with me all morning, and now on the drive home, makes the thought of telling her that much worse.

She has kept a hold on my hand ever since she opened her eyes this morning. I don't question her about it; I just give her the closeness, the security that I'm here and I'm not leaving. I can't tell her. Not now. Not when she's vulnerable like this.

Thinking about what sparked the whole conversation with Candace yesterday, I say, "I hate that your tattoo makes you feel the way it does." I hate the way it makes me feel too. It's hard for me to look at because almost every time I do, I see the girl from that night, and I can't stand thinking of her like that, the way she looked lying there unconscious. There have been a couple times in the past where I've had to cover it with my hand while we make love because it hurts too much to look at.

"I thought about having it removed once."

"Have you thought about changing it?" I ask as I glance over at her, giving her hand a little squeeze.

"I just don't know what I would do. I don't want anything bigger than it is now," she explains.

"Did Roxy's boyfriend do it?"

"Jared? Yeah."

"When we get home, why don't we talk to him, see what he can do?"

"I guess," she says, unconvinced.

"I just think if it looked different, or you could add something to it that was meaningful to you, that you could associate it with something new, instead of what you're doing now. Give it new meaning."

"We can go talk to him," is her only response, and I don't say anything else about it because I know it's a difficult thing to talk about.

When we arrive back in Seattle, I take Candace to her house to spend a little time with her before I have to run to the bar to take care of some work.

Setting her bags down on the bed, Candace quietly says, "I don't want you to go to work."

I hate that she's feeling like this today, and that she doesn't want to be alone, but I tell her, "Baby, I have to. It's Saturday night, and I've been gone all week."

She leans into me, sliding her arms around my waist. She's needy, and I don't want her to be alone either, so I offer, "Come with me."

"What?"

"You don't even have to be around everyone. Stay with me in my office."

I'm not expecting her answer when she says, "Okay."

"Really?" I question, stunned that she would agree so easily, especially for a Saturday night.

"Just park in the front, okay?"

chapter thirty-seven

I WAS RELIEVED to see Candace enjoying herself when she went with me to the bar. I was nervous because Saturday nights are really busy, but I had Max with her the entire time. Jase was there to hear Mark's band play and was able to talk her into going downstairs with him while I got my work done. Once I finished up, I hung out with her for the rest of the evening. Aside from meeting Max, she also met Mel. Candace has always been a mystery to them, so to have them finally meet her was nice since they know what a big part of my life she's become.

When Candace walks down the stairs, I ask, "You ready?"

"Yeah, I just need my coat," she says as she walks towards me.

"I got it," I tell her when I stand up and help her put it on.

We head out into another rain-filled night to go spend the evening at Max's place. He invited us over when he met Candace at the bar last week. Zane is back in town for a few days, so he and Mel will be there as well.

It's an odd transition to be coupled off and doing things like this tonight, but it's a welcome change that seems to better suit me now.

When we pull up to Max's place, I help Candace out of the car and then head inside and out of the cold. We walk in, and I introduce her to Zane and Traci, who is now very pregnant. We sit around and talk for a little bit until Traci takes Mel and Candace back to see the baby's room, leaving the guys alone in the living room.

"Dude," Zane says as he nudges me with a smirk.

"What?"

"Who's the chick?"

"Candace?"

He laughs when he says, "Yeah, man. What's going on?"

Last I spoke with Zane, I was still into going out a lot with Gav, so I clue him in when I tell him, "We started dating soon after you high-tailed your ass to L.A."

"What?!" he exclaims, nearly spitting out his beer. "What the hell have I missed around here? Seriously, I come back and you're settled down with some chick, and this guy," he says, pointing the neck of his beer bottle towards Max, "has his girl knocked up."

Max laughs at him and says, "That's what happens when you ditch town and don't check in."

"I guess," he says and then turns to me. "Just never thought I'd see you with a chick." Taking a swig of his beer, he asks, "Are you guys serious?"

"Yeah, man. Pretty serious."

Max butts in, and asks Zane, "Tell us what's going on with you and Mel."

"I have no idea. She refuses to come to California, but I'm not giving up this opportunity so that she can stay close to her family."

"Stop bullshitting," I say, calling him out. "She said you told her you didn't want her to go with you."

"Why would I?" he responds. "I mean, she has done nothing but bitch about all of this, so why would I want her to tag along with her piss-poor attitude?"

Our attention is distracted when we hear a burst of laughter coming from the girls in the back of the house. In this moment, I smile. I just can't help it. Candace doesn't have any girl friends aside from Roxy, so to hear her laughter spilling through the house is infectious, and I let out a light chuckle.

Looking back over at Zane, I tell him, "She was upset when you left."

"When I left? What about now?" he questions. "Seems to me that she's doing pretty well on her own here."

"God, you're hard to talk to," Max interjects.

"Can we not talk about my shit?" Zane says. "What about you?" he asks as he eyes Max. "I can't believe you're gonna be a dad. How are you not freaking the hell out right now?"

"I did when I found out, but it's all good now," he states simply.

We continue to catch up for a while until the girls eventually join us again. Candace has a smile on her face when she sits next to me on the couch as she continues to talk with Traci and Mel. Max and Zane are in their own conversation while I find myself focused on Candace. She's happy and light-hearted tonight in this new circle of people. She's so tight with Jase and Mark, but I'd like to see her widen her group of friends. She needs it even though she doesn't see it.

On the drive home, I look over at her and ask, "Did you have a good time?"

"Yeah, Mel's pretty funny."

"She definitely keeps things entertaining at work," I say with a grin. "So what did you talk about? We kept hearing you all laughing."

"Traci was just talking about her pregnancy. I was a little shocked with some of the things she was telling us," she says with a dramatic shudder.

Laughing at her, I ask, "Like what?"

"Stuff I had no clue about," she tells me in a high-pitched voice, reeling with disbelief. "She told us that she has hemorrhoids!"

"What?!"

"Yes!" she squeals.

"I don't wanna know about that shit," I say, disgusted.

"Well, I don't either, but I do now, thanks to Traci!" she says as she begins to laugh, and I join right in with her. "She said that most pregnant women get them! It's so gross!"

"Shit, are you serious?"

"Mel said it was true too."

We both continue laughing as she fills me in on more than I ever wanted to know, and the theatrics of Candace telling me all of this and freaking out is completely entertaining when I'm not cringing at the unwanted information.

Once we have quieted down and composed ourselves, I look over as we're stopped at a red light and ask, "Do you think that's something you want?"

"What? A baby?" she asks.

"Yeah."

"I don't know," she says softly. "I've always been scared to be a mom."

"Why's that?"

When she leans her head back against the seat, she tells me, "Because I'm not sure I know what it is to be a good mom. I mean . . . how would you know if the choices you were making were the wrong ones? I wonder if my mom thought she was making the right choices with me."

She says this and I understand her fears. I get it because they're my fears. Scared to become what we are products of. But I know that she would have nothing to worry about because she's the most non-judgmental person I know.

"But I don't have to think about that for a long time," she adds.

"Why's that?" I ask, when I pull up to the loft and park the car.

"Because dancers don't have babies until they are done with their professional careers. Your body changes too much, so the likelihood that the way you dance would be impacted is high. It's just not something you toy with if you want longevity," she explains. "What about you?"

"Me?"

"Yeah," she says as she shifts herself to face me.

"I've always wanted what my cousins have, but never saw it in the cards for me," I tell her. "But when I really think about it, it scares the shit out of me too."

"Because of your dad?"

I nod my head and when she smiles up at me, she says, "I don't think you have anything to worry about."

I lean over and kiss her before giving her sentiment right back. "I don't think you do either. You're amazing at everything you do."

Making our way inside, she turns to me and asks, "You wanna camp out and watch a movie?"

"Anything you want." I tell her as we head upstairs to change clothes.

When we return to the living room, I get the fireplace going while Candace tosses a bunch of pillows and blankets onto the floor and flips the TV to TCM. I love sharing my black and white movies with her, and lately, I'm finding that she's starting to get into them as well.

Lying down, pulling Candace into my arms, we relax and watch 'Bank Holiday.' I lazily comb my fingers through her hair, and we fall asleep before the movie ends.

Waking up in the middle of the night, Candace is sleeping along my side, and the fire is almost out. When I pick up the remote to shut the TV off, the screen reads that it's almost two in the morning. Setting the remote down, I roll over to look down at Candace, and my shifting causes her to stir awake.

It takes a moment, but when her eyes flutter open and she focuses on me, we stay silent as we watch each other in the faint glow of the firelight. When I lean in to kiss her, she runs her hand behind my neck, pulling me down to her. I slide my tongue across her lower lip before sucking it into my mouth, and she grips my neck tighter. Her body is flush against mine, and I begin to lift her shirt so that I can feel the warmth of her on my skin. Discarding her top, I reach back and remove mine as well before bringing her back to me. The room is silent as our bodies begin to move as the haze from our sleep dissipates.

When I roll on top of her, I drag my head down the center of her body, letting my lips move along her smooth skin. Licking and sucking my way down, her hands are holding the sides of my head, and when I hit her pants, she lifts her hips, allowing me to pull them off, keeping her lace panties in place.

Taking her leg in my hand, I kiss my way back up, giving her soft sucks behind her knee before I lower myself down on her. I want to feel every part of her, but she has always been so skittish with some of my touches. Needing the closeness in the moment, I break our silence and whisper, "I want to touch you."

I see the reluctance when she looks at me, and I reach my hand back to hold her knee as I say, "Let me touch you."

I catch her faint nod and take my time as I let my hand fall along the inside of her thigh, but as soon as I reach the edge of her panties, she clamps my wrist with her hand and jerks her hips away from me. I want to show her that it isn't disgusting and that she doesn't have to be scared of my touch, so I move my hand back to her knee as I rest my body on top of her. With my forehead against hers, I take her lips with mine. Her hand rests on my cheek while she keeps her other locked around my wrist, not letting go. I stay close to her when I move my hand back down her leg, and this time, she doesn't startle.

Her breathing is shaky when I touch her and cup her in my hand, holding still as her legs are clutched to my sides. My lips continue to move with hers as I take in the warmth of her before I gently run my hand up the edge of her panties then tuck my fingers under the lace of the fabric and run them back down.

She lets out a whimper as I feel her smooth skin under my fingers.

"Just relax, baby," I breathe as I drop my head to her shoulder.

Keeping my wrist clutched in her hold, I bring my hand to the top of her underwear and then slip it under the fabric, moving the back of my fingers down the seam of her. I know this is hard for her, but I also know that no one has ever touched her like this, without hate and force, so I keep my touches soft as she gives me this. After a little time, her body begins to respond to me, and I feel her relax as she grows hot in my hand. Her forehead becomes damp when I sink my fingers inside of her, breaths heady, and bodies on fire as we move in this new way together.

We spend a good amount of time like this before we make love in the darkness of the room. The only noises are the ones that are products of the pleasure we give each other and eventually the moans that come from us losing ourselves completely to the other.

chapter thirty-eight

"YOU OKAY?" I ask while I drive us to the tattoo parlor. She's fidgety and a bit vacant. Placing my hand over hers, I question, "Were you this nervous when you did this the last time?"

"No . . . well, kinda. I dunno. It was different then."

"You don't have to do this today. We can always call Jared and reschedule."

She shakes her head and then looks over at me. "No, it's fine. I'm sure I'd be just as nervous if it were any other day. Let's just get it done."

I hold her clammy hand for the rest of the short drive. When we arrive and walk in, Jared is the only one here. He came in early so that it would only be the three of us.

"You look like you're about to puke," he teases her and laughs. "You've been through this before. No big deal, right?"

"Right," she responds with a nervous smile as we follow him back through the shop and into his booth.

Candace takes a seat on top of the black table, and I stand next to her, still holding her hand.

"So, what are you thinking about doing?" he asks her.

"Umm . . ."

Jared squeezes her knee, and soothes, "Relax."

She looks over at me, and then looks back, telling him, "Can we just fill it in?"

"That's it? Damn, girl, by the way you're acting I thought you were gonna tell me to wrap a skull around it or some shit," he jokes, and it's just what she needs as she laughs with him.

Jared gets everything set up, and when he slips on his black latex gloves, he instructs her to lie back and shift her pants down.

"So, no more empty heart," he mumbles as he slips the paper cloth under the edge of her pants, and she laces her fingers with mine as I stand over her.

"No more empty heart," she repeats as she looks up at me.

We talked about what she was going to do with the tattoo the other day when she told me that she wanted to keep it small. She said that she wanted to simply fill it in, and I was worried that it wouldn't be enough of a change for her. But she assured me that it would be, and I know it holds a new significance for her. I'm glad she sees her heart in this way now—full—no longer empty.

Once the gun starts buzzing, Candace squeezes her eyes shut, and it takes less than a minute for him to be done. Jared and I both laugh when she opens them back up.

"You guys are evil," she tells us as she sits up after Jared applies a small bandage over the area.

"Let me know when you're ready for that skull," he says with smirk.

Candace hops off the table and says with joking aside, "Thank you."

He smiles at her, saying, "Anytime," followed by a wink. "This one's on the house, so I expect a few hook-ups with those scones."

Returning his smile, she tells him, "Of course. See you later."

"Later, guys."

Walking outside, the mist still fills the air. When I open the door and help her up into her seat, I ask, "Happy?"

"Happy," she confirms with a kiss to my lips.

I hope now every time she sees that tattoo, she is no longer taken back to that night.

Three weeks have passed and Candace has been tied up at the studio almost daily, preparing for the production in May. She has the lead in all of the ensembles she's dancing in, plus a duet and her solo.

She's yet to mention what might happen after she graduates. It's nearing the end of April, so we only have a couple months until she's finished with school here. I know she doesn't know where she'll be, but offers should start coming in after her performance next month.

I don't want to stress her out with everything she has on her plate right now, so I haven't broached the topic, but I know it's on her mind. It has to be. I know she loves me, but I wonder what she's thinking and what she wants, because I'm so clear with what I want.

Max has really stepped up and gotten the bar under control since I brought him on as manager. I'm confident with leaving him in charge if I have to move. It's the best situation for the time being, but she has no idea that's the reason why I promoted him.

Tonight, Max has arranged for one of the bands Gavin represents to put on a concert at the bar, and Candace agreed to come along. We met up this morning for a quick run, but then I had to spend the day up at work. I left a little while ago to go pick her up since she left her car at my place last night.

When I get to her house and walk into her room, my stomach drops. There are a few cardboard boxes packed up with her belongings. I wanna ask her. I wanna know where we stand in the mix of everything that is about to happen, but that's gonna be a long conversation that we don't have time for right now.

"Babe, you ready?" I ask, no longer wanting to think about any of this shit.

"Yeah, I just need to grab my jacket."

As she walks into her closet, I feel like I should prepare her for what the bar will be like tonight, so I tell her, "So, it's going to be busy. A lot busier than the past few times you've been. You sure you're okay with that?"

Walking out of the closet, she looks at me and says, "I mean, if it's too much then I can always go upstairs until you're ready to leave."

Grabbing her hand and yanking her flush against me, I suggest, "Or we could just stay here and break in your bed a bit more," remembering our sweaty sex session this morning after our run.

"I think we should go now and break in the bed later," she says with a blushing smile.

Leaning down, I playfully nip on her lips before we head up to the bar.

The place is packed when we arrive. We park out front, and Candace eyes the crowd of people waiting to get in. Walking to the door, Max sees us and comes to Candace's side, holding on to her as he walks us in. I keep her hand in mine, and she grips it tightly as Max leads us through the throngs of people. The band is already playing, and the music blasts through the building as we round the back of the bar and spot Jase, Mark, Gavin, and a few of our other friends.

"Hey, guys," Jase hollers and then takes Candace in his arms. I watch as he orders them some shots, and I call out to Mel for a beer.

We have this area cornered off, so Candace is relaxed with it only being our friends around her. I hang out and bullshit with Gavin and Mark while Jase and Candace take their shots and start goofing around with each other.

After a while, I turn to see Candace chatting with Mel who is working behind the bar. They've started talking on the phone, and the two of them have gotten together to hang out a couple of times. I know Mel is going through some shit, but Candace says that she isn't letting it take too much out of her. It's great that the two of them are starting to become friends and to see Candace coming out of her shell a little bit more.

A couple hours pass, and Max leaves us when the band takes a break. I catch Candace standing a few feet away from me, leaning over the bar, whispering something to Mel and making her laugh. She looks incredible in her dark jeans, fitted grey v-neck sweater, and her hair pulled up on top of her head from the heat of all the people in here tonight. She's simple and stunning. She doesn't even have to try, she just is. When she turns and catches me ogling her, she shoots me a smile before walking over to me and into my arms.

"What are you doing?" she asks.

"Staring," I give her blatantly as I lower my lips to hers.

She smiles up at me, and the band returns to the stage, playing their next set. It's loud when I tell her, "Hey, I need to run up to my office to grab some papers for Mel before I forget. Do you want to stay down here?"

"I'll go with you," she shouts over the music.

Max hasn't come back, so I grip her hand and pull her in close as I start pushing us through the crowd. She clings tightly to me as we bump shoulders with nearly everyone we pass, and I know she must be freaking out with the contact. I pull her a little when I feel her stumble, but then her body goes rigid and she starts shuffling back against my hold.

"What are you doing?" I holler over the crowd.

Her eyes are focused on something, but I can't figure out what it is in this chaos. She tugs against my arm, and when I turn, she falls out of my hold and onto the floor. Terror streaks across her face, and she panics, stumbling back on her hands. I grab her, and when she makes it to her feet, she turns and starts to bolt. Quickly, I link my arm around her waist from behind, leaning over her shoulder, shouting, "Babe, what's wrong?"

"It's Jack!" she yells in a panic, trying to pry my hands off of her to get away.

"Who?"

"Get me out of here!" she shrieks, thrashing to get out of my hold. "I can't breathe! Get me out of here!"

I don't even question her; I tuck her under my arm and rush her, as fast as I can, to the door. Spotting Jase through the mass of people, I call out to him, "Jase!" but I don't wait to see if he heard me or not because all I'm focused on is getting Candace out. She has her hands clutched to my arms that are holding on to her.

Making it past the door and outside, she's shaken and barely breathing when she breaks away from me and runs to my jeep.

"Babe, what the fuck happened in there?" I ask, when we get to my car, her whole body shaking. "Who the fuck did you see?"

She falls with her back against the side of the car and grabs on to my shirt as she's crying, gasping for a decent intake of air.

"Jack is in there. We have to leave."

"Who's Jack?"

"Him! Jack is . . ." Her cries are strained when I see Jase approach, asking in shock, "Candace, what happened?"

"Jack's inside."

"Oh, shit!"

"Who the fuck is Jack?!" I scream, confused as fuck with what's playing out in front of me.

"The guy that attacked her," Jase tells me.

Everything stops.

Grabbing on to Candace's shoulders, I demand, "Get in the car. Now."

I pull my keys out of my pocket and hand them to Jase, yelling at him, "Get her in the fucking car!"

Everything tunnels as I turn from everything good in my life and walk away.

One second. That's all it took.

Suspended in a false reality where actions and consequences no longer exist. Where rage boils so deep inside your veins that you'd do almost anything to drain them. I'd bleed it all out for her.

Chaos. I'm in it when I slam through the doors and bark out, demanding only the way a feral animal would, "Where's Jack?!"

When the guy to my left points him out, I come unleashed.

Without a conscious thought, I grab ahold of the hair on the side of his head and drive him with unrelenting force as I smash his face into the brick wall, blood splattering everywhere. The screams around me are nothing but hollow echoes as I keep my hand fisted in his hair and with one fluid movement, jerk him back and throw him to the floor, hearing the crack of wood as his head clips the edge of the table on his way down.

I watch his eyes roll back with heavy lids as I slam my fist into his face. Over and over. Blow after blow. I'm ravaged with hate, feeding this guy his own blood as I knock another punch into the side of his jaw, giving him only a small piece of what he gave my girl. I'm blinded by the rage that pounds in my chest. I'm gonna fuckin' kill this piece of shit as I ram my fist into him until I'm suddenly pulled back.

I can't feel anything besides the strain in my muscles, tense with fire.

"Breathe, man!" I hear Max yelling in my ear from behind me. His large hands are clamped to my arms, pinning them to my sides as I try to jerk out of his grasp. When I peel my eyes off of the sorry fucker lying there, spewing blood, I see Mark in front of me, hands against my chest, holding me back. Everything moves in slow motion around me when suddenly the noises start to filter in clearly. No more static. Everything in full force around me.

"Get the fuck off of me," I seethe at Max.

"What the hell is going on?"

Yanking myself out of his grip, I turn and lean into his ear, forcing out the words, "He raped Candace."

His head snaps up as he looks at me, and I see the fury in his eyes grow.

"Get the fuck outta here, man," he tells me in a low growl.

Looking down, the guy is starting to come to, when I say, "No way, man." I'm not even close to being finished with him. "This guy's dead," I spit out, and before I can propel myself on him again, Max pulls me back, and says, "You left her outside. Go!"

"Dude, she's outside, hysterical!" Mark shouts.

That's all he needed to say to grab me. To suck me out of this tunnel.

Looking at Max straight on, I give him my hard words, "Finish him off, and throw this piece of shit out by that dumpster." I feel my tears well up as he nods at me. "I'm not fuckin' kidding, man!"

"I hear you, boss," he says when I turn to Jack, draw my foot back, and kick the living shit out of him, cramming my boot into his balls. The pained shriek that rips through his throat is the last sound I hear as I storm out, fists still clenched when I spot my girl sobbing in the front seat of my car.

"Keys," I quietly demand as I pass Jase.

Hopping into the car, I keep my eyes to the front. I'm still fuming, and my racing heart is making it hard to take in a solid breath. I need to get the hell out of here before the cops show up, but all I want to do is go back and destroy every little piece of that sack of shit.

I know I'm scaring Candace; I know how sensitive she is, but I also know that if I open my mouth right now, I'll probably really upset her. So I stay quiet and focus on bringing my heart rate down and calming myself. I don't even realize how firm my grip is on the steering wheel until I feel the blood from my knuckles running down the back of my hand.

By the time I pull up to the loft, my breathing has slowed, and I'm in a daze with all that just happened. Everything that I never wanted to do in front of her, I just did. And without a single second thought. Completely shut down, letting my anger get the best of me. I wouldn't have been able to control it even if I wanted to. And the sick thing is, I'm still not satisfied.

Parking the car, I get out and walk around to her door. When I open it, I see her reddened face, soaked with tears. I grab on to her hips and turn her towards me as I drop my head onto her lap and cry. It hurts too much to keep it in, so I let it out. I feel her body as she leans down and drapes it over mine.

I hate every piece of me that I got from him. Pounding my fists into someone else to try and make myself feel better when all I feel is worse. It's as if I could stand in front of a mirror, and the reflection I'd see would be that of my father.

Candace holds on to me, hands threaded in my hair, but not even her touch can take this misery away. Knowing that I can't escape what's in my blood. I hate that I scared her, but I don't hate what I did to that guy. I'd do it again, and worse. I just hate that this asshole has infected what Candace and I have. That he holds this power over both of us and has the ability to stir up so much pain.

When her grip loosens on me, I lift my head up, and I can see the torment in her eyes as she wipes the tears from my face. There's blood on her fingers as I reach for her hand to hold, and I know it has to be Jack's, so I walk her inside and straight to the bathroom. As she cleans her hands in the sink, I hop into the shower and watch the muddled, red water running off of me, taking his blood down the drain.

I can hear Candace crying, and my heart just crumbles to have her so upset. I'm terrified to see what this has done to her. She's always been nervous of crowds because she's always feared running into him. Now that it's happened, I'm worried she's going to shut down. Worried about what this has stirred up and awakened inside of her.

I quickly finish up, throwing on a pair of boxers, and slide into bed with her where she's curled up, crying into her pillow. I scoop her in my arms, and it isn't but seconds before I feel her tears running down my chest. Sliding us down in the bed and under the covers, I hold her close, and her loud cries begin to soften.

She draws her head back and then presses her lips to mine, but my stomach is in knots so it's hard for me to do much of anything aside from keeping myself still.

"Make love to me," she whispers before covering my lips with hers again.

I can't do this. Not now.

"Baby, you're crying."

"I don't care," she says when she tugs me in and starts kissing my neck, but I don't want to do this. It feels wrong, and she's so upset. Pulling back to look at me, tears still spilling out, she says, "Kiss me."

"Candace, you're upset."

"I need to be close to you right now. I want to get him out of my head, and you're the only one who can do that for me."

I roll on top of her, hating what I'm about to do because it feels so wrong when she's hurting so bad. "Are you sure, babe?"

"Yes."

The thought of making love to her in the shadow of him makes me sick, but if this is what she needs, I won't deny her. As soon as I slip my hand under her top and take her breast in my hand, she starts pulling my boxers down. Rushing.

"Candace," I plead, wanting her to slow down.

"Please, Ryan."

Hearing her desperate voice, I take off my boxers and then sit back as I remove her shorts. She quickly strips her top off and pulls me down to her, urging me, so I go ahead and slide inside of her. Nothing about this feels right. With her eyes closed, she grabs my hips, wanting me to move faster, so I do. As she clings to me, and I give her a part of me that I never wanted to experience with her. She won't look at me, and I don't feel like I could even ask that of her. Holding on to my hips, she encourages me to thrust myself inside of her. I never wanted it to be this way with us. So disconnected and too fast.

I watch as she cries. She's cried while we've made love in the past but for completely different reasons. It kills me to know that it isn't me behind her closed eyes; it's chaos mixed with me. It's *him*, it's that night, it's this night, it's everything I never wanted to bring into our bed.

Moving at the speed we are, it doesn't take long for both of us to come, and when I roll off of her, I pull her close to me and cling to her, hating what we just did. My chest is heavy, and my throat is achingly tight. I reach down and find her hand, locking my fingers with hers.

"I'm so sorry," she whispers on a broken voice. "I shouldn't have done that."

And even though I never want to do that again, I would if it was really what she needed, so I tell her, "Don't be. You take whatever you need from me," because I'd give it all no matter how much it hurt me just to take away an ounce of her pain.

Waking in the middle of the night, I open my eyes to see light filtering from underneath the bathroom door. Candace isn't in bed with me, and when I walk over to the closed door, I can hear her soft cries on the other side. Slowly, I open the door to find her sitting on the edge of the tub with her head in her hands.

Kneeling down in front of her, I rest my hands on her legs. She doesn't respond to my presence, she just keeps her face covered as she tries to control the sobs that are breaking through.

"Talk to me, baby. Please."

"It's . . . I just, I can't get it out of my head now." When she lets her hands fall, her eyes are so swollen and red. "I don't know what to do anymore."

Her wrecked voice penetrates me, and I feel my throat begin to restrict again as I fight my own tears back.

"I'm so sorry," I release on a hard breath. "I'm sorry I lost it like that and scared you." I pause for a moment, and then admit, "I scared myself."

She catches her breath and looks at me. She's worn out, but I continue to talk.

"I wanted to kill him." Those are the words that break me and cause the tears to escape. "I would have killed him if it weren't for Max pulling me off of him. I've only wanted to kill one other person in my life, and he's dead. And now I wonder if I'm turning into him."

When I drop my head onto her lap, she lifts it back up and holds my face in her hands as she says through her tears, "You're nothing like him. I don't have any doubt about saying that. And I'm not scared of you. I never have been."

"I completely lost control. Wasn't even fully aware of what I was doing."

She slides off the edge of the tub and onto the floor with me as we wrap each other up in our arms.

"I wasn't scared of you, Ryan. I was just so scared of losing you," she cries. "I was afraid you'd kill him and I wouldn't have you."

"Baby, I'm so sorry. But I'm here. I swear you're not gonna lose me," I assure her. "I promise you that he will never step foot in my bar again."

We cling to each other, and when we both calm down, she softly says, "I'm sorry about earlier. I just . . . I wasn't thinking."

"Don't be sorry, babe. I love you. I'd give you just about anything if you asked me for it."

"It was wrong. Selfish."

Brushing the hair off of her face, I tell her, "Do you know how much I love you?"

"Hmm," she hums.

"You don't ever have to worry about me because I've never wanted anyone the way I do you."

She kisses me, and I linger in it before picking her up and taking her back to bed. I can't help the worry that still consumes me. I wonder how she's going to feel about everything when she wakes up. I can only hope that tonight doesn't have a lasting impact on her because I feel like she was just starting to come out of herself. But all I can do tonight is hold on to her, hold on to my hope.

chapter thirty-nine

WAKING UP, I roll over to Candace but she isn't here. The bed is empty, and when I look over to the bathroom, the door is wide open and the lights are off. She's probably downstairs drinking her coffee.

"Candace," I call out as I sit up, still half-asleep.

When there's no response, I walk out of the room and see her cell phone lying on the floor at the bottom of the stairs.

What the hell?

"Candace," I call out again as my pulse quickens, wondering where she is. I rush over to the windows only to see that her car is gone. Panic and confusion start to tear through me. What the hell happened last night? Where is she?

I throw on a pair of gym shorts and a t-shirt before getting my shoes on and then I'm out the front door and in my jeep. I rush over to her house and figure if she isn't there then she must be at Jase's, but when I pull up, her car is in the driveway.

Thank God.

I knock lightly, and when no one answers, I check the handle to find it's unlocked. Worried about why she's here and not in my bed, I go ahead and let myself in, making my way back to her room. As soon as I open her door, she's in a frenzy, slinging the sheets from her bed across the room.

"Candace?"

She snaps around, and her face is worse than it was last night. Puffy with bloodshot eyes, and she's crying.

"Get out," she seethes, and my gut knots. I don't know what's going on, but the look in her eyes is freaking me out.

"Babe, what's going on?" I ask as I walk towards her, but she shoots her arms out at me, not wanting me to come any closer.

"Stay away from me."

"Baby, what happened?"

She begins to cry loudly as she backs herself against the wall, and I just want to know what the fuck happened and why she's acting so scared of me.

"You know exactly what happened. You know exactly who I am!" she screams.

I stand there, in the middle of her room, confused as shit while my mind races to find clarity in this.

Suddenly, it hits.

She knows.

But how?

She's freaking out, and I can't seem to find the right words to explain myself.

"How could you?!" she screams, and I don't know how I'm gonna calm her down. My heart is pounding, and the utter fear inside of me has me in a panic.

"Babe, let me explain."

"Explain what?! That you've been lying to me this whole time? That you've just been using me? Why?!"

"No! It's not like that. I didn't know."

"How could you not know? God, I'm so fucking stupid."

"I didn't know when I first met you. I didn't know until I saw your tattoo," I try telling her, but I see it in her eyes. She doesn't believe me, and I don't know what to do.

Fuck. What do I do?

"What?!"

"Babe, please let me explain."

"Get out! Get the fuck out! I don't ever want to see you again."

Her words pierce through me, and I choke in a breath as she falls to the floor, wailing, but I can't leave. My mind is racing, and I'm at a loss.

"Just leave me alone," she cries.

"I'm not leaving," I tell her because I don't know *how* to leave her. I can't. I've never seen her so mad and to have all that anger directed at me makes me terrified to walk away until I know we're okay.

I quickly move to the floor, kneeling in front of her, but she coils herself away from me.

I'm desperate.

"I fuckin' hate you," she throws at me, and it kills. "You made me fall in love with you, and it was all a goddamn lie."

"God, Candace. Please let me explain," I beg as I reach out to touch her.

"Get out! Get the fuck out!"

My head snaps back when I hear the door slam open.

"Get the fuck out and away from her before I call the cops," Kimber says as she stands in the doorway, but I don't give a shit about her as I look back to my girl who is falling apart on me.

"Babe, please. I love you so fuckin' much. Let me explain. Don't do this."

"I didn't do shit, Ryan! Just go. It's over!" She covers her face and won't even look at me. It's like a damn knife in my heart, and I feel like I'm drowning. I don't want to believe her words. She's just upset. She can't really want this to be over.

"I'm serious. After the shit from last night, you better get the fuck away from her and leave. Now!" I hear Kimber say from behind me.

I don't know how to fix this or what I can do. Every time I speak, I seem to only make it worse. So against everything I want to do, I stand up and walk away. It's like I'm losing her piece by piece with every step I take, but I love her too much to hurt her, and I'm so fuckin' mad at myself for lying to her.

Walking past Kimber, I can't even look back to Candace who's crumpled on the floor crying. It hurts too much to know I'm the cause of her pain. How could I do this to her? How could I have been so selfish?

"Fuuuck!" I scream, gritting it out of my lungs as I slam the door shut and walk out to my car. Getting in, I strike my palms against the steering wheel, pounding it over and over again, screaming. It hurts coming out, but I need to feel the pain because I feel like I just lost everything.

I've seen her cry and be upset in the past, but *this*... this is beyond just being upset. Instead of going back inside to be with her, comfort her, explain to her how stupid I am, I drive back home. I don't want to, but I do. I don't feel like I have a choice since I just ripped out my girlfriend's heart because I was too much of a coward to tell her the truth.

Walking through the door, I see her phone that remains at the bottom of the stairs and begin to wonder what the hell happened while I was asleep. How did she find out? I have a thousand questions swarming inside of me, but I'm just too far gone to concentrate to try to make sense out of all of this.

I don't know how to respond or what I should do. I figure I'll give her space to calm down before I try talking to her again. She has to understand. She has to listen and believe me when I tell her how much I love her. I can't lose her, but what if she doesn't believe me?

The agony ripping through me hurts so much, and I can't control the unrelenting tears that begin to pour out of me, taking every bit of happiness with them, until I'm nothing but numb, sitting on the couch and staring out at the rain.

Time doesn't exist right now. Nothing does. I don't know how long I've been sitting here in a stagnant melancholy when I hear a knock on my door. I hope with everything I have that she's standing on the other side. When I walk over and open it, I barely get a glimpse of Jase before his fist barrels into the side of my face, clipping my jaw, causing me to lose my balance as I stumble back.

"I told you not to fuck around with her."

Looking up, he steps inside and slams the door shut. I wish he would come back and bury his fist into me again. I deserve every hit. When I straighten myself up and wipe the blood from my split lip, he's pissed and has every right.

"What the fuck, man?" he slings at me.

I don't even try to defend myself. I'm a piece of shit and know it.

"You better fuckin' say something and give me a reason to not beat the shit out of your ass."

"Is she okay?" I ask because that's all I care about.

"No, man. She's not okay. She's a fuckin' mess right now, and I don't know what to do for her. What the hell were you thinking?"

"I don't know," I say as I walk over and flop down on the couch. "I didn't know it was her."

"Don't bullshit me."

"I'm not bullshitting you."

"Did you just feel sorry for her?"

"Fuck no. It wasn't like that."

"Then tell me what it was like, because right now, my best friend is falling apart," he says, completely pissed, as he sits down in the chair.

His words hit me hard, and I lose it. I don't even try to hide my pain from him because at this point, I feel like I have nothing left. I give him the honest truth when I tell him, "I was the one who called 911 that night. But that girl was unrecognizable, so when I met Candace, the only thing that struck me about her and that girl in the alley was their small size. I swear I didn't know it was her."

"But you did eventually."

"She has this tattoo. The same tattoo I saw that night. I had already fallen hard for her when I saw it, and it fuckin' killed me. I didn't know how to tell her at that point. I couldn't hurt her."

"So you lied to her?"

"It didn't seem like a lie, man. Not for a while. Not until she opened up to me about the rape."

"So why didn't you tell her then?" he asks.

"I was scared I'd lose her. It was selfish, but I love that girl with everything I have. I just . . . I didn't know how to tell her."

"When I met you at the bar that morning . . . you hadn't just found out, had you? You already knew."

"Yeah, man. I knew," I admit. "It was just the first time she opened up about it."

Jase leans forward, with his elbows propped on his legs when he releases a deep breath and says, "You should have told me. We could have figured out a way to tell her."

The two of us have become pretty decent friends, and now I see that I deceived him as well.

"I'm sorry, man," I tell him, completely defeated.

He stares out the window when he says, "She's devastated."

I want to help her, but I'm not even sure if I know how. "What do I do?"

I ask, desperate.

"I don't know. She feels betrayed and lied to. Like she was some project just to make you feel better about what you saw."

"She said that?"

He nods his head, and I ask, "You believe that?"

When he looks over at me, he says, "No. I know you love her. I get that you were trying to protect her."

"I just need to talk to her. I need her to understand."

"I don't know if that's gonna happen." He takes a pause before continuing. "You know how she is. She avoids and hides. I don't know if she's gonna want to deal with this pain."

Lowering my head, I choke out, "I can't lose her." I let the agony take over me for a moment before I sit up, and ask, "How did she find out?"

"She spoke with the detective this morning."

"What?" I ask in shock. "Wait. Is she pressing charges?" I ask.

"I think she was considering it, but now, I don't think so. I don't think she'd be able to deal with it right now. Not with how upset she is."

I had no idea that she was thinking about this. Enough to make a phone call. It's all I've ever wanted her to do. To take control and stand up for herself. Whether or not she wants me in her life, I need her to do this because I know it will help her deal with all of it, so I tell Jase, "You need to tell her to do it."

"I don't think it's gonna happen, man. Not now."

Guilt floods me. Knowing that I possibly ruined this for her. Ruined this opportunity for her to seek justice and to help herself fight through this. That my lie would take that away from her. I feel like I keep failing her. Hurting her because of my selfish decision.

"Talk to her. Tell her to not let what I did stop her from doing something about this. She needs to do something."

"I know that. Trust me, I do. But she's in a bad place right now, and I can't push her."

I take in his words, knowing that he's right, but it doesn't make it any easier.

Jase stands up and says, "She wants me to get her things."

His words take me by surprise. "Why?"

He doesn't say anything, but I can read his face. She's having a knee-jerk reaction, and I'm losing control. That she would be so quick to walk away from me. To want her things out of my house. The place she's been spending all of her time when she's not at school. How could she want me gone in an instant when I want to fight so hard to keep her? I want to throw him outta here. Not because he isn't a friend of mine, but because the longer he's here, the more I feel her slipping away. If he takes her things, he takes a reason for her to come back here. It's selfish, I know, but it's all I have.

"How much?" I ask, fearing the words that come next.

"Everything."

He follows me upstairs, and as I help him pack her clothes and dance stuff, it's like I'm packing up parts of me that she helped me find. Without her, I just don't know who I am anymore. I can't even wrap my head around what's going on right now.

I go into the bathroom to get her belongings, but I keep a few of her things, including her bottle of perfume. I can't let him take all of her away from me, so I leave them on the counter as I carry her other items out and pack them in her bag.

I watch as Jase zips it up and slings it over his shoulder. Before he walks out, he steps next to me and says, "I'm sorry."

Nodding my head, because I can't speak with the pain in my chest, he adds, "I'll try talking to her for you. You're a good guy and the only reason why she was able to be happy after what happened to her," before walking out of my room and out the front door to head back to where I left my heart—with Candace.

Turning to face the bed, I look at the mussed up sheets where I held her last night. I tell myself that she just needs time. That when she calms down, I'll be able to explain everything and we can work this out. Because we just have to.

Walking over to her side, I sit on the edge of the bed and see her necklace on the nightstand. She never takes it off, but here it lies. When I reach over to pick it up, I notice the chain is broken. I run my finger over the stamped words and wonder if we're broken too.

chapter forty

"BABY, PLEASE. I know you're upset with me, and you have every right. I fucked up, but I love you. Please call me back. Let me talk to you and explain everything. I miss you."

I hang up the phone after leaving another voicemail for her. I've been calling and texting for the past few days, but I get nothing in response. It kills me to think that I might not ever hear her voice again, but each day that passes without being able to talk to her confirms what I don't want to accept because it can't be over. This can't be it.

I went out yesterday to get her necklace fixed. I didn't like the idea of it remaining broken. I can only hope that she'll one day wear it again, but for now, it lies on the counter in my bathroom by her perfume.

I decided to come into work today because I'm going crazy at home. I need the distraction, and when I get here, I head upstairs. Max's office door is open, and when I stop in, he says, "Hey, man. Been trying to call you."

"Sorry. Things have been crazy," I tell him as I sit down in front of his desk.

"Dude, I don't even know what to say. Shit was insane when you left the other night."

"Yeah?" I ask, but that night feels like it was weeks ago instead of days. So much has happened, and my thoughts haven't been on anything but Candace.

"The cops came by later that night."

"What did you tell them?"

"Just that I didn't know who the fuck started the fight. That by the time I made it inside they were gone. There were so many people here that they weren't gonna waste their time asking around, so you're good."

"Thanks, man," I say. "What happened when I left?"

Leaning back in his seat, he tells me, "I dragged his ass out back and kicked the shit out of him before slamming him into the dumpster. He was fucked up. Bad."

I don't even know how to feel about all of this because it all just hurts. Every part of it. It all came crashing down so fast.

"How's Candace?"

"I don't know. She won't talk to me."

"Why? What happened?"

Dropping my head to the side, I rest it in my hand, telling him, "She found out about me being the one who found her that night. She bailed, and I haven't heard from her since the day after the fight."

He shakes his head, confused, and questions, "You told her?"

"No. I talked to Jase. He said she had spoken with the detective on the case, and he had told her who the witness was . . . *me*. She took the call while I was still asleep, and when I woke, she was gone."

"Fuck," he sighs out.

"I really fucked this up."

Leaning his arms on the desk, he asks, "What are you gonna do?"

"I dunno, man. I keep calling and texting, but knowing her, she's probably just deleting them."

"Maybe she just needs time."

"Yeah," I say as I stand up. "Maybe. I'll be in my office if you need me."

I spend the rest of the day buried in work that Max should be doing, but I need to keep busy, so I take it off his hands and work late into the night.

I finally talked to my mom last night after avoiding her calls. She was upset, hating that Candace had to find out from someone other than me. But I can't keep asking myself what if. It is what it is, and I can't go back because if I could, I would have done it all differently.

It's been two weeks—and nothing. I call her everyday—and nothing. I'm going crazy, practically living at the bar, hiding in my office, and doing what I can to keep busy. I wound up hanging out with Jase and Mark the other day when they came up for drinks.

They're my only connection to her, but they are also genuine friends and I don't want to let go of that. Aside from Max, they're friends that I've connected with on a more authentic level than I have in the past. I don't want to go back to what I had before I met them. Candace showed me what it was to connect, and I'm not going to trash that. I can't.

When there's a knock at my door, I open it to find Jase standing there.

"Hey, man. What's up?" I say as he walks in.

"Nothing. What are you up to?"

"Not a damn thing," I tell him. "Wanna beer?"

"Nah, I'm good," he says as he takes a seat in my living room. "How have you been?"

"How do you think I've been?" I respond as I fall back on the couch, kicking my feet onto the coffee table.

"I can't get her to talk to me," he admits.

"Join the club."

"I'm serious, man. She won't leave her house. I'm worried."

"Why are you telling me this?" I ask, because all his words do is hurt me.

"Maybe if she could hear you explain yourself..."

"You don't think I've tried? Dude, I call her every single day. She won't talk to me."

"Go over there," he says.

"If she's not returning my calls or texts, she's not gonna let me in."

"She needs to talk to you. Take my key and just go. She needs to hear you 'cause she's shutting us all out," he says. "You should see her. She looks awful."

I watch as he slides her house key off his key ring and then sets it on the table.

"I don't know, man. I don't wanna hurt her."

"She's already hurting. You're the only one who has ever really gotten through to her in the past. Just try?"

Staring at the bronze key lying there, I'd be an idiot to not take it. If only just to get a look at her. Anything. I'm desperate, so I take it.

"Thanks, man," he says before heading out.

Pulling into her driveway, I already feel my anxiety welling up. I don't know what I'm about to walk into, but I know she's inside, and I'm desperate to see her. When I ring the doorbell, it takes a moment before I hear that voice I've been missing so much, but her words are nearly lifeless when she says, "Go away."

"You won't return any of my calls, babe. Please, let me talk to you."

She doesn't respond, and when I use the key to unlock the door, she turns to me and yells, "What are you doing?!"

"Jase gave me a key."

She mumbles something under her breath before saying, "Ryan, please go. I don't want to talk."

Jase wasn't lying; she looks awful. She was small before, but I can tell she's lost weight by the way her clothes are hanging on her. And I know she isn't sleeping by the dark circles under her eyes. What the hell have I done to her? God, knowing she's hurting so much that she isn't taking care of herself is just another punch to my gut.

"I can't *not* talk to you. It's killing me."

"It's killing *you*?" she snaps. "What about me? Ryan, I can't do this. I can't even look at you. Please, just go." Her words are strained as she speaks.

"I can't stand to see you like this."

"Then go! I will do almost anything to make you leave."

"Just let me talk to you. Please, babe, just let me talk," I beg.

"Fine, say whatever you need to say, then leave me alone."

When she sits on the couch, I walk over and sit next to her as I watch the tears begin to fall from her tired eyes. I wanna touch her. I wanna pull her into my arms like I've done so many times before, but now I feel like I can't. Like if I tried, she would just reject me. I'm so close to her right now, but I've never felt so distant. I hate it.

"I'm worried about you."

"Don't," she says as she turns her head away from me.

"When was the last time you've eaten?"

"Ryan, don't. Just say what you need to say."

Reaching out to take her hand, she yanks it away from me. God, this is bad. Needing to get through to her, needing her to know, I just start talking—pleading. "I love you. I know you don't believe me, but I do. No one has ever affected me the way you do, babe. I swear to you . . . I swear I didn't know. I didn't, Candace. Not at first," I tell her when I start to choke up, and I just let it out. I let all the tears fall that I've been holding in because I feel like I'm losing everything I am at this point. She's all I have ever wanted in this life, and I'm losing her.

"When I saw you at the coffee shop, I thought it was you. I thought you were *that* girl," I tell her, nearly crying out the words because they hurt so much. "But then I kept thinking, 'What are the chances?' I didn't know because you looked so different than from that night. And then I found out that you were friends with Mark. Every time I saw you, I felt myself being drawn to you in a way I've never felt before. I had myself convinced that my head was playing games with me, and I honestly did not think you were that girl. It wasn't until I saw your tattoo when we were in bed. That's when I knew. When I found that girl, I saw her tattoo—*your* tattoo."

"Ryan, please," she begs, but I can't stop. She needs to hear this because I'm starting to wonder if I'll ever get this chance again.

She's trying to shut me out, so I continue, "When I saw it, I broke. I didn't want you to be her. I had already fallen so hard in love with you, and realizing that it was you fuckin' killed me," I explain through my tears as she sits there crying with me. "Everything started making sense to me. How scared you always were with me when we first met, how afraid you were when I tried to touch you. Everything made sense. But, I didn't know how to tell you. And then you told me you loved me, and I know how hard that was for you. I just couldn't hurt you."

"But you did," she sobs out. "You lied to me. I let you see all the parts of me that weren't pretty, but you knew all along. And when I finally opened up to you, you already knew." She drops her head and begins to cry harder when she says, "You let me give everything to you. You had to have known that you couldn't hold on to that secret forever. I would've eventually found out, and you still let me fall for you like I did. I feel so stupid and used, like you just felt sorry for me or pitied me."

"I never pitied you, babe. I have only ever loved you. I just didn't want to hurt you."

When I try pulling her into my arms to hold her, she shoves me back and gets up from the couch, stepping away from me.

"I can't do this. You can't say those things to me," she says.

Walking toward her, I stop right in front of her and confess, "I know I fucked up. I fucked everything up so bad. I know all you wanted was someone you could trust. I wanted to be that for you, and I fucked it all up. But I didn't know what to say; I was scared. You'll never know how fucking sorry I am."

"I knew better. I knew I shouldn't have let you in like I did. But I can't see you anymore. You have to stop calling and texting," she says. Her words tearing me apart as she continues, "I need you to just not exist for me because I can't do this. It hurts more than I thought anything possibly could."

"Candace, please," I beg. I can't fuckin' do this. I can't *not* have her in my life.

"Just go."

I see it. She means what she's saying, but I can't move. I don't how I'm gonna turn and walk away from her. So I stand here, a broken man, in front of the only girl I've ever given my heart to and I cry.

"Please, you have to go. I can't do this," she pleads.

"You have to know how much I love you."

Closing her eyes, she whispers, "Please, Ryan."

I wait for her to open her eyes, but she doesn't. I'm always gonna want her, but reality hits me like a brick.

It's over.

I've never felt pain like this before. It's one thing to get the shit beat out of you by a man you don't even like, but it's another thing entirely when the person you love the most in this world doesn't even want to look at you. I'd go back and take a thousand more beatings just to have her open her eyes and look at me.

But she doesn't, and I can't bear the agony, so I take one last look and absorb everything I can before I turn away from everything I never wanted to. She gave it all to me, and now I leave it behind as I walk out of her house.

The finality of what just happened starts to sink in as I drive home. How is this over? Ending faster than it began. I'm not sure what else I could have said to save what we had. I would've kept her forever if she would've let me. But it's done, and I'm not sure where I go from here. In my head I've been thinking that I was going to give it all up for her. Move to wherever she was going. Maybe I was just in too deep.

There's a black van parked in front of my place when I get home, and as I'm getting out of my car, I see a guy opening the back doors and pulling out a large, wrapped item.

Walking toward him, he asks, "Mr. Campbell?"

"Yeah. What's this?"

"I have a delivery from Thinkspace Art Gallery for you."

Her photo.

"Would you like me to carry it up?"

"No," I tell him as I reach out to take the piece, which is covered in a brown paper wrap.

"You sure?"

"Yeah. I've got it. Thanks."

Before getting into his van, he turns and says, "It's a beautiful piece, sir. Enjoy."

I watch as he drives away, but I don't think I could ever look at this photo—her photo. How could I enjoy something that has been torn to shreds because of me? Carrying the canvas upstairs, I lean it against the wall as I go to the kitchen to get a beer. Popping the cap, I turn and rest my back on the counter and look at it, just sitting there—masking away my happiness, knowing that she's underneath the paper. But being the masochist that I am, I need to see her. I set the bottle down and rip the paper off, revealing the white line of her back.

As I step away, I keep my eyes on her. Her smooth skin. Nothing ever felt better on me, and the thought of never having that comfort again makes seeing her painful. It's tearing out my fuckin' heart, and I need it gone.

Picking it up, I take it upstairs to my bedroom and into my closet where I shove it behind one of the racks of clothes. I hide it because I don't want to look at it, but I don't want to let it go either.

The memories of that day start to run through my head. That rainy afternoon with her in my bed. She was jittery, lying in the dark while I snapped her picture. She trusted me. But now that trust is gone, and she can't even look at me. I just want to touch her. Have her lips on mine, her body warm against me. She was so good at everything she was willing to give. I took it all, and no amount of pain could make me believe that it wasn't worth the fall because falling in love with her was the best thing I ever did.

chapter forty-one

SITTING HERE, NURSING my beer that has now grown warm, I watch as Gavin talks to some blonde who's wearing way too much makeup. I want to leave, but I don't want to go back home. Home and work, those are the only places I seem to find myself lately. But that's all it was before Candace, so why should I expect it to be any different after her? It feels different, but the routine is the same. I work, I go out with Gavin, and I go home—alone. I'm always alone. There was a time not too long ago that I liked it. Now . . . I hate it. So even though I sit here, miserable and bored in this bar, it's better than being alone.

Gavin keeps trying to sling girls at me, but the thought of touching anyone other than Candace is something that I just can't stomach yet. A part of me wants to. Desperate to do anything to get her out of my head, but then I get scared of losing her, even if my head is the only place she exists for me. I'm torn. Lonely, but unwilling to walk away from the girl who doesn't want me.

Another chick approaches, and as soon as she lays her hand on my knee, I'm out of my seat and walking away to go get another drink from the bar.

"Can I get another?" I ask the bartender as I set down my bottle.

"I don't understand why you keep coming out if you're just gonna be a dick," Gavin says when he slides up next to me at the bar.

Looking over at him, I ask, "Who am I being a dick to?"

"This place is loaded with chicks, but you're the biggest pussy in here."

"Nice," I say as I laugh with annoyance.

He turns to lean his side against the bar and gives me a serious look before saying, "She's gone, man."

When the guy from behind the bar hands me my beer, I take a long draw, but it hurts to swallow past the lump in my throat that reared itself at the mere mention of her. Setting the bottle down, I turn and say with irritation, "Yeah? And what if I don't want her to be?"

He sighs when he responds in a matter-of-fact voice, "It doesn't seem to be about what you want. She holds the cards on this one because you handed over that power when you fell for her."

He's right. I've always called the shots with chicks until Candace. It sucks to have someone else dictating your destiny, but with her . . . I wouldn't have it any other way. If this is what she needs, to be away from me, then I'll stay away.

"You wanna know what's gonna make you better? Make you forget?" he asks me.

"What's that?"

He lifts his arm, beer in hand, and points over the crowd of people as he says, "Take your pick." When he turns to look at me, he gives a smirk and adds, "Just like old times."

I might not know what my life is right now, but I do know that it isn't this. It vanished when I met Candace. She made me see this for what it is. She showed me a different version of myself—a version that I was happy to be. So this? This is nothing but a distraction that I no longer want.

Before taking a sip of his beer, he mutters, "I never understood what you saw in her anyway."

"What's your problem?"

"Nothing. Just being honest. She was just so different than your normal type. I didn't get it."

Tossing a few bucks on the bar, I get up and tell Gavin, "I'm going home."

"Ryan," he calls out as I make my way to the door, but there's nothing here for me. Who am I kidding? No matter where I am, my misery follows, so I might as well be home.

When I was hanging out with Jase the other night, he told me about his plans to go over to Westport for a day trip to get some surfing in. Needing the headspace, I decide to tag along. He met me at my place earlier this morning, and after several hours of driving, we unload my jeep and zip up our wetsuits before heading out into the water.

For the first time in a while, I feel good. If only for a moment, being out here in the water, my head finally settles as I simply enjoy the breaking waves as I ride them. The salt on my face and the sun that's starting to break through the clouds is freeing in a way. Being out of Seattle and away from the gloom that seems to follow, I take a break as I straddle my board and stare out over the endless water.

"The breaks are pretty decent today," Jase says as he paddles over to me.

"Yeah. The tide is starting to come in."

Shifting himself to sit up on his board, he asks, "You doing okay?"

I nod my head, but I know he isn't just talking about surfing, and curiosity gets to me when I decide to ask, because I just can't avoid it. No matter what she says or what she does, I can't forget about her. I can't stop caring about her, so I go ahead and ask, "How is she?"

Running his hand through his hair, he says, "She's better."

"Yeah?"

"She started seeing a therapist a couple weeks ago," he tells me. "She's been going a couple times a week."

"That's good." It relieves me to hear that she's finally talking to someone, but at the same time, it's hard to not be there to support her.

"Yeah. She's been working really hard, trying to sort everything out."

When I don't respond, he questions, "What about you?"

"I don't know, man. I'm fuckin' stuck. Like I'm just waiting for something I'm not sure is gonna happen."

"With her?"

Nodding my head, I ask hesitantly, "Should I be?"

"Waiting?" he questions.

"Yeah."

Looking out over the water, avoiding having to face me, he breathes out, "I don't think so."

It's the reality I've been trying to hide from. I've been hanging on to a thread of hope, but hearing those words from Jase, they hold an honesty that there's no more hiding from.

"She's working hard on pulling herself together, to make sense of the madness she's been living in. Maybe you should do more for yourself too. I hate to see you stagnant, waiting for something that doesn't seem likely to happen at this point."

I hear his words, and they're hard to take. I don't want to accept them, but he makes it clear what I should do when he adds a hard truth to my reality, saying, "I think it's time you just walk away from it. She seems to have."

How do you walk away from someone that still occupies so much of your heart? To be so certain about something just to turn your back on it? And how can she move on so quickly when I'm still in pieces over here? It sucks to have all these questions that I can't get any closure with. To constantly be wondering and hoping.

"I've tried talking to her, tried telling her how you feel about everything, but she shuts me down. She said she just needs to be on her own."

"No, I get it," I mumble. "You don't need to say anything to her. If she's happy . . . that's all I've ever wanted for her."

"Sorry, man."

"It's life," I say as I lie down on my board and paddle back out.

"So, I'm planning on leaving here next Friday morning," my mom tells me as I sit in my office at home.

"Mom, I don't know if that's a good idea."

"It's your birthday," she exclaims, but we both know that's not her reasoning for wanting to come.

"You never drive up here for my birthday. I know you're coming to see Candace dance, but I just don't know if that's a good idea at this point."

"I told her I was going to be there. I would feel awful if I didn't show up. This is a huge night for her, and I've never seen her dance."

"I just . . ."

"Her family turned their backs on her; I'm not going to do the same. I want to support her. No matter what happens with you guys, I'd like to at least offer my support."

"Nothing's gonna happen with us, Mom," I tell her as I shut the lid to my laptop.

"How do you know that?"

"Jase told me last week that she's done, and I should just walk away. So that's what I'm trying to do."

"I'm sorry, dear. I know you love her."

Having her so close, blending so nicely with my mom and me, it was perfect. It's something I don't think I'll be able to find again. Something I'm not sure I want to open myself up to again.

"You still there?" she asks when I don't say anything.

"Yeah, I'm here."

"Are you okay?"

Taking a hard swallow, I admit, "I don't know how to be okay. I don't how she's moving on when I can't."

"Maybe she isn't. Maybe she's hurting just like you are."

"Then why isn't she coming back?" I ask as my voice slips.

"She could just be scared."

"It's been over a month, and I wanna run to her every day, but I know if I do, I'll only be hurting her. She lives right down the fuckin' street from me, but it's like she's across the world."

My mother is at a loss for words, so I cut the conversation short, not wanting to talk any more, but as soon as we hang up, Tori's name flashes on my phone when it starts ringing again.

"Hey, Tor."

"Hey, how are you? I talked to Aunt Donna earlier today. Why didn't you tell me what happened?"

"There's not much to talk about," I clip out.

"Well, what happened?"

Leaning back in my chair, I say, "You were right. I wasn't honest with her and fucked everything up."

"What did you lie about?"

"It doesn't matter. I kept something from her that I shouldn't have, and it's done." I'm tired and just need to blow this off so she doesn't keep me on the phone. "Look, it was over a month ago, so there's not much to say about it. Moving on."

"Got it," she responds. "You coming back here for Memorial Day weekend?"

"Maybe. Haven't thought about it. But, hey, I'm gonna hit the sack, so I'll talk to you later," I tell her so I can hang up.

I'm about to throw the damn phone across the room when it starts ringing again, but this time when I answer it, all I hear on the other end is panic.

"Ryan?"

"Hey, Max. What's going on?"

"Traci's in labor. We're heading to the hospital." His voice is rushed, and I can't help but laugh at the fear in him.

"So why are you calling me? Shouldn't you be driving?" I ask with a chuckle.

"Because I know when I get there it's gonna be us and her crazy-ass sisters driving me insane."

"You better watch it," I hear Traci bark at him in the background.

"Dude—"

"Okay. I'll admit. I'm scared shitless," he tells me when Traci butts in, saying, "You're scared? Are you serious? I'm the one about to have a baby here and you're on the phone with your buddy because you're scared?"

"Shit, you've got your hands full," I laugh, and the next thing I hear is Traci as she says, "Ryan? You there?"

"Hey, Trace."

"Tell your buddy to calm the hell down and to stop being a pansy."

The dramatics of this late night call are cracking me up, and I do not envy Max with having his girl fed up with him.

The phone muffles and then Max says, "You coming to the hospital?"

"You need to relax before Traci rips your head off, but yeah, I'll be there."

Seeing Max with a baby is a head-trip for me. Traci went into labor quickly, and by the time they made it to the hospital, it was too late for her to get any drugs, so now Max has some god-awful scratches on his arms where she took her pain out on him. But in the end, they have a healthy baby boy.

The sheer happiness splayed across his face is something that any man would envy. Max is content, and I couldn't be happier for him, but I'd be lying if I said I wasn't panged with a slight sense of jealousy. I never thought that settling down and having a family was in the cards for me, but with Candace, I was starting to believe that it could be a possibility. So in my attempt to move on, I hold his baby in my arms and shut my selfish emotions out as I sit here with one of my good friends as he gushes over his new son.

chapter forty-two

"How was your drive?"

"Long," my mom says as she hugs me. "It's good to see you."

"Come in," I tell her as I take her bag and set it against the wall. "Max called a little while ago. He said that Traci is feeding Bennett and now would be a good time to come over, so if you still wanted to see the baby, we should head out."

"Of course I want to see the baby."

Grabbing my keys, we leave and make the drive over to Max's place. My mother has gotten to know Max a little over the years, and she never passes up an opportunity to hold a baby, so when we arrive, she melts at the sight of Bennett.

We settle ourselves in the living room, and Mom doesn't even wait for me to introduce her to Traci. She is already sitting next to her, making her own introductions, and before I know it, they're chatting away. My mom just has this way about her that can put anyone at ease. Candace loved that about her.

"So, what's been going on?" Max asks as he flops down on the chair.

"Just covering for you every day," I tease.

"Ha, nice, man."

"Got another band booked."

"Yeah? That's good. So what's going on with Mark and the guys?" he asks, and I'm momentarily distracted when I hear my mom talking gibberish to the baby.

Shaking my head and laughing at her, I turn back to Max and tell him, "They're gonna alternate Saturdays with the new band for the next four weeks, and then their contract is up."

"Is he staying here in Seattle?"

"Yeah. He and Jase had a few interviews at some firms in the city," I tell him.

"Nice."

"How have you been? You look like shit."

"Dude, this kid wakes up to eat every two hours. When we first brought him home he slept solid for the first few days, but now he's up around the clock."

"Sounds great," I joke when I turn to Traci and ask, "So how's this guy really holding up?" I laugh as I nod to Max.

She shakes her head and teases, "For such a big guy, you wouldn't think he'd be so squeamish."

"Don't listen to her. I've got this completely under control," he defends with a smile.

"Oh my goodness," my mother squeals as we all turn to look at Bennett when he lets out a massive fart.

"Holy shit!" I crack up, nearly doubling over at the insane gas that baby just released.

"Ryan!" my mom scolds. "Don't cuss in front of the baby."

"Are you serious, Mom? He's barely a week old. Little dude doesn't even speak English," I laugh out as she rolls her eyes at me.

"Speaking of having everything under control," Traci says to Max as she picks up Bennett and hands him over. "Why don't you take care of this issue your son has in his pants?"

"You think you're funny, don't you?"

She pats him on the back and mocks, "Try to control the gagging this time, huh?"

He plants a kiss on Traci's nose, and I follow him back to the nursery. I take a front row seat in the rocker as Max lays Bennett on the changing table.

"Dear Jesus!" he says in utter disgust when he peels the diaper off, and it only takes a second for the stench to hit me.

"Ugh! What the hell is that?"

Before Max can say anything, the baby rips out another rancid fart.

"For the love of God!" Max says, and I have to clutch my stomach because I'm laughing so hard at the visual of him being taken down by his own baby, one fart after another.

Max tries holding on to his tiny ankles, when he farts again.

"Dude," he snaps at me. "He's shitting everywhere. Traci!"

"Oh my God," I laugh out. "I'm dying."

"*You're* dying. This shit's right in front of my face."

"What is going on in here?" Traci exclaims when she walks in.

"Honey, there's poop all over me!"

"You boys are ridiculous," my mom says when she takes Max's place and starts cleaning Bennett.

"Donna, let me take care of that," Traci says.

"No worries. You go sit and relax," she tells her. "And you boys get out of here," she scolds as if we're kids and not grown men.

Once Bennett is cleaned up and changed, my mom returns to the living room and lays him on the couch between her and Traci. As she's rubbing his belly, Traci kicks her feet up on the ottoman and leans back into the couch, laughing.

"What's so funny?" Max asks when he returns with a clean shirt.

"You."

"Why is it that every time I change him, it winds up in a fiasco, but when you do it, it's just a simple pee diaper?"

"Payback for me having to be pregnant."

We continue to hang out and when Bennett falls asleep, we say goodbye and head out.

I've been anxious all day, knowing that tonight is Candace's production. I feel weird about going, almost like some kind of voyeur, but I couldn't miss seeing her dance on stage. I have only seen her in a couple of videos she had once shown me.

The whole time we were together, she was preparing for this night, so to finally have it here is bittersweet because I always thought I would be there with her. I should have wrapped her legs up last night in her crazy Saran Wrap. I should have been watching her walk around my loft all day, a neurotic nervous mess, helping her stretch and rub out her calves that had been bothering her, staring at her while she stood in the bathroom as she put her hair up in a bun with all those tiny hair pins.

This day should have been completely different; instead, I've been walking around with a knot in my stomach. I haven't seen her in a long time, and I'm not sure how tonight is going to affect me, but I have to see her.

"You ready?" my mom asks when she walks down the hall.

"Why don't you go on without me?" I suggest. I just think I should be alone tonight when I go. It's definitely not something I want to do with my mother right next to me.

Without a single question, she walks over and runs her hand down my arm as I stand, leaning up against the windows in the living room. "Of course."

When she turns to walk out, I stop her and say, "Mom . . ."

"Yes?"

"You look really nice."

"Thanks, dear. I'll see you later."

Leaning back against the windows, I look out at the darkened night sky and decide that after tonight, I have to be done. I can't keep questioning and wishing things were different. They aren't, and enough time has passed to know that she isn't coming back.

When I arrive at Meany Theater, most everyone is already in their seats, quietly holding their personal conversations. The theater is large with seating up in the balcony. The curtain is dropped, and I look at the program to see which numbers she will be in. She's one of the two featured dancers, so she'll appear throughout the night. I feel so disconnected even though we are probably closer tonight than we've been in a while, knowing she's in the same building as me.

She's in the opening number, so I quietly stand in the back of the room when the curtain draws up. The stage is filled with girls who all look the same, hair pinned up, short white tutus. It isn't until after the music has already started that I see her.

God, she's beautiful.

She's the only one wearing purple, standing out from all the others as she dances in front of the other girls. I've only ever seen her in leotards and tattered warm-ups. Never like this. She fits the part perfectly. Stoic and polished. Graceful and soft. And even on a stage filled with other dancers, she's all my eyes can see, captivating me in a way that only she can do. No one else exists in this room right now—it's only her.

But it isn't until her solo when it hits me. She stands center stage as the curtain goes up, and chills prick along my arms. She's perfection, wearing black with a short, full tutu, pale pink tights, and her pink toe shoes. Her skin is a striking contrast to the black, and she looks amazing. She isn't someone you simply look at; she's someone you admire.

I know her music by heart from all the times she played it at my place. It's a dark and intense piece that she struggled with for so long, but watching her work the whole stage, she's nothing but a natural as she bares her heart up there, making me feel the haunting pain of the piece. She gives it all, up on her toes, gliding through her movements. It almost hurts to look at her because I know this will be the last time I will probably ever see her. I can't take my eyes off her. I don't ever want to.

I'd hide back here forever if it meant I wouldn't have to stop looking at her. As tiny as she is, she made the biggest impact on me. I've never loved as hard as I did with her. I don't know how anyone could ever love her more. With everything we went through to get to the point we were at, knitted so tightly together, I never thought there could be a possibility of us unraveling like we did. But we did.

I don't blame her though. She hasn't made a wrong choice yet. I know she left me because it was the best thing for her. I talk to Jase often about her, and knowing how hard she's working in therapy, I know she wouldn't be doing that if she were still with me. She needed to be on her own. To do it for herself and not just because it was something I wanted. I'm proud of her, and even though it hurts me, I know she's doing everything right to try and pull herself out of the darkness that was consuming her.

The crowd is deafening when the music stops, and I finally see it. Her big, gorgeous smile with that cute dimple in her cheek. She soaks up the standing ovation, as she should, because she deserves every second of this. She's elated. I can see it in her eyes, even from this far away. Her instructor walks out with a huge bouquet of roses and hands them to her as she takes her final curtsey before the curtain drops, taking her away from me.

The pain hits hard as I blink back the tears. I'll never want to see her any other way than what I just did. That's the image I want in my mind. My girl, not a tormented thought in her head. Happy, free, and on top of the world. Filled with nothing but joy. She has a couple more numbers to dance, but I take what I just saw because nothing could possibly be better. She gave me perfection, and I decide to leave with that as I walk out, leaving a huge piece of my heart in that theater.

And now I start over because I can't look back. She's happy, and I have to be content with that, no matter how much I wish I could be a part of it.

I wake up the following morning to the smell of bacon and eggs. I lie in bed for a while before getting up to see my mom in the kitchen, fixing us omelets.

"There you are. I was starting to wonder when you would drag yourself down here," she says as she stands over the stove.

"Sorry. I didn't get much sleep last night," I respond as I walk over to fix myself a cup of coffee.

"Wait. Before you do that, you should open your birthday gift," she says with a smile as she nods her head to the dining table where a large box sits, wrapped in gold paper with burgundy ribbon. Tearing the paper, I note the store name on the box and question, "Sur La Table?"

"Just open it," she says as she fixes our plates.

Opening the box, I pull out the De'Longhi cappuccino machine. "This is perfect, Mom."

"Yeah? I figured you'd get good use out of it," she says as she walks past me and sets our plates down on the table.

"It'll give me something to do today, figuring out how to use the damn thing," I joke as I sit down.

"Happy twenty-ninth birthday, darling."

"Thanks."

As we start eating breakfast, she looks up and says, "So, I never saw you last night."

"Yeah, I crashed early. Sorry about that." After I left, I was too upset to even think about seeing my mom, so I spent the evening upstairs.

"Did you go?" she asks.

"I went."

"Do you want to talk about this?"

"No."

I get up and walk into the kitchen to fix my coffee, and when I return to the table, I tell her, "It's done with, Mom. I'm walking away, so there's no point in ever bringing her up again."

Nodding her head, she responds, "Of course, dear."

But I'm not completely walking away because her canvas is still in my closet, and a bottle of her perfume still sits on her side of the sink. It's pathetic, but even though I know I should, I'm not entirely ready to let her completely go just yet.

Another week passes, and while I'm cleaning up my home office, I come across the sheet of paper where Candace wrote down the information for the woman we met at the gallery showing. It's funny that I should run across this now because this past week, I started working more on some of the photos that were stored on my camera. Albeit photos of Candace, but the thought of trying to find someone else to photograph turns my stomach.

Needing to step out of the monotonous routine I have going, I pick up the phone and give this lady a call. She once mentioned being interested in seeing more of my pieces, so why not?

"Henry Gallery."

"Is Stacy Keets available?" I ask.

"One moment."

The line is picked up after a few seconds. "Stacy here."

"Stacy, this is Ryan Campbell. We met at Thinkspace a few months back."

"Yes. I remember. 'Nubile,' right?"

"Right."

"What can I do for you?"

"I have a few pieces that I've been working on if you were still interested in taking a look," I say.

"I'd love to. My time is a bit limited, and I'm about to go on vacation, but I'm free this afternoon, if that isn't too soon?"

"No, that works for me."

"Great. How about three o'clock?"

"Sounds good, Stacy. I'll see you then."

After running up to the bar for a few hours, I head over to the Henry Gallery.

Sitting down in Stacy's office, she says, "I'm glad you called. We actually just had two wall openings become available yesterday."

I hand over my samplings and while she studies them, she keeps her eyes down as she casually says, "Your girlfriend was brilliant last week. You must be so proud of her, huh?"

She says this not having a clue that we're no longer together, but for the moment, it feels good, so I don't correct her, saying, "Yeah. She's amazing."

"She's more than amazing. Sergej has always considered her a prodigy," she says as she flips to the next photo. "Has she gotten many job offers?"

"Umm, I don't really know," I answer honestly, and when she looks up, she says, "Well, I have no doubt that she's gonna have quite a few companies to choose from."

"I'm sure she will."

"And these," she continues as she takes her sleek glasses off and sets them on her desk, "these are really beautiful."

"Thank you."

"Are you being displayed anywhere else at the moment?" she questions.

"No. Didn't really think all too seriously about pursuing anything with these photos until this past week, to be honest."

"Well, I'd be interested in these two, if you'd like to discuss further," she tells me as she sets two of the samples aside and stacks the rest. "Are you optioning a sale?"

"No. I won't sell these," I respond. All these photos are of Candace, and I don't want any of them hanging in some random person's home. They're mine.

"Well, then. Let me look at something really quick," she says as she starts clicking away on her laptop. "I can do a six-week spot showing. It's a good slot because they will be on display during one of our invite-only showings next month. You'll have a lot of eyes on these that could help jumpstart some work if that's a direction you'd like to go."

"That sounds great."

"Perfect, then. Let me go grab all the necessary paperwork, and we can get everything secured for you right now."

Feeling like I've been needing to do something different, have a little more focus, this couldn't have come at a better time. Although I would never sell these particular photos, I'd love to have an opportunity to expand this and possibly take on some work. So we spend the next half hour getting everything set up before I head out, feeling good about this new door that could be opening for me.

chapter forty-three

AFTER STACY SELECTED the two pieces for display a few days ago, I went to have them canvassed and just got back home from dropping them off at the gallery. The wall had already been prepped, and they should be up by tomorrow. It's a good feeling to be doing something that will hopefully bring me some opportunities.

When I start heading back to my office, there's a knock on the door.

"Are you Ryan Campbell?" a guy questions when I answer it.

"Yeah."

He hands over several papers and says, "I've got some legal documents here for you. Are you active military?"

"No."

"Okay. Well, there's no signature required. Have a good day," he tells me before walking down the stairs.

Closing the door, I unfold the papers to find that I've just been served a subpoena, and when I see who the plaintiff is, anger that I haven't felt in a while kicks up. This fucker has a lot of nerve, and I'm about to put an end to this shit, pulling out my phone and calling Jase, who's out of town with Mark right now.

"Hey, Ryan. What's up?

"I need to know where I can find Jack," I demand.

"What?" he asks as I take him off guard.

"I just got served a subpoena, man. Tell me, or I'll just get on the computer and find him myself."

"What are you gonna do?"

"What should have been done months ago," I tell him as my annoyance builds inside of me. "Don't make me ask again," I nearly threaten.

Jase huffs out a hard breath before responding. "He lives at the frat."

"Which one?"

"The Lambda house on nineteenth."

I hang up without saying anything else and grab my keys.

My heart is racing when I pull up in front of the large brick house. There aren't many cars around, and with classes over for the summer, everything is in my favor when I knock and he's the one that answers. The preppy son of a bitch stands there in his white polo as my fist clenches around the court documents in my hand. Looking at his face, you can still see the slight greyish-yellow bruising around his nose and muted pink rings under his eyes where I beat the shit out of him nearly two months ago. There is no doubt that I seriously fucked this guy up.

His eyes are wide as he looks at me in shock, and I don't say a word when I push my way inside, kicking the door shut before I fist his shirt and slam him up against the wall, pinning him with my forearm square across his neck.

I'm seething, and the fear in his eyes is prominent.

"Candace Parker, you know her?" I grit out in pure hate. My muscles tense as I keep him locked against the wall.

He doesn't speak as all the blood drains from his face at the mere mention of her name.

"Yeah, you know her." Backing my weight off, I slam my arm into him again, causing his head to pound against the wall. "You're lucky I didn't fuckin' kill you at the bar."

"Dude," he faintly gasps out in distress, and his voice just adds to my rage.

"Don't think that I'm not still considering it because I'll kill you with my bare hands, and there's not a goddamn thing you can do to stop me because I know you don't want your dirty secret being exposed."

"I don't know what that bitch told you, but I didn't do shit," he spits at me.

Slamming him down to the ground, head smacking hard against the wooden floor, I grip his neck in my hand, yelling, "I was fuckin' there, you sack of shit. Who do you think beat your ass that night? I know everything you did to her, and there's a rape kit with your DNA all over it, so tell me again that you didn't do shit!"

Before he can respond, I pull back and hammer my fist into his nose as he screams out, blood running down his face.

"Don't worry, I'm not gonna kill you. But I am gonna let you go through your life every day wondering if that's going to be the day that I show up, because I'll never let what you did to her go. So you can live your life in fear just like she does every day, you piece of shit."

Striking my fist into his jaw, I stand and pick up the papers that I dropped. I step back over to him as he lies there, curled up in agony, and lean over as I smack the papers on the ground next to his face, telling him, "You're gonna drop these charges today and fuck off."

My veins are on fire with vengeance and knowing that I've got him by the balls on this, I ram my booted foot into his smug-ass face, listening to him heave in pain as I walk out. All my emotions about Candace that I've pushed down these past couple weeks flood back in a matter of seconds. I could kill that fucker, but it still would never feel like enough because even after all this time apart, the hard truth is, I still love her with every part of me. She's moved on, and I have been trying to do the same, but here I am, back in this.

Driving home, fueled by rage laced with sadness, I crack. I've never hated a single thing more than I hate that sick fuck for what he did to my girl. For what he did to us. I lost it all because he's the one that gave me the secret that I held from her. He's the one that inflicted himself on our relationship that no longer is. Without even trying, he continues to cause chaos in our lives.

After spending a good chunk of the day taking my lingering aggravation out at the gym, I'm finally able to settle my nerves and calm down. I have no doubt that the charges will be dropped, so I'll give it a few days before calling to make sure there isn't anything pending against me.

I've been trying to keep my mind occupied with anything other than Candace and what happened this morning, so when I'm completely burnt out from watching TV, I head upstairs to get ready for bed.

It's after one in the morning when I hear a knock on my door after brushing my teeth. When I make my way back down, I peek out the windows to see who could be here this late, but there's no car in the drive as the rain pours down. I unlock the door, and I swear to God, the whole world stops moving when I open it to see Candace. In an instant, she begins crying and falls into my arms. She's soaking wet from the rain, and I know she had to have walked here.

For this moment, I lose my breath in her as I feel the warmth I thought I would never feel again. A warmth that only she can give me. She clings to me as she cries, and I break for her, not knowing what to say because I'm afraid if I speak, she'll leave. She's here, and all I want to do is make sure that she stays.

God, just stay.

Reaching down, I slip my arm behind her knees and scoop her into my arms as I carry her inside. She keeps her head tucked into me, and I've missed this so much. Even with her hurting, for whatever reason, I miss it. The touch, the feel of her skin, the smell of her hair. I have it all wrapped up in my arms, and it's where I want to keep it.

I sit us down on the couch with her still in my lap, and I keep my arms tightly banded around her because I just can't let her go. I listen to her sobs as they begin to soften into whimpers, feeling the soft quakes of her body as she takes in tiny gasps of air.

"Baby, what happened?" I finally ask, and when she lifts her head and stares into my eyes, I fall for her all over again. It's in my heart, the heavy weighted emotion that's nothing but the love I have for this beautiful girl.

Needing to touch her, I reach up and run my fingers down the soft skin of her cheek.

"Jack died tonight."

What did she just say?

Suddenly my heavy heart takes on a pounding as questions brew inside. What the hell happened after I saw him this morning? Fuck! Did I do it? Did I kick him too hard in the head? I could have easily killed him. Panic shoots through me, cold like ice, but the sudden rush of fear is diminished when she says, "Kimber called and told me he died in a car crash earlier today. Drunk driving accident or something."

A hard breath thuds out of my chest. Relief. Maybe I'm sick, but there's not a single piece of me that feels bad about this. But her? She's so upset, and I have to wonder where her head is at with this.

She's so close in my arms, tears still streaking down her face, and when I rest my forehead against hers, greedy to take every touch I can, she begins to ramble, an emotional mess.

"I'm sorry. I didn't know where to go. I'm so confused. I don't know what's wrong with me."

"Slow down, babe."

"Should I be happy? Or relieved?" she asks as she pulls her head back and looks at me, pleading for answers I don't have.

"Well, what do you feel right now?"

"Sad. And hurt," she admits honestly before dropping her head and adding, "I don't know why. It's like all I can think about is Jack when he was good. Or when I thought he was. But I know he wasn't. I know I should hate him. But, if I'm sad, does that mean I don't hate him?"

Lifting her chin to look at me, I say, "I think you're just in shock. I think you need a little time to sort this out in your head." She rests her head back on my shoulder, and I feel her body lightly shivering under my arms. "Let me go get you a towel. You're freezing."

She slips off of my lap as I grab a couple of large towels from the guest bathroom, and when I return, I wrap one of them around her shoulders and then pull her back into my arms.

"You need anything to drink?"

She sits up, and I lose her touch as she clutches the towel around her, shaking her head no. I reach to her again and slowly pull her back against me. I'm selfish, but I don't care. I've missed her so much. No matter how hard I try to give up on her, I just can't. I bury it and keep myself busy enough to where I don't think about her. But she's always there, lying beneath, deep inside of me where I'm starting to believe she will always be. It's like she's the other half of me. The half that would make life miserable if I didn't have it, so I've always kept it. It's not even a choice.

"Talk to me," I urge.

"I'm sorry. I didn't even realize I was here until I was in front of your door."

"I'm glad you're here," I tell her before I move to hold her face in my hands, trying to keep myself together when I let her know, "I've missed you so much."

My words hurt coming out of me, a confession that shouldn't be because she should just know, but I tell her anyway. The thought of her walking away from me now that I have her here in my home, in my hands, and so fuckin' deep in my heart makes it hard to breathe right now. But she gives me hope, a hope I thought was forever lost, when I look into her eyes that are rimmed red with tears and she touches me. She gives me her soft hand as she places it on my face and runs it down my jaw, and then she crumbles. With her eyes shut, she chokes on the sobs that break through.

"Baby, don't cry."

Leaning in, I kiss her forehead, simply resting my lips against her. I need every second of this as I feel her coming back to me, until she pulls away, shaking her head, and then the knife strikes when she whispers, "I can't."

"Babe."

"I can't. It hurts so bad, I just can't."

"I swear to you," I beg because that's all I have at this point. "I will never hurt you again."

"But you swore you wouldn't hurt me before and you did."

Lowering my head to look her in the eyes straight on, I affirm, "I love you. God, I love you so much," as I move in, holding her face in my hands, and gently graze my lips across hers, tasting the sweetest thing I've ever had.

"I'm moving," she breathes against my lips, and her words echo in my head. A painful reality that I knew would come, but to have it here when I finally have her, is something I don't want to face.

I shift back to look at her, not wanting to accept her words, when she says, "I got a job. I'm moving to New York in two weeks."

Dropping my head, I feel the panic in me. The finality of this has never been more tangible than it is right now, and it's a sharp blade in my heart. A slow bleed that bears the agony of an unrelenting suffering.

"You can't kiss me," she says as a new slew of tears starts. "If you do . . . I'll never want to leave you."

"Then I'll come with you."

"Ryan . . . I just can't. I'm too scared you'll hurt me again. I just need to be on my own. I've been working so hard to pull myself out of the hell I've been living in."

"I know you have. I ask Jase about you all the time. He's told me how well you're doing. I just wish I could be around to see it, babe," I choke out around the knot in my throat that I can no longer fight as I drop my head and cry. Cry for what we once had. We were so good and happy. Completely in love and bound together in a way I never thought two people could be. But we were, and I don't think something like that comes around too often.

"All I ever wanted was for you to be okay, to be happy," I tell her.

"I'm okay."

She lets me hold on to her, so I do. Scared to let go of her because I know what it means when I finally do, and it's a pain I'm not ready to feel. So I let time pass as I keep her tucked into me, her head nestled in the curve of my neck, the feel of her damp hair against my skin, the smell of her soft scent that filters into my lungs . . . my senses consumed with her, and then comes sound as she finally speaks.

"Do you think you could drive me home?"

"Yeah," I whisper, wondering how you say goodbye to someone like her. But I find happiness in one thing, and that is, after all we have been through and all the time that has passed, she ran to me for the comfort that she needed.

I let my tears fall as I drive her home, and with each glance over, I see her own stained face. My gut is in knots, and with my eyes on the road ahead, I ask, as desperate as a man could, because I have nothing else, "Tell me how to fight for you."

"Please," is her only response, spoken softly, pleading for me not to push any more.

When I pull up to her house, I turn to her and ask, "Can I walk you in?"

"Ryan."

Nodding my head, I get it. I see the pain in her eyes, but when she turns to grab the handle, I give her my last attempt to let her know, "I'll never love anyone the way that I love you."

She looks back at me, tears streaming, and she nods. Without words I hear what she's telling me, and I hate that she's denying us something we both know is great. She feels my words too, and having the knowledge that she feels the same way about loving me makes this all the worse. With the click of the handle, she steps out as I hear her crying begin to crack though, and the sound is excruciating.

And that's it.

She's gone.

chapter forty-four

"HOW IS IT that you're so good with Bennett?" Traci asks me as I lay him down on the floor on his blanket.

"Because for the past five years my cousins have been pushing out babies," I tell her.

Max returned to work this past week, and he wanted me to stop by and check on Traci. He told me she was freaking out about being alone with the baby, so I decided to bring my camera along to take some photos of Bennett for her.

"Can you turn off the light? I just need the natural light right now."

"Yeah, sure," she says as she flips the lights off.

The sun is shining today, making it perfect for these pictures. Bennett is asleep as I adjust him before bringing the camera to my eye and taking a few shots then moving him into a different pose.

"Thanks for doing this."

"No problem. I wasn't doing anything today, so I'm glad I have the distraction," I tell her because I feel like I just went back in time a few months, and I'm feeling the loss of Candace all over again.

"Max is worried about you," she says, and when I look up at her, I say, "Is that so?"

Tilting her head at me, she adds, "Yeah, that's so."

"Tell him I'm fine. Life is full of shit. It's nothing that I'm not used to."

"That's a depressing outlook."

Sitting back on my heels, I scan through the photos I just took as I say, "Not everybody gets what they want, Traci."

"There's probably someone else out there that you're gonna want more; you just haven't met her yet."

"I'm not so sure about that."

"Ryan," Traci says to get my attention as she sits on the floor next to Bennett and me. "We've all lost someone we loved only to find that it wasn't as deep of a love as we had thought when we finally find *the one*."

"Is Max *the one*?"

She looks at her son and smiles when she says, "Yeah."

"And there's never been a question or hesitation about it?"

Turning back to me, she tells me, "No."

"And what about the others you thought you loved? Any hesitation there?"

When she nods her head yes, I add, "That's the difference here. Never was there a question or hesitation. And she wasn't just someone I loved."

She doesn't respond as I lie down next to Bennett with my camera to get some close-ups of his facial features. Traci and I have gotten to know each other better since the baby came along, and I started spending more time over here at their house. At first, I was just trying to keep myself busy, but in the process, I've connected with Traci, and Max and I have become closer as well. I have a good bond with Jase, and even Mark, but it's hard to be around them at times because it only reminds me of how it used to be. But having this with two people that don't have that connection with Candace gives me a reprieve.

I head up to the bar to give Max the prints of the photos I took of his son a few days ago, and when I walk in, I see Jase sitting at the bar, talking to Mel.

"Hey, Ryan. I didn't think you were coming in today," Mel says as I walk over to them.

"I just needed to drop some stuff off with Max," I tell her and then look at Jase, asking, "How are you doing, man?"

"Good. Just waiting on Mark to get out of an interview."

"How's all that going?"

"I got a job offer yesterday, so I'm good to go. Just hoping that Mark gets this one because it's the firm he really wants," he tells me.

"Congrats, man. That's great. So when do you start?"

"Next week."

Knowing that Candace should be moving soon, I ask because I guess I like to torture myself, "When does she move?"

I don't even need to say her name when he tells me, "Friday morning."

It's hard to imagine that she'll be in New York City, all alone, in three days. It's always been her dream to dance with the company that she signed on with, and I'm happy that she's doing this for her and no one else. It's something she's always wanted and to have this opportunity in life, to see your dreams through, is an amazing thing, and I'm so proud of her. I honestly never thought she would ever move away like she is, all by herself. It's hard for me to imagine her in a place where she's okay to do this on her own. The girl that was always so scared of crowds and going out. Timid and paranoid. I worry about her.

"Could you do me a favor?" I ask.

"Yeah."

"Are you taking her to the airport?"

When he nods his head yes, I ask, "Will you give me a call when she's gone?"

The pity in his eyes irritates me, but I expect it. There's no doubt that this girl makes me weak. She always has. She softened me up because she was so delicate, and I loved that about her, that she could do that to me.

"You sure?" Jase asks.

"I'm sure."

"Alright," he says as he stands up. "I gotta get going. Mark should be at my place soon."

As he walks out, Mel comes back over after giving the two of us space to talk.

"Mel," I sigh out on an exasperated breath.

"You look like you need a drink."

"When did life get so damn depressing?" I ask her with a slight laugh.

"You're asking me?" she responds as she hands me a beer. "All I know is, I'm over it."

Her expression mirrors mine, and I know something is weighing on her.

"Talk to me."

The place is dead with it being early in the day, so she takes a seat next to me.

"Zane wants a divorce," she tells me.

"What?"

She nods and says, "Yeah. I got the papers a few days ago."

"Shit," I mutter. "I'm sorry."

When she shrugs her shoulders, she tells me, "We just grew apart, you know? Maybe it was me. Music was always his life; I just never thought that he would make anything big out of it, so I never considered it in our path in life. But that's not the life I want."

"So now what?"

"I don't know," she mumbles.

Taking a swig of my beer, I say, "Yeah, me neither."

It's Friday, and I'm sitting around dreading the call that I asked for. *Why do I do this shit to myself?* I tried to keep busy by working on some photo editing from a shoot I was hired to do for a portfolio, but my head just wasn't in it. So now I'm killing the minutes, surfing around on the internet when my cell finally rings, causing a quick drop in my gut.

Seeing Jase's name on the screen, I take the call that I should have never sought.

"Hey," I say quietly.

"Hey, man. I just got back to my apartment. Sorry it took so long to call; I had to take Kimber back home."

"So you got her dropped off?"

"Yeah. She should be boarding now."

"How was she?" I ask.

"Nervous as expected, but this is what she's been working so hard for, so I know she's excited."

Feeling the welling of sadness, I rush off the phone, needing to just drown in this for a while.

"Thanks for calling, I'll catch you later," I tell him before hanging up and leaning back in my desk chair as I stare up at the ceiling.

I'm completely drained, and to finally have the book closed on this may be what I've been needing. With her on the other side of the country, maybe I can finally let it go. Let go of the hope that died months ago when I woke up to find her gone. The hope I was determined to keep alive when it was already dead.

Needing to get out of the house. I start heading upstairs to change my clothes for a run, but as soon as I hit the top step, there's a ringing at my door. I look out the windows and see a cab pulling out of my driveway, and when I go back downstairs to open the door, all that hope comes back to life.

She's beautiful, even though she's crying, as she stands on my doorstep.

"What are you doing here? I just got off the phone with Jase. He said he dropped you off at the airport."

"I can't go. I'm so sorry. I can't do it," she cries and with each word I feel the ever-vacant part of my heart filling up.

"What do you mean you can't do it?"

"Because . . . I love you too much to leave. And I miss you. And I made a huge mistake by leaving you. I'm so sorry," she continues to cry, and I don't even waste a second, pulling her into my arms where she was always meant to be.

"Baby, you didn't make any mistakes."

"I did. And I know I hurt you. But, I'm so sorry. I can't go because I can't leave you. I don't want to leave you."

Pulling her inside and taking her to the couch, I feel the weight of what she's doing pile on, and tell her, "I can't let you give up on your dream. I can't."

"But, it's not my dream," she says in her unwavering confessions. "I was just hanging on to it because I was scared to see that it really wasn't what I wanted. It's you. It's always been you."

Covering her lips with mine, I hold on to her as she climbs onto my lap, straddling her legs across me, and gives me what I've been dying for. I kiss her hard, in disbelief that this is even happening.

"I've missed you so much, babe," I tell her when I pull back and look into her eyes. "You have no fucking idea."

"I love you. I'm sorry I've been so stupid and wasted all this time when all I really wanted was to be here with you."

"You have nothing to be sorry for. I fucked up. I hurt you, and you'll never know how much I regret it."

"I don't blame you, Ryan. I did, but I don't anymore. I just want to be with you."

Her words mend all that was broken inside of me, and I cling to each one, desperate for this, and tell her, "I don't ever want to lose you again."

"You won't. I'm yours."

That's all I need to hear. I don't give a shit that it took her this long to realize it because I have her.

She's mine.

This time when I kiss her, I bring her in slow because I intend on taking my time to make up for all that we lost. With her soft lips pressed against mine, I'm taken back to a place where the pain of losing her doesn't exist. With her hands on my face, I stand, picking her up with me as she loops her legs around me. When I get her upstairs, I lay her down on the bed, needing the smell of her all over my sheets—all over me.

Hovering over her, I slip off my shirt, and when I do, she slowly sits up as I rest back on my heels. I watch as she takes her hand and brushes her fingers along my scar. A scar that doesn't even amount to the pain I felt when I lost her.

She tilts her head back to look up at me, and I tell her, "I couldn't breathe without you."

"I need you."

And so I give her me, every little piece. She doesn't even need to ask because I've always been hers, even when I tried so hard not to be, to move on and put her in the past. I could never do it because she's always had me.

Lying on top of her, I press the weight of myself onto her to feel her softness beneath me. She runs her hands from my wrists, up my arms, and to my shoulders before she lets them fall above her head. Comfortable, as if she's saying 'have me.' Taking the hem of her silk top, I slowly slip it off of her body and toss it onto the floor.

Everything about her is familiar, and I need the comfort of her as I use my hands to reacquaint. Sliding them down her neck, over her lace-covered breasts, and down her stomach. Her breathing quickens along with my pulse as I undo her pants and slide them down her legs. *God, her legs.* After discarding my pants, I return to her, pulling the sheets over us, needy to trap her heat to me. She slips her arms around my neck when I reach around to remove her bra.

The warmth of her naked body with mine, we linger in the moment, touching, kissing, and exploring what we've been missing with each other. I'd go through the ache of these past few months all over again just to be with her like this. Nothing compares to this feeling of peace that she's able to give me. She's the one who allowed me to find myself, and without her I didn't know who I was.

Dragging my head down the length of her, I kiss my way back up her stomach, underneath her breast, and I slide my tongue over her nipple before sucking her into my mouth, pressing my tongue against her pert bud. She releases a heady breath into the air, moving her body as the passion takes over us. When I reach down, needing to reclaim everything we had taken our time working up to, I gently run my hand between her legs, touching her intimately. She doesn't push me away when she lets go of a soft moan as I feel how ready for me she is.

Spreading her legs apart, I settle myself between the heat of her thighs. Gazing at her, naked beneath me, bared to each other and coming out of the agony that's loomed over us, I see all I'll ever want.

"God, you're so beautiful."

She pulls me down to kiss her, sealing her mouth with mine. Her kisses are deep and purposeful, laced with an intent that settles my heart in hers, filling up the joy that I've been without. She's my happiness. She's the light in my life and without her, I was lost, but now . . . having her giving this all back to me, it's elated every part of my soul. We're completely wrapped up in each other as I guide myself inside of her, never breaking our kisses. The connection is intense, both of us claiming the other as our own but in the most unselfish way a human can as we give ourselves entirely to the other.

Her grip tightens on me, and I push myself deeper inside of her causing her body to bow up into mine, head pressed into the pillow beneath her. As she rolls her head back, I drag my mouth up her exposed neck before I flip us over and sit up to keep our bodies close, with her legs draped on either side of me. Wrapping my hands around the back of her small shoulders, I press her down on me as she rocks her hips into me in response.

When she grabs my shoulders, she begins to slowly roll herself over me. My breathing is heavy as I drop my head down to her chest, kissing and sucking lightly. We move slowly, taking our time with each other.

Gripping her bottom, I guide her as she begins to stagger as emotions flood over. She tangles her hands in my hair and looks into my eyes as she begins to cry, but I have no worry because I know she's safe with me. Vulnerable, exposed, but entirely safe in my touch.

Our eyes remain locked as I feel her body trembling on top of mine. She rocks her hips over me as she's finding her release. And as my body parallels her, I reach the peak of my build.

"Let go, baby," I breathe out and she drops her head to mine, eyes hooded, tears falling, but they never leave mine.

Running my hand up her damp back, she falls apart in my arms. Body quaking against mine, and I explode into a thousand pieces beneath her as our moans fill the room, taking every bit of pleasure we can while we continue to move with each other, my fingers pressing into her delicate skin as she writhes against me.

Movements begin to slow and she kisses me, pressing her face, wet with tears, against mine. The beating of my heart is strong, and my emotions are in overdrive when I focus on what just happened. Making love to the girl I thought I'd lost. It overpowers me as I lay us down, keeping myself buried inside of her.

With my lips on hers, we continue to kiss as I hear her whimpers, and I know she feels it too.

"Babe."

Pulling back, she takes her time before choking out, "I never want to know what life is without you."

"You won't ever have to."

As I keep her folded up in my arms, she cries, releasing the pain we've been through to get here. I let her get it out, and she eventually grows tired, falling asleep in my arms, the only arms I ever want her to have around her because it's within them that she will always have a safe place to fall.

chapter forty-five

WHEN I FEEL the bed shift, I begin to wake, and as I open my eyes, I catch a glimpse of Candace walking into the bathroom, wearing my t-shirt. I'm not sure what happened to make her heart shift back to me. The whirlwind of emotions when she showed up at my door a few hours ago are now replaced with sated contentment, but also questions.

I watch her flick on the light, but she doesn't close the door. She stands there, and it isn't until I step out of bed and walk up to her, that I see what she's looking at. I couldn't ever get rid of her things that I kept the day Jase came over to pack up her stuff. I had the necklace repaired, and it has always sat on the sink counter next to her bottle of perfume.

I slip my arms around her waist from behind and she stands there, running her finger along the etched words: *And though she be but little, she is fierce.* Her eyes meet mine in the reflection of the mirror before I tell her, "I could never let you go."

I take her necklace and clasp it back around her neck, where it's always belonged. Turning around in my arms, she rests her hands on my chest as she hangs her head down, saying, "I'm so sorry."

Not wanting her to regret a single choice that she has made, I tell her, "Come here," as I take her back to bed. I sit against the headboard and pull her next to me before asking, "What could you possibly be sorry for?"

"Leaving you. Hurting you." She takes in a shaky breath as her emotions get to her and she tells me, "I hated every second I wasn't with you. I wanted to come back . . . I was just scared."

"I'm the only one who has something to apologize for."

"But I get it," she says. "It took me a while to see it, but I understand."

We sit there for a moment, quiet, with her head rested against me when she finally says, "I feel like I have so many questions."

"I know, babe."

"I never knew we had so many holes."

"So let's fill them in," I tell her as she looks up at me.

"I don't know where to begin," she says as she shifts down, and I move with her as we lie on our sides under the covers.

With her face only inches from mine, I brush her hair back and whisper, "I love you, babe. I don't want there to be any uncertainty about anything between us. You can ask me anything, and I swear I'll tell you whatever you want to know, but I also feel like I have missing pieces of you that I need."

She nods her head and closes her eyes when she softly says, "I didn't know anyone was there that night. That anyone saw me like that." When she opens her eyes, she asks, "What happened?"

I know we both need to hash everything out, and as hard as this conversation may get, it's one that needs to happen. I'll spend days in this bed with her, filling in all the blanks, just so we can have nothing between us but fleshed out honesty.

"I was working late that night," I begin as I hold her hand that's rested between our chests because I know this is going to be difficult for her to hear. "I heard noises outside but ignored it. There are so many people who cut through the back lot, and I figured it was just some drunken college kids." I take a moment as the guilt creeps in and then confess, "I'm so sorry. You were out there the whole time, and I just ignored it." The pain of my words to her is something I don't think I will ever be able to get rid of.

She's silent as tears begin to roll off the side of her face. Wiping them away, I continue, "It wasn't until I heard you screaming that I ran out. I swear I moved as fast as I could, but . . . by the time I made it out . . ." I'm scared to continue because I don't know if I should say anything else, knowing how bad this will hurt her to hear. "Baby, are you sure you wanna hear this?"

"I feel like I need to." Her hand is tightly clenched around mine when she asks, "What did you see?"

Letting out a sigh, I reveal, "You were naked and covered in blood and dirt." I choke around the words, and she begins to whimper as she tries to hold in her cries. "He had his hand between your legs, and you were screaming, then all of a sudden, he punched you in the side of your head and knocked you out. It all happened so fast. In a second, I pulled him off of you and beat the shit out of him, but I couldn't hold on to him and he fled. I stayed with you—"

"While I was naked?" she asks out of embarrassment.

"I had covered you up with my shirt. But I saw your tattoo. That's how I knew the connection."

"But how did you not know before?"

"I thought it could be you, but I had such a hard time after seeing what I did that I just figured my head was playing with me. Trying to trick me into thinking it was you," I tell her. "When I saw you the first time at your work, it was my initial thought. The girl from that night was so tiny, and so was the girl in the coffee shop. Max tried telling me my mind was just trying to put closure to everything."

"Max knows?"

Nodding my head, I gently tell her, "Yeah, babe, he does. I had told him about what happened at the bar because he was head of security and needed to know, and then I told him about the girl in the coffee shop because I was really screwed up about it. I never thought I'd fall in love with you; it wasn't like I told him behind your back, he just always knew everything. Then once I saw your tattoo and put it together, we never spoke about it again. And I swear we never have."

"God," she breathes out. "I'm so embarrassed."

"Babe, you have nothing to be embarrassed about," I try telling her, but I know my words are weak in comparison to her feelings about this.

"It's humiliating, Ryan."

Running my hand through her hair, I say, "You're the most beautiful person I've ever met. No one could even come close to how genuine you are, and I swear to you, that's all people see when they look at you, including Max."

"Does anyone else know?"

"Only my mom."

"Why would you tell her?" she cries, mortified.

"She heard us when we were at her house, and you were upset, telling me that you blamed yourself for what happened. She thought we were fighting. I was upset after you fell asleep, and we were talking downstairs. Again, she knew about what I saw before I ever met you, and I felt like I needed someone to talk to. I probably never should have said anything to her, but my own guilt about not getting to you faster was eating away at me, and then seeing how hurt you were, thinking it was your fault . . . it killed me."

I hold her close as she wraps her arm around my neck, clinging on to me as I continue to hold her hand.

"All I ever wanted to do was protect you, and the one moment you needed me the most, I let you down. If only I would have gone out there when I first heard the noises, but I didn't, and I'm so sorry, baby." I take a moment before I tell her, "I couldn't stop thinking about you and what had happened after the ambulance took you to the hospital."

She loosens her hold around my neck and wipes her face as she takes a deep breath.

"I know I shouldn't ask," I say. "But . . . what happened that night?"

"It was a mess," she quickly responds and then takes a pause before she continues. "I didn't even like him, and I had only gone out with him that night so that I could talk to him." Never letting go of my hand, she tells me, "There was a party at his frat house, and he had gotten mad at me for leading him on. He had thrown me into a wall and pinned me against it. We fought, and I ran out. But he drove me, and I didn't have my phone, so I . . ."

She trails off, and I suddenly feel bad for asking her. "You don't have to tell me."

"I need to."

"Why?"

She drops her head before she eventually brings it back up, telling me, "My therapist keeps telling me I should talk about it."

I don't say anything else. I just keep her tucked into me when she eventually starts to speak again, and I listen as she tells me how he chased her down, beat the shit out of her, and raped her. Hearing her tell me the hell he put her through is gut-wrenching. I don't know how anyone could ever come out of something like that without an insane amount of damage. Knowing how violent he was with her makes me want to hide her away forever, but I can't do that. So I lie here and cry for her. For everything that little shit took away from her.

"Were you going to press charges? Is that why you were talking to that detective?" I ask after a while.

"Maybe. I don't know. I never planned on it, but then when I was packing I came across his card he had given me in the hospital. I guess I was more curious than anything," she explains.

"After all of this, if he were still alive, do you think you would?"

"Would you think I was weak if I said no?"

"Baby, there's nothing about you that I find weak," I tell her. Of course I would want her to fight and press charges, but I'm not the one who was stripped of all my trust, so I understand the need to avoid it. Who'd want to go back and relive what she had to endure? She fights in her own quiet way. Most probably don't even see it. I didn't used to, but I do now.

I roll onto my back, and she shifts her head into the crook of my arm. "When did you start seeing a therapist?"

"A couple days after you came by to talk to me. I just . . . I was so miserable. I didn't know what else to do."

Kissing the top of her head, I tell her, "I'm glad you have someone you can talk to. You think it's helping?"

"I think so. I mean, she's helping me see things a little clearer. We've been focusing on my anxiety and pointing out my triggers. She wants me to put myself in situations that tend to make me panic. I've tried a couple of times, but it's hard," she says.

"It's gonna be, but it'll get easier, babe."

"She wants me to stop taking my sleeping pills."

I run my hand up her arm and around her shoulder, asking, "Are you going to?"

"I told her I wasn't ready. She said she wouldn't push it but that I should think about it."

"I know you're scared, but they're just dreams."

"Dreams that feel completely real. And stress always triggers all that stuff, and with everything that's been going on . . . graduation, packing, the production . . . *you*. It was all too much."

"I know. You don't have to explain. I get it," I tell her. "But what about

New York?"

"What about it?"

Turning to look at her, I say, "You don't have to give it up. I'll go with you. It's not a big deal. I was already planning on moving anyway."

"What?" she questions, confused.

"It's one of the main reasons why I replaced Michael with Max at the bar. I figured you'd be moving and there was no way I wasn't going with you."

"Why didn't you ever say anything?"

"I didn't want to stress you out. You had so much going on. I kept waiting for you to bring it up, but you never did, so I just started getting everything worked out on my end," I tell her as she shakes her head.

"I had no idea."

I let out a light laugh and say, "You didn't think I'd let you leave without me, did you?"

"Honestly? I didn't know. I didn't bring it up because I was scared I *would* have to leave without you. I didn't know what I was going to do, but I knew I wouldn't be able to leave you," she admits. "But I'm going to stay here. I called Pacific Northwest Ballet. I had originally turned down their offer, but I called them when I left the airport, and the spot is still mine. I go in on Monday to sign all the papers."

"You don't have to do that. You can still have New York."

"I'm not ready for it," she says softly. "I thought I was, but I think I was just forcing it. To prove to myself that I could go there on my own and be okay. But I need to be here. This is my home, with you, Jase and Mark, and everything that I'm used to," she tells me. "I want to get better, and I want to do that here where I have the support."

"Are you sure?"

"I'm not saying no to New York, I'm just saying no for right now."

I finally let go of her hand to cup her face before bringing her to my lips. She holds on to my wrists as I move my lips over hers, giving her only a couple long and slow kisses before pulling back, and saying, "I love you so much."

She runs her hand behind my neck and whispers, "I love you too," before our lips meet again. But before I can lose myself in her, she pulls away. "Oh my God," she draws out.

"What's wrong?"

"All of my stuff—everything—is already in New York. I've gotta call the landlord from my apartment there. I shipped everything last week."

"Don't worry about it. I'll take care of all that. Did you have luggage?" I ask.

"Yeah, I had already checked it," she says with worry.

"I'll call the airlines. Don't stress about it. We'll get everything shipped back," I tell her, but I'm not letting her move back in with Kimber. I have her here with me, and I don't want any more space between us, so I add, "But babe, when I arrange everything, I'm having it shipped here."

She nods her head, not picking up on what I'm saying, so I clarify, "Here to my loft." When I see her pinch her brows together, I say, "I want you here. With me."

"Move in?"

"Yeah. Move in. I don't want to be apart from you."

The smile that grows on her lips is beautiful, and I can't help myself when I kiss her.

"God, I missed that smile," I say. "It's been too long."

"So that's it?" she questions.

"That's it," I give her. "I want this to be your home. Here with me."

She wraps her body around me, hugging me close when she whispers in my ear, "Thank you."

"For what?"

"Everything."

After talking everything out this afternoon, Candace was drained and had a headache, so I gave her some aspirin, and she's been upstairs sleeping for the past hour. I go ahead and make all the phone calls to arrange for her belongings to be shipped back here. Her luggage should be at the airport tomorrow morning, so at least she'll have her clothes.

It's amazing how quickly everything can change. One minute, I thought I'd lost her and the next, she's back here and agreeing to move in with me. But I don't want to waste any more time. I want to pick up where we left off, and it seems she wants the exact same thing.

When I notice the sun starting to set, I call in an order for dinner at the little Italian place down the street that Candace likes so much, figuring she could use a solid meal after the day she's had. As I set the phone down, I hear a ringing from Candace's purse that's lying on the coffee table. I pull out her phone and answer it when I see that it's Jase calling.

"Hey."

"Ryan?" he asks.

"Yeah."

"Sorry, man. I thought I was calling Candace but accidentally dialed you," he says.

"No, this is Candace's phone."

"Huh?"

"She's here," I tell him, and I know he's completely thrown off when he questions, "What do you mean she's there?"

"After you called me this morning, she showed up at my door. She didn't get on the plane. She's been here ever since."

"What happened? Is she not going?"

Sitting down on the couch, I tell him, "No. She's staying. She took the spot at PNB."

"Is she happy?"

"She's happy," I say before letting him know, "She's moving in."

"With you?"

"Yeah."

He takes a pause before saying, "I knew she'd make the right choice."

Laughing, I say, "She nearly destroyed me in the process."

He begins to laugh with me, and then asks, "Can I talk to her?"

"She has a headache and is sleeping right now."

"Just have her give me a call later, okay?"

"No problem."

"I'm really happy you guys worked things out. She wasn't the same without you."

"Thanks, man. You've been a really good friend to me."

"No thanks needed. You guys have a good night and give her a kiss for me. I didn't know what I was going to do without her."

"Me neither. Talk to you later," I say before we hang up.

Walking upstairs, I step into the bedroom and look at the only love I ever want to know, curled up in my sheets. She's peaceful and quiet as she sleeps. She needs this after the emotional day she's had. We spent hours in this bed, hashing everything out, filling in all the gaps, and settling all the questions. But it needed to happen, and finally, for the first time, everything feels whole.

chapter forty-six

CANDACE AND I finally drag ourselves downstairs for some much needed coffee after making love all morning. I'll never get my fill of her, and I made sure she knew that.

She's a little needy this morning, but I like that. I've missed that—her need to have me close. It's to be expected with everything going on, so I hold her hand as we walk downstairs and into the kitchen.

"All I have is milk, babe. We'll have to stop by the store to get you your creamer and stock up on groceries."

"When did you get this?" she questions, and when I look over to her, she's checking out the cappuccino machine.

"My mom. She got it for my birthday."

"Birthday?"

Grabbing the milk to pour into her coffee, I say, "Yeah."

"When was your birthday?" she asks as I hand her the mug and head over to the couch.

"Last month. May nineteenth."

"Oh," she says with a twinge of sadness.

"Babe, don't let it bother you. It's really not a big deal."

Taking her eyes off of her mug, she looks up at me as she rests her back against the arm of the couch and says, "It does bother me. I feel like I've missed so much time with you."

"You weren't missing much. Nothing happened. Everything was literally in slow motion the whole time."

"I still feel bad that I wasn't here for your birthday."

Setting my coffee down on the end table, I take hers as well, setting it aside as I pull her over to me and fold her in my arms. "None of that matters, so just forget it, okay?"

"I can't just forget it."

"Would it make you feel better if I told you that I was with you on my birthday?"

She pops her head up and stares at me with question. "What do you mean?"

"I saw you the night before," I tell her. "I went to see you dance."

"You were there?"

"Nothing would have kept me from seeing you that night," I tell her and then kiss her forehead. "You were amazing. I couldn't take my eyes off of you."

"I didn't think you were there. I saw your mom afterward, but I had no clue."

"You saw my mom?"

"Yeah. I ran into her as I was leaving."

"She never told me that," I say, but then remember telling my mom that we weren't going to mention Candace again. I never gave her a chance to tell me.

"I felt awful."

"Why? What did she say?"

"All the right things, but it was hard to see her because I was missing her. She drove all that way and then I told her that I needed space. It just hurt too much," she explains.

"I know she wasn't expecting anything. She just really wanted to see you dance. I told her not to come, but she insisted."

"I miss her," she says as she rests her head on my shoulder. "I feel like I should apologize or something."

"For what?" I ask with a light chuckle. "You didn't do anything, babe. If anyone should be apologizing, it's me, so stop thinking that you did something wrong, 'cause you didn't."

She nods her head, unconvinced, but I don't push. Instead, I offer, "Why don't we go visit her in a couple of weeks for Fourth of July weekend?"

Her smile shows off her dimple when she says, "I'd like that."

"I'll give her a call later today."

"Speaking of calls, I need to call Kimber. My car is at her parents' house. We should probably go pick it up today."

"I'm gonna go grab a shower, so why don't you call her, and we can pick it up after we go to the airport to get your bags."

"I don't have any clothes," she tells me. "Maybe Jase can bring me some. Crap!"

"What?"

"I was supposed to call Jase when I got to New York last night. He doesn't know I'm here," she panics.

"He does. I talked to him yesterday when you were napping. I just forgot to tell you."

"You talked to him? What did he say?"

Giving her a smirk, I tell her, "He said he was glad you made the right choice."

She pokes me in the ribs as she whines, "No he didn't."

"I swear, he did," I laugh and then stand up. "Make your phone calls.

I'm gonna go get ready."

Once I'm out of the shower and dressed, Candace walks into the room and says, "Jase is on his way."

"Did you get in touch with Kimber?"

Flopping down on the bed, she says, "Yeah. Her parents aren't home, but she gave me the code to the garage," in a dull voice.

Walking over to the bed, I look down at her and ask, "What's wrong?"

"She just doesn't get it."

"Get what?"

Candace sits up and tells me, "She said that I was throwing everything away. She was annoyed when I told her I wasn't gonna move back in with her. It's just hard because she doesn't know you. All she saw was how upset I was when we weren't together. She knows that you kept that secret from me, but she doesn't know how far I've come this year and that it was mostly because of you. She never saw how bad it was, and now all she has is this tainted idea of you."

"Maybe she just needs time to get to know us together."

"But I feel like she doesn't even know me. We used to be close, but so much has happened this year, and she wasn't around," she says. "I'm just . . ." She drops her head when she admits, "I'm not the same person. I wish I could be, but I'm just not."

"That's not a bad thing like I know you're thinking it is. The cause of it is the only thing that's bad. But it's like I told you before, there isn't a damn thing about who you are now that you should be ashamed of. You're perfect to me," I tell her, and I can see that she still struggles with this concept, but I'll keep reminding her every day if I have to.

We're interrupted when the doorbell rings, and Candace jumps off the bed, saying, "Jase is here," as she flies down the stairs.

When I make it to the top of the stairs, she is already in his arms. I smile at the sight of her as I start making my way down.

"So what the hell happened after I dropped you off?" he asks her as I take the bag out of his hand and set it by the stairs.

"I realized that all my worries about leaving were more about my fears of losing Ryan than they were of moving to New York," she tells him as she sits on the couch, and I walk over to join her.

"So now what?" he asks as he takes a seat in the chair.

"I'm gonna sign with PNB on Monday."

"So, no New York?"

"Not right now," she says. "I feel like I need more time here, where I'm comfortable. I just want to put the past few months behind me and have things settled again."

"You talk to Kimber?"

"A little bit ago. She didn't seem happy that I was moving in here," Candace responds as I slip my arm around her.

"I think she just feels left out of everything. All of us have been through a lot, and she wasn't around. And let's face it, she has a skewed perception of Ryan, and she barely even knows Mark. And now Mark and I are about to move in together, and you and Ryan are too. She's just kinda out of the loop."

"You're moving in with Mark?" I ask, having had no clue, and both Candace and Jase give me a look as if I should already know this. "Why are you looking at me like that?"

"I thought you knew," Jase says.

"How would I have known if you didn't tell me?"

"Sorry, I guess with everything going on, I just never brought it up," he says.

"That's great, man. I just didn't know, that's all."

Candace gives me a smile and then turns back to Jase and says, "Anyways, I'm just not really sure where we stand."

"I suggested that maybe we should all get together so Kimber can get to know me. You and Mark should be there too, though," I tell him.

"That's probably the best thing to do at this point," Jase says as he looks to Candace.

"Okay, then. I'll call her later and see when she's free."

Jase leans back in the chair and lets out a long breath, saying, "I'm relieved, girl."

She lets out a giggle when she asks, "Why?"

"Because I hated the thought of not having you here. I've been a mess, and Mark has been stuck dealing with me."

"Mark isn't stuck. He loves you."

"Still. I'm just glad that you're staying and that you're happy."

Candace looks over to me and then back to Jase, saying, "Me too."

After picking up her car and getting her luggage at the airport, we stopped by the storage unit Candace had rented to keep all the stuff that she wouldn't have had room for in her apartment in New York. She doesn't need much since I have everything she could possibly want already at my place, but we picked up a couple of boxes, and now we are shifting things in my room so that all of her belongings have a place.

She's in the closet, hanging up her clothes, when I hear, "Ryan!"

Rushing in, I see her sitting on the floor, pulling out the canvas from behind the clothes where I had been hiding it.

When she looks up at me, she says, "I thought someone bought this."

I lean against the doorframe and tell her, "It was me. I bought it."

As she shakes her head, I say, "Did you really think I would let that hang in anyone's house but my own?"

"But why is it shoved back here?"

Walking over, I sit down next to her and look at the picture that I haven't seen in a long time and say, "Because it hurt too much to look at. It only reminded me of everything I lost." I look at her and slide the picture back against the wall before I kiss her, leaning into her as she lowers herself to the floor.

Grabbing on to my face, she pushes me back slightly when she says, "I can't believe you bought it."

I press my lips into hers, dipping my tongue in to caress hers as she fists my hair in her hands. Our lips move slowly together, as she pulls my weight wholly on top of her. She keeps me close, running her hands underneath my shirt and up my back. We move slowly as we lie on the floor of the closet, her clothes strewn everywhere in the midst of combining our belongings. Making this place ours.

We spend the rest of the evening situating her things, but before it gets too late, I tell Candace, "I'm gonna give my mom a call."

She acknowledges me as she continues to move things around, and I take a seat in the chair by the window while I call.

"Hey, Mom."

"How are you?"

"Actually, I'm really good," I tell her, and when I turn, I catch Candace grabbing her pajamas as she mouths to me, 'I'm gonna take a shower.'

I give her a nod as my mom says, "Well, that's good to hear."

"I have some news I think you'll like," I goad and she falls into it, saying, "Don't keep me in the dark. Tell me."

"Candace is back. She's moving in with me."

"What? How did that happen?" she asks in total shock.

"She showed up here yesterday, and we talked everything out."

"And she's moving in?"

"She *is* moved in," I clarify as I look at all of her things scattered around the room.

"That was quick."

"It feels like it took forever," I joke.

"You know what I mean," she says. "How is she?"

"Good. I think we're just both so worn out, but I was calling to see what your plans were for the Fourth."

"No plans really. Why?"

"Candace and I want to come down for a few days. I know she misses you."

"Of course," she exclaims. "I miss her too. Is she around for me to talk to?"

"She's in the shower, but I'll have her give you a call tomorrow."

"So . . . how are you feeling about all of this?" she asks in a more serious tone.

"Like this was how it was always supposed to be. Having her here with me. I felt completely lost without her, and now it just feels right again."

"I'm so happy for you, dear. For both of you."

When I hear the water shut off, I say, "Thanks, Mom. I'll talk to you later, okay?"

"Love you."

"You too."

I walk over and grab her empty luggage off the bed and take it downstairs to store it in the guest bedroom closet before heading back upstairs. Slipping into bed, I don't have to wait too long before Candace comes out and crawls under the sheets with me.

As she lets out a heavy sigh, she says, "I'm exhausted."

"It was a long day, huh?"

"Too long," she says with a breathy laugh.

"So, my mom said we could come out for a visit. She's anxious to see you. I told her you would call tomorrow."

"Oh . . . umm . . ."

Seeing the hesitation on her face, I ask, "What?"

She inches down and lays her head on the pillow, and I do the same as we face each other.

Reading her eyes, I ask, "What's going on?"

"It didn't feel weird to me until you called her."

"Is that why you rushed in to take a shower?"

I watch as her eyes drop and I ask, "Tell me what makes this feel weird?"

She moves her eyes up to mine when she says, "Because she knows."

"Knows what?"

"What you told her about what happened . . . to me."

Pulling her in close, I tell her, "Please don't let it make you feel weird. You know a lot of her secrets too, babe."

"But she doesn't know that. It's awkward because I'm aware that she knows this about me."

"I'm sorry."

"I hate that people know," she mumbles as she rests her forehead against my chest while I run my hand down her back.

Leaning down, I kiss the top of her head. "I'm sorry I told her, I—"

She cuts me off, looking up at me and saying, "Don't be sorry. I'm not mad about it, just embarrassed." She quickly moves her fingers to my mouth to keep me from talking, adding, "And I know you're gonna tell me to not be embarrassed, but there's no way around it. I just am."

I kiss her fingers and then take her hand, holding it against me. "She loves you. She has her own past that I know is embarrassing to her. She never wanted anyone to know either. That's all I'm gonna say," I tell her lightly and then put an end to all of the talking for some much needed kissing.

chapter forty-seven

"SHE'S LIVING WITH you?" Max questions before laughing and saying, "This from the guy who once gave me shit for Traci moving in with me."

"Go ahead, man. Get your laughs in, but I don't give a shit."

"I know you don't," he says. "I'm really happy for you. I was getting tired of your broody side."

Packing up my things, I let out a chuckle when I say, "Me too."

"You guys should come over. I know Traci would like the company. She's going a little crazy being at home every day."

"Yeah, that sounds good. I'll talk to Candace and call you. I gotta run though. She signed all of her contracts today with that ballet company, and I wanna be there when she gets home," I tell him as I start heading out.

"See ya."

When I get back to the loft, Candace's car is already there, and when I walk in, she's finishing up a phone call. I don't wait as I go to her and pull her in for a hug, lifting her off the floor.

"Okay, thanks. I'll see you then," she says and then hangs up before kissing me.

"How did everything go?" I ask when I set her down.

"Good. I start tomorrow."

"That soon?"

Smiling at me, she says, "Yeah. Auditions for the first performance run are in August."

"You're gonna have to explain how all this works, babe, because I don't know the first thing about what your job is going to look like."

We walk over to take a seat in the living room, and I reach out to set her on my lap as she explains, "Okay, so basically a season runs from September to June. I'll have typical rehearsals throughout the week with about five to seven performance runs that I'll have to audition for. Performance runs are around two weeks long with matinees and evening shows. Normally they have a two-month run around the holidays, but they cast two dancers for each role to divide up the schedule. So I'll have some time off for Christmas, hopefully."

"You seem excited."

"I am, but I'm mostly nervous. Most of these girls have done their apprenticeships up there and already know each other. I'm the only one coming from a university," she tells me.

"You'll be fine," I assure her. "I'm so happy for you, babe."

I kiss her dimple when she smiles, and then ask, "Who were you talking to when I came in?"

"Oh," she says as she sits up, looking a little flustered. "Um, that was Dr. Christman, my therapist. I needed to get back on her schedule. But . . . umm . . ."

"What is it?" I ask when she starts hesitating.

"Well, I told her what happened with the whole New York thing and moving in with you. She suggested that maybe you could come in with me for my next appointment, but you can say no," she says timidly, avoiding my eyes.

"Why would I say no?" I question. I've never done the whole therapy thing, but for her, I'd do anything.

"Because it's . . ."

"Embarrassing," I answer for her.

"I know you're sick of hearing that, but I can't help it."

"I'm not sick of hearing it, babe. I get it. You just tell me when, and I'll be there," I say, trying not to make too big of a deal about it for her.

Switching the subject, she tells me, "I invited Kimber to come over Friday night."

"Jase and Mark coming over too?"

"Yeah, if that's okay? I should have asked first."

"This is your home, Candace. You don't need to ask me if you want to have your friends over. It's fine," I tell her. "Max invited us over to hang out as well."

"What about Gavin?" she asks out of the blue.

"What do you mean?"

"You still talk to him?"

"I haven't seen him in a while. I think that friendship is dead. We're just on totally different wavelengths," I explain.

"When did that happen?"

"When he kept trying to sling chicks at me when all I wanted was you," I tell her as I run my fingers through her hair.

She looks uncomfortable when her only response is, "Oh," and knowing her so well, I go ahead and answer her unspoken question.

"No. I couldn't even bear to look at another girl. You were all I ever wanted even when I didn't have you."

She runs her hands along my jaw before she kisses me with an affection that only she can show. Slipping my hand under her knees, I cradle her in my arms as I carry her upstairs and lay her down in our bed. We move at a leisurely pace as we remove our clothes, feeling the need to connect with each other in this way. She normally keeps herself tucked against me, bodies close, when we make love, but to see her now, completely relaxed underneath me as I move inside of her, it's stunning. Her hair splayed around her face, her arms draped above her head, she's completely exposed to me as I move up to my knees and watch her.

Seeing her this comfortable with me, a level of comfort I'd yet to experience with her, is something I wasn't expecting. She's beautiful as I reach down and grab on to her hips, lifting them off of the bed and completely flush against me as I move deeper inside of her. She has her whole body bared to me, and I can't help but stare down at her and admire how perfect we look together like this. It's overwhelming, and when she grips my wrists and thrusts up to me, I let myself fall on top of her as we both come. Her hands never let go of my wrists, as if she needs them there for support as we both continue to move, greedy to prolong our release.

She holds my hand as we walk into the dimly lit office of her therapist and take a seat on the small leather couch. Pulling her hand onto my lap, I can tell she's nervous. Shit, I am too. I have no idea what to expect or what this lady plans on talking to us about.

"It's good to see you again," Dr. Christman says to Candace and then turns to me to introduce herself before saying, "It's nice to finally meet you. Candace has filled me in on a lot already about the two of you, but I wanted to take this time to not only talk with you, Ryan, but to hear from both of you together. First, Candace, tell me what happened."

"With New York?"

"Yes. Last we spoke, you were excited and happy to be moving on and starting something new. What changed?"

Her grip tightens on my hand as she adjusts herself, bringing her legs up onto the couch and folding them in front of her. I watch her as she begins to speak with Dr. Christman.

"I don't think anything really changed. I was sitting at the gate, about to board the plane, and all I could feel was sadness and regret. I was scared, but I realized that everything I was so scared about wasn't the fresh start, but what I was leaving behind. It was like I was trying so hard to focus on my dream of New York that I completely shut out my dream of Ryan. Like I was trying to switch one for the other. Somewhere along the way my dream of New York changed, but I never allowed myself to see it until I was about to leave."

It's a little strange for me to hear Candace being so open. I'm not used to her speaking so freely, so I'm taken aback by her candidness.

"So what did you do?"

"I left the airport," she tells her. "I felt like my world was spinning out of control, but in a good way. As soon as I got to his place and saw him, it was like all the happiness I lost when I lost him came rushing back. I just knew this was the choice I was supposed to make."

Dr. Christman turns to me, and says, "I bet that came as a shock to you."

"You have no idea," I tell her with a chuckle.

"So, Ryan, Candace and I have spent a lot of time talking about your relationship and how the two of you came to split. Have you had a chance to explain to her the reasoning behind why you withheld who you were?"

"I feel like I have. I mean, I hope I have. We spent a few hours talking the other day, unraveling all the questions we each had."

She looks over at Candace and asks, "Do you feel you got everything you needed from that conversation?"

"I think so," she says in a shaky voice, and when I turn to look at her, she's wiping her fingers under her eyes.

"Tell me why you're crying," she asks Candace.

"Because it was hard to hear. I've gone nearly a whole year without having to talk about what happened. And listening to him tell me what he saw that night . . . it's just hard to hear and to know that he saw me like that."

"Ryan, I'm curious. When you realized Candace was the girl you had seen that night, how did you deal with that?"

I wrap my arm around Candace while she dries her tears with a tissue and answer, "As soon as I knew, I wanted to tell her, but I didn't know how. Then I started thinking that if I did tell her, how much it would hurt her. She was in a really dark place at the time, and I was scared she would break. She hid a lot, but I always knew she was barely holding on. But it fucked with my head—a lot. I get these flashbacks. It used to only be of my childhood. I see something or whatever and my mind takes me back. But ever since that night she was attacked . . . it keeps playing back in my head."

"What do you normally do when that happens?"

"Nothing. I eventually just snap out of it. But it kills me that I have that in my head," I say before I turn to see Candace staring at me in disbelief with what I just said.

"I'm sorry," I tell her.

"Were you aware that he has these flashbacks, Candace?"

"No," she answers and then asks me, "So that's how you see me?"

"No. I denied you were that girl for so long. I fell in love with everything I had in front of me. But when I found out you were that girl, the visions were just so conflicting because I don't see you like that at all. I know it's you, but I still don't want it to be."

She's crying now, and I take her other hand in mine when I affirm, "That is *not* what I see when I look at you."

"I don't want that in your head," she chokes out.

"I don't either, babe. But these aren't our choices, and I've told you before that I love you regardless."

"It makes me feel disgusting."

She takes a moment to settle her tears and take in a few deep breaths when Dr. Christman asks me, "What's the biggest thing you feel you struggle with about Candace's attack?"

Letting out a sigh, I tell her, "That I let her down."

"How so?"

"I was inside and heard the commotion in the alley. I ignored it, figuring it was just people passing through, which happens occasionally. If I had gone out there, then maybe none of this would have happened."

She sits back in her seat as she looks at Candace and asks, "Is it okay if I share some of the things we've discussed in our previous sessions?"

"Of course."

Focusing back on me, she says, "One of the issues I've been working on with Candace is her feeling of blame. She believes that her behavior led to her attack, and she continues to hold herself responsible."

"Yeah, I know."

"Do you see the parallel here?"

Looking at Candace, I see what Dr. Christman is trying to point out, something I guess I never really saw before. I've always thought it was crazy that she could think she was to blame, but in turn, she probably feels the same way about my thoughts.

"Yeah," I answer.

"Neither one of you are to blame, yet both of you are holding yourselves responsible," she says. "Did you know he felt this way?" she asks Candace.

I watch as she nods her head, saying, "Yes."

"Just as Candace and I have been discussing, there's no way you could have known what was going to happen that night, so you can't hold yourself responsible for that."

She says this, I get it, but I can't accept it . . . not right now.

"Well, I want to be mindful of our time together, so I'd like to focus on Candace, simply because she's the one who I have been working with. But going forward in your relationship, it's important that you're there to help support her as she continues to process and heal. Being aware of her triggers and knowing ways you can help her cope and push her are key."

"I know that she shuts down and avoids. I like to get it out and talk, but it's a challenge to get her to open up. I notice she's been more willing since we've been back together this past week, but . . ." I let my words fall, but she picks them up when she says, "It's very typical of trauma victims to shut down. Candace has expressed to me that when she opens herself up to emotions, she panics and feels like they're going to flood her, and the loss of control is scary."

I look to Candace and ask, "But what do you think is going to happen?"

She shakes her head before turning to Dr. Christman, and when she blinks, tears fall.

"Babe, I need you to tell me because I don't understand."

"Can you tell me why you can't answer him?" she asks Candace.

She shakes her head as I move my hand to her back.

"Go ahead and take a moment, but I want you to tell Ryan what you have told me whenever you're ready."

I feel like we sit here forever in the silence when she eventually turns to me and takes a deep breath before revealing, "It feels like I'm losing control and that I won't be able to handle it."

When I shake my head, still unsure, she tells me, "In the moment . . . it feels like I'm going to die."

I can barely handle her words and to know that this is how she feels. I pull her into my arms, thinking back to all the times she's been so scared. The day she saw that dumpster, her nightmares, our fight, and so many other things.

As I keep her folded into me, Dr. Christman says, "I've been asking Candace to try and put herself in situations that will generally trigger these emotions but in a place where she feels safe. Trying to help her cope with living inside the emotions, feeling them and not shutting down. Understanding that even though it's scary, the emotions will eventually lessen, and she'll be okay. I think it's important for you to understand how she's feeling during these episodes so that you can help push her through them, but to also be aware of her limits. Also, encouraging her to talk about her attack will help lessen the power it has over her."

I give her a nod of acknowledgement as Candace pulls away and sits back.

We talk a little while longer about how I can help Candace and discuss some goals as we move forward. Before we leave, we agree I will come in with Candace twice a month, but the rest of her visits will remain focused on her.

I was proud of Candace before, knowing she was doing this, but to actually sit next to her and listen to her makes me realize how much strength it must have taken her to do this on her own. Honestly, I don't think she would have ever done this if it weren't for us being apart. She had to do it alone and for herself. And just from that one session, I learned things about her that I never knew before. It helped me understand her in a way I wouldn't have been capable of on my own.

Instead of going back to the loft, we decide to take the rest of the afternoon to relax, and we head to Fremont to grab some coffee at Peet's before roaming around some of the antique shops. We don't talk about what was said. Although it seems Candace is feeling needy with me, I let her be. She never takes her hand out of mine as we drift aimlessly in and out of the different shops, simply enjoying each other.

chapter forty-eight

THE PAST COUPLE of weeks have been disappointing for Candace. She's been trying hard to include Kimber in our lives, but she continues to have a crap-ass attitude with me. I'd never say anything to Candace about it, but she sees it, and it upsets her that her friend has been shutting me out.

Candace realizes that too much has changed in the past year and they've simply grown apart. She's been sad, thinking about the what-ifs and wondering how it would have been different if she would've just told her about the attack instead of hiding it. But what's done is done, and people grow apart. I have with Gavin, but along the way we've made new friends. Candace now has Mark and has also been getting together with Mel and Traci, and I've befriended Mark and Jase and even become closer with Max, who I continue to spend more time with.

Now as we drive to my mom's, Candace is sleeping. We invited Mark and Jase to come as well, and they plan on driving down later this afternoon. We thought it would be fun for the four of us to get away since everyone has been so busy with their new work schedules, and we haven't spent that much time together.

Candace has been avoiding my mom's attempts to talk on the phone. I understand her apprehension about it, and I know she's a nervous wreck about seeing her, so I'm glad she's finding some relief from the stress as she sleeps. It's a good thing that Jase and Mark won't be there until later, giving the three of us time to talk privately and hopefully help ease Candace's embarrassment.

When I pull up to the house, I run the back of my hand down her arm. Rolling her head to me, she slowly opens her eyes.

"We're here," I quietly say, and she turns to look at the front of the house, letting out a soft breath. I hop out of the car and walk around to her side, helping her out. Placing my hands on the sides of her face, I tell her, "I love you."

I take her hand and walk her inside, calling out, "Mom." We head back to the living room, and my mom is already making her way to us.

"Candace!" she squeals, not even acknowledging me, and I have to laugh when she pulls my girl into her arms.

I'm relieved to see Candace smile. I went ahead and told my mom a few days ago that Candace is aware that I told her about the attack because she was starting to wonder why Candace wasn't returning her calls.

"I'm so happy you're here," she beams and then turns to me to give me a hug. "How was the drive?"

"Candace slept most of the time, and there was a ton of traffic." Cannon Beach is a hot spot for the summer, let alone the Fourth of July.

"Well, I'm glad you two made it safely. When will Jase and Mark be getting in?"

Candace lets me do the talking while she stands close to me, holding on to my hand. "Jase texted me a while ago, so maybe five hours or so with the traffic." Wanting to get Candace alone for a moment, I tell my mom, "We're gonna take our bags upstairs. We'll be down in a couple minutes."

Closing the bedroom door behind me, I sit with Candace on my bed. "Babe . . ."

"I *hate* this," she lets out as she falls back on the bed, staring up at the ceiling.

"Just talk to her."

"What do I even say?"

"Come here," I tell her as I tug on her hand and draw her up to me. "Just like you and I have been doing, just talk. Clear the air."

When she nods, I offer, "You want me to go with you?"

"Yeah," she says, and then I pull her off the bed, not wanting her to stew on this any longer. I give her a soft kiss before taking her back downstairs.

Walking through the house, I find my mom in the study, sitting in one of the chairs, flipping through a book.

"Hey, Mom."

"That was quick," she says as she closes the book and sets it on her lap while Candace and I take a seat on the couch.

"I think we need to talk," I tell her and then look at Candace who's holding my hand with both of hers, keeping her eyes fixed on them.

"Has Ryan told you about his father?"

Candace looks up to my mom, answering, "Yes."

"So, I'm sure he also added me to that equation as well."

When she nods her head in response, my mom begins talking and opening up to her about things she hasn't even talked to me about.

"Richard was a horrible man who would beat me on a nearly daily basis. I have scars to remind me of it every day. When he drank, the fights would get even more violent. At one point, I had become pregnant, but I never told him. I was too scared," she tells Candace, and I stare at my mom in horror because I never knew this. "I saw what he was doing to Ryan, but at the time I was so terrified of the man, that I never defied him because I feared what he would do to me. But he eventually found out about the pregnancy. He was furious, dragging me by the hair all the way up the stairs and then kicking me in the stomach over and over."

She stops talking to catch her breath as she begins to cry, but I can't move because I'm in shock. It isn't until I hear Candace let out a shaky whimper that I turn and see her tears as well.

"After he was done with me," she continues, "I couldn't move because the pain was just so excruciating. And then he threw me down the stairs. I knew I couldn't go to the hospital. He never would have let me get away with it. It took almost four days for me to miscarry my baby."

Candace's grip on me is tight as I watch my mom wiping the tears from her face. I never knew that had happened to her. The secrets that these women keep are horrific, and I'm at a loss for words.

My mother keeps her eyes on Candace when she says, "We both have secrets, dear. And that's the secret I have always held on to . . . until now."

When Candace's cries start to break through, I wrap my arm around her as her tears roll down her face.

"Ryan told me that you were embarrassed, but you have *nothing* to be embarrassed about around me. I have your darkest secret, and now you have mine."

She stands and walks over to sit next to Candace, and I let go of her as she turns to my mom and hugs her.

"You are an amazingly strong woman," my mom says to her as she pulls back to look at Candace. "Watching you get through this year with everything you had to go through with the attack, your parents, and with Ryan . . . I don't know if I'd be able to come out of that with the poise you have. It's been eighteen years since I lost my baby, and it wasn't until just now that I was able to finally say it out loud. I've held on to it for all these years, and then I look at you . . ."

She takes a moment as she begins to cry again, before adding, "You are everything I wish I could have been. I see you with my son, and how you've opened your heart to him even after what happened to you. I've never been able to do that since Richard died almost eleven years ago."

Candace doesn't even need to speak, and I love my mom for what she just gave my girl. Gave it in a way that Candace didn't even have to talk because I know she was so nervous about what she would say. The two of them cry together, and at this point, I give Candace the space I feel she needs to spend time with my mom and talk without having me around. I kiss the back of her head before I leave the room and go outside to the beach to digest everything I just heard.

When Jase and Mark arrived later that day, we spent the evening grilling steaks out back and hanging out on the beach. Candace told me, that after I left, she and my mom were able to talk for a while. And seeing them now, in the kitchen, cooking breakfast, they seem closer than ever.

"Hey, Mom, where are your binoculars?" I ask after we eat.

"They're outside on the table," she says when I grab Candace's hand to take her out to the beach.

"Where are we going?" she questions.

"I wanna show you something," I tell her as we walk outside.

Picking up the binoculars, I walk her down towards the water, and when I look through the lenses, I spot what I want to show her. I hand them over and instruct, "Here. Look over there to that sea stack. I want you to look carefully for anything bright orange."

"Okay," she draws out slowly as she holds the binoculars up to her eyes. "There, I see . . . oh my God!" she squeaks out, and it's cute as hell, bringing a huge smile to my face. "Look! There's so many of them. What are they?"

Wrapping my arms around her from behind, I rest my chin on top of her head, telling her, "Puffins." She keeps looking at them as I say, "Every year around this time they nest over there on Haystack Rock. That's why we can't shoot off fireworks because they come here to mate, and it would scare them away. This is the only place on the coast where it's not legal."

"They are so cute."

I lean down and press my lips into her soft neck, taking kisses when she drops the binoculars and turns in my arms to face me. The wind kicks through her hair as the sun casts a glow on her face.

"Are you happy?" I ask. Her smile tells me she is, but I want to hear it.

"I never thought I could be this happy."

She runs her hands behind my neck and brings me into her, kissing me intently, but the moment is short-lived when we hear Mark say, "Break it up, kids."

"What are you guys doing?" Jase asks as they walk over to us.

Candace holds out the binoculars and tells him, "There are puffins out on that big rock."

"Give me those," Mark says as he snatches the binoculars out of Jase's hands and starts searching for the birds. "There they are," he mumbles before telling Jase, "We should totally get one."

Candace laughs while Jase says, "Dude, it's a bird."

Handing the binoculars back to Jase, he says, "They look like penguins. Haven't you ever wanted a penguin for a pet?"

I can't control my laughter as I watch the two of them.

"No," Jase answers in exasperation. "Who even thinks like that?"

"I do. People have that shit for pets."

"Who?"

"I dunno, just . . . people. I've seen it on TV," is Mark's pitiful explanation as the three of us laugh at him. He turns to Candace and tries to get her to back him when he says, "Why are you laughing? You once told me you wanted a pig for a pet."

"What?" I question through a burst of laughter.

Turning to me with narrowed eyes, she defends, "Not like a gross barn pig. A domesticated micro pig."

"What the hell is that, babe?"

"They're these tiny little pink pigs. They say they're cleaner and smarter than a dog. You can even litter train them."

She says this in complete seriousness, and she looks adorable doing it, but that doesn't stop Jase and I from laughing at her and Mark for their choice in pets.

Slapping my arm, she scolds, "Stop laughing at me," with a hint of a smile.

"Just so you know, we're not getting a pig."

"You don't even know what they are. You've never even seen one."

Looking over at Jase for support, I call out to him, "Dude, Jase, are you hearing this?"

"It makes more sense to get a pig than Mark's desire to snatch up a wild bird just because he's thinks they're *cute,*" he says with a chuckle while shaking his head.

"Hey, guys," Tori announces as she walks out with Bailey on her hip, and Connor runs around her, straight to me.

Squatting down, I give him a big hug, as I say, "Hey, buddy. When did you guys get here?"

"Just now."

Picking him up in my arms, I watch as my mom follows Tori and Bailey, who just turned two, out to the rest of us.

"Candace, it's so good to see you again," she says as she gives her a one-armed hug while still holding Bailey.

"Can you say, 'Hi, Candace'?" Tori asks of Bailey, but all Candace gets in return is a 'hi' followed by babble.

The two of them laugh as Tori says to Bailey, "We're just gonna have to change her name, huh? Something a little more simple."

Looking at Candace, I tell her, "Don't worry. She can't even say my name." Setting Connor down, I reach over and take Bailey, as she says, "Wy-wy!"

"See? I'm Wy-wy," I say to Candace as I keep my eyes on Bailey.

"Tori, these are my friends, Jase and Mark," Candace introduces as they all hug and greet each other.

"Where's Trevor?" I ask.

"I'm here," he hollers as he walks out. "Had to unload the bags."

"Hey, man," I say when he gets closer. "You remember Candace, right?"

"How could I forget?" he says before giving her a hug.

Everybody meets Mark and Jase and spends a good amount of time playing with the kids before Candace and I take Connor down the beach a little ways to show him the puffins. I watch as she is on her knees behind Connor, helping him with the binoculars as he looks through them. She's relaxed and happy. I love that I could give this to her. This bond of a family we are beginning to form with not only my family, but with her friends as well. It's only because of Candace that I have this right now. She's the one who showed me what it was to open up. To connect to others. That I was capable of having meaningful relationships. And since having her in my life, my relationships with Tori and Max have grown to a new level, allowing for an even deeper friendship than before.

The shift that life has taken is one that I never would have expected, but one that I would never change as I watch her and then look down the beach to see Mark and Jase making a sand hill with Bailey and Tori while my mom and Trevor sit back and talk. And when Candace looks up at me with her beautiful smile, I know I have everything I could ever want.

Mark has taken a keen liking to Bailey over the past couple of days, which Tori has appreciated since he pretty much has taken Bailey off of her hands, giving her a much-needed break. She and Candace spent a couple of hours yesterday shopping at The Landing while the rest of us played outside with the kids on the beach. This time of year the weather is nice, so we take advantage and ditch the indoors.

On the Fourth, we take the kids down to the local parade in the morning and then over to Seaside later that night, for fireworks. We've had a good visit, and it was needed in more ways than one.

When I wake up the next morning, Candace isn't in bed with me, so I slip my pajama pants over my boxers and head downstairs to find her. The house is quiet with everyone still asleep, and when I walk through the living room, I look out the windows to see Candace sitting alone, down by the water.

Walking out, she has the binoculars up to her eyes, and when I get close, I ask, "What are you doing out here?"

She looks back at me when she says, "Watching the puffins."

I sit down in the sand next to her, wrapping my arm around her shoulders, teasing, "You want me to swim out there and get you one?"

"Mark may get jealous," she says with a quiet laugh.

"Yeah. You're probably right."

She sets down the binoculars and lays her head on my shoulder, saying, "I love coming out here."

"Why's that?"

"Because," she says, waiting a beat before continuing, "I feel like I'm part of a family. I never felt that way with mine, but I feel it with yours."

"Have you ever talked to your parents? Did they come to your graduation or anything?" I ask.

"No."

Not wanting to dampen this moment, I lift her chin up to me and tell her, "I love having you here. The first time I brought you here, last year at Christmas, I watched you in the kitchen with my mom, and I knew I wanted to bring you back. I had been chasing you for so long, nervous that I would scare you away if I told you how I was feeling, but bringing you home with me, I knew I had to make you mine."

She smiles, saying, "You never seemed nervous around me. I always thought you were so sure of yourself."

"There wasn't a second that I felt sure of myself with you. You're the hardest person I have ever tried to read."

"Is that a bad thing?"

"No. There isn't a single thing about you that I would change. I love every piece of you."

chapter forty-nine

THE LEAVES LITTER the streets as I drive home in the rain. I've been on a job all afternoon after I was commissioned to photograph a model for a portfolio. The photography thing has really picked up for me, and I've been trying to get a few more of my newer pieces on display at a couple of galleries. The exposure has been great, and Candace is nothing but supportive, coming along with me to showings when she can.

She's been so busy with rehearsals lately for her first performance run that will start in a few days. The transition into the company has been a challenge for her. Most of the girls up there have been there for years, skipping the college route to go straight into their dancing career. Candace told me that it's not very common to go from a university to a company, but she did it mostly to appease her parents. It's been very competitive and some of the dancers haven't welcomed her into the program very easily, giving her a hard time at first, but my girl is determined and always keeps herself focused when she's dancing. It isn't until she comes home to me that she finally lets out her frustrations.

We've made a routine of having Jase and Mark over every Thursday night so that Jase and Candace can watch the new episodes of 'Ridiculousness.' I just have to laugh at the two of them and their taste for trash TV, but she redeems herself each time we camp out downstairs by the fireplace to watch our black and whites.

Candace is already home when I pull into the drive, and when I walk up the stairs to the front door, I spot one of my bowls sitting on the ground. Picking it up, I go inside and set it in the sink then head upstairs. I stop in my tracks the moment I catch sight of her. She's securing felted green leaves around the bun on top of her head, wearing a puffy red strawberry costume with green tights.

"Baby, what's this?" I question with a smirk while I enjoy the view.

Taking out the hairpin from between her teeth and sticking it in her hair, she stands proudly on display for me, saying, "My Halloween costume!"

She's fuckin' cute, and I smile as I step towards her and ask, "Where did you get this?"

"Marilyn, the seamstress at the studio. She made it for me."

"I didn't know we were dressing up."

She looks down at her costume, running her hands down the fluffy red fabric and says, "I never do anything for Halloween, so I figured since we're gonna be with the kids, I wanted to dress up."

Wrapping my arms around the pillowy costume, I pull her close to me and kiss her. I love seeing her playful and happy like this. We decided to go to Astoria to take Tori and my other cousin, Jenna's, kids trick-or-treating next week. I felt bad that I didn't go last year, so I'm making it a point this year, and Candace is excited to tag along and see everyone. My whole family has embraced Candace, and hearing Bailey call her Aunt Ce-Ce every time we video chat means the world to her.

"So you like it?" she questions when she breaks our kiss.

"It's adorable, babe."

I kiss her dimple before she says, "I'm gonna go take it off. I just wanted to put it all on to see how it looks. Give me a few minutes."

My eyes follow her green legs as she walks into the bathroom and shuts the door. Even after all this time, she's still modest with me, always shutting herself away to change and get ready. It used to bother me, but now it's just another thing I love about her. So I sit on the bed and wait for her to reappear, looking more sophisticated in a pair of black pants and a fitted sweater, hair still in a bun.

"You wanna go grab a coffee before our appointment?" I ask.

"Yeah. Can we go to Common Grounds? I haven't seen Roxy in a while, and I'd like to stop in and say hi."

"Of course," I respond as I tug her onto the bed and pull her between my legs before kissing her. "Oh, hey," I say when I pull back. "Why was there a bowl by the front door?"

"I put some food out for this cat I keep seeing."

"Babe, if you do that, we're gonna have a shitload of stray cats hanging around outside."

"She looked sad. I just couldn't let her starve," she defends. "She doesn't have tags or anything, and it's cold and rainy outside. The least I could do was leave out some food."

I laugh at her, but love her soft heart, so I don't say anything else about it.

Kissing the top of her head, I tell her, "Come on. Let's get out of here."

After we stop by and visit with Roxy for a while, we head over to Dr. Christman's office for our appointment. We've continued to see her twice a month, and Candace has still been keeping her weekly appointments on top of what we do together. She's been working hard and talking more to me about the rape and how she's trying to process it. She still blames herself, but I can't get down on her for that because I still blame myself as well.

She did come off of her sleeping pill back in the beginning of September, but a couple weeks ago, she had another terrifying nightmare and immediately started taking her pills again even though Dr. Christman wanted her to continue on without them. I understand Candace's fear of her dreams. That nightmare freaked her out, and she wound up making herself sick, vomiting several times afterwards.

After seeing Jack at the bar, she was scared to come back there. I wound up telling her about the subpoena and going to see him. She was having a hard time believing that he was really dead, so I found out where he was buried and took her to show her that she didn't have to be scared of him anymore—but she still is.

Candace has been busy ever since we got back in town from spending Halloween in Astoria with my cousins a couple weeks ago. It was a short trip, but Candace had fun with the kids, and I had fun watching my strawberry go door to door with Bailey, helping her fill her bag with candy. Candace even got some candy herself at a few houses that just assumed she was a kid. We all teased her about her size, and she took it like a champ, but she's used to it from Mark. The two of them banter like brother and sister, and I'm starting to see that same connection building with her, Tori, and Trevor.

This past week has been crazy while Candace has been having costume fittings and dress rehearsals. But tonight is her first performance, and seeing her meddle around the loft, trying to keep her nerves in check, I think back to the last time—the only time—I saw her dance. I was alone, miserable, fearing I'd lost her for good. I watched her dance for the first time while I was hiding in the back of the theater, wishing I could have been with her, and now I am. This is the way it should have been the day of her performance in college, but I'm getting my moment now. And savoring every minute of it.

We ran out of bananas this morning, so she sent me out to grab a few since she worries about muscle cramps. When I get back from the store, a tiny white and tan cat greets me. No doubt, Candace's little buddy, waiting for her next meal. I walk past it and let myself in.

"Your friend's out front," I say as I walk through the room and into the kitchen to set the bag of bananas down.

"Who?" she asks from the couch.

"That cat you keep feeding all of our food to."

"Ryan, she doesn't have a home. She's been hanging around for a couple of weeks," she says as I walk over to her and sit down.

"We can take her to the pound."

"Oh my God! You're crazy!" she squeals at me. "We're not doing that."

Looking over at her, I already know what she wants to do, but I ask anyway, hoping she'll surprise me.

"So what do you suggest we do?"

In the most timid way possible, she suggests, "We could keep her."

"I'm not inviting a feral cat into my home."

Narrowing her eyes at me, she says, "You act like I'm asking you to invite a vampire in."

As I laugh at her analogy, she defends, "And stop calling her a *feral* cat like she's some Dickensian orphan."

"Why do I have a feeling like this cat is going to become part of our family?"

She gets a huge grin on her face at the mere suggestion as I sit back and drape her legs over my lap. When she lies down, I ask, "You doing okay?"

She turns her head to stare out at the rain that's now beating against the windows, and says, "I've never danced for a crowd this big before."

"You'll be fine," I tell her as I start rubbing her calves.

"Hmm," she softly hums with her eyes shut as I massage her legs.

"When I finally got to see you dance the night of your solo, I never thought you could look so beautiful. You were all I could see even when the stage was filled with other dancers. You stole every bit of my attention as if nothing else in the world existed but you."

She looks up to my eyes when I tell her this, and then I say, "I know you work your ass off, but when I saw you on stage, it's like you didn't even have to try. That's how I know you'll be fine. You can't help but be captivating, babe."

Sitting up, she climbs into my lap, straddling my hips, and says, "I wanted you that day of my solo. I was a wreck, and I just wanted you there with me."

Tangling my fingers into her hair, I tell her, "You have me now, babe."

She leans down and kisses me, moving her lips slowly with mine while I tug her hips into me. Leaning my head back onto the couch, I guide her with my hands still trussed in her hair. I love the taste of her in my mouth, and we continue to make out for a while, just like this, before she drags herself off of me to get ready.

I spend a good amount of time sitting in bed while I watch her move around the room as she stretches and works her ankles, puts her hair up in her bun, and replaces the lamb's wool in her toe shoes. She's quiet, but flashes me a grin every now and then as I watch what I hope will become our routine. Tonight's her first performance, but she'll have two tomorrow and two on Sunday followed by a few throughout the week. This will last for the next three weeks, and I'm excited that I get to see her dance like this, performing for thousands of people every day. She's a star in the darkness that hovers over us—she always has been.

I say goodbye to her early because she has to be at McCaw Theater hours before production, so when I arrive, Jase, Mark, Traci, and Max are already there and seated. Candace was able to get them all tickets for opening night, which is nearly a black-tie affair.

Tonight won't be like the last time I saw her. With the company, she dances in what they call the corps de ballet, an ensemble of dancers that accompany the soloists. It could take a while for Candace to work her way up to being a soloist.

Dancing 'Les Sylphides,' my eyes stay locked on her throughout the whole night. She's the only one I see as she moves gracefully around the stage. Just like before when I saw her dancing, she gives me goosebumps. She's soft and stoic, taking each number with a focus that only she can make so effortless.

She loves this. It's who she is, and to see her take this passion and turn her dreams into reality is an amazing thing. She's known what she's wanted to make of her dancing, and she did it. I'm in awe of her. To see her suffer through so much, yet never lose her way with her goals is a determination you don't find all that often in people. But she has it.

I never thought a guy like me would be found at the ballet and actually enjoying it, but I like knowing that this is now a part of my life and that I get to watch my girl up on that stage throughout the year.

Once the curtain drops and the lights brighten, I visit with everyone for a while before saying goodnight. Candace told me to meet her in the dressing room afterwards, so as I walk out of the theater, I see the main lobby emptying out when my eyes catch a man with familiar silver hair walking towards me. As he approaches, I'm stunned to see it's Candace's father.

"Charles?"

He looks up and stops in his tracks when he recognizes me. I can tell that he can't place my name.

"It's Ryan," I say, reminding him.

"Ryan. How are you?" he says as he reaches out his hand, but I don't take it.

"What are you doing here?"

It takes him a moment, but when he lowers his hand, he shifts his weight, saying, "I came to see Candace."

"Does she know you're here?"

"No."

When I slowly begin to shake my head at the man who is sneaking out because he's too much of a coward to see his own daughter, he defends, "I love her."

"You don't know her."

He doesn't speak after I say this, and my need to protect her takes over when I continue, "I don't know what it is about her that you aren't able to accept or that you don't think is good enough. I've tried to understand, but I can't." Taking a step closer, I pause for a second before saying, "I wish you could see the amazing girl that I do. The girl who has dreams that she's able to make come true. The girl who loves harder than anyone I've ever known. She's got a beautiful heart."

"I know."

"Do you know what you did to that heart when you turned your back on her?"

"I love my daughter," he says. "But I love my wife too. I won't stand here and make excuses for her. She has her faults, but in the end, I love her."

"So where does that leave Candace? Because I'll be honest with you, sir, I love that girl and seeing how the two of you hurt her is something that I would be willing to look past if it meant that you could repair things with her."

Shoving his hands into his pants pockets, he turns his head to the doors before looking back at me and resolves, "I just wanted to see her dance. Maybe you shouldn't tell her that you saw me," and then walks out the doors.

I've never wanted to protect anyone the way I want to protect Candace, but I won't ever hold anything back from her. As sick as it sounds, it's probably best that her parents walked out of her life. This is a girl who apologizes for herself more than anyone I know because she feels she is always making a mistake simply by being herself. She's someone who is so determined to succeed, but I know it's stemmed from growing up with parents who never thought she was good enough and made it their goal to make sure she knew it. And when she opens the door to her dressing room and I see her big smile, full of life and satisfaction, I know she's going to be better off without them.

"God, you're amazing," I tell her as I pick her up in my arms and hug her.

Her smile's infectious and after I kiss her, she beams in excitement, "That was incredible." Setting her down, she shuts the door behind me and asks, "What did you think?"

"I think you're gonna be seeing me here a lot."

"So you liked it?"

"There isn't anything I don't like about seeing you on that stage," I tell her and then move in to cup her face in my hands. "Do you have any idea how proud I am of you?"

She kisses me and then tells me, "You're the one that made me want to feel again. That helped bring me back to life."

I could easily give those same words back to her because she did the same for me, only on a completely different scope, so I let her have those words. I love that we can give each other so much. That we can have the best of ourselves with each other. We continue to hug and kiss for a while longer, celebrating Candace's opening night at the ballet in our quiet way.

She is already out of her costume, so I sit on the small couch as she powders her shoes and begins to pack up.

Spotting a vase full of pink roses, I ask, "Who are those from?"

She looks at the vase and then back to me, saying, "Your mom had those delivered before the show. She felt bad that she couldn't be here."

"Babe, I need to tell you something," I say and then motion for her to come sit next to me, and when she does, I turn to her and take her hands in mine. I know she'll be okay when I tell her about her father because she has such a solid support system in the people that choose to be a part of her life. "I saw your dad tonight."

Seeing her eyes open up with hope, she asks, "He's here?"

"He was," I say gently. "I ran into him as he was leaving," Her face falls when I tell her this.

"Didn't he want to see me?"

Her head drops when I shake my head.

"What did he say?"

We've been nothing but transparent with each other, so I give her that respect when I say, "That he loves you, but he loves your mother too. He didn't want me to tell you he was here, but I never want to keep anything from you again, and I need you to know that."

The tears in her eyes are hard to look at as she sits here. "Don't doubt for a second that you don't have a family full of people that love and support you because you do. They might not be your blood, but they are your heart."

She takes a second before she speaks on a soft breath, "So that's it?" referring to her parents.

"I think so."

Defeat washes over her as her shoulders slump.

"I know it hurts, babe, but I also know that you haven't done a thing wrong here. It's them, not you."

"Can you just take me home?"

"Yeah," I whisper and help her gather her things before I drive us home.

She's quiet, and I hate that I had to dampen her night, but I swore to her that there would never being anything that I would withhold from her again.

It's cold and rainy when I open the garage so we don't get wet. Walking into the house, everything is dark and quiet until a faint, "Meow," from outside filters in.

Cocking my head at Candace and giving her a knowing look, she knits her brows together, silently pleading with me.

"No."

"Ryan, it's freezing outside," she says.

"We're not bringing that stray cat in here."

"You're being mean. She's a nice cat. I've never seen her be aggressive," she defends.

Shaking my head at her, she pleads, "It's pouring out there."

Candace is giving me the most pitiful look, and knowing she's already feeling defeated tonight, I give in and sigh out, "Fine."

She tilts her head and questions, "Really?" for clarity.

"For tonight."

She doesn't waste a second when she runs to the front door and opens it, bending down and picking up the tiny cat who huddles in her arms. I smile at her as she coos and starts walking over to me.

"I'm gonna give her a bath."

"What?! No, you're not. The cat is gonna sleep in the garage," I tell her.

"She's filthy."

"You do know cats hate water, right?" I say, but she ignores me as she starts walking back to the guest bedroom.

Not trusting this animal in the slightest, I follow her back and proceed to help her grab towels and run a little water in the tub. This cat is terrified as shit, so I take it out of her hands and hold it while it squeals and writhes in fear as Candace washes her. But it's when she begins thrashing in my hands that she slips out of my hold, jumping out of the tub and tears through the house, no sound but her claws clicking against the wooden floors.

"Fuck!"

Chasing after her, all I hear is Candace laughing, still in the bathroom.

"Help me find her!" I call out while I make my way upstairs.

I follow the dreadful meows to the bedroom and find her under the bed. Getting on my knees, I peek my head under, and see her curled against the wall in the middle of the bed.

"Come here," I say in a singsong voice, mocking my liking for her. Giving the floor a couple light taps, I call again, "Come here," when I see Candace's head poke down from the other side, giggling.

"This shit isn't funny," I tell her.

She rolls her eyes at me, and then calls to the cat, but she still doesn't budge. "Great," she huffs out. "You've scared her."

"What?"

"She knows you don't like her."

"You're kidding me, right?" I say as we continue to go back and forth with our heads underneath the bed. "You're the one that tortured this thing because you just *had* to give it a bath."

"I didn't torture her," she argues.

Tapping the floor a few more times, the cat slowly inches to me, and I can't help but look over to Candace with a victorious grin as I reach out and pick up the cat.

When we reemerge from underneath the bed and get up, cat in my arms, she stands, hands on hips, miffed.

We manage to get the cat dried off, and after everything is cleaned up, we head to bed. Lying there together, Candace stares at the cat that is sleeping down by our feet, purring softly.

"She's so cute."

"You're so cute," I tell her, and when she looks at me, she smiles.

"I bet she was the runt of the litter," she says. "She's so small."

"Hmm," I hum as I pull her closer to me.

"I wanna keep her."

"I knew this was coming."

"What?" she questions when she tilts her head up to me. "You can't tell me that you don't think Tatiana is adorable."

Laughing, I question, "What did you just call her?"

"Tatiana."

"I'm not calling her that," I say firmly, refusing to call the cat a name like that.

"Why not?"

"Because it's way too girly."

Candace laughs at me when she says, "Well . . . she is a girl, Ryan."

"She's a cat," I say. "And where did you get Tatiana from?"

"She's a famous ballerina that I've always loved. I like the name."

"What's her last name? Maybe it'll sound better than Tatiana."

Candace answers through her giggles, "Riabouchinska."

"What the hell is that?"

"She's Russian."

Sliding down in the bed to face her, I kiss her lips before saying, "I'll call her Ana."

She gives me a sweet grin, asking, "So we can keep her?"

"No. She can stay here until we can figure out what we're gonna do with her. But we're taking her to the vet as soon as we wake up to get her checked out before we bring her back here."

I kiss her again, slowly, lingering against her soft lips when she begins to mumble, "I'm glad I had this with you."

When I pull back, she adds, "Everything about today . . . I'm glad it was all with you."

Rolling on top of her, I spend a great deal of time letting her know, in my own way, how much I love her as I thoroughly kiss her.

chapter fifty

"BABY, MAKE SURE you leave enough food out for Ana," I call out to Candace who is upstairs.

The seasons have gone by fast and now we are packing up, getting ready to head to my mom's for Christmas. We were just there for Thanksgiving a few weeks back. I didn't get to spend a whole lot of time with Candace because she was too busy plotting Black Friday shopping tactics with my mom and aunts. It was fun to see her so into it, finding deals on toys she thought we should buy the kids for Christmas. She left me at home while she spent the whole night and half of the next day shopping just to wind up sleeping for the rest of the afternoon.

"Do you have everything?" Candace asks me as she walks down the stairs.

"Yeah, it's all in the car."

"Did you give Tatiana her new toy?"

"Yes, babe," I sigh. Candace insists that we buy that cat a new toy every time we leave her for a few days. Even though the cat has been living with us for over a month now, I still haven't fully agreed to letting it stay with us permanently. Life has just been crazy with Candace's performance schedule around the holidays; she's lucky she was allowed this time off to go out of town. Plus my photography has really picked up, and I'm now in several galleries in the city. Needless to say, trying to contact vets and whatnot hasn't been high on the list of things to do. I know she loves that cat, and it's so funny to see how they mirror each other. Tiny, quiet, and both very timid. I can't lie, the cat is adorable, and when Candace isn't around, she spends a good amount of time in my lap. But I love teasing Candace about my loathing relationship with Ana, so I keep up the charade because she's so fuckin' cute when she gets all defensive over that cat.

Picking up Candace's coat, I help slide it over her arms before we head out into the blistering cold. Once I help her into the car, I hop in, blast the heat, and start heading down to Oregon.

"Jase called this morning," she says as she takes my phone to sync it through the speakers. "Their connecting flight got delayed and they didn't make it to Ohio until after midnight."

"That sucks."

"Yeah. And then it took them over an hour to get to Mark's house. Said they are having a horrible snow storm."

When Candace selects The xx to play and sets the phone down, I take her hand in my lap, and ask, "So what do you wanna do while we're away?"

As she leans her head back against the seat, she responds with, "Nothing. I'm so worn out, all I want to do is lay around in my pajamas."

"So I get to keep you hidden away in my bed the whole time?" I say with a smirk, and she smiles back at me.

"No, but I think lying around, watching movies, and eating are all my top priorities."

Bringing her hand up to my lips, I kiss her knuckles as we sit back and listen to 'Angels.'

"I always think of you when I hear this song," she murmurs as she gets comfortable in her seat.

I give her hand a light squeeze as I listen to the love song that is laced with a haunting melody.

Candace and I continue to work together with Dr. Christman, still focusing on the events of that night with Jack, but since running into Charles, we've been discussing more of our childhoods and how they've impacted us as adults. I've learned a lot about what it was like for Candace growing up and how she taught herself to shut down emotionally so she wouldn't be forced into feeling worthless and sad all the time. She learned how to bury it and hide it away, to just move on through life by avoiding. But I do the same thing. Although we've dealt with two very different sets of parents, we both used masks to cope.

Candace still deals with anxiety around crowds. She continues to wake from night terrors, although not as often as she did a few months ago. I have a feeling these things will stick with her, along with the blame she carries. She's still my same Candace, but she's beginning to settle with herself, no longer living inside of her chaotic head all of the time, constantly haunted and shadowed. Her personality is starting to brighten, and I love seeing bits and pieces of the Candace that was so far destroyed when I first met her.

When we finally arrive at my mom's, it's a little after five on Christmas Eve. Trevor helps me unload all the gifts for the kids, and Candace, staying true to her word, is already in a pair of her long red and white polka dot pajama pants and a long-sleeved white shirt.

Walking over to her as she's sitting down with the kids, watching cartoons, wrapped up in a blanket with her glass of Merlot, I sit down next to her and kiss her.

"You move fast," I tease.

She settles herself into my arms as we lean back against the couch and says, "Your mom insisted I take it easy."

"Oh she did? Did she also insist on getting you drunk?" I joke as I eye her rather large glass of wine.

Her only response is a soft kiss with her hand wrapped around the back of my neck.

"Eww! Gross!" Maddie squeals from a few feet away, embarrassing Candace.

"Don't you kiss your boyfriend?" I tease her with a wink.

"I don't have a boyfriend, Uncle Ryan."

"That's not what your mom says," I say, continuing to egg her on.

She tilts her head at me, clearly in the know that I'm making things up, and says, "Boys are nasty," causing Candace to burst out laughing.

"This boy isn't nasty," Candace tells her quietly as if it's a secret she doesn't want anyone else to hear.

"Don't listen to her, Maddie," Tori pipes in as she sits down on the couch behind Candace and me. "Uncle Ryan has cooties."

"Maddie, do you know what crabs are?" I tease, knowing that the only crabs she's aware of are those in the ocean.

"Ryan!" Tori squeaks as she slaps my shoulder.

Laughing loudly, I turn to Tori and say, "Hey, if you're gonna tell her I have cooties—"

"Ryan, that's disgusting," Candace scolds while smiling at the banter going on.

"Aunt Donna told me that you guys got a cat," she mentions as she sits back, and we turn to face her.

"We didn't *get* a cat; Candace just decided to open our home to a feral," I say and then wait for Candace to get defensive, and it only takes a second.

"She's not a feral. She's super sweet," she tells Tori before looking at me, saying, "Admit it, she's sweet."

Tightening my arms around her, I confess, "Yeah, babe. Ana's sweet."

"Her name's Ana?" Tori asks.

"No, her name's Tatiana," Candace responds.

"So why do you call her Ana?"

Looking at Tori with annoyance, I tell her, "Because no man should have to call any pet 'Tatiana,' especially a random stray."

Tori shakes her head and laughs, "You guys are funny."

"It's a pretty name," Candace says. "But Ryan feels it impedes too much on his masculinity to have to acknowledge her full name."

"Are you guys talking about Tatiana?" my mom calls out from the kitchen. "That is the *cutest* cat."

"When did you see it?" Tori asks.

As Mom starts walking into the living room, she answers, "I visited them before Thanksgiving to see Candace dance since I missed her opening night."

Wrapping another blanket around the two of us, I tuck Candace's head under my chin as the four of us continue to talk.

It isn't long before everyone is finished with dinner and busy giving the kids baths and getting them ready for bed. Candace and I stay downstairs, cleaning up the kitchen and then settling in front of the fireplace with some wine. We enjoy the peace while we wait for my mother. Candace wants to stay up with her to fill the kids' stockings and put the gifts from Santa under the tree. My cousins appreciate her enthusiasm since it means they don't have to stay up and can go to bed.

"It's so dark in here," we hear my mom softly say as she walks into the room.

"It's quiet," I joke. "That's the most important thing."

She laughs and then eyes the bottle of wine, grabbing a glass before joining us. "Ryan, I have all the stocking stuff in the laundry room closet. Would you mind grabbing it for me?"

When I get the bags and return, Candace and Mom have all the stockings pulled from the fireplace and lying on the floor. I drop the bags and watch the two of them working together, filling them up with candy and gifts.

"So how have you been, dear? You're always so busy; I hardly get to talk to you," she says to Candace.

"I know. I'm sorry. Everything is good though. We've been really busy with the Nutcracker and also rehearsing auditions for our next run."

"What's that going to be?"

"'The Tempest.' It'll run in February."

"I'll have to get tickets for that."

"Mom, you don't have to come to all of her performances," I tell her as they continue to fill the stockings.

She sets one down to take a sip of her wine before saying, "I know I don't have to, but I want to." When she looks to Candace, she adds, "It's fun for me to go and to know it's you up there dancing."

Candace's face lights up as my mom says this. "Thanks, Donna. But you don't need to buy tickets. I can get you the same passes I get Ryan. It's not a big deal."

Once everything is filled, they hang the stockings back up above the fireplace when Candace says, "Did Ryan tell you about his newest shoot?"

"No."

"He was commissioned to shoot one of the lead principals in the company to be displayed at the Metro Gallery downtown for a special invitational showing," she brags with a huge smile.

When my mom turns to me, she nearly scolds, "Why didn't you say anything?"

"I just got the gig a few days ago."

"Apparently the director, Peter, is friends with one of my old college dance teachers whose girlfriend works at the Henry Gallery, who Ryan works closely with now. Anyway, a few of his pieces are being displayed and caught Peter's eye, and when he found out the photographer was my boyfriend, he commissioned him for this photo shoot."

"That's wonderful," Mom says. "It amazes me the things you two have going on in your lives."

I laugh at my mom's excitement as Candace continues to chat with her while we start putting the gifts under the tree. When everything is done, we say goodnight and Candace and I head up to my room to crash.

I wake up to the smell of Candace's shower and the commotion from downstairs. I lie there for a moment, trying to fully wake up, when she walks out of the bathroom, dressed and looking amazing for so early in the morning.

Reaching out, I grab on to her arm and pull her on top of me. "Morning."

She giggles and then wraps her arms around my neck, kissing me softly. Pulling back, she stares down at me, whispering, "Merry Christmas," with a hint of a smile.

"I love you," I tell her as I tangle my hands in her hair and bring her back down to my lips.

Remembering this day last year, I was at her house after her parents tossed her out the night before. She was upset and quiet, only wanting to come home with me to hide from everything going on in her life. And now . . . now she's mine, and that day seems like years ago. She's happy and content in my arms, with a whole new family that she fits into flawlessly. I'm happy to have another Christmas with her, and one that isn't buried under so much darkness. Not that the darkness isn't there, but the rim of light is promising.

"I'll wait while you get ready," she says as she shifts off of me.

After a quick shower, I toss on some clothes and we head downstairs into the madness.

"Uncle Ryan's up!" Connor yells out with excitement, making Candace and me laugh, as if Christmas couldn't start until I dragged myself down here.

"Morning, Mom."

"Good morning. You better hurry and grab your coffee because these kids aren't going to last much longer," she says, walking out of the kitchen, stopping to kiss Candace on the cheek before going into the living room.

Candace and I grab our coffees and then head into the other room. I make myself comfortable on the floor as Candace sits on the couch behind me. I lean my head back and she plants a kiss on my forehead followed by a wide smile before Bailey plops down on my lap.

"Wyan," she calls out, finally starting to get the hang of my name as she clings her tiny arms around my neck.

She squeals when I start blowing raspberry kisses on her neck.

"You ready to open presents?" I ask, and when her eyes widen as she nods, I call over to Trevor, "Find me a few for this princess."

After opening several gifts with me, she trades me in for Candace's lap. I sit next to them on the couch as she helps Bailey unwrap the tea set we bought her. They open gift after gift, and when a box wrapped in black paper lands on my lap with Candace's name on it, I interrupt her and Bailey, teasing, "So you can buy me a gift, but I can't get you anything?"

She shoots me a grin and then turns her attention back to Bailey as I peel back the paper to find that she bought me a big tintype kit for my camera.

"I saw you eying that tintype at the Metro Gallery," she says to me.

"This is perfect." I've been wanting to work with something a little bit different and for Candace to know that, picking up on the fact that I spent a little more time observing that piece than the others on display makes it clear how gelled we've become with each other.

"Candace," Mom says as she walks up to us from behind the couch. "Ryan made me tuck this away." She hands Candace the gift I ordered for her and was having my mom hang on to so that Candace wouldn't find out.

She takes the small, wrapped box from my mom and then shakes her head as she mutters, "Ryan, I don't . . ."

"Don't worry. It isn't for you."

She gives me a confused look when I clarify, "It's for Ana."

Her smile is warm, and when Bailey hops off of her lap, she folds her legs underneath herself as she gently unwraps the paper. Pulling out the sleek, brown leather, designer cat collar, her smile grows, showing off her sexy dimple.

"The collar isn't the real gift," I tell her. "Look at the tag, babe."

Laying her palm flat underneath the gold tag, she reads the name I had engraved on it: *Tatiana Campbell.*

"Campbell?" she questions slowly with a wary eye before asking, "So we're keeping her?"

"We're keeping her."

She wraps her arms tightly around my neck, laughing with excitement. "Thank you."

I laugh at her demeanor, planting a couple kisses below her ear, and when she pulls back to look at the collar again, Tori snatches it and teases, "This is a really nice leather collar."

"I would have tied yarn around its neck, but I saw Candace drooling over this collar when she dragged me into some frou-frou pet store."

Eying Candace, she cocks a brow at her. "Really?"

"Don't make fun of me. I think it's sophisticated," she defends.

"That's what's so funny about this," she jokes as she hands the collar back to her. "I've got to meet this cat if Ryan was willing to *bestow* his last name on her," she jokes with laughter.

"You should see the small four-post bed Candace bought her. It's ridiculous," I tell Tori.

She turns back to Candace, and says, "So Ryan has a tiny four-post kitty bed in his bedroom?"

Candace nods her head with a grin and Tori adds, "God, I love what you're doing to him."

Narrowing my eyes at her, I defend, "She didn't give me a choice. I came home from the bar one day and there it was."

"Regardless, it's still there."

"It's really cute," Candace tells her, and I laugh when I reiterate, "It's a four-post bed!"

"Oh my God, you guys," Tori bursts out laughing, and we all join in, even Candace, at the absurdity of it all. But in the end, my girl is happy and that's all that matters. She's never had a pet, and she adores having Tatiana.

Once the living room is completely demolished and littered in paper, my mom has everyone get the kids dressed and ready for the day while I do a clean sweep of the place. Candace takes a moment to call Jase and check in with him and Mark.

"I got her and Jase a little something for Christmas," Mom tells me as we take out all the trash.

"Mom—"

"I know, but I saw this cooking school that is down the street from your loft, and after seeing how much Jase likes to cook when he was here in July, I thought they would have fun taking a few lessons together."

We start heading back inside when I turn to her and say, "She's gonna love it. So will Jase. He's been coming over whenever he has free time and has tried teaching her a few things."

"Any luck?" she asks with a smile.

"We wind up going out," I admit with a light chuckle. "Thanks, Mom."

Walking back inside, Candace is standing over by the windows, looking out at the ocean. I step up from behind and slip my arms around her shoulders, resting my chin on top of her head. "Whatcha doing?"

"Just thinking."

"About?"

"Last Christmas."

Lifting my chin, I run my hands down her arms, and when she turns to face me, she says, "Thank you."

"What for?"

She wraps her arms around my waist as I cradle her face. "For being so patient with me."

"You may be slow to open up and hard to read, but you're not the type of girl you wanna rush anything with. I want every slow second."

When she lifts up onto her toes to kiss me, I pick her up off the floor as we seal our lips together, both realizing how far we've come since last year.

Candace and I decide to get bundled up and take a long walk down the beach alone, taking our time while the mist floats its way down from the dark, grey sky. We don't talk much, just keep close, stealing kisses along the way. When we finally get back to the house, Candace stays with my mom for most of the day in the kitchen, cooking, while I hang out with the kids, keeping them busy and out of trouble.

After dinner, everyone is getting ready for bed when Candace and I decide to do a replay of last year. When everyone finally heads to bed, we pile a bunch of pillows and blankets onto the living room floor in front of the fireplace, and then find an old black and white to watch.

We lie down, and I snuggle her into my arms, but this time, I can kiss her whenever I want, so I do. We make it through 'Swing Time,' and I think this one makes it to the top of Candace's favorites so far, but I figured it would since it's a love story about dancers. She keeps glued to the TV, but when 'I'll Be Seeing You' comes on next, our eyes drift from the screen to each other's. It's after midnight, and we begin to grow tired as we lie here face to face.

Candace slides her hand along my jaw before she presses her lips to mine. Running my hand down her back, I pull her in tight against me. She begins to bury her hands in my hair when I slip past her lips and revel in the sweet taste of her mouth. I fumble my hand in the blanket until I find the remote and shut off the TV, the only light coming from the burning logs in the fireplace.

I'm overwhelmed with her. Having her like this when a year ago I was so nervous around her. Now all I want is what we have. She's given me everything I thought I never wanted. She's given it in her own way, but the most perfect way for me. I used to be so disconnected and cold, but with her . . . she's taught me how to be soft because I can't be any other way with her. I never knew how much I needed that until I had her. It's because of her that I no longer worry about the fears that plagued me throughout my life. She showed me what it meant to provide for someone else. She's always been my priority. I never even had to think about it; she always was. And to see how happy she was today, I know I'm able to give her what she needs. That I can love, and I can do it well. It's because of her that I'm the man I never thought I could be, and she makes it so easy to do.

I'm never gonna stop wanting her—I know that. From the broken girl in the coffee shop on that rainy Halloween night to the vibrant girl who owns that stage at McCaw Theater every time she dances, I want every version of her—forever. I've never known beauty until her. I've never known how good life could be until her.

As I slowly drag my lips away from hers, she opens her eyes as she rests her head next to mine on the pillow. She runs her small hand from my shoulder down to my chest where she keeps it, and I wrap my hand around hers. Her soft skin glows in the flicker of the fire as I stare into her hazel eyes, and I see everything I'll ever want to see. It's all within her. She holds every part of me, and it's in this very moment that I feel it. It floods inside of me. A peace that only she can bring me.

No doubt. No questioning. No hesitation.

"Marry me."

chapter fifty-one
(Candace)

HIS SOFTEST WORDS are the most powerful and hit hard inside of my heart as it begins to race when shock takes it over.

"What?" I softly whisper because he's caught me so off guard with his question that my mind is spinning.

"Marry me," he repeats with a clarity I can't deny. With a certainty I've always depended on him for. He's the warmth I draw my strength from. My safe place to rest my head when it won't stop torturing me.

Each word falls right through me, and all I can do is give him a nod of my head.

His smile is perfection as he covers me in it, kissing me with his whole heart. The only heart that has been able to unravel me. The heart that showed me *my* heart could still breathe when I felt as if it was suffocating. He walked right inside of me and brought me back to life. He promised me he wouldn't let me fade. I didn't believe him at the time, but he fought for me. I thought I'd lost who I was, but with each day, he gives me a piece of my old self back. A playfulness I thought was gone. A happiness I never thought I'd feel again. A security I thought was forever stolen from me.

When he pulls back, his face is intent, looking straight through me to my core as he says, "Tell me, babe. Give me the words."

Taking his face in my hands, I can't hold in my emotions when the tears slip out. "Let's get married."

He pulls me to his chest as he loops his arm behind my knees, cradling me in his hold as he picks me up. The giggles slip out, the pure reflection of joy as he carries me upstairs to his room, shutting the door behind him. Laying me down in bed, he crawls over me and pulls the sheets over us.

"Tell me you love me," he whispers against my skin as he runs his hand underneath my top and gently squeezes my breast.

"I've only ever loved you," I pant as he slowly grazes my nipple with his thumb.

His lips find my neck, and he begins to kiss and nibble his way down as he grabs the hem of my shirt and slips it off of me. I know what he wants, and I want to give it to him, but knowing the house is full of people, my nerves take over.

"Ryan, wait."

Lifting his head, he looks down at me and reads me well when he says, "Baby, I wanna make love to you."

"But—"

"You're all that exists for me right now," he tells me, and my eyes fall shut with his words.

His warm lips cover mine, and I let go of the worry, handing it over to him because I know he'll always take care of me. Running his kisses down the center of my chest, he moves to my breast and drags his tongue over the lace bra that's still covering me. The sensation is powerful as he gently sucks my nipple into the heat of his mouth. He takes his hand and slides it behind me, unhooking my bra and dropping it to the floor. Ryan stares down at me, then meets my eyes, saying, "I never knew it could be like this."

His words bring a smile to my face when I respond, "Me neither."

We go slow, the same way we always do. He's never rushed with me, always taking his time, but knowing that he wants to be mine—to be my husband—creates an underlying intensity. A piece of the puzzle that we've finally found. A wholeness that we can bring each other. And when we have each other undressed, he quietly slips inside of me and holds himself there. Still. His breathing is heavy, and I can feel the swarm of his emotions take over him. I see it in eyes as he keeps them locked on mine.

I pull him down to me, needing the weight of him to cover me as I press my hands into his back to keep him close. Tonight is different. Bared in a way we've never been with each other. The love I feel for this man is more than my body can handle, and when I release a whimper, he begins to move inside of me.

His head is nestled in the curve of my neck, and I run my hands up his back and into his hair, holding his head in my hands, and when he draws his head back, I see his cheeks are damp with tears. I don't say anything; I know exactly how he feels because his tears reflect the ones that run down the sides of my face.

Rolling to the side, we lie face to face. He takes my leg and drapes it over his hip as he grabs me from behind, guiding me with him. I keep my hands on his face and hold him close, both of us quietly releasing our love and happiness through tears. The room fills with nothing but soft breaths of pleasure as we make love, giving ourselves entirely with the certainty that we are perfect for each other. Feeling secure, knowing that through it all our love has never stalled. It only grows.

Waking up in the morning, the room is cold, and I snuggle in tighter to Ryan who is just starting to stir. I watch as he slowly begins to open his eyes, and before he can fully wake, he has a cheesy grin on his face when he rolls me on top of him.

"Morning," he says in his sexy rasp before I lower my lips to his, giving him a gentle kiss.

When I shiver in his arms, he rolls me back onto the bed, and wraps his arms around me.

"Mmm, you're still naked," he teases with a grin, and I tuck my head down into his chest. "Why are you so shy with me still?"

"Ryan," I softly nag.

"I'm not complaining. I like that you're still shy and reserved around me."

Peeking up at him, he kisses my forehead, and adds, "But I'm not gonna lie, I love feeling your skin all over me."

"Stop," I say, feeling the blush heat my cheeks as he quietly laughs.

He runs his hands through my hair as he looks at me, saying, "Tell me last night wasn't a dream."

"Which part?"

"The part where you said you'd marry me."

Smiling, I tell him, "I hope it wasn't a dream."

"Do you have any idea how happy you make me?" he asks, not letting me answer when he kisses the smile on my face.

He keeps his lips on me as he starts running his kisses across my cheek and down my neck. Holding on to him, I close my eyes as he sends tingles down my arms. "I don't wanna wait," I whisper.

"For what," he mumbles against my skin.

"To marry you."

He pulls back to look at me, and agrees, "I don't either."

"Well, I was thinking . . . umm . . ."

"Just say it," he tells me as he brushes my hair back.

"What about Indian Beach?"

"To get married?" he asks.

I nod my head, saying, "I love it there." It's where we went this very day last year when he told me that he wanted to be with me. It's where he taught me how to surf. It's a place the two of us go together every time we come to Cannon Beach. And I know it's his favorite beach too.

"Sounds perfect."

"But . . ." I start hesitantly. "What if we just did it this weekend?"

"In two days?"

"Or three," I say coyly, wondering if he's thinking I'm crazy for suggesting doing it so soon.

"Babe, don't you want a big wedding and have everyone there?" he asks, concerned.

Letting out a soft breath, I tell him, "I never wanted a big wedding. You know me; I don't want all that. I just want us."

He gives me a kiss and then questions, "Are you sure?"

"I'm sure. Just us," I assure him before adding with a smile, "And a pretty dress."

"What about everything else?"

"There is nothing else. I just want you, but no cheesy tux. Promise me no tux."

He laughs at me and asks, "Why's that?"

"Because it isn't you."

"Okay, no cheesy tux," he agrees with a sexy smirk, and the smile on my face can't even reflect the happiness that I feel right now.

After he makes sure he is satisfied from thoroughly kissing me, he says, "We should go downstairs. Everyone is leaving this morning, so we should make an appearance."

"Can we not tell them?" I suggest, and when he tilts his head in question, I add, "I don't want all the fuss. Can we just tell your mom when everyone leaves?"

"Of course, babe," he says and then gets out of bed.

After we take our showers and get dressed, we head downstairs to visit before everyone heads home, except Tori, who is going to stay so that she can go shopping with Donna.

"Hey, Mom. Can Candace and I talk to you for a minute?" Ryan asks as she is finishing up a pot of tea for herself and me.

"Sure," she says with a curious eye as Ryan takes my hand and starts walking back to the study.

"What's going on?" Donna asks as the three of us stand there.

My stomach is filled with butterflies, wondering how she's going to react to this sudden news. I think Ryan and I are still in a bit of shock with the spontaneity of it all, but it's what we both want.

Ryan doesn't waste any time when he comes right out and says, "I asked Candace to marry me last night."

"What?!" she squeals and looks to me, and then down at my hand, and Ryan catches her eyes.

"No ring, Mom," he says.

She shakes her head, questioning, "So . . . ?" and I laugh as I assure her, "I said yes."

"Oh my God!" Donna wraps her arms around both of us, and I can't stop laughing at her reaction. Happy, joyful, and everything else you would wish for from a parent.

"Why didn't you say anything?" she nearly scolds Ryan when she pulls back. "And why didn't you get her a ring?"

"I don't need a ring," I butt in and tell her.

"Because," Ryan interrupts, "I never thought of asking her until last night. It just happened, and before I knew it, I asked and she said yes."

"This is just wonderful news, you two," she beams with an ear to ear smile.

"But we need your help," he says.

"Yes, anything."

"We want to get married here. Either Saturday or Sunday."

"*This* Saturday or Sunday?" she questions.

"Yeah," he says while I nod my head.

"What's this Saturday or Sunday?" Tori asks as she walks in.

Donna doesn't say anything and looks to me, but Ryan goes ahead and tells her as he steps behind me and wraps his arms around my shoulders. "Candace and I are getting married."

"What?!" She gives the same squealed reaction as Donna. "In two days?!"

"Or three," I mumble quietly, starting to feel a little embarrassed with the reactions.

"How are you supposed to plan a wedding in two days?"

"Tori, stop," Ryan tells her, and when she looks at me, she back pedals as I'm sure she can see the embarrassment written all over my face. "I'm sorry, Candace."

"No, it's fine," I tell her and then look over at Donna. "We don't want a big wedding or anything. We were just thinking we could go to Indian Beach in a couple days and simply get married. That's all."

Her warm smile soothes the anxiety that Tori was starting to give me and softly says, "I think that's perfect, dear."

"We just need someone to do the ceremony, so could you call the church you attend and see if one of the pastors is available? We'll work around his schedule," Ryan says to her.

"Of course. I'll call right now, but you two will need to go to the courthouse to get a license today," she tells us.

"What about flowers, or a cake, or—" Tori starts.

"Nothing," Ryan tells her.

"Really?" she asks, looking at me, and I tell her, "Really. I just want a dress. That's all I need." But then it hits me . . . it isn't all I need. Turning in Ryan's arms, I look up at him, and before I can speak, he reads the panic in me, asking, "What's wrong?"

"We have to call Jase. I can't get married without him. I just . . ."

"We'll call him, babe. No worries."

Jase is my family, the closest person I have in my life next to Ryan. I couldn't imagine doing this without him by my side.

"Well, then," Donna says. "I'll get on the phone and start making calls.

Why don't the two of you go ahead and drive to the courthouse and call Jase on the way. As soon as I get things figured out on my end, I call and let you know, okay?"

"Thanks, Mom."

Donna walks over to me and takes my hands in hers, saying, "You have no idea how happy you've just made me."

"Really?"

"We'll talk later, dear," she assures and then adds, "I'll get a list of dress shops together so when you get back, you can decide where to go first."

"I was hoping that you could take me," I say, and when her eyes rim with tears and she nods her head, she tells me, "I'd love nothing more," before hugging me.

After Ryan and I left to head to the courthouse, I called Jase to tell him what was going on. He was shocked, which I expected, but hopped on the computer and was able to switch the flights for him and Mark, and they will be here tomorrow evening.

When Ryan and I got back home, Donna had spoken with one of the pastors at her church, and he agreed to marry us Saturday at five. He wants to meet with the two of us later today, so Donna and I are going to try our best to find me a dress before we have our appointment at the church.

Walking into the first dress shop, I have a pretty good idea of what I'm looking for. So when one of the bridal consultants approaches and asks, I tell her, "Simple. I really like lace."

"Not a problem. You're quite small, so if you are looking to buy off the rack, you're limited," she tells me as she leads us through the mass of wedding gowns.

Donna and I begin to pull dresses. Most are pretty detailed, so I only take a small handful back to the fitting room to try on. I step out and show Donna a couple of the dresses, but it isn't until the third one that I know.

Stepping out of the fitting room and onto the platform in front of the mirrors, Donna stands behind me to tie the satin sash around my waist. Smoothing my hands over the ivory lace, I look at myself in the mirror and just know that this is the dress I want Ryan to see me in. It's sleeveless with a v-neck front and a plunging v-cut dip in the back with a champagne colored satin sash around the waist. It's form-fitting and simple with a tiny sweep-train and solid lace, which I know Ryan has an affinity for.

"I love it," I say as Donna steps to the side.

"It's perfect, dear."

The hem is a tad long, but it'll do. Everything else fits perfectly. I never saw myself getting married. I dreamt about it as a little girl, but never really considered it as I got older.

It's odd to see myself like this. As a bride. It even sounds weird; but I love him. Even when I wasn't with him, I never stopped loving him.

"What do you think?" Donna asks, and when I look at her in the mirror, I nod my head.

Thinking about Ryan seeing me in this dress, thinking about becoming his wife, thinking about this past year—it all overpowers me, and I quickly wipe the tears that begin to drop. Donna steps onto the platform with me and gives me a hug.

"I certainly hope these are happy tears," she quietly says, and when I pull back and see another bride walking in, Donna takes my hand and walks us to my fitting room, closing the heavy curtain.

"Are you okay?" she asks as we sit on the small couch.

"It's a lot," I tell her.

She gives me a questioning look and I assure, "Not like that; I love Ryan. Just . . . this past year has been a huge change. One I never saw coming."

"I can't even imagine."

And out of nowhere, I think about my parents. About my father, and how everything has decayed with them. I was about to leave for New York without ever telling them, and now I'm about to get married. It hurts.

"My parents don't even know," I mumble as more tears fall.

"Sweetheart," she says as she pulls me into her arms. "Well . . . do you think you should call them? I mean, when's the last time you spoke with them?"

Sitting back, I tell her, "Last Christmas. It's been a year. Ryan said he saw my dad several months ago at one of my performances, but he didn't even want to talk to me. He told Ryan to not tell me he was there."

"I'm so sorry."

"It just makes me sad."

"Of course it does," she says. "Love doesn't disappear just because the people do."

"I'm not sure they ever loved me," I choke out around the knot in my throat. "But it feels weird to move on without them."

"What does Ryan say?"

"What can he say?" I tell her with a slight shrug of my shoulders. "He's supportive regardless, but it's hard not to think about them right now. I know them well enough to know that it's done with and has been for a long time."

She takes my hands, and tells me, "I don't claim to have been the perfect mother to Ryan. I let him down in so many ways. I didn't protect him like I should have, and I know that. But I've never once *not* loved him with everything that I am. I don't know your parents, so I can't speak for them, but I feel like I have gotten to know you well this past year. And you have a beautiful soul. I couldn't imagine anyone better for my son than you. To be able to call you my daughter, I can't tell you what that means to me." Her tears fall along with mine, and I soak in her words. "I love you as if you were my own."

Wiping my face, I don't feel like I could possibly speak, but I force the words out because she deserves to hear them when I explain, "It's always been hard for me to talk to people." I stop, trying to take a breath through my shaky voice but then continue with my trembling, strained words. "I don't open up easily, I know that. But you made it easy. You and Ryan both. And when I told you, the night of my solo, that you were the best gift Ryan ever gave me . . . I meant every word. It killed me not to have him for those few months, but it killed not to have you either. I never understood what a mom's love felt like until you."

We spend a few minutes hugging each other before we dry our tears and have a good laugh at our emotional mess.

"Here, let me untie you," she says as we stand up and she loosens the sash. "Should we look for a wrap or something? You're going to be freezing wearing only this."

"This dress is beautiful. I don't want to cover it up," I tell her.

"But it's the middle of winter."

Looking back at her, I say, "Ryan will keep me warm."

When she steps out, I slip off the dress and put my clothes back on. Donna tried talking me into a veil and jewelry, but I politely declined. Unfortunately, there was no declining when she insisted on buying the dress.

The past two days have been a whirlwind. After we met with Pastor Andrews the other evening, Ryan ordered dinner in and watched the new episode of 'Ridiculousness' with me. Donna couldn't believe that I liked that show, and she and Ryan had a heck of a time teasing me, but I know it was all in good fun. It was nice to veg out in front of the TV with the two of them.

I decided to go by myself to pick up Ryan's ring yesterday. As much as he likes to tease me, he loves nice things just as much as I do, so I decided on a timeless, brushed-platinum band. I waited while they engraved it for me, and by the time I got back to the house, Jase and Mark had just arrived. They were exhausted from spending the day traveling, so we all crashed early.

When I stir awake, Ryan is already up. Threading his hands through my hair, he says, "Morning, babe."

"Morning."

Inching his way down in bed, and facing me, he smiles, saying, "I feel like an antsy kid."

"Why's that?"

"Because I get my everything today," he says. "You nervous?"

"No. You?"

He pulls me flush against him, whispering, "No," before kissing me.

When we finally make it downstairs, Donna and Jase are cooking while Mark drinks his coffee and watches. We all sit around and enjoy a long breakfast together before Ryan and I throw on our raincoats to take a walk along the beach.

The skies are dark and a heavy mist fills the air as we head down the beach and find a spot to sit. Settling between his legs, I lean back into his arms. "Talk to me," I request.

"About what?"

"Anything," I say, simply wanting to hear his voice.

He tightens his arms around me, and tells me, "I don't want you to worry about anything. Thinking that marrying me is going to change us."

I smile at his words because somehow he just knew what I needed to hear. "I'm glad you said that."

He shifts me to face him and says, "I love us just the way we are. I want to marry you because I want forever with you. I want it all, and I know you're the only one who can give it to me."

"I don't know what to say," I tell him.

"You don't have to say anything."

Running my hand along his cheek, I give him the only words I can find, "My only wish is that I can give you everything you've given me."

"You already have, babe. You're enough."

I cuddle into his chest as we sit in the cold, in no rush to get back to the house. I need the quiet with him. I always will because I've come to depend on the closeness.

Ryan is spending the afternoon with his mom and Mark, letting me have the next couple of hours alone with Jase before we head to the beach. I sit in Ryan's room while Jase changes in the bathroom. My dress hangs in front of the window, and I sit on the bed, staring at it, thoughts filling my head, wondering how I wound up here when it wasn't that long ago that I was wishing I had died by that dumpster.

And then there was Ryan. The stranger that sat with me while I lay there naked and unconscious on the ground. The stranger who is now about to become my husband.

Ryan is an amazing man. More than I ever thought I deserved. He's always loved me, and no matter what we have dealt with, he's never wavered. He's always held my heart above his. Always giving me a safe place to fall. From the start he saw through my walls, to the darkest part of me, and found my light.

"What are you thinking about?" Jase says as he walks into the room.

"How I got here."

He sits next to me on the bed and holds my hand. "Remember that morning when Mark and I were talking to you about Ryan? I was being way too protective, worrying that you two might be interested in each other."

Looking at him, I nod my head, recalling that morning. The morning after Ryan returned my leopard scarf I had left at The xx concert.

"And you remember when you told me that you thought you wouldn't ever be able to fall in love, and I told you that one day you'll get everything you deserve?"

"Yeah."

"This is that day for you."

His words make me cry. We've been through so much together. Jase has always been my heart. We've depended on each other for almost five years now. From the moment I met him, I loved him. I couldn't imagine my life without him. Ryan has never questioned our relationship, and neither has Mark. It was always Jase and I—for years—before Mark and Ryan walked in. They blended seamlessly with us, and Jase and I have found a way to open ourselves up to our boyfriends.

"I love you," I tell him.

"I know you do. And I love you."

Feeling extremely overwhelmed by today, Jase sits with me while I let the tears stream down my face. But it's when I see his own tears slip out that I turn to face him as he says, "Tell me that this won't change. You and me."

"Nothing will ever change you and me."

"I know that you're Ryan's, but you are always going to be my girl." He wipes my tears with his thumbs, but they're falling too fast for him to catch.

"You're my heart. You always have been. But now, Ryan holds that heart," I tell him. "My love for you will always be there. I couldn't imagine my life without you."

Jase holds me as we share this moment with each other. He was the first person I ever trusted. The first one I ever shared my heart with. Never once has anything come between us. He's my constant—I've never had to hide from him. But it's because of him that I was able to fall in love with Ryan, and for that, I love him even more. Jase always believed that I would find love, that I would find happiness when I thought my life had been too far destroyed for any hope of that happening. He believed it, and he pushed me when I was scared to open my heart to Ryan.

The tears finally subside, and I freshen up before Jase helps me get dressed. When he's done tying my sash, I turn to face him as he looks me over. He smiles, and when his eyes meet mine, he says, "You look amazing, sweetheart."

"Thank you . . . for everything you've ever been for me."

"It's just the beginning," he says as he takes my hand. "You ready?"

"Just one more thing." I walk over to the dresser and pick up the necklace that Ryan gave me. "Can you clasp this for me?"

I know it doesn't go with the dress, but I wear it every day, and today is no different. So when Jase puts it on me, I know I'm ready.

"Let's go," I say.

Jase helps me into his car and drives to Ecola Park, through the winding streets until we get to Indian Beach. He parks the car, overlooking the beach down below where I see the pastor, Donna, Mark, Tori, and Ryan. I smile when I see him down there, wearing black slacks and a dark charcoal button-up shirt.

"No tux?" Jase says from the driver's seat.

"I told him they were cheesy." Taking his ring that I have been clutching in my hand, I give it to Jase to hold.

Keeping my eyes fixed on the people who mean the world to me standing below, I hear Jase as he reads the inscription, "I see you in colors that don't exist."

I've never been so sure of my life until now, and all I want is to feel his touch, so when I turn to Jase, I say, "Will you take me to him?"

He gets out of the car and walks over to my side, opening my door. I take his hand as he helps me out, and when I smooth down the lace, he says, "Grab the umbrella."

"No umbrella."

"You're gonna ruin this dress, you know?"

"I know."

Taking my hand, I lock my fingers with my best friend's as he starts walking me over to the wooden steps that lead down to the beach. A thick blanket of grey covers the sky as the heavy mist falls from above. The sound of crashing waves fills the air, and when Jase gives my hand a squeeze, he begins walking me down the first flight of stairs. When we hit the landing before taking the last set of steps to the beach, Ryan turns to see me.

(Ryan)

My eyes hit her when I spot her on the stairs. God, she looks incredible, wearing nothing but lace with her hair down. She's clutched to Jase, and I know she's got to be freezing in this rain, but she's never looked more beautiful.

When Jase starts leading her down, she keeps her eyes locked on me, and I can already see the tears running down her cold, pink cheeks. My heart begins to race at the mere sight of her, and I feel like the luckiest man. Everything about her is everything I dream about now.

She walks across the dense sand, rain puddles everywhere, but she doesn't care. She walks right through them, dragging her dress through the water and sand. Before I can touch her, she turns to Jase and gives him a hug and kiss. When he gives her over to me, I run my hands down her soft, damp arms as she smiles through her tears. Pulling her into my arms, I take a moment and hold on to her, needing the closeness. I breathe her in, and when the pastor begins to speak, I keep my arms around her, giving her my warmth. We stand, wrapped up in each other, and no one else exists right now—only her.

We make our vows to each other, and when I take the ring from Tori, Candace keeps her eyes fixed on the vintage ring I found for her. When I saw the aged pearl, I knew it was perfect, and I love what it stands for because she's the purest thing in my life. The pearl is set on a weathered gold band with a stamped filigree pattern. It's simple, delicate, and when I slide it on her tiny finger, it couldn't be more perfect.

We may not have a fairytale meeting, and we may not always have sunshine and roses, but what we do have is a raw love that is honest and true. And when the pastor declares her as my wife, I take my sweet time kissing her cold, rain-covered lips, tasting a life that is so much more promising now that she's in it with me.

Wanting to get my girl warmed up, we say our goodbyes to everyone, and I take her up to my car. But before I open her door, I band my arms around her, and really kiss her. Moving my lips with hers as I run my hands down the smooth skin of her exposed back. And when I finally drag my lips away, I look down at her and ask, "Now what?"

"Let's go home."

Helping her up into the car, I tuck in the bottom of her lace dress, which is now soaked with rain and dirt. I grab her a blanket from the back seat and wrap it around her before I get in and start driving us back to Seattle. She holds my hand the entire way, and when we finally make it back to the loft, I carry her up the stairs and inside.

When I get her upstairs, we stand in the center of the room as I cradle her cheeks in my hands, saying, "You will never have to doubt your place in this world again because I swear I will spend forever making sure you're right where you belong."

I watch her eyes rim with tears while I run my hands down her neck and underneath the lace on her shoulders as I slowly begin peeling off her wedding dress.

I never knew that a person could be capable of falling as hard as I have for Candace. I spent so many years fearing the fall, but she made it effortless, taking all my fears away. With her, I know I'll never get enough. I'm always gonna want more, and as I make love to my wife, I know I'm gonna spend the rest of my life falling.

epilogue

AS I WAIT for the curtain to draw up, I turn to Jase and watch as he and Mark keep their daughter, Caroline, busy by showing the program to her, reading off the various performance titles. This is her first time at the theater, and I'm surprised with how well-behaved she's being.

Jase and Mark ended up getting married a few years after Candace and I. When they adopted Caroline, simply having Candace and I be her aunt and uncle wasn't enough, so Jase and Mark asked us to be her godparents. She's always been a huge part of our lives, and to see that she is fast approaching her fifth birthday is a test to how fast the years have flown by.

Candace has managed to have a successful career, quickly becoming a soloist at Pacific Northwest Ballet during her second year, and moving to principal her fifth. She's loved every minute of it, and getting to watch my girl dance the lead in so many shows has been amazing.

Shortly after we got married, I took her to New York to attend a performance by the American Ballet Theatre, the company she turned down to stay in Seattle. I wanted to remind her that we could still make New York happen, but she was firm on staying with PNB. I never questioned her decision to stay, but I know a piece of her has always been scared to leave everything behind.

Security has consistently been something she has craved, and Seattle offers her that. Having her friends and family close was also important while she was in therapy and trying to recover from her attack. She continued with therapy for a few years, but through it all, and after twelve years since the attack, she's never gotten over holding herself responsible for that night. It's not something I believe will ever change, so I've simply accepted it and no longer try to convince her that she should feel differently.

A few months after we married, nearly two years since the rape, she finally came off of her sleeping pill. It was a rough transition, but the doctor insisted. She had nightmares for a while, but I feel it was her anxiety that was triggering it. Eventually the nightmares lessened, and then the night terrors lessened. She still has nightmares, but those only happen a few times a year, and they aren't nearly as bad as they used to be.

Aside from a few lingering effects of that night, she's blossomed into a beautiful woman, and I've been lucky enough to watch it firsthand. She's a lot more spunky than I would have imagined from when I first met her. Her laugh is infectious, and she has brightened every aspect of my life.

I wound up selling a percentage of Blur to Max, making him a partner. We remain close friends, but my main business now is my art. When my photos started being picked up by galleries in different states, my commissioned work really took off, but the majority of my income comes from gallery sales.

Candace and I have transitioned through the years with ease. She remains the love of my life, and I spend every day making sure she never forgets it. I'll never be able to thank her enough for giving me this life.

When the lights dim, and the curtain goes up, Caroline is excited as she watches the dancers on stage. I have to wait a few numbers until I get to see my girl. When the music cues, she lights up, sending chills up my neck. She moves across the stage with her beautiful smile, enjoying every second. I can't take my eyes off of her even though there are other dancers on the stage. She captivates me, and I'm stuck on her.

She's the greatest gift in my life. I never thought I could love the way I love her. The music comes to an end all too soon. I could watch her on that stage forever. When she takes her curtsey, she beams at the applause. After the curtain falls, I just can't wait to see her, so I quietly tell Jase, "I'm gonna run backstage."

Making my way out of the theater, I head back to the hall where all the dressing rooms are, and when I spot her, she smiles as she rushes towards me. I hold my arms out for her and catch a glimpse of Candace off to my side as she smiles proudly before my girl bounds into my arms, squealing with joy, "Daddy!"

I See You In Colors

I am pretending you did not exist.
Ink nightly washes black
over my consciousness
and abandons me as morning seaweed
upon a foreign beach.

I am pretending we were simply
the sparkling imagination of some higher being,
our life together set below a singular epic sky
unrepeated
in future histories.

I am pretending I cannot taste you
each day as I do the sea air in my breath
when I am running,
my heart tied upon one foot,
ancient melancholy tied upon the other,
anxiously racing,
madly racing through lifetimes,
to find our brightened souls.

I see you in colors that don't exist.

It is all that I see clearly,
and why I run.

—P. Matsumoto

1 in every 4 women will experience domestic violence in her lifetime. 30% to 60% of perpetrators of intimate partner violence also abuse children in the household. Boys who witness domestic violence are *twice as likely* to abuse their own partners and children when they become adults. Only approximately 1/4 of all physical assaults and 1/5 of all rapes are reported to the police.

Candace and Ryan's story is simply one of example of how so many people live. Although both of them hid what they had suffered through, you don't have to.

National Domestic Violence Hotline
1.800.799.SAFE
Visit www.ncadv.org to find more information and resources.
National Sexual Assault Hotline
1.800.656.HOPE
Visit www.rainn.org for more information and resources.

BONUS MATERIAL

FINDING FOREVER

a short story

(Ryan Campbell's POV)
7 years after the wedding

PULLING UP TO the loft, I hate that Candace's car already here. She's supposed to be at the studio, so the fact that she's home makes my chest ache. I know what I'm about to walk into, and it kills me.

We've been trying to get pregnant for over a year now. Every month seems to be filled with stress and anxiety, wondering if this month will be the month Candace will get pregnant. The doctors say it's not out of the norm for athletes to struggle with this. I've known that she's always had irregular periods, sometimes going several months without one. She works her body so hard, has since the day I met her nearly eight years ago when she was still in college.

But it was a couple weeks ago when she finally tested positive. Fuck, her smile was incredible as she leapt into my arms, squealing with joy. I've never felt my heart beat like it did in that moment. And then last week, my heart beat in a completely different way when Candace woke up in the middle of the night bleeding. She curled up in my arms and cried, feeling like she failed and that somehow she was to blame. We learned the following day that what had happened was a chemical pregnancy—an early miscarriage. Life's cruel joke of finally giving us a baby long enough to get excited and then ripping it away.

When I walk in, I can hear her cries from upstairs. I drop my things and rush up to find her muffling her sobs in her pillow. Without saying a word, I crawl in behind her and tuck her in my arms. Her tiny body heaves against mine, breaking away pieces of my heart of what could have been. A baby. *Our baby.*

I've watched her with Jase and Mark's daughter. They adopted Caroline a few months ago from birth. She's only a tiny infant, but she's become everything to us. We were beyond thrilled when they asked us to be her godparents. I've seen how Candace is with my nieces and nephews, but when I saw her holding Caroline, this tiny baby, I knew I wanted to give her that. Give her a baby of our own.

I'll never forget coming home that night.

"*I still can't believe she is finally sleeping in that thing,*" I laugh, amazed that Ana, our cat, is finally in her own bed and not ours.

Candace hops up into bed and teases, "*See, aren't you glad we never got rid of her bed?*"

"*Oh, I still wanna get rid of it. Trust me on that.*"

Her furrowed brow makes me smile, and she smacks my arm when I can't hide my evil grin. She still gets so worked up whenever I make the slightest jab at our cat. I laugh at her attempted abuse on me and then snatch her around the waist, playfully tossing her onto her back.

"*You wanna get feisty?*" I goad with a smile, and she puts on the most serious face she can muster up, saying, "*Are you mocking me, Ryan?*"

"*Never. I want you to get feisty with me,*" I tell her, and then go in quickly before she can respond, running my tongue up her neck and behind her ear and nipping her lobe between my teeth.

Her hands weave into my hair and fists it, moving me to her lips, which I take with mine. Her soft moans drive me to sink my tongue in her mouth, needing to taste what's mine. She's amazing, wrapping her legs around me, locking me close to her.

Candace used to be so timid with sex and understandably so. We married quickly, only dating for a year before she became my wife. The year we dated was a dark time in our lives. I met her when she was nothing but a broken mess. The first time I ever saw my wife, she was being raped. I hate that I met her like that. Even though we tell people, when they ask, that we met on a rainy Halloween night at the coffee shop she used to work at, we both know it's a lie.

Candace has gone through the depths of hell to get to where she's at now. Every intimate part of our relationship has taken time and an insane amount of patience, but we're now able to give each other every single piece of ourselves. She knows she's okay and safe with me. My tiny fighter. God, I love this woman so much that I want to give her the final piece of me—a baby.

Pulling back from her lips, I look down at her soft face, cheeks flushed pink, whispering, "*Do you have any clue how beautiful you are?*" She runs her hand along my jaw, and I tell her, "*I love watching you when you're with Caroline.*"

"*She's so perfect.*"

Dropping my lips to hers, I say, "*I want to give you that.*"

As soon as the words are out, I get nervous. Dancing is her life and maintaining her body is imperative. I knew from the get-go that it would be just the two of us for a long time while she moved up the ranks in the company she dances with. But she's now thirty and I'm thirty-six, the only ones without kids in our group of friends.

As soon as I start doubting her response, she surprises me with a *smile.*

"Really?"

I give her a nod. "Really. But, if you want to wait longer, I'm okay with that. I just needed you to know that I'm ready when you are."

Her eyebrows cinch up and her eyes rim with tears. Candace has always been an emotional girl with me. She's so soft, and I love that about her.

"Talk to me, babe."

"I'm glad you said that, because I've been thinking about it lately."

"And?"

"I'm ready."

With a heavy sigh, I drop my forehead to hers, and she lifts her chin, sealing her lips with mine. I swear, I'm going to enjoy every single second it takes to get my girl pregnant.

"I'll stop taking my pills tomorrow," she breathes between our kisses before I start peeling her clothes off, tossing them aside to get her naked beneath me.

"I don't know what to do anymore," she cries, pulling me from my thoughts.

"We don't have to make any decisions right now, babe."

"Do we try?" she asks, referring to what the doctor had told us, that after a chemical pregnancy, Candace should be at her most fertile state. She told us, that if we were up to it, we should give it a go, but seeing how upset Candace is, I just don't know.

Tugging on her hip, I move to roll Candace over to look at me. Her face is splotchy and her eyes are thick with tears and bloodshot. She looks so tired as I run my hand down her cheek.

"Baby, if you're not ready, then we wait. I have all the time in world."

"What if I can't ever give you a baby?"

"Don't put this on you. This is us, not just you," I tell her adamantly. "But I believe we will."

"How? How can you believe that when we've been trying for so long?"

"Because I saw her."

"Who?"

Threading my hand through her thick hair, I rest my forehead against hers and close my eyes when I tell her, "Our daughter."

Candace grabs ahold of my wrist as her cries pick up, but I continue anyway, explaining, "I had a dream. You were there. We were in the kitchen making breakfast, but there were three plates. I was watching you cut an apple and divide the slices between the plates, and then you hollered a girl's name. When I looked up, I saw her. She looked just like you, and I knew she was ours."

"When did you have this dream?" she asks through her tears.

"A few weeks ago."

"Why didn't you tell me?"

Running my thumbs under her eyes, I tell her, "Because I didn't want to put any unneeded stress on you."

She tucks her head under my chin and remains quiet for a moment before asking, "What did I holler?"

"Hmm?"

"You said I called out for her. What name did I say?"

"Annabelle. You called her Annabelle."

Candace's arms band tighter around me when I tell her this, and I strengthen my hold on her as well.

"It's a beautiful name," she murmurs.

"Can I show you something?"

"What?"

She pulls back, and I look into her eyes. She's so beautiful, even in this moment, she's simply stunning to me.

"You're Valentine's gift," I tell her.

She nods, and I roll over to open the drawer to my nightstand. Pulling out the small white box, I turn back to her and lay it on the bed between us. She stares at it for a moment before sitting up and crossing her legs in front of her. Candace used to hate getting gifts, but through the years, she's learned to enjoy them, so when she picks up the box, I move to sit in front of her.

Candace removes the lid and the puzzled look on her face makes me laugh.

She darts her eyes to me, and with confusion written all over her face, she says, "I don't get it. I feel like I should since you're laughing."

"I'm laughing because you're adorable," I respond as I pick up the tiny bell charm from inside the box. "This is our hope," I tell her as I hold it up. "Take off your necklace."

Candace unclasps the necklace I gave her when we first started dating. She still wears it everyday after all this time. When she hands it over, I slip the bell charm onto the silver chain.

"Our Annabelle," I say as I take the necklace and fasten it back around her neck. "But I'm going to call her Bell."

acknowledgements

AS THIS SERIES comes to a close, I am taken back to the night I finally swallowed my doubts about writing a book, remembering the moment I turned to my husband and said, "I'm gonna do it." He's the one that, out of the blue, said I should write a book, and it took him time to finally convince me, but eventually he did. No amount of 'thank you's' will ever be enough. I'm not even sure he realizes this gift he's given me.

And so I start with him.

Thank you to my husband, who, through it all, has always seen the light within me. Seen the potential that lies beneath. Seen everything I'm not able to. Always believing and sacrificing to make sure I can act upon every opportunity that comes my way. It's been a crazy year while I have been writing this series, and watching you take control of everything to allow me the time to write these stories has proven to me how lucky I truly am to have you by my side. And just as Candace views Ryan, I also see you in colors that don't exist, because what we have together is a rarity. Don't doubt for one second that I don't see everything you have ever given me. I do.

Gina, what can I say? You have been my partner through it all. Being able to share this journey with you has been amazing. The time you have sacrificed for me is something that I can't thank you enough for. You've been there from the beginning to the end, and I love you for loving Candace and Ryan as much as I do. For believing in their story and believing in me. For all the late night phone calls and texting. Encouraging me when I felt defeated. Guiding me to the end with your constant support. These books would not be what they are if it weren't for you.

And to Lisa, my amazing editor and friend, you constantly push me to make my writing better. You are the queen of cuts, and with each book I resist you less and less. I love that we have been able to share this whole experience together. That you were always a part of it and in the passenger seat with me. It's an amazing thing when you can share the discovery of a dream and passion with a friend. You were by my side when I felt so lost in life a couple years ago, and I love that you were by my side as I dug myself out and found this hidden talent. You're a unfailing support, and I hope to create more and more wonderful stories with you!

Now my family. To my father and step-mother, having the two of you tell me how proud you are of me means more to me than you will ever know. It's something that every child craves from a parent, and something that you have always given me. I'm one lucky girl to have such amazing parents. Cathy, to have you so invested in my writing is so much fun for me. Being able to sit around with you to plot and bounce ideas off of is the best. Thank you for your enthusiasm and unwavering support. Kelley and Traci, my sisters, thank your for taking the time to read my stories and for all of your encouraging words! And to my brothers, Josh and Quentin, thank you for not reading my books because I just don't know how I feel about you reading my intimate scenes. Josh, you have been a great support even if you don't know it. I love that you can be someone I can discuss my writing with and that you offer ways to strengthen my stories. Thank you for showing me around Seattle and Oregon and for being the one who took me to a place I never knew existed—Cannon Beach. You changed the direction of this story from the very moment I set foot onto Indian Beach. It might not be that significant of a moment for you, but it was for me and for my characters.

I want to thank all of my betas for putting in the hours to read and critique my manuscript. You guys do it all, from encouraging me when I get stressed to helping me promote. Your honesty and support has become something I have depended on through writing this series, and I am blessed to have had such an amazing group of women be on board with me.

Last but not least, to Candace, Ryan, Jase, and Mark, I know you aren't real, but it feels like you are to me. It's been an amazing journey getting to know you all. To live inside each of you for the time I was able to affected me in a way I never thought was possible. To learn and grow with each of you has been a true gift. I have spent the past year with the four of you, and it's sad to say goodbye to your stories, but I thank you for giving them to me, because no matter how anyone else feels about these books, for me, you have given me the stories I have always wanted to read but could never find—until now.

e. k. blair

Website:
www.ekblair.com

Facebook:
https://www.facebook.com/EKBlairAuthor

Twitter:
@EK_Blair_Author

THE black lotus SERIES

books in series

bang
echo
hush

They say when you take revenge against another you lose a part of your innocence

But I'm not innocent

"E.K. Blair's boldest, most daring work to date. Twisted and completely brilliant. There's suspense and steaminess, hopelessness and hope, romance and hate. It's simply damn good."
          -*USA Today*

Made in the USA
Charleston, SC
02 September 2016